PRETENSE

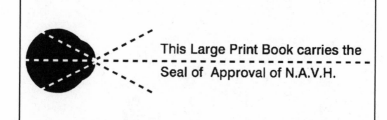

This Large Print Book carries the
Seal of Approval of N.A.V.H.

PRETENSE

LORI WICK

THORNDIKE PRESS
A part of Gale, Cengage Learning

GALE
CENGAGE Learning™

Detroit • New York • San Francisco • New Haven, Conn • Waterville, Maine • London

GALE
CENGAGE Learning·

Copyright © 1998 by Lori Wick.

Verses marked NASB are taken from The New American Standard Bible © 1960, 1962, 1963, 1968, 1971, 1972, 1973, 1975, 1977 by the Lockman Foundation. Used by permission.

Thorndike Press, a part of Gale, Cengage Learning.

LIBRARY OF CONGRESS CATALOGING-IN-PUBLICATION DATA

Wick, Lori.
   Pretense / by Lori Wick.
     p. cm. — (Thorndike Press large print Christian fiction)
   ISBN-13: 978-1-4104-1572-1 (alk. paper)
   ISBN-10: 1-4104-1572-4 (alk. paper)
   1. Family—Fiction. 2. Man-woman relationships—Fiction. 3. Sisters—Fiction. 4. Large type books. I. Title.
   PS3573.I237P74 2009
   813'.54—dc22
                                   2009004541

Published in 2009 by arrangement with Harvest House Publishers.

The nature of this book, the very way
I held it in my heart —
planning it, dreaming about it,
talking about it, and nearly living it
years before conception —
gives me a need for a special dedication.
This book is dedicated to my 18-year
marriage to Bob Wick.
No one in my life has portrayed Christ to
me more strongly than he has.

This one is for us, Robert.

May the next 18 years be as sweet as the last.

ACKNOWLEDGMENTS

Of all the books I've ever written, the journey toward this one has been the longest. So many people and places, so many years in my mind . . . Here is but a simple page to acknowledge the dear people who traveled with me.

Just a word of thanks to . . .

Mary Kay Deese and Kathi Mackenzie-Foster for the loan of your daughters' names, Mackenzie Rose and Delancey Joy. Such wonderful names. They literally inspired me to do this story.

Spencer, originally from New York, New York, who works at the Hyatt at Beaver Creek. Your gracious kindness as you gave us a tour has long been remembered. To this day I wish I'd given you a huge tip. Had my chance, muffed it!

Abby, who was a bright, fun, seven-and-a-half- and eight-year-old while I wrote this book. Thank you for all you are able to do and the help it was to watch you and see Mackenzie and Delancey in action. I'm so glad you're my girl.

Thank you, Matt, for being halfway between 11 and 12 during this book. It was such a help to see you in the sixth grade and to know what it was like and how you felt. It's so easy to forget that a sixth grader is not an adult but a wonderful, energetic child. Thank you for the way you reminded me. You are my sunshine, and I love you.

Thank you, Tim, for your eighth-grade year. I didn't see this part of the story coming, but there it was, and I needed you. Just little things — like your track experience and watching you do algebra homework — were such helps to me. You are so grown up, and I'm so proud of the wonderful big brother you've become.

Thank you, Matt, Sandy, Justin, and Tory Sommerfeldt. No one could ask for sweeter neighbors. The Bob Wick family is immeasurably blessed to have you so near.

Thank you, Cindi Fouch. This comes a little late, but I found myself using your words in this book as well as Sophie's. You shared with me from your own pain and enriched my knowledge. Thank you for your tender heart and spirit.

At last but not least, thank you to my readers. Over the years I've traveled far and wide in my subjects and locations, and you've hung in there and given me a chance. God bless all of you.

ONE

San Antonio, Texas
October 1976
Marrell Bishop worked on dinner with studied concentration, her dark blond bangs falling over her forehead in wispy confusion. As she stirred the muffin batter, she hoped the new chicken dish in the oven would turn out better than the last one she attempted. She was not the greatest cook in the world, but her husband loved variety, and she loved to try new recipes.

She was checking the recipe once again when her oldest daughter entered the room. Marrell watched eight-year-old Mackenzie Rose Bishop sit at the small kitchen table and stare out the window, her expression unreadable.

"What's up, Micki?"

"Nothing much."

"I thought you were going to play Monopoly with Delancey."

"She's in one of her moods."

She sounded neither angry nor put out, and suddenly Marrell didn't care if dinner was on time. She joined her daughter at the table and waited for her to look at her.

"Are your feelings hurt?"

"No, but she won't talk to me, so I don't want

9

to be in the room."

"Do you want me to talk to her?"

"No."

Marrell watched Mackenzie's face very closely. At times it was the only way she could tell when her daughter was upset, but at the moment she didn't seem too wounded. Marrell didn't want to make excuses for her younger daughter, but she still heard herself saying, "I wonder if Delancey might be upset about tonight."

"What's tonight?"

"Her big karate match."

"Oh. I forgot. What time?"

"Seven-thirty."

Mackenzie pulled a face. "I'll miss my show."

Marrell looked compassionate. "Sorry, Micki. Maybe they'll show it in reruns."

Marrell had no problem sensing that Mackenzie was upset about this. Although she said nothing, she was clearly not happy. And indeed, she *was* irritated, but not at her mother. She was rarely upset with her mother. Her sister, on the other hand, could be a great irritant. Mackenzie hated karate, and the fact that her sister's match was causing her to miss her favorite television program made it even less tolerable.

"I forgot to ask you about your whale story when you came in," Mackenzie's mother said, cutting into her irate thoughts. "How did your teacher like it?"

"She liked it a lot." Mackenzie was instantly diverted, her face lighting with a smile. "She asked if she could make a copy of it for her files."

"That *is* a compliment. Did you have a chance to read it to your dad?"

"No, but I brought it home with me."

10

"Good. He should be here in about 40 minutes, so don't forget."

"Okay. Can I help with dinner?"

"Sure. You can wash your hands and pour this batter into the muffin pan."

Mackenzie was happy to do just that and even happier when the aforementioned sister, Delancey Joy Bishop, came downstairs just minutes later. *Delancey* had not been asked to help with dinner. The satisfaction Mackenzie gained from giving her sister a superior smile was huge.

The first thing Lieutenant Colonel Paul Bishop did every night upon arriving home was kiss his wife. Over the years he had walked in to find company waiting for him, his daughters wanting his attention, phone calls from the base, and any number of other distractions, but he ignored all of these until he had taken Marrell in his arms and kissed her.

Paul Bishop had little time for church, but if anything could make him stop and thank God, it was his wife. It still amazed him that she had fallen in love with and married him. Marrell Bishop, Marrell Walker when he'd met her, was drop-dead gorgeous. Tall and curvy, blue-eyed and blond, there wasn't a male head that didn't turn when she walked into a room. Paul wasn't exactly a troll, but he knew he wasn't in Marrell's class.

At any moment Paul could recall the way he felt when he first saw her. She had been clearing the counter in a mom-and-pop diner in Colorado Springs, Colorado, when he had been stationed at Fort Carson. Her shy smile as she had taken his order had done his heart a world of good. His voice had been especially soft when he'd asked

11

her out the first time, his eyes kind as he worked to hide his anxiety. Months later, after they had become quite serious, she admitted that the only reason she'd gone out with him twice was because he hadn't tried anything on their first date.

"And the third time?" he remembered asking her.

"By our third date," she answered, blushing, "I was already in love with you."

With those words from 11 years ago now on his mind, he let himself into the apartment they called home. The smell of dinner assailed his senses, but with Marrell on his mind, he paid little heed. Finding her in the kitchen, he approached slowly, giving her a chance to take a pan from the oven. The moment she set it down, his arms went around her. Marrell had waited all day for his embrace and gladly returned it. The girls stood silently nearby, watching the familiar scene and knowing very well that no amount of noise or commotion would interrupt them.

"Hi," Paul said at last, his eyes smiling into hers.

"Hi yourself." Marrell's smile was content. "How was your day?"

"Long and hot. I'm glad it's over. Hey, girls!" It was now time for them.

"Hi, Dad." Delancey jumped toward him, her arms open wide. "Mom's gonna braid my hair for tonight."

"She is? You'll look beautiful." He bent low and hugged her tightly.

Mackenzie was close behind her sister, her arms going around her father's neck as he bent toward her. "I have a story to read to you."

"The one you wrote?"

"Yes." Mackenzie looked into his face and

smiled. She didn't know that he knew. "It's about a whale."

"Well, let's hear it, or is dinner ready?"

"It is," Marrell informed him, "but Mackenzie can read while I put the food on the table."

"It's a deal. Go get it, Micki."

The brown-haired Bishop girl did not need to be asked twice. She tore up the stairs in pursuit of her schoolbag and folder, her little legs carrying her at breakneck speed as she came back down. Paul was waiting for her at the kitchen table, Delancey in his lap.

"Okay, let's hear it."

Mackenzie did the honors with pride, telling of the little whale who saved all the whales living with him in the underwater village and thus became the hero of the day.

"What did you think?" she wanted to know.

"I think it's just as wonderful as you are."

Mackenzie smiled at him and sat at the table. Dinner was served, and to Marrell's pleasure, the casserole was as delicious as the muffins and fruit salad.

"You ready for tonight, D.J.?" her father wished to know.

"Yes. I practiced a little after school."

"What time shall we go?"

"She has to be there at 7:30," Marrell filled in. "I'd like to leave a little early if we could. I need to run into the mall and return those jeans Micki can't wear."

"Okay. What time will the match be over?"

"I'm guessing about 8:30 or 9:00. Last time we left after Delancey was finished, but I think that's frowned on by the instructors."

Paul smiled across the table at his wife but

didn't comment. Marrell caught his look and hid a smile of her own. The way Marrell hated anyone's disapproval had long been a joke between them. The very fact that Delancey's karate instructor was unhappy with Marrell would cause her to adjust her plans. Paul had been in the Army for more than 16 years. He was accustomed to taking orders every day of his life, but once he left the office, he didn't let anyone dictate his actions. Marrell was just the opposite. She wasn't a doormat, but she was most definitely happier when no one was frowning at her.

"Do you want to stay until everyone finishes tonight, D.J.?" Paul asked her.

"Can we? I want to see the black belts."

"We'll see how it goes. Tomorrow is a school day."

Now it was time for the girls to exchange a look. They both liked school but hated it when it kept them from doing what they really wanted.

They finished the meal in a normal fashion, with Marrell clearing the table and doing the dishes. Paul headed toward the newspaper he hadn't had time to read, and the girls found themselves back in their room. Delancey pulled her karate uniform from the closet, and Mackenzie sat on the bed with a book, the earlier incident seemingly far behind them.

"I can't find the belt," Delancey said, sounding almost panicked.

"It's right there," Mackenzie responded, pointing calmly. The important blue belt with the black stripe had dropped onto the closet floor. Two years ago Delancey had joined a karate studio that specialized in children's classes. She had worked hard, starting with a white belt and moving on to

14

gold, orange, green, purple, purple with a black stripe, blue, and then blue with a black stripe. Tonight she would graduate again, this time to the red belt.

"Is it straight in the back?"

"Um hm," Mackenzie told her honestly. "Let me see the front now."

Delancey turned for inspection, and Mackenzie smiled at her.

The room the girls shared was not huge, but each had a twin bed and her own small dresser. They shared the closet. There was also a desk, but schoolwork was usually done at the kitchen table. The Bishops had lived in this apartment for almost three years now, neither girl remembering much about the two other places they had lived.

As Mackenzie watched, Delancey put the finishing touches on her uniform and stood before the mirror that hung on the back of the door. She looked content with what she saw, but excitement about the coming event made it impossible to stand still. Only seconds passed before she was kicking imaginary opponents in the room, Mackenzie watching her in boredom. Not until she came close and sent a kick toward Mackenzie's face did the older girl raise an objection.

"Don't kick around my face, Delancey. I don't like it."

Delancey didn't listen, so Mackenzie glared at her and walked from the room. Delancey let her go, happy to have the room to herself. She planted herself in front of the mirror again, this time with a hairbrush in her hand.

"You seem preoccupied," Marrell commented softly to Paul from her place next to him in the

15

front seat of their car.

"Just thinking."

"Anything you want to talk about?"

He reached for her hand. "I'll catch you later."

"All right. Do you remember where to turn?"

"I think so. Holler if I start to pass it."

The girls, sitting in the backseat, had been almost silent for the ride to the karate studio, but their thoughts were strangely similar. Delancey was nervous about having to display her moves in front of so many people, and Mackenzie was thinking how nervous she would be if she were going up front tonight. Their father parked the car almost before they were ready.

Following their parents inside, the girls hung close as Paul and Marrell moved slowly inside behind other families who were looking for seats. Mackenzie looked over at one point and stared at Delancey. Thirteen months younger than Mackenzie and tall for her age, Delancey was eye-to-eye with her sister as she looked back, her little face pale. Mackenzie didn't notice her color; she only thought again about the way she might feel.

"Are you scared?" the older girl whispered.

Delancey was tempted to put her chin in the air and tell her no, but she confirmed Mackenzie's suspicions with a swift nod of her head. She had already tested for the red belt and passed, but this was different: This was in front of everyone. The girls continued to follow Paul and Marrell, and a moment later Delancey slipped through the crowd to join her class. Mackenzie's eyes took in everything, but they constantly strayed back to her sister.

Delancey looked every inch the professional. Her long hair, straight and blond, hung in a

16

perfect braid down her back. Carriage erect, back straight, and eyes ahead, she sat very still. Mackenzie stared at her before looking up at her mother, who had been watching her as well. They looked at each other at the same time.

"I think D.J.'s nervous," Marrell commented.

"She is," Mackenzie confirmed with confidence.

Both looked back at Delancey in time to see the owner of the studio step forward. He welcomed family and friends alike and praised the hard work of all the participants. Too busy watching Delancey to see if she was all right, Mackenzie heard only portions of his remarks.

First to show the curriculum they had learned were the little ones, whose ages went all the way down to four years old. The crowd was delighted with their small, earnest faces and even with their mistakes. Delancey's group was next, and although not the tallest, Delancey's proud carriage and expert manner drew many eyes. Marrell leaned close to her spouse.

"Oh, Paul, she's so cute."

"Yes, she is." His smile was huge as he watched his youngest daughter.

The decision to leave early on this night was taken from their hands. After Delancey received her new red belt, she was expected to stay with her class. It was rather late by the time everyone finished. The young karate student was flushed with pleasure, however, as compliments came from nearly everyone she passed. Her parents and sister were just as excited as they moved to the car, and any silence on the ride to the studio was made up for on the ride home.

"I thought you were the best," Mackenzie told her.

Delancey smiled with pleasure.

"Are you pleased with your performance, Delancey?" asked Marrell.

"Yes. I was a little scared, but then it was all right. I wanted to come and sit with you when I was done, but no one else was allowed to do that, so I didn't think I could."

"We understood."

At that moment the car passed an ice cream parlor, and Mackenzie immediately asked if they could stop.

"It's almost 9:30" was all her father said, but she knew the subject was closed. She finished the ride hoping that Delancey's next performance would be on a Friday or Saturday and that they could stay up as long as they liked.

"I tell you, Paul, they're so unpredictable," Marrell spoke when the girls were settled and they'd gained their own bedroom. "They were mad at each other before you got home, and now tonight they're the best of friends."

"That's kids for you." His tone was casual enough as he undid the buttons on his shirt, but still Marrell stared at his back, her mind only now having time to wonder at the preoccupied look she had seen on his face that evening. Unaware of her scrutiny, Paul took a moment to turn to her. When he found her eyes on him, he became very still.

"Are you all right?" she asked.

Paul stared at her, and without him having to say a word, Marrell had her answer. She sat down on the edge of the bed.

"We're moving on."

"Yes." He wasted no time in admitting it.

Marrell drew a deep breath.

"Where?"

"San Francisco."

"The Presidio?"

Paul only nodded and watched her. Marrell looked at the wall, her mind suddenly blank. She felt the bed move as her husband sat beside her, but for a moment she continued to stare at the wall.

"There's good news," he said softly as he waited for her to turn. "We don't move until June, so the girls can finish the school year here."

"That is good news," she said, her eyes looking into Paul's. "It just never comes easy, does it? I was not thrilled about a Texas posting three years ago, but now we've made a life here."

"And before this we made a life in Alabama, and before that, Colorado. We'll do it again."

"San Francisco," she whispered. "I don't know if I can raise my girls in San Francisco." With that she wrapped her arms around his arm and laid her cheek against his shoulder.

There was no need for Paul to say anything. San Francisco did not seem like a great place to raise children, but they were going and that was the end of it. They would both have to accept the fact. He wished he could tell her that they didn't have to live right in San Francisco, but the city was so expensive — he knew they couldn't afford to live anywhere but the Presidio. She knew it as well. The only question still in his mind was when would be the appropriate time to tell the girls.

"These are the reports you wanted, Colonel," the private said as he placed the papers in front of Paul.

19

"Thank you," the officer returned absently, nodding a dismissal. He stared at the papers, but all he could see was Marrell. She had not cried or been upset right after he'd told her of the move, but as the weeks passed she had slowly become more down. Feeling that he needed some time on his own, Paul went to a bar with a few fellow officers. There he made the mistake of telling them how hard Marrell was taking it.

"Sounds to me like you've got trouble, Paul, old boy," said a single man who was known for using and discarding women at will.

"How's that?"

"When a woman doesn't want to travel, it means there's someone she doesn't want to leave behind."

"What is that supposed to mean?" Paul's voice had grown very cold.

"Well, now, let me just put it this way — she wouldn't be pining for the dinky little apartment you live in or the other wives she talks to at the PX."

If the man hadn't outranked Paul, he'd have punched him in the face. Paul remained calm, however, and said only, "You don't know my wife."

The man was on the verge of saying he'd like to know her but finally looked at the cold gleam in Paul Bishop's eyes and let it pass. Paul had made it an early night after that. He wished he'd gone directly home from work, not because he suspected Marrell of infidelity, but because his wife needed him. In truth he was looking forward to the move, but it was selfish of him to go out when his wife needed his support.

The phone rang on his desk just then, and when he answered it, his commanding officer, Colonel

Mark Brinker, ordered him into his office. He saluted the man, who stood when he entered, but took a seat as soon as he was asked.

"I've got your transfer date all lined up," Mark began at once, handing a large envelope across the table. "Your duties terminate here on June 9, and you're to report for duty at the Presidio on June 20. Any problem with that?"

"Not at all, sir."

"Good." For a moment the other man stared at him. "How's Marrell liking the idea?"

"She's getting used to it," Paul said, hoping it was true.

"I saw her at the PX last week with the girls," his CO continued conversationally. "Originally from Colorado, isn't she?"

"Yes, sir, Colorado Springs."

The older man nodded. "They get snow at Christmas."

Paul smiled. "That they do."

"You won't find that in San Francisco."

Paul nodded, trying not to speculate over where his CO was headed with this.

"In the envelope," Mark spoke quietly, "you'll find that they have quarters for you at the Presidio. You won't need to rent off base for a time." This was great news to Paul, but he didn't have time to answer. "Correct me if I'm wrong, but don't you have some leave coming?"

"Yes."

"It's up to you, of course, but you could fly the family somewhere. Maybe some nice place where the girls could play in the snow on Christmas Day."

Paul smiled hugely, and Mark laughed.

"I'll give it some thought, sir. Thank you."

21

"You're welcome. I hope you go and have a great time."

Paul stood, as did the colonel. The interview was over.

Christmas in Colorado. It had been years since they had spent a holiday with Marrell's grandmother, the woman who had raised her. It didn't stop all the worries about moving, but the trip was sure to ease some of the hurt. Paul had to restrain himself from heading home to tell Marrell on the spot, but maybe it was better that he couldn't leave. Returning to his desk, he opened the envelope, searched inside, and picked up the phone. He had airline flights to book.

The boy in the seat across from the girls winked at Delancey, who turned and giggled in Mackenzie's direction. The two tried not to look at him, but their eyes were drawn back. He was already distracted, however and the girls continued the bus ride home in silence. They still had a ways to go, so Mackenzie pulled out a book. Delancey read over her shoulder, feeling free to ask about words she didn't recognize. Mackenzie put up with it for a time but eventually turned the book so her sister couldn't see.

"Come on, Mackenzie, just let me look."

"All right, but don't ask me any more words."

A good portion of the ride was finished in silence, both heads bent over the book. Mackenzie was a faster reader, so Delancey ended up just studying the illustrations that appeared every so often. The ride went faster that way, and before they knew, it was time to get off the bus and walk the short distance to their apartment on the base. As was her custom, their mother met them at the door. She had hugs and kisses for them and questions about the day.

"A boy winked at D.J. on the bus," Mackenzie said, laughingly.

"Well, now. Did you wink back, Delancey?"

This sent the girls into more laughter. Marrell told them to wash their hands for a snack. She then put apples and crackers with peanut butter on the table along with two glasses of milk. Even with this small act, Marrell felt that familiar ache steal over her and wondered at it. There was so much about Texas that was difficult — the heat and bugs, just to name two. So why did this move leave her feeling dejected? The weather was sure to be more pleasant in San Francisco, but for some reason the idea of uprooting again depressed her.

Maybe I can't be an Army wife after all. Maybe I need to ask Paul just how badly he wants to keep doing this. With this thought she was overcome with guilt. It had been weeks before she had even thought to ask Paul what his new job would be and if it was an advancement. Her selfishness had amazed her. He had been very understanding, but the very next night he had called to say he was going out with some friends. When he came home he'd been very attentive, but Marrell had begun to worry.

The phone rang just then, and Marrell started violently. She walked toward it, dreading the thought of Paul calling to say he would be going out again, but it was a wrong number. She could have wept with relief.

"Mom?"

Marrell turned at the sound of Delancey's voice.

"What is it, honey?"

"Are you gonna cry?"

"No," she said softy, "I was just thinking." She mustered a smile. "Eat your snack now."

It was a relief to have her daughter turn away. She and Paul had to talk tonight. He had been acting oddly, and she was sure it was over her mood. There were far worse places to be stationed than San Francisco. She'd never been there but knew there were people who found it very exciting. The phrase "It's a nice place to visit, but I wouldn't want to live there" leaped into her mind, but she pushed it away. She would talk to her husband tonight and tell him . . .

Tell him what? At the moment Marrell wasn't sure. She just knew things hadn't been good between them since that night, and she couldn't live like this any more.

It was already the middle of November. They would be gone from here in seven months, and Paul and the girls would be all she had. She could plan to make this move in anger and upset, or she could plan to look for new opportunities and friends. Shoving the ache inside her even deeper, Marrell determined that by the time Paul got home, she would accomplish the latter.

"It's bedtime, girls," Marrell announced several hours later.

"Bedtime?" Mackenzie felt as outraged as she sounded. "It's not even eight o'clock and —"

"Mackenzie!" Her father's sharp tone stopped her in mid-sentence. He was equally as surprised that his wife was putting the kids down so early, but unlike his daughter, he was not going to argue.

"Brush your teeth now," Marrell filled in, and both girls, their attitudes none too gracious, moved to do as she bid.

"Are you all right?" Paul wanted to know as soon as they were alone.

"Can we talk?"

"Yes. Actually, I was going to tell you some things when they went to bed anyway."

Marrell dreaded what he might say, and tears suddenly filled her eyes.

"Mary, honey, it's all right." Paul stood. His arms came around her. "I'll go up with you and make sure they're settled in. Then we'll talk."

Marrell was crying too hard to answer. Paul led her to the sofa and pulled her down beside him. He held her close, not speaking yet, even though she seemed to be quieting. Paul was bending his head to peer into her face when he noticed the girls. They had come back in their nightgowns and stood still at the edge of the room.

"What's wrong with Mom?"

"She's just a little upset. I'll tell you what," Paul said, standing as he spoke. "You come and kiss Mom right now, and I'll tuck you in tonight."

"But Mom always does it," Delancey argued.

"Well, you'll have to put up with me tonight. Come, now! Good soldiers always take orders."

He had put on his playful command voice for them, and even though they knew he could chase them up the stairs, they came over very carefully to kiss their mother and hug her. Marrell managed to dry her tears long enough to embrace them, and just as she expected, the girls charged for the stairs, Paul on their heels. It never made any sense to her when he stirred them just before they went up to bed, but she wasn't going to say anything. Suddenly it wasn't important at all.

Her mind wandered until he came back down,

and she didn't feel at all ready for talking when he gained the living room. He sat near her but not directly beside her on the couch, his body turned so he could see her. He picked up her hand and just stared at it. Marrell was quiet.

"Your hands were the first things I noticed about you."

"My hands?"

"Yes. Did I never tell you?"

Marrell shook her head no.

"You were cleaning that counter, and your hands were so slim and tanned, and the nails so long. I was captivated."

Marrell had long known that her husband was a romantic. His love and caring never ceased to amaze her. But lately she hadn't loved and cared for him; she'd only been thinking of herself. More tears came, and Paul changed positions to put his arms around her.

"Marrell, what is it? You can tell me. If it's the move or whatever, just talk to me."

"I don't know what's wrong," she got out, frustration punctuating every word. "I just feel so down all the time, and we haven't even told the girls we're leaving yet. You know they're going to be upset, and I dread it. I just feel so empty inside, Paul. What's the matter with me?"

He kissed her. "I think it's just what you said when I told you: At the beginning you weren't thrilled about Texas, but now we have a good life here. You have friends and know your way around, and the girls have done great in school. It's normal that you would fear the changes, but I'll be there, and the girls always adjust swiftly. We'll make it, Mary, you'll see. We'll be fine."

She looked into his face. "I've even been asking

myself if I can keep on like this. I've been horribly selfish, thinking that maybe you could do something else so we didn't have to move all the time."

"That's not selfish. I've asked myself that same question, but for now I think this move is a good one. It will probably be my last one before I have to go overseas again, and that won't happen for three more years. It's going to be all right."

"When should we tell the girls?"

"I think in March or April. That way they can say goodbye to their friends before school lets out."

"Have you been told yet what day you have to report?"

"June 20."

Marrell smiled, her heart still trying not to worry. "I wonder how Mackenzie will like spending her ninth birthday in San Francisco."

Paul smiled at the acceptance he heard there, but when he spoke, his voice was deliberately casual. "Did I tell you that I bought something for us today?"

"No. I didn't know you had planned to shop."

"I didn't have much notice myself."

"Where did you go?"

"I didn't need to go anywhere. I just dialed the phone."

Marrell looked at him. His warm green eyes stared right back.

"I have airline tickets for four in my briefcase."

Marrell's eyes grew. "Where are we going?"

"We are going to Colorado Springs for Christmas."

Mrs. Bishop's hand went to her mouth. "You wouldn't tease me about this, would you, Paul?"

"Not on your life. We fly out late on the twenty-third, and I don't have to be back to work until January 3."

Marrell's arms went around Paul's neck and pulled him close. She found his mouth with her own and kissed him deeply. "Thank you, Paul," she took a moment to say, then kissed him again.

They sat together, wrapped in each other's arms for the next two hours. Marrell didn't know when she had been so surprised and pleased. The girls were going to love it, and her grandmother would be ecstatic. All she had shared with her grandmother for the past year were letters and occasional phone calls. Now she would see her, and at the most special time of the year. By the time they went to bed, Marrell realized she wasn't feeling nearly as empty inside as she had been.

Two

Colorado Springs, Colorado

"It looks like they're going to build a snowman," Pearl Walker said from her place by the window. "Oh! Delancey just hit Paul with a snowball."

Marrell smiled from her chair by the fire but did not join her grandmother.

"Tell me again who you borrowed all the boots and snow clothes from?"

"I just put the word out at church, and they all came through." Pearl's eyes went back to the scene in her front yard. "I don't think Paul's boots fit that well. He can barely stay on his feet."

Marrell laughed. "He grew up in Florida, Grandma. He hasn't had much practice."

"Are the two of you going to ski?"

"I am certainly going to, and I hope he'll join me. We'll probably wait until next week."

"Did I tell you I was headed out to mail your Christmas gifts when you called to say you were coming?" Pearl's voice held wonder.

Only three times! The smile and serene nod from Marrell did a good job of hiding the tempestuous thoughts inside. *Oh, Grandma, please don't get old. Please don't change. I need something in my life to stay the same. Please let it be you.*

"And then I called Mavis to tell her, and we

29

laughed and laughed."

Marrell listened but felt an ache inside. She had told her all this on the phone just last week, in a letter before that, and several times since they arrived. Marrell sighed very softly.

"I know what I didn't tell you," Pearl said as she now sat across from her granddaughter and dug in a basket at the side of the chair. "I've had a letter from Barb Blankenship."

Marrell was suddenly all ears. Barb's granddaughter, Sharon, had gone to school with Marrell from the time they were small. Barb lived in Colorado Springs until five years ago. Her arthritis had become unbearable, and she had moved to warmer climes.

"She says Sharon is in San Francisco!"

"You're kidding!" Marrell had come upright in her chair.

"No, let me read it to you: 'Shay is on the move again, or should I say moved! Her divorce from Marty is complete and —' "

"Shay and Marty got a divorce?"

"Didn't I tell you?" her grandmother frowned.

"No. When was this?"

"It's been a year or better."

Marrell's heart sank. Sharon and Marty had been so in love. What had happened? Didn't anyone stick it out these days? She was on the verge of asking her grandmother to read on, but Mackenzie chose that moment to open the front door.

"Mom!" she yelled. "Can I have some more mittens?"

"I'll get them," Pearl offered, quickly standing. "You finish the letter on your own."

Pearl handed the paper to Marrell, who im-

30

mediately began to read.

Sorry it's taken so long to get in touch, but I've been extremely busy. I try not to promise to write when I know I can't, so even though we haven't even had Thanksgiving, this will probably be my Christmas letter.

Shay is on the move again, or should I say moved! Her divorce from Marty is complete, and as hard as it was for both of them, I'm glad she's made the decision to go on with her life, which right now means she's moved to San Francisco. Thank heaven there were no children involved. Much as I'd like to be a great grandmother, I can see what a mess that would have been.

What do you hear from Marrell? Shay asks after her every so often, but for the past few years she's been pretty involved in her own trouble. I've included her address. If you have time, you might want to drop her a Christmas card. I don't know if she has any friends out there yet, and she's trying to get her business off the ground.

Marrell sat back a moment and tried to remember what Sharon had been doing with her life. Marty was an architect, she remembered that much, and somewhere in Marrell's mind it seemed to her that Sharon had gone into those studies as well . . . or had she only been helping Marty with his business?

Marrell finished the letter, but other than having Sharon's address at the bottom, it said nothing more on the subject of her friend. Marrell studied the street address. As big as San Francisco was, the street could be miles from the Presidio.

Marrell thought she had best write the address down. She knew she could call and ask when she got back to Texas, but her grandmother might misplace it. Again she sighed very softly.

"Where is your mom?" Delancey asked very suddenly that night.

Of all the things the girls might be thinking about on Christmas Eve, this had never occurred to their mother. Marrell felt herself blink.

"Why hasn't she come yet?" the seven-year-old wanted to know.

"Honey, my mother's dead. She died when I was six. Did you think you were going to see her?"

Delancey nodded her fair head against the pillow.

"I tried to tell her," Mackenzie put in, "but she thought she would be here."

"Oh well, that's all right, D.J. We've talked about this, but you just don't remember. My mother died when I was six, and I came to live with my grandparents because my father was a salesman and traveled a lot."

"Is he still traveling?"

"No. When I was in high school, he got cancer and died before I graduated."

"Where's your grandpa?" This came from Mackenzie.

"He died just a few years ago. You would have been about four, and Delancey would have been three. I have pictures of you in his lap, but you would have been too young to remember him. Okay?"

"Okay," they both chorused.

"Sleep quick so morning will come."

The girls beamed at her. Marrell kissed them

and told them they were loved, but she was pre-occupied. Had she really spoken so rarely of her family that her daughters couldn't even remember the details, or was it that they were young and busy with their own lives?

"That's quite a frown," Paul commented as soon as he saw her. He was alone in the living room, and Marrell sat across from him.

"I was just thinking about how selfish we all are."

"Who?"

"All of us — all humans. We're really just wrapped up in our own little worlds with very little thought for anyone else."

Paul's brows rose. "I wouldn't go so far as to say none of us think of others, Marrell. I think you're right that man is basically self-seeking, but on the other side of that, if we don't take care of ourselves, who will?"

"That's a good point," Marrell admitted slowly, but even as she said it, she had doubts. Was man really just here on his own, stuck with making his way along and doing the best he could?

"How does popcorn and cocoa sound?" Pearl stuck her head around the corner and asked from the kitchen.

"Sounds great. Do you want some help?"

"No, I'll get it."

Marrell smiled and looked back to Paul. "Have I thanked you for bringing us here?"

"I think only about 30 times, so you probably should say it a few more times."

Paul patted the couch beside him, and Marrell joined him. Once she was snuggled gently under his arm, he picked up the remote control. Christmas specials of all kinds were on, and before long

33

the popcorn and cocoa made an appearance. The three of them sat up way too late, but it was worth every moment. This was going to be a Christmas they would never forget.

Mackenzie's eyes opened just moments before she suddenly sat up and looked at the digital clock. The LED glowed out a bright red 5:03, and she wondered how much trouble she would be in if she got up. No one had said anything about sleeping in, and this *was* Christmas.

She slipped from the double bed she shared with Delancey and out into the living room. The tree lights were dark, so she plugged them in, her face lighting with joy as she sank down to the carpet and looked at the gifts. She knew which ones were hers — she had inspected all of them the morning before. She picked up a small parcel for her mother and shook it. There was a little rattle inside, and for a moment she thought she might have broken something. She put it back with a careful hand and decided not to touch any more gifts.

A sudden movement at the edge of the room caused her to start. Her father came into the light, and she relaxed until she remembered she might be in trouble for getting up so early. She calmed completely when he sat in the big chair and said, "Merry Christmas."

Mackenzie was in his lap the next instant.

"Merry Christmas, Dad."

Paul hugged her close and pressed a kiss to her forehead, then bent lower and scuffed her cheek with his unshaved jaw.

"Shhh," he said on a soft laugh when Mackenzie began to giggle. "You'll have the whole house awake. Actually, I'm surprised D.J.'s not out here."

"I was quiet."

Paul didn't know that was possible, but he didn't comment. Mackenzie looked up to see his eyes almost shut.

"What are you doing?" she whispered.

"Haven't you ever done that? Squint your eyes until your eyelashes are together. See how the lights turn into rays that go all over the place?"

"Oh." Mackenzie's voice was awed. "It's like stars."

They sat and did this together for a while until Mackenzie needed to use the bathroom. The flush of the toilet right next to their bedroom brought Delancey out, and both girls snuggled with their father in the big chair. He tried to keep them quiet, but his effort was an utter failure. Soft giggles turned to full laughter, and before long both their great grandmother and mother emerged from their rooms.

"I'm sorry, Grandma," Marrell said apologetically.

"Oh, Marrell, for mercy's sake," her grandmother responded in soft rebuke, "I can sleep for a month when you're gone. How many times can I do this? Delancey and Mackenzie, you come with me to the kitchen. We've got coffee and sweet rolls to put on."

"And presents?"

"Presents are right after that. Come on now."

The girls didn't need to be asked twice. Marrell took their place in Paul's lap, and even from the living room they could hear the girls' delighted voices and laughter.

"I wish they could enjoy some of your family the way they do Grandma."

35

Paul stiffened for a moment but relaxed when Marrell said nothing else. Paul was the black sheep of the family; not because he'd run wild at any point in his life, but because he had joined the Army and not the family business. On top of that, there was his marriage to Marrell. The family had cast their disapproval before even meeting her, and when they did meet her, one of his brothers had made a pass at her.

Never very close to his two older brothers and one sister, Paul had written them off.

"It's their loss, Mary. They'll probably never know you or the girls, but that's their loss, not ours. I stopped sending cards and gifts to them a long time ago because they were never acknowledged. I'm not going to waste my time any longer."

"But what of Micki and D.J., Paul? I just ache that they've never seen where you grew up or played with any of their cousins."

"Have you forgotten what my brother said to you or the way he watched you?" he responded irritably. "I wouldn't trust him around the girls."

"He was drunk," Marrell said mildly. "And I'm sure he'll remember the broken nose you gave him for a long time."

Both of them fell silent. It was not the way they wanted to begin their Christmas. Marrell decided Paul was right. After all, it was his family. If he didn't want to push the point, then she didn't either. Her recollection of their time with them now came fully back to mind. Paul's mother was a strange woman. It had been very difficult indeed. Why would she want to put herself through that again?

"If you really want to, we can call them today."

"No," Marrell shook her head. "It's your family,

36

Paul. You do what's comfortable for you. I can't stand the thought that they might meet the girls, disapprove, and hurt them. I'm willing to let it go unless you want us to do something."

Paul reached up and pulled her head very close. He rested his cheek on the top of her head. "I have you, and I have the girls, Mary. That's all I need."

The words did Marrell's heart a world of good, but moments later, when Pearl and the girls paraded in with breakfast on a tray, the odd emptiness that Marrell often felt inside suddenly surfaced. She pushed it away. This wasn't a time to think about that. The hour was early, and she was tired — that was all. This was a day to be enjoyed to the fullest. All too soon it would be time to head home.

San Antonio
Early May 1977
"I've got the movers coming June 10. Does that figure right?"

"I think so," Paul replied, looking over Marrell's shoulder at the calendar of events. He knew that time would move swiftly, but it was hard to believe they would be gone in less than a month.

"How is the packing going?"

"It's all right. I really purged when it came to the girls' clothes, since it's not as warm there year-round. Anything too summery that I didn't think would fit them by fall went into the bag for charity. I wonder what the PX out there will be like?"

"I didn't think to ask. I did ask about karate studios though."

"You did?" Marrell replied, sounding very pleased.

37

"Yes, and there seems to be a wide variety. I think we'll just get out the phone book when we get there. Did you think to ask Mr. Schaller for a recommendation?"

"I didn't, but that's a good idea."

The words were no more out of Marrell's mouth than the air split with a scream. Their heads shot up, and they both made a dash for the living room. Delancey beat them to it. She was tearing down the stairs, hand over her face, her nose streaming blood.

"What happened?" Marrell cried as she guided Delancey into the kitchen and reached for a cloth. She wet it at the sink and tried to understand what her nearly hysterical daughter was saying. In the midst of the commotion, Mackenzie came into the room and leaned casually against the wall.

"Calm down, Delancey," Paul now tried. "What happened?"

"She punched me" were the first intelligible words they heard.

"What?" Marrell mouthed in stunned disbelief. Surely she had heard wrong. She continued to mop up the blood as well as stem the flow, getting ice from the freezer to help with that while Paul focused on a line of questioning.

"All right now, D.J., what really happened?"

"Mackenzie punched me."

Paul turned to his other daughter. Her arms were crossed over her chest, and she looked defiant.

"Is that true, Micki?" Marrell was the first to ask. "Did you punch D.J. in the nose?"

"Yes."

Marrell's mouth fell open for a moment.

"For heaven's sake, Mackenzie! Paul, what are

38

we going to do? What if it's broken?"

"It's not broken." The words came from Mackenzie's mouth before anyone else could say a word.

"You don't know that," Marrell snapped. She was angry now, at her daughter *and* at her husband, who had not said a word.

"Yes, I do. If I had wanted to break it, I would have."

With those words Marrell was shocked into speechlessness. While she watched, Mackenzie spoke rather calmly to Delancey.

"I told you I don't want you kicking around my face, Delancey, and I meant it."

"I won't do it anymore," Delancey responded in a subdued voice.

Mackenzie pushed off from the wall she'd been leaning against and left the room. Thinking she could scream, Marrell continued to mop up Delancey's face and clothes. A few moments of silence passed before she was sure the bleeding had stopped. Marrell stripped off her daughter's top in order to treat the bloodstains and then told Delancey she could go upstairs and put on something else. She looked to Paul as soon as Delancey was gone, and when she saw a gleam in his eye, she let him have it.

"Do not tell me that you think this is funny, Paul Bishop!"

He looked at her with maddening calm. "Not funny exactly, but I am a little proud of Micki."

"You can't be serious! She *punched* Delancey in the nose. What in the world is there to be proud of?"

"Marrell, Micki takes a lot off of D.J. and all of her moods. I don't think it's all bad that Delancey gets put in her place once in a while."

Marrell's mouth dropped open once again. "You're condoning this?"

"No, I'm not. I'll talk to Micki, but I could see by D.J.'s attitude that Micki had made her point. She would make a good soldier."

Marrell's eyes shot sparks before she whipped around and began to work on Delancey's top. Paul knew he would have to mend fences before the night was over, but for now he had a daughter to talk to — one with a mean right hook.

The air was hot and still as father and daughter left the apartment. Delancey had walked all the way downstairs to watch them go but wasn't invited. Paul planned to speak to her as well, but Mackenzie was first.

"Do you think you'll miss this base?"

Mackenzie shrugged. She was still trying to figure out whether she was going to be spanked.

"You must have some opinion."

"What's 'opinion'?"

"How you feel. Will you miss the base or not?"

"I will a little. I like my teacher."

"How about the apartment?"

"No."

"Why not?"

"Because I want my own room."

"I can understand that. Tell me, Micki, do you ever think about the work that goes on here?"

"On the base?"

"Yes."

"Sometimes."

"What do you think about it?"

"I don't know. Sometimes I wonder why. I mean you go to an office, and I don't know why you

40

need all these guns and stuff if you work in an office."

Paul smiled and reminded himself that he *had* asked.

"You make a good point, Micki. All these guns would be very dangerous if they weren't controlled." They had come to a fence. When they stopped Paul turned and looked down at his dark-haired daughter. "A person's fists can be dangerous too. That's why they have to be controlled."

"Like when I hit Delancey."

"That's right. I can already see that you would make a great soldier, Micki, but soldiers have to control themselves. They have to make themselves do things they don't want to do, *and* they have to stop themselves from doing what sometimes seems right."

Mackenzie looked up at him, her eyes on his face.

"Do you know what I'm talking about?"

"Yes."

"Good. Now what should you have done?"

"Come to you or Mom."

"That's right. You need to remember that for next time, or I'll punish you."

Mackenzie nodded. He meant it. Her mother did much of the discipline in their house, but that didn't mean their father never took care of it, and he spanked hard.

"We need to go back to the apartment so you can apologize to your sister."

"Does D.J. have to apologize to me?" There was a tone in her voice he didn't like.

"I will talk with D.J., Micki, but I'm telling you, no matter what she does, you do not punch her in

41

the nose. Do you hear me?"

"Yes. I hate karate."

"I know you do, but your sister enjoys it, and she's very good. You need to be glad for her and proud of her."

Mackenzie nodded. Delancey was good, and she was proud of her, but she didn't want to be practiced on.

Without further ado Paul led the way back to the apartment. He told Mackenzie to head to her room and then found Delancey. The three ended up in the girls' room and were sequestered behind closed doors for quite some time. Indeed, it got so late that they appeared in the kitchen, teeth brushed, and pajama-clad, to kiss their mother goodnight. Marrell was happy to see them getting along, but not for anything would she ask what happened.

Another ten minutes passed before she looked up from her magazine to see a white handkerchief waving around the corner.

"May I come in?" Paul stepped around the wall and stood at the edge of the kitchen, his face open and relaxed.

"Yes, but don't expect me to notice that white flag. I'm still mad at you." This was only a little bit true.

"Don't you want to know what I said to them?" Paul asked as he sat down across the kitchen table from her.

"No. I'm afraid you told Mackenzie that she would be a great soldier and to keep up the good work."

"I did tell Mackenzie that she would be a great soldier, but I would never tell her to punch people."

Marrell finally looked at him. "What did you say?"

"I just talked to her about control. And when I had them together, I told them what I would do to their backsides if in the future D.J. starts throwing kicks or Micki starts delivering punches."

"Did you know that D.J. had been kicking at Mackenzie?" Marrell sounded as confused and upset as she felt.

"No, and from what I gather, she's been doing it since she began to train."

"Micki's never said a word."

Husband and wife looked at each other. Both of their daughters were talented and special, and at times one of them was a little old beyond her years.

"The thought that they could hurt each other really scares me. We live in such a violent world, Paul, and I've wanted to spare them as much as possible."

"And you're doing a good job. D.J. cried. I'm not sure she realized how much Mackenzie hates it when she kicks toward her. And when Mackenzie said she was sorry, she meant it."

Marrell nodded.

"Still mad?"

"Furious."

"Maybe we should kiss and make up."

"Maybe we should."

After eleven and a half years it was still fun to flirt with her husband, who was already headed around the table. Marrell's heart warned her that she had better enjoy it now. In a month's time, when he was getting settled into a new posting, he would be distracted with the new job.

The Bishops' first day in the city that was to be their new home was spectacular. The June sun was warm over a cloudless sky, and for once the wind was tame. Planning to follow directions, they stayed on Highway 101, which swung them down Nineteenth Avenue and actually curved around part of the Presidio before their exit.

"Will we see the Golden Gate Bridge?" Mackenzie wanted to know. When her teacher had learned where she was moving, her class had done a short study on San Francisco. Mackenzie had been most impressed with the bridge.

"I think we probably will," her father told her, "so keep your eyes open."

Moments after he said this, they drove off the highway, sat for half a minute at the light with dozens of other vehicles, and then drove down Nineteenth where the sights grew a little more interesting.

"Look at that," Delancey said, pointing to a man on a corner. His blond Afro appeared to stand a foot off his head, and his face was painted in bold colors. He played the violin as if he were on stage at the Met.

"Don't point," Marrell reminded her, but her eyes were glued to the man as well.

Had they not been so distracted, they might have noticed the lush greenery along the way. A large variety of trees and bushes sprang up on either side, and in the midst of this lay their new home.

They were stopped at the gate, where Paul surrendered his papers and was handed a map and shown directions. The guard saluted and was very courteous, and the new officer at the post thanked

44

him before moving on. Marrell's and the girls' heads turned this way and that as they tried to take it all in.

They hadn't been told much about their new dwelling, but the base administration knew that Paul had a wife and two daughters. They had lived in some base housing that was very nice and other base housing that they were only too happy to leave. Their apartment in Texas had been very comfortable, but a third bedroom would have been handy.

Several minutes passed as Paul found his way around. Marrell and the girls waited in the car while he reported to the head office for his keys and directions, but it wasn't long before he was back in the car, a 1972 Mustang, consulting the map. After a few moments of study, he headed the car through the hilly terrain of the Presidio yet again. The girls' eyes were huge as they tried to take it in all at one time, but before they could anticipate much more, the car came to a smooth halt on Infantry Terrace. Their father had no more shut off the engine when they bounded out the doors. This was their new home and it looked *big!*

"Well, this is the place," Paul said to Marrell.

"It's beautiful, Paul."

"Yes, and big. They're expecting us at the hospitality barracks tonight, but shall we go inside and see?"

Marrell smiled. "No time like the present."

Paul picked up her hand and led the way up the stairs to the door. He tried to use the key, but the girls made this impossible.

"I'm going to be first, D.J.!"

"You are not!" Delancey answered back, but both girls suddenly found themselves grabbed by

45

the shoulders. When Paul had repositioned them behind their mother, he bent down and spoke firmly to them.

"Your mother is going to be first, and I don't want to hear another word."

He turned back to the door when both girls nodded. He unlocked the door, gave it a push, and looked down at his wife. Marrell smiled up at him and went through the door. Paul could not resist giving her a tap on the seat.

The house was a wonderful surprise. Although a bit musty-smelling, the odor was nothing a few open windows couldn't cure. The entryway was spacious, with hardwood floors that led to a high-ceilinged living room with huge windows.

The girls dashed up the stairs, and Mackenzie's voice could be heard as she shouted about finding four bedrooms. Her mother barely heard. She was in the large kitchen, thinking that her dreams had come true. Never had they had a kitchen this spacious. She opened cupboards and almost reverently touched surfaces and walls.

"The backyard is small," Paul stated as he came back to find her.

"That's all right," she said softly, causing her husband to smile.

The sound of a truck interrupted anything Paul might have said. He glanced out the window and said, "I don't believe it."

"What is it?"

"The moving truck."

"Is it really?"

"Yeah," he said on a laugh and moved toward the door. The men were just climbing from the cab.

"Are we glad to see you."

Marrell didn't go out with him. She had dreaded all of this, but suddenly her heart was very light. She leaned on the counter, a small smile on her face. They were going to be all right. In fact, they were going to be more than all right. They were going to be great!

THREE

"Did you forget my birthday?" Mackenzie asked very suddenly.

For Marrell the world was in an upheaval of boxes and movers, but she made herself stop and pay attention to her daughter.

"No, I did not. I shopped for you in San Antonio and brought everything with me."

"It's next week."

"I know it is. Were you worried?"

"A little."

Marrell smiled down into her eyes. They were an unusual color — a little green with a hint of gray. Her brows were perfect slashes of black, and her lashes, though not overly long, were very thick. Her nose was straight and even, and Marrell suspected that her pretty mouth would tempt many a man by the time she was grown.

"Well, I planned to make spaghetti and chocolate cake. How does that sound?"

"Yummy." Mackenzie beamed at her.

"Now, my almost nine-year-old, I need you to unpack the box that was put in your room. It says 'Toys.' Put everything on the shelves."

"What if they're D.J.'s?"

"Then take them to her."

"Okay. What do I do after that?"

"Come back and check with me when you're finished."

"All right."

Marrell went back to the boxes in the kitchen. She knew that if she didn't find some sheets, the family would never get to bed that night, but she had this "thing" about having her kitchen settled. An Army wife learned early in the game not to keep the superfluous, but in her kitchen she sometimes made exceptions. Paul came in while she was trying to hang a measuring cup rack on the wall. He took over and had it done quickly.

"Thank you."

"You're welcome. How is everything else going?"

"I think okay. Are the movers about done?" Her voice had lowered.

"Over halfway, I would guess. Why?"

"The blond guy keeps looking at my legs."

Paul's eyes dropped to the shapely length of leg that was exposed beneath her cutoffs and then back to her eyes. Marrell knew some men thought it very exciting when other men found their wives attractive. At the moment Mrs. Paul Bishop was never more happy that her husband wasn't one of them.

"I'll shut this door when I go out," Paul said, referring to the door that led out to the hallway at the front door.

"Thank you."

Only too happy to keep other men from ogling his wife, Paul kissed her cheek, exited, and shut the door. Marrell went back to work, only vaguely remembering that Mackenzie had never returned.

Had Marrell been able to see the daughter in question, she would have found her sitting on her

49

unmade bed, just looking around the room. Mackenzie had put her toys on the shelf and even delivered Delancey's to her. Now she just wanted to sit looking at her room. *Her* room.

Her eyes scanned the walls as she decided where she would put her posters. She had one of a kitten with a ball of string, another of a huge yellow smiley-face, an Army recruiting poster, and her favorite: a close-up poster of the Monkees. Delancey had one of a smiling Davy Jones on his own, but Mackenzie liked everyone in the group.

In planning what she would do with the four posters, the fact that her mother wanted her back slid from her mind. There was so much space on all the walls, and over her bed seemed to be a perfect spot. Her eyes even went to the ceiling. In the middle of this contemplation, her father walked in.

"Hey, soldier, why isn't your bed made?"

Mackenzie grinned at him. "I don't have sheets yet, Dad."

"I guess that's as good a reason as any." He sat down on her bed and looked around. "Your own room. Just what you wanted."

"D.J. has her own room too."

"Yes. I was just in there. She's still arranging her stuffed animals on her shelf. Why did you put your toys on only the bottom shelf?"

"Because the other shelves are for my books."

"Do you have that many books?"

"No, but I want those on before I move the animals up there."

Paul nodded. "Listen, I'm going to head off to the commissary and scrounge up some grub for dinner. Do you want to come?"

"Yeah. Can D.J. too?"

"Sure, go ask her."

An outing with Dad. *This* was a treat. Mackenzie found Delancey in the kitchen with her mother. The moving men had finally gone.

"Dad's going to get something for dinner. Do you want to come?"

"Yeah, sure. When are we going?"

"Right now. Are you coming, Mom?"

"No, honey. I'm going to stay here and try to put some more things away."

It wasn't an outrageous mess. They didn't have that much, but Marrell wanted the boxes cleared out and their contents put away. Paul had put all of their clothes in the closets and settled things in the dressers. That had been a great help, but the only one who knew how she wanted the kitchen was Marrell, who seemed only too happy to be left on her own to work.

"Can you get some Pepsi and ice, Paul?"

"Sure. What sounds good for dinner?"

"Chicken sounds wonderful. What do you think?"

"Chicken it is. Come on, girls."

"Are you going to get us set for breakfast too?"

"Yes. You can start a list for later, but I'll just get the essentials for tonight."

Marrell knew that the essentials would be doughnuts and chips, but she didn't care. There would be time enough later to shop for what they needed. She was thankful she had opted to put some canned goods, a box of rice, and bags of flour and sugar in one of the boxes so they would have a little to fall back on. A concern about the prices in California ran past her mind, but she pushed it aside.

Stop it, Marrell, she said to herself. *You have*

plenty to do without worrying over something you can't change. With that pep talk she began to attack the boxes in the living room.

Hours later the beds were made, dinner was eaten, and Marrell had heard all about the spectacular view of the Golden Gate Bridge from the parking lot of the commissary. Paul had cleaned the kitchen, and Marrell felt free to collapse on the sofa. There was an open box next to her, and on the top was a photo album. Tired as she was, the thought of paging through it made her smile. She picked it up and started at the beginning. As if by magic, her family joined her. Delancey first, then Mackenzie and Paul.

"What is that?" Delancey wanted to know as she looked at one of the pictures. It was a beach scene.

"That is a lifeguard station. Some beaches have lifeguards, and in order to see the water, they sit up high to keep a lookout."

"Look at that," Mackenzie giggled, her finger on another photo. "There's a dog on your skirt, Mom."

Marrell laughed too. "That is a poodle skirt I wore just a few years ago. Your dad and I were going to a costume party."

"Where is that skirt?" Paul asked.

"I think it's in the box I sent to my grandma's when we moved to Texas."

"We could have seen it last Christmas," Mackenzie said, sounding disappointed.

"Well, maybe next time we go."

"When will we go again?"

"I don't know. We'll have to wait and see."

"Where did you get it?" Mackenzie seemed the

most fascinated.

"I made it. Your dad's shirt too."

The girls peered at the picture again.

"Will you make one for me?" Mackenzie asked.

"Me too?"

"Well, maybe I will. They would certainly make cute Halloween costumes."

The girls exchanged smiles. While they would not have thought of this, neither were they going to argue.

They paged through the rest of the photo album, and when they closed the cover, it seemed like a perfect end to the day. It had been a full one, so neither girl argued when told to ready for bed. Had the truth been told, they were rather excited — their first night in their own rooms. Both Marrell and Paul kissed them, and within moments they were asleep.

The elder Bishops were just as tired, and once they retired, sleep held them completely unaware of the way Delancey awoke, somewhere near midnight, and sought her sister.

"Micki," she said softly.

"Um . . ."

"Micki, wake up."

"What?"

"I want to sleep with you."

"Um" was all Mackenzie could manage, but she still scooted toward the wall. Delancey climbed in, snuggled close, and was back asleep in just a matter of seconds. It was morning before Mackenzie would be awake enough to be indignant.

Paul's first day on the job gave him a headache. Army procedures were the same everywhere, but his job was new to him, and certain variations, as well as the basic need to learn new faces and names, made for a day of some stress. He worked two hours past his scheduled time, and by the time he arrived home, he was ready for quiet.

His daughters had other ideas. Map in hand, Marrell had taken the girls to see their new school building, for a walk across the Golden Gate Bridge, shopping on Pier 39, and for a visit to the Ghirardelli Square, where they had sundaes at the chocolate shop. Both small Bishops wanted to sit in their father's lap and tell him all about it. Paul was not overjoyed, but it was some time before the girls caught on to his closed eyes and still position.

"What's the matter?"

"I'm tired."

"Come on, girls." Their mother had come in in time to hear Paul. "Head to your rooms for a little while."

The girls obeyed, but both looked a little hurt.

"As bad as all that?" Marrell confronted him, none too happy.

"I just have a headache."

"And they just wanted to tell you about their day."

The two stared at each other.

Marrell was the first to offer the olive branch. "Do you want something to eat?"

"Yes, please. The girls can come and talk to me when I'm done."

The evening improved on that note. There was a children's special on TV, and they all watched it before the girls were invited to climb on Paul's back and be carried off to bed. Paul even apologized to Marrell for his mood when he'd arrived home. Marrell was sensitive and asked him all about his day. She was very pleased that, bad day or not, he knew he was going to enjoy his new posting and even like his commanding officers. The evening ended with talk about Mackenzie's birthday. It was just three days away, and Marrell wanted it to be extra special. The plans were made before they slept, and Marrell had Paul's word that he would be home on time.

Mackenzie was speechless as she stared at the pink Jeep in the box. She had wanted a Barbie Jeep for as long as she could remember. And there was not only a Jeep, but two new Barbie outfits from the store and five more that her mother had made.

She finally found her voice and threw her arms around her parent. "Oh, Mom, thank you. I love it."

"Look at this one, Micki," Delancey spoke up, fingering a tiny pair of shorts and a top their mother had made. "It's the same color as the shorts she made us."

"Oh, Mom," Mackenzie said again when Delancey held up some shoes that the older girl hadn't seen the first time.

"Looks like you scored big," Paul said from across the room, his left eyelid dropping in a wink.

Marrell smiled, but she was thinking about the way she'd almost gone blind making some of those outfits. She wasn't sure she would try it again, but it had been fun.

"Now is it time for cake?" Mackenzie asked.

"Yes," Marrell said indulgently. Her daughter's eyes had been like moons over the new things, but like a typical child, was ready to move on to the next event. Delancey was no different: While they were still eating their cake, she began to talk of her own birthday, which was just a month away. Marrell had to stifle a groan when she requested her own Barbie doll and homemade clothes as well. Marrell cleaned up the dishes, wondering if she'd created a monster.

The middle of July came and went, and as the month stretched on, Marrell thought of Sharon Elliott more and more. The thought of seeing her and being uncomfortable about her breakup with Marty was more than Marrell could stand, but on impulse and before she could change her mind, she wrote to her, explained their move to the Presidio, and even included her address and phone number. The call wasn't long in coming.

"Marrell, it's Shay."

"Oh, Shay!" Marrell felt as though she could cry. It had been years since she'd heard her friend's voice. "How are you?"

"I'm absolutely fabulous. I can't believe you're in San Francisco."

"Amazing, isn't it?" Marrell laughed. "When my grandmother told me you had moved here, I was stunned."

"When can I see you?" Shay asked, cutting right to the chase.

"Name a day."

"This weekend. Come to my place Sunday morning."

"All right."

"Your address is the Presidio — you must still be married to that handsome lieutenant."

"He's a lieutenant colonel now."

"Ooooh," Shay said with a laugh. "And you have two or three kids?"

"Two girls. Mackenzie and Delancey."

"Great names. How old are they?"

"Mackenzie was nine last month, and Delancey was eight on Monday."

"Bring them on Sunday."

"No," Marrell said in no uncertain terms. "You can meet them some other time. I want to catch up with you on my own."

"All right. Let me give you directions to my place."

Marrell found paper and a pencil with a chewed-off eraser and took down notes. She went over them again before ringing off, and after putting the phone down, reached for the map, her heart pounding in anticipation. In the midst of her excitement, she realized it had been weeks since she'd done something on her own. She had gotten together with friends before leaving San Antonio but hadn't really made any new friends here. She didn't know if Paul would be very excited about her leaving the family on a Sunday, but this was necessary.

Her daughters chose that moment to start shouting at each other. Marrell set her pencil down in order to look into it. She was calm enough on the outside, but inside her heart was vastly different. *Don't even think about telling me I shouldn't see Shay on Sunday, Paul. I need a break from this house and the girls, even if I have to take the bus to get it.*

Sharon Elliott's second-story apartment on Lombard Street was surprisingly easy to find, since Lombard Street was one of the streets that led directly into the Presidio. Marrell arrived right on time and was able to park without mishap, but her heart beat a little too swiftly as she rang the doorbell. She need not have worried. Shay looked older, but she was still the same — a bit zany in her dress and hairstyle but still lovely and warm.

"Marrell!" she cried, coming right onto the step to hug her. "How are you?"

"I'm fine." Marrell felt tears sting the back of her throat.

The women embraced for a long moment and the years fell away. Moments later Shay led the way inside, where Marrell was in for a surprise. Shay's apartment, actually the entire top story of a house, was beautiful. Shay's jeans were well patched, her shirt was a loud orange, and her red hair was as frizzy as a bird's nest, but her home was that of a professional with surprising style and taste.

"Come in. Sit down."

"Thank you," Marrell returned as she sank into an overstuffed leather chair, her purse going to the floor beside her. "This is beautiful, Shay."

Shay had settled across from her and now looked around in pleasure. "I like it," she admitted, "and I'm not far from work."

"What are you doing these days?"

"I can tell you're new in The City," she said with a proud smile, "or you would surely have heard of Elliott and Associates, San Francisco's finest new architectural firm."

"Sounds so professional."

Shay inclined her head modestly, giving complete lie to the way she'd just bragged. Marrell smiled at her, but with the mention of architecture, her mind shot to Marty. Marrell was asking herself if she should say something, but before she could, Shay started to question her.

"How did you end up in San Francisco?"

Marrell reminded Shay of the way she'd met Paul, and then explained how they had moved with his career.

"How many times have you moved?"

"Let's see . . . this is our third."

"In how many years?"

"We've been married eleven and a half years."

"So you just go wherever he goes?"

"Sure," Marrell answered easily, but she knew what her friend was thinking.

Shay studied her. "Not very progressive, but I can see you're happy."

"I am happy, Shay," Marrell told her. And she meant it.

A short but not uncomfortable silence fell between them, so Marrell took a moment to look around. In doing so she spotted a photo of Shay and Marty. A simple snapshot but beautifully framed, it sat on a bookshelf by the window. For a moment Marrell wondered if her grandmother had heard wrong.

Shay had been watching her and now spoke up.

"I can see you've spotted the picture."

"Yes," Marrell admitted. "My grandmother told me that you'd split up. Did she hear wrong?"

"No. We're divorced." Shay's eyes went to the photo. "I don't hate him, but I can't live with him."

"I'm sorry, Shay."

"Thank you, Marrell." She appreciated far more than she could say that her friend did not gush and carry on. "I was pretty shaken for a time, but I think I've got my head on straight now."

"That's good to hear."

"You don't know how good," Shay said ruefully. "You can't believe the crazy things I was into. Transcendental meditation, group therapy, drugs, water therapy, even a therapy that encouraged me to release my inner feelings."

"What did that entail?" Marrell asked, a bit afraid of the answer.

"It was weird. At the time I had a van that I drove, and when I just couldn't cope anymore, I pulled to the side of the road, got in the back, and screamed until I was hoarse. It helped for a while, but when I finally sold the van, it was a great relief."

Marrell was stunned speechless but managed to keep the surprise from her face. Shay went on as if this was all completely normal.

"Now I have a great therapist. He's a wonderful man, and he's helped me to see that none of this was my fault. It wasn't Marty's fault either. We just couldn't make a go of it, and there really wasn't much we could do about that. Right now my business is booming, and I'm happier than I've ever been in my life."

Marrell nodded, but she wasn't sure she agreed. Marriages didn't break up because no one was at fault, but she didn't think now was the time to voice that opinion.

"So what do you do with yourself all day?" Shay asked. "Hey," she cut in before Marrell could even start, sitting up very straight in her chair, "you were the best typist in class, Marrell. You wouldn't want a job, would you? I can't get good office help for love or money."

Marrell laughed. "I'm not looking for a job, Shay, but thank you."

"Are you sure? It wouldn't need to be full time. Not to mention that everyone in the office would love your accent."

Marrell ignored the part about her voice. "I'm

very sure I don't want a job in your office. I don't want anyone else seeing to my girls. Maybe when they're older, but not now."

"The salary's good."

Marrell shook her head. "It doesn't matter."

Shay pulled a face but then smiled. "I can see I'll never convince you. I guess I'll just have to offer you an espresso."

Marrell laughed at her change of thought and rose to follow her to the kitchen. This room was another surprise. It looked as if Shay enjoyed cooking. Marrell did not expect that. The architect had shelves of cookbooks, and pots and pans hung everywhere. As if it were an everyday occurrence, she pulled forth an espresso machine and began the process. Marrell felt immediately out of her element. She'd never had an espresso and wasn't sure she would like it. From the little Marrell had seen of San Francisco, she suspected Shay fit right in. She wasn't sure she ever would.

"Do you like espresso?" Shay suddenly asked her.

"I don't know," Marrell answered honestly, and Shay looked at her for a long moment.

"It's easy to see why you're happy, Marrell." Her voice was so serious that the other woman blinked.

"Why is that?"

"Your honesty. Anyone that straightforward has nothing to hide."

"You make it sound like you do."

Shay stared at her for a moment and then down at the machine. "I'm not as happy as I'd like you to believe." Shay wasn't prepared to go on, but when she looked up, Marrell's look was one of such compassion that she blurted the rest out.

61

"My therapist! It's getting serious between us, and I don't know what to do."

"You don't want to be married again?"

Shay looked utterly miserable as she said, "He's already married."

Marrell did nothing to hide her disapproval. "You can't do that, Shay, and that's the end of it."

"I don't even know why I'm telling you all of this," she suddenly burst out. "We don't even know each other anymore."

"We'll always know each other," Marrell insisted, "and besides that, you know what's right and wrong. Put yourself in his wife's shoes. How do you think it will make her feel?"

"I know how it will make her feel," Shay replied dully. "Marty already did it to me."

Marrell could have wept on the spot. "Turn that machine off," she ordered quietly. "Come back to the living room."

Expecting to be followed, Marrell walked out. Her voice was the one she used when the girls needed help but any comfort would dissolve them to tears. She had a few things to say to her friend, and she would say them even if they got her kicked out the front door. They took their original seats, and Marrell speared Shay with her eyes.

"You will call this man today and tell him you can't see him anymore. If he won't take you at your word, you change your phone number. If he has a key to this place, you get the locks changed. You can't do this, Sharon. It's wrong, and you know it is. You can call me naive or say I'm not progressive, but I know the type of thing that can destroy a person, and you're right in the middle of it."

"I don't know if I can do that." Tears had come

to Shay's eyes but were not spilling over.

"Yes, you can. Have you been intimate with him?" The question was fired like a shot.

"No, but we're going away next weekend together."

"Cancel it, Shay. Tell him you've changed your mind." Marrell's hand slashed through the air. "What kind of man takes advantage of his client? That's completely unprofessional."

"But he's helped me so much." Her voice was that of a lost child.

"Maybe he has, Shay," Marrell said, her voice softening as well, "but this is clearly wrong, or you wouldn't have told me you're not as happy as you'd like me to believe."

Shay lost it then. Marrell watched as her friend sobbed into her hands. She had come today not knowing what to expect but hoping they could renew their friendship. Never would she have imagined this. Marrell slipped across the rug then and knelt by Shay's chair. She rubbed her friend's arm and spoke with soft conviction.

"Right now it feels horrible, Shay, but it's the right thing to do. You don't want a man, no matter how wonderful he seems, who could treat his wife this way. Don't let him hurt you the way he's hurting his wife."

Shay cried some more but then began to gain some control. Marrell remained quiet until Shay turned angry eyes on her.

"I suppose you want me to leave."

"No." Shay's voice was tight. "I'm just so angry at myself. I do this every time. When am I going to get it right?"

When indeed? Marrell ached for her friend but didn't know what else she could say. She would

63

have offered to make the espresso herself but had no idea how. The phone rang in the middle of her thoughts.

"That'll be Dante."

"Your therapist?"

"Yes."

"I'll go, Shay."

"No. Please stay, Marrell. I'm going to tell him, and I would like you here when I'm finished."

Marrell nodded and watched while Shay rose and left the room. The ringing stopped a moment later, and Marrell could hear Shay's voice from another room, presumably the bedroom. She couldn't catch the words, but she didn't want to listen anyway. For the longest time she just studied the pattern on the oriental rug, still in shock over all that had transpired. To keep from pacing, Marrell finally picked up a glossy magazine from the coffee table and began to page through it. How much time passed she wasn't sure, but when Shay returned, she was pale and solemn.

"Are you all right?" Marrell asked, putting the periodical aside.

"Not right now, but I will be. When I heard his voice I almost lost it, but I told him it's over."

It was on the tip of Marrell's tongue to ask what he said, but she didn't feel it was her place. She had pushed in enough as it was. Shay surprised her by telling all.

"I don't think he believed me at first, but I was calm and finally got through to him. He's not angry, but I'm sure he's thinking I just need a little time to come around. I wonder what he'll say when I don't show up for our session on Tuesday night."

"Do you think he'll call here?"

"Yes."

"Come to dinner. Meet Paul and the girls. We'd love to have you. When you get home, unplug your phone."

For an instant Shay wanted to lash out at her. Marrell made it sound so simple, but Shay's world was falling apart. Deep inside, however, was a peace that Shay hadn't known since the first time she'd gone into Dante's office. They had been attracted to each other from the start, and the picture of Dante's wife and children on the desk only mocked her, even when she became practiced at ignoring them. But none of this was Marrell's fault, and Shay had no right to lash out at her. If she hadn't wanted her advice, she should have kept her mouth shut about the situation.

Before she could change her mind, Shay stuffed the pain deep inside and asked what time she should come.

"Come right after work. We'll eat at 6:00."

"All right. Shall I bring something?"

"No. Cooking is not my strongest point, but I won't poison you."

Shay smiled. "I'm ready for that espresso. How about you?"

"Only if you're up to it, Shay," Marrell said gently. "Maybe you'd rather I leave."

"I'll understand if you want to."

Marrell's head went to one side in thought. "I had hoped that we could renew our friendship, Shay, I had hoped very much. I must be honest and tell you I never expected this, but that doesn't mean I'm ready to walk away. We were best friends at one time, and I'll always love you. I'm sorry for this hurt in your life, but I'll be even more sorry if you need me and I'm not there."

Tears welled in Shay's eyes, but she bit her lip to keep them at bay. Motioning with her head, she led the way back to the kitchen. Less than an hour later the women sat across the table from each other — salads, rolls, and hot coffee in front of them. Their conversation had ranged to all topics, and even to the most painful one for Shay, but at no time did walls come up or uncomfortable silences fall.

After so many years, neither one could say that it was as if no time had passed — too much had gone on for that. They would never be girls again, but by the time Marrell was ready to leave, the ties were back in place.

"What will you do with yourself for the rest of the day?"

"Take a long walk," Shay told her, "and then cry the rest of the afternoon."

Marrell nodded and hugged her.

"I'll see you Tuesday night."

"Yes. I'll come right from the office."

Marrell turned with a wave, but not before Shay called to her.

"Next time you come, I'll actually make you that espresso."

FOUR

Marrell had been gone for only 20 minutes when Shay's landlady, who also lived below her, knocked on the door. Shay's plan had been to walk and then cry; it hadn't worked that way. As soon as Rose Cumberland saw her face, she knew something was wrong. Keeping her tone casual, she said, "Here's the bowl I borrowed."

"Oh, thanks, Rose. I have my rent check for you if you can wait a second."

"Sure."

The landlady stood patiently, her heart in quiet contemplation over what she'd seen on Shay's face. The lady in question was back just minutes later, and it was then that Rose noticed her running shoes and shorts.

"Are you off for a run?"

"Just a walk."

"I haven't gone today. Do you want company?"

Before Shay could answer, the phone rang. She turned and looked at it, but made herself look away.

"Can you go now?" She sounded almost frightened.

"Yeah. I just need to change my shoes."

Shay gave a decisive nod, grabbed her keys, and

followed Rose out the door.

Marrell could not get her arms around Paul fast enough. He met her at the front door, and as soon as the door was shut, she hugged him. The girls were trying to talk to her, but she just held on tight. Mackenzie and Delancey eventually wandered back to the living room, leaving their parents in the foyer.

"Bad time?" he whispered in her ear.

"Yes and no. I'll have to tell you later."

It was several more moments before Marrell moved back enough to see his face.

"We're not going to divorce, Paul Bishop," she said, her voice low and urgent. "And we're not going to cheat on each other."

Paul laid his forehead against hers. If the girls hadn't been in the next room, he might have tried to question her, but he would have to wait. He knew she'd been upset over Shay's divorce, but it must have been worse than either of them had suspected.

"Mom," Delancey finally got through; she had been calling from the living room. "Where did you go?"

Marrell made herself turn and address her. "To my friend's house," she answered patiently, even though she had already told them where she was going before she left. "You'll meet her on Tuesday when she comes to dinner."

Marrell glanced at Paul when she said this and watched him nod.

"What's her name?"

"Shay. Mrs. Elliot to you."

"Who's Mrs. Elliot?" Mackenzie wanted to know.

"A friend of mine."

"Does she have kids?"

"No," Marrell answered and changed the subject before they could go on. "What did you two do today? Did you take good care of Daddy?"

Delancey came uncorked, but Mackenzie was oddly quiet. The younger girl rattled on about something they had watched on TV. Marrell waited until she was finished and then asked Mackenzie how she was doing. She only shrugged in response. Marrell turned questioning eyes to Paul.

"D.J. broke Micki's Barbie Jeep. It's not completely ruined, but it has a big crack."

Marrell turned compassionate eyes to her oldest daughter. "I'm sorry, Micki. Did you cry?"

She hadn't, but tears that had been squelched then now filled her eyes. She came into her mother's arms, and Paul, with a hand to Delancey's back, took the other little girl from the room.

Marrell, dressed in nice slacks and a blouse, never hesitated. She sank down to hold Mackenzie right where they were.

"I don't like it when you're gone all morning," Mackenzie admitted when she could talk, her nose still drippy.

"I know, but I had a good time, and I haven't seen my friend in a long time. In fact, she offered me a job in her office, but I told her no because I wanted to be home with my little girls."

Mackenzie smiled, and Marrell kissed her cheek.

"Now, tell me something fun that you did."

"Dad took us down to play tennis. D.J. went first and then me, and then D.J. and I played each other."

"Are you getting better at hitting the ball?"

"Sorta. I think D.J. hits it more than I do." A competitive frown lowered the nine-year-old's brow, and Marrell smiled.

"Did y'all have lunch?"

"No, and I'm hungry."

With Shay's face suddenly in her mind, Marrell hugged Mackenzie. Remembering how painful the morning had been, she knew that no job she might need to perform for her children and husband would cause her to complain.

"So how was it?"

Night had finally come. Paul and Marrell were alone in the living room. Only one light burned. Marrell was on the sofa and Paul in an overstuffed chair. The light was on Marrell's face, and Paul was watching his wife, much as he'd done all afternoon. She had played with the girls and been completely normal for them, but he had seen the pain.

"It was hard, Paul," Marrell began softly. She was silent for a moment and then continued. "I was so afraid that it would be uncomfortable, and it was, but not because of the divorce. Shay's head is so messed up. She's been into all this trash, ridiculous psychotherapy, and even drugs, and now she's on the verge of having an affair with her therapist."

Paul nodded but wasn't too surprised. Something pretty serious had to have made his wife this upset.

"You probably wouldn't have recognized me," Marrell went on. "I told her how I felt. I decided that I would have my say even if she kicked me out."

A small smile lingered around Paul's mouth. He

would have loved to see her in action.

"What did you say?"

"I can't remember all of it," she admitted. "I know I asked her if they'd already been intimate, and when she said no, I told her to call and break it off with him. You wouldn't have believed it, Paul." Her face was shocked as she remembered it all over again. "He called in the middle of our conversation."

"You're kidding."

"I wish I were. I was ready to leave her so she could talk to him, but she wanted me to stay."

Marrell had run out of words. She laid her head against the sofa back and stared at the ceiling. Paul continued to watch her.

"How did you end up inviting her for dinner Tuesday?"

"I don't think she has anyone," she said before looking at him. "We don't have plans, do we?"

"No, I just wondered. She's not bringing this guy, is she?"

Marrell shook her head. "She broke it off. Right on the phone she told him. Their sessions are usually on Tuesday nights, so I invited her for that night specifically so he can't contact her."

Paul took a moment to compute all of this, remembering the way she had come home and hugged him, the almost desperate way she had held on. Paul wasn't close to anyone other than his wife and girls, but he hurt when they hurt and could well imagine how all of this had affected her.

"Still glad you went?" he asked.

"Yeah. I love her, Paul. And in so many ways she's still the same Shay. Even with all she's been through, I feel so lucky to be in the same town and able to see her." Marrell pulled a sudden face. "She says I have an accent."

"They're saying the same thing to me at work."

Marrell's mouth opened. The women she had met in Texas had had such pronounced accents that she never heard her own.

"Do the girls?"

"I'm sure they do. What's the trauma?"

"I just don't want them teased at school."

"Don't borrow trouble. The other kids may think it's fun."

Marrell was not convinced, but Paul was done talking about Shay, Texas accents, and his daughters.

"Are you tired?" he asked.

"A little."

"How tired?"

There was no missing his tone. Marrell smiled, and with that Paul rose and went to the stereo. Moments later the room was full of the soft sounds of the Glenn Miller Band. Paul held out his hand, and Marrell joined him in the middle of the floor. They danced slowly for the next 40 minutes with little need for conversation.

Not until Marrell had stood had she realized how tired she was, but the photo of Shay and Marty came to mind. *I don't hate the man, I just can't live with him.* With a huge sigh, Marrell moved a little deeper into her husband's embrace.

Marrell was nervous on Tuesday evening. Half of her expected Shay to call and cancel, and the other half hoped she would. How well did she know Shay now? What if she decided she wanted Paul?

Marrell felt horrible for the thought and pushed

72

it away. No matter what Shay had been into, she would not try to entice Paul. Marrell was sure of that. Not to mention Paul; he was not interested in other women. Marrell had always known that. A marriage built on suspicion was no marriage at all.

"How's it going?"

Marrell turned in surprise to find the man of her thoughts standing in the kitchen doorway.

"You're early."

"Yeah. I assumed you were working yourself into a trauma, but I must have been wrong."

"Why do you think you're wrong?"

He shrugged. "The table's set, the house looks great, the girls aren't fighting."

"Well, I'm glad to know that the surface looks good."

Paul came and put his arms around her for that. "What has your imagination dreamed up?"

"That she'll decide she wants my husband next."

"Oh, Mary." Paul's voice was low.

"I'm sorry, Paul. I'm going to give you a horrid impression of her. I love Shay. I wish I hadn't even thought of it."

"I'm sure we'll get along fine. And even if she did put designs on me, there's only one woman I'm interested in."

"I just finished telling myself that."

Paul kissed her. "Where are the girls?"

"They want Shay to see their rooms, so they're fixing them up."

Paul kissed her again. "I'll check on them on the way to the shower. Is there anything else you need?"

"No. You're home, and that's all that matters."

Paul smiled before moving on his way. The clock

73

read 5:20. Shay would be there soon. The lasagna was in the oven, and the salad and dressing were waiting in the refrigerator. She wouldn't do the bread until after Shay arrived. It was one of the few meals she never messed up, but she was still nervous. The sound of water came from upstairs, and she knew Paul was in the shower. The thought calmed her. She didn't have to face this alone. She was glad she'd met Shay again, but if for some reason it didn't work out, she always had her husband and girls. Telling herself she was finally ready to face the evening, Marrell went back to work on the pot she was washing.

"I can't believe how pretty they are, Marrell," Shay said several hours later.

Marrell smiled. Paul had just taken the girls off to bed, and the women had already started their coffee in the living room.

"We think so," Marrell replied, "but we're just a bit biased."

"Mackenzie's huge gray-green eyes and brown hair, and D.J.'s blond hair and blue eyes — I can't believe it. But then you've always been pretty."

Marrell laughed, but then she had been laughing all evening. She had expected Shay to arrive in a sad state, but in truth she'd been in a very good mood. There were moments when Marrell caught a look in her eyes, but Shay was swift to disguise it. Now, however, with no one else looking, Marrell caught sight of the pain that she had masked.

"How are you doing?" Marrell asked for the first time.

"All right." Shay's voice was soft. "He actually came to the office yesterday to see me, but I think

74

I made him see that I was serious. He was upset but didn't cause a scene. I wanted to cry my eyes out after that but didn't and found that I actually had done the right thing."

"I wondered about that. I was prepared to have you call at any moment and tell me that I should have minded my own business and that you never wanted to speak to me again."

"No," Shay shook her head, "I wouldn't have done that. In fact, on Sunday night I called my grandmother and told her everything. She said that little Marrell Walker was the best thing that ever happened to me."

"She's probably still picturing me in grade school."

"Probably, but she's still right, Marrell. I needed someone from outside to tell me to get my act together. My assistant was jubilant when Dante left. She asked me if we'd seen the last of him. It was good to be able to tell her yes."

"I'm so glad, Shay. I hate to see you hurting."

"Well, I do hurt, but I still know I did the right thing."

The women fell silent for a moment, and it wasn't long before Paul joined them. He fixed his own coffee and sat next to Marrell on the sofa.

"I'm impressed," Shay teased him, as she'd been doing to all of them the whole evening.

"With what?"

"That you get your own coffee. My friend Marrell is the most *un*liberated woman I've ever known."

Paul laughed but wasn't going to rise to the bait.

"Did she tell you I offered her a job?"

"Yes. She also told me that she informed you she already had one."

Shay shook her head. "I didn't think there were any couples like you left on the planet."

The Bishops only stared at her, causing her arms to go up in frustration.

"Come on, you guys! You know what I mean. Paul goes to work, and Marrell happily keeps house at a time when women are burning their bras and telling men off. I just don't get it."

Marrell could have told her friend that that was the very reason she was divorced. Shay Elliot didn't understand how love could change a person, but telling her would have been too cruel.

"I think you have a wrong impression of us, Shay," Paul surprised Marrell by saying. "I don't own my wife. She has her own life. I do come home expecting dinner, but if for some reason nothing's made, I don't go into a rage. I work hard to support Marrell and the girls, but I don't expect them to fall at my feet in gratitude every time they see me.

"I didn't tell Marrell that she couldn't work for you, but we both happen to think that our daughters are very important, and if we can make it on my salary, then we at least want one of us to be here with them."

Shay looked at Marrell, her face surprised. "I guess he told me."

"It's true, Shay. We do like things the way they are. That's not to say that the girls never drive me crazy, but don't forget, I didn't grow up with a mother. My grandmother was wonderful, but I want more for Micki and D.J. than I had."

Shay sighed. "Well, you've found something that few people do."

"What's that?"

"True happiness. I envy both of you."

76

"You'll have it too, Shay," Marrell said kindly. "I know you will."

Shay nodded. Paul was still sitting there, but it was as if the women had forgotten him. "You'll think I'm crazy, but I've scheduled an appointment with another therapist."

"Oh, Shay."

"This one's a woman," Shay swiftly put in, "and comes highly recommended."

Marrell's head dipped to one side. "What do you hope she'll tell you?"

The other woman shrugged. "I don't know. Often I feel so empty inside, and I just wish I knew why."

Marrell wouldn't have admitted it for anything, but she often felt the same way.

"Well, if she doesn't help you," Marrell suggested quietly, "don't prolong it. I think some of these counselors have more problems than their patients."

"I've met a few that have, but I'll tell you, Marrell, there's something very special about getting to talk about yourself for a whole hour every week. You don't have to compete with anyone or listen to their problems, and most of the time, I feel very good when I leave."

Marrell nodded, but inside she thought it sounded extremely self-centered. Paul changed the subject and rescued Marrell from having to reply. She refilled everyone's coffee, and the three talked of general things until almost eleven o'clock. When Shay left, they made plans for her to come again the next week.

Shay was all the way to the car before she gave in to her tears. *Why,* she asked herself all the way home, *can't I have a happy life like theirs? What's wrong with me that I'm always on the outside look-ing in?* No answers came to Shay's tortured mind, and she drove home in a fit of despondency.

The phone was ringing when she walked in the door, and without thought she picked it up. Rage exploded inside of her when she heard Dante's voice, and after calling him a few choice names, she slammed the phone back into its cradle. When she realized what she'd done, she burst into fresh tears, but her anger had done the trick. She did not hear from Dante Casale again.

"What if none of the other girls will play with me?"

"They will, D.J. You'll see." Marrell's voice was kind, but her heart was preoccupied. They had been shopping for the school clothes Marrell didn't care to make, and at the moment she was just plain tired.

"Can Micki come into my class?"

"No, honey, she's a year ahead of you. You know that won't work."

"I'll probably see you at recess," Mackenzie offered. She wasn't all that interested in comforting her sister, but with Delancey's surfacing fears came Mackenzie's. This was the first time they had ever been forced to change schools. She liked her school and her teacher in San Antonio. The year hadn't even started yet, but she feared it could be awful.

"Mackenzie, are you listening to me?"

"What?"

"I asked whether you tried these jeans on."

"Yeah. They're fine."

"Well, they have them in black. Do you want a black pair?"

"I do," Delancey spoke up.

"She asked me, D.J. Yes, I do."

Delancey's tongue came out the minute her mother's back was turned, but Mackenzie ignored her.

"Now, I think you need new nightgowns too. You can't go to Shay's looking like a rag bag."

"When do we go?"

"Saturday."

"This Saturday?" Mackenzie asked.

"What day is this?" Delancey wanted to know.

"This is Thursday, and you'll be staying the night at Shay's in just two days."

The girls' irritation was put aside. They exchanged smiles and thought about all that Shay had told them they would do.

Shay Elliot had become something of a fixture at the Bishop house. She came at least once a week for dinner and stopped by other times just to visit or bring ice cream and cookies. Their mother said she was getting fat with all of Shay's goodies, but the girls hoped it would never end. Now the big weekend had come.

Paul and Marrell's twelfth anniversary was Sunday, August 28. The girls were going to spend Saturday night at Shay's, her gift to the couple, so they could be alone for most of the weekend. Marrell was thrilled with the offer, and the girls were ecstatic over everything Shay had promised them — television for as late as they wanted and anything they cared to eat, even in bed. It was a little girl's dream come true.

"Okay, I think we're all set. We need to get home. Your dad will be arriving, and I forgot to leave a note."

Once in the car, the girls said they were starving. Too tired to even speak, Marrell didn't need much coaxing before she agreed to pick up fried chicken. Paul was glad to see them and always up for chicken. He teased his wife, however, when she told him how much money she'd saved shopping for the girls' clothes on sale.

"So you stop and buy take-out chicken and cancel out all your savings."

Marrell opened her mouth and shut it again. She had no argument, and all she wanted to do was giggle. He was still teasing her when the meal was over, but with a little food in her, Marrell was ready to fight back.

"I bought a new nightgown to wear on Saturday night, Paul Bishop," she said softly as they cleared the table. "But if you don't stop teasing me, I'll just take it back."

With two sentences, her eyes holding his, the issue was settled. Looking much like a Boy Scout, Paul's hand went in the air. "I won't say another word."

FIVE

The first day of school arrived as everyone knew it would. The school looked larger than ever, but unlike the mob scene in the girls' minds, kids were clustered in small groups, and some were even standing alone. Another misconception was put to rest when Marrell parked the car and got out with the girls. Delancey thought they would be dropped at the curb. Her mother walked calmly across the schoolyard, a daughter on either side of her, and moved toward Mackenzie's room. Checking the list of names by the door just to be certain, Marrell first dropped off Mackenzie and then a pale Delancey.

She made herself leave the girls in the hands of their competent teachers, relieved that she was meeting Shay in just a few hours.

"Well, how did they do?" Shay asked Marrell.

"Micki seemed fine, but D.J. was just about sick with nerves. It helped that her teacher was very kind and waiting right outside the door for the students."

The women were going to lunch. Marrell had gone to Shay's office, and now Shay was driving them to one of her favorite restaurants on the pier.

"Did Delancey ask to stay home?"

"Oh, yes."

Shay chuckled. "I remember doing the same thing. I was always so frightened on the first day of school."

"But you didn't change schools."

"No, I didn't, and that's the weird thing about it. I felt that way, you know, sick and nervous, at the beginning of every school year. I always had it in my head that all my friends had moved away and I would be all alone. I should have talked to Delancey and told her I know how she feels."

"Well, I hope everything goes well. Even as I said to her that everyone would like her, I remembered how cruel kids could be. At least she likes her teacher."

They were at the restaurant now, and since Shay was recognized, they were seated at a good table by the window, giving them a perfect view of the bay and the sailboats on the water. Several people stopped to speak with Shay, but Marrell was hungry and kept her face in the menu.

"What's good, Shay? I'm starved."

"The crab salad is excellent. It gives me fish breath, so I don't eat it if a client is coming in, but I love it."

"Sounds good." Marrell closed the menu. "That and iced tea, and I'm all set."

"I'll do the same, I guess." The women put the menus aside, and Shay asked, "What was Paul doing today?"

"I think the same as usual. He enjoys his work, and sometimes it takes him out of the office, but I don't usually hear about it until he gets home. He tried to set up a helicopter ride for the girls before school started but had to put it off until October. They don't know about it yet, but they'll love it."

"I'm so glad you mentioned October. My landlady, Rose, I think you met her —"

"Yes, I did."

"Well, her church is having a women's seminar, and she really wants me to go, but I don't want to. It would be easier if you would go with me."

"Shay, why would you attend something that holds no interest for you?"

Shay looked frustrated. "She's been a friend and a great landlady, and she's always so kind. I think if I just go to one thing at her church, she'll understand that I'm not into religion and won't ask anymore."

"I've done that," Marrell admitted, her nose wrinkling in self-disgust. "I've attended something just to get someone off my back. You know what you should do, Shay? Go to one service with her. That will do the trick. Why waste a whole Saturday or a weekend when you could take care of it with one service?"

"That's a good idea. Maybe I'll do that. Do you and Paul go to church?"

"No. I didn't grow up with it, and neither did Paul, so he's not interested. I want the girls to make their own choices and not have Paul and me preaching to them. Not too many years ago my grandmother started to attend church with a neighbor, but she doesn't speak of it much. We went with her when we were there for Christmas, but I think it's better if we all have our own beliefs. If there is a heaven and God can see us, He must know that we've tried hard and done our best on this earth. I don't think any one religion has all the answers."

"That's not what Rose would say," Shay commented as she put sugar in her tea. "She says the

Bible is the bottom-line authority."

Marrell shrugged.

The subject was cut short when the waiter delivered their salads, but the conversation stayed on Shay's mind long after they had eaten, driven back to Shay's office, and gone their separate ways.

"And there's a boy from my karate class, and my teacher, Mr. Austin, takes karate too."

Marrell smiled. Delancey had not stopped talking since she climbed into the car.

"And one of these days he's going to have Carl and me come and do a demonstration."

"I'm so glad, honey. I thought about you all day. How did things go for you, Micki?"

"Pretty good. Mrs. Grace says we do lots of reading — at least one book report a month and extra credit if we do more."

"You'll get extra credit, won't you, Micki?" Marrell said with a smile in her voice, and Mackenzie's little heart swelled with pleasure. She was good in math, reading, and writing, and loved it when her parents noticed.

"I need a paint shirt," Delancey said.

"Oh," Mackenzie put in as well, "I do too."

"Okay. We'll dig around in your father's clothes tonight and see if we can come up with something."

The girls were quiet after that, and Marrell found she was thankful. It was a lot of work worrying about her children. Delancey had been on her mind the entire day. A good first day did not mean that the entire year would run smoothly, but it was a relief. At any rate, the girls were off to a good start.

"Have you ever seen anything so cute in your entire life?" Marrell said softly to Paul, who could only smile.

Up at an amazing hour, the girls were ready for school and dressed in the red poodle skirts their mother had made them for Halloween. Thin sweaters — one white and the other a pale pink — white sneakers and socks, ponytails, and a bit of lipstick completed the ensemble.

"Where did you find those sweaters?"

"At a charity store for a dollar apiece."

Paul shook his head in wonder. The girls looked adorable. They had begged their mother to put a record on, and they were now in the living room doing their own version of "The Hop."

"Okay, you two," Paul called to them, "I'm going to get the camera, so get ready to smile."

In complete "ham" style, the girls struck poses that made their parents howl with laughter.

"Grandma's going to love these," Marrell said truthfully as Paul captured a few candid shots.

"I'll have to take them to the office with me. No one would believe me otherwise."

"Speaking of the office, you had better head out."

Paul looked at his watch, pressed the camera into Marrell's hands, moved to kiss the girls, and then back to kiss his wife.

"We never did get to finish our conversation last night," he said as she walked him to the door.

"No, I was too tired and emotional. Besides, I don't think there's anything more to talk about. It's all my fault. I told Shay to go to church with

85

Rose, and now she hasn't missed a Sunday. She just runs from one thing to the next, Paul. When is she going to grow up?"

"Maybe this will really help her."

Marrell shook her head. "She thinks it can help everyone. She wants us to go to church with her too."

Paul grinned. "Well, maybe we should just go one time and get her off our backs."

Marrell laughed before Paul kissed her and then stood in the doorway to wave him off. Her smile died swiftly when the door was shut, however. Shay's actions of late, or rather her lack of actions, were very hard for Marrell. She had thought their friendship was in full swing, but now Shay was coming around less and less. With the girls in school all day, she was just plain lonely. Paul came home for lunch often, but Marrell found herself with time on her hands and the familiar empty ache back inside her.

"Well, Shay has stopped seeing her therapist — maybe I should book an appointment."

"Who are you talking to, Mom?" Mackenzie wanted to know.

"Just myself, Micki," she answered honestly. "We'd better get ready to go."

The girls, so excited about their costumes, needed little urging. Ten minutes later they were on their way to the bus stop. They bounced up the steps with the other children, much too keyed up to hear their mother's soft sigh.

"You haven't mentioned your friend Marrell in a couple of weeks, Shay," one of the women in the circle said. "Is everything all right?"

"I don't know," Shay answered honestly. "She

86

has no interest in church or in Jesus Christ, and things are a little strained between us right now. I guess I felt it was best not to see her at all if it was going to be so uncomfortable."

Shay was part of a women's Bible study that met on Thursday nights. Just five weeks before, she had taken Marrell's advice and gone to church with Rose. What she heard had turned her world upside down.

All of the professionals had told her that nothing was her fault. The man at the front of the room that morning said that all people sinned. The counselors had told her she was a victim. The pastor said Jesus Christ was a victim by choice, and because of His sacrifice, we never had to pay eternally for our sins. Shay had been stunned speechless. Her plan to attend and divert Rose backfired in her face. She had kept Rose for hours that afternoon, asking her one question after another.

It had been her plan to ask Rose questions that were sure to put her on the spot, but all such arrogance left her. When she couldn't sleep that night, she opened the paperback New Testament the pastor had given her and read the book of Luke.

Sharon Elliot was never so taken with anyone the way she was taken with the life of Jesus Christ. He was amazing. She read with horror and delight, with tears and joy, to the last chapter, where Jesus Himself said in verses 25 and 26: *O foolish men and slow of heart to believe in all that the prophets have spoken! Was it not necessary for the Christ to suffer these things and to enter into His glory?* And further on in verses 46 and 47 He spoke again: *Thus it is written, that the Christ should suffer and rise again from the dead the third day; and that repentance for forgiveness of sins should be proclaimed in His name to all the nations.*

Shay had felt the air leave her in a rush. She was a sinner. It was clear to her for the first time. She didn't care how anyone else might take this. It was crystal clear to her. Jesus Himself had said that this was the very reason He had to die. How arrogant she had been! At the moment, however, Shay had never felt so small and unimportant. She was so proud of her business and her lovely furnishings and clothing, but in light of who God was and what His Son had done, they were nothing.

With a heart wrung with desperation, Shay had prayed and told God that she needed rescuing. She had told God she was ready to repent and be forgiven.

"All this time," she prayed softly as she sat on the edge of the bed, her eyes closed, "I thought that bad things just happened to good people, but there's nothing good about me. I need You, God, and I never knew it. Please forgive me; please let me share in the life You've given to Rose and the others at her church. Please, God, forgive my sins and make me Your child."

Shay hadn't slept for hours after that, but when the alarm rang she was not tired. She readied for work, hoping that Rose's curtains would be open and she would be up. Still in shock when she rang her neighbor's bell, Shay blurted out what she'd done. Rose had hugged her gently and not been able to stem the tears. After hearing the whole story, she had also advised her to get involved in one of the church's Bible studies. Just three days later Shay attended one for the first time.

"Does spending time with Marrell cause you to sin, Shay?" asked Mrs. Timm, the pastor's wife, who led the study.

"No, but it's like we don't have anything to talk about anymore."

The older woman was thoughtful for a moment. "There is a barrier between believers and the world, Shay, but we have to be careful not to cut ourselves off. If Marrell still wants to see you and be with you, that's wonderful. She'll learn more from watching you than anything else. For that reason, I think you should try to keep the friendship alive. If Marrell is involved in things that will drag you down spiritually, then you're wise to stay away. We'll be praying for wisdom for you. God will show you what to do."

"Thank you," Shay said sincerely, listening while a few more women shared. The routine was to start the evening with prayer and then continue on in their study of Romans. It was not the easiest book for Shay to comprehend, but she was learning things about herself as well as God. One of the greatest helps to her, however, was not in the study itself. It was listening to some of the women when they prayed.

Originally Shay had panicked. Between the day Rose had invited her and the night she was actually to attend the study, Shay told herself she didn't know enough to go, but one of the women there had rescued her. When prayer time came, the first two women had prayed with large words and a reverent tone. The third woman had spoken to God as though He were in the room. Shay had even opened her eyes and stared across at her when quietly, her voice utterly normal, she thanked God for all the things He had provided, and then asked Him for a mattress for her bed. Shay didn't hear anything else for a long time.

That night on the way home in the car, Shay found herself glad that she and Rose had not been able to share a ride. Shay poured her heart out to God, speaking to the windshield as though she could see Him sitting on her hood.

I've had so many wrong impressions. I've been so confused, and now I see how huge You are. You love all of us. You're big enough that we can pray to You in our own way. I've been afraid of not being good enough. I've been so selfish and wrong with so many things in my life, but Your forgiveness is bigger than all of that.

It was the start of a wonderful pattern for Shay. She fell asleep with her heart right before God and soon figured out that she could do that every night. Tonight she had done the same thing, but Marrell was on her mind more strongly than ever before.

I miss her, Lord. I miss her and the girls. I realize now that I rushed in and overwhelmed her. Help me to find a way back. She was here for me before I found You, and I love her so much. I know she thinks I've just run off on another spree; she couldn't think anything else. Help me to know how to approach her. Let her be receptive when I call.

This was the last thing Shay asked of God on this night. Her schedule at work and all the changes in her spiritual life were exhausting. She would be halfway to work before she remembered what Mrs. Timm had said, and in turn, figured out how she must approach Marrell.

"I don't know why I didn't try to talk to you before, Marrell. I guess I knew how you would respond, and I was just afraid."

"I don't want you to be afraid to tell me anything, Shay." Marrell's heart was in her eyes. She had missed her friend so much, and now they sat across from each other in the same restaurant Shay had first taken them.

"I appreciate that, Marrell, but I've handled this so badly. I know you think I'm just into my next 'thing.' But the truth is, I've been helped at Rose's church. I think that when I invited you to come, I made you feel that unless you did, our relationship was over. And that's not what I meant. I've just never seen things in my life so clearly before . . . my past . . . all of it. In my enthusiasm," she admitted softly, "I was overzealous and obnoxious."

Marrell reached across the table and touched Shay's hand. "Thank you for explaining, Shay. I've missed you terribly, and the girls ask about you a lot."

"After practically ordering you to church, I didn't think you would want to see much of me."

Again Marrell's look was compassionate. "Like I said, I'm not interested in your church, Shay, but that doesn't go for you. You'll always be welcome. In fact, I think you should come to dinner this weekend."

"I'd love to, but do you know what I just thought of? I've never had you guys over — at least not all four of you. Why don't you come to dinner on Saturday night?"

"We would love to," Marrell was very pleased to tell her. "Can I bring something?"

"Nope. The evening is on me, and I've eaten with you enough to know what you like. How's six o'clock?"

"We'll be there."

"Good, now what are we having for dessert?"

"I'm too full."

"I guess I am too, but I do want some coffee."

"When do you have to be back to work?"

"I don't. I cleared my calendar so that we could talk all afternoon."

"Oh, Shay," Marrell whispered with relief. "I'm so glad you called me."

"Me too." The new believer smiled across the table at her friend. She didn't know how and she didn't know when, but remembering what Mrs. Timm had said, Shay Elliot determined to witness to her friend by the life she lived. It didn't matter if it took ten years; she was going to show Marrell Bishop the way to Jesus Christ.

May 1980

"Oh, Paul." Marrell's voice sounded hopeful for the first time all day. Apartment hunting was proving to be tiresome. Paul's next posting was unaccompanied to Germany, which meant that Marrell and the girls would be alone for a year.

"It's so spacious and clean," Marrell said as she took in the nice living room, large windows, new carpet, and spacious kitchen, which had plenty of room for their table and chairs.

"Three bedrooms," Paul added rechecking the ad, "and the price is pretty decent."

Marrell looked around the apartment a little more. The bedrooms were nice-sized, and with three of them, the girls could still be on their own. The bathroom appeared to be freshly painted, and the vinyl on the floor looked new as well. The door and window locks, however, were the most important things to her.

"It seems pretty snug," she said as she pulled at the window edge.

"Yes, and the owner told me there's an alarm system."

Marrell nodded and then just stood looking at her husband.

"Where did the last three years go?"

"I don't know, but the next year will go just as fast. Before you know it, the girls will be out of school for the summer and then back in again. Then I'll be home for Christmas, and that will be the halfway mark. Not to mention, I don't leave for six weeks."

Marrell nodded and made herself look away. It was not the first time Paul had been given a posting overseas, but this was different. This time she had the girls' schooling to consider, and neither of them had wanted to move to Colorado Springs while their father was in Germany. After Paul left, they were going to visit her grandmother, but only for three weeks.

"I'll be okay," Marrell said, more for herself than Paul. "I've decided to ask Shay if she can use me in the office."

Paul's brows rose, and Marrell nodded.

"I didn't decide until yesterday, and by then I realized I hadn't even told you I was thinking of it."

It took Paul a moment to adjust, but as he thought about it, it sounded like a good idea.

"Do you think her offer still stands?"

"She's never asked me again, but she told me just last week that one of the secretaries wanted to go part-time, and that was going to leave the office short-handed. I'll wait until school starts again and probably just be part-time myself, but if I don't do something with you gone and the girls in school, I'm going to lose my mind."

Paul came then and slipped his arms around her. "It's a great idea. I'm glad you thought of it. And if for some reason Shay can't use you, I think you should look for work elsewhere."

"Thank you, Paul," Marrell whispered. She had needed his approval so much, and for an instant wasn't sure what he would say. He kissed her cheek.

"I'd like us to rent this and move here ASAP."

Marrell frowned up at him. "I thought you would want to stay at the base as long as possible."

Paul shook his head. "I need to live here with you before I go. I'll be able to picture you here, on the phone, in the kitchen, or in our bed. It'll help the ache when I'm so far away."

Marrell went up on tiptoes to kiss him again.

"Let's go talk to the owner." Paul took Marrell's hand in his and led the way toward the door.

Just an hour later they had paid the first and last months' rent as well as a cleaning deposit. They drove straight back to the base, knowing the girls would be home any time. Both younger Bishops had known their parents' plans for the day and didn't hesitate to ask what they found.

"Is the apartment in the same school district?" This came from Delancey.

"Yes. It's not that far from here or Shay's."

"Good."

"You'll even have your own rooms," Paul added.

Both girls shrugged over this, and Marrell smiled. Somewhere along the line they'd grown up a little. Mackenzie would be 12 the next month, and Delancey's eleventh birthday was in

94

July, but it was more than age. Neither girl had a single qualm about sharing the same room, each other's clothes, books, or anything else that came to mind. It wasn't that one never had a cross word for the other, but no grudges or bitterness lingered. Indeed, both were still strongly competitive, but not with each other. There were even times when Marrell heard them talking in one of the bedrooms and felt left out, but all in all, she was glad they enjoyed each other so much.

"How would you like to see it?"

"Yeah," Mackenzie didn't hesitate.

"Right now?" Delancey asked.

"Sure, why not?"

"I think Eric is going to call."

"Well, he'll have to try again." Paul speared her with a look. "I'm not sure I even want you getting calls from boys at your age."

Delancey had nothing to say to that. If she had to visit the apartment in order to have phone privileges with Eric, she would do it.

As it was, she had a wonderful time. Both girls did. They liked the apartment and even learned that a girl from Mackenzie's class lived in the complex as well. They returned home in high spirits, the thought of moving momentarily overriding the dread of their father being gone for a year.

Neither girl saw what Marrell saw — a year without her husband. And before that year could begin, three years of possessions had to be gone through as quickly as possible so the move could be made in a timely fashion. That night Paul stayed up late watching a movie. Marrell didn't join him. She turned in early, knowing the real work would start in the morning.

■ ■ ■ ■

"I think this is the last one marked 'Kitchen,' "
Shay said as she deposited yet another box on the
kitchen table. The movers weren't coming for two
days, but Shay and Marrell had decided to get a
jump on the boxes Marrell had packed and taken
over to the new apartment.

"Okay. Thanks, Shay," Marrell said tiredly as
she unpacked a box of odds and ends. Shay joined
her and looked down at the contents.

"What are you going to do without your spatulas
and spoons for the next few days?"

"At present we're living on peanut butter and
jelly sandwiches."

"You poor thing. I'll bring something over
tonight, okay?"

"Oh, Shay, Paul would love it. He's very patient,
but I can tell he's starting to loathe the taste of
peanut butter."

"What day did you tell me he's leaving?"

"June 13. Five weeks from tomorrow."

"And back at Christmas for a few weeks?"

"Yes. We'll probably head to Lake Tahoe to ski,
at least for part of the time."

"And you leave for Colorado on July 1."

"Yes. We'll be back the twenty-second."

"And what day do the girls go back to school?"

"Labor Day is early this year. I think they go
back September 2."

"And will you want to come to the office right
away or have some time to yourself for a while?"

"That's a good question. I don't know if I'll be
relieved to be on my own or not." Marrell suddenly shook her head. "No, I won't like being

96

alone. I'll probably come as soon as I can that week."

"Well, Marrell," Shay said as she pushed a few red curls from her face, "just know that no matter how much time you can give me, I can use you."

"How much will I have to answer the phone? My biggest fear is that I'll be asked for information I'm not familiar with."

"Not much, but you'll learn as you go along. Most of the questions concern buildings, and we design everything short of bars and nightclubs. A few months back we were even commissioned to put together a doghouse."

"You're kidding."

"No," Shay grinned. "The lady was thrilled with the work and even sent some business our way."

Marrell shook her head. "I can see why you enjoy it."

"I do that. Well, I'm going now. I need to get in a few hours at the office and then make dinner for some poor starving Army officer I know."

Marrell laughed. "What time will we see you?"

"About six o'clock."

"Okay. Thanks, Shay."

"You're welcome. Don't stay here and work too hard."

"I won't."

Shay let herself quietly out of the apartment but did not immediately rush away when she gained her car. With her eyes on the building, she began to pray.

I'm glad that Your timing is perfect, Lord. I would have had the whole family saved and turning the world upside down by now, but You've asked me to be patient. They all mean so much to me, Lord. Help me to keep on for them.

97

Lately I'm so lonely. I ache for companionship and someone to share my life, but You know all about that. It's been so long since I've been touched or held. I think I'm very vulnerable in that area right now, Father. Please protect me from myself. Don't bring anyone along who spins my head. I've got to think clearly.

Shay started the car and pulled from her parking place, but her mind was still prayerful. It would be very easy to envy Marrell right now. She had a husband who adored her. But Shay did not want to settle for envy and discontentment. If and when God had a partner for her, He would reveal it.

By the time Shay came to this peaceful conclusion, she was back at the office, her heart making a deliberate effort to turn her mind to business.

Six

"You can't have both, Shay," Paul spoke tolerantly. "If God is both loving *and* all-powerful, why is there so much pain in the world?"

They had had this discussion before, but Shay still patiently answered. "You want God to fit into your own plan, Paul. You believe you know what's best for this world, and you want God to put His stamp of approval on your blueprint."

"That's not true, Shay. Anyone with eyes can see what a sick world we live in. If God was all-powerful and all-loving, He would do something."

As with their previous conversations, they got nowhere. Shay's answers were the best she could manage, and she knew that Paul was not just being argumentative, but tonight she had nothing more to say. It was a great relief when the girls needed their father.

"Does it upset you that we disagree?" Marrell asked almost as soon as Paul left the room.

Shay tipped her head to one side and said softly, "Tell me something, Marrell. If you believed with all your heart that tomorrow San Francisco would have the worst earthquake ever, would you leave the city?"

"Of course."

Shay nodded. "Would you be upset if your own

daughters wouldn't listen to you? Would you be afraid for them if they refused to leave the city?"

Marrell didn't answer. It didn't take a rocket scientist to see where she was headed, but she still had one question.

"What is it that Paul and I should be so afraid of?"

Shay answered as best she could. "I mostly used that example to show you how strong my belief is. I know you haven't had your marriage break up, and you haven't made some of the foolish choices I have, but I still believe that all people need Christ. I also believe that someday God will return for His people, and that's where I think you need a sense of urgency. No matter what you believe, Marrell, I'll be your friend and love you, but I don't know how long God will wait for you to make up your mind. For all you know, you could die in a car accident tomorrow."

"But I'm not afraid to die."

"If you're counting on going to heaven because you're a good person, you should be."

This was the bluntest statement Shay had ever made about her beliefs. They had talked on many occasions, and Shay had always been very sensitive about giving Marrell time. Marrell listened to her friend but truly believed she was fine.

"I don't know what you mean exactly," Marrell finally said quietly, "but I'm not sure I want to talk about it right now."

A look crossed Shay's face that swiftly made Marrell say, "No, Shay, not because I'm upset with you, but because I'm tired, and to be honest, I just want to concentrate on my time with Paul right now. I don't have that many more weeks with him."

"I think I understand," Shay said kindly, remembering that before she came to Christ, this would have been exactly how she would have responded. She would have put God off for excuses far less valid than Marrell's.

"Will you do some special things before Paul goes?" Shay responded, tactfully changing the subject.

"Whatever we can fit into the weekends. We're trying to save the rest of his leave for Christmas."

"Well, count on me this Saturday for the big move. And also, if you and Paul want any time on your own, don't hesitate to bring the girls over."

"Thank you, Shay."

"You're welcome," Shay said and meant it.

Paul and Mackenzie came back to the room, and conversation moved to school. Mackenzie was more than happy to be almost finished for the year.

"How will you like the seventh grade?" Shay asked.

"A lot," Mackenzie wasted no time in saying. "I get to change schools and see some of my friends who are in the eighth grade. When I talked to them, they told me that junior high is really cool."

"I'm glad to hear it. Your mom tells me you also have big plans for the summer."

Mackenzie smiled. "We're going to see our great grandma in Colorado."

"That'll be fun."

"We can't ski because the snow is gone, but Grandma says there are lots of fun things to do."

"Like what?"

"I think swim mostly."

"Does she have a pool?" Shay's brow lowered in thought.

"No, but her next-door neighbor does, and she said we can swim any day we're there."

"Would that be Mrs. Healy?"

"How did you know?"

"I grew up in Colorado Springs."

Mackenzie's mouth hung open. "I didn't know that."

Shay and Marrell both laughed.

"Shay and I go back a long way."

"How far?"

"From the time we were little."

"My age?"

"Younger. I first met Shay in the second grade."

The older women exchanged a glance and laughed again.

"I think we've missed a private joke," Paul chuckled, winking at Mackenzie.

"No," Marrell replied, her voice fond with remembrance. "It's just that Shay found out on that first day that I would never be a nurse. She was so afraid of school that she was sick, and all I could do was laugh at her pale face. I don't know if we ever would have been friends, but the teacher asked me to take her to the nurse, and on the way I tripped and nearly fell. We both had the giggles after that, and by the time we reached the nurse's office, we were red in the face and hiccuping every few seconds."

"What did the nurse say?"

"Only that we looked perfectly healthy and should return to our room."

"After that, we ate lunch together and were inseparable for the rest of the week. We never decided to be friends. It just happened."

"What just happened when you were friends?" Delancey asked, having come into the room for

102

the tail end of the conversation.

Her mother gave her an abbreviated version but then announced bedtime.

"I still have homework," Mackenzie said.

"Then what have you been doing sitting out here?" Her father's tone left no doubt as to his displeasure.

Mackenzie made a beeline for her room, Paul on her tail, and Delancey was told to brush her teeth and head to bed.

"I'm not sure how I'll do when he's gone," Marrell admitted. "The girls are so much older this time."

"I feel for you," Shay said honestly, "but Marrell, I think the time is going to fly."

Marrell's brows rose. "Maybe on the other end it will seem that way, but tonight, a year feels like forever."

Shay nodded but said no more, although she felt she could relate. "Forever" was the way she'd started to see her progress with the Bishops. She had told the Lord that she would hang in there with this family no matter what, but at times it felt as though she were spinning her wheels. Several months ago she had even gone so far as to put some distance between them, but Marrell still sought her out. Shay worked to live her life before Christ, no matter whom she was with, always assuming that Marrell would be turned off and keep away, but that was not the case. If Shay made herself scarce for a few days, Marrell called.

"You look far away," Marrell remarked, cutting into her thoughts.

"I was," she admitted. "I'm suddenly very tired. Maybe I'll head home."

"Okay." Marrell smiled. "Thanks for dinner,

103

Shay. You're a lifesaver."

Shay grinned. "I'll see you Saturday morning. Do you want me here or at the apartment?"

"At the apartment."

"What time?"

Marrell pulled a face. "We're going to get going before eight o'clock, but that's your only day to sleep in, so come whenever you want."

"All right."

Marrell walked Shay to the door, everything seemingly fine between them. She waved her friend off and then thought some more about the conversation. What would Paul say if he knew she was thinking a lot about Shay's life compared to her own? Marrell shuddered at the thought, not because Paul would be angry, but because there was a slight chance he would be irritated.

Not this close to your leaving, Marrell spoke to Paul in her heart. *Whatever I've got going on right now can wait. I can't send you away on a fight. Nothing's that important.*

This settled in her mind, Marrell went back to the living room. Paul joined her soon after and turned the TV on. Marrell nearly sighed with relief that he didn't want to talk about the conversation with Shay. She could keep her thoughts private if he didn't ask, and she was determined to do that right up to the moment he left.

Colorado Springs

"It already feels like forever," Marrell admitted to her grandmother on the third day they were there. "And he hasn't even been gone a month."

"The girls seem to be doing well," Pearl Walker rejoined.

"They are now, but Mackenzie was inconsolable

right after Paul left."

"Mackenzie was? I'm surprised."

"Why is that?"

"She's grown up so much, Marrell. In many ways Delancey is still a child, but Mackenzie has become a young lady."

Marrell couldn't help but smile with pride. Mackenzie *was* growing swiftly. She had shot up in the last six months until she was within a half inch of looking Marrell in the eye. Her emotions had gone through some transformations as well. One minute she was open and ready to talk, and the next moment she was quiet or buried in a book. She wasn't what Marrell would term sullen, but it wasn't unusual to catch her staring into space with a dreamy look on her face.

"You didn't tell me how you like the apartment," Pearl cut into Marrell's thoughts.

"It's very nice. Quieter than I thought it would be, and that suits me just fine. About the only drawback is the lack of yard. There's no real place for the girls to play. D.J. often rides her bike in the parking lot, and I worry about that."

"I worry about San Francisco in general," her grandmother admitted.

Marrell's brows rose. "Some of the things I see in the paper and on the news make my hair stand on end. It's amazing that we really aren't all that affected by it. We have good friends and good neighbors."

"It's the Lord's way of taking care of you," Pearl said softly, and Marrell stared at her. Pearl didn't notice; her eyes were on the yard.

Never had Marrell heard her grandmother speak in such a way. Pearl Walker was not a religious person, so where had that come from? Marrell

105

was still staring at her grandmother when she looked back at her.

"I guess I'd better get a snack ready. I can see Delancey coming with a towel wrapped around her. They'll both be brown as berries by the time you leave." Pearl pushed to her feet and moved to the kitchen.

Marrell kept her seat, glad that no reply was necessary since she'd barely heard her grandmother's last comment. Shay spoke about the Lord all the time, but Marrell was used to that. Coming from her grandmother, it was just such a shock.

Why is it such a shock? Marrell asked herself. *Why would it upset you if your grandmother had a relationship with God?* Marrell didn't need to search far for the answer. How many years now had she been feeling left out? Marrell had lost track, but this much she did know: Not at any time did she feel included. The other officers' wives were kind and generous with their time, but Marrell never felt she fit in. Shay was a wonderful friend, but Marrell knew there was a huge gap between them. Even the girls at times seemed to need each other more than a mother. They loved her and most of the time got along famously, but at times Marrell felt left out. Paul was the only person who made her feel even remotely complete, and he was gone until December.

The thought of Paul had no more materialized than Marrell realized it wasn't entirely true. Lately not even Paul was able to make her feel needed and vital. So many women were trying to discover themselves. Maybe she was one of them. A long time ago Shay had looked at her as if she needed a doctor when Marrell had been proud to tell her she was a wife and mother and nothing more. But maybe she should have been more. She was looking to her husband and children to fill her life. Maybe she should have been looking to herself.

Well, you don't have long to find out, Marrell. You start at Shay's office in the fall. If you want a chance to find yourself in a "real" job, you're going to get your chance. Just before Delancey came in the door, Marrell's heart wondered why the thought gave her no excitement at all.

"Hello," Marrell said, picking up the ringing phone unsuspectingly.

"Hi, Babe," responded the deep voice on the other end. It sent Marrell's pulses racing. Her throat closed so fast that she couldn't even answer her husband. "Are you all right?"

"No." The word came out with a sob.

"It's okay, Mary," he said tenderly. "Just take a few seconds. It's all right."

"I miss you," she managed.

"Tell me about it." His voice was dry. "I spent last evening with the CO, and his wife is here. Every time he put his arm around her, I wanted to howl at the moon."

Even in her tears, Marrell laughed. It was the perfect thing for him to say. She snuffed and sniffled a bit more but managed to get herself together.

"What's he like?" she finally asked.

"The CO? Okay. I strongly suspect he's religious like Shay, but he hasn't brought it up, so I guess I can live with it."

Marrell shook her head. Was there any escaping people who thought they had all the religious answers? But that was not what she wanted to talk about to her husband.

"How are you, Paul? I mean, really?"

"I'm fine. *Really.* How are you and the girls?"

"We're all right. The girls are having the time of their lives at the neighbor's pool and with some of the kids here. I suspect one of the boys is interested in Micki, but she's taking it in stride."

"She has a good head on her shoulders."

"Yes. Something tells me she'll be the strong one when we get back to San Francisco and your absence is really pronounced."

"How's Grandma?"

"She looks great. Her energy is unbelievable. She hasn't let me do a thing, yet I'm tired all the time."

"It's the emotions. It was like that before."

"Was it? I guess I don't remember."

"It'll pass; you'll see."

"I'm counting the days, you know."

"You and me both."

Marrell heard a noise behind her and turned to see her grandmother.

"It's Paul."

Pearl smiled. "Tell him I said hi."

Marrell smiled at her and went back to her husband. They talked about several subjects — nothing too important, just any excuse to hear the other's voice. All too soon Paul said he had to go. They had been on for more than 20 minutes, but to Marrell it had felt like seconds. Paul confirmed the date Marrell and the girls were headed back to San Francisco, promised to write, and indicated he would call again soon. Not until she had set the phone back down did Marrell feel her fatigue. How did single mothers do it? A look at her watch said it was almost eleven o'clock.

108

Well, I know one way to survive this, Marrell. Try getting some sleep. She sought her grandmother out, kissed her goodnight, and took herself off to bed. Tired as she was, she shed only a few tears for Paul before sleep claimed her.

"I can't believe we have to go to church, Mom. I want to sleep some more."

"Well, you can't. I think this is important to Grandma, and we're going to go."

"Do you want to?" Delancey asked, but Marrell didn't answer. She was checking the girls' clothes over, and they were already running late. If the truth be told, however, she did want to go. A person would have to be living in a cave not to hear of all the churches taking advantage of old ladies and their money, all in the name of God. Marrell knew she would feel better about things if she could see for herself.

Both of the girls were groggy during breakfast and on the ride to the church, but Marrell found herself very awake and tense. As with a few days earlier, she wondered what had her so frightened and shaken up. It was more than just the thought that someone would harm her grandmother.

You're afraid, Marrell, and you know it. You're afraid you'll hear something that will cancel out everything you've ever done. You're afraid you'll find out that this emptiness inside is real and not imagined.

"This is the turn, Marrell," Pearl said. Marrell promptly put on the left turn signal and slowed down just in time.

"I guess you didn't go with me last time, did you?" Pearl went on almost absently.

"No, I don't think we did."

109

Marrell was pleased at how normal her voice sounded. Her insides felt like a bow that had been strung too tightly. It was a relief to get the car parked, find their way indoors, and slide into a seat. From there the morning was a blur. Marrell was so busy trying to find something that might be threatening to her grandmother that she heard little of the sermon or singing. She read every line of the bulletin, but other than showing the year-to-date giving and listing some special needs for the missionaries, there was nothing. In fact, when the plate was passed, her grandmother put nothing in.

"Should I have put something in?" Marrell heard Delancey ask Pearl.

"No, honey, you're a visitor here. That's not expected."

"But you didn't, Grandma."

"I do one check at the beginning of the month."

For some reason, Marrell did not panic over this. It was such a normal statement, and as she looked around, everything in the room looked normal too. Marrell felt almost ashamed when the pastor led them in a closing prayer. She missed all of it.

"Are you all right?" Pearl asked almost as soon as the man said, "Amen."

"Yes, just preoccupied."

Pearl eyed her keenly. "If you want to ask me anything about the church or the service, Marrell, I'd be glad to answer you."

Marrell stared at the older woman. Why had she thought her grandmother might be failing?

"Thank you, Grandma," Marrell said softly, smiling at her. She didn't know why, but a sudden peace filled her. She did have questions but now

110

believed the answers would be reasonable. She didn't have to wait long to find out. As soon as lunch was over, the girls wandered off on their own pursuits, and Marrell was left alone with the woman who had raised her.

"Grandma," Marrell plunged right in, "why did you start going to church?"

Pearl was on the verge of getting up to start the dishes, but she sat back in her chair. "I'm getting older, Marrell, and I can feel my body changing and weakening."

"So what does church do for your age?"

"Nothing directly, but for the first time in my life I realized I wasn't going to live forever. I watched your folks and your grandfather die, but it never touched me like getting old has."

"I still don't understand what going to church does."

"Going to church doesn't do anything. Believing that God's Son died for my sins does it all."

It was out. Marrell had asked and been told. Her grandmother believed just as Shay did. Marrell said as much.

"Yes, I know," her grandmother surprised her by saying. "We've had some correspondence."

"I didn't know that."

Pearl nodded. "She had heard that I was going to the Bible church and wrote to tell me she finally understood what she had needed all along."

Marrell looked stricken, and Pearl's heart broke.

"I haven't been a good example to you, Marrell. I've lived my life for myself."

Marrell shook her head but didn't speak. In her mind nothing could be further from the truth. She thought her grandmother the most selfless person in the world.

111

"I can't talk about this," Marrell finally managed. "Paul's not here, and I just can't."

Pearl backed off immediately. "I would never force my belief down your throat, honey. But if you want to talk again, you know we can."

Marrell thanked her and rose to clear the table. She and her grandmother worked side-by-side for the next 20 minutes but said little. Pearl's well-lined face was serene, but inside she was working to give her granddaughter to the Lord.

I've been a coward. I've been afraid to share with her. So many times I should have told her, Lord. I've failed You. Please show me how. I can't seem to get the words out. Please help me know what to say to a person whom I love this much, but who doesn't want to listen. She's afraid; I know she is. I know all about fear, Lord. You're the only one who can take it away.

Marrell was saying something about going into Denver the next week, so Pearl forced her mind to listen.

"What day?"

"What day is good for you?" Marrell asked with relief, glad to have the subject back to something she would call normal.

"Just about any day. I've cleared the calendar for you and the girls."

"Let's go Tuesday. D.J.'s birthday is right after we get back, so if I can find something for her here, you know, something that will remind her of our visit, that's going to be easier."

"Okay. I'd like to have a cake here and give her my present — maybe the Sunday before you leave."

"Oh, she would love that. What did you get her?"

They were interrupted before Pearl could

answer, so the subject was dropped. It was Delancey. She had gotten a hole in her swimsuit, one that was impossible to repair because it would only tear again. Swimming was all the girls had done since they had arrived, and this was the only suit she had. It looked as if some shopping would be in order even before Tuesday.

Marrell's life was one of adjustments and changes, so she took this in stride. She told herself to take her grandmother's religion in stride as well but found it wasn't that easy. It was nothing less than a relief to have the visit end before the subject came up again.

Seven

Marrell stared hard at the white envelope in her bag and then reached to pull it slowly toward her. She recognized her grandmother's handwriting and for a moment was unable to move. Winging its way toward California, the airplane had a few moments of turbulence, but Marrell never noticed. Having finished with their card game, the girls were wrapped up with their books, completely unaware of their mother's turmoil. Marrell pushed her straight blond hair behind her ears and, with a shaking hand, forced herself to open the letter.

My dearest Marrell,

This letter has been a long time in coming — too long. And for this I am sorry. I should have told you about my faith years ago. I have no excuse to offer, but I will tell you that I feared your response. You've had so many losses that I thought you would be angry with me if you learned I had turned to God.

I know that you thought me failing when you were here for Christmas more than three years ago, but in truth, I had just come to realize my need for a Savior and was so confused about how to tell you that I stumbled around like a fool. Since then God has urged me many times to call

114

or write you, and each time I have disobeyed. I can disobey no longer.

Please forgive me for not telling you right away. I am ashamed of my shame. I resisted God for so long, telling Him I was a good person and that surely He would not turn me away, but I finally stopped lying to myself. God alone says how I may enter His heavenly home. The Bible is very clear on this, and after reading the truth in that Book, I confessed to God that I needed His Son to save me.

Please do not hate this foolish old woman, Marrell. I have let you, Paul, and the girls down by not telling you before. All I can do now is beg your forgiveness.

I hope and pray that you will listen to Sharon. As I'm sure you must know, she has also seen her need for salvation. I sense that you have many questions, but I can see that fear holds you back. If ever you can gain the courage to seek answers, please call me or go to Sharon. I pray you will do so before it's too late.

"What's the matter, Mom?" Mackenzie's voice broke into Marrell's stunned mind. "You look sorta pale."

"No," Marrell said to her daughter, "I'm all right."

Mackenzie continued to look at her, and Marrell reached up to smooth her hair.

"What are you reading?"

"A letter from Grandma."

"Is something wrong?"

"No." The truth hit Marrell too late to act. "She's just telling me something that I wish we could have talked about while I was there."

"About her church?"

Marrell stared at her daughter. How much had she caught of the underlying tension that Marrell had experienced off and on?

"Yes, it is about her church."

"They're kinda weird."

"Do you think so?" For some reason her words hurt Marrell. By the third Sunday, she had started to enjoy the people.

"I don't know," Mackenzie shrugged. "I just don't like sitting there singing or trying to figure out what the man is talking about."

Her words so echoed Marrell's own thoughts on the subject of church that she was shocked all over again. *Well, what did you expect, Marrell?* she suddenly asked herself. *You and Paul have given the girls no reason to include church or God in their lives.*

Marrell's eyes went back to the last line she'd read. *I pray you will do so before it's too late.* Glancing toward Mackenzie and seeing that she had gone back to her book, Marrell swiftly read on.

I have always hated self-righteous people, Marrell, and I'm sure you feel the same, so I must tell you that I have one prayer for you: I pray that you will search this out for yourself. Don't let your grandmother's failings drag you down. I don't have all the answers, but God does. I'm praying you will have enough questions that you will search for answers no matter what you've seen or how far away God seems. I know you want Paul here, and I pray that he will search as well, but even if he doesn't, Marrell, you must come to this decision on your own.

Again, Marrell, I ask your forgiveness. I have

sinned against you and the Lord, and there are not enough words to tell you of my regret. Please tell the girls of my decision. I'll write to them in a week or so. I'll call you sometime next month, and if you want to talk about it, we can. If you never want the subject mentioned, I will abide by your wishes.

Please believe me when I tell you it was wonderful to see you. I'm so proud of you and the girls. You're doing a good job, Marrell, and my great grandaughters are the most beautiful girls I've ever seen. Don't spare me when you talk to them, Marrell. Tell them I've been a fool, but at 78 I'm still learning. Take care of yourself while Paul is away. I will be in touch.

All my love,
Grandma

Marrell made herself breathe very slowly. The shock was receding, but she still felt like she'd been shaken by a large hand. Three years! She had made this decision three, closer to four, years ago! How could her grandmother have thought that she would reject her?

Surprisingly enough, Marrell suddenly knew she was not angry with Pearl Walker. How could she be? Pearl Walker knew Marrell Bishop all too well. With just a few minutes of conversation at the dinner table, Marrell had asked her to stop. It wasn't any wonder that her grandmother didn't feel she could confide in her.

Marrell started when Mackenzie laid a hand on her arm. She looked over to find tears in Mackenzie's eyes. She knew that Mackenzie had seen hers.

"Mom," she said, her voice low. "What's

wrong?"

"I'm just upset because I wish I could talk to Grandma," Marrell whispered, glad that their three seats were on their own.

"What did she say?"

"She's become a Christian, but she didn't feel that she could tell me. I feel awful about that."

Delancey, who was by the window, peeked her face around her sister, and both girls listened while their mother briefly explained.

"So she's a Christian like Shay?" Delancey wanted to know.

"Yes. And we talked of it a little while we were at her house, but then I got upset. Now I wish I had listened to her."

"Do you want to become a Christian, Mom?" Delancey asked.

"I don't know, honey. Right now I'm too confused to know anything."

"If you do, Mom, do we have to?" Again this came from Marrell's youngest daughter.

"I don't know. Why do you ask?"

"Because the Christians at school are weird. They can't do anything fun."

Marrell sighed. It was like listening to her own thoughts.

"Does Dad know?" Mackenzie asked.

"No. I just found out myself."

"Are you going to tell him?"

"Of course. Why wouldn't I?"

Mackenzie shrugged. "I can't think he would be all too happy to find out you're going to be like Shay."

Marrell couldn't reply. Mackenzie had unerringly put her finger on the crux of the matter. She had never been able to tell Paul how empty she was inside. She had never been able to be completely up-front with him out of fear of what he would say.

The apple doesn't fall far from the tree, Marrell thought. *My grandmother was afraid of my reaction, and I'm afraid of Paul's.* With a deep sigh, she laid her head back on the seat. The plane would be in San Francisco in just 20 minutes. Marrell felt as limp as a rag, but tired as she was, she felt challenged. Her grandmother had told her to seek answers and hoped she was brave enough to do so. Marrell kept her eyes closed until they touched down, all the time asking herself if she really was that brave.

It felt so good to be home. Marrell would never have guessed that she could miss the apartment after having such a wonderful house on the base, but in truth, she was thrilled to be back among her own possessions and in her own bed. Shay had picked them up, and it had been wonderful to see her as well.

Marrell lay on her back, a book open on her stomach, but she didn't feel like reading. She had attended church three Sundays with her grandmother, and she had finally begun to listen on the last visit. Stories about Jesus, His birth, and even His crucifixion were not new to her, but the way He had interacted with the townspeople — these were insights that weren't so familiar.

The sermon that last day had been on children and the way Jesus had wanted them to come closer, even when the disciples would have held them off. She didn't remember what point the pastor had made, but in some ways she felt like a child — one who was trying to get close and

119

couldn't.

Maybe it's not that simple. I've run for a long time, and maybe it's too late. I'm ready to talk to Paul about this, but he's not here. The thought had no more formed when she realized what she could do. She left the bed and moved to the kitchen to find stationery and a pen. Pages later, through tears and fear, she folded the papers, put them in an envelope, and addressed the front. It would have been good to talk to someone in person, but she wasn't ready to do that with anyone here, not even Shay.

She had to go grocery shopping in the morning. On the way back to bed she put the envelope with her purse and made a promise to herself that she would mail her letter before she did anything else.

Heidelberg, Germany

Paul slammed the filing cabinet a little too hard and went back to his desk. The report he had retrieved was open on the wood surface in front of him before he realized he was being watched. He looked up to find his commanding officer, Brigadier General Allen Post, at the door, his face unreadable.

"I'd like to see you in my office, Colonel Bishop." With that he walked away, and Paul naturally followed.

"Shut the door," Allen ordered as he sat behind his own desk. "Have a seat."

Paul did all as he was instructed and worked at not showing his apprehension.

"You've been slamming drawers and barking at people for two days now. What's going on? Bad news from home?"

Paul had to stop just short of saying, *"You*

120

wouldn't think so." Instead he kept his voice respectful and said, "Not exactly."

"This is off the record, Paul." Allen's voice had softened. "I want to know if you're all right."

Paul took a deep breath. "I have heard from home and there's no emergency, but I'm a little confused about some things."

"Concerning your wife?"

Paul nodded.

"Can you call and talk to her?"

"I don't want to do that until I've calmed down."

"What exactly has you so upset?"

"With all due respect, sir, knowing how you believe, I don't think you want to hear what has upset me."

Allen actually smiled. "If it's what I think it is, you're very wrong."

Paul was completely flummoxed by such a reply, but he still answered. "Her grandmother has become a Christian." Paul said the word with difficulty. "And now my wife is asking a lot of questions herself, and I'm the last to find out that she has been asking questions for a long time." Anger had come into Paul's voice, and he momentarily forgot to whom he was speaking. "Is that what you *thought* it would be, General Post?"

To his surprise, Allen ignored the sarcasm. "Yes, it is, Paul. Shall I tell you why?"

Paul only stared at him.

Allen leaned a little way over the desk. "I've never met anyone so fascinated and yet still fighting it at the same time. I don't know what your experience was in San Francisco, but something has you scared. It would seem that it's the thought that your wife might need more than you can give her. I remember when I felt the same way. My

121

wife came to Christ before I did, and it was almost the end of our marriage."

"What did you do?" Paul, feeling desperate, asked without thought.

"The first thing I did was decide I didn't want a divorce. So I stopped being angry and listened to what she had to say, and do you know what? She was right. When she explained, I realized I couldn't give her all the things God did — the peace that I would be there for her forever. I'm just a man, and an Army officer at that. I couldn't promise to be there for her the next day. Neither could I give her the peace of knowing that she wasn't going to hell for eternity.

"I finally stopped fighting and listened to her, and in time I wanted that same peace. You have to do what I did, Bishop. Ask yourself if you love your wife. If the answer is yes, you can't hold her back. You can't make her feel guilty for wanting things you can't provide, no matter how much your pride says otherwise."

Paul couldn't have spoken if he had tried. He was so sick with worry that he wanted to board a plane for California that instant, but Allen was right. What would he say to Marrell? "I'm here now, you don't need God?" According to her letter, that wouldn't work.

And is Shay really so bad? Paul suddenly asked himself. Paul realized she didn't act weird or preach at them. Indeed, she was the best friend Marrell had ever had, bending over backward time and again to help out and show she cared.

"I have a Bible study with two men on Monday night, Paul. I can't help but think you should be there. All we do is discuss what the Bible says about questions the men have. You're welcome to

come and bring your own questions. There isn't a
one that God's Word can't handle."

Paul felt almost desperate inside to do just that,
but he only quietly thanked the other man and
waited to be dismissed. General Allen Post did
dismiss him just moments later, but not before
telling him they met at seven o'clock.

San Francisco
It was late on Saturday afternoon when Shay came
to see Marrell. Marrell had spent part of the day
at the Laundromat. One of the things she missed
most about the house at the base was room for
her washer and dryer. She was still ironing and
putting things away when Shay arrived.

"How are you?" Shay asked as she always did,
not letting on that Marrell had constantly been in
her thoughts.

Shay had begun to see someone from the
church. His name was Oliver Lacy. They had gone
out with some other people the night before. Shay
had had a good time, but even Oliver had seen
her distraction. Near the end of the evening, she
had admitted to him that her friend had been on
her mind. Then that morning she had to put some
time in at the office. Work was demanding more
of her lately, to the point that Shay was thinking
about selling and going to work for someone else.
Being the owner was getting more time-consuming
with every year. She'd come to Marrell as soon as
she was able.

"I'm all right," Marrell said softly. "I miss Paul.
Some days are worse than others, and since we
returned from my grandma's, it's worse than
ever."

Marrell turned her back on Shay to stack her

laundry baskets and hide her lying face. She hadn't planned to lie, but it was out almost before she could stop it. And she had no idea why.

"I've been thinking about you a lot," Shay told her, not having caught the deception. "I've wanted to come by for two days and couldn't get away until now. I came right from the office."

Marrell turned, sat on the sofa, and stared at her. "Why did you want to come?"

"I don't know. I just can't stop thinking about you."

"Did you think it would be hard for me when I got home?"

"I wasn't sure, but it makes sense." Shay studied her friend. She thought Marrell appeared strained and upset. "Is there something else, Marrell?"

The story came out then. Not all at once and not even in order, but bits and pieces emerged until Shay thought she had a fairly good idea of what her friend was going through.

"I feel so terrible, Shay," Marrell went on. "Like I plotted against my husband. I refused to talk about it before he left, and now that I've written to him, he hasn't replied. I did the same thing with my grandmother. She tried to talk to me, and I just put her off." Tears came to her eyes. "I don't know when my heart has been such a mess. I want to get close to God, but I don't want to sacrifice my marriage. I just don't see how Paul could live with that. He would never understand. And now he's so far away. I can't even talk to him."

Marrell talked as if Shay should know exactly what she spoke of, but in truth, it was becoming more unclear all the time.

"I want to be sure I understand, Marrell," Shay

broke in. "Why do you feel as though you've betrayed Paul?"

"Because until the letter, I never told him that I've been feeling empty for a long time. And then hearing my grandmother say how she couldn't tell me because she feared the way I would react . . . well, I realized I was just like her. I haven't been able to tell Paul. So then I do it in a letter, and it just feels so cheap. I'm such a coward. I don't want him upset with me, so I wait until he's an ocean away to tell him he can't give me what I need."

Marrell's own words were too much for her. She broke down and cried. Shay joined her on the sofa, and the girls chose that moment to come in. They sat across from the women on the chairs in the living room and just listened and watched with wide eyes.

Shay rubbed Marrell's back and hugged her from the side. She asked one of the girls to run for some tissue and then waited while Marrell got herself together. When her friend's red-rimmed eyes turned to her, Shay smiled gently.

"I have to say some things to you, Marrell, things that might hurt. Do you understand?"

"I think so. I can't think what would hurt more than this."

"Do you want the girls to stay?"

Marrell looked across at them. "They can stay."

"Paul loves you," Shay began when Marrell looked back. "I know he does, but he prides himself on being able to take care of you. I think that's some of the reason you've been afraid to tell him you're feeling empty inside. It would be a blow to his ego."

Marrell nodded her head, telling Shay they were

on the same page.

"I can't sit here and tell you that there is no cost to following Christ, Marrell. And that *is* what we're talking about, isn't it?"

"Yes. My grandmother told me she was praying that I would be brave enough to search for answers, and that's what I'm trying to do. I've got to find out why nothing ever satisfies me. I've got to find out why I feel so empty inside."

Shay squeezed Marrell's hand. "I can tell you everything I know, Marrell, but I can't make any promises about the way Paul will feel. I would never tell you to forget him and live your own life, but God has asked hard things of His children."

Marrell suddenly knew why Shay asked if she wanted the girls to stay. Marrell was careful not to look at them. Would God really ask her to give up Paul for Him? Could she do it? Would Paul really leave her if she wanted Christ in her life?

Oh, please, no, her heart cried, but at the same time she knew she must search on. How many more years was she going to wonder if there was more? So many things Shay believed sounded odd and unreasonable to her, but did she really know all the facts? There were so many things she wanted to ask her friend, but she looked up and saw her daughters still watching her. To send them out would only scare them and bring questions she might not be able to answer. Another avenue was needed.

"The girls and I would like to go to church with you in the morning, Shay."

"All right."

Marrell watched her daughters' mouths open in protest, but she put a hand up. "I need this right now, and you will not give me any trouble." Marrell used a tone they would never have argued with.

Shay was so proud of her, she could have cheered. She forced her voice to be calm as she asked, "Just church, or Sunday school too?"

"Both," Marrell answered on a deep breath. "I think both. I'm not going to learn if I'm not there."

Marrell looked into her friend's eyes, and Shay smiled. Was there any way to tell her what this meant? Was there any way to express how many years her heart had yearned and prayed for an opportunity?

"What time should we be ready?"

"Sunday school starts at 9:30, so I'll be here at 9:10."

"What should we wear?"

"Anything. Be as dressy or as casual as you like. If you're uncertain about it, call me. I'll wear pants or whatever you decide."

"Thank you, Shay."

"You're welcome. Are you going to be all right this afternoon?"

Marrell glanced at her girls. "Yes. I can see that Micki and D.J. and I need to talk, but I'll be fine. And we'll see you in the morning."

"Okay."

Shay gave her a quick hug and went to hug the girls as well. They loved Shay and accepted her embrace, but just as soon as the door shut, they approached their mother.

"I don't understand what's happening," Delancey didn't hesitate to say. Marrell had just hugged her, and now she felt as though she needed to cry.

"Mom?" Mackenzie asked, her voice filled with dread. "Is something wrong with you and Dad that you're not telling us about?"

"No," Marrell could honestly tell her, but she also knew it was time to explain. Mapping out her fears and feelings from the last several years, she knew that the girls' world was too calm and settled to know the unrest she had experienced.

"And you think you'll find help at Shay's church?"

"I don't know, Micki, but I'm going to start there. I don't even have a Bible, but I know Shay reads hers all the time. Her life is so peaceful even when things at the office are hectic. She's able to remain calm. I want that."

A look passed over Mackenzie's face that Marrell had to question.

"Are you angry, Micki? Are you hurt?"

"A little," she admitted. "I just think that Dad's feelings are going to be hurt. I mean, isn't he enough? Aren't D.J. and I enough?"

Marrell wrapped her arms around her oldest daughter and just held on. How to explain? How to make her see? Marrell didn't have a clue. She swallowed hard to keep from sobbing.

"I don't know what else to say to you, Mic, except that, no, you're not enough."

Tears filled Mackenzie's eyes, and Marrell took her face between her hands.

"Listen to me, Mackenzie Rose Bishop. This is not about you. No mother in all the earth has girls more precious than mine, but it's not about you. It's about me. *I* have something missing inside. I have a place that needs to be filled. You are wonderful, and so is D.J. I wouldn't trade you for anything."

Mackenzie nodded and laid her head on her mother's shoulder, much as she had done as a small girl. Marrell slipped an arm around her and another around Delancey. The three sat together like that for some time. Delancey was the one to break the silence.

"Do Micki and I really have to go with you?"

"Yes, honey. I don't want you to stay alone for that long."

Her small chest lifted with a large sigh. "It's going to be so boring."

Marrell opted against commenting, but she didn't think anything could be further from the truth.

There were no crashes of thunder or sparkling new revelations for Marrell on Sunday morning. She met a lot of kind people and listened attentively to everything going on around her. She watched Shay like a hawk but saw nothing new. Shay was still Shay — warm and smiling and listening as intently as she was.

Was there ever an end to what you could learn? Marrell wondered. Shay nearly hung off her chair, and she had been at this for several years. Marrell realized she was viewing this as one would college: Attend for three or four years, take your exams, and have your Christian diploma handed to you.

Even as Shay dropped her and the girls back at the apartment, Marrell knew it wouldn't be that easy. Shay was going to pick them up for church that evening and again for Wednesday night. She knew the girls were not thrilled, but Marrell was too busy with her own thoughts to give them much attention. She would go to church with Shay tonight and again Wednesday; of that much she was certain. What she would say to Paul, however, was still a complete mystery in her mind.

Heidelberg

"Don't make it more complicated than it is," Allen Post said to one of the men in the group. Paul hadn't asked the question, but he hung on every word.

"Salvation and a life lived for Christ are very basic — not easy, mind you — but uncomplicated."

The other man nodded and listened as Allen read a few more verses from the book of James. Paul hadn't taken in everything — his mind kept darting off — but what he had heard made more sense than he had expected. He was thankful that his CO had not pressed a bunch of questions on him. Indeed, after introducing Paul to the one man he didn't know, Allen had left him to listen in peace.

"Well, it's late, gentlemen. I think I'll close in prayer, and you can think on this and jot down any more questions you might have for next week."

"I can't make it next week, but I'll be here the week after."

"All right. How about you, Vince?"

"Next week is fine."

"Paul?"

"I'll be here."

"Okay, let's pray."

Paul bowed his head but didn't hear a thing. He was mentally figuring what time it was in California. Very early in the morning if his head was working right. It didn't matter. It was time to call his wife.

EIGHT

As soundly as Marrell slept — she'd been in bed only an hour — the phone ringing right next to her ear brought her instantly awake. She picked it up after only one ring, her heart beating a little too fast.

"Hello."

"I'm sorry it's so late." Paul's soft voice came from across the miles.

"It's all right," Marrell said, and she meant it. "I've been hoping you would call. It didn't matter when."

"I tried you for hours yesterday and then fell asleep."

"I'm sorry," she replied, sounding crushed. "We were out all day and into the evening."

"I shouldn't have taken so long to call in the first place."

Marrell swallowed, reached for the light, and pushed herself up against the headboard. It was just after midnight.

"Why did it take so long, Paul?"

"I was upset."

It was the worst thing Marrell could have heard, and she had no idea how to reply.

"I didn't call to tell you that though," he went on softly. "I called to apologize because I haven't

131

been honest with you."

Marrell's heart plunged. Those were the words a woman thought she would hear when her husband had been unfaithful. Marrell was so emotionally distraught that her imagination was lying to her.

"I was angry about your letter," Paul continued at last, "but then I stopped lying to myself and admitted that I've been searching too."

"Have you, Paul? Have you really?" Marrell felt as though she'd run ten miles.

"Yes. I went to a Bible study at my CO's."

"What did you think?"

"It makes more sense than I thought it would."

Marrell's breath left her in a rush, but she managed to say, "Paul, the girls and I went to church with Shay on Sunday."

"Did you, Mary?" He was as breathless as he sounded. "You went to church?"

"Yes," Marrell said on a sob, and Paul couldn't hold his own tears. Neither one could speak for some moments.

"I was just sick when you didn't call." Marrell pushed the words out. "I thought I had lost you."

"I'm sorry; I'm sorry. I should have called. I was upset, but I should have talked to you."

Marrell was overcome again. Tears poured down Paul's own face, but Marrell was aware only of her own.

"I'm already late for work," she finally heard him say.

"Oh, Paul, no!" she wailed softly. "We have to talk."

"We will. I promise you. I just wanted you to know that I love you. Do you hear me, babe? I love you."

"Yes," she answered, wishing desperately that

they could be together.

"I'll call as soon as I'm off. Just be home all morning and I'll get through. Promise?"

"Yes. I'll be here. I love you."

"Oh, Mary, I would do anything to see you right now."

She couldn't answer.

"I have to go."

"Okay," she said softly. "Call as soon as you can."

"I will. 'Bye."

Marrell just got the word out before the connection was broken. She felt like her heart would explode. He loved her! He was searching on his own! He was calling in the morning! She had thought he would never forgive her, but he still loved her. For the first time Marrell tried to pray.

Please let us both do this. Please let us end this search together. Don't let me lose my husband, God. I love him so much. The girls and I need him. If You love us, please help us.

Marrell didn't remember the last things she prayed before she fell back to sleep. She slept hard until almost three o'clock, when she woke and found the light still on. After a quick trip to the bathroom, she slipped back beneath the sheet, turned the light out, and eventually slept again. Her mind was so full that she wouldn't have believed it possible, but sleep she did, unaware of anything until she heard the girls getting breakfast.

Marrell allowed Mackenzie to answer the phone. She had warned the girls to keep the line open and then told her eldest, when she asked, that she could answer all calls. The one they had been waiting for came at 10:10.

"Hey, Micki!"

"Hi, Dad! How are you?"

"I'm fine. How are you?"

"I'm fine. Where are you?"

"At the base. In my room."

"You never sent us a picture."

"I'll do it soon. Are you getting ready to start school next month?"

"Oh, Dad, don't remind me."

Paul laughed. "How's D.J.?"

"She's fine. She's right here. Want to talk to her?"

"Sure."

"Hi, Dad!"

"How's my D.J.?"

"Fine. I miss you."

"I miss you too. Are you a foot taller?"

"No. Mackenzie is."

Marrell stood by patiently, letting the girls pass the phone back and forth until they had both had their say. She wanted no complaints when she took the phone and sent them on their way. It took several minutes, but she was finally in the privacy of her room and had the phone in hand.

"I think they could have talked to you all day," she said lightly, wondering at how tense she was.

"I can't believe how much I miss them. I show their picture to everyone. They all think the girls are beautiful."

"Well, don't you agree?"

"Yes, but whenever they say it, I always think, 'You haven't seen my wife.' "

"Oh, Paul."

She heard him sigh.

"I miss you," he said.

"I didn't think it would be this bad."

"Me either. You haven't written as much as I thought you would."

"I'm sorry. I've been such a mess, and until I sent that letter, I didn't know how to put it on paper."

"What did you think of Shay's church?"

"I liked it, Paul. I liked my grandmother's too. The girls think it's boring and the people weird, but I listened to every word. We went to Sunday school, church, and even evening church with Shay. We plan to go to the Wednesday night service tomorrow night."

"You'll have to tell me what it's like. I haven't quite made the leap to church attendance," he admitted, "but I told Allen Post that I would be back at Bible study next week."

"What did you talk about?"

"Well, there are two other guys besides the general and me, and one is really angry about something. I think he's lost someone and he's mad at God, but the other guy asks a lot of the same questions I have on my mind, like how do we know that the Bible can be trusted — you know, things like that."

"What did the CO say?"

"I was amazed, Mary. He had so many verses he turned to. I don't have a Bible, but he loaned me one at the house and even offered to let me take it with me."

"Did you?"

"No, I just wanted to talk with you, so I said no without thinking."

"I was thinking that I don't have a Bible either. Remember years ago when I took the Gideon Bible from that hotel? I felt so guilty I threw it away. I wish I'd kept it."

"I'll bet Shay would have an extra you could use. Actually," Paul said on a laugh, "it's not as if you're living in outer Mongolia. You could go buy one."

Marrell laughed. "What an idiot I am! I didn't think of that. You could do the same."

"Not as easily as you can. If the PX doesn't have one, I'm sure the Bibles in town would be in German."

"I didn't think of that either."

"Why don't you buy one for each of us and send mine here?"

"Okay." Marrell liked the idea, but doubts were crowding in. "Paul?" She said his name softly, and he thought she sounded like a lost child. "What are we looking for?"

"I think just what you said in your letter, Mary — peace. Shay has it; you and I don't. That thing you told me that she said, you know, about the city being destroyed and wouldn't we want to get out and get the girls out? I can't stop thinking about it. I feel like some huge hand is waiting to drop on me and destroy me. I've never felt so helpless in all my life. I don't know if the Bible has answers for those kinds of crazy thoughts, but I've got to start looking somewhere."

"Oh, Paul, Paul, why did this have to come up when we're so far apart?"

"I know. It's awful." Even as Paul said the words, he wondered at the chain of events. If he had stayed in California, would Marrell have gone to her grandmother's? If she hadn't gone to Colorado, would she have started to ask questions? Paul realized too that if Marrell hadn't written the letter, he might never have faced the fears inside himself.

"You're thinking," Marrell spoke into the silence.

"Yeah. I hate being away, but I must admit that it's forced me to do a lot of thinking."

"I hadn't thought of that. I don't always want to hear what's good for me, Paul. I've been angry at Shay because she says God has all the answers, and I don't always want to hear that."

"I know. I've argued with Shay so many times, but now I feel afraid. I've always believed there was a greater being out there. What makes me think I can get away with saying anything I want and believing anything I want? I can't stop thinking about it."

"So you're afraid most of the time?"

"Yes. How about you?"

"I'm more confused, Paul. I hate this empty feeling inside, and I can't understand why I would have it. I feel as though I have everything a person could want, but the hole inside me won't be filled."

"How much have you talked with Shay?"

"Not much. The girls are usually around, and I don't want to scare them."

"I'm glad you're being careful. Maybe this is just a passing phase for us, and there's no point in getting everyone shook up."

"Is that what you really think, Paul — that this is a phase?"

"No, but I'm trying to stay open."

They fell silent. Marrell's eyes dropped to her freshly painted nails. It was silly to fix herself up for a phone call with her husband, but she had. Her hair was brushed smooth and pulled back at the nape of her neck. She had even pressed her blouse and put on makeup.

"I think we've run out of things to say for right now," Paul said softly.

"I think so too. It's all so emotionally wearing."

"How are things at the apartment? You feel safe?"

"Yes, very."

"And money — are you guys all right?"

"Yes."

"Okay. Listen, I think I'll get off now and try to get my head together. I'll write to you."

"I'll write to you too."

"I'll call this weekend."

"I love you."

"Oh, Mary. I don't know when I've loved you more."

She didn't want to cry while he was on the phone, but when she said goodbye, her voice told him she would. Marrell hung up and tried to understand why it felt as though her heart was going to break. In some ways, this was the most exciting thing that had ever come into her life, but having Paul so far away in the midst of it took much of the joy from her heart.

"Mom?"

Marrell looked up to see the girls enter. She did nothing to hide her tears.

"Did you guys have a fight?" Mackenzie asked.

Marrell laughed amid her tears. "Micki, for heaven's sake, why would we fight?"

"I thought you might tell him about wanting to be a Christian, and I just thought that —" Mackenzie's voice died out, and Marrell's tears dried very quickly.

"Sit down, girls. I need to talk with you."

Mackenzie and Delancey were slow to obey, their feet dragging as dread filled their hearts.

Their mother had been so emotional lately, they didn't know what to think of her.

"Your father and I did talk about church," Marrell began when they finally faced her. "I told him that Shay took us to church, and he shared with me that he went to a Bible study at the CO's house." The girls' eyes grew huge with this announcement, but they remained quiet.

"I can't tell you exactly what's going on right now, because I'm not sure myself, but as I said to you before, Micki, it's not about you. Dad and I are not angry with each other or upset with you. This is about our need to find something more in our spiritual lives."

"What's a spiritual life?" Delancey asked.

"Well, it's the inside of you, D.J. Like knowing inside your heart that everything is all right or not all right."

"Do you know if everything is all right?"

"No, I don't, D.J. I've started thinking about life and death, and I have a lot of questions."

"Is it because Grandma's getting older?"

"Not exactly, although she did tell me that her own aging is what caused her to reevaluate things. I think I already told you about that."

Delancey nodded, and then Marrell found both girls staring at her. *What do they see?* she asked herself. *Have I really been so different? Would God ask me to give up my children for Him? I couldn't stand that, but if they want nothing to do with me if I become a Christian — if they think I'm odd — that's just what I'll be doing.*

"Are you all right?" Mackenzie asked. "You look like you're going to cry again."

"I do feel like crying, Micki, but I can't explain why. I'm just so full of emotion these days. I didn't think it would be this hard to have your dad gone, and sometimes my imagination runs away with me."

"Like how?"

"Like the worst that could happen — my girls not loving me anymore."

"Oh, Mom," Mackenzie said, sounding pained. "We love you. We just don't want to go to church."

Her voice sounded so chagrined on this last subject that Marrell smiled.

"It's not funny, Mom." Mackenzie's voice became testy.

"I'm sorry. But you make it sound like a prison sentence."

"Sometimes it feels that way," Delancey added.

There was so much Marrell could say, but she didn't know where to start. Their feelings were normal, but it would have been so good to have them excited with her. *Excited for what?* she asked herself. *I don't even know myself. How could I tell them? If only Shay were here.*

As if that very woman sensed she was needed, she called. Marrell smiled when she heard her friend's voice. Marrell hadn't finished with the girls, but she was at a complete loss as to what to say next.

"We'll talk later," Marrell said, holding the phone away long enough to tell them.

Both girls nodded, but neither was thrilled. Indeed, the day moved on, and evening and bedtime came, but their mother never brought up the subject. This suited the girls just fine. They both knew that Wednesday night would come soon enough. And at that time they wouldn't be talking about church; they would be attending it.

140

■ ■ ■ ■

"D.J.?" Mackenzie called softly from the doorway.
　"Yeah?"
　"Were you asleep?"
　"No."
Mackenzie came into her sister's room and sat on the edge of the bed. The light from the hall shone in, but the room was dark.
　"I don't want to go to church tomorrow night."
　"Me neither."
　"Let's talk to Mom again."
　"She won't listen, Micki."
　"She might. I don't think Wednesday night church takes as long as Sunday morning. Maybe she'll let us stay home."
　"I don't know." Delancey was quiet for a minute. "It's too bad we can't go to Shay's, but she'll be at church too."
　The girls sat in silence, not knowing that their mother was in her own bed thinking about the following evening's service too.
　The girls hadn't said much about Christianity; it was attending church they didn't like. At times like this Marrell tried to think of what Paul would do. It didn't take long to have her answer. She knew for a fact that if Paul were here, he would say the girls had to attend. She knew they weren't going to be happy about it, but she had made her decision.
　And Marrell was right. The girls, especially Mackenzie, were very unhappy. Indeed, when they climbed into Shay's car the next night, the oldest Bishop girl wasn't even speaking to her mother. For the first time in her life, Marrell had the

ungracious thought that she couldn't wait for school to start.

The letter started *Dear Grandma,* and it was Marrell's first attempt to tell her grandmother all that had transpired.

> It would be my wish to talk to you, Grandma, but I fear I will be too emotional. I know you plan to call, but we've been going nonstop, and you probably haven't been able to find us at home. With the girls going back to school next week and my starting to work for Shay, I thought I had better write while I had the chance.

Marrell chose her next words carefully, doing her best to explain how much her grandmother's example meant to her, how sorry she was for not letting her grandmother share with her before, and how much she hoped to find the truth on her own. In her heart, Marrell feared that all of these feelings would come to nothing and that her grandmother would have hopes of something that would never be, so Marrell walked on eggshells as she wrote.

> I guess I'm just trying to ask for your prayers. Paul is attending a Bible study on the base and searching as well. This time without him is more painful than I could have imagined. I've been to church with Shay four weeks now, and I just don't believe everything I'm hearing about God and the Bible. The world around me is so ugly, yet God does nothing. How can I put my trust in Him?
> Not to mention the fact that the girls hate going to church. It's a fight to get them out the door

each week. Sometimes I wonder why I bother.

Marrell could feel herself becoming excited and made herself calm down. She did not want to lash out at her grandmother or force her to defend her faith. Asking for prayer again, she closed the letter quickly and told her that she would be in touch soon.

She felt exhausted when she was finished. All of this was so tiring. To keep the girls happy, she took them just about anyplace they wanted and allowed them privileges they had never had before. All the running around, missing Paul, and trying to find a God who seemed to be hiding from her, made her feel ready to sleep for weeks. She thought about telling Shay that she couldn't start at the office right away but didn't know if she would be able to explain why.

As it was, she had no choice. The next week Marrell sent the girls off to school and went back to bed with a horrible flu. Shay, who had been waiting to do some serious talking with Marrell about what was going on in her heart, had to put her plans on hold.

Heidelberg

"It's so clear to me now," Paul said quietly. "I've fought this for weeks, but now I see how much I need to humble myself before God."

"When did you say this was, Paul, last night?" Allen double-checked.

"Yes. I couldn't sleep. I told God I knew I would be miserable, but if He still wanted me, then I would do my best to live for Him." Tears clogged Paul's throat, and he couldn't go on.

Allen put a hand on his shoulder. "I've done

143

nothing but pray for you since you arrived. I can't remember when I've had such a burden, Paul. You looked like a desperate man."

Paul gave a small laugh. "Two months ago I'd have laughed at you, but since I got my wife's letter, my life has been turned upside down."

"How is she doing?"

"She was sick last week. The girls went back to school, and she was in bed with the flu. She continues going to church with a friend of ours, but she still has so many questions."

"That's good."

"Yes, but she's not satisfied with the answers."

"You can relate, can't you?"

"Yes." Paul couldn't say any more. He was desperate to be with her, but even if he could get leave now, that would shorten his time at Christmas. Something told him he would be sorry if he did that. "I'd better get back to work."

"All right. Come back around 11:45, and we'll go to lunch."

Paul stood. "Thank you, sir."

Allen only smiled and sat in his desk chair when Paul was gone. His eyes closed over the joy he felt inside. *I knew he needed You, Father, but I didn't know how long it would take. You are so gracious, so holy. Thank You for this new life in Paul.*

Allen Post went back to work then, but his heart was still on Paul and what God had done in that man's life. He also prayed for Paul's wife, so far away, who needed to come to the same decision.

San Francisco

"The decision is yours," Pastor King spoke from the pulpit. "God won't force you to accept His Son. That's the kind of loving God we have."

With those words, Marrell shut down. How many weeks had she sat here — Mackenzie angry with her most of the time, Delancey falling asleep — desperately working in her heart to understand it all? How many nights had she read her Bible without a clue? She was glad for Paul's decision, but even though they had talked on the phone for hours and written back and forth for weeks to follow, she still didn't get it.

Why was Paul able to understand and accept this gift of salvation, but for her, it was like some elusive dream? He would be home in less than a month. Would it be better then? Marrell didn't think so. They had plans to head to Lake Tahoe and ski for five days. The girls were ecstatic. Marrell wasn't even looking forward to it. She could well picture the strain. As he was on the phone and in his letters, Paul would be brimming with delight, and Marrell would still be groping to find her way.

Without warning the sermon ended. Marrell worked to hide the confusion in her face when her daughters, Shay, and Oliver all stood. Marrell stood as well, but she could feel her face heating. She let her hair fall forward when she returned her hymnbook to its rack and, for a moment, missed the way Shay turned to her.

"I'm so proud of you," her friend said softly.

Marrell looked up in surprise. "Why?"

"Because you keep coming." Shay's voice was still low. "You come week after week, and you ask questions and keep searching." This said, Shay wrapped her arms around her friend.

"I've never been so confused in all my life, Shay," Marrell admitted softly. "I just can't seem to believe. I want to. I want to do this for Paul

145

and for you, but I just can't."

Shay had heard this before, so she looked her friend in the eye and said, "You have to do it for *you*, Marrell. You have to see your need for a Savior for your sins."

"But what if I put all my trust in Him, and He lets me down, Shay? What happens then?"

"He's not going to, Marrell." Shay stopped for a moment while Oliver called to the girls. They had been standing in uncomfortable silence and now scooted around the women and went to the church foyer with Shay's boyfriend.

"Are you still reading your Bible?" Shay changed tactics.

"Yes."

"Just keep on. God's Word is powerful, and all that He has for man is written in the Book. Remember, it's God's Word about Himself to man, not man's word about God. Just don't give up, Marrell, and you'll find the way."

Marrell nodded, and Shay hugged her again.

"I think I embarrassed the girls."

"Too bad," Shay said ruthlessly.

Marrell's eyes widened as they looked at her.

"I'm sorry, Marrell, but Micki and D.J. are too worried about what people think and not enough about what God thinks. That's a miserable way to live on this earth and nothing short of torture in eternity."

"Oh my, Shay," Marrell said softly, but she was not angry. It was such a true statement. The girls *were* too concerned with their own little worlds.

"Come and join Oliver and me for lunch. He's taking me to Zim's for a burger."

"Oh, Shay, Oliver doesn't want that. He wants time with just you."

"We spent the day with his folks yesterday, Marrell. I know he would enjoy having you and the girls."

"Are you sure?"

"I'll tell you what. I'll go and ask him, and he'll be very honest. If I've blundered, I'll tell you."

"All right."

Marrell sat down when her friend left and just looked around the near-empty church. Paul would want to attend when he came for Christmas; she was sure of that. But whether or not it would be better once he was home, Marrell could only hope. The thought that he might be so different that he wouldn't want her anymore caused her throat to close.

I really am a very insecure individual, she thought to herself. *Paul tells me he loves me, but it's not enough. I read that God's Son died for the whole world, but I feel left out.*

"We're all set," Shay called from the end of the pew. "To Zim's for burgers and shakes." Even the girls showed some emotion. Shay's voice had turned wry.

Marrell managed a smile, picked up her purse and Bible, and joined her friend in the center aisle of the church. She was glad for the momentary distraction of her thoughts, but she couldn't say she was joyously happy. Right now it felt as though she'd never be able to say that again.

NINE

For a moment Marrell couldn't breathe. Her husband's arms were finally around her, and she was afraid to draw a breath lest she wake up and find him a wonderful dream. But then he was kissing her again.

"Your plane —" she managed as he lifted her in his arms and carried her to the living room sofa. "We were coming to get you at eleven."

"I had a chance for an earlier flight and took it."

"The girls are going to go ballistic when they see you."

"Don't wake them," he said softly. "Right now I just want you."

Marrell still wasn't sure if she was dreaming. The clock had read 3:45 when she thought she heard a knock. Her heart pounding in fear, she listened while it came again. Ready to call the police if anything looked suspicious, she turned on the outside light and peeked through the viewing hole. Her brain registered the uniform just a moment before Paul said, "It's me, honey."

Now a light suddenly came on in her eyes, and Marrell squinted against the glare. Paul had reached for the lamp on the end table and turned it on. He smiled at her disheveled appearance, a warm, intimate light in his eyes.

"I forgot that you wear my old T-shirts when I'm away."

"I have to, or you feel ever farther away." She studied him for a moment. "You're different."

"I am, Mary. I've never known how to love you and the girls before, and now I do."

"That's not true, Paul," she protested. "You've always loved us."

"Yes, I have, but not like I can now with this new knowledge."

A noise by the front door caused Marrell's head to turn. It was nothing, just night settling noises, but it caused her to ask Paul if he'd locked the door.

"I'll check it. You go climb back into bed, and I'll be right with you."

"Are we going to talk?" Marrell came right out and asked.

"If you want to," Paul answered, wondering at her tone.

"I don't."

Understanding came in a flash. His mouth spread with a smile. Marrell smiled right back. Paul was off the sofa and seeing to the door just a second later.

"Dad?"

Paul woke to the sound of Delancey's voice and smiled when he felt her climb onto the bed.

"You're here!" She was all but attacking him now. "I can't believe you're here. Micki!" she screamed. "Dad's home. He's right here."

"Oh no," Marrell managed just before Mackenzie made her connection. There were tears and laughter, as well as many hugs and kisses, while Paul tried to hold both of his daughters and hear everything they were saying at the same time.

"Look at you two. I can't believe how much you've grown."

"When did you get here?"

"I don't know. What time was it, Marrell?"

"Before 4:00," Marrell grunted as Mackenzie shifted and put a knee into her thigh. Gone were the days of two little girls who fit on the bed with them.

"We were going to come to the airport." Delancey sounded disappointed.

"I took an earlier flight. You're not sad, are you?"

"Not really. I just wanted to see you come off the plane."

Paul smiled at her. "You two had better get ready for school," he said, keeping his face dead-pan.

"School? Mom said we were taking off so we could get you!" Delancey was crushed.

"But I'm already here," he returned, stating the obvious.

The girls stared.

"He's teasing." Mackenzie was the first to catch the gleam in her father's eye. "You really had us for a moment."

Paul grinned unrepentantly.

"So what's on the schedule for today?" he asked of his wife.

"We were going to leave that up to you. If you want to eat lunch out, we could do that, or we can stay right here and sleep all day. We were going to let you decide."

"I am going to need a nap this afternoon, but why don't we go out to breakfast?"

There was no need to convince the girls of this idea. They darted off the bed and ran for the door, each one shouting for the first turn in the shower.

"I'm not sure we'll have any hot water once they're through."

"We might have to shower together so we'll have enough." Paul's eyes were so mischievous that Marrell could only laugh. "I've missed your laugh," he said softly.

Marrell leaned over to kiss him. "Part of me wishes they had gone to school so we could talk. As it is, I'll have to wait the whole weekend."

"We'll fit it in," he promised her. "You've been on my mind so much."

"I'm a confused mess, if the truth be told," she said, the pain in her eyes confirming the words.

"I can't think of anyone who can relate to that better than I can."

"But you found the way."

"And you will too, Mary. I believe that with all my heart."

Marrell couldn't say any more. Paul put his arms around her, and she was relieved that he didn't expect more from her right then. Maybe having to wait the weekend wasn't so bad. Maybe by then she would at least be able to explain what was going on inside.

That night over supper Paul explained to the girls in detail about the decision he had made for Christ. He had already written to them from Germany, so they were not taken completely unaware. Paul found them quiet, almost accepting, but he was not about to take that at face value.

"Now, I want five questions out of each of you."

"What?" Mackenzie frowned at him.

"Just what I said. I want D.J. to ask me five questions, and I want you to ask me five."

"Why?"

"Because I know you have some questions on your mind, and I want to answer them for you. Also, I want you to show some interest in my life. Other than wanting to know what my apartment looks like on base and what German food is like, the two of you haven't shown a bit of interest in what your father does."

Both girls stared at him.

"So you want us to ask you about your work?" Mackenzie asked, although she knew better.

"No, I just used that as an example. I want the two of you to pull out of your self-centered worlds and show some interest in what I'm telling you about Christ. This is the most important decision I've ever made. It's going to change the way we do things, and I need and want your feedback."

"If you've already made up your mind that we all have to change," Mackenzie replied bitterly, "then why bother with any questions?"

"Because I care about your input. I care what you think, and I want to share this with you, even if you can't see the point right now."

Mackenzie had expected her father to be angry with her question. When he wasn't, she was put off guard. Sitting quietly on the opposite end of the table from Paul, Marrell was experiencing the same sort of surprise. She didn't remember mentioning to Paul how self-absorbed the girls had become, but in less than 24 hours back in their company, he had them figured out. Maybe she had said something and forgotten.

"Okay now," he said gently, "let's have those questions."

"Did you get the Bible Mom sent you?" Delancey asked.

"I did, D.J., thank you. I read it every day." Paul smiled kindly at her and looked to his oldest daughter.

Mackenzie looked uncomfortable but managed to ask, "Are you still going to that Bible study Mom told us about?"

"Yes. There are four of us, and we meet every Monday night."

"What do you do?" Mackenzie went on.

"Three of us come with questions about God and the Bible, and my CO goes over them and answers them from Scripture."

"What's 'Scripture'?" This came from Delancey.

"The Bible, honey."

"Oh." She looked a little pale, and Paul wondered suddenly if he'd been too demanding of them. They were self-centered, but hadn't he taught them to be just that?

What a pressure it is when I have only a month here, Lord. There's so much I want to share with them before I have to go, but I can't plan to do that. Opportunities have to come in Your time. Help me to leave this with You.

In the midst of his prayer, Paul remembered his wife. She was the one who needed the nurturing right now. His girls were important, but he believed Marrell was more so. If he could help her to understand, she would be better equipped to handle the girls in his absence.

What Marrell didn't know was that Paul *had* read between the lines. Marrell had begun expecting the girls to attend church, but because their attitudes were bad, she had run herself ragged in the last months trying to entertain them. No more. That's not what his wife was there to do, and it was time the girls understood that.

153

"Do you have any more questions?" Paul asked gently, seeing that he didn't have to stick with five each.

"I don't," Delancey said.

"Not right now," Mackenzie replied.

"Okay. I want you to think of two more each, and we'll talk about them later."

They both nodded.

"Okay. You two take off for a while so I can neck with your mother."

His tone was just right; they knew they were not in trouble. Both girls had smiles on their faces as they took their dishes to the sink and went to the living room. The sound of the TV springing to life could be heard as Paul moved from his chair to the one right next to Marrell's.

"How are you?" he said softly.

"I'm all right. I'm just trying to remember telling you that the girls dealt with your being gone and my going to church by drawing into their own little worlds. Shay was the one to point it out to me."

"You didn't tell me, but every letter and call was filled with all these things you had done: shopping, having friends over, running around. You also made no secret of how much they dislike church. I could see that you were trying to buy them. I don't want you to do that, and I don't want them to expect it. I can understand how easy it would be, but it's not fair to any of you."

Marrell had never seen it in that light, but it was all too true. "I'm such a pushover, Paul. I can't stand to have them scowling at me."

"Well, that's going to change. Our girls have a million things to be thankful for, and they can start while I'm here."

Marrell stared at him. The change in him was remarkable.

"Have I upset you?"

"No, I'm just thinking that we're never going to survive when you leave again."

Paul sighed. It was so hard, but he had to trust. He had to choose to let God be God.

"I'll pray for you every day, Mary — the girls too. You'll see. God will bring us through this."

Marrell was extremely comforted by his words. She was reminded of Shay's confidence, and Pastor Timm's as well. *I'll just keep on,* she told the Lord. *I'll keep searching until I can have what Paul's found. I'll keep on if it takes the rest of my life.*

Shay worked to hide her emotions on Sunday morning. She knew all about Paul from Marrell and warmly returned the hug he gave her, but knowing how left-out Marrell and the girls would be, she did not comment on Paul's new birth. The evidence was all around him: the Bible in his hand, his warm smile, the way he listened and took notes during the sermon.

He and Oliver got into a discussion right after church while Shay and Marrell talked. It was hard to stay focused, because Shay wanted to get alone and cry, but she forced her mind onto her friend.

"I would like it if you could come for dinner at my house," Shay told Marrell. "I'm going to be with Oliver's family on Christmas Day, but could you guys come on Christmas Eve?"

"Oh, that sounds fun. I'll check with Paul and see what he thinks."

"I know you have so little time, Marrell. If he doesn't want to, or you change your mind, I'll

155

understand. What day are you leaving for Tahoe?"

"The twenty-sixth, and we'll be back on the thirtieth. The girls want to stay longer, but that was the best rate on the condo."

"Sounds like fun."

"I think it will be. Micki's getting to be quite good at downhill, and D.J. has to keep up with Mic, so she pushes herself along."

"D.J. is the most fascinating creature, Marrell. When she puts that karate uniform on with that black belt around her waist, I'm awestruck by her poise and confidence. But then she gets in a crowd, and she all but stands behind Micki."

Marrell shook her head. "It's true, isn't it. Mackenzie can be just as bad, only I'm the one she hides behind."

Shay laughed. "And that's not working so well anymore since she now tops you by an inch."

Marrell shook her head in wonder. "I think I'm tall for a woman, Shay. I never dreamed that Mackenzie would pass me."

"How tall are you?"

"Five foot seven. Micki is five eight."

"I suppose D.J. will catch her soon. She's already got legs like a colt."

"Yes, and she's nearly wearing my shoes. She's not even eleven and a half!"

Shay smiled. The pride in Marrell's voice was very special. She knew that a mother didn't actually do anything to make her children grow tall, but somehow it seemed fitting that she take the praise.

"By the way, how are things at the office?" Marrell asked. Shay had given her Paul's entire leave off.

"The truth? We're falling apart without you.

You're the first person who has known how to do more than three things."

Marrell laughed at the look on Shay's face. A moment later the men joined them. The four talked until the girls showed up to say they were starving. With a promise to let Shay know about the evening of the twenty-fourth, the Bishops went on their way. Oliver could see the strain in Shay's face but kept quiet until they were in his car.

"You're ready to burst into tears," he said softly. "I could see that you barely made it through the sermon."

"Oh, Oliver." She laid her head back against the headrest. "I've prayed for so many years for Marrell and Paul, but mostly for Marrell. Now Paul is the one to believe, and I can't even talk with him for fear of hurting my friend. My heart is half joyful and half sad. It's giving me a headache."

She looked over to find Oliver's eyes on her.

"Not very good company, am I?" she asked.

"On the contrary, I've never loved you more."

Shay's eyes shut. He was so special. She didn't think she would ever get over Marty, but that had been immature ignorance on her part. Oliver not only loved God but understood how sin could lead a person into so many mistakes and horrible choices.

"I love you too," Shay spoke as she opened her eyes. "And one of the things I most appreciate about you, Oliver, is that you're not afraid to tell me."

"It's a risk," he said with the logic Shay loved. "All love is. Love puts people in a position to hurt each other, as you well know."

"I don't think we're going to hurt each other, Oliver. I really don't."

"No, I don't think so either — at least not in an irreparable way."

Shay nodded and smiled at him. He asked her whether she wanted to go for lunch but only tenderly kissed her cheek when she said she wanted to go home and cry her eyes out. After he had dropped Shay off, she realized that his tenderness was another one of the things she loved most about him.

South Lake Tahoe, California

"Do you think I don't know there's a difference, Paul?" Marrell whispered furiously, tears filling her huge blue eyes. "Do you think I don't see? I watched you with Shay and Oliver on Wednesday night, and even when Rose Cumberland came up for a few minutes. You all have God, and I don't!"

The girls were already asleep. It was only the second day of their trip, and husband and wife were talking on the rug in front of the huge stone fireplace in the condo they had rented. A fire crackled and burned, but right now neither one paid attention.

"Sometimes I'm so angry at all of you I could scream."

"I know, honey," Paul said lovingly, but Marrell was beside herself. She grabbed the front of his shirt with both hands.

"No, you don't! I just can't believe, Paul. I can't. Something is missing, and it's driving me crazy. I know I sin, and I know I don't have all the answers, but I just feel that God is holding me at arm's length."

She sat back now in utter defeat, and Paul stared at her. They had been talking off and on for two weeks, and still Marrell's heart raged on with grief and disbelief. Paul had no idea how to help her. He wished for a moment that Allen Post were there but then realized wishing for such things would be no help. He began to pray. Where the words came from he knew not, but he began to speak, and Marrell listened.

"Mary, do I make you feel that unless you come to Christ I won't love you anymore?"

"No," she said. But her voice was sad. "I thought that at one time — before you came home — but now I know better."

"You've told me that you believe that Jesus Christ is God's Son. Is that right?"

She nodded her silky blond head.

"And you've also told me that you know you're a sinner who needs a Savior."

"Yes."

"But you're afraid."

"Not exactly, Paul. I guess I would just call it a lack of belief. I don't know how much fear enters into it anymore. I used to be afraid of what God would ask of me, but I don't care any longer. If He'll just let me find Him, I'll do anything He wants." The defeat in her voice frightened him, but Paul went on.

"Mary, have you ever asked God to help you believe in Him?"

Marrell stared at her husband.

"Have you ever prayed and asked God to give you the belief?"

"No." Her voice was whisper-soft. "I didn't know I could. I thought I had to believe first."

Paul shrugged, feeling helpless in the face of his wife's confusion and pain. "I don't know for sure, Mary, but the Bible says that the very faith with which we believe comes from God. Why don't you ask God to help you believe, honey? It wouldn't hurt to try."

Marrell stared at Paul for a few more seconds before her head fell back, and she looked high on the stone mantel. She didn't focus in on the rocks but mentally knelt at the throne of grace and asked God, her heart wide open, to help her believe.

All this time I've tried to find You on my own, but I can't. Please help my sin-filled, unbelieving heart. Please help me to believe.

The truth was suddenly so clear to her that it took her breath away. With a gasp she looked at her husband, her eyes wide.

"Oh, Paul! It's all so clear to me now. He died for *me.* Not just for you and Shay, but for me. Jesus Christ died for me, for *my* sin." Paul's arms came around her, and he openly sobbed against her hair. Marrell clung to him. The girls had wanted to sleep in the loft above the living room, and Paul had never been so glad that he had said no. They were sure to have been right beside them if they had heard their tears.

"I believe You, Lord Jesus," she prayed as Paul held her. "I believe You died for my sins. Please take hold of me and never allow me to let go of You."

The tears would not be stopped. Lowering Marrell back against the pillows they had stacked up, Paul held her and let her cry. He felt like a limp rag. It was only too easy to understand how she must feel.

"I have peace," she finally whispered from where her head lay on his chest. "I'm so tired that I can't move, but I have peace at last."

"I never dreamed that God would rescue you

160

before I went back," Paul admitted. "It makes it so much more bearable, Marrell — I can't begin to tell you."

"So much makes sense now. I mean, I've been listening to Pastor Timm for weeks, but so often I was completely confused. Now I can't wait to hear more."

"You'll have to call Shay."

"Oh, Paul," Shay's name was enough to make her sit up. "What time is it? Can I call now?"

"It's late." He looked at his watch. "After twelve. We'd better wait until tomorrow."

"Okay." She looked down at him and smiled. "She's going to tell me how long she's prayed."

Paul chuckled. "I'm sure you're right."

Marrell's face brightened again. "Let's get blankets and sleep here tonight."

"You're on. You get the blankets, and I'll stoke the fire."

Marrell was back before Paul finished, and just before he joined her back on the pillows, he opened the curtains over the huge picture window that sat to the right of the fireplace. The lights were off inside, and they could see that it was snowing. Paul slipped beneath the blankets and snuggled close to his wife. They watched the snow in silence.

"God's blessings will be just like that snow, Mary. If we're obedient, His blessings will come down on us like snowflakes in a blizzard. The girls will come to Him, and we'll be fruitful and please Him all our days on the earth."

"And then eternity with Him," Marrell added.

Paul looked at her. "The peace is beyond anything I've ever known. I can't begin to explain."

There was no need. Paul knew just what peace

she spoke of, his own having increased in the last few minutes as he knew his precious Marrell had humbled herself before God.

It's going to be easy to be on an unrealistic high over this, Lord, he prayed as he remembered a warning from his CO. *Don't let us do that. Help us to have joy in You that goes deep enough to reach out to others, especially the girls.* Paul fell asleep asking God to help him remember his responsibility as father and husband, and to save Mackenzie and Delancey.

While Paul and the girls watched, Marrell called Shay and the two spent some emotional moments talking on the phone. The girls sat quietly at the kitchen table and watched their mother. In truth, they were very happy for her. They didn't understand this horrible emptiness that she talked about, but even that day on the slopes and while they'd eaten lunch at the lodge, they could see she felt better about everything. They sat patiently watching it all until Shay had news of her own.

"Oliver proposed."

"Oh, Shay," was all Marrell could say.

"It was so romantic, Marrell," Shay went on, even though her voice wobbled. "It was Christmas Day at his folks'. Everyone had gone home, and he asked me to go for a walk. Since he'd already given me a gift, I never suspected a thing."

"Where were you?"

"In his folks' orchard. Oh, Marrell, I couldn't believe it. The moon was shining, and he put a diamond ring on my hand."

Marrell gasped in an effort to control her tears.

"Oliver proposed," she told the room's occupants, "and gave Shay a diamond."

This got the attention of the girls as nothing else could. They left the table and begged their mom to let them talk with Shay.

"Just a few minutes," Marrell warned as she handed the phone off.

Questions about the wedding date, her colors, and the ring, took several minutes. Paul, who would never have thought to ask such things, was rather stupefied. How did his 11- and 12-year-old daughters know about such things? He didn't know if they had ever even attended a wedding. He said as much to Marrell, who only laughed and called him a man.

Marrell eventually took the phone back and spent a few more minutes with her friend. Paul had to leave again for Germany on Friday of that week — just five days. It had been Marrell and Shay's plan not to see each other until after he left, but the changes in their lives were too special. Before she hung up, Marrell set a date to meet Shay for a brief breakfast on Wednesday morning, the last day of 1980. It was sure to be a time they would never forget.

Ten

Heidelberg

I can't believe how much there is to learn, *Paul wrote to Marrell at the end of March.* Allen Post is unendingly patient with me. I wish I were as patient. I ache to be home with you and the girls. I wait like a schoolboy for each and every letter and then pore over your words a dozen times.

I've had several letters from Grandma. You can tell she's elated over our decisions for Christ, but she tells me she's been tired lately. Has she admitted that to you? She's got amazing fortitude for a woman her age, but since she's fallen twice in the last few months, I sometimes wonder how long she'll be in that house. It might help if she didn't have all those little rugs everywhere. If you feel a need to see her, go. We'll manage it. Maybe you can make some suggestions about her taking it easy. See how she reacts to that on the phone. Let me know what you want to do.

The ladies' Bible study sounds great, and I'm so glad you have Shay at the office for fellowship. Has she had any offers on the business? Part of me wonders if she shouldn't hold off a bit. If it sells right before she and Oliver get married, that's a lot of change at one time. Ah well, God knows best, and I know Oliver will advise her. He wrote to me recently. The letter was very welcome, as the longer I'm here, the farther I feel from home.

Have the girls shown any interest in spiritual things? I know I ask this in every letter and during every phone call, but at times I feel so out of touch. Talking on the phone doesn't tell me what their faces are doing. You reported that their attitudes have improved about church attendance, and I am thankful. I've been praying about that for all three of you since I left.

The space between us — the miles, and even the hours on the clock — are still strong on my mind. Nothing has ever made me consider leaving the Army more than the thought of having to be gone from you again. I've never seriously considered it before, but how can a man lead his family from across an ocean? He can't. I don't know if I'll reenlist for '83 or not.

Paul sat back, thinking about what he'd just written. After being in the Army for 21 years, he'd been almost afraid to write those words, but now that he had said them, he realized how true they were. This might be the time to call it quits, and having admitted it, he hadn't found it as frightening to think about as he once suspected.

What would I do? was Paul's very next thought. No answers followed, but he knew that didn't mean he shouldn't consider the possibility. Before he could start to worry, he went back to the letter.

I'm thankful that I'll be back at the Presidio. It's an excellent posting, and if God does want me to retire, at least I could finish out in an area that's become familiar and comfortable for all of us. Are you looking forward to being back on base, Mary, or are you dreading another move? Don't overdo before I get there. We'll put it all together as we always have. And at their ages, the girls will be more help than ever.

I have leave coming, almost a month of days. I thought it might be fun to go to Tahoe in the summer. Don't tell the girls yet. I want to surprise them. Maybe we could go up for the Fourth of July and watch the fireworks on the lake. Let me know what you think.

It's late here, so I'll close now. Tell Micki to run hard in track and she'll make the team; tell D.J. that I failed a lot of math tests in my day too. It's now one of my better subjects, and she just needs to keep trying. I can't wait to hold you in my arms again, Marrell. The thought alone makes me dream about you.

Love to you and the girls,
Paul

With those long legs of yours, Mackenzie, you should be running hurdles. It had been such an innocent remark on her mother's part, probably made six months earlier, but Mackenzie had not been able to get it out of her head. That must have been the reason she was standing with the 60 other seventh graders, looking for all the world as though she could drop through the earth with embarrassment and waiting for the track coach to call her name or give some sort of instruction. At least the coach was Miss Kane. She was Mackenzie's English teacher, and they already got on very well.

"Okay, everyone, come around me now until you can hear." The coach waited until they were

166

gathered a little closer. "At this level, we ask that you each try a little of everything to see where you might best fit in. Even if you want to throw the discus, I want to see your running form. If you're out here because your grandfather says you've got a great running stride, I still want to see you try the long jump. You get the picture, I'm sure.

"To make this easier we'll just do it alphabetically. Last names beginning with *A* through *N,* come to my right; O through *Z* to my left." She waited until kids were somewhat separated and then went on. "*A* through *N*'s go with me to the track. O through *Z*'s go with Mrs. Fenton to the long jump pit."

Mackenzie noticed right away that Mrs. Fenton was accompanied by one of the aides. Her math teacher, Mr. Frank, was with Miss Kane. She followed along with the rest of the kids, and only after they had started to walk did she see her friend Stacy.

"Mackenzie, I didn't know you were going out."

"I thought I told you, and you said you had changed your mind."

Stacy pulled a face. "My father changed it right back. Are you being forced too?"

"No, I wanted to give it a try. I don't know if I'll make the team though."

"There's no cut."

"There isn't?"

"No. Everyone who comes out for track can participate."

Mackenzie thought this was good news, but she wasn't sure she was good enough to do this. Coming out and making a fool of herself was not her idea of fun. Cut or no, if she couldn't do a good job for the team, she would be too embarrassed to keep showing up.

In the middle of all this speculation, she almost ran into the back of the boy in front of her. His name was Dan, and he was pretty cool, but at the moment Mackenzie wanted to avoid all attention. Just moments later girls and boys were separated and taken to opposite sides of the track. Miss Kane then explained how the girls would run.

They did some stretching — Miss Kane was very firm on how it was to be done — and then almost before she knew what was happening, Mackenzie found herself in the first group. She lined up with seven other girls and listened while the group was told that the race would end a quarter of the way down the track.

Miss Kane clapped twice, their cue to run. Mackenzie shot down the track, her legs pumping hard in long strides, not really aware of anyone near her. As she'd been instructed, she ran past the finish line and stopped to catch her breath several yards away.

Her shorts had crept up, and she was trying surreptitiously to pull them down when she realized that Miss Kane, along with several other kids, were shouting, "Good job, Mackenzie." To her utter surprise she had won, and if the times Miss Kane was shouting could be counted on, by more than a little.

"Nice run," Miss Kane complimented, having come up close.

"Thank you," Mackenzie breathed, still slightly winded.

"Be sure and give the low hurdles a try, Mackenzie. I think you would do well."

"All right."

The older woman moved away to work with the next group, and Mackenzie found herself glad for a few moments alone. Her solitude wasn't to last. She hadn't been aware of anyone else, but suddenly the other girls came over to congratulate her. Mackenzie was still visiting with them when a group of eighth-grade boys walked by.

"Nice run, Mackenzie," Brett Cooper spoke up, and a few of the other guys nodded in agreement.

"Thank you," she said kindly and smiled, but she could feel her already flushed face heating again.

"I think he likes you," Marie said.

"I do too," added someone else. "I've seen him watching you."

"Brett?" Mackenzie asked in surprise.

The other girl was nodding, a big smile on her face, when they heard Miss Kane clapping. It was a relief to turn and cheer the other girls on.

"Come on, Stacy!" Mackenzie yelled and watched her friend come in second. Mackenzie went right to her, and from there the time sped by. More races followed. Some she ran in, and some she cheered for. As Miss Kane had predicted, she did do well in the hurdles. Before she knew it, her coach was telling them to be on time the next day and dismissing them. Mackenzie spotted her mother's car just a few minutes later and climbed into the backseat. Delancey had the front.

"How'd it go?"

"Great. No one is cut from the team, so I'm on. I even won two of the races I was in."

"That's great," Marrell said.

"Who's that guy who just waved at you?" Delancey wanted to know, her eyes on the tall

169

blond boy.

Mackenzie finished smiling and waving back before she answered.

"Brett Cooper. Isn't he cute?"

"Yes. Does he like you?"

"According to Marie Overton, he does."

"He looks older." This was Marrell's only comment on the boy.

"He's in eighth grade."

Delancey turned to smile at her sister, who shook her head in playful exasperation. Delancey's boy craziness was getting to be something of a joke between them. That her mother didn't find it so funny was a fact both girls tended to ignore.

I need so much wisdom, Lord. They still have no interest in You, yet they obey me, and most of the time we get along very well. What can I expect? Marrell wondered if perhaps she didn't expect enough. *Please bring Paul home safely to us,* she finished. *We need him.*

"What's for dinner, Mom?"

"Omelets. I haven't shopped yet, so it's not going to be very exciting."

Until their mother went to work part-time, both girls had been guilty of taking her work around the house and in the kitchen for granted. They didn't always have the clean clothes they wanted now, and about once a month they had to settle for whatever was in the cupboard.

Remembering what her father had said about thankfulness, Mackenzie bit her tongue against complaining and asked, "How was your day at the office, Mom?"

"It was fine." Marrell was pleased to be asked. "Things have picked up for spring, but the busyness makes the day go faster."

"Do you have to work on our Easter break?"

"No. I already told Shay I would need it off. It's going to make things more hectic both before and after, but it'll be worth it to be home."

"I wish Dad could be here."

"Me too," Marrell said with a sigh. "I sat outside on my lunch hour today and counted the days."

"How many?"

"He's done there June 26, so he could be here as early as the twenty-seventh."

"He'll miss my birthday," Mackenzie said wistfully.

"Um hm."

"So how many days is that?" Delancey still wanted to know.

"Eighty-nine."

Delancey groaned. "That's forever."

At the moment Marrell felt the same way but stayed quiet. She had done so much growing since Christmas and continued to be hungry for the Word, but the job of single parenting and seeing to so many needs on her own was a hard task.

Help me to be thankful that I have a husband, Lord. So many marriages don't even make it. Help me remember to thank You that my husband is coming home in less than three months.

"Oh, look at that car," Mackenzie said. "It looks fast."

"You and your fast cars, Micki," her mother replied with a small chuckle. She liked sporty cars herself, but they didn't turn her head the way they did Mackenzie's. "Makes me dread the next three years."

"In California you can get your permit when you're 15, so it's only two years and three months!" Mackenzie's tone was nothing short of triumphant.

"Thanks for the warning. I might start riding the bus."

Mackenzie laughed. "Dad will take me out. He can do anything."

Marrell threw a smile over her shoulder. "A 15-year-old girl behind the wheel? I don't know if any man is that strong."

Both girls found this very funny, and Marrell was still smiling as she pulled into the parking lot of the apartment building.

"Will you girls enjoy getting back on the base?" she asked.

"I will," Mackenzie said. "I want a place for a basketball hoop."

Delancey, who had a crush on one of the boys in the apartment upstairs, said nothing at all.

Sebastopol, California

They spent Easter Sunday with Oliver, Shay, and Oliver's family in Sebastopol. The day was warm and sunny on the Lacys' farm, where the couple grew a variety of apples. In the fall they would be sold by the bushel or bag. They were also made into pies or caramel apples, or pressed into cider. The girls loved getting out of the city, and Marrell especially enjoyed the fellowship at the church they attended.

For most of the day, the talk was on Oliver and Shay's upcoming nuptials. The wedding was scheduled for May 2, just under two weeks away, and naturally everyone was excited. Mackenzie was happy for Shay and Oliver but tired of wedding plans. She wandered out onto the front porch and dropped into the padded glider, the seat moving gently beneath her. The rocking chair looked comfortable too, but it was in the sun, and Mackenzie was already hot. She had been on the porch for only five minutes when Oliver's father, Greg Lacy, appeared.

"May I join you?" he asked congenially. Mackenzie smiled. He was so like Oliver with his dark red hair and kind smile. He was just the way she'd always pictured a perfect grandfather — warm and caring, but not too old to be in touch.

"Sure," Mackenzie agreed. "Is the game over?"

"Yes, and they've got the bridal magazines out again, so I made my escape."

Mackenzie laughed.

"I've got something to show you, Micki." Greg held a book in his hand. "Do you have a scrapbook?"

"No. My mom has one, but I've never started one."

"Well," he sat on the other end of the glider from her and put the book between them, "I thought you might like a little of this." He opened the first page. "My mother was very good at keeping things, and I was in track from the time I was your age."

"Oh, Mr. Lacy," Mackenzie breathed reverently as she took in the old newspaper photos and articles. "You did hurdles."

"Yes, ma'am, I did. Just the way you do now."

"Oh, I didn't know. Oliver's never said."

Greg smiled humbly.

"Now, which one are you?" Mackenzie asked as she studied the photos.

"Here, and here again." He pointed to pictures as he went, giving a brief history. The pages mapped his career from junior high through his high school years and into college. He lingered a bit long on one of the middle pages, but when he turned it, his eyes were on Mackenzie's face. He had the headline memorized.

"The Olympics!" Mackenzie's mouth was agape. "You ran hurdles in the London Olympics?"

Before she could even see him reaching toward his pocket, Greg was dangling a medal in front of her.

Mackenzie gasped as he handed it to her. "A bronze. You won a bronze medal in the Olympics!"

Greg smiled at her enthusiasm.

"This is so cool." She fingered the medal and studied the scrapbook articles. Oliver came out to the porch then, and Mackenzie brightened at the sight of him.

"Oliver, isn't this cool?"

"Yes, it is. I've been meaning to tell you, but it just kept slipping my mind. Did you show her my favorite picture, Dad?"

"The one with your mother? Not yet."

Greg flipped through the book and came to a photo of the award ceremony. Seated in the front row of the stands, in a startling clear shot, was a very young Carol Lacy.

"How wonderful," Mackenzie said softly, "that she could be there with you."

"I didn't know her," Greg inserted, his eyes on Mackenzie's face again.

"You didn't know who?" Mackenzie lowered her brow in confusion.

"I didn't know Carol," Greg said. "We hadn't met yet."

Mackenzie's mouth, which opened but made no sounds, was fun to watch.

"You had better tell her, Dad." Oliver's voice was amused.

The 12-year-old could only stare at the older Lacy.

"There was a small party that night for those of us who had medaled in the track and field events. I was still floating on a cloud from the race, but I noticed this young woman sitting against the wall. The chairs all around her were empty, so I took my glass of punch over and asked if I could sit down. I can't say I did it because I felt sorry for her, but I was ready to wind down a little, and she didn't seem to be busy. We were joined by two other girls right after that, and after we exchanged names and the towns we were from, we got to talking.

"The two other girls were both English, but Carol Wagner was an American and from California to boot. We talked for more than an hour, and when the other girls got up to speak with someone, I asked Carol if I could see her the next day. She had to work. She was a nurse at a hospital over there, and by the time she was going to be off duty, I had to return to California. But we exchanged addresses and started to write to each other."

"Wow." Mackenzie looked at the picture again.

"It was weeks before I saw this picture and made the connection," Greg told her.

"Yes, by the time he saw it, Mom had moved back to California and they were engaged," Oliver added.

"It's like something you would read in a book," Mackenzie said, and both men could see that the wheels in her head were turning.

"Hey, Micki," Delancey called from behind the screen door, "we need someone for hearts. Do you wanna play?"

175

"Oh, sure. Thank you for showing these to me, Mr. Lacy."

"You're welcome."

Mackenzie handed the medal back and stood, but for some reason she didn't want to leave. She started to move away and then looked back at her host.

"Do you still run, Mr. Lacy?" she asked shyly.

"Yes, I do." That was all he said, enjoying the spectacle of his young guest trying to get the words out. She couldn't do it, so he rescued her.

"I don't do hurdles anymore."

Mackenzie laughed a little. "It's really not my business, but I did wonder."

Greg Lacy winked at her then, and she swung around to head inside. The men exchanged smiles the moment she left the porch.

"How was your Easter break?" Brett Cooper asked Mackenzie Monday after lunch. The seventh grader tried to answer him without staring; he was so tall and good-looking.

"It was fun," Mackenzie replied, thinking of the day before at the Lacys'. "We didn't do too much, but that was okay. How was yours?"

"Boring," Brett answered, and Mackenzie mentally flinched. She knew that he sounded like everyone else, but her father had finally gotten through. There was always so much to be thankful for, but most of the time the kids she knew were bored and bent out of shape about something. She had been too, until he had started getting on her. In every letter and phone call, her dad asked her to tell him at least five things she had to be thankful for. He also had a habit of sending home news clippings and photos from around the world

176

— articles of people who didn't have it so good. It had really started her thinking.

"We didn't do anything," Brett went on, his voice bitter. They were still walking toward Mackenzie's locker, and when she didn't say anything, Brett told her he had an oral report due that day.

"What's it on?"

"Germany."

"Oh, my dad is stationed there right now."

"He is? Why?"

"He's in the Army."

"Oh. When is he coming home?"

"This summer."

"Will he be stationed there again after that, I mean, in Germany?"

"No, he'll be back at the Presidio."

"Will you still go here?"

"Yes. It's the same school district."

The smile on Brett's face caused Mackenzie to blush. She was glad to be able to turn to her locker and spin the combination. The bell rang, and again Mackenzie was relieved. Brett waved to her as he walked away, but Mackenzie was torn inside.

Why does my heart leap when I see the guy, but when the bell rings, I'm glad he's leaving? With a mental shake of her head, she wiped her sweaty palms down the legs of her jeans, picked up her math book, and walked to class.

"What is your *problem*, D.J.?" Mackenzie nearly screamed at her sister several weeks later. "I'm sick of your mood. Now I want my book back, and I mean *now!*"

D.J. threw the book at her sister, and Mackenzie had started toward her when Marrell showed up

177

at the door.

"That's enough, Mackenzie!" Marrell's voice was a lash, stopping the older girl's fist in midair. "To your room. Right now!"

Marrell waited until her older daughter had stomped from the room before going in to address Delancey.

"You've been sulking all evening, Delancey. What is going on?"

"Nothing." Her voice was sullen.

Marrell only looked at her. The maturity was coming. The baby-smooth cheeks were gone, and now oily places around her nose and chin, along with a few pimples, were plainly visible. Her eyes were still like huge blue flowers, her lashes dark and long, but thick blond hair that could go for a week without a washing was now hanging limp around her face after just three days.

"Delancey," Marrell said softly this time, waiting for her younger daughter to look at her. "If you don't want to talk about what's bothering you, then I won't push you, but neither will I put up with your mood."

Delancey looked away for a moment, so Marrell waited. She thought she might share, but Delancey only looked back at her.

"Do I make myself clear?"

"Yeah."

"Are you sure you don't want to talk?"

Delancey shrugged. "There's nothing wrong, really, Mom."

"Then why are you so cross?"

"I just wish Dad were here."

Marrell nodded, but she had the feeling there was something more. Delancey had been touchy and down since Shay's wedding almost two weeks

178

before.

"How many days is it now?" Delancey's question brought Marrell back to the present.

"Forty-four."

Delancey's sigh was huge.

"Are you all right?"

"Yeah."

"I'm going to talk to Micki now, but if you want to talk, D.J., we still can."

"Thanks, Mom."

Delancey let her mother walk from the room. There was no point in stopping her. Something felt wrong, but she didn't know what it could be. If her mother had pressed her, she wouldn't have known what to say. Mackenzie was reading the only book she wanted, so Delancey reached for her sketchpad. All her recent drawings looked stupid to her, so she turned to a fresh page and started over.

"You will not hit your sister," Marrell wasted no time in saying.

"Mom, she's acting like such a brat today," Mackenzie defended herself. "She threw this book at me, and it belongs to the school."

"Right now I don't care what she did. I'm talking about your hitting her. I won't stand for it, Mackenzie Rose Bishop. Do you hear me?"

"Yes." Mackenzie's tone was none too gracious, but Marrell let that go. She had another bone to pick between them.

"You had a call when you were in the shower."

"Who was it?"

"He didn't leave his name."

"It was a boy?" This brought Mackenzie to the edge of the bed, sitting up now instead of lying down.

"Yes, and there's something we need to get straight right now, Micki. If they're not going to give a name, I won't hand the phone to you, even if you're free."

"Oh, Mom, you've got to be kidding." Mackenzie's face was thunderstruck.

"Not in the least, I assure you. Your father and I talked it over, and he told me to handle this any way I'm comfortable."

"Why do you have to know, Mom? A phone call is private."

"I didn't say I had to listen on the other line, Mackenzie. I just want to know who it is. If you're not doing something to be ashamed of, what's the big secret?"

"It's just so embarrassing. I mean, it's hard enough for a guy to call, let alone have to talk to the girl's mother."

Marrell smiled. She had said *mother* as though it were some specimen under a microscope.

"Not talk to a girl's mother," Marrell gasped. "Anything but that!"

Mackenzie, who had a pretty good sense of humor, smiled a little too.

"Are you really serious?"

"Yes, Mic, I am," Marrell's voice answered gently. "All I would have wanted him to do was say, "This is Clem Hinklewart. Can you please tell Mackenzie I called?""

A full smile came to Mackenzie's mouth at this, but she wanted to blush at the thought of telling a guy he had to give his name.

"His name is Brett Cooper."

"Well now, that's a much nicer name then Clem Hinklewart. He should feel no embarrassment in telling me that."

Mackenzie bit her lip to keep from smiling, and Marrell stood.

"Are we all set?"

"I think so. It doesn't look as though I have much choice."

Marrell shrugged. "Maybe your father will handle it differently, Mic, but with three women living here alone, I want to know exactly who owns the male voice of anyone who calls."

Mackenzie nodded. This made perfect sense. She had no way of really knowing whether Brett had called and wouldn't bring it up unless he did, but the reason her mother just gave made complete sense. If Brett did say something, she knew just how she would reply. In fact, she spent the time before bed writing it all down — what he would say, where they would be, how she would smile — all of it.

She didn't know until the next day that it was all a waste of time. Brett was on a trip with the eighth graders, and she wouldn't see him until Monday.

ELEVEN

Paul did not surprise his family in the night this time. On June 27, four days after Mackenzie's thirteenth birthday, Marrell and the girls stood at San Francisco International Airport and waited for Paul Bishop to deplane.

Marrell's palms were damp with excitement, and the anxiety that she would burst into tears and not even be able to talk to him was mounting. The girls' faces were pale like her own, each daughter looking as if she could cry too.

A moment later he was there. Dropping his bag, he tried to hug them all at once. As they clung to him, tears poured down everyone's face. No one could speak. They hugged for several minutes, and then for privacy Paul gently moved them to the corner of a nearly deserted waiting area. He bent and kissed his wife's wet cheek, his arm going around her, and smiled at the girls.

"Hi, Dad," Mackenzie managed. They all stood very close.

"Hi, Mic. Hi, D.J."

"Oh, Dad," was all his youngest could say. It felt as though he had been gone forever.

"Your eyes are running down your face," Paul teased Mackenzie, and she wiped at the makeup on her face as he leaned to kiss her brow.

182

"I wasn't going to do this," Marrell finally spoke, her cheek still laid against his chest. "It just feels so long."

"Doesn't it, though? They had some difficulty with my first plane, and I dreaded calling you and telling you I wasn't on the way."

"Oh, I'm so glad I didn't know about that," Marrell said fervently.

Paul laughed. "We'd better get down to the luggage carousels. Are we up to it?"

The females nodded, but all looked drained and emotional. Little talk was shared as they walked through the airport and down the escalator to retrieve Paul's two bags. But the walk to the car took some time, and everyone perked up a little on the way.

Marrell told him that since her last letter Shay had accepted an offer on her business, and that she would need to put in only a few days of work in July. Delancey shared about the garage sale she wanted to have, and Mackenzie wanted permission to go to Great America with a group of friends. Having just spent the last 27 hours on a plane and in airports, Paul forced himself to at least tell the girls that he would think about their requests.

They were almost home when his brain clicked into gear, and he said out of the blue, "D.J., we don't have a garage."

Marrell laughed at him and shook her head as Delancey launched into the perfect way to have this sale in the parking lot of the apartment building. By the time she finished, he was glassy-eyed again but managed to get them safely into the parking place. The girls scrambled out, taking the keys to get the luggage and heading inside. Marrell sat looking at her husband for a long moment.

"I've never felt for you what I do now," she said softly, thinking that God had blessed her beyond measure.

Paul smiled. "I've been thinking about that too. How about we get married again?"

Marrell's mouth dropped open. "When?"

"August 28."

"Our anniversary! Oh, Paul, what a wonderful idea."

"I think so. It just seems so natural after all the changes. We'll think about it, okay?"

"Okay."

They leaned simultaneously and kissed before climbing out of the car. The girls had made some things for their father, so as soon as he was inside, they presented him with a picture Delancey had drawn and a cake Mackenzie had baked.

"Oh, thank you. This picture is super, D.J. You're getting better all the time."

She smiled shyly but with great pleasure.

"What kind of cake, Mic?"

"Chocolate."

"That's my girl. In fact, I could eat some of this right now."

"Can we, Mom?"

"I wouldn't argue with that. Don't forget the ice cream."

It was a perfectly normal thing to do on their father's first day back. They visited some, but mostly ate in silence, and then Paul produced some gifts he had purchased, including a late birthday gift for Mackenzie. No one was hungry for supper just an hour later, and jet lag was catching Paul fast.

"A nap or an early night?" It was six o'clock

when Marrell asked.

"I don't know if I can make it until tonight, and if I nap now, I might not be coherent afterward."

"Don't try. Just go to bed now and sleep the night."

Paul hated to do it, but that's just what he did. He didn't remember his fatigue being this bad in December, but he was nearly dragging as he kissed his wife and girls and headed to the bedroom. Undressing and stretching out on his back, and even sighing with the pleasure of being in his own bed, he remembered nothing else until almost six o'clock the next morning.

Marrell rolled over and for an instant thought one of the girls had climbed into bed beside her. It took a second for her to remember that Paul was finally home. She squinted through the hair that had fallen in her face to find him lying on his side watching her. She smiled.

"How long have you been awake?" she asked, her voice rusty.

"Just a little while. You're beautiful in the morning, did you know that?"

She groaned a little. "You sound like a man starved for the sight of his wife no matter how bad she looks."

Paul chuckled and pushed the hair from her face. He kissed her, and Marrell realized he'd been up to shave.

"Are the girls up?" she asked.

"I don't think so. It's only about 6:20."

"Did you sleep well?"

"Very well. I didn't even hear you come in."

"How was your bed in Germany? I never asked you."

185

"It was fine," Paul said before a smile lit his eyes. "But I never got to wake up next to my wife — a keen disadvantage, I can tell you."

"Oh, Paul, I didn't know anyone could miss someone the way I missed you."

He kissed her again. "I assure you, the feeling is quite mutual. Tell me again, what time do we need to leave for Sunday school?"

"About 9:10."

"Perfect," he said as his arms went around her. "Plenty of time to cuddle with my wife."

"Hell is a very real place," Pastor Timm said later that morning. Delancey didn't like the sound of that, but unlike previous Sunday mornings, she wasn't able to shift her mind to other things.

Did people really burn forever? Would God really make someone do that? The thought was so awful to her that she refused to believe it. One time, while she was still quite little, her mother had been baking a cake. Delancey had touched the pan and burned the side of her small finger. She remembered thinking the pain would never go away. She hated it and had a mark for days after.

What would it be like to feel that all over? Delancey felt sick at the thought. She chanced a look at Mackenzie, but she was looking bored and disinterested. Delancey knew she couldn't talk to her. She could talk to her mother but hoped by the time the service ended that she would have forgotten all about it. Delancey finally distracted herself by thinking about a dress she had seen at the mall. After a few moments her mind was as far away from the sermon as Mackenzie's.

The following week was busy. On Monday and

Tuesday the four Bishops packed. They threw out, cleaned, sorted, threw out some more, and loaded every available box with possessions. They woke up Wednesday morning to go at it again.

"Where did we get all this stuff?" Paul asked at one point, having just lifted a very heavy box and set it by the wall in the living room.

"That box holds books," Marrell admitted. "I probably buy two or three a month."

Paul nodded. He had been doing more reading as well.

"Do we need to keep them, or can we donate them to the church library?"

"Oh, I never thought of that. Maybe I should go through them again."

"Not now; they're packed. We'll leave those boxes and sort them once we're on the base."

"All right. Did you hear back about housing?"

"Yeah," Paul's face brightened. "I forgot to tell you. We're back on Infantry Terrace."

"Are we really?"

"Yes. I don't know the number, but that's what I was told."

"Oh, that's the best news I've had all day."

"What's the best news?" Delancey wanted to know.

"Our house on the base is right back where we were on Infantry Terrace."

"Oh, cool," she said calmly as she headed into the kitchen to attack the fruit bowl. She wandered past with an apple and two oranges in her hands, and Paul stared after her.

"Is she about two feet taller than she was yesterday, or is it me?"

Marrell laughed. "She shot up right after Easter, and it hasn't stopped yet. All she does is eat and stretch out more. She's already in some of Micki's clothes, and she can't wear my shoes any longer."

"She looks like pictures I've seen of my mother when she was in high school — tall and lean."

They were silent for a moment as they worked. Paul had written to his family after his conversion, but the response had not been good. He hadn't even mentioned the Lord, but his father's letter back to him had been scathing, blaming Paul for the distance between them, hurting his mother, and thinking only of himself. Paul had written twice more, but no answers came.

Marrell had a sudden thought. "Did you ever try writing to just your mom, Paul? I wonder if she wouldn't be more receptive than your father."

Paul realized how true it was. His mother had never been as angry as his father; hers had always been the kinder approach.

"Do you know what I'm going to do?"

"What?"

"Call. My father would still be at work right now, and I think I'll just call. If she doesn't want to talk to me, I'll leave them alone. It can't hurt any more than it does now, so what have I got to lose?"

"Oh, Paul." Marrell was anxious as she followed him to the phone in the kitchen. It was all so sudden. He dialed the number without hesitation, and Marrell stood by, begging God to let Mrs. Bishop be home alone. She didn't think she would be able to breathe when Paul said, "Mom?"

Paul listened intently as there was a long hesitation on the other end and finally a tentative, "Paul?"

"Yes, Mom, it's Paul. I didn't mean to frighten you."

188

"It's all right. I'm just . . ." Arlene Bishop was too overcome to go on.

"I'm sorry, Mom. I'm sorry I've made you cry."

"It's all right," she gasped. "Just don't hang up. I have to get a tissue."

Paul glanced at Marrell, whose hands were over her mouth. Mackenzie came in and asked what was going on.

"He's talking to his mother," Marrell whispered.

Mackenzie's eyes grew on this announcement, but she made no comment.

"I'm here," Paul said into the phone once his mother had returned. "I wasn't sure if I should call. Dad's letter was pretty final."

"He's at the office," Arlene said softly.

"I figured he might be."

"He's sorry he sent that letter, Paul, but he'll never take it back." She wasted no time in saying the very thing she didn't think she could admit to anyone. "He's read your other two letters a dozen times."

"But you don't think he'll change his mind?"

"No, he's too stubborn for that."

"What about you, Mom? I mostly called to see if you feel the same way."

"No, I was just glad to know you're still alive." She gave a harsh laugh. "Do you remember how hard we were on you when you married Marrell? Well, yours is the only marriage that's made it. Tells you what we all know."

"Everyone's divorced?"

"Yes. Your sister three times."

"Oh, Mom, I'm sorry."

There was an uncomfortable silence then. Paul was at a complete loss.

"You still in Germany?"

"No, I'm back in San Francisco now. In fact, we're moving back to the base at the end of the week."

"How are Marrell and the girls?"

"They're great. It's good to be home with them."

"Is it really? You're still getting along with Marrell?"

"Yes. I'm thrilled to be home."

"I'm glad, Paul. Don't divorce. It's awful."

"I won't, Mom. In fact we're going to repeat our vows on our anniversary in August."

"I wish I could be there."

"You would be very welcome."

"Your father would have a fit. I don't want to think about it."

Silence came again before Paul found the courage to ask the only question on his mind.

"Would I be welcome if I came to see you?" he asked softly and could hear she was crying again. Tears gathered in his own eyes, and he could feel Marrell come up and hug him from the back.

"He would be so angry, Paul. I'm sorry, but he's never going to forget."

Arlene was sobbing, and Paul's own tears would not be squelched.

"I love you, Mom," he cried.

"Oh, Paul, Paul!" Arlene wailed.

Paul called her name, but she had dropped the phone. He waited, unsure of what to do next. He hadn't even said goodbye.

"Hello?" Someone had picked up the other end.

"Hello."

"Who is this?" a female voice demanded.

"It's Paul Bishop."

There was a moment of silence.

"Paul? Is it really you?"

"Tammy?" Paul had not even recognized his sister's voice. He didn't remember it sounding so gravelly.

"Yeah, it's me. Mom's sobbing, and I . . . Well, um, I mean, what are you doing?"

"I just wanted to talk to Mom and see how she is. I'm sorry she's so upset."

Paul heard voices in the background now, and a moment later his mother came back on.

"Are you all right?" he said softly.

"Yes. I'm okay. I didn't want you to hang up before I could say goodbye."

"Can I call you again?"

"Yes, during the day. He takes Mondays off now."

"Okay. I'll call again after we're settled on the base."

"Okay."

"Mom?"

"Yes."

"You can tell him I called. I don't care if he knows, as long as he won't take it out on you."

Arlene sighed. "I'll think about it."

"Tell Tammy I said hello. Art and Lance too."

"I'll do that. You tell Marrell hello. And those girls."

"Okay. Take care, Mom. Don't forget what I said."

"I won't."

Paul hung up the phone a moment later, amazed at the conversation he'd just had. Ten minutes ago his mother had not even been on his mind; now he had spoken to her. All she had cared about was that he was still alive. Marrell was still clinging to his back, which left Paul's hands free to wipe at the tears coming down his face.

191

I miss her, he told the Lord. *I miss my mom. It's been so long. I made some bad choices, but now You've given her back to me. I may never see her again, but I know she still cares. Even my father cares. I'll write again, and this time I know he'll read it.*

He turned now, ready to take his wife into his arms.

"How is she?" Marrell asked.

"She's okay. She said Dad's sorry about the letter, but he would never admit it. I can call back, and I plan to write again."

"Oh, Paul." Marrell still felt as though she could bawl. "When I suggested contacting your mother, I didn't know what I was getting us into. I thought I would die when I heard those tears in your voice."

Both Delancey and Mackenzie were on the scene now. In an apartment with a short hallway and the bedrooms right off the kitchen and living room, there was very little privacy. Mackenzie had never moved, and Delancey had joined them when from her bedroom she had realized things had gotten very quiet.

"Are you all right, Dad?" Delancey asked.

"Yes. Your grandmother said hello."

"Does she know us?"

"She knows your names, but that's about all."

"Who's divorced?" Mackenzie asked, having heard all of Paul's side of the conversation.

"Both my brothers and my sister."

"Is Tammy your sister?"

"Yes," Paul told her and wondered at how little the girls knew about his family. "Come in the living room for a few minutes, and I'll tell you about them."

They pushed boxes out of the way to get to the sofa, reminding them that time was getting away, but Paul believed this was important.

"I don't know what you know about my family, but they live in Florida. My father grows citrus fruit, a business he started with his own brother who's dead now. My brothers, Art and Lance, work with him. I was expected to follow along, and when I didn't, they all grew angry with me, but mostly my father."

"Maybe you should tell them your siblings' names and ages," Marrell suggested.

"My sister Tammy is the oldest; she's 8 years older than I am. Next is Art; he's 46. Lance at 43 is just two years older than me. I was pretty close to Lance, but he got into some wild things in high school, and my mom started keeping us apart. It was as if she was saying, 'I can't control your wild brother, but I'll keep you away from him so you won't turn out the same.'

"I graduated from high school at 18 and went to work in the orchards. My father didn't believe in playing favorites, so I had to start at the bottom. I had done some work in the summers but always knew I'd be able to get out of it in the fall when school started. I hated the job I had. I hated it so much that all my father and I did was fight.

"I stuck it out for two years, but when he threatened to cut my pay, I quit. I was terrible to him. I called him all sorts of awful names, and he did the same to me. I got so angry that I joined the Army. He didn't believe me when I told him. He didn't take me seriously until I showed him my papers and bus ticket. He told me to get out and never come back."

Paul paused here. It was such a painful memory.

"So was today the first time you talked to your mom in all these years?" Mackenzie asked.

"No. I did go home at times, but I was never very welcome. My father couldn't stand the sight of my uniform, and when I told them I was going to Officer Candidate School, you'd have thought I was joining the mob. My father never dreamed I would make a career out of it. I sent them invitations to everything. I let them know every time I was promoted, but they never responded.

"Then, as a newly commissioned officer, I walked into a diner in Colorado Springs and met your mother. From that point forward she became my life. We visited my parents only twice after we were married because they didn't approve of the marriage. The last time we visited, I had a fight with my brother over something he said to your mom, and we've never been back."

"Why did you call her today?"

"I can see now as never before how wrongly I've treated my parents. I'm trying to make amends. I wrote to them when I was in Germany. My father wrote back, as angry as ever. I hoped my mother would feel differently, so knowing that my father would be at work, I called just to talk with her."

"Was she glad?"

Paul smiled, his throat closing again. "Yes. She even admitted that they had been wrong about your mom. All my siblings married local people, and none of the marriages has lasted."

"Will we go see her?" Delancey queried.

"No, honey, I'm afraid not. My father still won't welcome me, and I wouldn't want to put any of you through that."

Delancey had tears in her eyes.

"What is it, honey?" Marrell asked.

"I don't know," she shrugged, looking miserable. "I would hate it if I couldn't see you and Dad."

"Oh, D.J." Paul's heart felt as though it would break. How did he explain a man like Otto Bishop to his innocent daughter? "I'm sorry we can't see him. It hurts me too. It did help, however, that my mother said he was sorry he had written the letter, but she made it very clear that he wouldn't want to see me."

"I'm going to pray that he changes his mind," Marrell put in softly.

"As will I," Paul seconded.

"Did I hear you tell your mother that you're marrying Mom again?" This came from Mackenzie.

"We're talking about it, yes. On our anniversary."

"Why?" Mackenzie asked in genuine confusion.

Paul sighed. "I know that the changes in our lives have not really affected you, Micki. If I had come to Christ while this marriage was on the verge of breakup or from a life of constant drinking and fighting, you might have more to go on. The truth of the matter is, I've always loved and provided for you guys, but I know there is more. Your mother and I are new creatures in Christ now, and we want to celebrate that by standing before God and our friends and rededicating our lives to each other. I'm very excited about it."

"Will there be a lot of people there?"

"Hundreds," Marrell jumped in. "And you and D.J. will stand up with us and be in the ugliest dresses ever made. It's sure to be covered by the evening news. You'll be so embarrassed you'll never be able to show your faces again."

"Mom!" Mackenzie tried not to laugh.

"In fact," the older woman continued, not letting her say a word, "you'll both have to write speeches, memorize them, and recite them to the whole group. I'll see to it that every boy you've ever had a crush on will be there to watch from the front row."

Both girls were laughing now.

"This is serious, you two," Marrell went on, refusing to let up. "I think I want you each to sing a solo."

"Dad," Delancey choked out, "will you stop her?"

Paul and Marrell exchanged a smiling glance.

"Seriously, Mom." Mackenzie was not done. "Will it be like a ceremony?"

"We don't know yet, Micki. We're still just thinking about it, and long before that time comes, we have a houseful of furniture and stuff to move."

The phone rang. Mackenzie ran for it, coming back to tell Marrell it was Shay.

"Hi," Marrell spoke into the phone.

"How's it going?"

"Pretty good. The movers come for everything Friday morning. I just got the good news that we are right back on Infantry Terrace."

"Oh, that is good news. Which house?"

"Paul isn't sure. Hey, did you find that note I left on your desk?"

"Yes. That's why I'm calling you. Closing is Friday, July 31."

Marrell just about squealed with delight. "Oh, Shay, I could dance. Are you ecstatic?"

"I am, but not just about that."

"Why? What's up?"

"Marrell," Shay said softly. "I'm going to have a baby."

Marrell's eyes slid shut. "Oh, Shay," she whispered, "my dear friend Shay. No one could be happier for you than I am."

"I think my mother would disagree with you."

"What did she say?" Marrell smiled.

"She screamed for a full minute and then ran through the house like a wild woman trying to find my dad. She left the phone dangling, and I had a stitch in my side from laughing."

"Oh, Shay, I'm dying to give you a hug. Let's get together tonight."

"Okay. By the way, we're not telling everyone yet. I mean, this is my first baby at 36 years old, and I've got all the way to March to go, so I want to keep this low-key right now."

"That's fine. I'll just tell Paul."

"Okay. What time tonight?"

"Well, do you want to come here, or should we pick up something and come to you?"

"Come here. I'll make a salad and dessert, and you come up with something to go in the middle."

"Okay. It'll probably be a bucket of chicken. You know what I'm like. Hey, are you sick at all?"

"Not really. Coffee doesn't interest me right now, and raw meat makes me feel a little weird."

"I'm glad it's no worse than that."

"Listen, I've got to run. I'll tell you all about it tonight."

"Okay. 'Bye."

The girls had wandered off, so Marrell was able to tell Paul in privacy. His smile was huge.

"Well, since I can't hug Shay until tonight, I'll hug you."

"It's a secret," she whispered into his ear.

"Okay. Even from the girls?"

"Yes. I told her I would tell only you."

"Okay."

They went back to work, and by the time they left for Oliver and Shay's, they felt things were under control for the next day and pickup on Friday. Paul was to report to the base first thing Tuesday morning, so all was looking well.

Oliver and Shay lived in Shay's apartment. They were hoping to buy a home when her business sold, but right now her place had been more centrally located for both their jobs. Shay had confided in Marrell many weeks before that as soon as the business sold, she would sleep for a month, but then was a bit worried about what she would do after that. This was one of the first things Marrell brought up when they were alone.

"You certainly won't be at a loss now."

"No, not in the least. I probably have more planned than I'll get done. I can already tell that I'm going to need more sleep. It will be nice to baby myself for a while before I have someone I have to baby."

"I'm so excited for you. I've been walking around on a cloud all day."

"God is so good to us, Marrell. I don't have any guarantees that I'll carry this baby full term or that everything will be 'all right,' but God has shown us that we can have children, and that's such a special thing. Even if the unforeseen happens and we never hold our baby, we'll know that he or she is with the Lord."

"That's so special, Shay. I was terrified when I was pregnant, scared that something would go wrong or Paul wouldn't be there. Only God can give the kind of peace you're talking about."

The men came into the kitchen. They had been talking of the business and closing date. Paul

198

wasted no time in teasing Shay.

"I understand, Mrs. Lacy, that you're soon to be a woman of leisure."

Shay gave as good as she got. "I'll have you know, Colonel Bishop, that I'm the only person in this room who can be doing absolutely nothing and still be totally productive. Top that."

"I guess she told you," Marrell mouthed off.

Paul started toward her, but she darted away. Shay stood as well.

"I think if the guys have this much energy, they ought to help with the dishes."

No one complained as they went to work. Paul had to see what the girls were watching on TV but then pitched in to help in the kitchen. They all worked swiftly, and Shay even served coffee, but the Bishops did not remain long. Shay was clearly tired, and Marrell felt as though she had put in a 20-hour day. Before nine o'clock they were on their way, knowing that tomorrow there was more packing to be done.

TWELVE

Time rushed on after the move back to the base. The Bishops moved in the middle of the July Fourth weekend, and from there the summer seemed to disappear. Paul and Marrell celebrated their sixteenth wedding anniversary by writing and reciting new wedding vows before a few friends and surprising the girls by taking them along on the second honeymoon to Lake Tahoe.

School started just a week after they returned, and by mid-September Marrell felt as though she had never left the Presidio.

One afternoon, the date was September 17, her grandmother called.

"Marrell?"

"Grandma! Hi. How are you?"

"I've got cancer, honey."

Much later, Marrell would thank her grandmother for not drawing it out or trying to play word games to prepare her, but at the moment she didn't know where her next breath was going to come from.

"I've seen two doctors," Pearl went on softly, "and they both agree to let it run its course."

"Run its course?" Marrell managed. "What does that mean?"

"Not to operate or do chemotherapy or any-

200

thing."

"Grandma, where is it?"

"All through me."

Marrell couldn't cry; she couldn't do anything.

"Is anyone there with you, Marrell?"

"Paul just went back to work. The girls are at school."

"I'm going to ask a big favor of you, Marrell."

"All right."

"I want you to come now. I want you to visit me while I still have some strength and feel like me. I don't want you to wait and come near the end to try and get in one last visit. That's a horrible way to live. Come now and see me, and if we can't be together again, it will be all right."

"Oh, Grandma."

"It's all right, honey. It hurts now, but it will be all right."

"I'll come. I'll leave as soon as I can get a flight. I don't think I'll bring the girls, though. I think I just want the time with you alone. Will that bother you, Grandma? Did you want all of us?"

"I just want you," she said softly, and Marrell could speak no more. Her grandma. She was the strong one. She had buried the rest of her family. Marrell thought she would die from the ache. How could she lose this precious part of her life?

They talked for a few minutes longer, Pearl telling of the symptoms that had made her suspect. She admitted being in shock herself, since she still felt good, and also admitted that she had been testy with the doctor when he wouldn't tell her how long she had left.

Marrell almost laughed when Pearl said, "How am I supposed to get my affairs in order when I don't know when I'm leaving?"

"You've always been too organized for your own good," Marrell said, enjoying the sound of her grandmother's chuckle.

"You'll call me?" Pearl asked.

"Yes. It might be two weeks before I can come."

"Whenever you can will be fine."

"All right. I love you, Grandma."

"And I you, sweetheart. Bye-bye."

" 'Bye."

Marrell knew she must not wait. She picked up the phone before any tears could come and dialed Paul's number. She spoke the moment she heard his voice.

"My grandma has cancer, Paul."

"I'll come right home," he stated calmly, and Marrell was actually able to hold herself together until she saw him. All she could do was tremble from the shock. It was so painful. She tried to pray and did, forcing her mind to ignore the numbness stealing over her. Even Paul's arms around her were strange. It helped to hear him start to pray.

"Thank You, Lord, that You are sovereign. Thank You that Your plan and will are perfect. Put Your hand on Grandma right now. Touch her and comfort her with Your presence and love. Give us wisdom so we know what to do and when to go to her."

"She wants me now," Marrell interrupted. "She's asked me to come now, and I told her I would." She began to crumble.

Marrell sobbed until she thought she might be sick. Every fiber of her being ached with this news. She forced herself to stop crying so she wouldn't be ill. Paul left her on the sofa after a time, telling her that he would call the travel agent so she could get back to her grandmother with the plans.

The earliest flight Marrell could take and not be penalized for late booking was nine days away. Paul scheduled it, getting her out as soon as he could that morning, and then returned to sit by her. Marrell stared at nothing across the room.

"Would you like me to call and tell her what I found out?"

"Okay. What day do I go?"

"A week from Saturday."

"What date is that?"

"The twenty-sixth."

"All right. I think one of the girls has a dentist appointment next week. I can't remember. What time is it? Are the girls coming soon?"

"It's only 1:30. I'll call Grandma."

Marrell didn't try to listen to the call. She was glad he went into the kitchen.

She'll be with you, Lord. I know this, but I'm selfish, and I want her here. She'll be out of her pain and earthly body and be at Your side. Nothing else gives me comfort like that does. I'm so glad You saved us, Lord. I'm so glad she found You. My heart feels bruised, but it's not broken, because I know she'll be with You.

Paul was back in the room before she even realized he was done.

"She's not supposed to drive right now because they're still doing two more tests, but she will meet you with Mavis in her car."

"All right. Do you think the girls will be upset about not going?"

"They might be, but it's reasonable for you to go alone, honey. Don't feel you need to take them. We will be fine. You just go and take care of Grandma while you can."

"How long will I be there?"

"Two weeks."

"You're sure you and the girls will be all right?"

"Very sure. Don't worry about us."

"I have a headache."

"Do you want something?"

"No. What time did you say it was?"

"About 1:30."

Marrell couldn't think any more. She wasn't sleepy, just weary and in shock.

"Paul, call Shay, will you? Let her know, and tell her I'll talk to her later."

"I'll do that."

He must have made several calls or been on the phone to Shay for a long time, because the girls came in before he returned. Marrell met them at the door, and Mackenzie, after seeing her mother's pale face, didn't hesitate to ask what was wrong.

"Great Grandma has cancer," she told them as gently as possible, still standing by the front door.

"Will she die?" Delancey asked quietly.

"Yes. We don't know when, but the cancer's all through her, and they're not going to do anything."

"Why not?"

"Come into the living room," Marrell urged them, amazed at how strong she could be when it was her turn to be mother. "She's 79 years old, almost 80," Marrell spoke when they were seated. "She's strong, but the cancer has spread all through her. She could try chemo, but it would make her very sick, and she's decided she doesn't want that."

"Did you cry, Mom?" Delancey asked. Mackenzie could see that she had. Paul came into the room and sat next to Marrell.

"I did. I cried a lot because I'm sad for her and for me, but I'm also thankful."

A look came over Mackenzie's face that neither of her parents could miss. Paul spoke kindly to her, his heart praying for patience and wisdom.

"Micki, don't be angry at your mother because she's choosing to be thankful."

"But how can she be?" Every ounce of Mackenzie's frustration came out in those words. "Mom loves Grandma, and now she's going away. It just makes me so mad. *I don't feel thankful at all!"*

"Your mother and I could be feeling the same way," Paul said, keeping his voice even. "We've chosen otherwise. That's not to say we won't ever be angry and upset, but if we're thinking well, we'll see that God has been in control all this time, and that's what thankfulness is all about, honey — understanding that God is sovereign, and trusting that the things He brings into our lives are His best for us."

"I don't think I could ever have that much trust," Mackenzie said softly, and Paul worked at not letting defeat rush through him. He reminded himself that the time had not been long, but right now it seemed that Mackenzie's heart would never soften.

God is sovereign, Paul. Remember what you just told her.

"I'll be praying for you then, Micki, just as I always do," Paul said. "I'll pray that God will help you to trust in His Son, since He's the only One worth putting your trust in."

"You're not mad at me?" She was feeling guilty about being snotty when her parents were upset.

"No, I understand exactly what you're think-

205

ing," Paul said.

"Trust is hard, Mackenzie," her mother spoke up. "It takes a lifetime to get it down."

"Is Grandma scared?" Delancey's voice sounded for the first time in some minutes.

"No, honey, I don't think she is. I'll be going to see her next week, and that's what she wants more than anything else right now."

"Are we going?"

Delancey cried at the small shake of her mother's head. Marrell was certain it was the events of the last half hour and the news of her grandmother, as well as the knowledge that her mother leaving. Delancey looked more like a young woman with every month that passed, but she was still a 12-year-old girl inside.

"Come here, honey." Marrell held her youngest daughter next to her side. No longer did she fit into her lap. "It's going to be all right. We're going to hurt and cry, but God will take care of us."

"Will we see Grandma again?"

"I don't know. Maybe."

And that was all the promise Marrell was willing to give. The days that followed were hard. The girls dealt with their pain in separate ways: Delancey shadowed Marrell's every move, but Mackenzie distanced herself from everyone. Paul spoke with her on many occasions, even taking her to dinner — just the two of them — in an attempt to draw her out. By the time Marrell left, she felt her daughter was coming around.

Colorado Springs
"This is another one of your mother." Pearl held up yet another picture for Marrell.

"Why have I never seen these?"

"I think they were just tucked away. I'd completely forgotten about them until I started going through things."

"I knew you would do this."

"Do what?" Pearl asked, looking innocent.

"Sort everything in the house, planning to get it done before I arrived."

This was so close to the fact that Pearl laughed.

"Do you have diet restrictions or anything like that?" Marrell asked suddenly.

"No, why do you ask?"

"Because I'm hungry for something from the Mexican restaurant that we went to last time I was here."

"Oh, I know the one. Sounds good to me."

"All right. Why don't we move some of these photos to the kitchen table? I think it would be more comfortable."

"All right. You'll have to do the big box."

"I've got it."

This was the way they spent most of their days. They turned out closets, went through old photos and letters, and in the evening watched old movies and musicals while they ate popcorn and drank tall glasses of Pepsi over ice. Marrell didn't know when she had been so rested. The phone seldom rang, and few demands were made on her time, freeing her to spend time with her grandmother.

Like a long walk down memory lane, Pearl and Marrell sorted through boxes of memorabilia, threw out what they didn't want, and repacked the containers, marking them clearly for future reference. And through all of this activity, they talked of the Lord. Pearl had started a study on heaven, and the things she shared with Marrell delighted her.

"Did you know that there's no need for the sun?"

"In heaven? No, I didn't know that."

"God shines so brightly that He is all the sun heaven needs."

"Where does it say that?"

Pearl got her Bible and showed her the place in Revelation 22. She even read it out loud.

"Listen to this: 'And there shall no longer be any night; and they shall not have need of the light of a lamp nor the light of the sun, because the Lord God shall illumine them; and they shall reign forever and ever.' "

"I've never read that." Marrell's laughter was soft with wonder, as she sat in silence and looked at her grandmother. "I don't think I could leave here in four days if I didn't share your hope now. I would be devastated."

For the first time since Marrell arrived, Pearl cried. "I can't tell you what it means, Marrell. To know I'll be with you and Paul again . . . I just can't tell you. I pray for the girls every day."

"We do too. I know that God will reach them. Someday in His time and way, He will save my girls."

"And your coming —" The older woman was still overcome. "I can't tell you what it means to have you here. Thank you for coming, Marrell. Thank you so much."

Marrell went to her, and they hugged for a long time. This was the woman who had raised her and loved her. When she should have been able to put her feet up a little, she found herself with a young girl to raise, but Marrell never felt any bitterness from her. Pearl had made Marrell's wedding dress, and when the girls were small, sewn outfits for them every month. It was like losing a part of herself to think of Pearl gone.

However, Marrell was able to leave with a clear heart. If she didn't see her grandmother on the earth again, she would know nothing but peace. A small corner of her heart told her that she would have more time with her and that Paul and the girls would see her again. She told Paul as much when she was finally home, tucked in for the night in her own bed. Paul kissed her and said that he hoped it would work out that way. But Marrell was wrong. Their plans to be with her grandmother for Christmas that year were radically changed. Pearl Walker was gone on December 15.

Delancey ignored the other girls' conversation, even though she could hear every word. She bent a little farther over the math book that lay on the library table and tried to concentrate.

"She's such a snob. I can't stand her."

"She has such cool clothes, though, and they all look so good on her."

"I heard someone say she looks like a model. Tell me how many models have zits on their faces."

"She doesn't have very many, Darcy — not as many as Kay Parks."

"We're not talking about Kay Parks!" the other girl snapped, and Delancey was relieved to have the other table fall quiet. The temptation to reach up and touch the pimple on her chin was nearly overwhelming, but she wouldn't give them that satisfaction. She knew who the girls were and why they hated her, but it wasn't her fault. She wasn't interested in Kevin Bains and never asked him to break up with Rosa Castro to go with her. Rosa even knew that, and she and Delancey were still friends.

"Hey, D.J." Mackenzie was suddenly beside her. "I got a note to come to the office and call Dad. Mom's gone with Shay to the hospital. Her water broke."

"When?" Delancey's smile was huge.

"Just now when she was at the house with Mom. Dad said he would come home and let us in if Mom's not back by the time we get out of school."

"I hope she has a girl."

"Yeah, but a boy would be cool too. When Mom and I were out shopping on Tuesday night, we saw the cutest little jeans."

"Shh." This came from the table of malicious girls.

"Shut up, Darcy," Mackenzie wasted no time in saying, her voice not all that soft. She turned back to her sister. "I think the administration office should check birth certificates more often. Some of your classmates act like they're in the third grade, D.J. I'll see you at the bus."

Mackenzie left with that parting shot, and Delancey had to bite her lip to keep from laughing. She forced herself not to look at the other girls. She was almost three inches taller than her sister these days, but she still felt loved and protected when Mackenzie stood up for her. She had just gone back to her math paper when Rosa sat down at her table.

"Hey, Rosa."

"Hi, D.J." The other girl's face was sad.

Delancey was about to say something else when she realized the girls from the other table were staring at them.

"May I help you?" Delancey's voice was at its most sarcastic.

The other girls just stared.

"Come on, Rosa," Delancey started to gather her books. "Let's move over here where Big Ears and Company can't hear."

It gave Delancey great satisfaction to have her friend accompany her and sit with their backs to the other girls.

"It's a girl," the doctor told the redheaded couple in the delivery room. "Red hair too."

He put the baby on Shay's stomach, and she gasped in delight. Oliver was kissing her, and she looked up into his eyes.

"A girl. Delancey will be thrilled."

"Yeah. You did it."

"I feel as though I've run a marathon."

Shay felt the nurse's hands take the baby as the little person was whisked away for a few minutes. Shay had torn quite badly, so the doctor worked to repair her, and Oliver went to help with the baby. He was back just a short time later to hand Shay her daughter.

"Oh, Oliver, she's perfect, just perfect."

"Look at this hand."

"Is Marrell still here? I want Marrell to see her."

"No, honey, she went home before midnight."

"Oh, that's right. Call her."

"It's four o'clock!"

"She won't mind." Shay looked so convinced that Oliver laughed.

The nurse wanted to take the baby to the nursery, and since Shay was still being worked on, Oliver went along. Shay lay with her eyes closed, thinking about the miracle of birth.

It's so amazing, Lord. Your design is so perfect. I hurt, but I have a little girl. We made it, Father, the

211

whole pregnancy. I'm not a kid anymore, but You had her for us. She's so precious, and You gave her to us. Thank You for Marrell — thank You that she could be here — and for Oliver. He's going to be a wonderful father. Help us to show her You. Help her to see her need for salvation and not to fight You as I did. Provide the right house for us in Your time, Lord. Lombard is so busy. Shay stopped then and nearly laughed out loud. She'd just had a baby, and here she was being distracted by the home she and Oliver hoped to find. Talk about obsessive!

Suddenly Shay was tired. The attendants transferred her to another bed, and she was drifting off as they wheeled her to her room. After adjustments and checking the chart, the nurse assured Shay that she would inform Oliver where she was. And then she was gone. It was nice to be alone.

Shay's hand went to her stomach. It would probably never be flat again, but she didn't care. She had a baby . . . a wonderful baby girl . . .

Thirteen

The track runner in Mackenzie that showed promise as a seventh grader emerged as a team leader in the eighth grade. Delancey was trying out as well this year, and if the length of her legs was any indication, she would be as swift as her sister.

From where she was standing, Mackenzie looked over to where Delancey was getting instruction from the coach and wondered how she was doing. Brett Cooper, now at the high school as a ninth grader, chose that minute to walk by. Irritated over the fact that he would even visit the junior high, Mackenzie only glanced at him without a flicker of interest.

A year ago was a long time, but she still remembered the way he had given her the cold shoulder when she wasn't able to date or agree to meet him without her mother's knowledge. If rumor could be trusted, he was interested in Delancey, but Mackenzie knew her sister. As soon as Delancey found out the way Brett had treated her, she wouldn't think him cute anymore. Mackenzie would be surprised if Delancey even gave him the time of day.

"Okay, Bishop," the coach called. "Let's see your jump."

Concentrating on the distance to the sand pit, Mackenzie stepped up to her mark and took off. Running was her strong point, and if she hadn't overstepped the takeoff line at the pit, it might have been a school record. The person watching for just such a mistake held her flag in the air, and Mackenzie groaned before the coach called her over.

"I can't seem to get this," she complained. "I think I should stick to the relay and hurdles."

"You need to keep practicing," Coach Frank disagreed with her. "The only eighth-grade girl who can jump farther than you is Stacy. Now I want you to go again."

"All right." Mackenzie jogged back down the grass next to the lane and stood in line for her next try. She heard people cheering at the track and looked over to see Delancey come across the line. It was almost her turn to jump again, or she would have gone to her. Delancey finished in second place, but it looked as though she was flailing her arms too much.

"Delancey had a good run," Stacy spoke from in front of her.

"Yeah," Mackenzie smiled. "It's those long legs of hers. But she's flapping like a bird, and that's going to slow her down."

Stacy laughed a little. "Doesn't it feel good not to be a seventh grader?"

Mackenzie grinned and couldn't help but agree.

"Here's the track schedule," Mackenzie said, putting a piece of paper down on the kitchen counter and wandering away. "The meets are usually right after school, same as last year."

"All right. Do you want dessert?" Marrell spoke

214

to her retreating back.

"What is it?"

"Lemon cake."

"No thanks," she called from the other room.

Delancey was just finishing her own supper and stood to leave, her lemon cake in her hand.

"You're welcome, D.J."

"Oh yeah, thanks, Mom."

Marrell looked back to Paul, who was still at the table. "She towers over me," she said dryly. "Have you noticed?"

"Considering the fact that she's nearly looking me in the eye, how could I miss?"

Marrell sat back down at the table. "It's our own fault. We keep feeding her."

Paul found this highly amusing and smiled across at his wife.

"When's the first track meet?"

Marrell consulted the paper. "Not until after Easter break. Whenever Mackenzie hands me something, I have to ask myself how long it's been riding around in her backpack, but this time we have it with plenty of notice."

"She's not strong on organization," Paul said of his oldest child.

"Unless it's something important to her, like her books or story notebook."

"That's true."

"Have you thought about what you want for your birthday?"

"Is that coming up?" Paul's eyes were all innocent. Marrell had been asking him for suggestions for a week, and he still hadn't replied.

"Paul, it's less than three weeks away. It would be nice to have an idea."

"No man wants to be reminded that he's going

to be 42. I think I'm in denial."

"Oh," Marrell brightened, ignoring his last statement, "I just thought of something."

"What?"

"I can't tell you," she chided him. "I'll be right back. I've got to go write something down."

Paul started the dishes after she left, his mind on the months to come. He still didn't know if he should leave the Army, or at what point. He'd already made up his mind that he couldn't leave his family again for another year, and if he stayed in the Army, he would be expected to do just that. But when did he call it quits? He was stationed here at the Presidio until August of 1983, which meant he had approximately a year and three months left in San Francisco. Unless he decided to call it quits — then he could stay in the area with his family, friends, and church family. A very appealing idea.

Since he had arrived home close to a year ago, he had been meeting with the pastor and one other man for Bible study. Each week they met in a corner booth of a restaurant at 6:30 on Tuesday morning. Paul had asked them to pray with him on the subject, and they talked of it often, but he was still no closer to a decision. He realized suddenly that he hadn't spoken to Marrell about it for some time. They had talked about it almost nonstop after he got back, but without having come to a final decision, the subject had rather died down.

"That's quite a frown."

"Just thinking."

"You're getting water on the floor."

"Oh." Paul shook himself and grabbed the towel. "We need to talk tonight about my career."

"Okay." Marrell sounded uncertain. "Has something come up?"

"No, but I need to figure out a plan, and I realized suddenly that we haven't talked for a while."

"Are we including the girls?"

"Not yet. They know we're talking about it, so it won't come as a huge surprise, and right now I wouldn't have anything to tell them anyhow."

"I've thought of it from time to time, but part of me is afraid, so I push it away."

Paul turned from the sink, leaned one hip against the counter, and stared down at her.

"I didn't know that," he said softly.

"I didn't want to tell you. I hate being afraid of things like change, but I am. The Army is so secure, Paul." She made a face, clearly disgusted with herself. "As you can see, I'm not trusting very well."

His hand came up, and he tucked her hair behind one ear, letting his finger trail down her cheek. She was so precious to him and a frequent surprise to boot. He had watched her strength and growth through her grandmother's death. And now here she had a chance to remain in the area, and she was afraid.

"Come here."

Marrell didn't need to be invited twice.

"We'll talk, okay?" He bent to speak into her ear. "When the girls go to bed."

Marrell nodded and looked up at him. "That's getting later all the time." Marrell stopped. "Do you know what I just thought of? This is D.J.'s dish night."

"Well then," Paul said firmly, "she can finish."

That was the last thing said on either subject for several hours, but finally the house became quiet, and husband and wife sat across the living room from each other.

"What is it that scares you? The lack of security?"

"Much of it, yes. I can't think of another employer who is going to take care of you the way Uncle Sam does. I know the Army has its problems, Paul, and I know you're trained to go into several different fields, but I can't help but wonder how we'll make it on the outside. You're accepted here. As a civilian, you'll have to prove yourself. I get frightened for you. Unless you get passed over, they don't fire you in the Army."

"I can't say as I haven't thought of it, Marrell, and it does concern me, but going overseas for another year, and even moving from this church family, bothers me more."

"Those bother me too," she admitted softly. "I guess I do need to do some weighing. I can't have it all. Have you talked to Gene?" Marrell asked, referring to his present CO.

"No. It's time I did, but he's going to ask me what I want to do, and I would like to have some answers for him."

"Can you wait until this summer? That would be about a year's notice. Do you think that's reasonable? It would give us a little more time to think and plan."

"I think that's a good idea. I can keep talking to friends and praying for wisdom. In fact, I forgot to tell you that I got a letter at the office today from Allen Post."

"How is he doing?"

"Very well. He's scheduled to be stationed back in the States by September. I was thinking of writing to him about my plans too."

"Maybe you should. I would think his counsel would be a great help." Marrell covered a yawn. "My body is telling me to go to bed."

"Yeah, it's that time."

Paul checked the doors and hit the lights before heading to the bedroom. Marrell was already in the bathroom when he spotted a stack of papers on the bed.

"Mary, what's this stuff?" He opened the door to show her.

"Oh, it's the mail. I was so rushed after I picked it up, I forgot where I set it down. Where was it?"

"On the bed." Paul's voice was preoccupied as he sorted through it. "There's a letter here from my mom."

Marrell swiftly finished brushing her teeth and went to join him on the edge of the bed. She read from his side, scanning his mother's words as he read.

Dear Paul and Marrell,

Thank you for the letter and pictures of the girls. I've shown them to everyone, but one day I couldn't find them. They reappeared mysteriously after your father came home from work, and I strongly suspect that he took them to the office. Still no word from him about how he feels.

How are the girls doing in track? It looks like they're both tall enough to make those long jumps. I enjoyed your call last week. Lance came in just after you phoned, and I got the impression he was sorry to have missed you. I told him I could give him your number, but he declined.

Mrs. Barry's cat had kittens three weeks ago now. So cute. I found myself wishing the girls could have one each. Impractical thought, but then I've been practical for too many years. I'm sending a birthday card next week sometime. Do you have big plans for Easter and your birthday? I feel old having my baby turn 42.

Best close now. Your father will be home soon. I would like to say he sends his love and to visit anytime, but it hasn't happened yet. I have hope. Call again soon.

Love,
Mom

Paul put the letter on the bed and sat very still. "The girls have to know that I love them, Mary. If nothing else, they have to know how much I care."

"They do, Paul. They love you. Girls who call you back to their rooms to make sure you'll be at their track meets are not girls who want nothing to do with their father."

He nodded and continued to stare across the room.

"I have to admit to having some fears, Mary, but I also have to tell you I'm excited about having a regular job." He turned to look at her. "I'm excited to move on and experience things in civilian life. Every move we've made has been hard on you, but you've done it. Don't let me push you into this, babe. If you really want me to stay with it, I will."

"Oh, Paul." Marrell put her arms around him. "No, I don't want it that badly. I have fears, yes, but excitement too. I know you'll take care of us." She leaned forward and kissed him.

"Toothpaste."

She smiled. "I just brushed."

"I'd better brush too." He wiggled his eyebrows at her and slipped into the bathroom. Marrell picked up the letter and read it again.

Please let his father welcome him home, Lord, Marrell prayed. *Please work a miracle in Otto Bishop's heart.*

"Look at her smile," Delancey said with a laugh.

"That outfit is so cute. Hi, Jana," Mackenzie cooed.

The Bishops were making fools of themselves. Ten-week-old Jana Lacy was spending the evening with them, so her parents could go out for their first anniversary. Someone watching them would have thought they had never seen a baby before.

"My turn," Paul proclaimed, taking Jana from Marrell's arms without permission.

"Isn't she precious?" Marrell breathed.

"It's hard to believe D.J. and Micki were ever this size." Paul looked up at his daughters. "You were, you know."

"I think it's coming now, D.J. — a teary walk down memory lane."

Both Paul and Marrell laughed. Mackenzie often had that effect on them.

"You just wait," her mother warned. "Someday when you present me with a grandchild, I'll remind you that it's no big deal — just a baby."

"I think she's doing something," Delancey said, her face looking horrified.

Paul laughed down into Jana's red, scrunched-up features and asked Delancey where she had put the diaper bag.

"*You're* going to do it?" Mackenzie was amazed.

"Did you think your mother did all of it?" His tone was telling. "We had an infant and a 13-month-old. Trust me when I tell you there was plenty of teamwork."

221

Delancey handed the diaper bag to her father and stood aside while he headed to the bathroom.

"That baby is so cute," Marrell said. "Tempts me to have another."

"You wouldn't really, would you, Mom?" Delancey asked, looking unsure.

"Why would that be so awful?"

"It wouldn't. I was just curious."

"I think it would be cool," Mackenzie said. "A little brother."

"I would want a girl."

"Should I be told about this?" Paul asked as he returned with a clean baby.

Marrell laughed. "No, the girls are just dreaming."

"About a baby."

"Of course."

Paul smiled. He had a sneaking suspicion that the girls' feelings would change, and he wasn't far wrong. Jana was happy for about an hour before deciding she needed her mother. Shay had pumped some breast milk, but Jana was not used to the bottle and would not be comforted. Marrell walked her and worked to feed her, but it was quite some time before she could get her to eat. The girls had lasted only a few minutes, both disappearing into their rooms and closing their doors.

"We do an activity every month during the summer," Sheila Carver said to Marrell over the phone. "Most schools are out now, or nearly so, and the June activity occurs on the nineteenth. I really think Delancey and Mackenzie would enjoy it."

"I think so too. And their father isn't giving

them a choice in the matter. I know you won't have trouble with them, but they're going to be embarrassed and probably keep to themselves. What is the June activity?"

"Marine World Africa USA."

"Oh, we haven't been there in years. I think they'll love it."

"I hope so. I need to tell you, Marrell, they're not the only ones who will be coming who aren't regulars. There are several new families with teens, and I've been calling all of them. The parents are very enthusiastic, and the young people who do come regularly know this is an opportunity to reach out. Your girls are very well liked and welcomed when they come, Marrell."

"They've told me as much, but their hearts still haven't grasped their own need, Sheila, and I'm sure that's the biggest problem."

"We'll keep praying, Marrell. You know that."

"Thanks, Sheila."

"I'll let you go now. Watch the bulletin for more details."

"All right. We'll probably see you tomorrow at church."

"Okay, bye."

Marrell had no more hung up the phone when she heard a knock on the door. She wondered if the knocking had gone on long, so she rushed to answer. Gene Barlowe, Paul's CO, was standing on the porch.

"Oh, Gene. Come on in. Paul's not here right now, but he should be right back."

Gene stepped into the foyer area, his hat in his hand.

"Are the girls here, Marrell?"

"They're playing tennis," she answered.

The CO took a breath. "Marrell, Paul is dead."

Marrell started, shook her head a little, and almost smiled.

"He just ran to the commissary, Gene. He was out of razor blades. He'll be right back."

"There's been an accident. It wasn't his fault. He's gone, Marrell."

This simply couldn't be happening. Marrell refused to believe it. He couldn't be dead; he just couldn't be. She shook her head again.

"I think there's been a mistake, Gene. He just needed to go to the commissary. He wasn't even leaving the base."

She stopped when she saw tears fill his eyes.

"I'm sorry," he whispered.

Marrell began to tremble. Her chest felt so tight that she thought she wouldn't be able to breathe.

"The girls," she gasped. "I need the girls."

"Did you say the tennis courts? I'll get them."

"No, no," Marrell begged him. "I mean, if you call them they'll be afraid that something's wrong. I've got to go."

"Let me, Marrell. I can do it."

"No, no. Just give me a minute, and I'll get them."

Marrell's hand fumbled with the doorknob, so Gene had to open it for her. She made herself walk down the steps and out to the street. She spotted the girls at the tennis courts that sat below street level and cleared her throat in an attempt to call down to them.

"Micki, D.J."

It wasn't loud enough.

"Girls," she tried this time, and Delancey spotted her.

"Did you call us, Mom?"

"I need you to come in."

"Now?"

Marrell nodded and motioned with her arm, turning away only when she saw they were coming.

Watching her, Gene made himself stay back, knowing she didn't want the girls spotting him. He waited only until she was back on the front walk before taking her arm and leading her inside. He felt the trembling and took her right to the living room sofa. Shock was setting in fast.

The girls came through the front door minutes later, both tall young women, blooming with good health. Gene's heart clenched over the news that would destroy their world. Thinking it was his job, he stood, but he wasn't given time to begin.

"What is it, Mom?" Delancey asked. There was no missing her pallor.

Marrell stared at them and made herself say the words. "Your father is dead."

Mackenzie shook her head much the way Marrell had done. "He just went to the store."

"There was an accident," Marrell began but then looked to Gene. She really didn't know a thing.

"Yes," Gene filled in. "There was nothing Paul could do."

"Where?"

"Right on Old Mason. We don't know what happened yet, except people watching said it was the truck's fault. The driver's door was hit," he said to the widow. "Paul's neck was broken. He died immediately, Marrell."

It still wasn't getting through. She looked up into the faces of her girls. Was her face as pale? Mackenzie and Delancey were both dripping with sweat. Had they been playing that long? Hadn't Paul just left, or had she been on the phone longer than she realized?

"I want to see him."

"I'll arrange it." Gene didn't hesitate. "In fact, I'll use your phone right now."

Marrell nodded. After he left, the girls came closer and sat down. Marrell absently thought she would break if someone touched her.

"Is it true, Mom?" Delancey asked. "Do you believe it?"

Marrell looked at her. "It is true, honey, but I don't think I believe it yet."

Mackenzie was the first to break down. She covered her face with her hands and sobbed. Marrell moved close to sit beside her, her arm going around her, but she did not cry. She was too numb. Gene came back into the room.

"I can take you right now, Marrell . . . if you want."

She nodded and stood. "Come with me, girls."

They were in Gene's car a moment later, but Marrell didn't remember how she got there. The street, the other houses, the tennis courts — all so familiar, yet Marrell felt as though she'd never seen them before. The girls were just as silent in the rear seat, and suddenly she felt too far from them. She turned to glance back but found she had nothing to say.

Gene stopped the car outside Letterman Hospital. She hadn't been thinking about where they were going, but this surprised her. This made her think that Paul had been brought there for medical attention.

"You did say he died right away, didn't you, Gene?"

"Yes, Marrell, I swear to you."

Gene waited until Marrell made the first move and then climbed from the car. In full shock now and clearly taking their cue from their mother, the girls followed suit. As they went in through the door, Marrell realized she had never been there. She didn't see anyone as she came in, but many people saw her. Word had traveled swiftly, and dozens knew that Paul Bishop was dead.

Gene took them down a few halls and then had them wait for him outside the door marked "Autopsy." Marrell glanced over at Delancey and Mackenzie, but their eyes were closed as they leaned against the wall. Gene was back in a moment, but Marrell hesitated.

"Gene, does he look —" She couldn't say it.

"He looks just as you remember him," Gene assured her.

Marrell's legs and feet didn't feel like her own, but she moved forward mechanically. Partway in she stopped and reached for the girls' hands. They approached the table, vaguely aware that a man in a white smock was backing away.

"Oh, Paul." Marrell's soft voice quivered as she looked down at his still form draped with a white sheet. Her heart told her it couldn't be real, but the evidence was right before her eyes.

"Oh, Paul," she said again. "Please don't leave us now." The girls were sobbing, each clinging to a different arm, but Marrell could see only her husband's beloved face.

How will I survive this, Lord? How will I carry on? I love him. He's the only man I ever loved and wanted. Please help us. Right now I can't think what we'll do, but You know. Only You know. Help us.

With a trembling hand, she reached forward and

brushed the soft brown hair from his brow. His skin was cool. With the girls still clinging to her, Marrell bent over and kissed his forehead and felt herself falling apart. She turned and pulled the girls to her as they sobbed, joining them in their tears.

Gene Barlowe stood in the hall, his head back with agony as he listened to their cries. A family man himself, the thought of his own wife and children in this same situation was almost too much for him. He hated this. Nothing was confirmed, but several reports had come in that the other driver, a young enlisted man, had been drinking. He was still out cold when Gene had left for the Bishops' house. The thought of having to tell Marrell about that made his gut clench.

Inside, Marrell was working to gain some control. The girls were inconsolable, and she had no idea what to do next. What would she say to them? How would she act? What was the best action to take right now? She was still working on it when Mackenzie took the decision from her hands. As she watched, her daughter pulled from her embrace and approached Paul's body.

"I love you, Dad," she cried. "I love you so much. I don't want you to go. I can't live without you."

Delancey joined her sister, and Marrell stood to the side and let them talk.

"I love you, Dad. I love you" was all Delancey could manage.

Marrell let them have their say. Her grandmother's body flashed into her mind. Had it really been less than five months ago? Marrell could hardly deal with it. She felt herself begin to tremble all over again and only barely heard the door behind her. She glanced to see Dr. Peck, one of the base physicians.

"I'm sorry, Marrell," he said softly, his eyes taking in the whole scene.

"Thank you," she replied automatically.

"I have something for you that might help you sleep in the next few days," he wasted no time in saying. "I'll be in the hall and speak to you when you come out."

"All right."

She waited until the doctor had gone and then moved close to speak to the girls. They were still standing close to their father.

"I don't know how, but we're going to make it." Her voice was soft, but her faith was strong. "We'll get through this with God's help."

"I feel like it's all a bad dream, and I'm going to wake up any minute," Mackenzie admitted.

"I think it might feel that way for a long time." Marrell spoke from experience. She was still not over her grandmother. "I want to see Shay," Marrell went on. "Let's go home so I can call her."

"Are you going to call Grandma Bishop?"

Marrell nodded. "Yes. Allen Post too." Marrell was suddenly overwhelmed. "We'll have to make an appointment with the funeral home."

"Like we did with Great Grandma." Delancey's voice was flat. She had hated that.

"Yes."

Marrell moved close to Paul again, and the girls moved aside some to let her get close. "I'll always love you, Paul Bishop. You were the most wonderful husband any woman could have asked for." She kissed him again and moved away. The girls kissed him as well, which started their tears again. Marrell couldn't stay any longer. Tears and all, she moved them toward the door and out into the hall. Dr. Peck came right to her side and pressed a prescription bottle into her hand.

"These are very mild sleeping pills, Marrell. You could even give them to the girls if you thought it would help."

"Thank you."

"This paper has my number at home. If you need me and can't get me here or at the clinic, don't hesitate to call no matter what time it is."

"All right. Thank you."

He squeezed her hand, spoke briefly to the girls, and moved down the hall.

"Are you ready to go home?" Gene came close to ask.

"Yes."

"The car is still out front."

"Okay."

The numbness was stealing in again, but Marrell ignored it. All she wanted to do was get home and call Shay. Nothing else mattered right now.

On the ride home Gene told her that Army Relief Services would be calling her the next day and not to worry about anything; he would be there to help. Marrell said little. Her mind was busy going over the people who would need to be informed and how best to go about that.

At the Lacy home they were just talking about what to have for dinner. Jana was on the floor, surrounded by toys she ignored while gnawing on her fist. Oliver answered the phone when it rang.

"Hello."

"Oliver, it's Marrell."

"Hi."

"Oliver, Paul's dead."

"Oh, Marrell, no."

"Yes. He's gone. Can you come? I need to see Shay. Can you bring her?"

"We'll leave right now."

"Okay. I'll see you."

By the time Oliver replaced the phone, Shay was behind him.

"Oliver?" Her voice was frightened.

He turned and stared at her. "That was Marrell. Paul is dead."

Shay's hand flew to her mouth.

"I have to go to her," she gasped.

"Yes. She wants you."

For a full minute, she couldn't think. She put toys in the diaper bag and then realized there were no diapers.

"Maybe I'd better go and let you come with the baby."

"No." Oliver was adamant. "I'll drive you."

As if in a cloud, they worked together to gather the baby's things and headed down to the car. Shay could hardly believe what they were doing. Her last thought as Oliver pulled from the curb was thankfulness that they'd never found a new house. The apartment was just a few minutes' drive from the base.

FOURTEEN

The sleeping pills were no help to Marrell because she couldn't bring herself to take any. The girls were still crying at 10:30, so Marrell had insisted they each take a pill. Oliver and Shay were still at the house. The girls had roomed together and given Delancey's room to Oliver, Shay, and the baby.

From her place by the window, Marrell looked back at the bed. She had lain down for a while, but it felt too lonely and cold. She had such a headache and knew she needed a little something to eat. The bowl on the table had peaches and apples in it, and suddenly a peach with milk and sugar sounded good to her. Not bothering with her robe, she moved to the door. She stopped as soon as it was open. Someone was lying in the hall.

"Marrell?" It was Shay's voice.

"Are you sleeping there?"

"I thought you might need me."

"I'm going to the kitchen."

"Okay." Shay pushed to her feet, picked up her pillow, and followed her friend. "Do you want me to fix you something?"

"I'll get it." Marrell flicked on the light.

Shay sat at the kitchen table and studied her

hands where they lay on the top. Marrell brought a knife, bowl, milk, and sugar over and then reached for the fruit bowl and a napkin. Shay watched her as she began to cut.

"Do you want something to drink with that?"

"Ice water sounds good."

Shay rose to get it without comment. Marrell ended up at the sink to rinse the juice from her hands, but she eventually sat back down and had a few bites of food. The milk was cold with the combination of sweet peaches, and she felt a little better.

"Do you know what my grandmother told me?" she asked her friend. "She started this study on heaven when she learned of the cancer, and she said there's no need for the sun in heaven. God's glory is that bright."

"And Paul's there."

"Yeah. Oh, Shay, I would never have survived this if he hadn't come to Christ. Think of the peace I have. I know where he is and that I'll see him again."

Shay's throat was too tight to let any words out. She listened to her friend sigh.

"I can't quite figure out what I'm going to do without him. I never thought about having to be on my own. I mean, he was in Germany just a year ago, but I knew he was coming back."

"Oliver and I will be here for you."

Marrell nodded. "Did he get the baby to sleep?"

"Yes. He emptied one of D.J.'s dresser drawers and put it on the floor. Jana thought she was in her crib and fell sound asleep."

Marrell played with her bowl of peaches, no longer hungry. She drank a bit of water, and Shay watched her eyes fill with tears.

"I don't think a week went by that he didn't tell me a new verse he had found." Her voice shook uncontrollably, but she went on. "He was so excited about his study in Romans." Tears made a steady path down her cheeks. "He was the most romantic man I've ever known, Shay. Just the other night he brushed my hair for an hour and then painted my toenails. Did you know he used to do that, paint my toenails?"

"I think the girls mentioned it one time."

"Oh, Shay, what am I going to do?"

Shay moved close, and they clung together and cried. Marrell didn't know when she had felt such pain. There had been no argument as to whether or not Oliver and Shay should stay; Marrell had only been relieved. Oliver had gone home to pick up a few things, and the girls had been glad to have the baby to distract them.

"I think I'm finally tired now," Marrell confessed, sitting back and wiping at her face.

"Okay," Shay handed her a tissue. "I'll clean up in here for you."

"Or you can leave it. I can get it in the morning."

Shay didn't answer but said goodnight, waited for Marrell to leave, and then quietly put the kitchen to rights. Her pillow was in her hand as she put out the lights and headed back down the hall. Marrell's door was already shut, so she was unaware of the way her friend once again lay down in the hall to be near her.

"Mrs. Bishop," Marrell spoke tentatively into the phone, "this is Marrell."

"Oh, Marrell." She sounded surprised. "How are you?"

"Mrs. Bishop, Paul is dead." Marrell knew no other way to say it. "There was an accident, and he died last night."

"Paul's dead," she heard the woman whisper.

"Yes. I'm so sorry."

The cry of anguish and suffering that came from the other end of the line brought Marrell's heart into her throat.

"I just got him back." The voice of Paul's mother rose to a wail. "How can God do this to us?"

Marrell's hand was on her mouth as she heard the phone being dropped and voices in the background. Her mother-in-law's screams could be heard as well as the voice of another person. Marrell was on the verge of hanging up when someone barked on the line.

"Hello, who is this?"

"It's Marrell Bishop," she said softly. "Is this Mr. Bishop?"

"Yes."

"Paul is dead." She was forced to say it again. "There was an accident on the base, and he died last night."

The silence was almost too much for Marrell's bruised heart.

"My boy is dead?"

"Yes." Marrell began to sob. "He died very quickly. There was no suffering. We haven't made arrangements yet, but I can call you again."

"Yes. All right."

Marrell didn't know what to say next. She could still hear Arlene Bishop in the background, her lament sounding inconsolable.

"I'll let you go now, Mr. Bishop."

"Yes. All right."

"Goodbye."

"Goodbye."

Marrell put the phone down and sat with her head against the headboard. She didn't think anyone else was up; it was only nine o'clock in Florida. Marrell had finally fallen asleep around two but hadn't been able to make it past five-thirty. Her eyes felt gritty, and she wanted some coffee but let it go for now. Shifting around so the light would be right, she reached for her Bible.

"Are you awake?" Delancey whispered a little after six o'clock.

"Yes."

The younger girl breathed deeply, fighting tears. "It's all my fault, Mic. Dad's death is all my fault."

Mackenzie shifted around in the bed to look at her. Delancey was flat on her back, her eyes on the ceiling.

"That's not true."

"It is. Dad wanted me to believe for so long, and I wouldn't. This is God's punishment for me."

"Do you know what Dad would say if he heard that?"

Delancey hadn't thought of that, so she didn't answer.

"He would say God's not like that. I don't need Jesus the way Mom and Dad did, D.J., but they still love me. I know they do."

"What if we do need Jesus, Mackenzie? What if we do?"

"That's fine," her sister said. "You do what you need to, Delancey, but Dad loves you no matter what. Don't you forget that."

Delancey might have been comforted by those words if she'd had any idea what she was supposed to do, but she was at a painful loss. She rolled on her side and stared at the door, her mind registering only one thing: *My dad is gone.*

Hundreds of mourners attended Colonel Paul Bishop's funeral on June 9, 1982. The service was held at their church, although the theme was military, and Marrell was overwhelmed by the support. The base relief group, along with dozens of church family members, came along to see to almost every need. Shay and Oliver had been at the house every day since the night Marrell had called them, but now the funeral was over. Marrell and the girls were alone.

"Why didn't Grandma and Grandpa Bishop come?" Delancey asked.

"I just don't think Grandpa Bishop can handle it, D.J. He cut himself off from your dad for so long, and then when he had a chance to have him again, he pushed him away. I'm sure his regret is huge."

"I think I hate him. How could anyone treat Dad that way?"

"Your dad hated him for a lot of years too, but he eventually learned there was no point in that."

For a time they ate in silence, but Marrell had things on her mind, and the girls had to hear them.

"We have to be off the base in 30 days," she plunged right in. "Oliver has checked on our old apartment building, and the woman is going to call him back. If she has room, you could stay in the same school district."

Delancey didn't think she ever wanted to go to school again, but she kept her mouth shut. When Mackenzie didn't reply either, Marrell went on.

"I want us to try and get back to that apartment building. I feel better about that than anything else. What do you think?"

"Why do we have to move so soon?" Mackenzie asked.

"SOP," Marrell shrugged, giving the military reply the girls had grown up with. Standard Operating Procedures. "I wish we could have longer, but in some ways that might be harder."

The girls thought about this for a silent moment.

"Has Colonel Barlowe gotten back to you yet about the other driver?"

"With something new, no. He was heavily intoxicated with no insurance at all."

"Are you angry with him, Mom?"

"No, I'm not. I'm not happy about it, but there is no use hating the man." Secretly Marrell thought about God's sovereignty. That perfect attribute was the only reason Marrell didn't hate anyone. Her husband was gone because it was God's time, not because a drunk had hit him. But right now that type of comment only upset the girls, so she let it go. Besides, there were other things she needed to bring up that were going to be upsetting enough.

"I'm going to wait until we've moved," Marrell plunged in again, "but just as soon as we do that, I'm going to start looking for a job."

"Why so soon?" Mackenzie was clearly not happy.

"Because I want to leave as much of our savings intact as possible."

"You said Dad was insured."

"He was, but I want to leave that for big things. My getting a job is going to come sooner or later, Micki. We've got to face that. If you girls were already out of school, I probably wouldn't work

238

for a long time, but this way I can provide for our monthly needs and leave the insurance money for your college education, special things, and unexpected large expenses. I spoke with Oliver about it, and he thought it a sound idea. Soon after the Fourth of July, I'm just going to start looking for a job. If nothing comes up, then we might have to dip into the insurance money, but like I said, I won't if I don't have to."

The girls were surprised speechless. Their mother was a constant presence in their lives. She cooked, ran them places in the car, cleaned the house, did the laundry, and loved them unconditionally. But their father had paid the bills and been the one to read the fine print when anything was in question. They never thought their mother stupid, but both found it surprising that she had given this much thought to the insurance money.

"Is it a lot of money, Mom?"

"Yes."

"How much?"

"I don't want to tell you that right now. If people question you — and some are rude enough to do so — then you can honestly say you don't know."

The sisters looked at each other.

"We'll be fine," Marrell said softly. "I believe this with all my heart."

No one was hungry for any of the many desserts people had brought, not even Mackenzie for chocolate cake or brownies. The three did the dishes in near silence, and just as they were finishing, the phone rang. It was Oliver for Marrell.

"Hi," she said after she took the phone from Delancey's hand.

"Are you in the middle of dinner?"

"Just finished."

"Good. I just got off the phone with your former landlady. She has an apartment opening up in August. It might turn out to be July, but she promised no later than August 1."

"Oh."

Almost a month after they had to be off the base. Marrell tried to think, but Oliver was talking again.

"Before I could call you, the phone rang again. It was my father. He asked if I thought you and the girls would like to come and stay with them for two weeks — just come to be waited on and relax at their place. I asked him if a whole month would work, and he said, "Absolutely." I told him I'd call you and get back to him."

"Are you serious, Oliver — a whole month? Would they really want that?"

"You bet. They love you and the girls, and as my mother said, they have two bedrooms that sit empty most of the year."

"Oh my." Marrell was overwhelmed. "Let me talk to the girls. No, wait, first tell me what apartment is available. Is it like that one we had?"

"Yes, it's just on the other side of the complex. The rents have gone up a little." Oliver named the new rent, but Marrell still thought she could swing it.

"What do you think, Oliver? Am I working too hard to keep the girls with their present schoolmates?"

"No, I think that apartment building is perfect for you. Paul chose that for you originally, so you know he was comfortable with it, and you're only ten minutes from us."

"Okay. Let me get off here and speak with Mic and D.J. Should I call back tonight?"

"Yes. The woman has others interested, and since she's had you before, you'll have first choice, but I don't think you should wait too long."

"All right. I'll call back as soon as I can. Oh, one other thing, Oliver. What will we do with our stuff for a month?"

"We'll cross that bridge when we come to it."

"Okay. I'll call you."

Marrell was not surprised to turn and find both girls waiting to hear what was going on. Not only did they hear her side of the conversation, they wanted to be close to her at all times these days.

Marrell gave a quick rundown of the situation, and Mackenzie was the first to speak.

"That was a nice apartment, Mom. Are you sure it won't be the same one as before, because I wouldn't want that."

"It's not, Micki. It's the same floor plan, I guess, but that's all. The rent has gone up a little, but as Oliver pointed out, that's to be expected."

"What if after we get to the Lacys', we just wish we could be on our own?" Delancey insightfully asked.

"Well, I guess we could take a drive for the day."

"We don't have a car."

"The insurance company is looking into that. And we're talking about July now, which is still three weeks away." It didn't feel very long once she heard herself saying it, and she worked on trusting the Lord in this too.

"I don't want to sound ungrateful, Mom," Mackenzie said softly, "but I don't know if we have any choice. Maybe the apartment will open up soon and we won't have to stay away a whole month."

"Does that mean you think we should take the

apartment?"

"Yes," Mackenzie voted.

Delancey also nodded her head in agreement.

Marrell walked back to the phone, telling herself not to sob. That she was even having to think about this was nothing short of amazing to her.

My husband's gone, she thought as she dialed Shay and Oliver's number. *He took such good care of me, and I don't know if I ever thanked him. Tell him, Lord. Tell him I now know what a good job he did.*

The weeks passed in a blurry sort of confusion. Some days rushed by, and others dragged. Nights lasted forever for Marrell, but she was able to nap almost every afternoon.

With the aid of many people, their furniture and possessions were packed up and stored in a warehouse belonging to one of the church families. Mackenzie's fourteenth birthday passed in a very low-key fashion, but Marrell still managed to find her a gift and bake a cake. A nice-sized check came in from the insurance company, and Oliver found a car for Marrell. Cramped as they were, Shay and Oliver made them welcome through the Fourth of July weekend, and the three Bishop women left for the Lacy farm on Monday, July 5.

It was better than any of them could have imagined. There was no set schedule or demands. The fellowship for Marrell got her through some rough days, and the girls even opted to work in the orchards a bit. Shay and the baby visited often, and Marrell wouldn't have traded the time for the world. Not at any point did the Bishops feel crowded or anxious to be away, and they were actually surprised to have Oliver call one night and say the apartment would be available on the twenty-fourth. The surprise was even greater when, upon their return, they discovered that all of their furnishings had been moved in.

Shay and Oliver remembered how the other apartment had been set up and simply arranged it the same way. Marrell forced herself to get up in church the next Sunday during testimony time and thank everyone for their help. It wasn't without pain, but as she looked out at their smiling faces, she was glad she had made the effort.

For the girls the summer passed all too swiftly, and it was with something akin to panic that they realized it was almost time to go back to school.

"I can't," Delancey said flat out. "I can't go back — I just can't."

"Why, D.J.? What is so upsetting about returning to school?"

"Just everything, Mom. School is just one more thing!" came the angry, tearful reply. "You wait until your birthday comes and see if you like having it without Dad."

Marrell held her. Mackenzie's birthday had been bad enough, but Delancey's, just a month after her sister's, had been awful. Marrell shopped and did a special meal and cake, but Delancey's birthday fell on the first weekend they spent in the apartment, and the very reason they were there seemed to scream at them all day long. Now August had come upon them, and Marrell had mentioned school clothes, only to have Delancey run from the room in tears.

Have they even remembered that I was going to look for a job, Lord? I put it off so I wouldn't have to leave them at the Lacys', but we have to eat and pay the rent. If I don't have something by the end of

243

October, I'll be forced to dip into our savings.

Marrell looked up to see Mackenzie at the door.

"Would you rather not even shop for school clothes, Micki? Tell me what's going to make this easier."

She shrugged, tears in her eyes. "I don't know, Mom. It's so hard. You think that all the kids can tell, just by looking at you, what's happened. We saw some of our friends at the grocery store. They didn't say anything. They probably don't even know. But it just felt so weird. And everyone at church smiles at us in that sad way. It's so awful."

Marrell couldn't have agreed more. *Yes, it is awful, and right now it feels like it always will be.*

Marrell waved her over, and she came and sat on the other side of the bed. Delancey still had her head bent and her hand over her eyes.

"I'm going to pray," she said softly, "and you're going to listen. 'Father in heaven, we hurt so much right now. It feels as though we're going to drown in this pain. Thank You that Your ways are perfect, Lord, even when we can't find our way. Thank You that You never stop loving us and doing what's best. Help Micki and D.J. not to be angry with You. Help me to be there for them, but also for us to realize that we have to move on.' " A sob broke in Marrell's throat, but she kept praying.

" 'I want everyone to stop and realize that my world has just fallen apart, Lord, but that's not the way it works. The sun still rises and sets, traffic lights still work, babies are being born, and other people are losing loved ones and starting their own time of grief. I only know one thing right now, Lord, and that's the fact that You love me and know what's best. Help us, Lord. Help us as only You can.' "

Marrell couldn't say any more. She was spent with emotions, burdened over the job that must be found and how hard it would be for the girls to return to school.

"Come on, D.J. Let's look in your closet and see how you're doing on clothes."

Delancey didn't argue, and Mackenzie stayed close and helped as well. Delancey needed jeans and a few tops, but new shoes, socks, and underwear were the most pressing needs. Mackenzie's room was next. Delancey found a few of her tops in there, because Mackenzie's were not in the best shape. She had plenty of jeans and shorts, but her shoes were in sad repair. Marrell made notes as she went and then made her way to the kitchen to balance her checkbook, but not before telling the girls that they would be headed to the mall in the morning.

It had finally happened. Male heads turned from every direction to look at Delancey Joy Bishop, but she didn't care. Five-foot ten, slim, blond-haired, and blue-eyed, she was as lovely as her mother, attracting the attention of old and young alike, but not one ounce of joy came with that fact. Only vaguely aware that anyone else was in the stores, Delancey shopped with her mother and sister and looked at herself in the mirror only long enough to see if the clothes fit.

Marrell could see that she was miserable and disinterested and even offered to buy her a 49ers T-shirt. Delancey was a big fan of the current Super Bowl champs. Today, however, the shirt did not look good to her.

"I think I need to see Jana," Marrell confessed hours later as they climbed into the car. For not having had much fun, they had accomplished quite a bit. The girls, at any rate, had no argument over a visit to Shay's. They liked their new clothes and thanked their mother, but little could cheer them these days the way the six-month-old baby could. Sitting up now and even scooting a bit, Jana was constantly full of smiles and laughs for the two teenage girls.

"Come in." Shay wasted no time in welcoming the weary shoppers. "Jana got up from her nap just a little while ago."

The girls went right to the baby on the living room floor, but Marrell hung back and accepted a hug from Shay.

"Does coffee sound good?"

"How about iced tea? Would that be too much trouble?"

"Not in the least. Come on in the kitchen. Hey, D.J.," Shay called as they passed, "she just ate, so you might want to watch the bounces."

"Okay."

The women disappeared into the kitchen. Marrell sat at the table, and Shay glanced at her before getting out tall glasses for tea.

"Just out and about today?"

"We went school shopping. No one was very excited, but I think we got everything we needed. I keep asking myself if I'm always going to feel so apathetic."

"I did after the divorce. I didn't use makeup or an ironing board. I just didn't care."

"What pulled you out of it?"

"Moving out here and wanting the business to make it. It will be something different with you, Marrell. Just give yourself time."

"I have to find work, Shay. At this point I might

246

as well wait until the girls go back to school, but I have to start looking. I think I already told you, but I planned to do that in July."

"But you ended up in Sebastopol."

"Yes. I'm glad for that time, but it's thrown things off a little."

Shay busied herself with ice and tall spoons, but she was thinking. Two weeks ago she had put in a call to a friend about a job for Marrell but hadn't heard back from him. It was the perfect position if it came through, but Shay didn't want to build Marrell's hopes up if it didn't. She wisely kept silent.

"Do you want some pretzels?" Shay asked as she handed her the glass.

"No, I'm not hungry. Maybe I'll check with the girls." But she didn't. She took a sip of the tea and just sat. "It's like I'm not really here, Shay. It's like I'm watching someone else, an actress maybe, going through the motions and living my life."

"Weird, isn't it?"

"Yeah. Before my grandmother died, she did a study on what the Bible says about heaven. I've started the same study. It's very comforting, but heaven also feels so far away. Knowing Paul is there means everything to me, but in some ways I feel cheated that I've been left behind."

Shay nodded. Oliver had said something very similar the night before — that being left behind when someone goes to heaven could give a person a very empty feeling — but then he went on to say something much more helpful. Shay now shared it with Marrell.

"Oliver agrees with you, Marrell. He said as much last night, but he also had a good slant on heaven and the death of someone near. His grandfather was the first person whose death really affected him. The two had been very close, and he said it gave heaven a new significance. Even knowing that we're going there to be with the Lord and worship Him, it's been comforting to Oliver to have his grandfather there and know that he's waiting. I thought that was pretty neat."

"Yes, it is." Marrell's face brightened. "I think of Paul walking along and talking with Jesus, and even being able to ask Him questions, but I don't think of him waiting for me. I like that thought. Tell Oliver thank you."

"I will," Shay said with a smile.

"I guess we'd better take off," Marrell said as she finished her tea. "I should run a load or two of laundry."

"Do you hate sitting down there with the machines?"

"It's not my favorite, but the girls take turns with me. We manage to make it work."

"Feel free to come here and do some too, Marrell. You could stay as long as you like."

"Thanks, and thank you for the tea."

"You're very welcome."

Marrell pushed to her feet and went to join the girls in the living room. She spent some time with Jana, who was a little sweetheart.

"Watch this, Mom," Delancey said, holding a pink bunny up in front of Jana's face. The little girl squirmed with delight.

"Oliver bought that," Shay said with a laugh, "at the grocery store, no less. He went for eggs and bread and came back with a bunny and milk."

The Bishop women thought this hysterical.

"Are you serious?" Marrell asked.

"Yes. It was right after she was born, and he was so excited that he just forgot."

It was a sweet note on which to leave. The girls laughed about it off and on all the way home.

The first weeks of school were nothing short of torture for Mackenzie Bishop. She was in ninth grade, and that meant high school. The high school was bigger, combining her junior high school with two others. There were many kids she didn't know. At any other time, having Brett Cooper as a lab partner would have made her groan, but since she was in a sophomore science class, and he was one of the few kids she knew, it was almost a relief. The first day they sat at their lab stations, Mackenzie steeled herself for his scorn, but she didn't get it. He had a steady girl now and had clearly done some maturing.

"I saw you in gym class yesterday," he said one day at the end of September.

"I didn't see you."

"The guys were in the weight room."

"Oh, yeah. I'd heard that Coach Pullman was starting you guys on weight training."

"Yeah. We'll be at it all the way through basketball. I think you should go out."

"For basketball?"

"Yes, the girls' team. I saw you shooting yesterday, and your lay-ups are good."

Mackenzie stared at him. He was the third person to say something. She had never played any serious basketball and didn't think she was any good, but her gym teacher had been one of the people. It was getting harder and harder to ignore the compliments when she shot baskets, especially from the free-throw line.

"I don't know" was all she said.

If Mackenzie had known the truth, Brett was aware of the way her father had died. He had seen it in the paper. He had hated Mackenzie when she wouldn't go out with him, but after reading about her father, he hated her no longer. The compliment was sincere about her basketball skills. At 6'1", he played a lot of ball himself and knew what to look for.

"You don't have to decide today. I don't think the girls' tryouts start until next Monday."

Mackenzie only nodded because they had to get back to work, but he had certainly gotten her attention. Indeed, she mentioned it to her mother that night during dinner.

"Why, Micki," Marrell said with pleasure, "I think that's a great idea. When would you do this?"

"Tryouts start Monday. I just have to be there after school for a week of practices, and then Coach will post the team on Friday when we're done."

"What if you don't make it?" Delancey asked.

Mackenzie shrugged. "Coach was one of the people who said I should try out, so I don't know if that means something or not."

"What time will you be done each day?"

"I think about 4:30."

Marrell looked uncertain, and Mackenzie picked up on it.

"What's wrong?"

"I don't think anything, but Shay called today, and I have an interview tomorrow — something she set up."

Marrell had had several interviews since the girls had gone back to school, so they didn't know why this was any different.

"I don't understand what the problem is," Mackenzie pressed her.

Marrell shrugged. "There isn't one, but Shay is
sure I'll get this job, and if I do, I'll probably have
to start right away. If that's the case, I don't know
if I'll be free to pick you up at 4:30."

Mackenzie finally understood, and she didn't
like it. Once again she'd been taking her mother
for granted. She was always there for them, dropping everything to see to their needs. Mackenzie
was ready to say she would forget basketball, but
Marrell had second-guessed her.

"I want you to do this, Micki. If I end up at a
job next week, we'll figure out a way."

Mackenzie agreed, completely unaware of the
way her mother was silently begging God to let it
be true.

FIFTEEN

Marrell's palms were so damp the next day that her purse nearly slipped from her grasp. None of the other businesses had called her back. She had interviewed for two receptionist jobs and even gone back to Shay's old office. Nothing had panned out. Now she was headed into Bayside Architecture and had no greater hopes than before.

It was a square building, three stories high, and as soon as she entered the elegant lobby, she told herself it would never work. Shay would have given her a lecture for this, but she didn't care.

"I've got something for you" had been Shay's excited call to her.

"What is it?"

"A job."

"A job? What are you talking about, Shay?"

"It's with another architect in town, Marrell. It's a great firm, and the man whose secretary needs an office assistant is a wonderful Christian man. He goes to our church."

"Oh, Shay, I don't know. I don't really know anything about architecture, and I can't pretend that I do."

"You don't have to. I've talked with Jack, and it sounds like the job is just what you were doing at my office."

Marrell had sighed. "Whom do I call?"

"You don't. I already set up the interview. It's for Wednesday at 11:30. You'll fill out a job application when you get there, so take everything you need. Then you'll go to lunch with his secretary, since you'll be working mostly with her. If she likes you, you'll interview with Jack. They are very good about calling one way or the other." Shay had thrown in this last part because Marrell's biggest complaint was employers who said, "We'll call you," and never did.

Had it just been yesterday that she had the conversation with Shay? Marrell now asked herself, absently reading that Jackson Avery's office was on the second floor, Suite 6, and then making her finger push the elevator button. There were mirrors on the walls inside the elevator. Marrell thought she looked pale and pursed her lips together to spread her light pink lipstick a bit better. She had opted for a pale blue suit and pulling her hair back in a neat chignon. She hoped she didn't look too stuffy or more professional than she really was. Her handbag and low-heeled pumps were navy.

The elevator was much too fast. The door opened onto the second floor before she was ready, and with just ten steps across the second-floor lobby, she was at Suite 6. *Jackson Avery, Architect,* it said on the door. Marrell smoothed her already-smooth skirt, tugged at the bottom of her jacket, and opened the door.

The waiting room was not huge but richly carpeted and wallpapered in dark green and navy. At the end of the rather long room sat two desks, side by side, behind which were two very large windows looking out over the city. Marrell's own feet seemed to find a life of their own as she approached the desk where a young, dark-haired woman sat.

"Hello," she greeted Marrell with a smile.

"Hello, I'm Marrell Bishop. I have an appointment. I might be a little early."

"No, you're just right," the woman said as she stood, extending her hand. "I'm Taya Albright. Did you find us all right?"

"Yes, I wasn't sure about the parking."

"We have a lot under the building. If things work out, you'll be given a sticker for your car and be able to park there for free. Why don't you have a seat and fill this out for me," Taya went on. "Let me know when you're finished, and we'll go to lunch."

Lunch went well. Taya's questions were kindly put and Marrell found herself relaxing more and more. Not until the end of the meal did Taya take some time to tell Marrell what the office was looking for. By the time Marrell actually stood back in the lobby of Suite 6, she was ready to run for her life.

Taya had used terms like *facade* and *quoins,* and Marrell thought her head would spin. Then she had referred to CAD seats and massing studies. Marrell had no idea what the younger woman was talking about.

Taya moved back inside the inner office, and Marrell stood by the desk, her mind going a hundred miles an hour. *I can't do this,* Marrell's panicked heart told her. *I've got to find a way to explain.* But it was too late.

"Mr. Avery is ready to see you now, Marrell." Taya was back much too swiftly. "Come on in, and I'll introduce you."

Marrell followed but called herself every type of fool. She knew the job was from 8:30 to 5:00 Monday through Friday, and that she would be expected to type some, answer the phone, and file, but she realized now that she should have asked more questions — many more.

"Marrell Bishop, this is Mr. Avery."

A tall man stood and came around from behind his desk. He had a dark mustache and a head full of brown hair, although Marrell noticed the graying at the temples. His suit was dark blue, but his jacket was off, showing a pale pink shirt and light rose and navy striped tie.

"Hello, Marrell. It's good to meet you."

"Thank you," Marrell responded. She could feel her face blushing. How did she explain without making a complete fool of herself?

"Have a seat," Jack invited and went back to sit in his desk chair. Marrell was vaguely aware of Taya leaving and shutting the door.

"I've read your application over. How did you like working for Sharon Elliot?"

"Very well. It was interesting work," she was able to say honestly, but knew she couldn't leave it at that. "I don't think I learned much about architecture, Mr. Avery, but Shay said it was always nice to have an extra pair of hands in the office."

Jack smiled before saying, "Tell me a little about yourself."

"Well, I live with my two daughters here in the city." She paused and then made herself admit, "I'm recently widowed, so I'm looking for a job. I don't have a lot of experience."

"Have you done much office work?"

"I did take business classes in high school, but that's been a number of years ago now."

"How long were you with Elliot and Associates?" he asked while scanning the application.

"About a year."

Jack nodded, his eyes still kind as he looked up at her and asked his standard question. "Tell me, Marrell, why should I hire you?"

Marrell's hands were so slick she thought she could use a towel, but none of that showed in her face when in a low voice she said, "You shouldn't, Mr. Avery."

Jack was so stunned that he blinked at her and sat forward in his chair.

Her voice was still soft as she took a deep breath and continued. "I would never want you to think I can do the job if I can't, Mr. Avery, and after talking with Taya, I just don't think I'm qualified."

Marrell started to gather her purse.

"Marrell," Jack said compassionately but was ignored.

"I'm so sorry to have wasted your time. You've been very kind."

"Marrell," he said again, but she was now on her feet.

"Goodbye."

Jack finally caught her at the door.

"Marrell, please stop."

Marrell did but wouldn't turn to look at him. She could feel that tears had gathered in her eyes, and she would rather die than let him see.

"I ask everyone that question," he exclaimed, his eyes on her profile. "It's not meant to intimidate or put you on your guard. It's just a standard question, and I can see now that maybe it shouldn't be."

256

"I'm not who you want for this job, Mr. Avery."

"I need to tell you that you come very highly recommended, Marrell. Shay Lacy couldn't say enough about you." He didn't mention that Taya had termed her "perfect."

"You need to know," Marrell turned without thinking, showing him the tears he already knew were there, "that Shay is a very good friend."

"Be that as it may, she would never lie to me. She's ethical and too much of a professional for that. If you don't want this job, Marrell, I would never push it on you, but anyone as honest as you are can start in the morning."

Marrell blinked up at him. "You're willing to hire me?"

"Yes."

"What if I can't do the job?"

"Then we'll figure out why and talk about it. Taya is a very good teacher, and I think you'll find many of your duties will be just what Shay expected."

Marrell licked her lips, thinking her heart would stop.

Jack named a salary and said, "You can start at 8:30 in the morning, or if you need the weekend, Monday will be fine."

"Thank you," Marrell said simply.

"Thank *you*," Jack returned. "We've been looking for the right person for quite some time. If you'll just go out and see Taya, she'll get you all set."

"All right."

Marrell was so stunned that she forgot to thank him again or even to say goodbye, none of which Jack noticed. He closed the door as soon as she walked out and stood very still. He had never let on that he knew exactly who she was, or that he had been in church the morning she went up front and bared her heart in front of the congregation, thanking them for their help after Paul's death. He had felt his own heart sink with hurt when she had stood and almost run for the door.

To lose your husband and be forced to take work just months later must be pain beyond anything he had ever known. There had been three such women in the church in the last few years, suddenly widowed and in need of support. Jack had been burdened to pray for each of them. He'd even anonymously given some money to the first widow so that she could eventually move to the Midwest to be with her family. Then Shay Lacy had called and told him that Marrell Bishop needed a job. Jack had determined to find one for her, even going so far as to look into some other positions in case Taya found her unsuitable.

Jack was able to return to his work, light with the knowledge that he hadn't hired someone because he felt sorry for her, but that in being able to give her a job, he had helped a sister in Christ. He got an amazing amount of work done that afternoon.

Taya looked up from her work to see Marrell standing outside Jack's office door. She watched her come forward very slowly, stop, and stare at her.

"He hired me," she said, wonder filling her voice.

Taya beamed at her. "I was hoping he would."

Tears filled Marrell's eyes. She couldn't stop them. "I'm sorry," she whispered, her hand over her mouth.

"It's all right," Taya said.

"I just didn't think I'd find anything, and now that Paul's gone, I have to take care of my girls."

"When did he die, Marrell?"

"June 5."

"Of this year?"

Marrell nodded, reaching for a tissue from her purse. Taya was stunned. That wasn't even four months ago.

"We'll do fine together, Marrell," Taya said bracingly. "You'll see. I think you'll like the job."

"Thank you, Taya. I can't tell you what a help you've been."

"I am the one who's going to be helped. Jack gets more work all the time, and it's just too much for one person. We had a good team, me and another gal, but her husband's job transferred them out of the city. We've been shorthanded for about three months. What day does Jack want you to start?"

"He said tomorrow or Monday, whatever works for me."

"Oh, okay. Uh, let's see. How about you come in for a few hours tomorrow and a few hours Friday and start full-time next week?"

"Oh, that would work. I need to figure out what I'm doing with the girls after school, so that would be very helpful."

"Great. Have you got time to fill out some insurance forms right now?"

"Sure."

Marrell did so with a feeling of unreality. She had a job! Shay had been right, and as soon as she was done, she would head to her apartment and tell her.

"My only problem," Marrell was able to say when

259

Shay stopped dancing around the living room, "is what to do with the girls. I won't get home until 5:15 or 5:30, and to top it off, Micki's going to go out for basketball, and she isn't finished with practice until 4:30. Now, there's only a week of that if she doesn't make the team, but I don't know what to do, Shay."

"I do," Shay said calmly, forcing herself not to volunteer for everything. "We let the church family know and see if anyone can help. Maybe one of the other ninth-grade girls from the youth group will be on the team, and they can drop Mic off. As for D.J., couldn't she go to Mrs. Baker's until Mic gets there?" Shay was referring to Marrell's neighbor, a kind woman in the apartment complex who babysat her own grandchildren four days a week. "The girls would only be on their own for an hour or less before you arrived. They've proved themselves responsible enough for that. And if they did need something, they could always go back to Mrs. Baker's."

"How would I know they've arrived?"

"Well, Mrs. Baker would call you if there was no sign of Delancey, and likewise, Delancey could do the same if Mic didn't show up."

It sounded like a good plan, and Marrell was so muddled that she knew she would never have thought of it.

"Do you think D.J. will be upset about going to Mrs. Baker's?"

"She might be, and you might find out that she would do fine at home alone, but this way you have a backup."

Marrell nodded. It was all so much. God's Word promised that His yoke was light, but lately Marrell seemed to forget this truth so easily. Oliver had recently reminded her that she needed to stop doing God's job.

"You're just not that good at it, Marrell," he'd said, only half kidding.

She had laughed but understood his point, and now she was at it again.

I feel as if the world has been placed on my shoulders. That's not true, but some days I don't know how I'm going to keep on.

"I think I've lost you," Shay broke into her thoughts.

"Oh, I was just praying and working at understanding what my job is, so God can do His."

"I forgot to ask you what you thought of Jack Avery. Isn't he a nice guy?"

"Very. I'm embarrassed over what a fool I made of myself, but he still offered me the job."

Shay looked surprised, and Marrell realized she hadn't told her. The redheaded woman was in stitches when Marrell described the way she had told Jack not to hire her and bolted for the door.

"Oh, Marrell, please stop. I can't take any more. You actually said that?"

"Yes, and it wasn't funny, Sharon Lacy! It was humiliating, and then I went out to Taya's desk and cried like a baby."

"Oh, Marrell, what a time this has been for you. Do you know how well you're doing?"

Marrell shook her head, clearly not believing her.

"You are, Marrell. You've been such an example to me. I would be tempted to crawl in bed and never come out, but you still go to everything and praise God for His love."

Marrell didn't see herself in this light. She thought she was the weakest woman who had ever

261

lived: weak, faithless, and troublesome.

"I can see by your face that you expect too much of yourself, Marrell. Be careful that you don't put standards on yourself that God doesn't."

Marrell knew Shay was right. She had been expecting things of herself that God was not expecting. The verse in Matthew 6 about seeking God's kingdom and righteousness and leaving the rest to Him jumped into Marrell's mind. She would study those verses tonight after she told her girls the good news.

"I thought you would be so pleased," Marrell said as she looked into her daughters' stricken faces. "It's a good job with kind people, and that means I'll be able to take care of you."

"You won't be taking care of me; Mrs. Baker will be," Delancey said bitterly.

Marrell was stunned. "D.J., did you really think I wouldn't have to get a job? Because if that's the case, you haven't been listening."

"None of the others have worked out," Mackenzie said, as if that explained everything. "We don't like coming home and your not being here."

"I don't like it either, Mic, but right now I don't have a choice. I could try and find something part-time, but I don't think we can live on that. We'll have to look for a cheaper apartment, that's for sure."

The girls felt utterly defeated, and their faces said as much. Marrell was glad that she'd had time to be in the Word before they arrived home. The things she had read in Matthew helped her to remember that God was in control and that worry was a sin.

"What's it to be, girls?" she asked, her feelings

262

well under control. "I can call Bayside tomorrow and tell them I can't take the job, or see if they'll allow me to go part-time. We'll have many changes ahead of us, but that's not all bad. I'm thankful for this job and think I should take it, but I'm willing to listen to other ideas."

"I don't have any, Mom," Delancey said, again sounding bitter, "but I still don't like it."

"Tell me, D.J.," Marrell tried to push down the thought that her youngest daughter was being completely unreasonable, "did you really think I wouldn't have to work?"

"I guess I just tried not to think about it."

"I've been doing the same thing," Mackenzie admitted. "It just seems so unfair."

There was little Marrell could say to that. She had felt that same way at their ages, and after her father died, she was convinced of it.

"I'm going to take the job," Marrell said after a few seconds of quiet. "The pay is good and so are the benefits. There's no base hospital or clinic to visit now; we've got to cover this on our own. If something else should ever come up that would let me be here, I'll look into it, but you need to understand that I won't work nights and leave you here alone. I'm thankful I found a job that has almost the same hours you do."

"I just remembered something," Mackenzie spoke up. "I have to have a sports physical to join basketball."

Marrell nodded, taking it in stride. "All right. Get the information for me, and we'll take care of it."

Mackenzie wandered off to get her book bag, and Marrell said, "Are you all right, D.J.?"

"Yeah." She wasn't, but as usual she had no idea

263

how to explain. "What's this place like?" She came from her shell just long enough to ask.

"Bayside Architecture? Nice. The building is three stories high, and I'm on the second floor. The parking garage is under the building. I'll have a desk in the reception room and be working with Taya Albright, who works for Jackson Avery."

"Jackson is his first name?"

"It must be. That's what the door says."

"What will you do?"

"Probably a lot of the same things I did at Shay's — typing, files, the phone too. I think it's going to work very well. Taya and Mr. Avery are nice."

"Can we call you?"

"Yes. Taya said that would be no problem."

"I'll be sending notes with you tomorrow so the offices will know where to reach me, and you can write my number somewhere on your bag."

With that Delancey was lost again in her own world of pain. She told her mother she had homework — which she did — but when she got to her room, she only lay on the bed and stared at the ceiling. Her eyes strayed to the dresser where a picture of her father and mother had been. She had put it facedown under her old T-shirts in her drawer. It hurt too much to see his face.

When does the pain end? she asked God. *When do You help someone stop hurting? What is it You want me to do to prove to You that I know it's my fault?*

But there was nothing humble about Delancey's prayer. She was furious with God. At times she understood what her mother and father believed, but most of the time she felt it was too risky. There had been a few times when she had been tempted to believe, but before she could follow through

264

with the idea, her father died. Delancey felt nothing but relief that she'd never made the mistake of trusting such an undependable God.

Almost three weeks at Jack Avery's office told Marrell it wasn't going to work. Mackenzie had made the basketball team, and her games started at the end of October. Delancey, however, was drawing deeper and deeper into herself. By the time Marrell got home each night, Delancey was in her room, the door shut. The 13-year-old had to be ordered to come to the dinner table each night, and none of her chores were being done. It was with a sinking heart that Marrell approached Taya at the end of her third week.

"Something wrong, Marrell?"

"Yes, Taya, there is, and I don't know how to tell you."

"You're quitting." Taya said flatly.

"It's not the job, Taya," Marrell went on without asking how she knew. "I'll give two weeks' notice, but my younger daughter is having a very hard time, and I don't get home for two hours after she does. It's just not working."

Taya looked upset but didn't say anything right then. Marrell thought she was mad at her and wished she had waited until the end of the day to say something. She hated the thought of Taya frowning about the situation for the next three hours. And then the worst thing happened: She was called into Jack's office. Marrell knew he would have to find out, but she was hoping it would be after she left for the weekend. Her heart sank with dread as she made her way across the room to his desk.

"Sit down, Marrell." His voice was as kind as

ever, which only made Marrell feel worse. A gentleman, he waited until she was seated and then resumed his own seat. "Taya tells me you feel you have to quit."

"I'm sorry." She wanted to bawl but didn't. "You've been so kind, but I have to be there for D.J."

"What if you had different hours?"

"Different hours?"

"Yes. When do the girls leave for school?"

"D.J. goes at 7:15, and Micki at 7:30."

"What if you came in at 7:30 and left at 4:00?"

Marrell stared at him. "But what about the phones? How can I help with that?"

"Coming in at that time of the morning means you'll have done so much of the paperwork that Taya will be freer to answer the phones until five. This was Taya's idea, by the way."

"I don't know what to say."

"Will it work, or will the girls just feel they're losing you in the morning too?"

"I don't know, but I can't think why they would. We would be heading out the door at the same time. Well, D.J. and I would. Mic would be on her own for a few minutes, but she hasn't had the problem. It's been Delancey."

Jack watched her concentrate and tried not to comment. The desire to tell her that they would work this out no matter what was strong. This is where she needed to be. She worked hard and never complained, but there wasn't a day that she didn't remind Jack of a lost child. He didn't know how she would be treated if she worked elsewhere; here he had control. On top of all that, Taya loved her.

"Why don't you talk it over with the girls?" Jack

forced himself to say. He thought it a fine idea to *tell* the girls her hours were changing, but he wasn't involved enough to know if that was a good idea or not.

"No," Marrell surprised him by saying, a small frown between her brows. "You're gracious enough to offer this to me, and I accept. If Delancey isn't happy with this, then she can just learn to deal with it. It's been like living with a hermit these last weeks, and I'm sick of it. It's been completely unreasonable on her part to think that I didn't have to go to work. *I'm* the one who should be having trouble with it, but I've chosen to be thankful."

Marrell sat there for a moment and stewed. Jack wanted to laugh, not because he found the situation funny, but because Marrell Bishop was adorable when she was mad.

"I'll just tell her," she went on with new resolve. "She can live with Mackenzie and me or she can move out. I'm doing the best I can. Paul always said to me that I don't like people to be mad at me, and now I've let Delancey run things because I can see she's upset. Well, I'm upset too! Does she think she's the only one involved here? I know she's only 13, but I've taken all I'm going to."

Marrell was on her feet now, pacing in front of the desk. She had become quite loud, and Taya had even gone so far as to peek in the door. Jack had a chance to shake his head at her before Marrell turned and pointed her finger at Jack.

"I'm not even going to tell her about my change in hours — not right away. First I'm going to tell her that she will start making more effort and that Micki and I are not going to tiptoe around her anymore."

267

Marrell finally caught herself. Her hand went to her mouth.

"I'm sorry, Jack. I don't know what came over me. You must think I've snapped."

"No, I don't. It's hard to have your children upset with you, and it must be a relief to know that this job will still work."

He was so understanding that Marrell felt embarrassed.

"I'd better go tell Taya about the change and find out what she wants me to do before she gets here Monday."

"All right. Have a good weekend, Marrell."

"Thank you." Marrell's voice sounded normal, but she was still humiliated. Delancey would be waiting at home, in her room no doubt, and Marrell would have to go to war. Nevertheless, she was still glad to have five o'clock come. She could escape the office and having to think about the way she blew up in front of her boss.

SIXTEEN

"I want to talk to you, Delancey." Marrell had wasted no time in going to her daughter's room that night and opening the door. Delancey was on the bed with a book.

"Is dinner ready?"

"No. Come out here immediately."

Delancey's sullen face and long-suffering sighs left no doubt as to her feelings. Marrell had worked through her anger, but she would have her say, and new expectations would begin today.

"Have a seat," Marrell directed when the younger Bishop arrived in the living room.

Delancey dropped into a chair but didn't look at her mother.

"Can you tell me what has you so upset? I would like to know."

"No, it's nothing."

"You're not upset about anything?"

"No."

"All right, then you've got exactly 24 hours to change your attitude, or you can pack your bags and get out."

This was enough to bring Delancey's eyes to her mother. The young teen looked up in shock to find her mother's angry face. Marrell had tried to hold it in, but Delancey's belligerence had proved too much.

"Do I make myself clear, Delancey?"

"Mom, what's the matter with you?"

"Do I say 'nothing' like my daughter does, or should I tell the truth?"

The barb hit home. Delancey hung her head.

"Do you think you're the only one to feel pain, D.J.?"

"No."

"But that's the way you're acting, and I'm not going to put up with it anymore."

"I can't help it, Mom."

"Yes, you can, and you will. Micki and I hurt just as much as you do, but we're not shutting the world out. If you don't want to turn to God for forgiveness and comfort," Marrell hadn't mentioned this in a long time, "that's your choice, but you're going to start talking again, doing your jobs, and making it easier for us to live with you."

Delancey didn't say anything. She didn't know how she would do as her mother asked when she felt so dead inside. And that wasn't all of it.

"Delancey, I need to hear from you now. Do you understand?"

"Yes. I'm not sure what to do. I mean, I just don't have a lot of interest in anything right now."

"Not even your sister and your mother? That's all I'm asking, D.J., that you join the family again."

"All right," Delancey said after a moment.

"I quit my job today," Marrell said almost conversationally.

Delancey stared at her mother, her mouth agape. "You quit? Why?"

"Because I know you need me home sooner than 5:30."

Delancey took a moment to compute this before

saying, "What will we do?"

"Well, as a matter of fact, Mr. Avery offered me other hours. I'll go in now at 7:30 and be done at 4:00. Does that sound like it will work better for you, Delancey?"

"You did that for me?"

"Um-hm. Contrary to popular belief, honey, I love you."

With those words, Delancey cried. Marrell had tried to be there for her as soon as she got home, often fighting the fatigue that threatened to overwhelm her come evening, but it still hadn't been enough. Her daughter needed more of her.

"I'm flunking two classes," Delancey sobbed. "I just don't know what I'm doing anymore. I used to ask Dad for help on my math, but he's not here. I've even hidden the teacher's notes from you and gotten in trouble over that."

"Oh, honey." Marrell's heart broke. She'd had no idea. In some ways she didn't know what she was doing anymore either. "Go get everything and let me see it, notes and all."

Mackenzie had been in her own room for all of this but emerged when she heard the voices die down and her sister in the hall.

"You all right, D.J.?"

"I don't know. I don't know anything."

"Is Mom going to help you?" She had known her sister was struggling in math and English.

"I don't think she can."

Mackenzie followed Delancey when she went back to the living room and watched as their mother read the note and then looked at the homework Delancey could not get done. Marrell wanted to sob. Delancey was right: She needed Paul.

"We've got the weekend," Marrell said softly. "We're both tired tonight, but tomorrow we'll figure some way to do this. Here, give me that pen." Delancey looked on while Marrell signed the notes to her two teachers — English was involved too — and then jotted notes of her own, including her work number in each of them.

"Now, you return these Monday, and by then we'll have this work done."

"I'm way behind in the algebra book."

"I can see that." Marrell said and prayed for a miracle.

"Mom?"

"Yes." Marrell was still looking at the book.

"Would you have really made me move out?"

Marrell glanced over at Mackenzie and then looked Delancey in the eye. She thought for a moment before saying, "I tend to be soft, D.J. — a pushover. Your father would have been on you about your attitude the first day it surfaced. I should have been, and I'm sorry for not doing my job. I've let things go, and now you've become the parent, telling me with your attitude and actions when you'll do your chores or join the family. It would break my heart, but I must have final say in this home. If you and Mic don't like my rules, you can move in with a friend or whatever you can find and see for yourselves just how good you have it here."

Delancey nodded, her heart feeling better already. She would never choose to move out, so there was no fear, and when her mother took charge the way her father used to, she found it strangely comforting.

Marrell wasn't comforted at all. At the moment she was so drained she thought she could sleep for a week. She asked the girls to work on dinner with her and reminded Delancey that first thing in the morning she would make some calls.

To her surprise, she woke up at 6:00 the next morning. Tired as she was, she could not get back to sleep. Pulling on grubby jeans and a sweatshirt and scraping her hair into a ponytail, she wrote the girls a note, pinned it up in the kitchen where they wouldn't miss it, and went to the grocery store. The note said she would be home in one hour. Not until after she arrived at the market did she realize that wasn't enough time. List in hand, she found herself tearing through the market until she nearly ran into someone.

"I'm sorry," she said without even glancing up.

"Where's the fire?"

Marrell's head came up. "Jack! I'm sorry."

"That's all right." He took in her harried expression. "I take it you're in a hurry."

"Yes, the note I left the girls said I would be back in an hour. It takes ten minutes to get home, and I still have half my list."

"Will they even be up this early to see the note before you get back?"

Marrell gave a little laugh. "Probably not, and I just realized I didn't say when I left. It could be an hour from any point."

Jack smiled at her. "How was the news received about your new hours?"

"All right. I mean there were some other things, but I think Delancey was pleased."

"Is there anything I can do?"

Marrell's smile was lopsided. "How are you in pre-algebra?"

"Top of my class."

"Are you serious?"

273

"Yes, math is a strong point for me. Who's having trouble?"

"D.J."

"So that would be eighth grade?"

"Yes."

"Piece of cake."

Marrell's mouth opened. She was terribly in awe of anyone who was good with numbers and those awful letters, but it was more than that.

"Are you actually saying you'd help Delancey?"

"Sure. I'm free today or even after church tomorrow."

"Jack, are you really serious?"

"Absolutely. What time shall I come?"

"Oh, I don't know. You tell me when you're free."

"How about 10:30?"

"Okay. Are you sure about this?"

"Yes. Tell me where you live."

Marrell gave him directions, and they parted company, but many items were left off her list. She was so stunned she couldn't think. She actually held together all the way home but then sat in the apartment parking lot and prayed.

I hadn't even remembered to ask for Your help, but You sent Jack anyway. Thank You, Lord. Thank You for seeing to every need. Help Delancey to accept Jack's help. I can't do it for her, and Shay and Oliver already do so much.

Still sniffing with emotion, she lugged bags of groceries up the stairs to find that Jack was right: Both girls were still sound asleep.

"Do I have to, Mom?" Delancey asked for the third time, but she was not angry, only embarrassed.

"Yes, honey. You'll find that he's very nice. Mackenzie's been trying since nine o'clock, and it's just not working. You certainly know I can't help you." Her tone was dry. "At least listen to what Jack has to say. Maybe it won't be any clearer, but we can say we tried, and I'll let your teacher know if you need extra help."

Delancey nodded but felt her face heat all over again. The thought of some strange man coming in and showing her how to do something that confounded her was nothing short of humiliating. She had tried so hard to understand what Mackenzie was saying, but Mackenzie was naturally good at math and had a hard time telling anyone how she did what came so easily to her.

As was Delancey's habit when she was nervous, she sought out food. She had just dished up a huge bowl of ice cream when the doorbell rang. She heard her mother answer but couldn't make herself leave the table. She was stunned to see a man from church come around the corner to the kitchen table. She barely noticed her mother in the background.

"Algebra and ice cream," he said with a smile. "That's a winning combination."

"Do you want some?" Delancey offered without thinking.

"Sure." Jack answered and sat down at the table to peruse the math book, noticing that Marrell had quietly slipped away. "I'm Jack, by the way," he called to the tall blond in the kitchen.

"Oh, right. I'm Delancey."

"Nice to meet you."

"You're my mom's boss?"

"Guilty as charged."

Delancey found herself smiling. She liked the way he said things.

"I didn't know how much you wanted." Delancey set a small bowl down in front of him. It was piled high with chocolate ice cream.

"This is fine. Tell me, Delancey, is this where you are?" He pointed to a page in the book.

"Yes. Well, I'm not, but the rest of the class is."

"Okay, so we need to back up to where?"

And with that they were off. Forty-five minutes flew by, and Delancey was still frowning in confusion. Jack was the soul of patience, calmly explaining concepts until, more than an hour later, Delancey knew what she was doing. Jack was careful never to let on how delightful it was to have her face dawn with understanding and her eyes roll with impatience that it had taken her so long.

"Can we do one more?" she asked a little before noon.

"We can do the whole book. I love anything to do with numbers."

"Then why are you an architect?"

Jack laughed. "I can tell that you don't really know what an architect does."

Delancey blushed all over again, but Jack only grinned at her.

Marrell had been back and forth a few times, but while they had been busy in the kitchen, she and Mackenzie had cleaned the rest of the house. It was getting on to lunchtime, and she thought she should at least make the offer. As long as Jack had been there, Marrell expected him to decline. He surprised her.

"Sure, I'll stay. Anytime I don't have to cook suits me fine."

Until that point Marrell had not been sure he was single.

"Well, good," she said sincerely, hating to send

276

him away hungry. "It won't be fancy, but since I just shopped, you should get enough."

"Don't forget to warn him, Mom." Mackenzie's voice came from the edge of the room.

"Of what?" Marrell asked, but she knew.

"You know," Mackenzie replied indulgently.

Marrell tried not to smile and turned to find Jack watching her.

"This is Delancey's older sister, Jack. Mackenzie, please meet my boss, Jack Avery."

"Hello."

"Hello." Jack held out his hand. "Are you going to tell me what that was all about?"

"No, she's not," Marrell cut in, still fighting laughter. "We'll suffice it to say that my cooking gets little respect in this house."

Mackenzie grinned at her mom and took a place at the table.

"How'd it go, D.J.?"

"Good. He's a better teacher than you are, Mic."

"That's no surprise. I don't even work with a partner at school."

"Hopeless," her sister said, writing all the while.

Jack checked her progress but then turned to Mackenzie.

"I think your mom told me you play basketball."

"Yeah, this is my first year."

"But you made the team."

Mackenzie smiled. "Um-hm. I can't think why."

"She's being modest, Jack. She never misses from the free-throw line."

"Impressive."

Mackenzie smiled again. She had felt sorry for Delancey when she heard he would be coming, but he seemed pretty cool, and Delancey was as relaxed as a cat in the sun.

"Mic, wash your hands and shred this lettuce for me. D.J., if you're done there, please clear the table, wash it, and set it."

"Are you going to put me to work?" Jack asked.

"I think you've worked enough."

He was not convinced and came further into the kitchen to ask again.

"What can I do?"

"Well, you could wash your hands," she said automatically, "reach up into the cupboard, and get four glasses. The ice is in the freezer, and the Pepsi is on the counter."

"Will do."

They sat down to lunch about 20 minutes later, and Jack offered to pray. Marrell did not expect to feel the way she did. It seemed as though she hadn't heard Paul pray in years. Hearing a man's voice, she suddenly missed him so much that she had to force herself to eat. No one at the table seemed to notice, and by the time everyone's plate was full, she had managed to compose herself.

"I've seen you at church, haven't I?" Delancey asked.

"Yes, I've seen you too."

This was news to Marrell, so she kept quiet. She wondered if she might be too wrapped up in her own little world, and not just since Paul died. Jack had probably been going to the church for years.

"Do you live in a house you designed?" Mackenzie suddenly asked, and Marrell was a bit alarmed, thinking it wasn't any of their business.

"No, I've designed some nice homes, but I live in the top story of a house that's been converted into an apartment."

"Do you wish you could live in a house you designed?"

"I will someday, but right now this is easier. Reasonably priced property is hard to come by in San Francisco, and I don't have time to take care of a lawn and yard. When I retire in 25 years, I'll look into it."

"You're going to retire young," Marrell said before she thought and stopped herself.

"At 65? I don't think that's too young."

Marrell's mouth hung open, and she blushed when he grinned at her. With that boyish smile and smooth face — not a crow's-foot in sight — he did not look 40. Marrell wasn't sure if he was having one on her or not.

"He was nice," Delancey said to her mother an hour later. Jack had just left.

"He is nice, D.J. Easy to work for too. I'm glad he was able to help you. Do you think you have it under control?"

"The algebra, yes, but I'm still way behind in English."

That was a little more Marrell's speed, so she told her to get it out. It wasn't what the younger Bishop wanted to hear, but as Marrell pointed out, she had already had her time off. It was time to get to work.

"I think you'd better get that look out of your eye, Sharon Lacy," her husband told her firmly the next day. They had just driven out of the church parking lot. "It's way too soon."

"I know, Oliver, but Jack Avery is a doll, and I just can't stand the thought that Marrell would be alone for the rest of her life."

"But you saw her face when she said he had been there. It meant nothing to her. She probably doesn't even see him, and if she did, at this point

I would be telling her to go slow. A woman in grief does not think as she normally would."

Shay's sigh was huge. "I can't help wishing I could see his face when *her* name is mentioned."

"I assure you, there wouldn't be anything to see."

"How do you know what he feels for her?"

"I don't, but I've been in the same prayer breakfast with Jack for more than three years. He's not a man who wears his feelings on his sleeve."

Shay sighed again. She knew it was too soon for Marrell to be interested in anyone, and that had not been her intent when she had steered the new widow toward the job at Bayside. But since then it had occurred to her that it might be a wonderful thing for Jack and Marrell to find each other. Shay said nothing else to Oliver, but she couldn't help but think that it was a very good idea.

For some reason New Year's Eve was the hardest. Thanksgiving, Christmas Eve, and Christmas had all been rough, but the last night of 1982 was almost more than Marrell could take. Mackenzie had been asked out, but Marrell said no, so the three of them had popped corn, drank soft drinks, sat in front of the TV until midnight, and then watched the rerun of the ball dropping on Times Square.

But midnight was long past and she was still awake, the queen-size bed feeling huge on her own. Marrell missed her husband so much her skin ached. January 5 would be seven months, but right now it felt like forever.

Thinking she was the only one awake, Marrell was surprised when Mackenzie knocked softly on her door and came in.

"Mom?"

"Yes."

"Are you asleep?"

"No. Come in."

Mackenzie came forward and sat on the end of the bed.

"I can't stop thinking about Dad." There were tears in her voice.

"Come up here." She patted Paul's pillow and waited for Mackenzie to crawl beneath the covers. Marrell put an arm around her and lay close, Mackenzie's head on her arm.

"I was just missing him too. It feels so much longer than it is." Marrell was quiet before saying, "I know I've told you about Grandma studying her Bible for clues about heaven, but I don't know if I told you that I've been doing some of that myself. And the thing that jumps out the most to me, Micki, is not to feel sorry for your dad."

"I don't know what you mean."

"Remember that great time we had at the Lacys' orchard for Thanksgiving? I had to force myself to remember that your father didn't envy us. He's in heaven. He's able to talk with God and be at perfect rest. He wasn't looking down at us and thinking, 'Why couldn't I have stayed and gone to Sebastopol too?' "

Mackenzie's shoulders moved in silent laughter. It was such a funny image.

"It's me I feel sorry for," Marrell said. "I'm the selfish one for wishing your father back to this awful earth."

"I wish him back," Mackenzie admitted. "Sometimes I get angry. If he could leave, why can't I? I guess I'm just glad to know he was such a good person."

"He would be the first one to tell you he wasn't, Mackenzie," Marrell said softly, opting not to give her a sermon. There was so much she could say on that subject.

How could her two girls be so blind and stubborn? Marrell knew that a person couldn't sit in the church she attended and not hear the one and only way to heaven, but the Bishop girls would have nothing to do with it. They didn't complain about going, but one look at their faces when anything spiritual was mentioned, and Marrell knew they were a hundred miles away.

"Mom, why couldn't I go out with Jay Murray tonight?"

"Oh, Mic, I can't handle that right now. Jay might be a very nice boy, and I'm not trying to keep you a little girl, but having you dating is not something I'm willing to deal with right now. Do you like him a lot?"

"He's pretty nice. I wasn't all that disappointed. Mom?"

"Yeah."

"How much dating did you do?"

"I started dating when I was 15, and at first I went out a lot, but it slowed down after that."

"Why?"

"Because every guy tried something. I didn't want to play around, and every guy wanted to end our date in the backseat of his car."

Mackenzie turned to see her mother's face. "Did that really happen?"

"Yes. Then word got out that Marrell Walker 'didn't,' and guys stopped asking. The only reason I went out with your father a second time was because he didn't try anything."

"What was it like, Mom? What happened when

you first saw him?"

"Um," she replied, smiling with remembrance, "he was so handsome, and he looked as lonely as I felt."

"Why were you lonely?"

"I just was. Some of my friends had gone off to the university, and some were married. I felt totally out of touch."

"And without even knowing Dad, you went out when he asked you?"

"Yes. It was very stupid of me."

"Because it could have been dangerous?"

"Exactly. Thinking back, I can see that my grandparents were not aware enough. Your father turned out to be a wonderful man, but more than one woman has done that and never been heard from again."

For a time they were quiet. Marrell's thoughts had drifted to Paul when she realized Mackenzie was crying.

"Oh, honey, it's all right."

"I'm going to be 15 this year," she sobbed. "I always wanted Dad to take me out driving, but right now I'm not even interested. Mom, things are never going to be the same again. I just can't stand it."

There was so little Marrell could say to that. It was true that things were not going to be the same, and Marrell knew the only reason she was still surviving was because of God's Son. But the girls hadn't chosen Him.

They need You so much, Father. Help them to see. Break through their stubborn pride and show them how You're waiting to forgive and take care of them.

Mackenzie fell asleep in Marrell's bed, and all three Bishops slept soundly until late in the morning. Marrell fixed a lavish breakfast that was eaten with good fun and talk. It was impossible to know how the year would go or what it would bring, but even with the pain in her heart about Paul, Marrell was confident of God's care. The girls, Marrell knew, did their best not to think about the weeks and months to come; they believed it made things less painful.

SEVENTEEN

Why are we doing this? Mackenzie's question leapt into Marrell's mind as she and the girls walked back into the terminal at San Francisco International. Going to Florida to see Paul's family had been such a mistake. She looked forward to telling Shay all about it.

"Jack." Mackenzie was the first to spot him in the terminal, bringing Marrell's head up in surprise. Not having expected Marrell's employer, the three women went toward him, their faces curious.

"Hi. What happened to Shay?"

"Jana got sick," he spoke as he took Marrell's bag and slung it over his own shoulder. "Nothing too serious, but this was the only time she could get an appointment."

"Poor little thing," Marrell said with compassion, also wishing she could have seen her friend.

They started down the terminal but hadn't gone 15 yards when the girls needed to use the restroom. Marrell and Jack waited outside for them, and Jack asked the question that had been on his mind since he caught sight of Marrell's disquieted face.

"Are you all right?"

Marrell looked up at him. "Yes and no. It was

such a mistake, Jack. I don't know if the girls will ever get over it. I mean, it ended well, but my husband's family is not normal, and I don't know why I thought that might have changed."

"Want to talk about it?"

Marrell looked so frustrated. "They like to drink" spoke volumes, but Marrell wasn't finished. "I realize the girls are pretty, Jack, but their own cousins and uncles stared at them in such a sick way."

"And at you too?" Jack guessed wisely and watched tears flood her eyes. She looked away in an attempt to stop them. "I'm sorry, Marrell. It must have been awful for you."

She nodded, careful to stand in a way that gave her a modicum of privacy in the busy airport.

"It's my own fault for thinking they would be different."

"So you've had this happen before?"

Marrell nodded. "A long time ago."

"Mom, are you crying?" The girls were back.

"Yes," she admitted, irritated with herself. "Jack was asking me about the trip, and I'm mad at myself all over again." She dashed at the tears on her cheeks.

"She thinks it's all her fault," Mackenzie explained.

"Well, it is." They were walking again. "It was my idea to go."

"Yes, but Oliver, Shay, and I all encouraged you," Jack said logically, "so why aren't you mad at us?"

Marrell looked up at him. He was much more than a boss. He was a friend too, and right now Marrell wanted to laugh with the pure relief of being home.

"Maybe I am," she said softly. "I may never speak to you again for advising me to go."

Jack smiled in understanding. She was ready to change the subject. "I believe some restitution is in order here. I think I should offer to take you to dinner. Shay was going to have something ready for you, but with the baby sick, she couldn't do it."

"I'm all for that," Delancey's voice was fervent. She did not like airline food.

"Okay. Let's head to the car. I think a steak and baked potato work for me. Any arguments?"

As he expected, there wasn't a one.

It had finally happened. Delancey had not been planning on it, nor had Mackenzie, but it was there. Fourteen-year-old Delancey Bishop was the hottest freshman for the 1983–84 school year. She had been well-liked and admired in junior high, but now young men as old as seniors checked her out and made no secret that they liked what they saw.

Many times she wished she had her sister's smart-alecky wit that could get her out of any uncomfortable situation, but at least one boy, a junior by the name of Jace Booth, liked Delancey's shy smile and the fact that she didn't have an answer for everything. That she had a body like a model and a face to match didn't hurt his opinion either.

He was starting to sit with Delancey and Mackenzie at lunch each day, and twice he had taken Delancey's hand when he walked her to class. He hadn't kissed her yet, but that would come. He didn't know if she was able to date yet, but the football season was around the corner. He had injured his arm as a sophomore and couldn't play anymore, but he was quite confident that Delancey's parents would at least agree to a home football game for their first date. At least that's what he was banking on. If she could date . . . well, better and better.

Jace, however, had not banked on Mackenzie's intuition. Mackenzie said little when he ate lunch with them, and since she also talked with her own friends, she oftentimes didn't even hear what they were saying. But Mackenzie had been in the school a year longer than her sister, and in her opinion, guys who wanted just one thing stuck out a mile. She thought Jace Booth a classic case. For one thing, he went over to the same group of guys almost every day after lunch and before he walked Delancey to class. Mackenzie had the impression he was giving a report.

Delancey, who truly liked Jace, never noticed. She was too busy trying not to show him that she cared, so she worked at not looking at him too much. Mackenzie was well aware that Delancey needed protection and was also aware that Jace really didn't see how close the two sisters were.

"Did Jace ask you out yet?" Mackenzie asked when they got off the bus that very day.

"Yes."

"What did you tell him?"

"I didn't really give him an answer. It's embarrassing to have to say I can't yet."

"Have you asked Mom?"

"No, but you couldn't date at 14. She's not going to let me."

"Where did he want to go?"

"To a movie. When I didn't answer, he suggested that we wait and go to a home game for our first date."

Mackenzie was quiet as they let themselves into the apartment, but Delancey caught her look.

"What's the matter, Mic?"

"What do you mean?"

"I think you're not saying something. What have you heard? Does he like someone else?"

"Oh, he likes you all right, D.J. Be assured of that." Mackenzie cocked her head to one side. "But doesn't it strike you as odd that he always goes back to his group of guys?"

"No, I go talk to my friends."

"But your friends aren't the same. Your friends don't use people. Jace hangs out with guys who are known for only dating girls who will go all the way with them."

Delancey's chin went in the air. "Well, maybe I will. Lots of girls do."

"True, but be prepared to be dumped. Jace and his friends always take what they want and move on. I watched it last year with my classmates, and now you're one of the freshmen they like to work on. Not to mention, he'll tell all the guys you've done it. Just be warned."

Delancey watched Mackenzie go into the kitchen for a snack, but she couldn't move. She knew very well that most people thought her sister smarter, and she probably was, but Delancey was no fool. She had, however, spoken with more bravado than she'd felt. Jace Booth was cute, but even the thought of taking her clothes off in front of him made her face heat right there in her own living room.

She moved to the kitchen for her own snack, found a note from her mom about gathering the trash, and opened the fridge for the milk. She didn't want to talk about it anymore to Mackenzie, but she would be careful in the future. A football game with Jace sounded like a dream come true, but where would he want to end the evening? A sudden case of nerves pushed Delancey to eat more cookies than she wanted.

Marrell had taken to writing in a journal. She didn't write often — not anywhere near as much as she had planned, but from time to time she enjoyed going back and looking at the entries. About midsummer she had been in a panic, afraid the girls were on their own too much, but then Delancey had been offered a babysitting job four days a week with Mrs. Baker, and Mackenzie had decided to take a correspondence course on creative writing and spent the summer with her head buried in a book or her notepad. And almost before she'd been ready, the girls had gone back to school.

Her eighteenth wedding anniversary was another day when she chose to write, and although it hurt her to look back, she was glad that she had been so honest about her feelings on that day. It was hard to believe that so much time had passed, but there was some healing to her own heart as well as the girls'.

She had worked at Bayside more than a year now and was even considering another position in the building. Jack had told her about it — a secretarial position for an architect down the hall. It meant leaving Jack and Taya, but because the other architect was a great guy and it meant an increase in wage, they both thought she should go for it. The only problem was the hours. Telling them she would have to work 7:30 to 4:00, Marrell interviewed and prepared to wait several days.

They called within a matter of hours, and yes, she could have the job. She was their first choice, but her hours would have to be 8:30 to 5:00. Marrell thanked them and declined. She found Taya and Jack in Jack's office and told them of her decision, only to be surprised by Taya's reaction. She looked shaken when she swiftly rushed out. Marrell had the impression that she was upset with her. She turned to her boss when it was just the two of them.

"Have I done something that's made Taya wish I didn't work here any longer?"

"No, Marrell, that's not it." Jack's heart broke a little over her hurt face.

"But there's something."

He nodded.

"Can you tell me?"

Jack weighed the choices and opted to bare his heart. "I believe she's upset because she thought if you no longer worked in this office, I would feel free to ask you out."

Marrell's mouth opened. "Why would she feel that way?"

"Because after all these years, she knows me very well."

Marrell could only stare at him.

"What she doesn't realize is that your working here has nothing to do with my not asking you out."

Marrell tried to take this in and eventually asked, "What does it have to do with?"

"Jack?" Taya's voice suddenly came through on the intercom.

"Yes."

"Marrell has a call."

"All right, thank you. Why don't you take it here?" Jack had punched the button and was holding the phone out for her, but Marrell shook her head.

"That will be Arné Northrup about that lake house. I need to be at my desk."

Marrell forced her mind back to work. She took care of the call, and was ready to go back and finish her conversation with Jack, but someone else called. Four o'clock was on top of her before she could breathe. She might have gone back then to find out what was going on, but his door was shut.

Marrell picked up her purse, said goodbye to Taya, who seemed to be herself again, and headed out the door toward the elevator. She was so glad it wasn't the weekend where she would be forced to speculate about Jack's response for two days. She would do everything she could to talk with him tomorrow.

It was clearly a simple case of miscommunication. She and Jack were good friends; he had been there for her many times. She would talk to him and find out what needed to be done. If it would help, she would talk to Taya as well. Marrell shook her head. Married less than a year, the younger woman still had stars in her eyes. Intent on getting to her car and how she would handle things in the morning, Marrell didn't hear Jack until he was beside her. She started a little but didn't allow Jack to apologize before speaking.

"Your door was shut, so I thought I would catch you tomorrow."

"I'm sorry I handled all of that so badly."

Marrell shook her head in confusion. Handled what so badly? Suddenly she was not so confident.

"It must be true," she made herself say. "Taya

292

does want you to ask me out, but you don't want to."

Jack shook his head. "I do want to ask you out, very much, but I'm trying to be sensitive to your feelings and what you've been through in the last year and four months. Taya is under the impression that your working for me is what's stopping me. That's not it. I admit that business and pleasure don't usually mix, but where you're concerned, I don't care."

Marrell could only stare at him. This was Jack — her friend, Jackson Avery. Was he really saying he wanted more than friendship?

"Tell me, Marrell," he said softly when she remained so quiet, "how does a man let a woman know, especially when that woman has become a good friend and has already been so hurt by the death of a husband? How does it work? How does he tell her he would like to see her on a more personal level and not have her quit or never be able to look him in the eye again?"

For the first time in her life, Marrell saw how hard this was for the man. She also wondered how insensitive she might have been over the last year, or was she even now understanding what he was saying? *How much plainer could it be, Marrell?* Her chin went in the air. She would never hurt him by quitting or being ashamed to face him. They were both too old for such childish games.

"A man tells a woman just like you've done, Jack. You've never played games with me, and I hope you never do. Thank you."

Jack worked to keep his emotions from his face. She might never care for him, and in time he would get over that, but if she was ashamed to face him, he felt as though he would die. He

293

forced himself to ask the next question.

"If I asked you out, Marrell, would I be overstepping my bounds?"

"No, but I must tell you that I have to speak with the girls. I think we all take you for granted, Jack. You're always there to help out and offer friendship, and I'm sure at times we've looked right through you. If there's any type of change in our relationship, I wouldn't want it to be a surprise to Mic and D.J."

"Of course not. I appreciate your telling me. I'd better let you go. The girls will be calling."

Marrell nodded but she couldn't move. He wanted to date her. She found that quite amazing, and without thinking, said so.

Jack smiled. There was so much he could say to that, but not now. "Why is it a surprise?"

"I don't know," she shrugged, laughed a little, and looked embarrassed. "It just is."

Jack smiled to make her feel more at ease, but there was so much in his heart. He could have told her right then that he found her beautiful, that he had wanted to ask her out on the day he interviewed her, and that she was the sweetest woman he had ever known, but he knew it had to wait.

"I'll see you tomorrow." He released her with those words.

"Right. Thank you, Jack."

Jack stayed in the garage until she had gone on her way, and then made his way slowly back up to the office. It was a waste of time; he didn't get another thing done.

Eighteen

Marrell drove home in a fog. Jack wanted to date her, but Jack was Jack: her boss and a good friend. She had never seen him in any other light. She had certainly never thought of dating him or anyone else. And what if she did? What did it mean? Did it have to mean anything?

Marrell nearly shook her head at her stupidity. *He's a man, Marrell. You can't expect to date him and just remain friends. If that's all you want, don't go out with him.* She needed that pep talk, but mostly she needed Paul. *How can I think of going out with someone when I'm still in love with you? I miss you, Paul,* she said softly, and she stared at the side of the apartment in front of her parking place.

She knew if she sat in the car too long the girls would call the office. They would think she had smashed the car or something, but she was filled with a desperate need to be alone. She never was these days. She was either at the office or home, and the girls tended to be there when she was. She took a breath, tried to pray, and went upstairs.

"Hi, Mom," Delancey greeted her from the living-room sofa.

"Hi, D.J. How was your day?"

"It was all right. You sound tired."

"I am. Where's Mic?"

"Mrs. Baker called and needed to go to the store. The baby was still asleep, so she went over to stay with her. I was over there for a while, but I was too lazy to write you a note, so I came back."

Marrell could hardly argue with that; she was feeling pretty lazy herself. Delancey was preoccupied with a television program, so Marrell went to her bedroom, climbed into sweats and a T-shirt, and lay on the bed.

"I have no idea what to do here, Lord. If I follow my heart, I would run so far and so fast. Love has started to scare me. Jack is wonderful, but what if I can't be the person he needs? What if I fall for him and he leaves like Paul did?"

Marrell's whispered prayer was interrupted by the phone ringing. She didn't bother to answer it, knowing it would be one of the girls' friends. She was trying to bare her heart to the Lord again, when Delancey opened the door.

"For you, Mom."

"Oh, thank you." Marrell sat on the edge of the bed, reached for the phone, and said hello when she heard Delancey hang up.

"It's Jack, Marrell."

"Oh, hi, Jack. Is something wrong?" He rarely called her at home.

"That's what I'm trying to find out. I can't stop thinking about you and the fact that I've probably upset you terribly."

"Well —" Marrell admitted quietly, "I'm just so confused, Jack, and so very afraid."

"Of me?"

"No, no, never you. I'm afraid of hurting you or you hurting me. The thought terrifies me."

"I'm such a klutz," Jack said softly. "I don't

know how to do this, Marrell. The last thing I wanted to do was upset you."

"It's not you, Jack. It's the fear. I did realize something though."

"What's that?"

"I can't talk to the girls until you and I have talked. If they were to ask any questions of me, and I know they will, I wouldn't know what to tell them. Can we talk sometime?"

"Yes, definitely, anytime you'd like."

"Do you know what, Jack?"

"What?"

"I'm never alone these days. I'm at the office or here with the girls. Sometimes I just want to go someplace and stop. Isn't that selfish of me?"

"Not at all. It just means you're human."

"I never realized how much time I had to myself before Paul died. I would never have said I was a person who needed solitude, but that was before I didn't have any. Oh, listen to me, Jack. All I do is complain when I have so much to be thankful for."

"That's true, Marrell, you do have a lot to be thankful for. But you're also still trying to adjust to being mother, father, and breadwinner. It's a lot of work."

"I'm finding that out. Everyone says the first year is the hardest, but I'm starting to doubt that, Jack. I was in shock the first year. Now this year I'm starting to see the *foreverness* of the situation."

"Did I ever tell you that my mother was widowed when I was still young?"

"No, you didn't."

"She was. And that's exactly what she said to me: The second year was worse."

"How old were you?"

"When she said that, or when my father died?"

"Both."

"I was 13 when my father died, and she told me about the second year when I was an adult."

"Is she still living, Jack?"

"No. She's been gone about ten years."

They had so much more in common than she would have guessed, but then Marrell had always been sensitive not to intrude into his life or bring her problems to the office. She had cried the day she was interviewed and determined never to cry at the office again. She didn't think the front seat of her car in the parking garage was the office.

"Mom!" Mackenzie's voice could be heard from the other room.

"Just a minute, Jack." Marrell got the words out just before Mackenzie opened the door.

"What's for dinner?"

"Oh, I don't know yet. Probably eggs. I'll be out in a minute."

"Can I cook something?" Delancey looked over Mackenzie's shoulder and asked.

"Be my guest," Marrell said and waved them away. "Sorry about that."

"It's all right. I should let you go."

"Yeah, I guess I'd better make sure they don't burn down the apartment."

Silence fell between them for a moment.

"You know, Jack, you've always been the easiest person to talk to."

"Have I?"

"Yes. Whom do you talk to?"

"Oh, I don't know. Sometimes Oliver."

Marrell sighed. "Men don't need to talk as much."

"We do, but we're just not good at it. I'll see you tomorrow, all right?"

"Okay. Thanks for calling, Jack."

"My pleasure. 'Bye now."

"Goodbye."

Marrell hung up but didn't immediately leave the room. Never had she felt so confused and inept. She was still talking to him like he was a friend, but he wanted more. But he still was a friend; indeed, his tone gave nothing away. It was as if they had never had the conversation. So what did she do? Was it his place to set up a meeting or hers? And would that time of talking be considered a date? As though Oliver were in the room, Marrell heard him reminding her that she was not to do God's job. Marrell got off the bed to check on the girls.

"I need a favor without a bunch of questions," Delancey said to Mackenzie as soon as they got to school the next day.

"What is it?"

"At lunch today I just need you to mention my being in karate. If a lot of the girls are there, then don't, but if you can bring it up in, you know, a subtle way, then do."

"I take it you want Jace to know?"

"Yes. Here he comes. Just do it, okay?"

Mackenzie nodded, smiled at Jace as he passed her to get to Delancey, and then headed into school.

"What are you smiling about, Mackenzie?" Rosa asked.

Mackenzie laughed. "Why, first period science, my favorite hour of the day."

Rosa laughed and let it go, which was just what

299

Mackenzie wanted. She would never tell anyone she had just discovered that Delancey was smarter than anyone else in her class.

It didn't look as if Jace was going to join them. Delancey and Mackenzie were through eating and getting ready to head on their way when he sauntered in and sat down. The look he gave Delancey was nothing short of territorial. Seeing it, Mackenzie didn't care who was around; she was determined to mention the karate.

"How are you?" Jace asked Delancey in that soft way of his.

"Fine," Delancey told him, thinking he really was the best-looking guy in school. "I wondered where you were."

"Oh, something I had to do." His voice was a bit too casual for Delancey's taste.

"Hey, D.J.," Mackenzie said from across the table.

"What?" Delancey looked across to find her sister's eyes across the table.

"Isn't that Adam over there? Wasn't he in your karate class?"

"I can't see his face from here." Delancey went along very well.

"Karate?" Jace said but was ignored.

"Oh, he just turned — no, I guess it isn't Adam." With this act, Mackenzie could have been on the stage.

"No, I don't think it is," Delancey agreed and made ready to leave the table. "I'd better get going. The bell's about to ring. 'Bye, Mic."

" 'Bye, D.J. See ya at the bus."

Delancey rose, well aware of what she was doing. Jace came right after her, but she made a

300

point not to let her hand be free. She tossed her milk carton out, left the lunchroom, and moved toward her locker, leaving it up to Jace to keep up. They were silent all the way to her locker, but Jace regrouped as he went, and, hoping to get Delancey's attention again, he leaned against the locker next to hers in what he thought was an eye-catching stance.

"Mackenzie's some joker, Delancey."

"How's that?"

"Some kid in your karate class. Come on."

"What makes you think I've never taken karate?"

He laughed a small, mocking laugh. "Because you're a nice girl, Delancey. Anyone can see that."

"And nice girls don't do karate, is that it?"

"I don't know," he replied, his voice turning testy. He was feeling foolish now and didn't like it. After all, Delancey Bishop was only a freshman. "You haven't, so I don't know why we're talking about it."

Delancey gathered her books, closed her locker, and said she had to get to class.

"I'll walk you."

"Okay." Delancey agreed but kept her arms wrapped around her books. She did not want him touching her right now.

"Are you mad at me?" he asked when she was so quiet. She was never a chatterbox, but this was different.

"No, but I was thinking about how little we know each other."

They were almost to her class, and the halls were getting crowded, so he stopped her with a hand to her arm and directed her to the side of the hallway. The moment her back was against the wall, he put his hand on the wall above her head, leaned close, and said, "I would like to get to know you better, Delancey."

"Like in the backseat of your car?"

She surprised him, but he hid it. "I wouldn't mind."

"Well, I would," she said very softly, and for an instant she saw anger in his eyes and knew this had been his intent all along. He knew a lot of people in this school. She would probably never get a date with anyone, but right now she didn't care. "And for the record, Jace, I'm a black belt. Don't ever make me prove it to you."

"Delancey —" He sounded almost hurt, but the tall blond would not let him go on.

"I've got to get to class."

She slipped away and into her English class door just moments before the tardy bell rang. It was a tremendous relief to sit in the back. She had a better chance of hiding her tears.

"What's wrong with D.J.?" Marrell asked that night. "She hasn't been this quiet in a long time."

"Have you asked her?" Mackenzie's look was instantly guarded.

"No. She just went in to take a bath. Is it something or someone at school?"

"Yeah."

"Which is it?"

"Mom, that's not fair," Mackenzie wasted no time in telling her. "She might not want to talk about it."

This was all too true, but Marrell wanted to know. It was so hard being a parent at times. When did you respect your child's privacy, and when did you push the point so you could help?

"All right. I'll ask her when she comes out, but I

might be back to see you."

Marrell was not joking, and Mackenzie knew it. Delancey had been doing very well lately — both girls were — but the younger Bishop girl had wanted three bowls of ice cream and solitude. The signs were classic Delancey.

"D.J.?" Marrell spoke through the bathroom door.

"Yeah."

"I want to talk to you when you come out."

"All right."

"Come find me in the living room."

"Am I in trouble?"

"No, not at all, just come."

Marrell had quite a while to wait. She made out a grocery list, filed her nails, and tried not to think about another Friday night at home. Her daughters had stopped asking her if they could go out; she always said no. They were amazing girls, and it had to be the Lord. They didn't argue with her, tell her lies, or sneak around behind her back. They liked music that she couldn't understand, but when she asked them to turn it down, they did so. Right now she felt they deserved better than Marrell Bishop for a mother.

I'm so down lately, Lord. I'm not thankful and I'm not content. How can I ask my daughters to do the things I'm not willing to do? How will they ever see their need for You if I don't live a life of joy? It was so hard to be near Jack today and not be able to talk to him. I don't know when I thought we would talk, but having things unsettled was miserable today. And then I come home and D.J. is upset. She hasn't been lately, so this makes me think something is very wrong. I feel like all I do is work and sleep. When am I supposed to be a mom?

Marrell was nowhere near done praying when Delancey came in. She sat across from her, and Marrell wondered at a mother's love. There was no way to describe what she felt for this child.

"I'm going to ask you how you're doing and what's wrong, D.J., and you're going to want to say nothing, but I want to know — so prepare yourself."

Delancey's hand went to the back of her wet hair, and for a moment she didn't look at her mother. Marrell was not to be put off. She was opening her mouth to get some answers when Delancey spoke up.

"I did something today that I'm ashamed of."

"Okay." Marrell's face was open even though her heart pounded in alarm.

"There's this guy, Mom." Her voice was so soft. "He likes me . . . well, he did until today." Tears filled Delancey's eyes. "Dad told me he would tan me if I ever used my karate to hurt or even threaten someone."

Marrell's heart felt as though it would pound out of her chest. Had Delancey struck someone?

"You can tell me, D.J.," Marrell managed.

"Oh, Mom, it's such a mess. Mackenzie said he only wanted one thing from a girl, and I started to believe her, so I tested him. I know I hurt him; he'll probably never speak to me again."

"If he only wants to use you, Delancey, then I find that rather a relief," Marrell admitted. But she knew there was more to this. "Was Mackenzie wrong, or is he just interested in something sexual?"

Thinking about what he had said to her in the hall, when they hadn't even had one date, Delancey only looked miserable and didn't

304

answer, which in fact gave Marrell more than enough answer.

"I'm going to tell you something, D.J., that I don't know if you and I have ever talked about," Marrell said with soft remembrance. "My first date was just two weeks after my fifteenth birthday. The boy was a little older — he was a friend of a neighbor and my grandparents — and I thought everything was fine. You know, girls wore more dresses or skirts in those days, and this guy was taking me to dinner and a movie, so I was dressed up. I felt so grown-up. He was so cute and treated me so well. Dinner was wonderful, and so was the movie. But he didn't take me right home. He pulled off in a wooded area because he said he wanted to talk."

Marrell shook her head. She had been so naive and foolish. "He didn't want to talk. I pushed him away just long enough to get out of the car and run back to the main road."

"Oh, Mom," Delancey was horrified.

"It was awful. I was almost home by the time he found me, and even then I refused to get back in the car. My grandfather was so angry that he nearly went for his gun, but I'll tell you what helped me the most was something my grandmother said.

"She said she was proud of me and that I had done the right thing, but at some point the memory of that night would fade. A boy was going to kiss me, and I would like it. She said the temptation to do more than we should would be very strong but to remember one thing: I deserved better than that.

"That was all she said. After that I didn't do as much dating as my friends did, but through their

305

lives I saw what she meant. In time I realized that girls sell themselves short. They think the only way to hold a guy is to climb into the backseat of his car, and that it's worth doing. Well, I didn't. If a guy asked me out and tried something, I never went out with him again."

Delancey was looking more stunned than ever, but Marrell just kept on.

"My grandmother was right. It took a long time, but I eventually forgot how awful that night was. And when I met a man who was wonderful, I wanted him, D.J., more than I can say. He was the only one who hadn't tried anything, and when he did finally kiss me, I was ready to do anything, but I didn't. So many of my friends were stuck remembering their first time in a car or under the deserted bleachers after the football game. My first time was in a beautiful hotel room with no shame because the man was my husband, D.J. I've never been sorry that I waited or wasn't experienced. So now I'll say to you what my grandma was saying to me: I don't care who the guy is. If he's only after one thing, you deserve better."

Delancey was astonished. She had known the reason her mother was drawn to her dad was because he'd been such a gentleman, but she had never known about her mother's first date.

"You're a beautiful girl, Delancey. This boy, what's his name?"

"Jace Booth."

"Jace Booth is only the first. Unless you meet a boy who's determined to wait, he's going to have expectations of you. You're the only person who can make it clear that you don't want to do anything you would be ashamed of. You've never given me reason not to trust you, D.J., but with as much as I work, you could easily choose to see someone without my knowledge. It would be a horrible mistake, but you could."

"It's just so hard," the younger girl finally admitted. "A lot of guys look at me, and he's a junior, Mom. All the other girls think it's so cool that he likes me, and some of them have, you know, done it. They say it's wonderful."

Marrell nodded and heard Mackenzie in the hall.

"Micki?"

"Yeah?"

"Come here, please." Marrell waited until she came and took a chair. "I want to talk to both of you, and I want you to listen. All through the Proverbs a young person is admonished to listen to his elders and those who are old enough to have wise counsel. Fathers and sons are mentioned often. Dad's not here, so I'm going to translate that to mothers and daughters. I'm going to speak bluntly to you, and I don't want you to pretend to be listening and then blow it off as soon as you leave the room. This is very important." Marrell looked at them, unaware of how fierce her look was.

"Delancey, has this boy kissed you or touched you?"

"He's held my hand."

"Did you like it?"

Delancey nodded yes and bit her lip in embarrassment.

"That's the way a woman is, D.J. She likes romantic things — small touches, flowers, loving looks, and long talks. I'm not saying that men don't like those things, but they are created differently. Men would rather get to the main event than hold hands and walk along talking. It's worse for young men — high school boys, especially — when their hormones can control them if they let them. Am I making myself clear?"

"Sorta," Mackenzie frowned at her. "I don't like anyone right now, Mom, and D.J. hasn't been proposed to or anything like that."

"But you were the one to warn D.J.," Marrell pointed out, and Mackenzie nodded. "That's why I said don't blow this off. You both need to be aware. Men respond differently, and a woman can give out signals and not even know it. I don't want you to be known as a tease; that's a cheap trick on any woman's part." They still looked a little at sea, so Marrell knew she would have to keep this brief and be more to the point.

"The best example of men and women I've ever heard is that women are Crockpots and men are microwaves."

"What?" Delancey frowned at her.

"Okay, D.J., Jace is holding your hand, you think it's wonderful, but do you know what Jace wants to do? He wants to put his arms around you and kiss you. You're perfectly happy to hold his hand, but he wants much more. Am I getting through to you?"

Both girls nodded, their faces serious. Marrell saw that they were with her now and calmed a little. *I can't believe I'm doing this. I'm talking to my 14- and 15-year-old about sex. How did we come to this? They seem so young, but they probably know more slang than I do.* She made herself continue and not get emotional.

"I know what I did and what my friends did, and I know what God's Word says about sex

308

before marriage. It's always a mistake. God knew what He was talking about when He called it a sin. I'm not going to hate you if it happens, but I'm telling you there will be a price to pay. It may not be a baby or a sexually transmitted disease, but there will be a price. I would be wrong not to tell you what I know. If this is too soon, I'm sorry, but you're both in a caldron of temptation at high school, and like I said, I'm not around enough to know everything. Delancey's friends are already telling her it's great. They're wrong. I'm not saying they're lying to you, but if they find it's great for them now, they won't think so for long."

Marrell was silent for a moment, trying to read their thoughts by their faces. "Have I overwhelmed you?"

"No," Delancey said, but Marrell wasn't convinced.

"Mom?"

"Yes, Micki."

"Was Dad, you know, nice to you?"

"Oh, Mic, he was so tender. Your father was the most romantic man on the earth." Marrell's eyes grew moist. "And that's just the way it should be."

"Did he wait, Mom?" This came from Delancey.

"Yes. He had dated a girl pretty seriously in high school, and they came pretty close a few times, but he waited. He told me after meeting me that he wished he'd never touched her. And that's something else you need to remember: Boys can have regrets too, but their drive is so strong. Regret is usually the last thing they're thinking of. D.J., can I ask you something?" Marrell slipped a question onto the end.

"Sure."

"Did you kick Jace today or anything?"

"No," she said softly, "but when he walked me to class, I made sure he knew I was a black belt."

Part of Marrell wanted to laugh. Delancey was so feminine and usually rather shy. Marrell would have loved to see it.

"Are you laughing?" Delancey frowned across the room.

"I was thinking how nice it would have been to be able to tell my date that night that I was a black belt. And part of me is laughing because you don't look like you could be threatening."

"That's because most people haven't seen those ten-foot-long legs flying in the air at them." Mackenzie gave a false shudder. "It's no pretty thing."

Delancey didn't even want to smile, but Mackenzie gave her no choice.

"Shut up, Mic," she said to try and cover it.

Mackenzie went on to make grunting noises and kick her leg in the air. Marrell and Delancey couldn't hold their laughter.

"You kick like someone who thinks it's easy but hasn't had any training," Delancey said, her tone superior.

"That's all right. Airline pilots don't need to know karate."

"Is that what it is now?" Marrell was amazed. Just a month ago she was going to be a doctor, or was it a writer?

"Yes, and this one I'm staying with. I might become a nurse too. That could come in handy."

Marrell smiled at her, and Mackenzie grinned back.

"What's your latest, D.J.?"

"I still want to run my own karate school, but I'm thinking lately that teaching might be fun too."

"What age group?"

"Little ones, like kindergarten or preschool."

"Or a whole room full of Janas," Mackenzie suggested. "Wouldn't that be great?"

"Yeah. We never see them anymore." Delancey sounded sad, and Marrell was overwhelmed with guilt. Shay spent her days chasing a toddler, and Marrell felt as though she lived at Bayside Architecture. They hadn't had a good long talk in many weeks.

"Call them up," she said suddenly. "Ask them to dinner Monday night and to watch the football game."

"Really?" Delancey looked overjoyed.

"Yes. Call now before it gets much later."

Delancey rushed to do the job, coming back only long enough to ask what Shay could bring.

"How about a pan of her good brownies?" Marrell threw out the first thought that came.

Delancey danced back into the room just moments later and surprised Marrell by running over to hug and kiss her.

"Thanks, Mom!"

"You're welcome" was still leaving her mouth when Delancey danced her way out of the room and down the hall. Mackenzie disappeared as well.

I've got to do something, Lord. We're completely cut off from everyone who loves us. It's so easy to remember to ask the widow over right after the husband is gone, but more than a year later, when the loneliness and grief are still fresh, the widow is sometimes forgotten.

Even as this thought formed, Marrell knew that some of it was her own doing. She was tired all the time — that was a very real fact — but did that mean she had to give in to it? Too often she used her weariness as an excuse. Too often she found it easier to read a book or watch television than get up and do something. Even going for a walk was too much of an effort.

She glanced toward the window: too dark to go out now, but in the morning she would do better. Marrell stood with renewed purpose and walked to the girls' rooms.

"Hey, you guys," she said from in the hallway between their doors. "Let's do something tomorrow. Let's go somewhere and do something."

"Where?" Mackenzie came to her door.

"I don't know, but let's think of something and run away for the day. I'm going to grocery shop in the morning, but when we get back we'll take off. I'm entertaining all suggestions."

"I know," Delancey called from her bed. "Pier 39. We haven't been there in ages, and then down to the bay to watch the kites."

"Mackenzie?"

"Sounds good to me."

"All right. It's all settled. We leave at nine o'clock."

No one bothered to check the forecast; it rained buckets. But Marrell didn't care. She took the girls anyway, at least to the pier, and even treated them to lunch on the bay. They had a wonderful time, Marrell included, but she had to work on herself all over again not to miss Paul.

NINETEEN

Marrell didn't even see Jack until Delancey called his name and rushed across the foyer to him. Marrell and Mackenzie followed a little more slowly and only got there in time to hear Jack say, "I have time this afternoon. Will that work for you?"

"Yeah. What time should I be ready?"

"Why don't I come right away?"

"Sure," Delancey smiled at him. "We have plenty of chocolate ice cream."

Jack laughed and walked with them into church. He sat on the other side of the girls, not an unusual thing, but it was uncomfortable for Marrell. On the outside he was the same old Jack, but Marrell couldn't help but ask herself if he was all right inside. She had said she needed to talk to him. Did he feel no sense of urgency? For her part, she could leave church on the spot and sit down face-to-face with him, but he seemed so calm. Maybe she had misunderstood.

Marrell mentally shook herself when she realized she was missing the sermon. *This is not the time for it, Marrell. Now listen up, girl.* That was all she needed — that and shifting her body so she couldn't see Jack from the corner of her eye.

"Is right now going to work, Marrell?" Jack wasted

no time in asking. "Or is that going to mess up your lunch? I can come later."

"I take it Delancey needs help with her algebra?"

"Yes. She says it's not much, but she wanted to get on it this year before she falls behind."

The girls had disappeared. Sunday school had been great and the church service very encouraging and challenging, but for Marrell, one of her biggest challenges was seated on the pew beside her.

Her eyes were to the front when she said, "We use you, Jack. Have you ever noticed that?"

"I don't know what you're talking about." He was a big man, but he sat forward in the pew so he could see her face. Marrell looked at him and wanted to sob. How could they use him this way?

"Are you ever lonely, Jack?"

"Yes, I am at times," he admitted, his voice telling of his confusion.

"So what does *thoughtful, sensitive* Marrell do? She rattles on about wanting to be alone, about never being alone. We use you."

"Stop saying that," he commanded, his voice low but firm. "You do not."

"Yes, we do. D.J. is struggling with numbers, so she calls on Jack. Shay can't come to the airport, so Jack has to pick up the Bishops. I can't get into the office because I forget my key, and who's stuck coming down an hour early? Jackson Avery. Without thought for your feelings, we use you."

Marrell looked away from him again, and Jack thought he would give much not to be in a semi-crowded church sanctuary.

"Look at me, Marrell," he commanded softly.

She did so reluctantly.

"I'm going to be coming over right from here

314

and helping Delancey. You can feed me some lunch, and when all of that is out of the way, we're going for a long walk and having a much-needed talk. Do you understand?"

"I'll probably cry," she told him in disgust. "That's all I do anymore."

"That's *not* going to bother me."

"I told myself I would never do that again, and here I've done it twice."

"Do what?"

"Cry in front of you the way I did the day you hired me."

Jack's hand went to the back of his neck in a long-suffering move.

"That's something else we'll talk about," he said softly, since Delancey and Mackenzie came looking for their mother.

"We're starved, Mom," Delancey proclaimed.

"All right. I'm coming."

"I'm going to run home and change my clothes," Jack decided suddenly. "Do you want me to eat while I'm there?"

Marrell glared at him. "Of course not. I just shopped yesterday."

"You look fierce," he told her.

"Do I?" she fired back, still put out. "Why are you going home to change?"

"Because I have to wear a suit five days a week, so as soon as I can get out of it on Sunday, I do."

"Oh." The fire had gone out of her. "We'll see you at the apartment."

"All right. I made a cake yesterday and only ate one piece. Do you want me to bring that?"

"What flavor?" Mackenzie wanted to know.

"It's a yellow cake with chocolate frosting."

"Lots of frosting?"

"Mackenzie!" Her mother's voice left no doubt as to her mood. Marrell looked up at Jack as if to say, "See what I mean?"

"We would love to share your cake, Jack." Her voice was soft and sad. "Thank you."

Jack knew he couldn't comment without showing his frustration, so he bid them goodbye and headed to his car. His heart, however, was determined: Marrell Bishop would know where he stood before the day was over, or his name wasn't Jackson Avery.

"Mom, should I not have asked Jack to help me? Are you mad about that?"

They were in the car on the way home.

"No, that's fine, D.J. I just want us to be a little careful as to how much we take Jack for granted. He does have a life of his own with better things to do than constantly help out the Bishops."

"I shouldn't have said that about the frosting."

"No, you shouldn't have. We need to be thankful that we'll have dessert at all."

"Especially after Mic's last cookie-baking venture," Delancey reminded them.

"They weren't so bad, D.J. You're just picky."

"The raisins were like chewing on rocks, Mic," her sister argued. "Don't give up your day job."

The girls got a good jolly out of this, but Marrell was having a hard time with levity. She went to work on lunch the minute she got in the door, but since they had run off the day before and had fun, the apartment wasn't as clean as she liked. The carpet was far from new, so a week without vacuuming made it look all the worse. She tried to pull out of her awful mood, recalling the sermon, and praying and singing hymns in her mind, but suddenly Jack was there, and she was still bent out of shape.

"I can tell it's going to be fun walking with you," he said when they had a moment alone at the front door. "You're still frowning at everything."

"Maybe I won't go on a walk with you."

"Oh, yes, you will." His voice was soft, but there was no missing his tone.

Marrell's head whipped around to glare at him, and he calmly returned her regard. She had a dozen things to say to that, but needing Marrell's help, Delancey called from the kitchen.

"We'll just see," she told him and would have turned away, but he bent low and said, "By the way, what are we fighting about?"

For the second time in under an hour, the fight went out of Marrell.

"I don't know."

"Well, we'll figure it out and pick it up again on the walk."

It was such a "Jack" thing to say — outrageous, straight-faced, and funny. Marrell smiled, shook her head, and led the way into the kitchen.

They ate just 15 minutes later, and while Marrell and Mackenzie did the dishes, Jack and Delancey attacked her homework. In truth, she hadn't spoken to him soon enough. The end of the first quarter was just weeks away, and she was barely pulling a C grade. It took longer than Jack had anticipated, but about 3:00 he finally got Marrell out the door for a walk. The park he had in mind was quite a ways away, but Marrell had told the girls that they would be back when they were back.

"Are we going to church tonight?"

"If we get back in time. Go to Mrs. Baker's or

call Shay if there's an emergency."

"What if we want to go somewhere; should we leave you a note?"

"You both have homework," Marrell reminded them. "Just plan to stay here and do it."

"But if we do?"

"You can't, Mic. You have to stay here."

"All right."

"Goodbye, girls. Take care of each other."

" 'Bye," they both called and stood for a minute after Jack and Marrell were gone.

"Have Mom and Jack ever done anything alone before?" Delancey asked.

"I don't think so, unless it was something at work."

"Why do you suppose he's taking her for a walk without us?"

"I think for the same reason Mom's sorta crabby. She needs some time alone or with adults."

"She gets that at work."

"That's like saying we get time with our friends because we see them at school, D.J. Nothing could be further from the truth."

Delancey had nothing else to say on the subject and plenty of school subjects waiting for her attention. Both girls got to work without further ado.

Jack and Marrell were fairly quiet on the way to the park. It was a brisk San Francisco day, so they walked along swiftly, slowing only when they reached the paved path of the park and finally found an empty bench. Marrell was slightly winded.

"You're not even breathing hard," she accused him good-naturedly.

318

"I have more time to work out than you do."

"What do you like to do?"

"Walk mostly, some biking."

"I was just thinking about that on Friday night — that I don't get any exercise these days. Some of the other women bring walking shoes and head out during their lunch hour. I should do the same."

"It might give you more energy."

"I was thinking the same thing." Saying this, Marrell thought how easy it would be to skirt the main subject, but she didn't want that. "I was so crabby at you this morning, Jack. You offered to come and help Delancey, and I took your head off. I'm sorry."

"I appreciate your apology, Marrell, but you still feel that I'm being used, don't you?"

"I guess I do," she admitted, turning her head to look at him. "I can't believe you don't see it."

"Do you hate me, Marrell, or dislike me in some way?"

"No," she said with surprise.

"Then you're not using me. You're a friend who needs occasional help, and you ask me. I can always say no, and Marrell, where have you gotten to thinking that you're calling on me every few seconds? In my opinion, you never ask for anything."

She looked away in confusion.

"And since when is it wrong to cry? If I've made you feel bad, then the shame is on me."

"It's not you, Jack, but it's so embarrassing. Do you realize that I cried in your office when you interviewed me? How humiliating. I was so amazed you offered me the job that I could have walked into a wall."

319

"So I should have thought you were some type of emotional nut and sent you packing?"

"At the very least, yes."

"That's funny," he said with a chuckle. "All I wanted to do was ask you to dinner."

Marrell gaped at him. "Jackson Avery, you did not!"

He looked her in the eye and smiled very tenderly. "Yes, Marrell, I did."

"Oh, Jack, it's just not fair to you. I'm still in love with Paul Bishop."

"I know you are," he said calmly.

"But you still wish we could have something more. I mean, is that what you're saying, Jack?"

"That's exactly what I'm saying. And if someday you can care for me —"

"I already care for you," she interrupted, "but I'm not in love with you."

They were quiet for a moment.

"There isn't a young person on the planet who would agree with me," Jack spoke as he looked across the park, "but I think love is a choice. Now if everything about me repulses you, or my touch makes you shudder, then we have a problem. But if you care, then we have something to work with. A place to start."

When he looked down at her, Marrell searched his deep brown eyes and saw nothing but honesty and kindness.

"I'm 41 years old, Marrell, and very patient. I've waited a year already, and I see no reason to rush you now or make you feel obligated in any way."

"But you want to marry me?" She had to make sure she understood.

Jack nodded. "And take care of you and the girls

for the rest of your lives."

"Oh, Jack." She didn't know what else to say.

"Have I horrified you? I'll not say another word if you don't want me to."

Marrell put her hand on his arm for a moment. "No, no, that's not it. I'm just so overwhelmed. I mean, I don't even know what you see in me. I was such a crab today, but beyond that . . ." She stopped and looked up at him. "Jack, I was going to grow old with Paul Bishop, and sometimes I can't believe that's still not going to happen. I'm not even one of those women who feels unfaithful. I mean, Paul would laugh at that. If I wanted to remarry, he would be the first to say 'go for it.' And even that!" she burst out suddenly. "All I do is talk about Paul. When are you going to tell me you're sick of hearing about Paul Bishop?"

"I'm not ever going to say that."

"Then you're too good to be true."

"No, Marrell, I'm not. I have plenty of faults, but I'll never try to erase Paul from your memory or take his place. I just want the opportunity to love and cherish you as I dream of doing." He brushed a tear from her face. "And to be honest with you, I think you need someone very badly."

"What if I can't ever do anything but care for you?" She looked tragic, but he smiled.

"Then I know you'll do that with all your heart, since that's the type of person you are. Marrell Bishop is the sweetest woman I've ever known."

She cried then, and he put an arm around her and brought her close. He had a bulky sweater on, and Marrell cried right into the front of it.

"I never carry handkerchiefs," she heard him mutter. "Here, use my sleeve."

A watery chuckle escaped Marrell, and she used

321

her own sleeve.

"What are we going to do?" she asked.

"That remains to be seen."

Marrell looked up at him and realized she was sitting very close.

"You don't need to move on my account."

His arm was on the back of the bench now, but Marrell's heart was not on that. She had suddenly remembered the girls.

"How do we do this, Jack? How do we find out if we have anything here without the girls knowing? I don't want them hurt."

"I don't plan to stomp off and never speak to you again if you don't want to marry me, Marrell. We can tell Mackenzie and Delancey what we're thinking of because I'm still going to be there for the three of you."

"So we should talk to them?"

"If you're comfortable with that . . . if you want us to pursue this, yes. If not, then I'll just go back to being friend Jack."

"And you could actually do that?"

"Yes, Marrell, I can. For you, I can."

"I don't want that," she said almost immediately. "I'm not sure exactly what I do want right now, but I don't want you to fade into the woodwork." She looked up at him. "Are you really 41?"

He laughed. "Yes."

"You don't look it."

"Well, then we're even, because you don't look like the mother of teenage girls."

She pulled a face. "Most days I feel like one." She sighed. "When do we talk to them?"

"No time like the present."

Marrell bit her lip. "Okay."

They left the bench then and started down

the path.

"Just a minute." Jack caught her arm and led her back to where they were. "I think we need a little help before we do this." He held out his hand and Marrell put hers into it. Jack prayed and Marrell listened, her heart settled and at peace. She didn't know what God had for them, but when a man was willing to pray as Jack was doing, she felt that was a very good start. If the girls felt the same way, that would answer just one of the many questions rushing through her mind. The rest would have to wait on the Lord's time, and as Jack let go of her hand and didn't touch her all the way home, she knew he was willing to wait as well.

"Okay you two," Marrell came right at them from the front door. Jack had only been gone a few seconds. "What did you really think?" Marrell sat down and tried not to look as anxious as she felt. If they felt she had betrayed them or been sneaky, she would be so hurt and upset.

The Bishop girls stared at her, both a little shocked. Jack Avery had just sat in their living room and said he was in love with their mother and hoped to marry her someday. Jack — Jackson Avery — their mother's boss.

"Did he mean that, Mom, that he's not trying to take Dad's place in your heart?"

"Yes, he did. Jack is a very special man, and he knows that I still love your father."

"Then how could you marry Jack?" Mackenzie cut to the point.

"I'm not sure I can, but I will tell you this: There are different kinds of love. I must admit to you that whenever I've thought about remarriage, I've never outright dismissed it or told the Lord no. I don't believe I'll ever love again, but there are marriages built on caring and trust."

"Would you sleep together?" Again Mackenzie went for the bottom line.

"I would not marry Jack otherwise. That's not fair to either of us, and he's not proposing that type of marriage."

"Has he actually asked you, Mom?" Delancey asked.

"No. Right now he just wants to know if I care enough to move in that direction. If you girls are totally against it, I'll tell him. He'll understand."

"Would that upset you?"

"It would, but I'm not going to sacrifice you two for anyone or anything. I would want to talk about it, not just have you tell me no. I would want to know why."

"I like Jack," Delancey said. "I like him a lot. I'm just not sure I want him living here."

"I doubt if it would be here," Marrell said, "but I don't think that's what you meant."

Delancey had never imagined living anywhere else, so this got her attention. Marrell read her look.

"D.J., there would be many changes — where we live would only be one — but that's not what I'm asking you right now." Marrell stopped because she had to rethink this. What was she asking? It came to her very suddenly.

"I just realized I want to give this a chance. Like I said, I care for Jack, and I want to see what the Lord might have for us — not just Jack and me, but you two as well. There will be lots of questions along the way, and I will answer what I can. Some answers you may have to wait for. But all I want us to concentrate on right now is how you feel about my seeing Jack."

"Would you have children?" Again this came from Mackenzie.

"I've had my tubes tied, Mic, and although the process is reversible, I need to keep in mind that I'll be 40 next year. Jack and I have not discussed that, so I can't say how he feels, but I strongly doubt that would be an issue."

The girls fell quiet. Indeed, they were quiet for so long that Marrell apologized.

"I'm sorry," she said with soft regret. "I shouldn't have thrown this at you. I miss your father, but I also don't love being alone. Jack is so kind and caring, but I don't think it's fair to ask this of you. I'm sorry."

"I don't want Jack to be out of our life," Mackenzie said.

"He won't be, Mic; he assured me of that."

"But he might not come around as much."

Marrell shrugged. She had thought of this, but what could she say?

"Would you marry right away?" Delancey wished to know.

"No. We would take things very slowly — as slowly as we all need to go." As soon as Marrell said this, she knew they could never give her permission. It was just too much for the girls to put into words. Very gently, her eyes on their faces, she made the decision.

"I'm going to start seeing Jack. I don't know exactly what that's going to look like, but we'll just take this as it goes. If at any time we feel God is directing otherwise, through you, through Oliver and Shay, or anyone, we'll step back and reevaluate. You must come to me at any time. I will always listen, but unless you have an objection right now, I'm going to talk it over with Shay and Oliver. If they think it's a good direction, I'll let Jack know."

Both girls nodded immediately. Not for the first time, Marrell was amazed over the relationship they had. It was true that Paul had worked hard with them on their attitudes and appreciation for their parents, but it was more than that. Marrell was sure that God had been at work in their hearts. The girls were at an age when many of their friends hated their parents and wanted nothing to do with them. The Bishop girls were ready to be with their mother almost any time or place.

"It's too late for church," Marrell now said softly. "How about pizza for dinner?"

"What kind do we have in the freezer?" Delancey asked.

"I meant go out."

The girls looked so surprised that Marrell wondered about it. Did her girls think that she was a slave to the church's schedule of services? She went to church as often as she was able because she loved fellowship with the local body, but since the girls only came to church to please her, she could see how they would not view it that way. As they moved out the door for the car, Marrell prayed that her life, not her church schedule, would make an impression on her daughters, and that God would be able to reach them through some open door in their hearts.

The next day Jack asked Marrell how the girls had been, and she had been able to give him a positive report. She also told him that Shay and Oliver were coming that night and that she wanted to talk to them. She wasn't sure why she was nervous about this, except that Shay's opinion was so important, and Oliver had been an unending source of comfort and help. At this point in time, Marrell could live with the thought of not marrying Jack. The thought of hurting him, however, made her feel as though she had a knife in her side. That thought was still so heavy on her mind that it was a relief that evening to have the kitchen clear out so she could talk to her friend.

"Am I imagining things, or do you have something on your mind?" Shay came out with what she was thinking.

"I do have something on my mind, but I wanted to wait until the girls were out of here."

"Should I get Oliver?"

"No, you can tell him later. The girls like him watching the game with them."

"Who's playing tonight?"

"I'm not sure."

Jana waddled her way into the room — she walked everywhere now — and wanted to climb into her mother's lap. Marrell reached across and tickled her knee, smiling when she squirmed and grinned.

"Should I take her out to Oliver?"

"No, I don't think she'll be a problem."

The words were no more out of Marrell's mouth when Jana tried to put her hand in the butter.

"On second thought," Shay said good-naturedly, "I think she really wants to see her dad."

While Shay was in the other room, Marrell worked a little on the table, stacking the dishes on the counter for later. She was just washing the table down when her friend returned.

"Do you want some coffee?" Marrell offered.

327

"No thanks, but don't let me stop you."

"I don't want any either."

Marrell sat down at the table, but for a moment she said nothing. Shay waited, hoping they could talk before Jana looked for her again.

"I want to tell you something, Shay, but I don't want you to be too excited."

"All right. I take it that I'll think it's good news."

"Yes, and maybe someday it might be, but right now I need to go real slow."

"Okay."

Marrell took a breath. "On Thursday of last week, Jack told me he would like to see me on a personal basis."

Shay's heart stopped and plunged on again like a rocket. She worked to keep the feelings from her face and said only, "How do you feel about that?"

"I don't know yet. I talked with the girls last night — we both did — and I told them I'm going to give this some time and attention and see what happens. It's important to me that you and Oliver know, Shay, because if you have any objections, I need to hear them. I don't want to do anything the Lord wouldn't want me to do, and part of the way I'll know is how my friends respond."

Shay nodded. "I see your point, Marrell, and you're right, I do want to get excited. But first of all, I want to know how *you* feel. You sound more like you're talking about a business arrangement than a relationship."

"I know I do, Shay, but in truth, my heart's not as involved right now as Jack's is."

"He loves you?"

Marrell nodded. "He told the girls last night."

"In front of you?"

"Yes, right in the living room."

"Oh, Marrell." Shay's heart was tender with compassion. "Can you tell me how this came up?"

"It was Thursday — I think I told you that. Uh, let's see . . . oh boy, Shay, it's been so long since we've talked."

"Tell me about it. I'm into 'Sesame Street' these days and loving it, singing every song, but I do miss our heart-to-hearts."

Marrell had a good laugh over that.

"Go on now," Shay leaned forward. "We'll talk about me some other year. I want to hear this. He talked to you Thursday."

"Yes. You see, I had this job interview in the building, but I didn't take it because of the hours, and well, that led to Jack telling me he would like to ask me out. We talked about it after work that day and even that night, because he called to see if I was upset. That led to us deciding we needed to do a lot more talking. Then D.J. asked him to help her with her algebra, and he came yesterday. After that we went for a walk, and he said he's wanted to ask me out since the day he gave me the job."

Shay's eyes slid shut and a warm smile came to her lips. When she opened her eyes, Marrell was just looking at her, an expression of hopelessness on her face.

"Oh, my dear Marrell. What did you say?"

"Well, Shay, that's the strangest thing about all this. He's still just Jack. He's kind and funny and so easy to talk to. I even told him he was going to get sick of hearing Paul Bishop's name, and he said it wouldn't happen. He's so patient, Shay. I've never known a man quite like him."

"What did the girls say?"

"They were surprised, but when I told them I was going to do this, they had no objections."

"And what exactly are you going to do?"

"Get to know Jack Avery. Unless," Marrell said the word firmly, "you and Oliver don't think I should."

Shay shook her head no. "That's not going to happen. A long time ago I told Oliver I wished the two of you could get together, and he said it was too soon and to stay out of it. Then, just two weeks ago, you called over something, and he said you sounded so tired and that he wished you could find someone and not have to keep working the way you do. Not to mention the fact that Oliver thinks a lot of Jack — has for a long time."

"But you just stated the problem, Shay. I can't marry Jack because I don't want to work anymore. I'm terrified of hurting him or using him. I can't marry the man because I feel sorry for him."

"I quite agree with you, Marrell, and if you were marrying him this week, that's what I would be saying to you, but as you stated, you're taking it slow and seeking counsel. It doesn't sound as though you're deliberately going to hurt anyone."

"I don't want to unintentionally hurt him either."

Shay looked very understanding. "If he's already in love with you, Marrell, you might not have a choice, but he's not the type of man to pout and never speak to you again."

"No, he's not. I just need to keep my head about all of this, that's all."

"What if you do fall in love with him?"

"I think that would be great, but right now it doesn't seem likely. I even asked him what happens if my feelings never go beyond caring. He made it sound as though he could live with that."

"But could you? Could you marry a man you weren't in love with?"

Marrell smiled. "Do you know what Jack said to that? He said love is a choice."

Shay whistled. "He's certainly given you a lot to think about."

"Yes, he has. Please talk to Oliver, Shay, just in case he has any cautions."

"I will. I think he would only congratulate you for going slow, but I'll check with him."

Again silence fell for a moment before Marrell asked, "What do you think, Shay?"

Her friend's smile was warm. "I hope you tip head over heels and never recover."

Jana was looking for her mother again and the conversation was over, but for the moment that was fine with Marrell. As Shay had stated, she had quite a bit of thinking to do.

TWENTY

Delancey worked at not showing her surprise, but it took an effort. For the second day in a row Jace Booth was at her table, eating lunch with her and Mackenzie and acting completely normal. Well, maybe not completely. He was actually a bit kinder, Delancey thought, with no attempt to gain intimacy and no air of proprietorship. She was completely stumped. The day before he hadn't walked her to class but had met her at the bus to say goodbye. Now today he walked her to class. Class itself was actually a waste of time; Delancey heard little of what the teacher said.

If public opinion could be trusted, women were normally thought of as baffling creatures. Delancey knew better. She had practically threatened a boy with harm if he tried anything — a boy who was known for his interest in the physical side of relationships — and now he was hanging around and acting as if they were the best of friends. *No, indeed,* Delancey told herself as she tried to get into English literature, *women are not the difficult creatures. Of this I'm sure.*

You can't buy her, Jack said to himself. *You can't and you know it. Just look the other way. You know she's not starving. Now just ignore it.* But it wasn't working. Marrell's small lunch — half a peanut butter sandwich, a carrot, and a cup of water — were driving him crazy. He had been in her house. They ate fine, but there were never any extras. About the only thing she seemed to splurge on was Pepsi and the occasional meal out.

He knew he was probably taking his cue from Taya, who had a new outfit every week, but it bothered him a little that the dresses Marrell had worn when she started to work for him a year ago were the same dresses she still wore — nothing ever changed. The girls had new things on occasion, but Marrell's blouses, slacks, and blazers from before still remained.

As if Jack's thoughts were not bad enough, he glanced down to see that the cuff of her blouse was wearing. He could see where she had patched a small hole. He had so innocently asked her to have lunch with him outside on the bench. Right now he couldn't eat a thing.

"Are you all right, Jack?" Marrell suddenly noticed.

"I worry about you," he said softy.

Marrell sat looking up at him. "For any particular reason?"

"Just a lot of little things." He looked over at her. "Do you have enough lunch today, Marrell, or will you be hungry this afternoon?"

Understanding lit her face. "We're doing fine, Jack, I mean, most of the time. Well, that is, sometimes things come up, or I don't think well and spend more than I should, but most of the time we're all right."

"How about this month?" he asked, not willing to let it drop.

"This month is different," she defended herself.

"Why? What happened this month?"

"Just some things." She didn't want to tell him.

"What?"

Marrell busied herself with her napkin and wouldn't look at him.

"Tell me, Marrell."

He wasn't going to let it go. Marrell saw no choice. "We had some car repairs, and then I forgot and took the girls out to eat twice." She shrugged and looked guilty. "I just forgot."

"So because you forgot, you don't get enough to eat for lunch?"

"I'm fine," she assured him, and it was true. "This will be plenty. We just have to be a little more careful."

He didn't believe her, and in fact he looked so stern that Marrell looked away. It was then that she spotted her own worn blouse and understood a little more.

"I've been thinking of taking a little money out of savings and getting myself some new things. I know it's important to look professional here at the office."

She looked up when she heard him exhale on a frustrated sigh.

"You could wear your bathrobe to the office for all I care, Marrell. I'm talking about the things you *need.*"

"Then you're spoiled, Jackson Avery."

He gawked at her.

"I have everything I need," Marrell told him quietly, not wanting him to scowl at her. "I don't have all my wants, but as far as needs go, I have plenty."

Jack thought about this for a moment. He knew

she was right, but it didn't change the fact that he wanted to see her with more.

"Tell me something. Why did the car repairs tax your monthly budget if you have savings?"

"Because I try not to touch the savings. Most of it is insurance money from Paul's death, and I want the girls to be able to attend college and have some of that money to establish themselves someday."

Jack continued to look down at her. "I'm going to do something now, and you're not going to argue." He reached for his wallet.

"Jack," she began.

"What did I just say?"

Marrell bit her lip and said nothing when he pressed some bills into her hand.

"This is not because I don't think you look good at the office — most days you look so good I can't concentrate. Take this money and buy yourself something that you've wanted or needed. Whatever."

Marrell thanked him quietly and sat looking at her lap. Only when she glanced up did she realize his eyes were on her.

"And while you're at it, you're supposed to be working on falling in love with me. Don't forget that."

Marrell's hand came to her mouth to cover her smile.

"It's not funny," Jack told her, but knew the effect he was having: Her face was turning red with suppressed laughter. He didn't smile right away but winked at her before saying they had better get back inside. It would be some time before Marrell understood that he oftentimes joked with her to stop himself from saying what was really in his heart.

"Well, Jack," Shay said that very night, "come on in."

"Thank you. Is this a bad time?"

"Not at all. We're just sitting in the living room hoping to wear out this active baby so we can go to bed at a reasonable hour."

Jack laughed. "Keeps you up, does she?"

"Well, we put her down, but if she's not sleepy, she sings and keeps us awake."

"Oh, no," he laughed again. "I've never heard of that before. She doesn't cry?"

"No, and she doesn't climb out. She just sings."

"Hello, Jack," Oliver greeted, coming forward to shake his hand. "Come in and sit down."

"Thank you. Hi, Jana," Jack said when he sat in a chair near her. She smiled at him, and Jack laughed. "You are a cutie, did you know that?"

Her answer to that was to come over and drool on his tennis shoe. Jack didn't mind and to prove it, he scooped her up and hugged her. Her hand went right for his mustache. Jack took the keys from his pocket and jingled them in front of her, and she was instantly diverted. He shifted her onto one leg, and she played with the keys and never moved.

"I have a feeling you're here for a reason," Shay said after watching him.

"I am, but I still don't know if I have the courage to ask what I want to know."

"Marrell," she accurately guessed.

"Yes. I want to help, but I don't know what I'm doing. And I don't know if it's unfair to ask you without her knowing."

"It's completely fair," Oliver spoke up, surpris-

336

ing his wife and guest. "I'll tell you anything you want to know."

Shay's mouth opened in a way that Oliver couldn't miss.

"Honey," he turned and said tenderly, "Jack loves her, and she's good about coming to us, but she's not going to tell Jack just anything. She also said she's willing to give this a try, which means she is ready to open her life up to him, at least to some degree."

Shay nodded, still in shock. "Do you want me to leave?" she finally asked.

"No, I don't." He smiled at her. "If Jack asks something you don't think we should share, you can tell me. Okay, Jack," he turned back to the man, "shoot."

Jack laughed a little and looked uncomfortable but still said, "What's her financial status? She said something about car repairs, but she didn't want to touch her savings to take care of them."

"No, she wouldn't use her savings for car repairs," Oliver confirmed. "The only thing she's touched that savings account for was to take the girls to Florida, and then her father-in-law sent them money to cover the flights, so she put it right back."

"How bad is her car?"

"It could be worse. It did very well for the first few months, but then she started driving to work every day, and although it's not far, the car wasn't new to begin with."

"And she won't use savings to buy a newer one?"

"She will," Oliver assured him. "We've already talked about it. But not before this one dies on the side of the road. Those are her very words."

Jack's head went back, and he stared unseeingly

at the ceiling. "I don't want to buy her," Jack admitted. "I never want her to feel that way, but I want to do more than the time allows."

"What do you mean?" Oliver didn't know.

"It's too soon," Jack explained. "We're not to that point in our relationship where she would freely take money from me. And in truth, I have no guarantee that we ever will be. I did give her some money today, and she took it. Maybe that's a good sign."

"Did you have to scowl at her?" Shay asked.

"What do you mean?"

"Were you at all upset with her? Did you order her around or frown at her? If you did, that's why she took it."

"Why would that make her take the money?"

"Because Marrell doesn't like anyone to be unhappy with her. She doesn't like confrontation. She works hard to stay firm with the girls, but for a time Delancey ran things with her bad attitude. Marrell finally got the spunk to take her home back, and everyone's been happier for it."

Jack was shaking his head. "She's stood up to me on many occasions. Shay, are you sure about this?"

"Yes. I mean, she's better than she was, but she hated for Paul to be unhappy with her. It crushed her."

Jack was quiet on the outside, but inside he knew that he had bullied her. Now what to do?

"Was she upset with you?" Shay asked quietly.

"No. I made her laugh, but I still didn't handle things well."

"Don't be too hard on yourself, Jack," Oliver suggested. "You can't believe the mistakes Shay and I made. It takes a while to get this communication thing down, even after marriage. I'm thinking maybe a lifetime, if you know what I mean."

"I don't know what you mean, but I'm willing to take your word for it." Jack looked at both of them. "How do you feel about this thing between Marrell and me?"

Shay's smile was huge, but she let Oliver answer. "We think it's wonderful. She needs someone, and you're the perfect person."

"Why am I the perfect person?"

"Because you're patient, and that's what Marrell needs."

"That's your way of saying I need to give her lots of time."

"Yes. Paul's memory is still very fresh, and the longer she goes without him, the more she understands that he won't be back. Repairs on the car, the toilet backing up, or just the fact that they no longer live in the security of the base, are all stark reminders that Marrell and the girls are alone. Marrell has done a tremendous amount of growing in the last year, but because of the job, she's not able to be in Bible study with the women on Thursday mornings. I know she feels cut off. Days, weeks will go by, and she and Shay won't even speak on the phone."

"So you're saying that if she does fall for me, it will be out of desperation." Jack's face and voice were deliberately comical, and Oliver laughed, but both knew there was a serious side to this.

"I guess you've summed up my problem," Jack went on. "If I could help her financially, then she could go part-time and have a chance to regroup and figure out if she wants marriage again. But if I help her, she'll feel obligated, and I'll find myself with a wife who feels she had no choice but to marry me."

"I don't think so," Oliver said quietly. "I mean, I can see why you would feel that way, Jack, but Marrell's a better thinker than that. She might hurt over her decision if she said no to you, but she's not going to marry a man to whom she only feels obligated."

"So you think I should help her financially?"

"Well, she is doing all right. She was telling you the truth about that. But if you want to give her things or help out on small matters — take her to dinner, whatever — that's just courtship."

Jack felt like he had been set free. He honestly hadn't known what to do about this. Before he talked to Marrell he would have said that was all that was needed. He would tell her he was interested, and the ball would either get rolling or never start. It hadn't been that simple.

Jana was still very happy in his lap, the keys wet from her mouth, but when Jack looked down at her, he caught sight of a picture cube on the table. He picked it up and found a picture of Shay and Marrell in front of a Christmas tree.

"I think she's beautiful," he said softly.

"She always has been," Shay said without jealousy.

"I tend to forget that the two of you grew up together. How old were you?"

"We met when we were in the second grade."

"What was she like?" Both Lacys could hear the smile in his voice.

"She was shy around big groups, but gutsy if she had to be — protective of those she loved."

Jack wasn't surprised. That sounded like her, but right now he couldn't get her face from his mind. Not the smiling, serene face from the photo, but the one that looked sad and uncertain on the bench outside the building that afternoon.

"I just thought of something I need to do," Jack said. "Will I be welcome back if I run off with so little notice?"

"That's a silly question," Shay teased him. "Come here, Jan," she said, moving to talk to her daughter. "Let's rinse these keys off and say good-bye to Jack."

"Are you going to be all right?" Oliver asked when Shay left the room.

"Yes. I thank you for your help."

"Anytime. We are praying for you, Jack. I hope you know that."

"Thank you."

A moment later Shay was back with the clean keys, and Jack was on his way. Shay began to speculate as to what Jack was headed to do, but Oliver's mind was taken up otherwise. He was busy praying as he told Jack he would.

Marrell had no more settled in at her desk the next morning when Jack walked in. It wasn't that it never happened — he oftentimes worked early — but he hadn't come in this early in a long time.

"Good morning," she greeted him softly.

"Good morning." Jack's voice had an early-morning growl to it. He came directly to her desk and set a bag in front of her.

"Oh," she said, looking up at him, "what's this?"

"It's for you."

"Okay. Something for the office?"

"No. Open it."

Marrell stood and opened the top of the bag. She reached in and drew out a small cedar box.

"Oh, Jack, how beautiful! This looks like a tiny cedar hope chest."

"That's what it is."

Marrell stared at him.

"I want you to put your hopes in that box, Marrell."

Marrell was still working this out in her mind when he went on.

"I want you to write your hopes down and slip them into the box. Anything you hope for. That the girls will come to Christ, that the girls will go to college, that you won't have to work here forever, that Jack would shave off his mustache, that you could go back to women's Bible study, that you could take more time in your own study of the Word, that you could have a new dress. Anything, Marrell, anything at all."

Marrell looked down at the box, still too stunned to speak.

"You can even put a piece of paper in there that says, 'I hope Jack doesn't scowl at me anymore and make me take money I don't want.' "

"I don't feel that way," Marrell was able to say. "I very much appreciate you giving me the money. I'll spend it very wisely, Jack — not like I did this month."

"You're too hard on yourself, Marrell. If you want to put the money toward car repairs, that's fine, but if you want something completely unpractical, that's okay too. I gave it to you without strings."

"Thank you, Jack, but can I ask you one thing?"

"Of course."

"What am I to do with the papers?"

"Bring them on our dates. I'm hoping you and I can start seeing each other every week — a walk to the park, an evening out for dinner — or just lunches here — times that would give us a chance to talk about Marrell and Jack."

Marrell cocked her head to one side. "You're a very special person, Jackson Avery."

"I'm glad you think so. Did you open the box and smell it?"

She hadn't but did so now, her eyes closing with pleasure.

"It's beautiful. I don't know what to say."

Jack didn't reply to that; he just enjoyed watching her pleasure. She had been in his dreams the night before, and just before morning they had been so vivid it was a surprise to wake up and not find her there. He prayed for patience and also a love for God's timing and plan.

"I'd better get to work," she said now. "Taya will wonder what I've been doing."

"Did I hear you say yesterday that you misplaced a file?"

"Oh yes, I had forgotten about that. Can I check on your desk?"

"Sure."

Marrell put the chest away, thanking him as she did, and then got to work. Jack could have easily taken the day off and talked to her for hours, but this was best. Getting his mind back on work was the only way he was going to survive this ordeal.

Once again Delancey had followed in her sister's footsteps. Both the Bishop girls had made the junior varsity basketball team. Tonight was their first game, and it was at home. Jack accompanied Marrell, who asked to get off a little early, and sat beside her about halfway up the bleachers and off to one side. It was a bit quieter there since many

343

of the kids chose to sit behind the team.

"D.J.'s first game, right?"

"Yes, but not Mic's. She played last year, and her coach was very pleased."

"How tall is Micki?"

"Five-foot-8."

"And D.J.?"

"Five-foot-ten. Most of the time I think she plays center or forward. Mic was a guard last year. I was never athletic, so it's a little amazing to me."

The girls were amazing to Jack in every way, or maybe it was God's work in their lives. He knew that both girls had never made commitments for Christ, but their love and caring of their mother was a sight to see. Neither girl dated anyone or ever gave Marrell a hard time about not going out all weekend long.

He knew from the busy signal he would get for hours that they occupied the phone with their friends, but other than the occasional mood, he rarely saw them out of harmony. Their faces told him they were bored with church, just putting in their time, but he never heard them say they wouldn't go.

Both so attractive, athletic, and intelligent — the girls were very special to Jack. Now he was to watch them play basketball, and it was quite a performance. Delancey's height was a strong advantage in the center of the key, and Mackenzie was remarkably aggressive, yet she did nothing more than stare impassively at the ref when she was called for a foul.

Indeed, she was the coolest player of the game, taking in stride the different problems until Delancey was elbowed in the chin by an opposing team member and went all the way to the floor.

Mackenzie was on the bench at that time, and it took the assistant coach to keep her there. Marrell's right hand was on Jack's arm while her left was at her mouth. Things calmed quickly. A foul was called, and Delancey went to the free-throw line. She took two shots and made one. Only then did Marrell start breathing again.

"Mic is protective of D.J.," she said by way of explanation.

"I've noticed that," Jack said, deliberately keeping his voice light. "They're both rather protective of each other and someone else I know."

Marrell looked at him. "Are they protective of me?"

Jack only stared at her, and Marrell tried to think of what he could be talking about.

"Are they, Jack?"

"Yes, very."

"In what way?"

"Just little things, like if you look like you're going to cry, they watch you until they can see you're all right. And I had eyes on me at all times the first few Sundays I visited."

Marrell's mouth opened. It was true, but she had never even seen it. "How did that make you feel?"

Jack smiled. "I didn't take it personally. I was rather proud of the girls for caring so much."

Marrell shook her head, a small smile on her mouth. As she had been coming to realize, this man was very special. And she was proud of her girls as well. A cheer rose up in the crowd then, and their attention went back to the game. They ended up losing by just two points.

It was a school night, and even though they lost, Jack still took them for ice cream when the girls came from the locker room. They laughed and talked until way too late, but Marrell didn't mind. She was starting to see that something very special was happening in her life.

The days turned to weeks for Jack and Marrell, and as Jack had asked, they saw each other every week. He often asked Marrell and the girls for dinner out on Friday night, but the most regular time was Sunday afternoon, when he would come to lunch and go for a walk with Marrell. At times they would watch the football game together or work on homework, but even if only for a half an hour, Jack would manage to get some time alone to talk with Marrell.

And Marrell was starting to feel things she didn't believe herself capable of. In all the weeks Jack had never stopped being a friend, but now he was becoming something decidedly more. By the time he asked Marrell and the girls to come to his place for Christmas Day, Marrell was well on her way to feeling more than just deep caring for Jack Avery.

"Mom?" Delancey chose that morning to tell her mother some things.

"Yes."

"I need to talk with you a minute."

"Okay. What about?"

"Jack."

Marrell stopped fussing over the salad she was making and turned fully to her daughter, but the younger Bishop was quiet.

"Go ahead, Delancey."

"Well, I think I want to tell you."

"Are you afraid I'll be upset?"

"I don't think so, but I don't know."

346

Marrell shrugged. "You don't know unless you try."

Delancey nodded. "You know a long time ago, Mom," her voice was soft, "back at the beginning when Jack came and said that he would never try and take Dad's place?"

"I remember."

"Well, I didn't believe him."

Marrell nodded.

"But I just realized it's true. I mean, he really hasn't tried to be Dad. I think it's so cool that he came to two of our away games without you. And well, I guess I'm wondering how you feel about him these days, because I don't want him to leave and not be around anymore."

Marrell hugged her youngest daughter. "I don't want that either."

"So you're going to marry him?"

"I would like to, but I still need to hear from Mic, and I haven't figured out yet how to tell him I've fallen for him."

Delancey smiled. "You could just throw your arms around him and kiss him."

Marrell laughed. "I don't know if that's a good idea."

"Mom." Delancey was serious again very suddenly. "I was talking to one of my friends recently, and she was sorta critical of you when I told her you were seeing someone. She said, 'Your dad just died, Delancey. Why is she doing that?' I felt terrible when she said that, Mom — not because you're seeing Jack but because I'm not upset about it. Why is that?"

"I don't know, D.J. I guess it's just the Lord's way of taking care of us. The thought of living with another man — becoming his wife — does feel a little funny. But then I think, 'It's not just anyone; it's Jack,' and he loves me and he loves you girls. It won't ever be the same as it was with your dad — that's impossible — but that doesn't mean it can't be special and all part of God's plan."

"Are you talking about Jack?" Mackenzie had come in.

"Yes. D.J. was telling me how she felt. Would you like to tell me how you're doing with it these days?"

"You'll not get anything mushy out of her," Delancey cut in. "Will she, Mic?"

"Mushy about what?"

"Jack."

"Oh." She frowned a little and spoke with hysterical logic. "It's not me who's going to marry him, so why do I have to get mushy?"

"What makes you think I'm going to marry him?" Marrell asked, a smile on her face even though she knew she had not discussed this with her oldest daughter.

Mackenzie's mouth hung open. "How much time do you have?"

"Mackenzie, I don't know what you're talking about. We haven't discussed this."

"No, but how about the way you blush when he smiles at you, and the extra time you take on your hair and clothes lately? I don't need to discuss those with you to see them, Mom."

For some reason Mackenzie's words hurt her mother, probably because Mackenzie hadn't shown any enthusiasm at all. Marrell frowned at her daughter.

"Will you excuse us a moment, D.J.?"

"Okay."

348

Marrell waited until Delancey had walked from the room before saying, "What happened just now, Mic? You sounded a little too blasé about the whole thing. Is there something you're not telling me?"

Mackenzie hesitated. "I don't know. I'm just not sure I can deal with your loving Jack. I still love Dad, and I don't know if I can handle your marrying Jack and our living together."

Marrell found herself wishing they had talked of this earlier, not on Christmas morning. She decided not to let this get into a full-blown discussion.

"I'm glad you told me," she said instead. "You say the word and I'll stop."

Mackenzie shook her head. "I don't want that either. I feel so selfish."

"Help me here, Mic." Marrell kept her voice gentle. "Do you have any objections to Jack?"

"No."

"Have your friends made comments?"

Mackenzie remained quiet, and Marrell knew she had her answer.

"D.J. had the same thing happen."

"What did she do?"

"I think she just blew it off, but let me ask her."

"No, don't," Mackenzie said swiftly, feeling angry at herself. "It's none of my friends' business. I don't even know why I listened to them. It hasn't been that long, but that doesn't mean you didn't love Dad."

"Is that what they said, Mackenzie?" Marrell was outraged. "I think you had better find new friends."

"Right now that's not a bad idea," she responded, still put out at herself. "I'm sorry, Mom.

I never meant to make this hard for you."

"I'm glad you told me, Micki, but there's something else you need to know. I meant what I said. You say the word and I'll stop. I won't think you're selfish and neither will Jack. I'll just tell him we have to slow way down and maybe even quit."

"No!" Mackenzie was adamant. "I want Jack around, and I'm glad we're going to his place today. Have you been there?"

"No, but are you sure, Mic? We can still talk about this."

"We don't need to. I'm not going to let my friends hurt Jack, and that's what I would be doing if you stopped now. Just kiss him or something, and tell him you love him so we can get on with this. I don't like things being up in the air. I want to know where we're going to live and all that."

Marrell wanted to laugh. Her daughter's pendulum had gone from "against" to "all for" in a matter of seconds.

"You're trying not to laugh." Mackenzie had caught her.

"Well, Mic," Marrell chuckled, "you did do a pretty good 180 just now."

Mackenzie went over and hugged her mom. "Have I ruined your day?" she whispered.

"No. You don't know how much you mean to me, to Jack too. We would never want to do anything to hurt you."

"Does he know how you feel?"

"No. Things have been so busy at the office the last few weeks, and I just realized it myself."

Mackenzie nodded and looked her mother in the eye. "Tell him today, Mom. Give him the best Christmas present in the world. Tell him you love him on Christmas Day."

Marrell gently kissed Mackenzie's cheek, thanked her, and tried to figure out how she could do just that.

TWENTY-ONE

The Bishop girls loved Jack's apartment. It was spacious and laid out in classic styles and colors. And since the man himself had a "thing" for electronic gadgets, it wasn't long before both teenagers were totally absorbed with his stereo and new videodisc player.

"You turn it on right here and slide the disc in here," Jack explained just moments after they arrived, holding a disc that looked like a record. He proceeded to show them, and they watched as *The Sound of Music* sprang to life on the large TV.

"This is so cool," Delancey said.

"It is, isn't it?" Jack agreed. "The only drawback is there aren't many movies I'm willing to buy. Video recorders that take regular tapes have a wider selection. Maybe I'll get one of those someday."

Marrell heard only part of what was going on. She was too busy looking around his beautiful home. Like Shay and Oliver, he had the top floor of a house as his apartment, but it was much larger than the Lacys'. The living room was spectacular, with a huge picture window that looked out over the bay and allowed him to see the sailboats lining the docks along the waterfront.

The apartment didn't have a formal dining

room, but that didn't seem to matter. The kitchen was huge. Its table and six chairs did not crowd things at all. There was an island with a range top on it in the middle of the kitchen. The eye-level oven was to the side, and a microwave was next to it. A turkey was in the oven and Marrell could see the stuffing, but the counters were neat as a pin. Marrell was still taking it all in when Jack found her.

"What do you think?" he asked from across the room. She looked so good today that if he got any closer he was going to have to touch her.

I think I love you was the first thought in Marrell's mind, but she looked away so she couldn't see his face and said, "It's beautiful. The whole place is lovely. Tell me how long you've lived here."

"Twelve years."

Marrell shook her head in wonder. "I can see why. I would never want to move. How much decorating have you done?" she asked as she took in the wallpaper and perfectly coordinated countertops and appliances.

"I've done most of it. My landlord is elderly, and as long as I don't burn the place down, he doesn't care. He hasn't raised the rent in five years."

"Hey, Jack," Delancey called from the living room. "Is this a picture of your mother and grandmother?"

Jack went to the living room, a smile on his face. He joined Delancey by the photo on the wall, took it down, and held it in his hand. "These are my sisters."

Delancey's mouth opened. "Your sisters?"

"Yes. I was an afterthought. My mother didn't have me until she was 49. The woman on the left is my sister, Kate," Jack said, pointing. "She's 68. The one on the right is Anne. She's 72. They both live in Eugene, Oregon, where I grew up. They never married."

"Never?" Mackenzie asked after she had come on the scene.

"Nope. They live in the house I grew up in, and they've only been down one time to visit me in all these years. I grew up with three mothers," Jack offered fondly.

"How often do you go see them?" Marrell asked.

"Only about twice a year."

Jack showed them some other photos, and the three women were delighted with the pictures of him as a baby and from grade school. At one point he slipped away to put the pies in the oven, but not long afterward he said it was time to open gifts. He had such a look of childish delight that Marrell laughed at him.

"What?"

"You look just like a big kid."

He wiggled his eyebrows up and down.

"Wait until you see what I've bought. You might feel like a kid yourself."

Marrell smiled but tried not to feel anxious. She hadn't been able to do much for Christmas and had really struggled with how inadequate her gifts seemed. She and the girls had opened theirs after the Christmas Eve service the night before. Both girls had been pleased with their gifts, but Marrell had wanted to give them so much more.

Mackenzie was wearing her new watch today, and Delancey had on her new sweater — but other than a new book each and a favorite candy bar, that had been all.

You've told Jack in the past that he's spoiled, and

now listen to you, Marrell chided herself. *You and the girls got him what you could afford. Now leave it at that. It doesn't honor God when you buy gifts on the birthday of His Son with money you don't have.*

"What's the matter?" Jack asked softly, having come close.

"I was just giving myself a pep talk because I'm not being thankful. I'm still having a hard time with not being able to give the girls everything I want, and we have gifts for you, but they're not very fancy or special."

"Then I think you should go shopping right now and find something else for me. Spare no expense."

Marrell bit her lip, but he did not let up.

"Did I tell you I have my eye on a bike? Mine is more than 20 years old and getting tired. Why don't I give you the directions to the store? You could go now."

"Stop," she finally laughed. "You asked and I told you. I didn't say it was right."

"I wasn't expecting anything, Marrell," he said, growing serious. "I shopped for the three of you, but I didn't expect you to buy me anything."

"Thank you," she said softly, still working to push down the feeling of disappointment that she didn't have more. She had almost accomplished this when Jack told the three women to gather around the tree. After doing so, Marrell realized that every gift beneath it was for her or the girls.

"Jack." Marrell was shocked. "What have you done?"

"I've had fun," he said without apology. "I never have anyone but my sisters and a few colleagues to buy for, so this year I splurged. Here we go." He ignored their shocked faces and passed a gift to Mackenzie.

"You first, Micki."

"Okay," she responded, looking a little over-whelmed. "Thank you."

"Oh, wait a minute," he stopped her. "I want D.J. to do hers at the same time."

He handed an identical package to Delancey and sat back with a huge smile. "You're going to like these," he told them, obviously feeling proud of himself.

The girls looked at each other and then tore open the paper. They gasped when they saw the boxes.

"Mini stereos!" Mackenzie exclaimed.

"You'll love 'em," Jack jumped right in. "You see, they have speakers for your room, but the players themselves are portable with headphones and all. You can play the radio or a tape, and these little speakers sound very good. They're really clear."

"Thank you," they said quietly, both so surprised that it took a moment for them to smile.

Jack smiled as if he'd received the gifts himself.

"Okay, now one for your mother." With that, Jack put a heavy box at Marrell's feet.

She eyed him suspiciously even after he winked at her, and she tore back the paper. "Jackson, what have you done?" she asked again.

"I've been in your kitchen, Marrell," he said practically. "You need one of these."

Inside the box was a Kitchen Aid mixer with every possible attachment. Marrell didn't know what to say. She wasn't given a chance. Jack was handing out gifts again, and the women soon learned that this had been only the start. The girls got necklaces and a basketball. Marrell received a bracelet, candy, and a pile of books. The last gift for her was two tickets to the theater to see *Fiddler on the Roof* in January.

It was such a lovely surprise and made better when the girls jumped up, feeling none of their mother's attitude, went to the bag by the door, and brought Jack's gifts to him.

"Well now," he said, looking delighted, "two gifts. Which shall I open first?"

"The smaller one," Delancey wasted no time in saying.

"All right." Jack tore the paper away and moments later brought forth a navy silk tie.

"This is beautiful," he said seriously.

"We made it," Delancey filled in, and Jack looked over to see the girls smiling at him.

"You made this?"

"Mom helped," Mackenzie explained, and Jack looked to that woman.

"I'm amazed."

Marrell smiled shyly at him, and Delancey ordered Jack to open the other one.

"That one is from Mom."

Jack smiled at the younger girl before pulling a shirt from the box. It was a fine wool plaid in navy and green. Jack had never had anything like it. It took a moment for him to see that there was no tag in the collar.

"Did you make this?" he asked.

Marrell nodded, her lip tucked in her teeth again.

"You told me you sewed, but I had no idea, Marrell. I'm astounded."

"Put it on," Delancey ordered. "We want to see if it fits."

"I'll do it."

A moment later he was gone, and the women looked at each other.

"I can't believe how cool all this stuff is." Mackenzie's voice was wowed. "I can't believe he shopped for us."

"Isn't he funny —" Marrell shook her head. "He just went slightly crazy."

The girls laughed, and then Jack was back, looking wonderful in his new shirt. Marrell went right to him and fingered the collar and touched the shoulders for fit. She liked what she saw.

"How does it feel?"

"Perfect. This fabric is incredible. Thank you so much."

Marrell smiled.

"Why don't you two work on cleaning up the papers in here?" Marrell suggested to the girls. "I'll head into the kitchen and see how things are coming." She left as soon as she said this, missing the way the girls came forward, kissed Jack's cheek, and thanked him. He grinned at them in delight, wiggled those mobile eyebrows again, and said he was going to help their mother.

"Oh, Jack," Marrell sighed when she saw him. "You made everything so nice."

"It was my pleasure. Did you put the bracelet on?"

Marrell looked at him. "No, I'll get it before we eat."

She went back to the salad dressing she was mixing, not even turning when she felt him move beside her. But a moment later Jack's hand curved gently around her jaw, and he moved her face so he could softly kiss her mouth. He'd never done anything more than touch her hand or arm, so she was quite surprised.

"Why did you do that?" she whispered.

"I was rather hoping it might help you say what I've been reading in your eyes since you arrived."

Marrell looked up at him, her heart in her throat. For a moment she was at a loss, and then she remembered. She suddenly dug into the front pocket of her jeans and pulled out a scrap of paper. She handed it to him. It smelled of cedar.

Jack opened the folded note and read to himself, *I hope I can find a way to tell Jackson that I've fallen in love with him.*

Jack took her in his arms; he could do nothing else. Marrell felt him tremble with emotion. Her own arms clung to him until he shifted so he could see her face.

"I love you, Marrell Bishop," he finally said.

"I love you, Jackson Avery," Marrell told him, tears filling her eyes.

Jack kissed her cheek and nose and then her mouth before wrapping his arms around her again. They were still standing in each other's arms when they realized they weren't alone. Both turned their heads to the room's other occupant.

"You're hugging?" a vulnerable-looking Mackenzie asked.

"Come here, Mic," Jack turned, beckoning to the 15-year-old with one arm around Marrell. He hugged her with the other arm, but her eyes were on his face.

"Please don't leave us, Jack," she said softly, her lips trembling uncontrollably. "Please don't leave us like my dad did."

"Oh, Micki." Jack's whisper was tortured as he put both arms around her. "My sweet Mackenzie. I'll be here for you," he told her, because he believed with all of his heart that he would.

Mackenzie cried against him, aware that her mother was hugging him from the back.

"Are you all crying in there?" Delancey's wobbly voice came from around the corner.

"Yes," Marrell managed, "Come in."

"I don't want to cry on Christmas Day."

"Well, come anyway."

Delancey tried to hold back, but she couldn't. She had to go in, and once she saw the tears in Jack's eyes, her own would not be stopped. He hugged her on her own before trying to get his arms around all three of them. They broke apart only when the oven timer began to buzz. Jack went to turn it off but came right back. He brushed the tangled mess of hair from Marrell's face and pressed a kiss to her brow before turning to the girls.

"Are you all right?" he asked, taking time to touch them both and smooth their hair as well.

They nodded, not able to speak yet. It was all so new and a little strange, but exciting too. Jack had such a confident air about him. He always seemed to have an answer, and whenever they were with him, they felt safe and cared-for. Both girls had been waiting for the adults' relationship to get physical, but it never had. Now that Jack was not just touching their mother but them as well, they were strangely comforted about the future.

"Why don't we put this meal on?" he suggested. "It's a bit early for dinner, but I'm hungry."

No one was ready to argue with that. The gravy was made, the stuffing scooped out, the potatoes whipped, and the salad dressing finished — all to *The Sound of Music* coming from the player in the living room. By 4:30 they were at the table, Marrell's gold bracelet in place, the girls in their necklaces, and all of them ready to eat.

Jack prayed, and Marrell realized the way he talked to God was one of the first things she had loved about him. His prayer was confident yet reverent. At the moment he was thankful for the food and for her and the girls, but Marrell's heart had another prayer.

Nineteen eighty-four is just around the corner. Let this be the year, Lord. Let D.J. and Mic find You this year. Maybe through Jack and his love for You, or through some way I've never thought of, but please move this year, holy Father, and save my girls.

February 1984

"I don't know how you can even think about giving up your apartment, Jack. It's too much to ask."

"Marrell —" his voice was patient without effort. He loved her and understood her fear. "I would not trade my wife and daughters for an apartment. Think about what you're saying. I'm ready to do this. Just come and look at this one."

But Marrell was having a hard time moving from the car. It had never occurred to her that they lived so differently until she had seen his apartment. She had never had a place to herself, and now she was in a panic that Jack would not have enough space to himself.

"You haven't seen our place except when we know you're coming," she explained. "It's like a girl's dorm most of the time — pantyhose and brassieres hanging in the bathroom to dry. Delancey and Mackenzie can be slobs if I don't keep on them."

"This apartment has two bathrooms — one in the master bedroom for us and one in the hall for the girls."

"Well, what if you find that it drives you crazy to share a bathroom with me? What happens then?"

In Jack's mind that was like panicking because they were going to sleep together: ridiculous. Something else was wrong, and it had nothing to do with the bathroom. Without speaking he got out of the car, came around to her side, and opened Marrell's door.

"Come on," he said firmly.

Marrell did so but frowned at him.

"We're going to go for a walk."

Marrell thought he was marching her up to the apartment and was so surprised to find out otherwise that she didn't protest when he took her arm and led her through the cars and down the sidewalk. They walked for some time in quiet. Marrell was the one to finally speak.

"I'm sorry I panicked back there. I'm just so sure you'll need your space, not be able to find it, and then leave the girls and me and break our hearts. After all, Jack, you have lived alone for a long time."

"I appreciate your caring about that, sweetheart, but I want you to make sure you're going to be all right. Is there a little corner of your mind that's afraid you won't have *your* own space? Are you afraid to live intimately with me?"

Marrell stopped. "No, I'm not. At first I was afraid I would think of Paul, but I don't. When you kiss me or hug me, I don't think of anyone but you."

"And how about the rest of it? Are you upset about having to share the same bed and bathroom with me? Do you feel I'm going to have expectations and be disappointed?"

"No," she said, but she didn't sound sure even to her own ears. "I have worried a little bit about the fact that I'm not 19 anymore, but you've never made me feel anything but desirable, so I've told myself to forget that."

"I'm glad, Marrell, because I don't want a 19-year-old. I want you. And in case you need to hear it outright, you have a wonderful figure."

She didn't look convinced. "Clothes can cover a lot of little imperfections."

"It's the same for men."

That statement was very freeing for Marrell. She didn't know why she thought he wouldn't understand.

"Marrell," he went on, "I think you'll be surprised by this place. I haven't looked at an apartment yet that fits our needs the way this does. I want you to see it. If you still want to talk about my space, we will, but I want you to see this first."

Marrell agreed. She had run out of steam trying to explain herself. They had taken the afternoon off to look for a place, and now she was wasting it by arguing with Jack. She went willingly back to the apartment, and just as Jack hoped, was in for a surprise. It was gorgeous.

Marrell had never seen the like. The kitchen, living room, and dining room were set up with a great-room effect. Large windows gave lots of light, and there was a huge stone fireplace in the living room. Marrell could only stare at it.

"Come this way," Jack invited her, standing back while she went down the hall and found two nice-sized bedrooms across from each other, a bathroom next to a bedroom on the right, and a laundry room across the hall from that. Marrell did not see what Jack considered the most important feature until they got to the end of the hall. He opened the master bedroom door, let her precede him, and began to speak.

"I'm trying to start a new life with a woman who has nearly grown daughters. I believe with all my heart that it's going to work beautifully, but we need our privacy, and the girls still need to feel that they have access to us, especially you."

Marrell took in his words even as her eyes gazed about in amazement. The bedroom had a sitting room and stairs up to where the bed would be. Also up on that level was a huge walk-in closet and bathroom.

"If I get up and want to dress, I can go in here and shut the door. The girls can still have access to you if they need it. We can just tell them that if the hall door is shut, they should knock; otherwise, they're welcome."

"This is why you wanted me to see this. It's perfect."

"I think so. The girls have privacy without being too far away, and so do we."

"It must cost a fortune."

"About a hundred dollars more than I pay now."

"Is your place as high as that?"

"It has a bay view," he reminded her. She needed no other explanation.

Marrell took another look around, checking out the closet and bath fixtures, and moved back down the hall.

"A laundry room." She stopped and stared. "How wonderful."

Jack smiled. He didn't have to ask her if she liked it. Her approval was written all over her face.

"I want you and the girls to move in as soon as

possible."

"Then you're going to feel as though you're moving into our place," she countered. "That's what I wanted to get away from. You move in first."

"Then you'll feel as though you're moving into my place. I think it's best if you three come here first."

Marrell thought for a moment. "We'll just wait. We'll move what we can, and since the girls are going to stay with Oliver and Shay while we go away, the four of us will all sleep here the first night we're back and not before."

Jack smiled. "Have you figured out a date?" It was something he asked her every day.

"Not yet, but I'll have one by the end of the week."

Jack kissed her and told her he hoped it would be soon.

Selecting a wedding date should have seemed like such an easy task, but there were so many associations to avoid: her birthday, Paul's birthday, the date of Paul's death in June, and if they waited for summer, the girls' birthdays and her wedding date to Paul in August.

The decision took until the end of the week, but Marrell finally made it. They would be married May 5. May was always a busy month, but this year they would just make it work. And then they would be husband and wife.

As they sat together and marked the day on the calendar, making little plans as they came to mind, Marrell's heart knew nothing but peace. God had blessed her beyond measure — to be loved by two men whose lives were sold out for Christ. The girls were another blessing. They hugged their mother when she told them they had

set a date and laughed in delight with her when
she told them the best was yet to come.

TWENTY-TWO

January 1986

"I want to join the Army."

Jack and Marrell Avery looked across the table at Mackenzie but didn't comment, the food on their plates momentarily forgotten. Delancey had been about to ask for the car so she could run to the mall, but she changed her mind, her own food ignored.

"What made you decide that?" Jack, who was the first to find his voice, asked.

"Well, everyone's been asking me what I'm going to do after I graduate, so I've been thinking about it a lot. Then today there was a recruiter at school. I got to talking to her, and, well, I just know this is what I want to do."

"Your life is not your own in the Army," her mother put in. "You're a very independent person, Mic. Are you ready to have someone telling you where you can be and when, when you will stand and sit, and where you'll live?"

"I've thought about all of that, Mom. I know it's not always easy, but if it was so bad, why did Dad stay in for more than 20 years?"

"Because he loved it," Marrell said simply. "But you know very well that we were thinking about his leaving the service. In fact, not just thinking

367

about it but trying to determine when. He was not willing to be away from us again, but if he had stayed in, he would have had no choice."

Mackenzie nodded, but she still wanted to do this. It was a sudden announcement for Jack and her mother, she knew, but not sudden for her. Things had been in an upheaval before Thanksgiving when her mother had started to sort through some boxes of things that had been more or less forgotten. Most were her grandmother's things and a few boxes from Jack's sisters, who, he said, were always cleaning. But some boxes held many of Delancey and Mackenzie's remembrances, and they ended up needing to go through their own paraphernalia. That's when Mackenzie found her old Army recruiting poster. She hadn't been able to get it from her mind.

"Where would you go?" Delancey asked.

"I'm not sure right now. All those details will come out later when I join."

Both adults caught the fact that she said *when* and not *if.*

"How long have you been thinking of this, Mic?" Jack wanted to know. "This isn't the type of thing you do on a whim."

"It's been on my mind for a few months," she admitted. "I even had a chance to talk with Trina's mom one day after basketball practice. She was a Wac, and she said she wouldn't trade those years for anything."

Marrell forced herself not to look at her husband. They didn't have anything going on tonight, so she would have plenty of time to vent her spleen in the privacy of their room.

"Are you still going to the mall?" Mackenzie suddenly asked her sister with a maddening

368

change of subject.

"I want to."

"I'll go with you."

"All right," Delancey agreed, pleased to have company and even to let Mackenzie drive.

"How long will you be gone?" their stepfather asked.

"Well, it closes at 9:00 and we'll come right home."

"All right. Whose night is it for dishes?"

Marrell almost volunteered for duty but stopped herself. She needed to stay controlled, and if the girls left right now, she would be crying within seconds of their leaving.

"I think mine," Delancey spoke up. Jack studied her serious eyes and knew she was thinking about her sister's announcement.

They all helped clear the table, as was their pattern, but then each wandered off on his own pursuit. Jack wanted to be near Marrell but held off until the girls left, moving to the bedroom instead. Mackenzie went to her room to get ready to go, and Marrell headed to the living room to try and get her mind into a magazine article she had been reading. The idea didn't work, but it gave her time to think.

I'm not ready for this, Lord, and I thought I was. I've known for so long that she would grow up and leave me, but now that it's here, I'm stunned. Would it be easier if I knew that she was taking You along? I don't know. And D.J. — her face was as shocked as mine. Mic has been bringing home college information but not doing anything about it. I thought she was headed to the junior college. She could end up anywhere and be gone for months at a time. Last Christmas might have been the last one with her for who knows how many years. She'll take her leave where she wants to, and it might not be here. I can hardly stand the thought of saying goodbye.

"Goodbye, Mom." Delancey was suddenly beside her, bending low to kiss her cheek. Mackenzie was right behind her.

"Have fun," Marrell said sincerely.

"Okay. Did you want me to look for that cookbook you wanted, Mom?" Mackenzie asked.

"Sure. If you spot it, let me know."

"Okay. 'Bye."

Marrell waved, waited for the door to close, and then put the magazine aside. Jack was with her just moments later.

"It's a lot of things living with Mackenzie, but boring isn't one of them." Jack's humor was still in place.

"I'm still in shock," Marrell admitted. "I was prepared to have her go away, even live on campus somewhere, but this never entered my mind."

"I suppose it's ridiculous to think that she might not get in."

Marrell's look was telling. "She's a picture of health, drug free, and one of the most driven and mentally strong people I've ever known. She's her father's child from the toes up."

Jack had little to say to that. "I could hardly look at Delancey. I think she's utterly crushed. Do you think they will talk about it?"

"If D.J. has anything to say about it, they will. Left up to Mic, it wouldn't happen. But Delancey needs to talk about everything."

The Bishop girls were a remarkable blend of contrasts and mixtures. With her blond hair and blue eyes, Delancey had her mother's coloring, but her figure, the willowy length of her, was all

370

from Paul's side of the family. Mackenzie had her father's coloring, the dark hair and unusual gray-green eyes, but the curves that filled out jeans and sweatshirts were her mother's all the way. Both were attractive, but Delancey was a beauty, catching the eye of most who saw her. She also laughed easier. Mackenzie was usually the one to make her laugh, and there was often a glint of humor in her eye that warned Marrell she was about to say or do something outrageous. But from all outward appearances, Mackenzie had the more serious nature.

Mackenzie could go for days without talking about a problem, and no one would be the wiser. With Delancey, Marrell knew within minutes or hours if something was wrong. Delancey could not let an upset or an argument go unsettled. Mackenzie could walk away from a fight, even believing she was right, and never mention it again.

"What are you thinking?" Jack asked the woman he loved.

Marrell smiled at him. "About how different they are."

Jack laughed.

"What?"

"I was just going over how much they're alike."

"Like what?"

"Both so creative, and when they love, they love with their whole hearts. I mean, D.J. tends to say the words more often, but Mic is never afraid to hug me or put her arm around you. And their love for Shay and Oliver's kids is so special. They're both nuts about Jana and can't get enough of her brother Josh. They're still very protective of you and even me to a point. Both are good athletes and students." Jack finished and looked at her.

"I guess I was thinking more of their looks and personalities."

Jack nodded. There was no denying the differences there. A moment later he rose from the chair, started a fire, and joined Marrell on the couch. She fit so nicely under his arm and always smelled so good. He said as much.

"It's that new cologne you gave me for Christmas."

"I must have very good taste."

Marrell kissed his cheek. "I don't want to over-react, Jackson, but this is a big step on her part."

"Yes, it is, but I do have one question for you."

"What's that?"

"How good of a soldier would she be?"

Marrell could only stare at him, and Jack smiled tenderly at her.

"You need to let her be who she is, sweetheart, even if it breaks your heart."

Tears filled her eyes. "I think it might."

Jack hugged her close and didn't ask any more questions. He was sure there was much more on Marrell's mind, as there was on his own, but for the moment, he didn't ask.

"You'll have to wear that ugly green," Delancey now said, and Mackenzie laughed. "And the pants are always so baggy. They won't do a thing for your figure. You'll look gross, Mic, and we both know it."

It wasn't like Delancey to be so comical, but at the moment Mackenzie couldn't speak for laughing. The conversation hadn't started out so lightly. Delancey had flat-out told her sister that she was being ridiculous and to stay home. When Mackenzie didn't answer, Delancey got angry. But before they actually gained the mall entrance, Delancey had apologized and asked her sister if she was really going to go.

"Yes, I am. I know it seems sudden for everyone, but I feel very good about this. I want you to be happy and excited for me, D.J., and try to put yourself in my place. In just a year, you'll be in your last semester of high school and wanting to get out and do something too."

Delancey hadn't answered, and in order to cope with her emotions, she had taken a page from Mackenzie's book and started to joke. If she hadn't, she might have cried in the mall.

"Well, there is one great advantage," Delancey finally said.

"What's that?"

"How does the song go? 'A million handsome guys with longing in their eyes.' "

"Leave it to you to think of that."

"Don't tell me you haven't."

Mackenzie only smiled, but in truth, the men who might be joining with her, or any male commanding officers she would encounter, were the last thing on her mind. If she had really been pressed to answer, she wouldn't have been able to say exactly why she wanted to join the Army. Her father had done it, but beyond that, she only wanted a change. She loved Jack and her mother, but she was ready to get out and do something on her own. The pictures in the brochure looked wonderful. Mackenzie was wise enough to know that it wasn't all fun and games, but her father had seen some of the world while stationed in Germany, Korea, and various parts of the United

States. Mackenzie wanted that same opportunity to travel and see the world.

Wrapped up with their own thoughts, both girls wandered through Stonestown Mall, not really looking at anything in particular. Delancey tried on a jacket, and they both had ice cream before leaving, but it wasn't long before they were on their way home.

In the living room of the apartment, Jack was watching television and their mother's nose was buried in a crossword puzzle. The four talked for a few minutes, and Delancey even joined Jack in front of the television, but it wasn't long before Mackenzie headed to her room. Marrell wasn't far behind her.

"May I come in?" the older woman asked after she knocked on the doorjamb.

"Sure."

Marrell found Mackenzie lying back on her pillows, but her eyes were wide open. She had a book close by, but it wasn't open. Marrell came in and sat on the chair. For a moment she only stared at her daughter.

"I love you. You do know that, don't you, Mic?"

Mackenzie smiled. "Yeah. I love you too, Mom. Are you upset about the Army?"

"I was at first, but I know what a good soldier you'll be, Mic, so that's not my reservation."

"What is it then?"

"A few things. The distance is a big factor. It's hard to think of you being so far away."

Mackenzie nodded, but then Marrell opted to be as honest with her daughter as she always had been. "The hardest part is the spiritual aspect, but I know I'd be feeling that way no matter where you went."

Mackenzie did not immediately reply, but it wasn't because she didn't know to what her mother referred. It was merely something she didn't feel she needed. She clearly remembered the day her father had come home from Germany and explained his salvation experience to them, and then just after that at the cabin in Tahoe when her mother had come to the same conclusion.

In conversations she'd had with Jack and her mother over the years, they had told her that her choice not to believe was rebellion against God. Mackenzie didn't agree. She wasn't saying anything against God, she just knew she didn't need Him the way her mother and Jack did.

"I know what you're going to say, Mom," Mackenzie said softly. "I know you're going to tell me that I'm rebelling and that I need to turn to God."

"Actually I wasn't," Marrell stated honestly. "I just wanted you to know that I'm praying for you and to tell you one other thing. No matter where you go, Mic, be it here in the States or overseas, God is there. That might sound like an obvious thing, but I still wanted to say it. You might find yourself very alone and very far from home at some point. God can be found everywhere, Mic. Don't ever forget that."

"Thanks, Mom. Is Jack upset about this?"

"No. In fact, he's the one who reminded me what a good soldier you'll be. His words helped me a lot. The Army needs good enlisted personnel on whom they can depend. I have no doubt that no matter what area you end up in, you'll be one of the finest in your rank."

"Thank you, Mom," she said softly, her heart filling with warmth.

Marrell's words did a world of good for Mackenzie. She wasn't uncertain about her decision, but it wasn't something she wanted to do with everyone frowning at her. She knew her sister had covered her own feelings with jokes and laughter. Indeed, when the time came, it would be hard to leave everyone. But the excitement of this venture outweighed any fear of the unknown or the ache of separation.

"Are you doing this for your dad, Micki?" her mother suddenly asked.

Mackenzie's head tipped to one side. "Yes and no. I mean, I'm doing it for me, but I would want Dad to be proud of me."

"He always was."

"Yeah." Mackenzie's voice was soft with remembrance. "I still miss him."

"I know what you mean. It won't be four years until June, but it feels so much longer."

"I dreamed about him the other night. It was weird because he was here in this apartment, and of course he never was. Jack was even a part of the dream, which was really strange."

"But not all that surprising. After all, Mic, they're two men who have played key roles in your life. Did it keep you awake or bother you?"

"No, I didn't remember it until morning, and then I didn't think of it again until just now."

Marrell nodded but then realized she'd gotten slightly off course. "Mackenzie, I need to ask you something that might seem clear to you, but I want to be sure I've got this right."

"Okay."

"Are you definite about the Army, or are you still thinking?"

"I'm definite."

"Okay," Marrell said softly. Having expected

this, she wasn't upset. "What's the next step?"

"A trip to the recruiter's office to start the paperwork and physical."

Marrell nodded. "I trust you'll keep us informed?"

"Yes. They strongly encourage the family's involvement, and because I'm not 18 yet, I would need you along anyhow." Mackenzie stopped for a moment, her mind working. "Mom, do you want to tell me no? Do you wish I was still a kid so you could just put your foot down and say, 'Absolutely not'?"

"In the first few seconds I did, but right now I honestly don't wish that. I can't say that I'm used to the idea yet, but I wouldn't want to forbid you even if I could. I know you'll have tremendous opportunities in the Army — chances you wouldn't have in college — but as I said at the table, your life will not be your own, and I wonder how you'll do with that."

"I guess I'll find out," Mackenzie said softly. Marrell thought it was a good note to end on.

"I'd better let you get some sleep. If you don't graduate, you won't be going anywhere."

Mackenzie smiled at her. Marrell came close to hug and kiss her goodnight before joining Jack in the living room. He was still engrossed in the TV special, so she sat quietly beside him. Thinking of the evening and how swiftly life could change, her mind drifted far and wide. It was a great surprise to have Jack touch her arm.

"Did I fall asleep?"

"About 20 minutes ago. Why don't we head to bed?"

"Okay. I didn't kiss D.J."

"She kissed me and told me to give one to you."

Marrell nodded and Jack kissed her, but she was too groggy to respond. She came to her feet and realized that the television was off. Jack's hand was at her back as they moved down the hall, and with little preparation for bed, Marrell climbed beneath the covers, still trying to work out why she felt so spent. It was morning before she fully remembered that her oldest daughter was joining the Army.

March

"You would think I'd be used to this," Marrell commented softly to Jack as they followed the girls into the recruiting office.

"This is not your husband, Marrell. It's your daughter, and it's not going to feel the same. As you reminded me, you weren't around to experience any of this firsthand."

Marrell nodded and reached for his hand as they continued down the hallway. She had not met Paul Bishop until he was an officer. He had certainly told her about his training and all the places he'd been stationed, but it wasn't like living through it with her daughter.

"Mackenzie, come in," Sergeant Clare Wallace said as soon as she saw her new recruit.

"Hello, Sergeant Wallace. I want to introduce you to my family. This is my mother, Marrell Avery, my stepfather, Jack Avery, and my sister, Delancey."

"It's a pleasure to meet you," she said as she shook their hands. "Please have a seat."

There was no missing Mackenzie's excitement. She didn't even let her back rest against the chair.

"Well, Mackenzie, have you and your family read over the pamphlets I gave you?"

"Yes, we've read everything, and I did write down some questions. My mom did too."

"Okay. Let's go over them."

The questions were standard fare for Sergeant Wallace. Where was basic training? When would Mackenzie join? How would she get to the training base? How long would it be before she qualified for leave? Did she need to join for a certain amount of time right now, or could that decision wait for a while? And on it went. The sergeant answered everything they asked and more, and when they ran out of subjects, she had questions for Mackenzie.

"There is something important I want you to understand, Mackenzie. A fact many people miss is that while the Army needs capable men and women who can perform their jobs with competence, it's also true that the Army has something special for you. It's important that I know about your interests and strengths."

Having read this in the brochures, Mackenzie only nodded.

Sergeant Wallace asked her about her hobbies and even more personal things, such as whether she had a boyfriend, what type of grades she got, and if she'd ever been in trouble with the police. It took quite awhile, and interspersed with all of the sergeant's queries were more questions from Mackenzie, her mother, and Jack.

"At this point, Mackenzie," the Army recruiter said after almost two hours of interview, "you need to tell me what you want to do. You are welcome to go home and think about your decision and discuss it with your family. Or do you want me to start scheduling appointments for your aptitude test and physical exam?"

Mackenzie looked over at her mother and Jack.

Marrell smiled at her, and Jack said, "If this is what you want, Mic, your mother and I will support you."

She smiled at them before turning back to Clare Wallace.

"Please schedule the exams."

"I'll do it. Because you won't be 18 until June, you'll be entering the DEP, which is the Delayed Entry Program I spoke with you about. We'll get everything else out of the way so that when the time comes you can proceed as smoothly as possible."

Again, all Mackenzie could do was nod. They were at the office for another 30 minutes with the scheduling. Mackenzie was quiet on the way out to the car, but she was thinking. A number of things could block her chances, but she was confident of her grades and athletic ability. She hadn't said much about her father being in the Army, even though the sergeant had asked why she wanted to join. But right now her father was heavy on her heart. Mackenzie would have loved some time alone just to think about him, but at the moment someone else needed her.

"Are you all right, D.J.?" Mackenzie asked after Jack started the car and began to drive home. There was no missing the younger girl's tears.

"I don't know. I just can't believe you're going. I'm not mad or anything. It's just so strange."

Mackenzie nodded, and the adults in the front seat said nothing. "You know," the older girl said softy, "it's not as if I can't come home, or you can't come to see me. You could visit me, D.J. It's not the same, I know, but we can still talk on the phone and write and stuff."

Delancey looked over at her. "Do you remember when we were all set to go get Dad at the airport, and he came in early and was there in the morning?"

"Yeah. That was fun."

"You could do that, couldn't you? Fly in and surprise us?"

"I could, yes. In fact, military personnel get a discount."

The short conversation seemed to help for the moment. The girls fell silent, but it wasn't an uncomfortable lull. Jack thought that lunch out might be a nice treat, but he hadn't counted on Marrell's reaction. One look at her profile told him that she wasn't so at ease. He kept his mouth shut and drove straight home.

"You do know that she's searching, don't you, Jack? It's so clear!"

Jack watched his pacing wife but didn't comment. The girls were in front of a video with a huge bowl of popcorn, and husband and wife had retreated to the bedroom.

"She's just like me — so stubborn and headstrong. If only God would get ahold of her."

"Do you want me to answer any of this or just listen?"

The deep, quiet tone of her husband's voice stopped all movement. Marrell came over to drop into a chair across from him.

"What would you say?"

"I would say that if she's so much like you were before you came to Christ, then you know exactly how to pray. I would say that if you remember what it's like, then you know very well that all the talking in the world isn't going to change anything.

She has to do this on her own, and just like you at one point, she doesn't believe she needs a Savior right now."

He was right, of course, and for a moment Marrell only looked at him.

"It's true," she confessed. "Shay came to Christ, and I just thought she was off on another tangent. I was certain it wasn't for me. Then the hole inside of me — the one that seemed impossible to fill — got so big that I couldn't push it away."

"Sounds to me like you know just how to pray," Jack told her. "And if you think that getting mad at her or the Lord will help, you're in for double the pain."

"I have been angry. At times I've been furious. I would have said it was with Mackenzie, but we both know better."

"God can take your anger, honey. He can handle it. I'm glad you're not shutting Mic out or acting cold toward her, but at the same time, you need to see the anger as a sinful response. You're just a little quieter these days, and that's fine, as long as you're not simmering with anger."

Marrell nodded.

"Take all the time you can with her, Marrell," Jack advised. "When someone leaves home and breaks your heart in the process, there's a strong temptation to wall up your heart so it won't hurt so much. Don't do it. Enjoy your daughter and love her with all your heart. I'm not saying that because I don't think you'll see her again, but when a child leaves home, it's never quite the same. It might be better, but no matter what, your role will change. Mackenzie doesn't need a mother so much as she needs a friend. Be that friend to her."

As if Jack had called her, Mackenzie knocked and stuck her head in the door.

"Mom, we've got the movie paused at your favorite part — you know, where Tevye gives Tzeitel permission to marry Motel, and they sing that song in the woods. Come watch."

"I'll be right there."

Mackenzie disappeared, and Marrell came to her feet and went to Jack. She leaned over and kissed him.

"Thank you," she said softly before walking out to join her daughters.

TWENTY-THREE

Fort Leonard Wood
Waynesville, Missouri
August 1986

Mackenzie could not remember how she'd gotten there or even what her legs felt like. She had been so excited to join. She had volunteered — no one had forced her — and now they were trying to kill her. She didn't know when she had felt such pain. Her legs and feet were throbbing, and the heat and bugs were enough to send her screaming into the night. She wouldn't, of course — not because she was afraid of the repercussions, but because it was too painful to stand.

At least the day is over, she thought, her body a mass of aches. *I can sleep.* But it wasn't that easy when she was two weeks away from home and in a strange bed. Only a week and a half of actual training had taken place, but it felt as though she'd been gone forever. She could still see Delancey's tear-filled eyes and her mother's wobbly smile. Jack's hug had been especially warm, and at the moment Mackenzie couldn't remember why she had left.

You'll have to wear that ugly green. You'll look gross, Mic, and we both know it.

Delancey's words from so long ago leapt into

384

her mind. Mackenzie wanted to laugh, but a small sob broke in her throat. Sore as she was, the young Army recruit managed to turn over so that her cries could be muffled by her pillow.

Mackenzie woke up with Jack on her mind. It was the first Sunday in September, his forty-fourth birthday. She wished she could have seen him, or at least talked with him or been a part of the party they were sure to have with Oliver, Shay, and the kids. Mackenzie realized at the same time that things did not look quite as grim as they had. She received word from her mother every week, twice from Jack, and from Delancey every other day. Mackenzie had actually found time to write a letter herself, and she now made plans to walk to the base post office to mail it. She didn't have to. She could put the envelope in the mailbox outside her barracks, but she had three hours before she had to report for inspection and opted to get out for a time.

The next day started her fifth week of training, so she didn't want to overdo. Still, she could already feel a difference in herself. Some of her platoon mates had been quite sedentary before they joined, and they were still feeling pretty sore, but Mackenzie had a very active lifestyle. Indeed, just before she had graduated, she'd gone to state with several other girls on the 4 x 200 relay team. They hadn't won, but not one girl was ashamed of the second-place medals they all received.

"Hey, Mackenzie!" a voice called from behind her. She turned to see one of the women from the barracks rushing her way. Kim Rivers, a petite blond, caught up with her and fell into step.

"Tatum said you were going to the post office.

May I walk with you?"

"Sure."

Mackenzie didn't know this woman very well — her bunk was on the other end of the barracks — but she didn't mind the company.

"Where are you from, Mackenzie?" Kim asked, and Mackenzie had the impression she was desperate to talk. Mackenzie wasn't, but neither did she mind a little conversation.

"San Francisco. How about you?"

"Dallas."

Mackenzie smiled. She had caught the soft accent, and as she glanced over, also noticed a swift, vulnerable look in the other girl's eyes. It strongly reminded her of Delancey, and for the first time since she arrived, she allowed herself to open up to someone.

"I lived in San Antonio when I was a girl. My father was stationed at Fort Sam Houston."

"Your father is in the Army?" Kim sounded delighted.

"He was. He died a few years ago."

"I'm sorry, Mackenzie. Is this hard for you?"

"It is a little. I haven't thought about it too much, but I'm starting to. He did all this long before I was born — you know, basic and all that — but he was stationed here. It's easy now to see what it must have been like. Before this I never knew what he faced, and now that I'd like to ask him all about it, he's not here."

Silence fell between them for a few moments. Mackenzie could have stayed quiet, but realizing what she'd just revealed, she knew she would have to be the one to speak first or Kim would feel she had intruded.

"What field are you hoping to go into, Kim?"

386

"I've thought a little about finance and administration."

Mackenzie nodded. "My scores were high in math too, but I'm still thinking about where I want to head."

"I'd like a listing overseas."

This surprised Mackenzie, but she admitted, "I would too. My father was stationed in Germany, France, and Korea. France was before I was born, and we didn't get to go with him to Korea or Germany. I don't feel like I've been anywhere."

"My family travels a lot, so I have been to the Continent and all over, but I'd still like to get out of the Lower 48. I could live with Hawaii."

Mackenzie laughed. "Kayla Bolton — she's in the bunk next to me — says she prays for a posting in Hawaii every night. She's from there, and it just about killed her to come to Missouri."

"I think it kills *Missouri* people to be here." Kim's voice was dry, but Mackenzie had to agree with a small laugh. In truth, she'd never felt such humidity. Florida had been bad, but not like this.

They were finally at the post office. Mackenzie disposed of her letters, Kim did the same, and Mackenzie bought stamps. They talked of nothing in particular on the way back to the barracks and nothing at all when the time got away and they nearly had to run. Being late was something they didn't want to think about.

"Do you call that a shot, Martin?" Sergeant Waxley shouted at the woman next to Mackenzie.

"Sir, no, sir," Tatum Martin responded from her position on the ground.

"Try it again," Waxley barked, moving on.

Mackenzie remained quiet, concentrating on her

own firing and thinking about how uncomplicated it seemed to her. For some reason Mackenzie had taken to shooting. She wasn't perfect, but compared to the three other women with whom she was assigned to the rifle range, she was an expert. In truth, the gun did not frighten her as it did some recruits. That she was comfortable with it from the moment it was handed to her seemed to go a long way. It also went a long way with her companions, two of whom approached her that night.

"She takes you apart about your wall locker, Micki," Tatum complained, "but you can do no wrong on the rifle range."

Both Tatum and Kayla were sitting on Kayla's bed. Mackenzie was on her own across from them. The three were speaking in hushed tones.

"You both did better today," Mackenzie encouraged them. "And she didn't yell as much at the end as when we first got out there. I think you're too hard on yourselves."

"Maybe, but we still want to know your secret."

"I don't have one, and stop looking at me as if I'm holding out on you. I'm just comfortable and accurate, that's all. I certainly can't say that about everything, and you both know it. You saw how I was with the map. I thought Waxley would have apoplexy. You got us out of that swamp, Kayla, or I'd still be out there."

The women would have laughed, but a "lights out" shout came from the other end of the room. Waxley was on the way, her eyes missing nothing. Tatum swiftly slipped over to her own bunk, and Mackenzie and Kayla made a point of not looking at her or each other before they climbed beneath their own covers. And not a moment too soon:

Lights out came just moments later.

Mackenzie had to smother the laughter that bubbled inside her. The cartoons that Delancey had drawn on her letter were hysterical. A caricature of Mackenzie in fatigues was the funniest thing Mackenzie had ever seen. D.J. had done a remarkable job with the bayonet that "Private Bishop" was using to pick her teeth. She only had time to skim the contents of the letter, and in so doing caught Delancey's line about "a million handsome guys . . ."

Mackenzie was not able to finish. It was the final week of basic training, and graduation started in two hours. The instructors had tried again to run them to death during the week with a 15-mile march, field training exercises, and practice for graduation, but Mackenzie had made it. Kim, Tatum, and Kayla too.

In just two hours their unit would be presented to the commander. Having grown up with an Army father, Mackenzie had never before noticed just how much ceremony was involved in the military. It didn't matter what was accomplished, it was done ceremonially. Now it was her turn.

If you can see me, Dad, or hear me — I did it. I made it through basic. I did it for both of us.

Mackenzie didn't have time to think of him again. Never a day where it mattered more, her uniform today needed to be in perfect order, and she hadn't even started polishing her shoes. Some of the other women were obviously feeling the same way. Several who had also been going through their papers and mail began to ready for the ceremony. Indeed, the time was flying. Inside of 90 minutes, she would be on the parade

389

grounds.

Mackenzie had just given Tatum a hug and watched as she joined her family farther down the grass when someone called her name. She turned to see Kim heading her way.

"We made it!" Kim exclaimed, and the women hugged.

"That we did. Doesn't it feel good?"

"Yes. I was so proud of you when they called your name for that expert marksmanship badge, Micki. You'd think I was the one getting it."

Mackenzie laughed. Kim had become a good friend over the last weeks.

"Listen, Micki," she said suddenly, "I want you to meet my folks."

"Okay."

Kim smiled hugely before she turned to the couple that approached. Seconds later Mackenzie met Madeline and Kenneth Rivers. She smiled kindly and spoke with them for a moment, but her throat felt clogged with tears. It never occurred to her, until it was too late to get flights, to ask her mother and Jack to come. Right now she couldn't even think about Delancey, or she would be in tears. It was a relief to have the Riverses do most of the talking. Ken had been in the Army before his marriage to Maddy, and it was interesting to hear how procedures had changed.

They asked Mackenzie to join them for a meal, but she was ready to be alone. Kim seemed to understand, and Mackenzie was glad. She thought about her friend even as she walked away. It was hard to say if they would see each other much in the future, if at all. It would be another few days before she learned that her hunch was right. Kim was headed to New Jersey, but Mackenzie's next assignment was at the Army's finance center and school — Fort Benjamin Harrison, Indianapolis, Indiana.

San Francisco
November 1986
"What's in this?" Delancey held up a large manila envelope for her mother's inspection.

Sitting at the desk in the corner of the kitchen, both women were looking through old photos and papers.

"I don't know." Marrell squinted at it. "Open it and see."

The 17-year-old pinched the clasp, pushed up the flap, and drew forth a stack of papers.

"*Micah Bear in the Rain,*" she read out loud.

"Oh, that would be one of Micki's stories. She was looking for those. I wonder how they got into my desk."

Delancey glanced through them. Remarkably prolific, Mackenzie had filled every page with her messy scrawl, and Delancey found it too depressing.

"I feel like she's been gone forever."

"I miss her too."

"She doesn't write as much as I thought she would." Delancey's complaint was not new, but Marrell was not going to indulge her. A high schooler, at least *this* high schooler, had no real idea of what hard work could be like.

"She's not on vacation, D.J. The Army is a lot of work. I know that doesn't make her silence any easier, but I can tell you that she's very busy learning new skills. It's much like being in college."

Suddenly Marrell was very glad she hadn't met

391

Paul until after he was commissioned as an officer.

Delancey's thoughts were elsewhere. Her sister had joined the Army for three years and been gone only four months. Right now Delancey didn't know how she would survive the time. Had she known it, her parents were just as concerned about her.

"I never considered the girls' relationship a problem, Jack," Marrell had mentioned to him just two days past. "I mean the girls have always been very close, and I never felt it was a problem, but now that Delancey's on her own, she's lost. From Mckenzie's letters, I don't know if she is much better. The girls have never been good at making girlfriends, and I'm just now seeing that. I wonder what I could have done to have avoided this."

Jack did not have an immediate answer for her, and Marrell would not have said anything to Delancey, but it was true. She prayed for Delancey right then, but for the moment decided to keep her mouth shut.

"I'd better get something to eat," Delancey said as she put the envelope aside.

"Oh, that's right. I forgot about your babysitting job. When does Shay expect you?"

"At six o'clock."

"All right. You'd better call and remind them you'll need a ride home. I don't want you driving that late."

"It might not be that late — probably between ten and eleven o'clock."

"Well, either way they can bring you, or Jack can come and get you if that would be easier."

"Are you going to take me there or is Jack?"

"I probably will, why?"

"I want to stop at the grocery store, and Jack might not get home from work in time to stop."

"All right. Go call Shay and then eat. I'll get you to the store and to Shay's on time. Don't forget your homework."

"I won't," Delancey answered tiredly, but she would have loved to. Babysitting Jana and Josh Lacy was about the only bright spot on her calendar these days. She would do her homework, but only after she'd played as long as she could with Jana and Josh.

The no-smoking signs had come on, and the pilot had already asked the flight attendants to prepare for arrival. It wasn't as early as Mackenzie had hoped it would be, but at least this way she knew her family would be home. By the time she deplaned and caught a taxi, they might be in bed, but Mackenzie was quite certain they would forgive her the late hour.

Missouri and Indiana seemed a long way off. In truth, she hadn't been away from home that long, but a lot had certainly happened. She missed her mother, Jack, and Delancey terribly and could laugh with sheer joy just at the thought of seeing them, but she was not sorry she had left. At times she was so lonely for family that she would have quit if given the chance, but those moments were rare. And now with this latest posting . . .

The plane bounced a few times on landing, but Mackenzie barely noticed. She was in the eleventh row, so she was off the plane swiftly. With nothing to check, her kit bag dangling from one shoulder, she walked through San Francisco International Airport in better shape than she'd ever been.

Within minutes she was hailing a cab and giving her address. The ride home wasn't going to be cheap, but it would be well worth the investment.

The eleven o'clock news had just started when Marrell realized she was too tired to watch. She wanted to go to bed, but Jack was bringing Delancey home, and after her daughter's depressed reaction to Mackenzie's absence earlier that day, she wanted to have a word with her. Marrell was reaching for the remote control when the doorbell rang.

"You could wait for Jack to park the car, D.J.," Marrell muttered under her breath. "I might have been in the bathroom."

Marrell froze when she saw her oldest daughter. Not until Mackenzie raised her hand and saluted did Marrell respond.

"Private Bishop reporting for duty."

"Oh, Micki," Marrell cried, her arms reaching to hug her. Both women were instantly awash with tears. Mackenzie had the foresight to close the door, but after doing so they just stood with their arms wrapped around each other.

"Look at you," Marrell gasped. "This uniform. Your father would be so —" she couldn't go on.

Mackenzie wiped at her own tears, her face more lean than Marrell had ever seen it.

"Where are Jack and D.J.?" Mackenzie finally managed.

"Oh, quick," Marrell said suddenly. "Into the kitchen. We'll surprise them."

"Where are they?" she asked, even as her mother pushed her along.

"D.J. was babysitting for Jana and Josh."

"Here." Mackenzie pushed a tissue into her

394

mother's hands. "You'd better dry up or they'll know."

"That's true," Marrell said, but she couldn't manage it. When they heard the front door open not five minutes later, she stayed where she was.

"Is that you, D.J.?"

"It's Jack."

"Where's D.J.?"

"Right behind me."

"Can you send her into the kitchen?"

"Sure. Did you hear that, D.J.?"

"Yeah. What did you need?" Delancey asked as she came around the corner.

Jack was about three steps ahead of his stepdaughter, so both he and Marrell were able to see her face and hear her scream. A minute later the two girls were hugging, and for long moments neither one tried to speak.

Marrell had gone into Jack's arms, and Jack patiently waited for Mackenzie and Delancey to break up before claiming his own hug.

"Hi, Jack," Mackenzie smiled up at him.

"Hi, Mic. Nice surprise. You can do this anytime."

"All right."

"How long can you stay?"

"Until Saturday."

He hugged her again when he realized she would be there for Thanksgiving. They had been invited to spend Thanksgiving in Sebastopol with Oliver's folks but had wanted to stay home this year. At the moment Jack was very pleased with their decision.

"You look so different," Delancey said.

Mackenzie grinned. "It's a lot of work."

"But you like it," her mother stated.

"Yes." Her eyes were alive with excitement. "I love it."

Marrell cocked her head to one side. "Wasn't the finance school scheduled for twelve weeks?"

"Yes, but there's been a change."

Marrell's brows rose. "Going to tell us about it?"

"Just as soon as I change into jeans and get a huge glass of Pepsi."

Marrell laughed. Some things would never change, and at the moment that was a tremendous source of comfort. The confident young woman who had left home had come back with more poise and awareness than Marrell had planned on. For a moment her mother hadn't known her, but then out came the jeans and Pepsi. This was her Mackenzie.

"Why don't I get your drink, and we'll talk in the living room," Jack offered.

"I won't pass that up," Mackenzie answered and made to leave.

"Do I have to go to school tomorrow, Jack? It's only two days until Thanksgiving break."

"We'll see. Did you get your homework done?"

"Yes."

"All right. Let me discuss it with your mom. Maybe we can take your homework in, explain the situation to the office, and then get your work for the rest of the week. We'll just have to see."

Delancey looked as though she could burst and swiftly followed on the heels of her sister. Marrell turned to find Jack's eyes on her. He was always so careful with her feelings.

"Is she really here, or am I dreaming?"

"Want me to pinch you?" he asked and used those mobile eyebrows of his.

"I think I do," she smiled back. "I'll take a Pepsi too, if you're offering."

"I am, but aren't you afraid you won't sleep?" As soon as Jack said it, he shook his head. With Mackenzie home, sleep was the last thing on their minds.

"I drew something for you when I was at the Lacys' tonight," Delancey said as she came into Mackenzie's room without knocking.

"Let's see it," Mackenzie responded, pulling up the zipper of her jeans.

In soft colored pencil, Delancey had done a teddy bear. His tummy was round, and he was a bit on the scruffy side. Sporting a dark-blue bow tie and a matching vest, his face was turned to look at the viewer with an expression that was all at once confused and determined.

"Micah Bear," Mackenzie said softly.

"How did you know?" Delancey was shocked.

"How did *you* know?" Mackenzie stared at her younger sibling.

"We found some of your old stories, but how did you know it was Micah Bear?"

"Because this is exactly the way I would have drawn him if I had the talent. I can't believe how good this is."

Delancey looked very pleased.

"Can I keep this?"

"Sure."

"Thank you. It's wonderful. Do you still have the stories?"

"In my book bag."

"I've got to see them. It was so long ago. It'll be a riot to see what I wrote."

"Actually, some of them are very good. I think

you might be surprised."

"I don't know about that."

"So what's going on, Mic?" Delancey couldn't stand it any longer. "Why are you here?"

"I've been transferred," Mackenzie said as she pulled on a pair of thick socks. "Come on. I'll tell you all at the same time."

TWENTY-FOUR

"I'm headed to Arlington Hall Station in Virginia," Mackenzie told her family, a huge smile on her face.

"What's the work?" Jack wanted to know.

"Army Intelligence and Security."

Marrell had already known this but the realization finally struck her.

"What's the matter, Mom?" Delancey asked, having just caught her mother's look.

"Your sister is going into national security," Marrell said softly.

"Is that what it is, Mic?"

"Yes, D.J."

"Can you tell us how this happened, Mackenzie?" Marrell asked. "Or is it hush-hush?"

"It's not hush-hush at all, Mom. I would have written you, but I had a chance for leave. I don't know when I'll get my next one, so I just came to tell you in person."

"Explain to me why it's such a surprise, Marrell," Jack asked. He thought he might understand but wanted a full picture.

"It's more the honor of the situation than any type of danger. For obvious reasons, national security is a tight field." Marrell looked at her daughter and smiled. "You might not have as much to write about in your future letters."

Mackenzie nodded. "It is an honor, and I'm excited about it, but you're right — it's not without its limitations."

"Tell us how it happened, Mic," Delancey pressed her.

Mackenzie nodded. "It was going well in Indiana, but it wasn't anywhere near as challenging as I had expected. One of my instructors asked to see me, and that was the first of four interviews. I know they reviewed my records, and I was certainly asked a lot of questions. Then they asked if I was willing to cut the finance training short and go to Arlington. I made myself think about it, but I wanted to say yes on the spot."

"When do you report?"

"The Wednesday after I get back."

"Thank you for coming home, Micki," Jack said softly. "This wouldn't have been nearly as special to learn about in a letter."

She smiled at the stepfather she adored and asked, "Will you come to visit me?"

"Yes, we will. We'd even talked about coming to Indiana but then thought it might be better to wait until after your schooling."

"I didn't think that," Delancey put in firmly, and Mackenzie laughed.

"You have too much time on your hands, Deej."

The younger girl looked thunderstruck, but Mackenzie did not let up.

"Now if you join the Army, you won't have time to miss anyone."

"All right, Mic," her mother cut in. "Let's not overdo this."

Mackenzie only grinned unrepentantly.

"You've got some nerve, Mackenzie Rose

Bishop," Delancey came back at her. "You wrote back and told me that we would probably never see each other if I joined."

"And that's true, D.J., but at least you wouldn't have time to miss me."

Delancey snorted. "That's a great consolation."

"What was your favorite part about basic training?" Jack interjected, stemming the other conversation with a well-timed question.

"Graduation," Mackenzie joked. "No, I think I liked the fact that my dad was stationed there. It gave me time to think about him, although not much time, since they keep you so busy. But when I'd see troops of men somewhere, I would picture him, and I liked that."

"Do you have any idea how long you'll be in Virginia?" Marrell asked.

"No, not right now. There is a chance that I won't be what they're looking for, but that's all speculation at this point."

"What exactly are they looking for?" Delancey asked.

"I think someone who catches on to things swiftly and can analyze information in an orderly fashion. I'm not sure what they saw in me at Ben Harrison, unless it was the fact that I understand how systems work. Numbers weren't a problem either." She stopped for a moment. "I hope it works out. I'm not sure what else I'd be interested in right now."

"Weren't you interested in finance?"

"Yes, until they offered me intelligence."

Marrell nodded with understanding. She was certain that most people would feel the same way. A glance at her younger daughter gave her pause. Staring at the flames in the fireplace, Delancey seemed deep in thought. Could she be taking Mackenzie seriously? Marrell forced her mind not to dwell on that possibility. If Delancey was thinking of enlisting, it would happen and that was all. Worrying and telling God what to do would accomplish nothing, and on top of that, it would be a sin. However, Marrell did ask God to help her cope, all the while reminding herself to be thankful that He was in control.

Arlington Hall Station, Virginia
March 1987
Mackenzie had not expected a job in the files. She knew from her father that the military required mounds of paperwork and that her rank was very low, but when Mackenzie heard the word *intelligence,* her mind had run off like a gleeful child's. It wasn't that she was bored — there were always a dozen things to do, and some of the case files were fascinating. But the inactivity and the hours every day that she spent at a desk or in front of a file cabinet were driving her nuts. She had even gone so far as to join a health club. She was headed there right after work, when three of her female coworkers, who also happened to be her roommates, stopped by the file room on their way out. While all the same rank as Mackenzie, the others had various duties, none of which included the files.

"You're not going to sit at home this evening, are you, Micki?" Janelle Price asked. Janelle was older, and Mackenzie knew she liked to be in charge.

"I haven't had a better offer," Mackenzie said lightly. She had yet to open up to any of these women.

"Well, your luck has just changed. We're going out in search of male companionship, and we want you to join us."

Mackenzie had to laugh.

"Come, Micki," Aimee Langford said softly. She was as young and wet behind the ears as Mackenzie. Beth Hughes was just the same, but she was quiet. Aimee and Mackenzie had their own rooms, and Beth shared a room with Janelle.

Janelle didn't bother with an answer. "How long before you can be ready?"

Mackenzie took a moment to reply. She might have to bow and scrape to those who outranked her, but that did not include her contemporaries. "Maybe 20 minutes," she said at last.

"Make it 15," Janelle ordered.

Mackenzie watched them wander off and shut down her computer for the weekend. She wouldn't be ready in 15 minutes, but they would wait. And if they didn't, that was all right too. Yes, it was a Friday night, and yes, she'd been on her own every night all week, but right now that was okay.

Why did I think this was going to be the answer to every problem? Mackenzie asked herself, not for the first time. *Why did I think that being out on my own was just what I needed?*

No answer floated out of the air, and Mackenzie felt herself rushing. Suddenly she didn't want to be left alone tonight. She didn't know these women very well and wasn't sure she wanted to, but the thought of being alone right now scared her to death.

The East Coast was vastly different from the West. Mackenzie had been noticing this for weeks, but it was never more evident than this night. In the

20 minutes the women had spent at the apartment, the other three had transformed themselves into elegant creatures. Two wore black pantsuits, and another had on a deep green jacket and matching slacks. They were dripping with jewelry.

Mackenzie had freshened her makeup a little and put on navy slacks and a light blue oxford-style blouse, but she added no extra jewelry, and in fact, she'd used only the bare necessities on makeup. Her earrings were nice, a Christmas gift from Jack and her mother, but she hadn't even bothered with a necklace. Her watch was more functional than elegant.

They had gone to Serge's. It was a little on the pricey side, but the food was wonderful, and the bar area always had good music. At least that was what Mackenzie had been told. She had never been there.

Thinking back on it, the food had been good, but Mackenzie had never been into the bar scene and felt terribly out of place. Janelle and Beth had been asked to dance, and Aimee had gone to the ladies' room. Mackenzie sat alone, a ginger ale in front of her, and felt more 8 then 18. So deep in thought was she that it took a moment for her to realize someone was standing next to the half-circle bench that enclosed the booth.

"Do you have the time?"

A man, probably in his thirties, was standing at her table. He looked tall from where she was sitting, and his hair was very blond.

"Sure." Mackenzie was on the verge of raising her arm when she spotted his wrist. She stared at him for a moment. "You're wearing a watch," she said softly.

He grinned charmingly, revealing a surprising

pair of dimples that made him look younger. "You're right, I am, but I was hoping to talk with you."

Mackenzie laughed and automatically shook the hand that was held out to her.

"Paxton Hancock," the man stated.

"Mackenzie Bishop," she filled in.

"Any chance I might join you?"

Mackenzie gestured across the table. "Suit yourself. Some of my friends will probably be back soon," she explained.

"Will they mind?" Paxton asked from the seat across from Mackenzie.

"I don't think so." Mackenzie took a sip of her drink, appearing more relaxed than she felt. She wasn't worried about her personal safety, the Army had seen to that, but she wasn't sure she wanted to talk to a strange man in a bar.

"You look intent," Paxton cut into her thoughts. "Are you figuring out how to give me the brush-off?"

Mackenzie studied him. He was too good-looking to have experienced the "brush-off" very often. And the sparkle in his blue eyes told her he knew it.

"What if I was?" she chanced a flirtation.

"I'd have to do something fast. I can't let you get away."

"Why? There must be dozens of women here with whom you could talk."

"I'm sure you're right, but they don't all look like you."

Mackenzie's look was nothing short of skeptical. She decided to ignore his flattery.

"Where are you from, Paxton?"

"Pax, by the way," he said easily. "My friends

405

call me Pax, and I'm originally from New York, but I've lived here for almost ten years. How about yourself?"

"San Francisco, and I've only been here a few months."

"What's your line of work?"

"I'm at Arlington Hall Station."

"The Army?" He looked stunned.

"Yes," Mackenzie returned, very amused.

"I'm being laughed at," Paxton guessed correctly. But he didn't seem too offended.

Mackenzie could have said many things to that but didn't. Aimee chose that moment to come back.

"Oh, Micki, I —"

Ignoring her coworker's embarrassment, Mackenzie moved over in the booth and introduced her as she was sitting down.

"Aimee, this is Paxton Hancock. Paxton, this is Aimee Langford, also one of Uncle Sam's finest."

Paxton stared at them in amazement.

"You're in the Army too?"

Aimee nodded shyly.

"Well, Uncle Sam sure knows how to pick 'em."

Aimee smiled in pleasure, but Mackenzie, thinking it was a line, looked bored, unknowingly making her all the more fascinating to the man at their table.

"Oh," Aimee said suddenly. Mackenzie followed her gaze.

"It looks as if Beth is trying to get your attention," Mackenzie noted.

"Should I go?" Aimee asked, looking uncertain.

"Sure." Mackenzie smiled at her. "Maybe she wants to introduce you to someone."

Aimee looked more than a little apprehensive

but still rose and left the table.

Paxton was more than happy with this turn of events, but something told him he was going to have to move slowly.

"Can I you buy a drink?" he offered.

"Sure," she said, trying to sound casual. She watched him stand.

"What'll it be?"

"Ginger ale."

Paxton blinked and waited for her to laugh. She didn't.

"Ginger ale?"

"Yes, I'm not much of a drinker, and beyond that, I'm only 18."

For a full five seconds Paxton only stared at her. "Ginger ale it is," he said softly and moved off toward the bar.

Mackenzie had no idea what to think, but she felt better. She had the impression that he had been under the *wrong* impression since he sat down. It was good to have the air cleared. If he did have ideas, he now had the facts. Not that Mackenzie would be interested. Even if he was younger, the last thing she wanted in her life at this time was a man.

Paxton was back surprisingly fast. He set Mackenzie's drink in front of her and took his same place at the table. Mackenzie was relieved that he didn't try to sit closer. It would have forced her to cut the evening short.

"So tell me, what do you do for Uncle Sam?"

Mackenzie was sure he was at his most charming. She smiled. "A lot of filing and paperwork. I haven't been at it for very long, so I'm not a lot of use to anyone yet."

"And you would eventually like to do what?"

"I like what I'm doing, but I hope to get a little more hands-on with the material — see the reports before they come for filing, have a chance to think, analyze, and search out possible problems; that kind of thing. What do you do for a living?" she asked abruptly, hoping the conversation would move away from her.

"I'm an editor at IronHorse." Paxton named one of the largest publishers in the world.

Mackenzie immediately thought of Delancey.

"Children's books or adult?"

"Adult." His head dipped to one side. "What made you ask that?"

Mackenzie opened her mouth but shut it again.

"Not going to tell me?" He watched her closely.

"It just occurred to me that your job must be a little like being a doctor: You go to a party and everyone expects free medical advice."

"Are you really only 18?" he asked, looking stunned.

Mackenzie laughed. "Yes."

Paxton shook his head in wonder. "Go ahead and ask me."

"It's just that my sister draws beautifully, and I was curious as to how an illustrator gets started."

"How old is she?"

"Seventeen."

"Her best bet is to contact some children's magazines. If she met someone who was writing a book and could collaborate on that, that would also help. But if she just wants to get started, she should be sending her work to children's magazines. And if she's already doing that, she should keep trying."

"No, she isn't. In fact, she'll probably be surprised that I even asked you. I don't know if she's ever considered doing anything with her work." Mackenzie shrugged. "I didn't think about it until you said you worked with IronHorse. What exactly do you do?"

"I have certain authors with whom I work. Editing their books is part of the job."

"How many authors?"

"I have about 10 whose books I do every year, and then another 10 to 15 first-timers. The market is always changing, but that's about right."

"Anyone whose name I would know?"

He proceeded to list three authors whose names made Mackenzie's mouth fall open. They were some of the biggest names on the New York Times Bestseller List.

"There are people who would go to great lengths to meet some of my authors, which, if they make the connection to me, only makes my job miserable. So if you could keep that to yourself, I would be pleased."

"I will, certainly," Mackenzie said, wondering why he had confided in her. Maybe it was all a big line. Maybe he would say anything for a date.

"You know," Paxton said suddenly, "I haven't met a woman who's as hard to read as you are in a long time."

Mackenzie took a moment to reply. Delancey was always telling her that she didn't wear her emotions on her sleeve, but she had never paid much attention to her.

"Why would you want to read me?" Mackenzie asked. It was the first question that came to mind and reminded Paxton just how young she was.

"Just to get to know you."

Mackenzie barely held herself from asking why again. She glanced out over the crowd and had the firm impression that her friends were deliberately leaving her alone. She had to get out of there.

"I hate to be rude," Mackenzie said softly, checking her watch, "but I think I'm going to call it a night."

"Any chance I can see you again?"

"There might be if I could figure out why you want to, but since I can't, no."

Paxton laughed. She had a remarkable way of fielding everything he said.

"Are you heading home, Paxton?" she now asked congenially, her purse in hand.

"I'm planning on it, yes, but I'm open to a better offer."

Mackenzie only smiled and stood. "Well, I hope you get one. Goodnight, and thank you for the drink."

Paxton watched her walk away with his mouth slightly agape. He stared after her until she disappeared into the crowd. He wasn't a stalker; neither was he a man who pursued a woman who wasn't interested in him. But even though 19 years separated them, he thought that if they could get to know each other, Mackenzie might like him. His ex-wife would disagree, but then she disagreed about everything. Paxton sat back and signaled the waiter for another drink. "Ginger ale," he heard himself say, even as he tried to figure out a way to stop thinking about Mackenzie Bishop.

Mackenzie's ponytail bounced against her neck as she went from a jog to a walk on the indoor track. She'd just put in 11 miles and needed to cool down a bit. She was not particularly winded and realized she had the Army to thank. Actually, she had the Army to thank for several things — the least of which was being in good shape; the most of which was that it was causing her to grow up a little.

She hadn't planned to come to the gym tonight, but a letter waiting for her when she arrived home had forced her to get out of the apartment and find some think-time. Delancey was joining the Army. Mackenzie had only just teased her about that very thing, but until she'd had a chance to ponder her sister's decision, she hadn't known how to react.

I'm selfish, Mackenzie concluded. *I want to go off and live my own life, but I want to know that my family is safely home in San Francisco, waiting for me whenever I decide to visit. Sorry, Deej. I've been unfair.*

With this little pep talk, Mackenzie knew it was time to go home and call her sister. For the first time she had an inkling of what her mother had felt when she left, but that wasn't what was important. There was no reason not to support Delancey's choice, and Mackenzie would go home, call her, and do just that.

"Good evening, Miss Bishop."

Mackenzie's head came up, and she found herself looking into Paxton Hancock's light blue eyes. He was leaning against the wall outside the men's locker room. Mackenzie had been headed to the women's showers.

"Hello, Paxton."

"How are you?"

"I'm fine."

"Just finishing?"

"Yes. You look like you've had a workout."

"A long one. I'm getting flabby in my old age."

411

Mackenzie smiled but thought he might be serious.

"There's a great coffee shop around the corner," Paxton volunteered. "Can I buy you a cappuccino?"

For some reason Mackenzie could not say no. She wanted to call her sister, and she did not want to encourage this man, but she still said, "All right. Will it work for me to meet you there in about 30 minutes?"

"That's fine. Do you know the place?"

"Yes."

"Good. I'll get a table and wait for you."

"All right. I'll see you there."

For a moment Paxton stayed where he was. He thought his heart would stop when he had come from the weight room and seen her on the track. He knew he was foolish. Asking her to coffee was no way to get her from his mind, and if he thought her desirable in slacks and a blouse, she was downright distracting in a tank top and shorts, and her face flushed and moist. Paxton finally walked into the showers, thinking he'd better make it a cold one.

"I just got a letter from my sister," Mackenzie found herself confiding when Paxton asked her about her day. "She's joining the Army."

"Is that good or bad?"

"I don't know. I'm still a little off-balance. I'm going to call her and congratulate her, but inside I'm still trying to deal with it."

"Do you regret your own decision?"

"No, but there's something secure about knowing that my sister is home safe with Jack and my mother."

"Jack?"

"My stepfather."

"Did your parents divorce?"

"No, my father's dead."

"I lost my own father about 18 months ago. It's awful, isn't it?"

"Yes. Especially the first few years. It does get easier, but there's always a hole that no one else can fill."

"Is your stepfather okay?"

"He's wonderful," Mackenzie said softly. "I don't know if I'd have ever left home if he hadn't been there for my mom."

"That doesn't surprise me about you. You seem like the type who would naturally take care of others."

"That was a nice thing to say."

"I have a lot of nice things to say to you if you would let me."

Mackenzie's eyes were direct. "I can't say that I'm not flattered, Paxton, but if you're talking about a dating relationship, I don't have time for a man in my life right now. My career is very important to me, and I want to focus all my energy on that."

He studied her for a moment. "I don't scare you or anything like that, do I, Mackenzie? There are a lot of weird people on the streets today, and you might be thinking I'll attack you. If so, you might be saying that to hide your fear of me."

"No, Paxton, I'm not. And I have to be very honest with you about that as well, which means telling you that if you did try something, I'd take you apart."

She was completely serious, and Paxton knew he couldn't let her get away. It would kill him to keep his distance, but he desperately wanted to be as close as she would allow.

"What about an occasional date, just as friends?"

"Does that ever work? I didn't think men and women could be friends."

"Was that a nice way to tell me to get lost?"

"No, just an honest question. You've shown interest in me — at least I think that's what you're saying — and now you want to know if I'll go on casual dates. Just what is it that you want?"

"You do like to ask the hard ones, don't you?" His voice was so chagrined that Mackenzie laughed.

"I'm sorry. I don't mean to be so intense, but I want to see what the Army has for me. A man in my life would only be ignored so I could pursue this job."

Paxton looked at her for a moment, reached for his pocket, and pulled out a card. He wrote something on the back, turned it over to the front, and slid it toward her.

"This is my business card. You have only to say it's Mackenzie calling, and they'll put you through. On the back is my home number. If you can't find me at work, try me there."

"And what am I calling about?"

Paxton shrugged, working to keep this casual. "I doubt you'll give me your number, so I'm giving mine to you. If you find yourself alone some evening and want to go to dinner, just call me."

"Paxton, don't you have someone *you* can call, a more sure thing?"

"Not right now, and just so we're straight, I'm not looking for marriage or anything like that. I've done that, and I'm not ready to do it again. I would like to get to know you better, and I'm even

414

willing to allow you to call the shots."

Mackenzie nodded, a little overwhelmed at his open attitude.

"Frank Biddle was in my office today," Paxton added, knowing they both needed to be rescued from the moment.

"Frank Biddle?" Mackenzie repeated. "*The* Frank Biddle?"

"One and the same." Paxton reached into the bag that was by his chair. "I thought you might like to have a copy of his latest book."

"Thank you." Mackenzie was so taken aback that she could only stare at the hardcover that featured an old-fashioned pocket watch. *The Time-piece* was its title.

"Open the front cover."

Mackenzie obeyed and saw that the author had signed it — to her!

"Paxton," she began, then stopped. "I mean, you asked him? That is, how did you know you would see me?"

"I didn't, but I hoped I would at some point."

Mackenzie stared at him. Did she really just meet this man in a bar a few weeks ago? She was not romantically interested in him — she had been honest about that — but neither was he a man you could ignore. There was something so worldly and sure about him that Mackenzie was fasci-nated. That he was interested in her only added to the captivation.

"Please thank him for me, and thank you again. I know I'll enjoy it."

"He even included me in the dedication this time." Paxton flipped the pages so she could read.

"Wow," Mackenzie said softly, "you must feel honored."

Paxton smiled. He had been mentioned in dozens of books over the years. It was nice to see it through her eyes. Maybe he had started to take this distinction for granted.

"You must be good at what you do, Paxton," she surprised him by saying. Indeed, he could think of nothing to say.

"I hate to run," Mackenzie offered apologetically, "but I need to call my sister."

"How old did you say she was?"

"Seventeen."

Paxton nodded. "You must have gone into the Army just as soon as you turned 18."

"Yes. My birthday is in June, and I left for basic training last August."

"Now your sister will do the same?"

"Yes. She'll be 18 in July, and even though her letter didn't say so, she'll probably be headed off in the fall. I shouldn't be too surprised. Our father was in the Army for more than 20 years. But I guess an older child always thinks of her younger sister as needing protection, and now she'll be out of the nest. It just feels a little weird."

"Will you say that to her?"

"No. I'll just tell her I'm proud of her and then try to call again sometime when she's not home, so I can see how my mom's doing."

Paxton was again reminded that she was protective of her loved ones. And for an instant he allowed himself to think about what it would be like to be included. He nearly shook his head. He didn't even know her, and yet he was having this kind of emotional response.

You need a vacation, Pax; you need one badly.

Mackenzie was on her way just after that, and Paxton forced himself not to dwell on her. He got

416

home and put on the weather channel. He had a sudden need to see just how warm it was in Florida this time of year.

TWENTY-FIVE

Mackenzie could not believe where she was. She racked her brain, trying to remember exactly how the conversation had gone, but at the moment she could not remember why she had agreed to attend church with Aimee.

I always go at home. Aimee's words now came to mind, but not much else.

"Micki," Aimee whispered suddenly from the pew beside her.

Mackenzie turned to her.

"Did you go to church at home in San Francisco?"

"Yes, with my mom. She went a lot."

Aimee nodded and looked back to the front, but Mackenzie watched her profile. The service hadn't started yet, so Mackenzie felt free to ask, "Why did you want to come to church, Aimee?"

"I just felt so guilty," she admitted, her tone as hushed as Mackenzie's. "Ever since I was in the bar last month with the three of you, I haven't felt right."

"And you think that being in church today will help?"

"I don't know, but I hope so. Don't you feel better when you go to church, Micki?"

People were rising to their feet as a man came

418

in from a side door, so Mackenzie was unable to answer. She did, however, start thinking.

A glance at her watch told her it was early in California. Her family would still be sound asleep, but she knew her mother would go to church that morning, and not out of guilt. She would go because she was delighted to be in the house of God and to fellowship with believers. Mackenzie had heard her say so often enough.

So what am I doing here? Aimee asked me, of course, but I've always told my mother I didn't need God.

It was a lame thought, even to Mackenzie. For the first time Mackenzie could remember, she wouldn't allow herself to think about God or her mother's salvation beliefs. She barely heard the sermon, so busy was she working to think of other things. And as soon as she arrived home, she disappeared into her room and started the Frank Biddle book that Paxton had given her. She didn't come out until lunchtime, and then only long enough to find something to eat. She read all day, and when Monday arrived, gladly immersed herself in her job once again.

San Francisco
April 1987
Jack woke up abruptly, thinking for an instant that someone had broken into the apartment. He lay very still for several moments and then realized Delancey was up and in the bathroom. The clock read 2:15 A.M. He turned over to get comfortable again but then realized his stepdaughter was not going back to her room. He shifted again, and this time woke Marrell. He felt her lift up and look toward the open door. A light came from down

419

the hall.

"I think D.J. is in the bathroom," he said quietly.

"Okay." Her voice sounded sleepy, but she stayed on one elbow. When a few more seconds passed, Jack made a move to get up.

"I'll go," Marrell stopped him. "It might just be that time of the month."

Not bothering with a robe, Marrell slipped out of bed and met Delancey as she came from the bathroom.

"You all right?" the older woman asked.

"My stomach is upset." Delancey sounded subdued as she moved across to her room. Marrell followed and saw in the dim light that Delancey did not lie back down. She sat up against her pillow, and Marrell took a chair by the door.

"Do you want something?"

Delancey said no, but Marrell didn't move.

"Mom," the girl said softly after a few moments of silence.

"Yeah, honey."

"I don't want to do this." Her voice shook with emotion.

"Don't want to do what?"

"I don't want to do the Army testing. I don't want to go into the Army."

She broke down, and Marrell moved to the bed. She put her arms around Delancey, and her daughter clung to her, sobs racking her slim frame.

"Oh, Mom, what will I do? What will Mackenzie say? I just can't stand to hurt her!"

"Delancey . . . Delancey . . ." Marrell's voice was soothing. "It's all right. You can't do this for Mackenzie or anyone else. You have to do it or not do it for you. Your sister would never wish this on you. She would tell you to stop right now."

"But the process is already started."

"Just barely," Marrell reasoned. "Now is the time to tell them you've changed your mind. They've heard it a thousand times, and this is when they want to hear it, not after you're on your way to basic training. You can call on Monday, ask for Sergeant Wallace, and explain that you've changed your mind. You can call Mackenzie in the morning and tell her. She's only going to say she loves you and understands."

Tears were coming again, but Delancey felt better. She hadn't known how to deal with this, and even though she'd gone to bed a little after 10:00, she'd not slept. She had even tried to write a letter to her sister to explain but ended up feeling worse.

"Do you know what I want to do, Mom?" Delancey sniffed a little.

"What?"

"I want to draw and illustrate. That's all I've wanted to do for so long, and if I go into the Army, it might be years before I can pursue that. Do you think Mackenzie will really understand?"

Marrell flicked on the bedside light and waited for their eyes to adjust.

"Look around this room, D.J.," she commanded softly. "Just look at the walls covered with your artwork and tell me your sister's not going to understand. You draw like a master, and Mic has been your biggest fan for as long as I can remember. She'll do nothing but cheer when you tell her you're going to chase your dream."

"Oh, Mom." Delancey's voice held relief. She had never thought of it that way. She did dream of illustrating — it was all she ever dreamed of —

and now her mother was saying it was all right.

"Can you sleep?"

"I think so. I was tired when I went to bed, but then I just lay here and made myself sick."

Marrell stood. "Slip under the covers."

Delancey obeyed, and Marrell bent to hug her.

"What will Jack say?" Delancey asked suddenly.

"Jack will say 'I love you, D.J.' just as he always does."

"Thanks, Mom." Delancey's sigh was great.

"I love you, Delancey Joy."

"I love you too."

"Go to sleep."

"All right."

Marrell smiled down at her daughter before turning out the light. She moved slowly until her eyes adjusted and then sought her own bed. Her husband did not wake up, but Marrell had been right. As soon as Jack heard the news the next morning, he hugged Delancey, told her he was proud of the way she had come forward with her change of mind, and also said that he loved her.

Arlington

"I've got tickets for a show this Saturday night," Paxton said as soon as he heard Mackenzie's voice. "I have to go and I don't want to, so you're going to have to doll up and go with me or I'll lose my mind."

"You know," she said dryly, working not to laugh, "this is the third time you've called this week. Unlike some people who have the cushy life of an editor, most of us have to work for a living."

"Cushy?" He sounded outraged. "Do you know how much rewriting was required on Brett Kirby's last book? I didn't think we'd ever get done."

"Did you ever go out with his sister?" Mackenzie asked.

"Yes."

"Was she nice?"

"No. The evening couldn't end swiftly enough. All she did was talk about the book she wants to write. Save me from aspiring writers."

Mackenzie laughed, but inside she was cringing. Never in a million years would she tell Paxton she'd been playing with a story of her own — not just playing, but writing in earnest on a personal computer she had splurged on and bought the month before. She hadn't done any serious writing since the summer she took a writing course, but after reading *The Timepiece,* a book she enjoyed, she felt vaguely dissatisfied. Most of the book was fabulous, but she would have written a completely differently ending, and there wasn't a need for the sex scenes, or for that matter, the swearing.

Mackenzie was no prude, but in high school she'd had a teacher who was very firm on several things, one of which was "cut the superfluous." She could still hear him: "If the scene doesn't add to the story, cut it. I don't care how well-written you think it is, cut it. I don't care if it's your favorite part, cut it."

To say such a thing to Paxton would hurt him. After all, he was the editor, but Mackenzie would have probably cut a good 50 pages from the book. The finished length was well over 700 pages, and in her opinion, no one would have missed the scenes she didn't like.

"Are you still there?"

"Yes."

"So are you free Saturday night or what?"

"I think so. Just how dressy is this?"

"Very. I'll be in a tux."

"Are you serious?"

"Um-hm." He sounded too satisfied by half.

"Pax, I don't have anything that dressy, and none of my roommates is the same size."

"Go shopping."

"For a dress I'll wear one night?"

"You buy a dress, and I'll see to it that you wear it again."

Mackenzie wasn't sure she found that a deal, but Paxton Hancock was turning out to be a great friend. His expectations of her were next to nothing, yet he was always ready to give of himself.

"Come on, Mackenzie," he coaxed. "You'd look good in black."

"I'll be sure and look for red."

"Mmm, red would work too."

"I don't know, Paxton. Can I think about it?"

"No. Now tell me you'll go shopping tomorrow and be ready with bells on Saturday night."

Mackenzie heard herself agreeing. It was the first time he'd ever demanded anything of her, and a sudden desire not to be so self-centered caused her to acquiesce.

"Six o'clock" were the words he rang off with, and for a long time Mackenzie stood looking at the kitchen floor. She would shop, but not before she ruled out her roommates' closets. Hoping one of them had the perfect dress, she moved to the living room to give them the third degree.

"Mackenzie," Aimee breathed when Micki came from her room four days later. Aimee's reverent voice brought the other two women from the kitchen. They were headed out as well, but with

424

something more casual in mind.

Mackenzie was anything but casual. The dress she'd bought at Jones was deceivingly simple. A deep green velvet with a rounded neck and long sleeves, it hit just below her knees, and, although not skintight, showed her figure to perfection. She wore her best gold earrings and a thin gold chain. Beth had loaned her a dressy watch and bracelet. Her high-heeled pumps were black and so was her small clutch. With her hair pulled back in a loose chignon, she looked like she had just stepped out of a mansion.

"Are you sure Paxton is just a friend, Micki?" Janelle wanted to know. She still liked to be in charge, but Mackenzie had learned that her heart was big.

"Yes, he is. It's some sort of show, so he'll be in a tux."

"When will he be here?" Beth asked.

"At six o'clock."

"Are you nervous?" This came from Aimee.

"No. It's just Pax, and we never run out of things to talk about."

As if on cue, the doorbell rang. Mackenzie moved to get it, but Janelle beat her to it. She opened it with a flourish but was let down when Paxton did little more than spot Mackenzie and ask if she was ready to go.

"Sure. Goodnight," she called to her roommates and headed out the door. Janelle was there to close it behind her. Paxton and Mackenzie walked down the stairs in silence. Not until they were next to his elegant Mercedes did Mackenzie speak.

"You look nice, Pax."

He opened the door but didn't speak, and Mackenzie had the sudden fear that his silence was over the fact that she was dressed all wrong. She stepped between the car and the curb but didn't get in. She looked back to find him watching her.

"This was my idea, wasn't it?" he said before she could question him.

"What was?" Mackenzie asked in genuine confusion.

"You don't have time to go back and change into fatigues?"

Mackenzie laughed. "I don't think so. Is that what you really want?"

"No, but I'm going to pay for it."

Mackenzie let that one go and stepped into the car.

"What do you hear from your family?" Paxton asked after a short silence.

"Everyone's fine. D.J. has been looking into several art schools. Most are pretty close to home, and I can tell she is ecstatic."

Traffic was heavy, so Mackenzie fell quiet as Paxton drove them into the downtown D.C. area. He pulled into a parking garage a little off the main route, so parking wasn't impossible. Thankfully they weren't that far from the theater, since Mackenzie's shoes were not made to walk for miles. A few elevators and a long walkway, and soon they were in front of the theater. Mackenzie's mouth opened.

"You're taking me to see *Les Miserables*?"

"Uh-hm," he responded, sounding bored.

Mackenzie came to a stop.

"Why don't you want to see it?"

"Because I've seen it twice."

"Then why are we here?"

Paxton gestured toward the curb with his head. A black limo had pulled up, and with it, enough pomp and ceremony to welcome the queen. A man and a woman were emerging from the deep rear seat.

"Who are they?" Mackenzie asked.

"I don't know who she is, but the man is Carson Walcott. We're trying to lure him away from Bancroft for his next book."

Mackenzie gripped his arm with bruising strength. "Do you mean to tell me we're watching *Les Miz* with Carson Walcott?"

"Yes."

"You could have warned me." She glared at him.

"But then you wouldn't have come. You would have been nervous and upset instead of relaxed and beautiful."

Mackenzie opened her mouth and shut it. He was right. She would have been sick with nerves. Paxton smiled at her before taking her arm and moving forward. She was introduced to Carson Walcott, a bestselling mystery author and playwright, as though hobnobbing with celebrities was an everyday occurrence. Mackenzie hoped she did everything right because ten minutes later, when she was seated in a private balcony seat, she couldn't remember a thing.

"Do you work with IronHorse?" Carson turned to ask her.

"As a matter of fact, I don't," she said softly, hoping it didn't matter and wishing that Paxton wasn't seated on the other side of Ruthie, Carson's companion. Mackenzie would have gone on to tell the famous author where she worked, but he put his hand on her knee and slid it up her leg a little. She was stiff as a poker by the time he stopped. When Ruthie touched his arm and spoke to him, he moved his hand.

The show hadn't even started, but Mackenzie was ready to leave. For the next few minutes, Carson was in deep conversation with Ruthie and magnanimous with his tips to the man who brought them drinks and hors d'oeuvres. Mackenzie shifted away from him in her seat and pulled the hem of her dress over her knees as far as it would go. She thought everything would be all right, but without warning Carson turned to her, his hand landing so high on her thigh that she jumped to her feet and moved toward the door. The hallway where she emerged didn't look familiar, but escape was Mackenzie's only intent. She turned left and had to stop herself from breaking into a run.

Mackenzie didn't know that Paxton was on her heels. He made the mistake of not speaking as he caught up to her and grabbed her by the arm. Mackenzie reacted without thinking. She whipped around, caught her attacker by the neck, put a leg behind his knees, and none-too-gently landed him flat on his back. Not until Mackenzie looked down into the stunned face of Paxton Hancock did she realize what she'd just done. She straightened, shifted her dress into place, and moved down the hallway to lean against the wall. Her whole body felt suffused with heat, and for a moment she closed her eyes. She heard movement and steps but did not look at Paxton until he stepped directly in front of her.

"The show has started," Paxton said softly, amazed that none of the ushers had seen the display and called security. "Will you please come back inside?"

"Sure, Pax." Mackenzie's voice was low with rage. "I'll come back in, and when Carson Walcott puts his hand on my leg again, I'll break his nose and you can kiss your book deal goodbye."

It was on the tip of Paxton's tongue to tell Mackenzie to grow up, but he was glad he held his words. Mackenzie was the victim. He noticed absently that she didn't have a hair out of place.

"Promise me you'll stay here, Mackenzie. I'll be right back."

Mackenzie only stared at him.

"You don't even have your purse."

Again the stare.

"Can I help you, sir?" An usher had appeared.

"Please," Paxton recovered smoothly, "my date would like a tall glass of ice water. We're in the Jefferson box."

"Very good, sir."

Paxton leveled Mackenzie with a look and steered her back down the wall in the direction of their box. She hadn't promised to stay, but in truth she was too shaken to move from where he left her. He returned in a surprisingly short time.

"Ruthie has moved to your seat," he wasted no time in telling her. "I'll sit next to Carson, and you'll be on my right."

Mackenzie knew that if she didn't get her mind off what had just happened, she would burst into tears. She nodded and allowed Paxton to take her arm. Moments later he took a seat, effectively blocking her from the lustful author, and waited for her to sit down. As soon as she did, his arm went around her shoulders.

Very aware of her trembling, Paxton said nothing and hoped they could make it through the next few hours. The usher came several minutes later with the ice water, but Mackenzie didn't reach for it. Paxton took it from the offered tray.

When the man moved away, the editor leaned close and spoke to her.

"Don't you want a little?"

"I'm shaking too much right now to even hold the glass."

Paxton took a drink himself and suddenly found Carson leaning close. His breath smelled of wine.

"I wanted Mackenzie to sit by me."

"Come on, Carson," Paxton responded, keeping his voice light, "you can't expect to have my woman. No book contract is worth that."

The mystery author grunted but then laughed at something that occurred onstage. A glance to Paxton's left told him Ruthie's leg was getting some of Carson's attention, but she didn't seem to mind. His arm told him Mackenzie was still upset. He leaned close.

"It really is a fabulous show. If you can relax, you might enjoy it."

"I don't even know why I'm here. Where's my purse?"

"Under your chair. I'm sorry, Mackenzie. I won't let him at you again. Try to enjoy this."

"Do you tell everyone I'm your *woman?*"

"No, only when the man is trying to take advantage of a situation *I* put you in."

His voice was so contrite that for the first time in many minutes, Mackenzie was able to let her back relax against the seat cushion. The music coming from the orchestra pit was beautiful, and even though she wasn't as interested in the stage performance, she did allow herself to enjoy the music.

By the intermission she was enjoying both. There was a moment of panic when Carson stood and came toward her, but he did so only to tell

Paxton that he and Ruthie were leaving. Paxton saw them out, and Mackenzie sat with her eyes on the curtain of the balcony box and waited for him. She stood as soon as he appeared.

"Are they really leaving?"

"Yes."

"Is it because of me?"

"No, Carson is a restless man, and something in the second act gave him an idea."

"Will you get the book contract?"

"I think so. He's offended some pretty big names in the business, and although most publishers will put up with a lot, he is aware that his reputation is becoming muddied. Tell me, Mackenzie, would you like to see the rest of the show?"

"We don't have to, Paxton. You've seen it so many times."

"But you are enjoying it?"

"It's beautiful."

"We'll stay."

"No, Pax, come on. We'll go."

He would not listen to her, so Mackenzie felt she had no choice. He sat down and she took her seat again. Before the production was over, Mackenzie was glad that he had talked her into staying. The rest of the play was incredible, and Mackenzie was very moved at the tender ending. She was speechless as they moved from the theater and walked to the car.

"I take it you enjoyed the production?"

"Yes," she said softly. "It was so special. I had never realized it was all about redemption."

Paxton left her in silence to think about it, and it was some time before Mackenzie understood that they weren't headed back to her apartment. She looked at him questioningly when he pulled into the parking lot of the Watershed.

"You didn't think I was going to let you starve, did you? We have a ten o'clock reservation."

"I guess I haven't eaten. I hadn't realized it until just now."

"Well, come on. Dinner awaits."

Hunger hit Mackenzie the moment she walked in and smelled the lingering scents of fresh vegetables and steaks. It didn't take long for her to order off the menu.

"I must say, Mackenzie," Paxton began softly, "I don't know when I've been so taken by surprise. I had no idea you could protect yourself so well."

"I am sorry about that, Paxton. It was purely automatic, and I'm embarrassed."

"I'm the one who should apologize." He paused for a moment and then admitted softly, "I hadn't planned on Carson trying anything like that, but I can't say as it surprised me. I have to be honest and tell you that you're the first date I've had who didn't laugh it off or give as good as she got."

Mackenzie looked down at her bread plate and took a sip of water before looking him in the eye.

"I'm going to be 19 next month, Paxton. I know that I'm sheltered in many ways, but if that's the way your business is — if that's what women are expected to put up with from big-name stars — then you can have it. I won't ever live that way, and I'm amazed that you choose to."

Paxton was still staring at her when their salads arrived. They were several bites into their meal when he said, "Are you still planning to head home to see Delancey graduate?"

So that's to be the end of it. The thought went through Mackenzie's mind, but she let it go.

"Yes. I fly out in about ten days and should be

gone for two weeks."

The conversation continued from there, and there was no mention of the incident with Carson Walcott again. Paxton took Mackenzie home a little after midnight, and he even called to tell her goodbye before she left for the West Coast.

Mackenzie was thrilled to be on her way, but after seeing a big-name author up close and personal, she had no more desire to work on her book. The days before her leave had dragged, and only the thought of seeing her family kept her from feeling like throwing in the towel completely.

Mills College
Oakland, California
"This is it," Jack said as he pulled the car close to the large Spanish-style buildings, all empty with their red tile roofs and white stucco walls.

The Bishop sisters exchanged glances in the rear seat. Never had Mackenzie seen Delancey so full of peace and delight. D.J. had done a lot of growing up in the last six months. They both had. It was hard to imagine what the future might bring, and Mackenzie didn't know if she would ever grow used to being so far away, but it did her good to know that Delancey was following her heart.

Jack parked the car, and the four of them piled out. It was hot, but Delancey didn't notice. This was her school. This was where she'd been accepted. She never dreamed to hear back so soon, but her letter concerning their art program had been very passionate, and someone must have taken her seriously. Now it was happening.

Ten days ago she had graduated from high school. At the end of the summer, the day after Labor Day, she would start college as an art major.

433

"You look like you're walking on a cloud," Marrell said softly.

"Oh, Mom, I can't believe it. And if I hadn't heard back so soon, Mic wouldn't have been here to see it."

"Shall we try to get inside?"

Delancey surprised her by shaking her head no. "For today I just want to look around the grounds. Does that make sense?"

"Yes, it does." Marrell squeezed her arm.

The four traversed the grounds and buildings, finding something new to see everywhere they looked. The paths were lined on both sides with tall eucalyptus trees that acted like tunnels. The smell was heavenly. Marrell and Jack walked these, and when they had a few minutes alone, Marrell reached for his hand.

"Are you all right?" she asked. The big man looked shaken.

"I was the strong one when Mic left, but now with D.J., I feel as though my heart is breaking."

"She's closer to home too. I wonder why you feel that way."

"Probably because she hasn't come to Christ. Remember the way you prayed that Mackenzie would make a decision before she left? I've been doing that for Delancey. God gives me peace, but sometimes I choose to fret and worry."

"It will come," Marrell said from experience. Indeed, she had been forced the hard way to leave her daughter in God's hands. Being 3000 miles away gave her little choice. It had been a time of growth for her, and she knew that she would be strong for Delancey because of it.

"I'll say this much about the Army," Marrell commented, "it was a lot cheaper."

Jack chuckled.

"Oh, well," she went on. "I'm just thankful we've kept Paul's insurance money set aside."

Jack stopped on the path.

"I'll pay for Delancey's schooling."

"Jackson, you don't have to do that. That's one of the reasons I've been so careful."

"That's great, but I'm still going to do this. And if Mackenzie ever needs school money, I'll take care of hers as well. I want you to leave that money in the special accounts we set up two years ago. Do you hear me?"

"Yes, sir," she said as he leaned to kiss her.

"Now, now," Delancey spoke as she came toward them. "Enough of that. This is an all-woman college. Someone might be looking and faint."

Jack looked at her indulgently, but Marrell aimed a swat at her backside when she passed by.

"Where is Mackenzie?" Marrell called after her. Delancey didn't hear. She was taken with something else she had seen and was off in hot pursuit.

TWENTY-SIX

Arlington
June 23, 1987

Two nights before Mackenzie left California, her parents and sister had an early birthday party for her. The Lacys, Rose Cumberland, a few of the neighbors, and even some of Mackenzie's schoolmates had come. She'd had a wonderful time catching up with all of them, but nothing could have prepared her for spending her actual birthday alone. She had never mentioned to her roommates that her birthday was coming up, and they had joined an exercise class that met on Tuesday nights. She thought Paxton might know, but he hadn't called, not since she'd returned almost two weeks before.

Mackenzie knew she had a choice. She could fall into a depression or face the fact that at 19 you didn't have the same type of surprises that you did at age 10, then simply get on with the evening. She opted for the latter. As she made some dinner for herself, one of her mother's favorite Bible verses from Psalm 32 kept coming to mind. The verse spoke about the godly praying to God at a time when He might be found. Mackenzie pushed the Bible reference away, thinking it would only make her more lonely for her mother. Having started writing again, she ate her food and headed in to boot up her computer. An hour later she was so deeply involved in her story that the ringing phone was almost ignored, but it would not be silenced, and she eventually moved to the kitchen to get it.

"Mackenzie?"

"Paxton?" She was still trying to come back to reality.

"Welcome home," he said absently, and Mackenzie dragged her mind to the present. She'd been in a rather hair-raising part of the story that took place in Paris — a foot chase around the Eiffel Tower, guns and all.

"Thank you. Um, how are you?"

"I've met someone, Mackenzie," he said so softly that the distracted writer almost missed it.

"You what?"

"I've met a woman . . . well, actually, I've known her but never noticed her."

Mackenzie began to smile. He sounded like a boy.

"What's her name?"

"Jodi. Jodi Spence. She works here in the office — well, not my office, but down on the second floor — and we ran into each other at a party just a week ago."

"Have you gone out?"

"Yes. We just spent the weekend together. She would be here tonight, but she's taking a class and it goes until ten o'clock."

For a moment Mackenzie didn't respond. It was still a surprise to her when people treated sex so casually. Not that she thought of Paxton as being flippant; indeed, he sounded quite smitten, but she remembered back to their first meeting. He had come right out and said he was looking for a better offer, and he'd known her less than an hour.

Mackenzie and her roommates had agreed when they got their apartment together that no men would spend the night. They also outlawed heading into the bedrooms with the doors closed. But Beth had met someone, and it wasn't unusual not to see her all weekend. Janelle's dating life wasn't as steady, but she was known not to come home until morning either.

"I want you to meet her," Paxton said.

"Sure," Mackenzie was able to say without anger. She had never been in love with Paxton and wasn't now. "When?"

"Maybe this weekend. You'll really like her, Mackenzie. I know you will."

"I'm glad you think so, but it's more important that you like her, Pax."

"Yeah."

His voice was so dreamy that Mackenzie had to smile. For a full minute he didn't speak. Mackenzie stayed quiet just to see how long the silence would last.

"How was your trip?" he suddenly blurted, and Mackenzie took pity on him, telling him briefly that she'd had a great time and then letting him get off the phone. He said he would ring again soon, but when he didn't, it wasn't hard for Mackenzie to guess why.

Mills College
September 1987
"Oh, Delancey," her roommate said softly as she studied the drawing in Delancey's hand. "What did Mr. Brinks say?"

Delancey's smile was huge. "He gave me an A."

438

Lovisa grinned at her, the freckles on her nose standing out all the more.

"I'm not surprised. It was your best one."

Both girls looked down at the perfect drawing of the campus art building with the two Chinese lions flanking the entrance. Delancey's way with pen, pencil, chalk, or charcoal made people stand and stare. Her drawings were all so soft but never impressionistic. The viewer could always tell exactly what Delancey was trying to say.

"How was your chemistry test?" Delancey asked Lovisa.

"I think I did all right. I could have used some more time with the lab test — you know how wordy I am, so I aced the essay."

"I hate essays," Delancey admitted. "My sister is the wordy one in the family, when she puts her mind to it."

"How's the book coming?"

Delancey reached into a folder she had by her bed. She drew forth a thick stack of sketch paper and handed the sheets to Lovisa. The first page said *Micah Bear and the Rainy Day.* Lovisa paged through the sheaves, looking at the sweet drawings of an adorable bear, pencil-drawn and then filled in with colored pencil, and read about the way he coped with rain when he had planned to go to the park. Delancey had been very creative with Micah's mother. The mother bear sometimes spoke, but you never saw anything but her legs and sometimes the apron over her round tummy. The whole story concentrated on this small bear, whose brave little face melted Lovisa's heart.

"And she doesn't know?"

"No," Delancey shook her head. "I plan to give it to her for Christmas."

439

"Are you going to try to have it published?"

Delancey shrugged. "I don't think it's good enough for that."

"Delancey," Lovisa began, but the tall blond was shaking her head. "What would it hurt to try?" she ended up saying.

"I don't want it changed all around. I love it the way it is, and the only person I'm interested in pleasing is my sister."

Lovisa nodded, although she didn't agree. Only about half done, the book was beautiful. But she could hardly argue with Delancey's logic. After all, they were her drawings.

"Are you going down to dinner?" Lovisa, who was always hungry, asked.

"Yes. What are we having?"

"I think pot roast."

Delancey made a face. She was in the mood for chicken.

"Do you ever wish we had a car?"

Lovisa laughed. "Only every weekend."

Arlington

Mackenzie took her job very seriously. She had from the day she started, and she knew that would never change, but not until very recently — the summer, actually — when she began to write very steadily on her story, did she understand how helpful her work would be. For years she had forgotten how fun and exciting it was to create a story. She had done some work as a kid, and in fact, was using parts from an action story she'd written then. With the computer as a tool and the plot so clear in her mind, Mackenzie was amazed at how swiftly it was all going down on paper. She had more than 300 pages completed and still so much more she wanted to write.

To work in the filing office of the Army's national security center only added to the depth of her story. Nothing classified would ever go down in print, but in her position she was privy to details and terms that lent credence to her tale. And now it was about to get better. Mackenzie had just been informed that she would be headed to the Pentagon in February. She'd been called into her CO's office and given the news. While in the presence of her superior, she had acted every inch the professional, but once back at the files, Mackenzie hid behind a tall cabinet so she could grin like a fool and bite on a finger to keep from shouting.

The Pentagon. More paperwork, yes, but also more opportunity for advancement and more insight to the nation's security and defense system — subjects that fascinated her and helped her to love her job. On top of that, it wouldn't hurt Mackenzie's feelings to have an excuse to leave her roommates. It wasn't that she didn't like them. She just didn't want to live with anyone any longer. She had very little seniority in her job at this stage, but when the transfer came, she was going to try living at Fort Meyers. The barracks there might be even less private, but on the chance that she could get a room to herself, she was willing to risk it.

It was also time to think about getting a car. Since her office was within good walking distance, she didn't need one, but with the move in February, that would change. As a rule she was careful with her money and thought that if she really budgeted, she could swing a fairly nice vehicle. She'd always liked fast, sporty models but realized the vehicle would have to be more serviceable than classy. Her mind began to play with some ideas. There were some very nice cars on the market these days.

Insurance. Thinking of the word stopped Mackenzie in her tracks as she remembered that a car needed more than gas and maintenance. Not living at home meant she couldn't ride on her parents' policy, and that would be costly. Mackenzie was making a mental note to check into just what it might cost when the phone rang.

"Hello, Mic," her mother's soft voice came over the line.

"Hi, Mom. How are you?"

"Jack just handed me an early Christmas present, so I'm doing very well."

"It's the twenty-fourth of September, Mom." Mackenzie's voice was comical and fond. "I tell you, he's like a kid in a candy store."

Marrell laughed. "That he is. Don't you want to know what it is?"

"Sure."

"He just handed me three round-trip tickets to the East Coast."

"For Christmas?" Mackenzie nearly shouted.

"Yes!"

"Oh, Mom, the time is going to drag until then."

Marrell felt much the same way. June, the last time she had hugged her oldest daughter, felt like years ago. The plan had been to visit often, but Mackenzie had managed to get home often enough so they never went east. Marrell had been tempted to go a few times on her own, but that hadn't worked out either.

"What day?" Mackenzie was asking.

"We come in on the nineteenth and leave the

twenty-eighth."

"I wish you could stay here, Mom, but there isn't room for anyone but Deej, and she'll have to share a bed with me."

"We understand, Mic. We've already booked rooms at a Holiday Inn right there in Arlington. It even has an indoor pool. Maybe you'll want to stay with us."

"Oh, Mom, it's going to be so fun. I already have D.J.'s gift, and she's going to love it."

"What is it?"

"It's one of those miniature easels that's almost like a music stand. You can sit down and set in right in front of you."

"Oh, Mic, she was just looking at those."

Mackenzie heard Jack's voice in the background and told her mother to say hi for her.

"Here, tell him yourself."

"Hi, Micki."

"Hi, Jack. I can't wait to see you."

"Tell me about it. It feels as though you've both been gone for years."

"It'll be the best ten days of the year. I'll show you everything."

"Well, be sure and take some leave to shop for your Christmas present."

"Oh, what's that?"

"I think it's time you had a car."

"Oh, Jack." Mackenzie was stunned. "I was just told today that in February I'm headed to the Pentagon, so I've got to have one. I don't know what to say."

"You don't have to say anything. Just look around and check on insurance and that type of thing. I can have our agent call you and give you some phone numbers of people to talk to there."

"Oh, Jack." Mackenzie said again. He was so loving. She didn't write home or call home anywhere near as much as she had planned, even though she missed them all, but Jack never reproved her. He always just loved her.

"The Pentagon?" he suddenly asked, and Mackenzie laughed.

They talked for close to an hour. Delancey was doing well, and the Lacy children asked about both girls every week. Mackenzie had been playing with the idea of going home for Christmas, and she would miss not being in San Francisco, but having her family coming to her was very special indeed.

"Will we be able to do a proper Christmas dinner in the apartment?" her mother asked as soon as she got back on the phone.

"Sure. I don't know what everyone's plans are, but we can shop when you get here and do it up right."

"Will you have a tree?"

"I think so." Mackenzie sounded uncertain, and Marrell laughed. Her daughter was not strong on her domestic skills. She liked things clean, but if pictures didn't get hung right away, or if a cardboard box was used for a nightstand, well, that was just life. Her roommates didn't sound much better. Marrell thought about suggesting they all eat Christmas dinner together, but she could tell from Mackenzie's few letters and comments that she was not close to the other girls. Her daughter was no child. If she wanted to include them, she would.

They rang off with reluctance, both feeling a need for the other. Marrell was thankful that very soon they would be together, but Mackenzie could only think about the fact that it was three whole months away.

Mills College

"Hey, Delancey," Mr. Brinks called to his favorite student after class one cold October morning. The beautiful blond turned back and joined him at the front of the classroom when he motioned to her.

"My brother is coming into town at the end of this week," he wasted no time in explaining. "He, along with my wife and me, is going to the football game at the junior college Friday night. Are you free to join us?"

Delancey looked at him for a moment. "Would I be your brother's date?"

"Yes," his brows rose, "I guess you would be."

A blind date. Warning bells sounded in Delancey's head. Her art teacher had no difficulty reading the signs, and in fact he didn't blame her. That she was a nice girl was one of the reasons he'd asked her.

"He's a great guy, Delancey. He was 20 in the spring and goes to USC."

"How tall is he?" Delancey asked, bringing a smile to Kevin Brinks' mouth.

"As tall as I am."

Delancey nodded. She could live with that. Mr. Brinks was over six feet tall and handsome to boot. Half the class was in love with him, herself included.

"What's his name?"

"Kyle. He asked me if I knew anyone who would like to join us, and I immediately thought of you."

"Why me?"

"I'm just not sure you get out much, and I

445

thought you might enjoy it." Which was true, but inside he was thinking, *My brother's going to take one look at you and think he's died and gone to heaven. Not to mention you're the sweetest girl in any of my classes.*

"Can I think about it, or does that put you on the spot of not being able to ask anyone else?"

"No, not at all. I don't have anyone else in mind, so just let me know, even if it's not until Friday."

"All right. Thank you, Mr. Brinks."

Delancey moved on her way, but her mind was still very much in the classroom. That this was an honor was not lost on her, but it didn't mean she wanted to go. She had allowed a fellow classmate to talk her into a blind date with her brother the second week of school. She should have been warned when she learned he was a senior in high school, but to please her friend, she went. It was a mistake. All he had done was stare at her, and after not saying two words the whole evening, expected to kiss her goodnight. Delancey's hand in the middle of his chest had given him the message, but not for several seconds. She'd had all she could do not to practice a little of her training on him.

Now she didn't know what to do. Kyle Brinks sounded nothing like the senior in high school. After all, he was 20. But Delancey was still uncertain. She hadn't reckoned with Lovisa.

"Of course you have to go!" the other girl said immediately.

"Why do I have to?" Delancey asked from where she had flopped on her bed.

"It's Mr. Brinks." Lovisa's tone indicated it should have been obvious. "He would never let you be hurt, and even if his brother is a troll, you can spend the whole evening looking at Mr. Brinks."

She hadn't thought about the fact that her teacher wouldn't let anything get out of control, but had he actually said they were going to be together the whole evening? When it came to protecting herself, Delancey was not nervous, but such situations were always unsettling, and she simply didn't want to go through that.

"You have to," Lovisa now told her. "It's Mr. Brinks."

"You make it sound like he'll cut my grade."

"No, I'm making it sound like you don't pass up this kind of opportunity."

"I'll keep thinking about it."

"What if he asks someone else?"

"He won't. I mean, I was the only one. I don't have to tell him until Friday if I don't want to."

In Lovisa's mind this settled it all the more, but she knew she had said enough. She wondered whether her roommate had any idea how pretty she was. She didn't spend tons of time in front of the mirror, and she never acted too good for the other girls on the floor, but there was a confidence about her that you couldn't miss. Maybe it came from being stared at. She had known girls who let it go to their heads, but Delancey didn't fall into that category. On the other hand, Lovisa had the impression that if she were ever backed into a corner, she would be a different girl entirely.

Lovisa shook her head. She had studying to do. She was, however, almost ecstatic when Delancey said yes, and when Kyle Brinks came to call for her on Friday night, Lovisa was just as thrilled as if she were going.

■ ■ ■ ■

"Are you warm enough?" Kyle asked Delancey as soon as they climbed from the car.

"Yes, thank you. I just hope it doesn't rain."

"Was it forecast?"

"Yes, but only about a 40 percent chance."

Kyle searched the sky. "Maybe we'll luck out."

Mr. Brinks and his wife, Marty, had already started across the parking lot. Kyle and Delancey fell into step some 20 paces behind them. So far Delancey liked Kyle very much. He was attentive, but he didn't act as if he'd never been out with a girl.

"Because you have my brother, can I assume you're an art major?"

"Yes. I'm trying to stay on top of all my other classes, as I wouldn't mind teaching art someday myself, but my main interest is drawing."

"What type of subjects do you like? Have you had to draw the art building yet?"

Delancey smiled. "Yes, we did that, and Old Mills Hall, but my taste runs to children. I love children's books and anything to do with making small animals come to life."

"Kittens and bears and such?"

"Exactly." She smiled again. It was so nice to be understood.

They were at the gate then, and Mr. Brinks was buying their tickets. Marty smiled at Delancey as she captured her arm and invited her to precede her into the stadium. This act gave the brothers a few moments alone. Kevin looked at his brother, his brows raised in question.

"Wow" was all Kyle had to say. Kevin smiled in

satisfaction.

Kyle was feeling pretty satisfied himself. Since the beginning of the month he had been thinking about transferring up to Stanford at the semester break. His reasons were purely academic, but Delancey Bishop would not be hard to add to the list.

Indeed, the cold was starting to turn her cheeks red by halftime, and with the white turtleneck she'd worn under a navy blue sweater, she looked good enough to eat. Kyle could feel himself falling and thought he needed a bit of a diversion.

"How about something from the concession stands?"

"Oh, sure."

"Do you want to come, or should I bring you something?"

"I'll come." Delancey stood, not wanting to mention that her feet were getting cold.

"Do you want anything, Marty?" Kyle asked of his sister-in-law. His brother had wandered off to talk to someone.

"Thanks, Kyle, but I'll wait for Kev."

"Okay."

The two descended the steep stairway, weaving in and out of noisy fans and food containers.

"What'll it be?"

"Anything hot," Delancey told him.

"Hot chocolate?"

"Yes, please."

Delancey used the bathroom and then waited by the wall until Kyle returned. It took about ten minutes, but it was worth it when he handed her a hot dog, a huge bag of popcorn, and a large mug of hot chocolate. She thanked him with extreme pleasure, but not wanting to presume, asked kindly if he wanted her to pay for hers.

He shook his head and smiled. "My treat, but you know, by the time we walk back up, these hot dogs will be cold. Why don't we eat them here?"

Delancey didn't need to be asked twice. The aroma had made her feel famished. She was just finishing her mustard-covered dog when Kyle surprised her.

"I'm not as bad as you thought I would be, am I?"

Delancey's face heated. She hadn't thought herself quite so transparent. "I'm sorry, Kyle, but I had a bad experience with a blind date last month."

"Let me guess — he wanted to kiss you."

Delancey nodded. "I didn't want that no matter what, but it certainly didn't help that he didn't say ten words the entire evening and all he could do was stare at me."

Kyle could relate to the guy's feelings, but he had a little more control.

"Well," he kept his voice casual and kind, "just so you know, I won't try to kiss you. I'd like to," he added, which made Delancey smile, "but I won't."

"Thank you."

"If you change your mind," he had her laughing now, "just let me know."

"I'll do that."

"Tell me, Delancey," he said, suddenly serious. "If I find myself in town on a weekend when you're free, would you go out with me again?"

Delancey didn't even need to consider. "I'd like that, Kyle."

She let her eyes meet his. With his sandy brown hair and brown eyes, he was really quite handsome, and sweet in the bargain. She also loved it that he was a few inches taller than her 5' 10″ frame.

"You're going to make it hard to go south on Sunday afternoon," he said softly, and with the way his eyes dropped to her mouth, Delancey knew he wanted to kiss her. She chose not to comment but smiled at the compliment, offered him some popcorn, and allowed him to take her arm and lead her back to their seats.

Arlington
Delancey is seeing someone, Marrell's letter to Mackenzie started out.

We haven't met him, but he's the brother of one of her teachers. They met on a blind date, and I can tell by the way she talks that she cares for him. Not since Jace Booth, who ended up being a friend more than anything else, has Delancey liked anyone enough to do much dating, but Kyle Brinks — that's his name — comes up every other weekend, and they go out all weekend long.

Mackenzie sat back and thought about her sister. She was a beautiful woman, but her mother was right — she hadn't dated much at all in high school, even opting to miss some of the big events like homecoming and prom. Mackenzie had usually had a date to the main events, but she wasn't asked out all month long like Delancey was. Mackenzie didn't want to analyze it anymore and read on.

I trust she's thinking well about what she

wants, and she's very good about telling us where she's gone and what they did. We met Mr. Brinks one time — he's the teacher — and he seems very nice. I only hope his brother is as well. I'm not worrying that D.J. will make a foolish choice so much as I don't want her hurt or getting serious at 18. You're probably calling me a worrywart right now. I'm trying not to be, but all these things come to mind when your daughter is dating.

Enough of that. How are you, dear? Have you seen much of Paxton these days, or is he still immersed in Jodi? Is it lonely for you? I hope not. I know that the move to the Pentagon is on your mind, and I also know that you're good at your job, but I can't help wishing you could get out and have some fun too.

Do you ever think about going to church, Mic? I'm sure you could find one that would have sound Bible teaching, and I wish that . . .

Mackenzie began to skim but finished the letter before going back to the part about Paxton. She smiled. She had seen him that very evening. She had just been getting started on the indoor track when she looked up to find him watching her. He had finished his workout, so she stopped and went over to him.

"I'd hug you, but I haven't showered yet," he said with a smile.

"I'll take one anyway," Mackenzie said back, grinning and accepting his embrace.

"You're just getting started?"

"Yes. Are you on your way out?"

"Yes, but I had to get a little time in — too much of Jodi's cooking."

"You worry too much about your looks," Mackenzie told him with a shake of her head.

"Spoken like a 19-year-old."

This had made her laugh, and for a moment, and even after she left the spa, she missed him. Her roommates led their own lives these days. Aimee grew more religious with every week. Both Beth and Janelle had steady males in their lives, and Beth was on the verge of engagement.

Mackenzie's writing was starting to flag, not from lack of ideas, but because she was tired of sitting in her bedroom night after night. Her job was still fulfilling, but with the transfer around the corner, she was restless. At least her family was coming in three weeks.

Mackenzie's eyes skimmed back over the letter and caught the question about church. It wasn't that she hated the thought of going, but Sunday was one of the few days she could sleep in. Aimee went to church on Saturday nights, but Mackenzie knew she didn't want to do that. She didn't know *what* she wanted, but at the moment, she found it easier not to think about it at all.

Twenty-Seven

Mackenzie took the Metro to the airport. She knew that Jack had planned to rent a car, but she could not wait to see them. It took a little walking, but she was at their gate in plenty of time. It was dark outside, so she didn't try to stand at the glass but positioned herself where she could see them come up the jetway from the plane. It felt like forever, but was in fact only moments later that they were all trying to hug her at once.

Mackenzie was so glad to see them that she didn't care that they looked older. It was the first time she ever remembered noticing their age. Her mother still looked like a woman in her thirties, but she had changed her hairstyle, and that had matured her. Jack's hair and mustache were getting gray. Even Delancey, who had cut her hair to right below her ears, had an older look. It made Mackenzie wonder how they saw her.

"That was the longest plane ride," Delancey wasted no time in saying. "I forgot just how much I hate airline food."

Mackenzie laughed. "Well, don't expect much at the apartment. I live on cereal and the occasional meal out."

"A bowl of Cheerios will do just fine."

"Let's get our luggage," Marrell suggested.

Mackenzie caught her sister's arm and started her down the terminal. Marrell watched as the girls walked close together, their mouths and hands going faster than their legs.

"I think that's one of the things I miss the most," Jack said as he too watched them. "They have such a special relationship."

"I think they bring out the best in each other."

"It runs in the family," Jack said in his romantic way. "You bring out the best in me."

Marrell smiled up at him.

"For some reason, it's at times like this that I think about Paul. He would be so proud of all of you."

"Isn't that funny," Marrell countered. "I think more of you at times like this because of the way you treat the girls. You love them as if they were your own, and I don't know how normal that is."

"Who told you I was normal?" he asked, crossing his eyes.

Marrell laughed and let the matter drop. The airport suddenly seemed crowded, and with the girls out of sight, the time shorter than ever. They rushed to catch up with the visiting sisters.

The family went out to dinner and checked into the hotel. Then Jack and Marrell dropped the girls off at the apartment with plans that they would pick them up in the morning to go car shopping.

"What's with Aimee?" Delancey whispered, once the door of Mackenzie's room was closed. The other girl had met her but then immediately gone back to her Bible reading.

"I think she struggles with being so far from home," Mackenzie answered, trying to be kind. "I went with her to church one Sunday. She told me it makes her feel better to go, but I'm not sure why. All they did was listen to a man read from a book and do a lot of repeating."

Mackenzie's room was a little bit of a surprise, until Delancey remembered that her sister had never been into shopping. Her double-size bed had a nice spread on it, but she had no headboard or chair, and her dresser was very small. About the only thing that gave evidence of caring was the computer desk and chair, and the computer itself. She didn't even have a printer. Somehow it felt good to know that she had not changed.

"How do you like your computer?" Delancey asked.

"I like it."

"Does it make you want to start writing again?"

Mackenzie was so quiet that Delancey looked at her.

"Mic," she said, her voice low, "what have you not told me?"

Mackenzie looked embarrassed. "I'm sorry, Deej, but there's no privacy on the phone here. Someone is usually around, and I've just become so accustomed to not talking about it to Pax that I haven't told anyone."

"What are you writing?"

"A full-length novel, sort of an action-thriller."

"Mackenzie!" Delancey threw her arms around the older girl. "I can't believe it. Tell me about it."

"Well, I'll tell you one of the exciting parts, not all the lead-up with his military career and all that." Mackenzie's voice and face became all at once animated. "My protagonist is named Vaughn Ramsey."

"I like the name, but tell me the title first," Delancey said anxiously.

"Access Denied."

"Oooh." Delancey was awestruck. "Okay, go on!"

"I will, D.J., but you need to understand that I'm not even willing to talk to Mom and Jack about it. This is really private for me."

"Okay. I won't say anything. Just give me the overall rundown."

"I think Vaughn is a little like Dad — you know, a great soldier and dedicated, but after 20 years in the service, he gets passed over for an advancement that he really wants. It's only the first time, so he's not automatically out of the Army, but he's so frustrated that he gets out as soon as he can and goes to work for a man named Doyle. Vaughn is so low about all that's happened that he doesn't really check Doyle out. If he had, he would have found out that Doyle's dealings are not all that clean. When Doyle sends Vaughn to France, supposedly to escort his daughter home, he ends up running through the streets of Paris with this woman and trying everything in his power to keep them both alive. He doesn't find out for five more chapters why they're even running."

"Why are they?"

"A microchip."

"What's on it?"

Mackenzie smiled. "Actually stored on the chip? Nothing. But on the chip itself is the number of a private bank account holding money stolen in the 1930s."

"How much money?"

"By now, millions."

Delancey could only stare at her sister.

"Oh, Mic, I can't believe you're doing it. I'm

mean, you're *really* doing it. You've got to talk to Paxton. With his connections, you're a shoo-in."

"That's just it. I can't talk to Pax. He's such a good friend, and you wouldn't believe how many times he's told me how he hates it when he gets roped in by an aspiring writer and has to listen to him carry on."

"But you'll have a book to show him, not just some story in your head."

Mackenzie shook her head. "I still won't. Even if Pax was interested, there's a side to the industry I can't stand. In some ways I don't want to have anything to do with being published."

"What do you mean?"

"I don't think I ever told you this, but I met Carson Walcott."

"The playwright?" Delancey was stunned.

"One and the same. He's nothing but a lech."

"You're kidding." Delancey looked completely deflated.

"No." Mackenzie actually managed to smile. "We were sitting in a theater together, his date on the other side of him, and he actually ran his hand up and down my leg. I dashed out of there, and Pax followed me. He grabbed my arm, and since I thought it was Walcott, I put him flat on his back."

Delancey had had a long day, and as the scene formed in her mind, she started to giggle. She let herself fall back on Mackenzie's bed, laughter overtaking her.

"I don't suppose Paxton thought it very funny."

"Not at the time, but he's teased me since."

"And because of Carson Walcott, you don't want to do this?"

"It wasn't just Carson. Pax was very understanding, but he basically said I was the first woman he

458

had dated who didn't see that kind of flirting as business and was actually bothered by the incident. I told him I would never live like that."

Delancey sat up suddenly. "There are ways around it, Mic."

"Like what?"

"Like a nom de plume. No one need ever know the work is yours. I just got done reading about Franco Bershevea, who died earlier this year."

"I've never heard of him."

"You would have if you had studied art, and he is a she. Her real name is Frances Butts. She was an American woman, not a Frenchman, and no one even knew until she died. Her painting style is known all over the world."

Mackenzie thought the idea intriguing but still wouldn't consider talking to Paxton Hancock about her book. She wasn't sure her sister would understand, but it just wasn't worth it to her.

"I think I just want to do this for me," Mackenzie finally said, her voice soft but sure.

Delancey nodded and gave no argument. She'd used those words to Lovisa and understood completely. Thinking of the illustrated story that was sitting in the bottom of her suitcase made her want to rub her hands together. If she started laughing or smiling, she was going to give herself away. She opted to say she needed to use the bathroom, which was true. Mackenzie never suspected a thing, but all the way out the door, Delancey told herself this was going to be the best Christmas they had ever had.

The time between Christmas and Mackenzie's move to the Pentagon went by so swiftly that she could barely remember it. The first half of March

459

was over before she could even draw a breath. She hadn't booted up her computer since she moved, but she loved her new job and enjoyed her CO, Captain Engel.

In the first week she caught a mistake that could have grown quite serious if left undetected. A file was marked closed when in fact the man in question, a man who disappeared after a huge shipment of guns was reported missing in Colombia, was still at large. Mackenzie would probably never know the outcome, or whether or not she had actually helped, but it was good to know that her captain was proud of her.

And if she wasn't feeling good enough about her job already, she had an appointment today, one that she hoped would turn out to be everything she dreamed of and more. This one was not work-related, at least not Army work-related, but she didn't know when she had been so excited about something.

The appointment was at Cary's, a restaurant in D.C. Mackenzie was early and had taken a booth by the window. Her coffee cup had been refilled twice, but she was too nervous to eat. At last she saw him: Paxton Hancock was coming her way, a big smile on his face. Mackenzie stood up so they could hug.

"Hello, stranger," he teased her as he slipped into the booth.

"Hi, yourself. How have you been?"

"Busy." He nodded his head when a waiter approached with a mug and a pot of coffee. "I thought it would all slow down when Christmas passed, but we're already gearing up for spring and summer."

"How is Jodi?"

"Great." Paxton smiled contently. They were living together now. "Just had a promotion, so she's at the top of the world. How's the Pentagon?"

"I love it." Mackenzie's smile matched his own. "I thought Arlington Hall was interesting, but it can't compare."

"How do you like being at the Fort?"

"It's fine. I have a very small apartment, which is a miracle, but privacy was all I wanted. My folks bought me that little red Jeep parked right out there for Christmas, and I've never had so much fun."

"It looks brand new," Paxton said with his face to the glass.

"It's two years old, but there's not a scratch on it. I've even taken some weekend drives. Parts of the East Coast are beautiful."

"I think so, but then I grew up here."

Mackenzie smiled but didn't comment. She suddenly realized how awkward this was going to be. She had been so excited when she called him that she didn't stop to think about this part.

"All right, Mackenzie," Paxton rescued her, "out with it. On the phone you sounded like someone had just proposed."

"No, it's not that, but I —" She paused. "I've never taken advantage of our friendship, have I, Pax?"

"Oh no," the man said with a laugh. "That sounds like a setup with a capital headache."

"Come on, now," Mackenzie coaxed. "I'm not doing this for me. Will you hear me out?"

"Of course I will."

"Okay." Mackenzie took a deep breath. "You have to understand that this is not for me; it's for my sister."

"Okay."

"She doesn't even know about it. That way, if nothing ever comes of it, she won't be hurt or feel rejected."

"I understand." Paxton smiled at her earnest face. He was quite in love with Jodi, but Mackenzie would always hold a place in his heart.

Mackenzie bit her lip and looked at him for a moment before reaching for a large folder that lay on the seat beside her. She pulled a stack of bound papers from it and placed them on the table between them. She watched Paxton's eyes go down to the top page: "*Micah Bear and the Rainy Day,* written by Mackenzie Bishop and illustrated by Delancey Bishop."

"My sister put this together for me for Christmas. The writing is nothing, just something I did as a kid, but I think her artwork is good. Will you look at this and tell me if you think anyone at IronHorse would want to take a look at it?"

Paxton smiled into her anxious eyes. "Of course I will," he shocked her by saying. "I would have been upset if you'd gone to anyone else."

Mackenzie beamed at him and carefully watched his face as he opened the front, studied the illustrations, and then paged through and read every word. Almost as soon as he saw the first picture, his face grew serious. Not one smile of delight crossed his features, and Mackenzie's heart sank. She had wanted him to be as thrilled as she was and see the potential her sister had. At last he looked up at her.

"These are incredible," he said softly.

Mackenzie's breath left her in a rush. "Do you really think so?"

"Yes. When you told me a long time ago that

Delancey wanted to illustrate, I had no idea. And the story, Mackenzie — it doesn't read like a child's work."

Mackenzie waved her hand in dismissal. "It's not really the story I'm trying to sell, but outside of this I don't have a large collection of Delancey's artwork, and I wanted someone in the business to see what she can do."

"You did the right thing. Tell me again how old she is?"

"She'll be 19 in July. She's studying art at Mills College in Oakland right now."

Paxton nodded and took a napkin to write out the details. He looked up and said, "I think I'm a pretty good judge, Mackenzie, but as you know I'm not a children's editor. Why don't I take this with me and show it to Tom Magy? He's head of the children's book department, and he would be the one to say if they could use it."

"You'll be careful, won't you, Pax? I would never be able to explain it to her if I lost this book."

"I'll be very careful, Mackenzie. You don't need to worry."

Mackenzie didn't know what to say. A chance to have her sister's work recognized was what she had hoped for, but she could hardly believe it would ever happen. And now that the opportunity had come, she couldn't tell anyone. She couldn't call her sister with the good news because it might not go anywhere. Would it be fair to tell her mother? She didn't think so. She would be all happy and excited, and it still might not get off the ground.

"Can I buy you some lunch?" Paxton asked bringing her back to earth.

"Oh, I couldn't eat a thing. I'm so excited."

"Well, try to relax. Like all of us, Tom is a busy man. He might not get back to me for some time."

"Okay. I'm glad you told me. Otherwise I would be expecting to hear next week."

"No, no." Paxton adamantly shook his head. "Nothing moves very fast, and when we're this rushed, established authors get top priority. If you don't hear from me for three months, then call and ask me."

"Three months?" Mackenzie's mouth hung open.

Paxton nodded reluctantly.

"Okay," she sighed. "Again, I'm glad you said something. I would have been wondering if you'd dropped off the face of the earth."

"No, just buried under mounds of paperwork." He looked aggrieved. "I haven't had any fresh writing cross my desk for a year. It makes me wonder if it isn't time for a change."

"What would you do?"

"I don't know. Some agents make good money."

"But wouldn't you have to read more new authors than ever?"

Paxton's light brow quirked. "Yes. I keep forgetting about that."

Mackenzie laughed. The two talked for almost two more hours, and in that time they did share a meal. Paxton walked Mackenzie to the Jeep, giving genuine approval on the leather seats and new tires. The top was cloth, and he teased her about letting the wind blow through her hair come summer. They parted on amiable terms, and as Mackenzie always did, she missed him for a time. However, life for Mackenzie never stayed in one place. Before the day was over, her mind was on something else, mainly that she hadn't been to the gym to work out in over a week. She ended the day at the gym on the base and exercised until she could do nothing more than return to her apartment and sleep like the dead.

"Mackenzie?"

"Jackson?" Mackenzie asked in astonishment and some fear. She would have said her family didn't even have her work number.

"Yes, I'm sorry to alarm you. Nothing is wrong, but I need to tell you something."

"All right." She heard the calm in his voice and relaxed. "I was just about to go for a cup of coffee."

"You're such a woman of leisure," he teased.

"Oh, yes." Mackenzie went along with the gag. "There's so little to do around here. We all come in late and go home early to make up for it."

He laughed before asking, "Have you got plans for the evening?"

"No, none at all."

"Can you meet someone at the airport?"

"Sure. Who?"

"Your mother."

Mackenzie said nothing for a moment. Then understanding dawned.

"April Fool's, right?"

"No, honey, she's really coming."

Mackenzie's voice dropped. "You're serious?"

"Yes. She decided she needed to see her girl."

"Oh, Jackson," Mackenzie said on a giggle. "I can't believe it. What time?"

"Six-thirty."

"Oh, Jackson," she repeated herself. "I can't stand it. My mom is coming."

Jack laughed over the line, wishing he could see

the reunion.

"She said she felt a little rushed at Christmas, and she just wants you to herself for a while."

"I'm so excited. I'll see if I can get some days off."

"Well, if you don't have any more than the weekends off, she'll be fine. She just wants to be with you and catch up on her rest. She's weary these days, says it's the change of life. The only problem is, I'm tired too, and I don't have the same excuse."

Mackenzie wanted to laugh but remembered where she was.

"I wish you were coming too," Mackenzie said, pleasing him with the compliment.

"I'm swamped with work, and I know the two of you will have a great time."

"How long can she stay?"

"Her return ticket is for the tenth."

Mackenzie sighed. This was like a dream come true. She wanted to talk with Jack for the next hour, but she still had work to do. They closed the phone conversation, Mackenzie telling Jack she loved him, and Jack telling her to have a great week with Marrell. Mackenzie made herself work and not look at the clock. Unfortunately she could manage that for only five minutes at a time. The next hour dragged, and when it was finally ten to five, Mackenzie went to Captain Engel's office, explained the situation, and requested a few days off. He was glad to oblige her.

"Thank you, sir," Mackenzie said gratefully before she slipped from his office. It was time to finish with the computer and last-minute paper-work. Just as soon as she was able, Mackenzie dashed home, cleaned up a bit, changed clothes, and tried not to speed as she drove toward Washington National.

"What would you like to do today?" Mackenzie asked Marrell in the morning. They had both slept rather late.

"Not too much," Marrell admitted, her coffee cup going back to her mouth. She had been quiet the night before, unlike Delancey, who would have been willing to talk until the wee hours, but Mackenzie understood. Flights across the nation could be very taxing.

"How is Deej?" Mackenzie asked. "I should pick up the phone and call once in a while, but I just don't. And I'm terrible with letters."

"Tell me." Her mother's voice was dry. "Your sister is a fascination. She's still seeing Kyle, and they seem to get along well. That's just judging from the one time we met, but I don't think she's very serious about him. Her grades are fabulous, which means she's working hard, and she attends every art lecture and seminar she can get to. If it keeps up, Jack thinks she'll be wanting a car come fall, so she can get to even more events."

"Does someone as good as D.J. really need to do all this studying?"

"I don't know, honey. She loves it, I can tell you that, but as for how good she is, I've seen some pretty miserable stuff for sale. I think she's fabulous, but I wouldn't be the first person to be blinded by love. Not to mention the fact that I'm no art expert. Her teachers seem to think she's wonderful, but she's in no hurry to exhibit her work. I wonder if she ever will be."

Mackenzie's face immediately gave away her thoughts.

"What is it, Mic?"

"Oh, Mom, I don't know if I should tell you. I mean, nothing may come of it."

"Come of what?"

Mackenzie hesitated. Marrell patiently waited for Mackenzie to make up her mind.

"Two weeks ago I gave Paxton the book D.J. did for me. Pax was so impressed that he's passing it on to a children's editor at IronHorse. I didn't say anything in case nothing happens. I didn't want her hurt. I did it for Delancey."

Marrell gawked at her daughter. "But you say he liked the illustrations?"

"Very much. He was wowed."

"Mackenzie." Marrell was stunned.

"I'm sorry, Mom. I just thought if someone could see them . . . I didn't know that D.J. had already said she didn't want this."

"That's not what she said exactly, Mic. Don't be upset. I can see why you did it this way. Like you said, if it falls through, she need never know. And a part of me wonders if maybe Delancey isn't like all of us — not willing to step out in case of rejection. Maybe she would love to be published but she's afraid of hearing that her work is no good."

"I can try and get it back if you want."

"No, don't do that. I mean, you haven't signed anything, right?"

"No, no. I probably won't even hear back for weeks."

Marrell gazed off into space and then back at her eldest daughter. "Tell me, Mic, what's it like having a friend in the publishing world?"

"Oh, Paxton? It can be interesting."

"But you never fell for him — I mean, before

Jodi came on the scene."

"No. He's 19 years older than I am, and when we met, I was so new here that all I could see was my career."

"You think that's changed now?"

"A little. I'm still very serious about my job, but if I met someone now, someone who was interested, I think I'd be more willing to find time for him."

"Is there someone?" Marrell asked gently.

"No."

Marrell tucked a lock of blond hair behind her ear and leaned intently toward her daughter. "Then tell me, Mic, what do you do on weekends and in the evenings?"

Mackenzie saw no help for it. "I told Deej at Christmas, but I didn't want her to tell anyone. I'm writing again."

"Oh, honey," Marrell smiled. "You were always so good with words. Is Pax going to help you?"

"I don't like that assumption, Mom." Mackenzie frowned as she said this. "It's like expecting Jack to design houses for his friends in his spare time. I've never even told Paxton. I mean, he knows I wrote the words in the book D.J. illustrated, but that's all. Just because we're friends doesn't mean he wants to be saddled with one more person trying to use him to get published."

Marrell had been put in her place, but she had one more question. "If you feel that way, why did you go to him about D.J.'s work?"

"That was for D.J.," she said softly. "I would do anything for her, and Pax was glad I did. But I can't do the same for me."

"I should have been more sensitive. Is there some reason you didn't want me to know you were writing?"

"No," Mackenzie answered honestly. "I'm not ashamed of it, but at this time I don't plan to do anything with it. I don't even have a printer. As a matter of fact, I haven't written since I moved, and I'm not even excited to get back to it right now."

"But that is what you do on your weekends and evenings, or at least what you have been doing?"

"That, and work out at the gym or run on the track."

"You look great," her mother said honestly.

Mackenzie smiled. "Thank you. I'm sorry if I took your head off."

"No, you didn't. It's good to be reminded. I mean, it would seem so perfect to go through Paxton. But you're right: He's your friend."

"Mom, you won't say anything will you?"

"To Paxton?" She looked shocked.

"To anyone," Mackenzie corrected softly.

"No, dear, I won't. I'll probably tell Jack, but you know he'll not breathe a word." Marrell stopped. "Is it for the reason I mentioned before — fear of rejection — that you don't want this discussed?"

Mackenzie thought for a moment. "I think there is some of that, but mostly I just want my privacy. I didn't know how hard it would be to live with so many strangers, Mom. I love being here on my own. I had my own room at the apartment, but I didn't even feel as if I could talk on the phone without someone listening. Does that make sense?"

"Yes. I remember I was never alone after your dad died. I was at work all day, and then I came home in the evening and needed to be a mom. I thought I would lose my mind. I told Jack when we were first getting to know each other that I had taken my solitude for granted. I'll never take it for granted again."

"I'm so glad you have Jack, Mom. I'm not sure I could have left if you'd been alone."

Marrell smiled. "He's wonderful."

"Do you think about Dad much anymore?"

"No, at least not every day like I did for the first two years. Jack will sometimes have your father on his mind and want to talk about him. He's surprised me a few times. Purchasing the Jeep was one example. He's become more tender as we've grown older. He actually cried the day we bought it for you. Your smile did that to him."

"But why did he cry?"

"Because you were so pleased, but also because he wants to do what your father would have done."

"You know," she reminded her mother softly, "when you asked me if I had met someone?"

Marrell nodded.

"Just know that when I meet a young Jackson Avery, I'll be calling to tell you."

Marrell reached and hugged Mackenzie. Mackenzie warmly returned the embrace. They spent the day listening and sharing, hugging and laughing, and not feeling a need to do much else.

TWENTY-EIGHT

Marrell knew she should get out and take a walk, but she just didn't have the energy. Mackenzie was at work, and she knew it would be good to get some fresh air, but the book she was reading and the lassitude she felt got the best of her.

She was very glad it did. Five minutes after she decided to stay in, Mackenzie's phone rang. It was Jack. Marrell was thrilled to hear his voice.

"I miss you," Marrell said softly, "but I'm having a wonderful time."

"Tell me what you've done."

Marrell obliged him, rattling off the hours of the day and having him laugh over how lazy she was.

"So how are you?" she finally asked.

"Other than having broken my ankle, I'm fine."

"Jackson! No!"

"I'm afraid so."

"When?"

"This morning. Oliver just brought me back from the emergency room."

"And I'm not there to take care of you!" Marrell wailed.

"Well, Shay called D.J., and even though I told her I'm fine, she's getting a ride home tonight."

"I'm so glad. I wish it was me."

"Honey, it's just a little broken ankle."

"Are you in pain?"

When he didn't reply, Marrell had her answer.

"Oh, Jack."

"It's okay. *I'm* okay. I've been burning the midnight oil since you left, so this is just the Lord's way of slowing me down."

"Well, at least D.J. is coming. And she's a better cook than I am."

Jack grunted. "By the time I can get active again, I'll have put on ten pounds."

"I won't mind. Sunday already feels like years away."

"Well, I'll be at the airport even if I have to come by ambulance."

She told him he didn't have to, but when all was said and done, she was glad he would be there with Delancey.

The conversation wore Marrell out, and Jack admitted that he was ready for a nap as well. Husband and wife, 3000 miles separating them, each climbed into bed and slept for the next two hours.

"He tripped on the stairs?" Mackenzie was incredulous when Marrell told her the news that evening.

"Yes. He said it's not a bad break, but the doctor put a cast on it that won't be off for at least three weeks."

"Is D.J. going home to be with him?"

"Yes. He says he doesn't need her, but I'm glad."

"I am too. Jack is always taking care of us. It's awful to think of him being there on his own."

"Don't say that, Mic." Marrell's eyes had already filled with tears. "You'll have me crying."

"I'm sorry." Mackenzie saw the tears, and her

own eyes began to flood. "Call him, Mom."

"We talked this morning."

"Call him anyhow. You'll feel better, and then I can talk with Deej too. I haven't in weeks."

Marrell took only a moment to concede. She called and learned that Jack was resting comfortably. Even though Marrell did feel better after talking to him, when she gave the phone to Mackenzie, she still wanted to sob. Sunday did indeed feel like ten years away.

San Francisco

Delancey was on a cloud. The decision to attend the lecture by Arnaud Fortier from the Chicago Art Institute was made on a whim. She was tired of drawing and restless about school, not to mention the fact that Kyle wanted to be with her every weekend, *all* weekend. That was not what she desired. She never saw her friends anymore and hadn't been home to see her mother and Jack since Jack broke his ankle. The Saturday morning lecture was really just an excuse to get away. She hadn't banked on Arnaud Fortier being one of the most exciting lecturers she'd ever heard or two of her classmates being there, one of them bold enough to approach the speaker when he was done.

Delancey had never met anyone like him. So sure of himself, he was like a handsome grandfather with a touch of arrogance. He was nevertheless generous with his conversation and time. He spoke to the girls for nearly 20 minutes.

"Delancey is very good," one of the other girls said near the end, causing Delancey to blush. "Maybe she should study with you in Chicago. Do you have anything with you, Delancey?" the

474

girl asked, turning to her. "Show it to Mr. For-tier."

Still red in the face, Delancey pulled out her sketchbook. She opened to the first page and hoped it would be one of her better works. It wasn't, but she wasn't given a chance to change the page. The gray-haired lecturer had reached for the pad.

"You are good," he said softly, and even turned to the next page and the next. "Very good." Smiling, he returned Delancey's sketchbook to her and handed her a Chicago Art Institute brochure.

"Just include any of the drawings I just saw. If your grades match your artwork, you'll get in."

"I'm at Mills right now."

The older man nodded. "They have an excellent art program, but I will go out on a limb and say we can offer you more. You will not fail at Mills, not in any way, but I naturally believe that Chicago is the place you should be." His smile warmly encompassed the three of them. "I must go now."

The other girls began speaking as soon as the lecturer walked away, but Delancey's face was buried in the brochure. She could hardly believe he found her artwork acceptable. A moment of panic filled her. Maybe to recruit students he said something similar to everyone, but that didn't make sense. According to the brochure, he still taught. If he lured her there under false pretenses, he would have to face her.

She accepted a ride back to campus with the other girls, but when she got to her room found that Lovisa had left her a note to call Kyle. She ignored it and phoned her parents.

"Jack," she asked after a few minutes, "is there

any chance you can come and get me? I want to come home and talk to you guys."

"Sure I can," he agreed as he always did. "Your mom ran to the grocery store, so as soon as she comes back, I'll tell her. If something comes up, I'll let you know. If not, look for us about noon."

"Thanks, Jack."

"D.J., are you all right?"

"I'm fine, but I'm thinking about changing schools and want your opinion."

"Okay," Jack said calmly. This was not the first time she'd talked about this, so he wasn't too surprised. And although they were pleased with Mills, he was more than willing to hear her out.

As he'd hoped, Marrell accompanied him, and they had Delancey with them just a few hours later. The conversation didn't wait until they arrived back at the apartment but started as soon as Delancey got into the car and thrust the brochure at her mother.

"How sudden is this?" Jack wanted to know.

"Very sudden, but I feel better about this than I have about any of the other schools I've considered."

"Why must you leave Mills at all?" Marrell asked.

"I don't have to, but I've been feeling down about my work lately. Then this morning, really on a whim, I attended a lecture by Mr. Fortier. He's listed right in the brochure, and I'm just so excited."

Marrell firmly believed that Delancey needed to be leading with her head and not her heart and said so.

"I am, Mom. The year is over in just a few weeks, and now is the time to get going on another

476

school. I'm not a quitter, so if I get there and hate it, well, I'll stick it out. But I want to try these things now when I'm young."

Marrell smiled. She made it sound as though her life would be over when she got older.

"Besides, I need to put some space between Kyle and me."

Marrell turned to look at her daughter.

"I know, Mom," Delancey shot in, "that's not a reason to go across the country to school. But he's getting rather persistent."

"As in marriage?"

Delancey's eyes widened. "No, he hasn't said that. He just wants to be with me all the time, and I'm feeling smothered. I never see my friends, and I haven't seen you guys in weeks. How's your ankle, Jack?"

"It feels good. The doctor was pleased at how fast it mended."

"Does it hurt to walk on the stairs?"

"It did for a few weeks, but not much now — just the occasional twinge. I'm riding my bike for exercise, and when I do that, I don't feel anything."

"Good. What's for dinner, Mom?"

"We were going to grill hamburgers. Sound good?"

"Yes," Delancey said fervently, and a moment later she'd settled in the back and gone to sleep.

"I think she should do this," Jack told Marrell much later that day. Delancey had called some friends and gone out for the evening, but before she left they had talked at length, her ideas and reasons sounding quite sane. The school's cost was lower, which was nice, but it was more the

Chicago school's reputation that made Jack think it would work.

"It's so far," Marrell said, voicing her first thought.

"It is, but if that's the only thing holding you back, we can't try to talk Delancey out of it."

"Are you concerned about this thing with Kyle?"

"Not from Delancey's standpoint. By her own admission she doesn't want to settle down. I worry about his feelings and whether she's been careless with his heart."

"Do you think she would do that?"

"Intentionally, no, but she's a fun, beautiful girl, and I can see how he would be very drawn to her. Not to mention that if they're at all physical, she's giving him all sorts of ideas."

"The last time I asked her, which was months ago," Marrell said with regret, "they weren't."

"Let's hope she's kept her head over that."

"Let me see that brochure again." Marrell took it from Jack's hand and read.

"It's the same as we've talked about with both girls, Marrell — they're searching and believing that they'll find what they want outside of Christ. You and I both know better, but before they see it, we need to let them grope their way along. If I felt that Delancey would be in danger or come to any harm, I would be shouting my objections from the rooftops, but other than the distance, I can't find a thing wrong with the plan.

"The very idea that she keeps coming up with other colleges to attend worries me about her finishing college anywhere. She wouldn't be the first student to move around and change majors several times. It looks as though all her credits will transfer, but who knows what she may find in

478

Chicago?"

"It's such a big city."

"Marrell," Jack said patiently, "we live in San Francisco."

Marrell nodded. San Francisco wasn't as big, but Jack had a point.

"So you think she should apply?"

"If she wants to. If she wants us to tell her what to do, I don't think we should. But if she wants to do this, I think we should stand behind her. You heard what I said to her about her spiritual state. Maybe one of us will feel there's more we can say about that, but for now, I think we should let her do as she wants."

Marrell nodded. "Are we ready to have her come home for the whole summer?"

Jack smiled. "Ready or not, she'll be here in less than two weeks."

Delancey didn't come in the door until almost 2:00 A.M., waking up both her parents. Jack made sure she was all right but then knew that almost-19 or not, they were going to have to have some rules for the summer.

Arlington

"The editor from children's division, Tom Magy, wants to see you."

Mackenzie heard the sound of Paxton's voice but couldn't answer. She was at work, but even if a call for a national disaster had come through at that moment, she couldn't have responded.

"Mackenzie, did you hear me?"

"Yes. What does that mean?"

"It means he's interested."

"Honestly, Pax, I mean, they don't talk with you if they're rejecting it, do they?"

479

"No, they don't have time for that. He'd like to see you as soon as possible."

Mackenzie's mind raced. "I'm not off until the weekend. Is that too late?"

"I can check with him. He knows you work full-time. I would like to see you before you talk with him, so when can you and I get together?"

"Anytime." She came back to life.

"Come to my place tonight. Jodi and I will feed you dinner, and then you and I need to talk business."

"All right. Pax?"

"Yeah."

"Do you know what he's going to say to me?"

"Not exactly, so you and I will talk over the possibilities. Then I'll give you some instructions."

"Okay. Oh, I've got to get off here. What time tonight?"

"Seven o'clock."

"See you then."

She was off the phone a moment later, taking the papers that Captain Engel was handing her. She thanked her lucky stars that the documents were routine. She wouldn't have survived otherwise. A glance at the clock told her it wasn't even lunchtime. Mackenzie began to type, bringing the files she needed up on her screen and adding the new information. At the same time she asked herself how she would make it until seven o'clock that night.

"I've thought it over, and I'm not going to go over the possibilities with you," Paxton began.

"But I want you to," Mackenzie argued with him. She had sat all the way through dinner and was not going to be put off now.

480

"Mackenzie, that's not what you need to know right now."

"Just humor me, Pax. Just tell me what *might* happen. I won't get my hopes up, but this is all so new that I feel like a kid on her first day of school."

"Come on, Paxton," Jodi encouraged from the edge of the room where she was making coffee for the three of them, "tell her what you think."

Paxton exchanged a look with the woman he loved and turned back to Mackenzie. Mackenzie was more beautiful than Jodi, but not the soul mate to him that his girlfriend was. Every so often he dreamed of Mackenzie, but her youth and inexperience right now made him feel like a big brother. Feeling all at once tender toward her, he capitulated.

"I wouldn't be asking to see an author unless I thought the book was publishable."

"The whole book — not just the artwork?"

"Mackenzie, I'm just telling you how I would handle this, but something tells me that if he only wanted the artwork, he would have told me that he needed to talk to you so he could get Delancey's number."

"I can't believe it."

"Well, there's nothing to believe yet, because I don't know what he wants. But at least he didn't return it and say, 'Thanks but no thanks.' "

Mackenzie could only stare into space. Jodi came in and set a mug of coffee down in front of her, but she didn't even notice. She wanted to jump and dance; she wanted to shout and sing; but mostly she wanted to call her sister.

You've made it this far, Mic, don't blow it now. You don't know what this man is going to say. You could call D.J., get her hopes up, and find out Saturday

481

*that they want to ruin the book. Delancey would
never stand for that.*

Mackenzie was repeating all of this to herself as
she sat outside of Tom Magy's office on Saturday
morning. She and Paxton had gone over everything from how to dress to what to do with her
face.

Remember, Mackenzie, he had said with a smile.
*Remember that soldier's face you gave me the night
we met? You just do that with Tom. Don't even act
excited. Just listen, ask a few questions, but remember that I can explain the contract to you. Whatever
you do, don't sign anything! Come and see me the
minute you're done and tell me what happened.*

Mackenzie mentally reviewed his instructions
even as she adjusted her knee-length navy blue
skirt for the tenth time. Her blouse was white and
her jewelry, dark red. She looked as American as
apple pie.

"Mackenzie Bishop?" A tall man was beside her
before she heard his steps. His dark brown hair
was cut in the latest style, longer on top and short
on the sides. His hazel eyes didn't seem to miss a
thing. He was younger than Mackenzie expected.

"Yes." Mackenzie stood.

He put out his hand. "I'm Tom Magy. None of
the secretaries are in today, so you'll have to make
do with me."

Mackenzie smiled easily but was feeling anything
but relaxed as he shook her hand and led her into
his office.

"I like the book," Tom told her as soon as they
both took seats in front of the desk. Mackenzie
had expected him to sit across from her, but his
style was more casual. She was also glad that he
skipped all the small talk.

"Okay." Mackenzie had no idea how to reply and so left it with her one-word answer.

"In fact," he continued smoothly, thinking that he liked the fact that she didn't fidget or chatter on, "I'd like to publish it. I've even prepared a contract for you and your sister."

Mackenzie could only stare as he handed her a stack of papers. She could feel her hands grow damp.

"I would like some changes," Tom went on. Mackenzie came crashing back to earth.

"Changes? In the artwork?"

"No," he shocked her by saying, "and I shouldn't have even said changes. What I really want is more words. Not many more," he rushed to add, "but I think the story needs a little more filling in. Is that possible?"

"Yes," Mackenzie said, regaining her composure.

"Good, because there's one other thing. The contract is for this book and four others like it. I want a Micah Bear series."

"You can't be serious," Mackenzie wasted no time in saying.

"I'm very serious. You see, Mackenzie, you can't get enough of this bear in one book. Children and parents alike will be looking for more. They'll want to know about Christmas, his birthday, a trip to Grandma's, the first day of school, anything. Do you see what I mean?"

"Yes, and I would like to say yes we can do that, but since my sister does the artwork, and she doesn't even know about this, I'll have to —"

"She doesn't know about this?"

Mackenzie could see that she had stunned him. Her voice a bit cool, more to protect herself than anything else, she gave him a swift rundown on what had transpired. She relaxed again when he smiled.

"That was a neat thing to do. How do you think she'll respond?"

"Since you're not tearing the art apart, I think she'll be fine. But I'll certainly have to speak with her."

"Well do, by all means. Tell her I'm very impressed. We'd like to start production ASAP. You'll both have to sign the contract, which means we'll have to send it to her. In fact, if you want to sign now, I can mail it to her. She can look it over and call me with any questions."

Mackenzie almost smiled. She could see why Paxton had warned her; they probably gave all new authors the rush-act.

"I believe I'll take some time with this," Mackenzie countered smoothly, watching the editor smile.

"All right. Can I expect to hear back from you in say, a week?"

"I'm not sure." Mackenzie suddenly felt very much in control, and again Tom smiled. He liked her; he liked her a lot. When Paxton had told him that she wasn't 20 yet, he'd expected a kid. And she was young, but she was not someone to be pushed around.

"Here's my card," Tom said, taking one from his pocket and handing it to her. "Call me after you've talked with your sister, and we'll see if we can come to some sort of agreement."

"All right. Thank you, Mr. Magy, for your time."

"Call me Tom, and may I return the thanks. It really is a great book. You and your sister are very talented. I hope we can work together."

He saw her to the door, and Mackenzie walked

to the elevator, out of the building, and to her Jeep in a state of shock. It had all happened so quickly. Statements from Paxton earlier in the week about the way contracts work were the only thing that had kept her from peppering the man with questions. Mackenzie broke every speed limit getting to Paxton's place.

TWENTY-NINE

"A contract," Mackenzie said for the twentieth time. "He gave me a contract."

Paxton was still reading it. Jodi was out, and Mackenzie had no one to talk to. She paced around like a caged animal while the editor sat relaxed on the long sofa.

"It's standard IronHorse fare," Paxton said at last. "I just have a few suggestions for you."

"Okay. What are they?" She sat close to him like an eager puppy.

"I think you should ask for more books, you know, the freebies. This number is too low. And I'd go up a percentage point on the royalties if I were you, maybe even two. He won't balk at that, but then I'd also ask for —"

The figure he named made Mackenzie's pretty mouth swing open. "You can't be serious. He's already offered so much. If I do that he'll say, 'Forget it,' and I'll lose the whole deal."

"No, Mackenzie, he won't. I've already told you that all contracts are negotiable. He'll just —"

"No, Paxton." She wouldn't let him finish. "It won't work. I'm a nobody. No one's heard of Micah Bear or Mackenzie and Delancey Bishop. He'll laugh and tell me to get out."

She was on her feet again, pacing and waving

her arms. She had kicked her shoes off and even dropped her earrings on the coffee table. Paxton let her flap around and spoke calmly when she finally turned to him.

"I don't think he'll give you all the money up front, but, Mackenzie, it's not that much per book."

"What if the books don't sell? We'll have to give it all back."

"That's not the way it works. Advance money is an advancement against future royalties. If books don't sell, it's the publisher who's out. You wouldn't get any more money, but you wouldn't have to give back what they've advanced you either."

"Oh." Mackenzie understood for the first time.

"Listen, Mackenzie," Paxton went on, "we could hash this over for a week, but the thing you need to do right now is call Delancey."

"Oh, right. I'll run home right now and then —"

"Call her from here."

"She lives in California."

Paxton smiled. "Call her from here, and if she has questions, I'll be able to answer them."

"Oh. All right."

Mackenzie went to the phone, not realizing her hand was shaking until she started to push the buttons, made a mistake, and had to start over. She listened to it ring, hoping someone was home. It was wonderful to have her sister answer.

"Hello."

"Hi, Deej."

"Mic! I was just thinking about you. I went in and stole a sweatshirt from your closet."

"What sweatshirt did I leave?"

487

"That old Cal Poly one. Where did you get it?"

"I can't even remember. You're welcome to it."

"Thanks! So, what's up?"

"Well, I've done something that I'm not sure you'll be happy about. Just tell me you'll hear me out."

"Sure I will. Hey, you're not engaged, are you?"

"No, nothing like that. Just listen."

"All right."

Mackenzie took a deep breath. "I showed the Micah Bear book to an editor, and his company wants to publish it."

"What now?"

"The Micah Bear story that you illustrated for me for Christmas, I gave it to Paxton, and he took it to a children's editor. They want to publish it."

"Mackenzie, are you serious?"

Her voice was soft, almost hurt, and Mackenzie thudded to earth.

"We don't have to, Deej; we don't. I just thought your artwork was so good, and I thought maybe someone would be impressed with that and want to put you on staff or something. Maybe not even now but when you finish school. But then they wanted the actual book, the words — everything." Mackenzie's voice ended on an apologetic note.

"Oh, Mackenzie! You're serious. Someone thinks it's that good?"

"Yes," Mackenzie laughed. "And that's not all. He wants a series. He wants four more books with Micah Bear."

"Who's 'he'?"

"Tom Magy with IronHorse."

"IronHorse wants this?"

"Yes."

"Mackenzie!"

Even Paxton could hear the screams, right up to the minute Delancey dropped the phone and ran off shouting for her mother and Jack. Mackenzie looked over at Paxton and shrugged. He only laughed.

"If you'd have called from home, I'd have missed all this."

Mackenzie smiled at him.

"Micki?" It was her mother's voice.

"Hi, Mom."

"So it's true?"

"Yes. I have a contract right here."

"I can't believe it."

"I'm not sure I can either."

"Here, talk to Jack. I can't think."

As it was, no one had questions Mackenzie couldn't answer. She didn't want to stay on too long and eventually got Delancey back on the line long enough to say she'd call later. After hanging up, she felt totally drained. Paxton had to leave, so he handed the contract to Mackenzie and gave her some last-minute instructions.

"This is all pretty straightforward. Read it, write down any questions you have, and we'll talk later today or tomorrow. When you make a change, do so in ink and initial it. Don't even bother having Delancey sign it until you've talked with Tom about the changes. Then when he signs it, make sure he's initialed the changes as well. Got it?"

"Yes, thank you, Pax. I think I'll go home now and take a nap."

He laughed as he hugged her.

Just as she had left IronHorse a few hours earlier, Mackenzie now walked from Paxton's in a cloud. She drove back to the base, this time at a normal speed, and lay down on her bed. She didn't fall asleep right away. Her mind was a rush of emotions. But she must have dozed off, since she woke to the ringing of the telephone and her sister's voice.

"Were you *sleeping?*" Delancey was amazed.

"Yes, the whole thing's worn me out." She felt grumpy and had a headache. "Give me a minute to get my eyes open."

"Oh, Mic, I can't believe it," Delancey began, and for several minutes Mackenzie had no need to speak.

"Tell me how this all started," she demanded at last.

Mackenzie recited the story for her, explaining why she had handled it the way she did. She wasn't in the mood to talk about this — she still felt half-asleep — but she wanted to fill Delancey in. By the end of the conversation, she felt better, and when her sister thanked her, tears in her voice, Mackenzie's own heart burgeoned with pleasure.

"How do you want to do this, Deej?" she had the foresight to ask. "Do you want to draw some pictures and let me put words to them or what?"

"I can't, Mic. I just don't think in terms of words. I never look at a picture and see a caption, but as soon as I see the words, my mind starts drawing pictures. Can you do the words first?"

"Sure. I'll call you as soon as I have some ideas, and then I'll write the story out and put it in the mail."

"Go fast, Mic. I don't know how much time I'll have in the fall, so I want to do this this summer."

"Any word from Chicago?"

"No, but I'm hoping they'll let me know soon."

The sisters talked for another ten minutes. Mackenzie, who had wanted to sleep so badly earlier, hung up the phone and only sat at her small kitchen table staring at nothing.

Why am I not more excited? My sister is over the moon, and I feel nothing. Mackenzie decided she needed some fresh air and exercise. Determined to push all melancholy thoughts from her mind, she climbed into shorts and a T-shirt and went for a run.

San Francisco

"D.J., is that you?" Marrell called from the kitchen when she heard the front door open and close.

"Yes," Delancey choked out.

"What's the matter?" Marrell asked as she came around the corner, but by the time she reached the living room, Delancey was already sitting on the sofa, her back to her mother. Marrell studied her still pose, put the towel she was holding on the table, and went to sit across from her daughter. Delancey had tears in her eyes, but she looked more angry than anything else.

"You and Kyle weren't gone very long." Marrell's voice was soft.

Delancey looked at her, raised her eyes in frustration, and shook her head.

"I take it he wasn't as excited about Chicago as you are."

Another shake of the head. "He wants to marry me, Mom. Can you believe that! All this time he's been pretending to be happy for me, and today he tells me he's been begging God not to let me be accepted."

More tears came now, but they were out of rage.

"I just turned 19, Mom. I don't want to get married! I'm doing what I've dreamed of: illustrating

491

books with my sister and going to study in Chicago. Why does he have to ruin all of that?"

"What exactly did he say?"

"Oh, only that he's serious and he thought I was too, and that we could be married right away because he's graduated and has two interviews next week. Both look very promising, and I could still be at Mills and teach like I've talked about. I don't know! He had it all so planned, but he's never talked to me like this before."

Marrell hated to see her daughter upset, but not for one minute did she believe this was all Kyle's fault.

"So you never gave him any indication that this was a forever thing for you?"

"No!"

"You didn't tell him you loved him?"

"No, Mom, because I don't — not in that way."

"And you've never let him kiss you?"

Delancey stared at her mother, and Marrell's brows rose.

"D.J.," she said very gently, "how physical is your relationship?"

"Hugging and kissing."

"No more?"

"No, honest, but I see what you're talking about. He always holds my hand and puts his arm around me, and when he kisses me goodnight, it can get rather intense." The fire had gone out of Delancey Bishop.

"I'm glad to know, sweetheart, that he didn't just want to use you and move on. He's ready to commit himself to you, but it's like we've always talked about: Things move faster for men. And Kyle is older than you are. It's not too hard to understand that he's ready to settle down and support the woman he loves."

"He said that unless I come to my senses, he doesn't want to hear from me again." The tears in Delancey's eyes this time were from pain. "I don't want it to end like this, Mom, but I am going to Chicago in three weeks."

"Maybe he'll calm down and call you, and you can explain and apologize."

"I don't feel that I need to apologize. He made all these assumptions and then got mad at me for not reading his mind. Remember when I told you I needed to put some space between us and you mentioned marriage? Well, I was serious when I told you he'd never talked about that, and now he's already started looking for an apartment close to Mills, so I won't have to commute far."

Marrell sighed. "Men can be horrible communicators, D.J. Your father used to assume he had told me things when he hadn't, and then he would get upset with me when I wasn't thrilled over last-minute plans. For the last two Christmases, Jack has forgotten to tell me about the company Christmas party, and I've had two days' notice. We don't get into big fights about it, but I make it more than clear that I would like more warning."

"I remember last Christmas. You were in a panic about your dress."

Marrell shook her head. "I'd put on weight and couldn't wear the one I liked, so I made a mad rush to the mall where I found nothing, only to end up wearing something that I had in the closet."

"But Jack didn't expect you to marry him until he asked."

"True, but it sounds to me as though you've

been distancing yourself from Kyle, and he's trying to get you back. As I said, he isn't the first man to silently plan and not communicate."

They sat in silence for a few minutes before Delancey reached up and removed the necklace she was wearing.

"I think I'll return this to him. Maybe he can get his money back."

"I don't think he'll want that, D.J."

"I don't know . . ." Her voice was sad. "But if we'd had this fight before my birthday, he wouldn't have bought me an expensive necklace."

Marrell had no idea what to say. She had only met Kyle twice in all these months, which was not the way she would have chosen to handle it. Clearly that was because Kyle was in love and Delancey wasn't. The whole thing made her tired.

I feel ashamed, Lord, for wanting Delancey to go back to school, but in truth, I'm ready to go back to my quiet life. This has been the most exhausting summer of my life. I want Bible study to start up again, and I want to be in this apartment alone with my husband. I'm sorry I'm so selfish. Help me to be there for D.J. but not to forget You or Jack. I need wisdom, Lord — more so than I did when the girls were little. I would have thought it was just the opposite, but I've been naive and —

Delancey stood very quietly, her eyes on her mother's sleeping face. She wasn't angry that she'd fallen asleep during their conversation. She still didn't know what to do about Kyle, however.

Delancey chose not to think about it. She'd already illustrated three of the four Micah Bear manuscripts Mackenzie had sent before learning that the first two wouldn't even be out until the next year. She didn't need to rush the last one at all, but it was a way to take her mind from her problems. She settled down at her easel for the next two hours, the manuscript to *A Snowy Day for Micah Bear* open on the desk beside her.

There didn't seem to be anything else to say. The doctor had sat at his desk and told Jack and Marrell that the cancer was all through Marrell's body and then explained their options. The Averys didn't say much, not to the doctor and not to each other, as they went to the parking lot, got in the car, and drove home. Jack opened the door quietly and went to the fireplace as soon as Marrell said she was cold. The fire lit, he turned to find her sitting on the sofa just watching him.

"Why doesn't cancer ever figure into anyone's plans, Jack?"

"I don't know." He stayed where he was by the fireplace and just looked at her.

"I was so excited to have Delancey go back to school. It's been fun to have the place to ourselves."

She stopped then as though she were out of words.

"Maybe this is what God is going to use to finally get their attention," he said quietly.

Tears filled Marrell's eyes, and she motioned to him with her hands. He came right to her, sat close, and put his arms around her. Her tears let him have his own.

"I can't stand it that you'll be here on your own, Jackson; I just can't bear it."

He moved until his forehead lay right against hers.

"I'm so glad you married me, Marrell Ann Walker Bishop Avery. Never doubt that for a moment. My life has been so sweet and so blessed with you beside me."

"Oh, Jack, just hold me."

It was so sweet not to need words. She'd been tired for the whole year, but a serious illness had never entered their minds.

"I can't call them," Marrell told him softly, her mind just realizing it. "I can't call the girls."

"I'll do it."

"Will you, Jack? Will you really?"

"Yes. Right now."

"Jack!" Marrell's voice was urgent, but the hands she put on his face were tender. "Do it like my grandmother did. Don't set them up or drag it out. She called and said, 'I have cancer.' That was it — no beating around the bush."

"I'll do that, just the way you said."

"And Jack, ask them to come now. Ask them to visit while I still feel good."

"Did your grandmother ask that as well?"

"Yes. The girls won't remember all the details, but I went on my own and we had two weeks together. It was wonderful. Then we all planned to go for Christmas, but she died just a few days before. At the time I was angry, but God is good, Jack. He knew the timing would be perfect, and she could have been ill for months or years. God was so merciful."

"You chose to rejoice."

"Yes, and as much as I hate to leave you, I'll choose that this time as well."

Jack kissed her. "We both will."

Marrell sat where she was when he went to the phone and prayed as she never had before for the daughters God had given her, knowing with all her heart that He was the only one who could help them now.

"Who is this?" Mackenzie held up a photo for her mother to see. Marrell smiled.

"That's Grandma Bishop."

"It looks like Delancey."

"Yes. Amazing, isn't it?"

It was all so reminiscent of Colorado. Marrell felt as though she'd spun backward in time, only in this scene she was the one with cancer, and her daughters had come to her.

"I forgot to ask you what Grandma Bishop said," Delancey mentioned, the old photo in her hand.

"Jack spoke with her. She wasn't able to stay on the line very long, and then Otto called back to confirm that it was terminal. I wrote her a letter, but she would have just gotten it, so I haven't heard from her yet."

Delancey kept looking at the photo, but inside she was shocked and amazed. During the day they were all so normal. But for three nights she had cried herself to sleep. During the days they had sorted through photos, cleaned boxes out of closets, even carted stuff off to charity. The talking was nonstop. She felt as though she had stepped into someone else's nightmare but didn't admit that to anyone until later that night when she was alone with Mackenzie in her room.

"I'm not going to survive this," she said softly. Mackenzie was sitting in the chair, and Delancey was on her sister's bed. "I feel like I'm dying inside, Mic. How can God take both our parents? I just don't understand."

"I don't either," Mackenzie admitted. "But what seems worse is that I don't feel anything. I just can't find any emotions at all."

The sisters stared at each other.

"This is the first time I've ever felt like asking God for help, Mic. I mean, really asking."

"Then ask, D.J., but don't expect —" Mackenzie cut off, realizing suddenly that there were more emotions inside her than she thought. She took a deep breath. Now was not the time to give way to the tight rage that coiled within her.

"Girls." Their mother's voice sounded at the door as she opened it a crack. "Is Delancey in here, Mic?"

"Yeah."

Marrell joined her daughters. She had fallen asleep on the sofa after dinner and awakened to find Jack asleep in his chair, Delancey's room empty, and Mackenzie's door shut.

"Are you all right?"

"Yeah," Mackenzie answered.

"Mom, are you afraid of the pain?" This came from Delancey.

Marrell sat on the floor next to the open doorway. "No. There could come a time when it takes me by surprise, but right now I'm just tired all the time and feel a little odd. If the disease was confined to my uterus, they would do a hysterectomy, but the cancer is so widespread that Jack and I decided to let it go."

"I've heard that chemo can make it more tolerable, Mom," Mackenzie put in. "Did you consider that?"

"Yes, but as you know, it can also make you pretty sick, so I don't think I want that. Shay wants me to do it, just on the chance that they could be wrong about its finality, but she understands my decision."

"I forgot to ask you how she took it."

"Hard. She's taking it very hard. We go back a long way."

"How many years?"

"Well . . . second grade." Marrell laughed a little and shook her head in wonder. "I was so tired all the time, and considering I'd turned 44 in March, I thought the weird symptoms were just the change of life. I especially felt that way when Shay started going through the same thing, and her doctor told her that's what it was and to ride it out. I should have gone in sooner, but the oncologist said that this has probably been going on for quite some time. Going sooner might have helped, but he wasn't overly optimistic about that."

"Do you think about waking up in heaven, Mom?" her youngest daughter asked. She didn't want to think about tests and doctors right now.

"I think about heaven, D.J., but not waking up there. Second Corinthians 5 talks about how temporary our bodies are. It calls them earthly tents. At death we just don't need them any longer. I won't fall asleep and then wake up in heaven. I'll be in my earthly body and then with the Lord, just that fast. No falling asleep and waking up — just one place and then the other."

Delancey, who found this very comforting, smiled at her mother, but Mackenzie was almost catatonic. Her mother couldn't help but notice.

"Are you all right, Mic?"

"No, Mom, I'm not. I can't feel anything. It's the weirdest thing I've ever experienced. I just can't feel anything."

Her mother smiled at her. "It's going to take some getting used to, Mic."

"You've always been here," the girl said as

though just realizing it. "I've never even tried to imagine life without you. I guess after Dad died I may have thought of it, but it was just too inconceivable. I wish I could think straight. I just feel numb."

"I recall feeling the same way when your father died — just numb."

"What will Jack do?"

Marrell smiled a little. "He'll keep on. Knowing he will keep on is one of the things that helps me. We talk all the time, and we cry a lot, but he will be here for you girls, so I know you'll be in good hands. We're also working on legal matters so that things will be as uncomplicated as possible. Oh, I almost forgot —" Marrell came to her feet. "I'll be right back."

She rushed out and was back so fast that the girls' eyes were still on the door when she returned.

"Okay, this one is D.J.'s, and this one is Mackenzie's." She handed them brown leather bankbooks. "Remember those accounts we set up for the two of you after your dad died? Well, you're old enough to have charge of them, so here they are."

"You can't be serious," Mackenzie said when she saw the total. "Where did this money come from?"

"Your father's life insurance. You didn't need it for college, Mic, and Jack has paid for all of D.J.'s schooling."

"I don't want this right now, Mom." Delancey had started to cry.

"Well, you don't have to do anything with it, but I've wanted you to have the books for a long time and just kept forgetting to give them to you. Don't spend it all in one place," Marrell finished, but her little joke fell flat. Delancey was in tears, and Mackenzie looked shell-shocked. Marrell moved close to the bed to touch her daughter.

"I'm sorry, D.J." Tears came for her daughter. "I'm sorry I won't be here to see you walk down the aisle or hold your babies, but please believe me when I tell you that God is in control. If I didn't believe that, I would never survive."

"Oh, Mom" was all Delancey could say. Her tears came in such a painful way. Delancey clung to her mother, and Mackenzie moved close to touch her as well. Mackenzie wished she could cry. She thought it might help. But no tears came. Not then, and not even when they gathered the next month for what was sure to be their last Christmas.

Her tears waited until Jack called in the middle of February, and Mackenzie Bishop rushed to California to stand by her mother's hospital bed. Jack was beside her, but Delancey hadn't arrived in time. Mackenzie wasn't aware of anyone else. She had eyes only for the mother she adored, the mother she didn't feel she could live without. Beside herself with pain, she held Marrell Avery's hand as she slipped away, and at the same time told God she would never forgive Him.

THIRTY

"You could wear a lot of these, Mic," Jack said gently. They were standing on Marrell's side of the walk-in closet. Delancey had left the day before, urged by both her stepfather and sister not to change her flight and miss any more school. But Mackenzie was taking a little more time.

"Are you in a hurry to have them out of here?"

"Not at all. I just wanted you to take what you wanted, especially since you're the same size."

Mackenzie fingered the sleeve of a long-sleeved dress but didn't take it down.

"I'm going to come back this summer, Jack. Maybe then."

"All right. Anytime."

Mackenzie looked at him. "Will you stay in this apartment, Jack? I mean, it's so big."

"It is big, but right now I just want to be here. I think I'll move at some point, but the advice everyone gives is not to do anything sudden for at least six months or even a year."

"I can't even picture myself a year down the road."

"I know what you mean."

Marrell Avery had been buried just four days, and already life seemed strange and incomplete. Mackenzie was leaving in two days' time, and the thought was so odd to her that she couldn't quite reckon with it.

I'll be in Virginia, but Mom won't be here. I can't pick up the phone and talk to her. It's not the same with Jack.

The phone rang as they walked toward the living room together, and Jack answered it in the kitchen. From the way he began to speak about the Lord's provision, Mackenzie knew it was someone from the church. For this reason alone she was eager to leave on Sunday. She had sat so still during the service, listening to every word from the pastor and asking herself how anyone could believe that God loved people. She concluded that Pastor Timm had never said goodbye to his mother.

"How about some dinner?" Jack asked after he hung up.

"I'm not very hungry. How about you?"

"Actually, I have a headache, so I think food is just what I need. Come talk to me."

Mackenzie accompanied him to the kitchen and watched as he pulled several casseroles from the depths of the refrigerator. She had to say that much for the church family: They had certainly been caring. Mackenzie's disinterest in food changed when she smelled something like lasagna. She rose from the table to serve her own dish when Jack moved from the microwave. The sight of the Kitchen Aid mixer that Jack had given her mother the Christmas before they were married was too much for her. She turned her back on it and tried to swallow the tears.

"I think I'll have it easier, Jack," Mackenzie said softly as she turned to him. "I think staying here, seeing all her things, would be harder."

Jack looked around. "You might be right, but whatever you do, Mic, let yourself grieve. Don't try to stuff it down. When you hurt, let yourself cry."

"I want to cry every time my mind sees Delancey's face when she learned that she had missed Mom by a few hours."

"That was pretty awful." Tears filled Jack's eyes. "There's something about seeing that person one more time. My sisters were really shaken when I called them."

"Did I hear you tell Oliver that you'll be going to see Kate and Anne?"

"Yes. I've taken three weeks off work, and I'll be there for about ten days. Your mom and I were there last summer and had a great time. Anne, especially, is very upset."

"Who's older again?"

"Anne. She's 78 this year."

Mackenzie worked at picturing herself at 78 and couldn't manage it. *Don't kid yourself, Mic. You won't make 78. Cancer runs in the family. You've seen that with your own eyes.*

If Mackenzie had voiced her thoughts to Jack, he might have helped her, but she kept them tucked neatly away in a painful little pocket that made her ache at all times. She didn't know how to deal with pain and loss, and in most ways she had no desire to try.

It turned out to be a myth that handling her mother's death would be easier in Virginia. Ignoring Jack's advice to let herself grieve, Mackenzie dealt with the pain inside her the only way she knew how: She threw herself into work by day and writing by night. She was on a destructive path but didn't care. Her CO could see she was hurting and even tried to talk with her, but he could not get past the respectful expression she kept plastered on her face. She had already informed him that she would be leaving the Army in August.

Surprisingly enough, a month after she returned to work, rescue came from an unexpected source. Tom Magy had asked to see her. She had known when she got off work at 5:00 Friday evening that he wanted to see her the next morning, but she had worked on her novel until the wee hours.

"You look awful," he wasted no time in saying.

"Thanks, Tom. It's great to see you too."

Gone was the upright, well-dressed woman from their first meeting. Mackenzie had dropped into a chair, swung her blue-jeaned legs over one arm, and stared at him. If she hadn't been wearing a navy blue sweatshirt — a color she always looked good in — she would have appeared totally washed out.

"Long night?"

"Yeah."

"Hot date?"

Mackenzie snorted but didn't answer.

"You know," Tom said as he watched her, "it occurred to me right before you arrived that I'm already here five days a week. Would you possibly agree to going to my place to work on these manuscripts?"

"Does your wife mind?"

"No, my wife doesn't mind at all."

Mackenzie shrugged. "Sure. Where do you live?"

"Not far from Pax." He stood. "Just follow me so you'll have your car."

Mackenzie was more than game. Indeed, she thought if she didn't keep moving, she would fall asleep on her feet. She hadn't planned to write so late, but the story, now down to the last quarter of the book, was pouring out of her. She was afraid that if she stopped, she would lose her train of thought.

She almost missed Tom's turning off because her mind had drifted back to her story. Getting her act together in time to see where he was motioning to her to park, Mackenzie got out and followed him to his door.

The condo was much like Paxton's and only a few buildings away. Mackenzie followed on automatic, so it took a few moments to realize that although they'd stepped inside his place, he hadn't moved forward but only stood staring at her.

"Do I really look that bad?" she questioned.

"No. I was just trying to figure out what goes on behind those incredible eyes of yours."

Staring back at him, Mackenzie had no idea how she should reply. As though fascinated with these new surroundings, she glanced around and asked, "When do I meet your wife, or is she out?"

"I don't have a wife, Mackenzie."

Mackenzie turned to look at him and laughed a little at his amused eyes. "The picture on your desk . . . ?"

Now Tom laughed. "That's a joke picture. It's actually one of the receptionists at IronHorse. One of my authors had it out for me, so Chris had a glamorous picture done of herself and put it on my desk. It worked, and that was all I cared about."

Mackenzie's mouth had opened. "You're just a bundle of surprises, Mr. Magy."

"That makes two of us," he said bluntly. "Here,"

he said, shoving some papers at her. "Look at these and I'll make some coffee, unless you'd rather have something else."

"Actually Pepsi or ice water sounds better."

"Coming up."

Mackenzie moved to the sofa, dropped the manuscript pages on the table beside the sofa arm, and decided first to scrutinize the place. His condo was a pleasant surprise. It was laid out with modern furniture and art. Although contemporary interiors were not her taste, she noticed that it still managed to be cozy and warm. Opposite the sofa was a huge recliner, and against the far wall was an entertainment system, the likes of which most people could only dream. She thought Jack would have drooled a little had he seen it.

The kitchen was set back and away from the front door. She could see a small chrome dining table and four padded chairs. Nearer to the kitchen than to the living room was an opening that presumably led to the bedrooms and bathroom. Feeling as though she could move right in, Mackenzie told herself she would have a townhouse or condo like this someday.

"You're in luck," Tom said as he entered with two glasses. "I just shopped last night, so I have plenty of Pepsi."

"Thank you," Mackenzie said fervently as she took the glass. Tom started to take the recliner, but the phone rang.

"I'd better get that," he said as he moved to the kitchen.

Mackenzie settled back. She had been a bit tense but was now feeling tired all over again. She knew she should get up and move around the room, but she was just too lazy. She worked on the liquid in her glass, eventually setting that aside as well.

Tom came back about five minutes later to find her sound asleep. She started to waken when he lifted her legs onto the sofa and put a pillow under her head, but when he stopped his movements, she went back to sleep. She didn't stir at all when he spread a blanket over her; neither was she aware of the way he stood and stared down at her for quite some time.

Mackenzie woke slowly. She felt a little stiff and frowned when she heard the sound of a baseball game. For a moment she thought she was in the apartment in San Francisco with Jack. Almost at the same instant she felt someone's eyes on her and looked over to see Tom watching her from the recliner. She sat up in one move.

"How long have I been asleep?"

"About three hours."

"Why didn't you wake me?" She swung her legs off the couch, embarrassed and disoriented.

"I thought you could use the rest."

Mackenzie looked at him, blinking slightly.

"You called for your mother a few times."

Mackenzie let her head fall against the sofa back. She felt as though someone had dropped her on her head. A glance down told her Tom was still watching her.

"I'm sorry, Tom. I've taken up your whole morning, and we haven't gotten a thing done."

He shrugged. "I just wanted to be home today, Mackenzie. I didn't care what I did. Right now I'm more concerned about you."

"I'm all right."

"I doubt that, and I'm a man who recognizes the signs."

Mackenzie wasn't sure of his point. Was it the late night or losing her mother? She didn't want to ask, but he wasn't saying anything either. She was still debating the issue when the doorbell rang.

"That'll be our pizza," Tom said simply, moving to answer it.

Mackenzie was thunderstruck. She didn't know this man very well — at least not on a personal level. Their meetings had always been over business. The last time she had even taken a day off to work on the books, so they had met in his office. Mackenzie's foggy mind was still trying to find its bearings when he handed her a plate with three pizza slices on it and put a fresh glass of cola on the table beside her.

"Thank you," she said automatically.

"You're welcome. Do you like baseball?"

"Sure — whatever. Tom —" she began, but with the remote control in his hand, he turned up the sound and looked at her, his eyes amused.

Mackenzie looked down at the pizza and realized she was hungry. Concentrating on her food, she tried not to cry. She didn't even know why she wanted to cry but could have sobbed her eyes out. It took her a few seconds to realize that the sound of the TV was low again. She didn't have to look up to know that Tom was watching her again. She hadn't thought him this sensitive.

"Why don't you have a wife, Tom?" she asked. It was the first thing that had come to mind.

"I've come close," he told her without hesitation. "In fact, I just broke off with someone, or rather, she broke off with me, about six months ago."

"Is it still hard?"

"Yes. It's worse than a death — not to be

509

insensitive to your loss. It's just that I know where she is and who she's seeing now, so the hurt takes even longer to work itself out."

"I've heard people say that about divorce, so I think I know what you mean."

"Your parents weren't divorced?"

"No, my dad died two and a half weeks before my fourteenth birthday."

"And you're how old now, 21?"

"Not until June."

"And you lost your mom . . ."

"A month ago."

"So is it just you and Delancey?"

"Pretty much. We have a stepfather and some family in Florida, but we don't have much contact with the family in Florida."

"Because they don't want to see you, or because you don't want to see them?"

"We don't want to see them. We've met them only once, and it wasn't very much fun."

"I think what you need is a boyfriend, Mackenzie."

"The last thing I need is a boyfriend," she told him bluntly.

"How do you figure?"

"I just know me, and I don't need a boyfriend."

"How many have you had?"

Mackenzie didn't answer.

"Tell me what you think it would be like?"

Mackenzie shook her head, more out of exasperation than denial.

"Come on, tell me why you dismissed it so quickly."

"For one thing," Mackenzie leapt in, "I can't just go out and rope some man and drag him home. On top of that, I'm not very domestic. I'm not into cooking and cleaning, and most of all, I'm not interested in sharing some man's bed."

"Not all men are like that, Mackenzie. You must know that."

"So you mean to tell me that your girlfriend didn't do those things for you?" He was being nosy, so she felt no hesitation in turning the table.

"Mackenzie, I was going to marry Brita," he explained patiently. "It wasn't some fling. I was in love with her."

"Well, you'd have saved yourself a lot of pain by marrying her *before* you moved in together."

Tom gawked at her, and Mackenzie wished she could rip her tongue out. She put her pizza aside and stood.

"I'm sorry, Tom. I shouldn't have said that. I've got to go."

Tom stood but didn't try to stop her. Mackenzie was at the door before she remembered the books. She spoke without looking at him.

"I forgot about the manuscripts. Can I just take them with me and get back to you?"

"Come back here tomorrow at ten o'clock."

This brought her eyes up. "You already said you have to do this all week, so now you want me back here on Sunday?"

"But I didn't have to do anything today, Mac-kenzie — nothing that I didn't want to do."

Mackenzie didn't reply.

"Ten o'clock, or I'll come looking for you, Miss Bishop."

Mackenzie nodded but didn't say anything else. She exited silently, her stomach growling as she climbed behind the wheel. She wondered absently how her stomach could be growling when she felt as though she could be sick. Some minutes later she walked into her apartment on base, briefly wishing she'd learned to drink. Anything to take her mind off what had just happened.

Mackenzie tried not to blush the next morning but couldn't pull it off. Tom noticed as he let her back into his condo but didn't comment. He could tell by her face that she planned to get done and get out as fast as she could. He wanted to smile. He was in no hurry; neither was he inclined to make Mackenzie's getaway easier for her.

"Coffee?" he offered, his voice casual.

"No, thanks. Where are the papers?"

"Oh, I'll get 'em."

But he didn't. He went to the coffeepot and began working as though he had all the time in the world.

"I would have thought you would be anxious to get on with this."

"Not as anxious as you are evidently," he said, his back to her.

Mackenzie could have thrown something at him.

"Black?" He was holding a mug out to her.

"Actually," she replied, her voice tight with anger, "I take cream and sugar — lots of it."

Tom turned back and prepared the coffee and then set it on the table in front of a chair. He took the seat opposite, and Mackenzie felt she had no choice but to sit. She did so with ill grace, making no attempt to mask her displeasure.

"It's really quite a comfort to see that you're human," Tom commented, taking a sip from his own mug.

"How's that?"

"Well, up until yesterday I wasn't too sure."

Mackenzie only frowned at him, her mood no

better.

"Yesterday you called for your mother, and today you're in a snit like a five-year-old. Makes me think there's hope."

If he expected anger over these statements, Mackenzie was going to surprise him. Her shoulders slumped a little, and she actually raised her cup to drink. They were silent for several minutes before Tom spoke.

"Are you going to make it, Mackenzie?"

"I don't know," she said softly, her chest rising and falling with a huge sigh. "I can't believe she's gone. I just don't even know what to think or do. She's gone, and all I can do is pour myself into my writing to escape the pain." The words were no more out when Mackenzie's eyes shot to Tom's. This action more than anything else told him she was not talking about Micah Bear books. He knew he had to rescue her.

"I'll tell you what, Mackenzie. When you're ready to talk about what you're writing, come to me."

Mackenzie licked her lips. "All right."

"Shall we get started on the books?"

"Sure. Tom?" she said when he rose. "You won't say anything to anyone, will you?"

"About what?"

Mackenzie took another deep breath and nodded. He did understand. "Thank you" was all she said, and the subject was dropped so they could get down to business.

Chicago
Delancey studied the subject at the front of the room, a barefoot blond male in blue jeans and a white T-shirt, before swinging her eyes to her

easel. It didn't take long to see that her imagination did a better job. When she had to copy someone, she was too much of a perfectionist, expecting the painting to look like a photo, not a drawing. She had a tendency to fix things until the person was distorted.

"Looks good, Delancey," Tab McDonald, one of the male students, commented as he walked by. He was a senior and also the teacher's aide.

"Thank you," Delancey said briefly before going back to her work.

"Rumor has it that he's dying to ask you out," a soft voice whispered from beside her. Delancey glanced over to find Mona Reeve watching her.

"Well, we mustn't believe everything we hear."

"But considering that his sister is on my floor, it's a pretty sure thing."

Delancey looked at her. "I'm still not interested."

"Is it Tab or all men?"

The teacher came by before Delancey could answer, and she felt only relief. She knew Mona pretty well — they had met the first day of classes — but she wasn't very excited to talk with anyone about men. She didn't count on Mona's persistence. As soon as class ended, the other girl snagged Delancey and walked with her to their dorm.

"Would it really hurt to go out with him, Delancey? He's the nicest guy. All the girls are crazy about him, but he's picked you, and you don't even notice."

"It's not that simple, Mona," Delancey tried to explain. "I'm not interested in getting serious with anyone right now, and not very many men as old as Tab are interested in casual dating."

"What if he was?"

Still able to see Kyle's angry face in her mind, she shook her head. "There's no way to know that, and I'm not willing to take a chance."

Mona had plenty of things she could say to that, but stark pain filled Delancey's eyes, causing her to remain quiet. For a moment she had forgotten about Delancey's mother.

"Okay, Delancey, but if you change your mind —" She smiled, letting the sentence hang.

Delancey watched as she moved off. Mona was a pretty girl. Why would she care who Tab dated? Delancey wondered if she was only making sure the path was clear for herself, but as Mona said, Tab seemed to have his eye on her.

Delancey let herself into her room and lay across the bed. She had a class first thing the next morning, but for the rest of the day she was free. Her stomach growled with hunger and made her look down. Her jeans were so baggy in the waist that she could have tucked in five shirts. She knew she should go down to dinner, but she wasn't sure she would eat much. She was just dozing off when the phone rang.

"Hi, Deej," Mackenzie said softly from the other end.

"Oh, Mic." Delancey was instantly in tears.

The girls couldn't speak for some minutes. Mackenzie ached to be with her sister, and Delancey hadn't known how lonely she was until she heard Mackenzie's voice.

"It's so awful," Mackenzie sobbed. "I just hurt so much, and I hate it."

"If we could just be together, it would make such a difference."

"When is your spring break?"

"Not for three more weeks."

515

"Why don't you fly here?"

"Oh, Mic, I want to, but I feel so awful for Jack. I feel like I should go home."

The tears came again.

"Why don't you come to California, Mic?"

"I don't know if I can get the time off."

Delancey felt so light-headed all of a sudden that she knew she needed to eat. She didn't know how she would manage to hold anything down, but she was fading fast.

"Can you try?" Delancey finally asked her sister in an effort to ignore the spinning room.

"Sure," Mackenzie told her, but it wasn't quite true. She didn't want to see Jack at the moment. Every time she remembered the funeral, she grew angry. It wasn't anything she hadn't heard before, but now his talk of God infuriated her. She'd even received a letter from Oliver and Shay, but she couldn't bring herself to answer and thank them for prayers she didn't want.

"Are you still there, Mic?"

"I'm here, but I have to tell you, D.J., I'm not real crazy about going to San Francisco right now. I'm going to go this summer and help Jack sort out some things, but I don't want to be around him right now."

"Why, Mackenzie?" Delancey was thoroughly shocked.

"I just don't want to hear anymore about God's love and God's will and God's being in control."

"Okay," Delancey said with complete understanding. She was not as angry as her sister, but neither was she buying what Jack and her mother had been selling for more years than she could remember.

My mother served You with all her heart and what

516

do You do? Give her cancer. Delancey was surprised at her own thoughts and wondered if she might be more angry than she realized. She calmed when she visualized Jack alone.

"I'm still going home," Delancey said. Jack still meant that much to her. "But I understand why you're not."

"Are you going home for the summer?"

"Yes, as far as I know. In fact, right now I'm not even sure I'm coming back in the fall."

"Oh, Deej." Mackenzie sounded pained. "I thought you loved it."

"I do, but I'll only come back if I can get an apartment by myself. I'm tired of dorm life and college food."

"Jack'll help you if you don't want to touch your savings," Mackenzie told her. "I know he will, and I also know that he will understand why you want to be alone."

"You think so?"

"Yes. And if I could just have that side of Jack, the one that cares for me, I would go home. But I can't handle the rest. If I'm there, I'm going to say something I'll regret."

Delancey understood, but she felt her throat close all over again. They needed to be together, and she wasn't sure she could wait until summer.

"Just make me one promise," she said through tears. "Promise you'll not change your mind about this summer. Promise me you'll come, Mic."

"I will, Deej. I'll be there. I want to go — I just don't look forward to it the way I did before."

"I can't believe she's gone," Delancey said softly, voicing both girls' thoughts.

"I've got to get off here, Deej," Mackenzie whispered. "I'll call you later this week."

517

"Okay." Delancey hung up feeling so awful that she had to lie back down. In the next few minutes she shoved the pain away, took a few deep breaths, and formed a plan for dinner. She worked at thinking about what sounded good to her in an effort to be prepared, but early as it was, she decided just to go and eat the first thing she saw. Her plan worked beautifully until she felt sick in line and almost dropped her tray. She didn't see who owned the hand that took it from her. Neither did she protest when that same someone led her to a table.

"Here, Delancey," one of her teachers, Mr. Fitch, suddenly said. "Drink a little of this water." He pressed a cup into her hand, and Delancey managed a few sips. She looked into his concerned face and shook her head.

"I'm just hungry," she said softly.

"What's that?"

"I'm just hungry," she said, a little louder this time. "I just need to eat."

He nodded. No one could miss the way she had dropped weight in the last month.

"I have to get to a class, Delancey, but I'm going to ask someone to sit with you."

"I'm all right, Mr. Fitch."

"I'm glad to hear it, but I'm still going to ask Tab to sit with you."

Delancey could have groaned. She opened her mouth, but he was already headed across the room. She glanced at her plate and saw food she didn't remember taking. However, it looked good. She picked up her fork and took a mouthful of mashed potatoes and then another. From there she moved to an unknown salad concoction that was also very tasty. Tab was at her table a moment later, a trayful of food in his hands.

"How are you?" he asked conversationally.

"Fine," Delancey answered, even as she glanced behind him. She thought Mr. Fitch would at least stop back.

"He was running late," Tab noticed, filling her in.

"Oh," Delancey said inanely, pushing some of her food with her fork.

"Have you tried this?" He offered her a small dish. "It's a Mexican casserole. They've made it before, and it's my favorite."

"Thank you." Delancey took the dish and tasted it. "Oh," she said when she realized she had put her fork in it.

"It's all right. I've got my own."

"Thank you." Needing to do something with her hands, Delancey took another bite. It was good. She ate half of what was on the dish before she realized Tab had added other things to her side of the table.

"This is a lemon bar," he said when she looked up, "or if chocolate is more your thing, these brownies are pretty good."

"Thank you."

"And you can stop saying thank you and just eat everything I shove at you. Mr. Fitch will ask me how you're doing, and I need to be able to tell him you didn't faint or anything."

For some reason Delancey giggled. She hadn't felt like laughing in weeks, but this was funny to her.

"I've never fainted."

"No? Well, you've probably never been so underweight before either."

Her mouth fell open. "I can't believe you just

said that to me."

"What? That you're underweight?"

"Yes."

"Delancey, your clothes hang on you right now. How could I miss it?"

"I didn't say it's not true. I just said it wasn't very kind."

Tab suddenly sat back and studied her. "I should get you riled up more often. This is the first time you've had color in your face in the last month."

Delancey's eyes narrowed. "Tell me, Mr. Mc-Donald, do you have any other *compliments* up your sleeve?"

"Yes, but I'm saving them for when you agree to go out with me."

"In your dreams," she wasted no time in telling him.

"You are in a lot of those," he said so softly that Delancey was momentarily disarmed. She looked down at her tray and picked up a brownie. She glanced up to find several people staring at her and wondered if their voices had been loud. Almost at the same time, she decided she didn't care. She raised her chin as she looked across at her dinner companion.

"Thank you for sitting with me, Tab, and for the food."

"You're welcome."

Delancey started to put her tray together.

"I'll walk you back to your room."

"No, thank you."

Tab smiled at her prim tone. He knew very well that she wasn't feeling like herself and wished desperately that he could have gotten to know her before her mother died.

"I will be calling to ask you out, Delancey. You

can count on that."

"Well, prepare to be disappointed, Tab. But then life is full of those little inconveniences."

Delancey stood, tray in hand, and moved to exit the room, Tab's smiling eyes still in her mind. Being unkind did not come easily to her, but she made herself not turn around. It helped to know that Mackenzie would have walked away without a backward glance and also that her sister would have been proud of her.

THIRTY-ONE

Arlington

"You're a hard lady to get ahold of." Tom's voice sounded in Mackenzie's ear after work one night.

"Am I?"

Tom snorted. "What have you been up to?"

"Nothing," Mackenzie said on a laugh, but she knew what he was talking about. She had started taking her phone off the hook. Jack had called on Easter Sunday, two-and-a-half weeks before, and the conversation had been very strained. Mackenzie did not wish to repeat the incident, so like a coward, she was keeping the phone off the hook and immersing herself in her writing. She called Delancey every few days to stay abreast of her state, but other than seeing Tom a few times, the rest of the world was very cut off.

"Come to dinner tomorrow night," Tom said. "I've got something to show you."

"All right. What are we having?"

"What do you want?"

"Anything but pizza. You've served that the last three times."

"That's gratitude for you." His tone was long-suffering.

"What are you going to show me?"

"You'll have to come and see."

"All right."

"What time?"

"About 6:00."

"Okay, but if the pizza man shows up, I'm leaving."

They rang off to the sound of Tom's laughter. Mackenzie went back to work the next day and did her best, but her mind was still on Tom's invitation. Not really thinking of herself as a curious person, she nevertheless arrived at his place early and found him just climbing from his car. Knowing exactly what she was about, he smiled and handed her a heavy envelope when she got out of her Jeep.

"What's this?"

"Open it."

Mackenzie did so and gasped, "It's early."

She reverently held the first copy of *Micah Bear and the Rainy Day*. Across the bottom it said: Written by Mackenzie Bishop and illustrated by Delancey Bishop.

"Oh, Tom, this is it," she whispered, as if speaking louder would ruin the moment. "This is our book. We did it. My sister and I did it."

"That you did," Tom said just as softly. It was old stuff for him, but the delight in Mackenzie's eyes was very touching.

"I've got to call her." Mackenzie began to turn away. "I've got to tell Delancey."

Tom took hold of her arm. "Come inside and do that. I've got to clean up so we can celebrate in style. Just call from here."

"Oh, Tom" was all Mackenzie could manage as she followed the editor inside. He handed the cordless phone to her, or she might have stood there fingering the book all evening.

"Call her and tell me what she says." He exited on those words, and Mackenzie dialed. It was a horrible letdown when Delancey didn't answer, but she kept the phone in her hand and went to the sofa. She sat down and slowly paged through the book, studying every detail. She had seen the artwork, the cover, and the galleys, but nothing could compare with the final package.

For Mom was all the dedication page said, and the excitement of the book fell a little flat. It wasn't enough that her mother had known they were to be published: Mackenzie was bitterly disappointed that she wasn't with them to see the finished work. Jack sprang into her mind, but she decided to let Delancey tell him. She heard the shower come on and knew that Tom was going to be awhile. She tried Delancey two more times but still couldn't get her. It took a few moments for her to remember she was on spring break in California. Sitting back on the sofa, Mackenzie felt depression stealing over her.

Right now she had a choice to make: She could thank Tom for the book and go home, or she could put her hurt aside and go out and celebrate with him. The edges of apathy crept in ever so slowly. After all, she had worked all week and was tired. For several minutes she didn't care what she did and had no desire to make a decision. She heard the water being shut off, and with an effort she pushed those feelings back as well. By the time Tom arrived in the living room, dressed and ready to go, she had resolved to make the best of the evening.

Mackenzie didn't expect the kiss, but neither did she fight it. She and Tom were back from the restaurant. They'd eaten at a small bistro on the waterfront, but it was late, and Tom had simply walked her to her Jeep. Mackenzie was getting ready to thank him when he bent and kissed her. His arms went carefully around her, and Mackenzie kissed him right back. He was only two inches taller than she was, and she fit very nicely in his arms. Even when Tom broke the kiss, he stood holding her for several minutes.

"You're certainly a nice little bundle to hold, Miss Bishop."

"You don't feel so bad yourself."

Tom looked down at her, the overhead lights casting a bluish glow on her lovely face.

"Now, I'll be expecting you to change the sheets on my bed tomorrow and iron my shirts. After that you can fix some dinner."

Mackenzie smiled, remembering what she had said to him that first day.

"I'd better let you go," he said as he stepped away. "If I know you, you'll head home to take your phone off the hook and start to do whatever it is that you do. And since you'll do it until the wee hours of the morning, I'd best say goodnight."

Still smiling, Mackenzie shook her head but didn't bite.

"Goodnight, Tom. Thank you."

"Goodnight, Mackenzie. And you're welcome."

The smiles they shared were warm and genuine, but as Mackenzie drove away, she thought about what he had said and finally understood why she never talked about *Access Denied.* There was simply no reason to discuss it. She had a story she had to get out of her head and onto paper, and that was about the end of it. What she hadn't figured on was Tom coming to visit her on base, something he'd never done before, and the way his friendship forced her to show her hand.

Chicago

Never had Delancey had so much fun *not* dating someone. The night she had been ill and needed Tab's help had been a turning point. Rude as she had been, he had taken her words as a challenge. Not a day went by that he didn't smile at her, wink at her, or gain access to the group she was walking or talking with and somehow end up right beside her. He'd knocked on her door at least twice a week and brought her treats — sometimes flowers, sometimes food. She would frown at him but always take what was offered, and if it was food, eat every bite. Indeed, she had gained the weight she had lost plus some. She accomplished this by thinking about her mother as little as possible.

Her time with Jack had been special, but he felt Mackenzie's absence keenly. Jack had confided to Delancey that he knew something was wrong but had no idea what. Delancey had not known how to respond and wondered all the way home on the plane if remaining silent had been a lie. She was still thinking about it when she disembarked at O'Hare and found Tab at her gate. She hid her surprise and nodded to him, careful not to assume.

"Hello, Tab," she said softly, starting right past him.

"I'm your ride, Delancey," he said to her profile, watching her halt.

She turned to him, her face expressionless.

"What happened to Mona?"

He tried to look angelic. "Would you believe

she's sick?"

"No."

"How about that her car broke down?"

"How about the truth?"

"I asked her if I could pick you up, and she told me when and where."

Delancey's eyes went heavenward.

"Tell me, Tab, do you have any idea why Mona seems to want us to date so badly? What's it to her anyway?"

Tab shrugged, glad that she wasn't really mad. "I don't think she has a motive beyond just being a little too busy for her own good."

Delancey shrugged ruefully. "I hope you didn't have to come too far out of your way."

It was an inane remark since the airport was some distance from the school, but Delancey had no idea what else to say. She didn't want to get serious with anyone, and Tab seemed to enjoy this cat-and-mouse game they had started to play. Something struck Delancey as soon as they began to walk from the gate, and the moment she got into the front seat of his car, she voiced it.

"I owe you an apology, Tab, and I need to make it right now."

"For what?"

"For taking the things you bring to my room. It's very sweet of you, but it's giving you the impression that we're going to start something, and we're not. I'm sorry I've been so insensitive."

Tab was quiet for a long time. He maneuvered out of the parking garage and through the busy Sunday-night traffic toward school. Delancey was not accustomed to having her apologies ignored, so she sat miserably beside him.

"Has someone hurt you, Delancey?" he finally

527

asked.

"Yes," she answered, telling the first person since she'd left California and finding it very therapeutic.

"Why did he break up with you?"

"He didn't. I broke up with him because he was ready for marriage and I'm not. I don't get into casual relationships, and seeing one person exclusively leads to intense feelings. I won't make that mistake again. I also want to do well in my studies, and that's hard to do with a boyfriend."

"So rather than risk things getting serious, you don't go out at all."

"That's right."

They were at a stoplight now, and Tab looked at her.

"Thank you for telling me," he said, working hard to keep the pain from his voice and believing he accomplished that. "I hope we can be friends, Delancey, but I won't pressure you again."

"Thank you, Tab. I'm glad you don't hate me."

"Not at all. I admire the fact that you know what you want."

Nothing was said to that, which suited both young people fine. The flight was catching up with Delancey, and she was hungry. She had some snacks in her bag but didn't want to eat in front of Tab. Tab, who had started to believe that there would be something more between them, just wanted to be alone. He was mature enough not to resent her or treat her badly, but Delancey Bishop was one he wasn't going to get over very soon. It was only the middle of April, but the end of the term, and with it graduation, couldn't come soon enough for him. For the first time since he had met her, he was glad that Delancey lived in

California and his home was in southern Illinois.

Arlington
"So this is where you live." Tom spoke kindly, but inside he wondered how she stood it. He had never thought Army life was for him, and seeing Mackenzie's small, aseptic apartment only confirmed that fact.

"Yes. It's not very fancy, but it's home."

"What happens in August?" he asked. She had already told him she would be leaving the military.

"I've already started looking for apartments, just checking prices. It's expensive here, so I'll probably head out of the area."

"Going back to California?"

Mackenzie shook her head. "Not now, maybe not ever."

Tom could see she did not want to speak of it. He was sitting at her kitchen table and now glanced around the room a bit more. He looked at the "living room" area and saw her computer and desk. Next to her new printer was a tall stack of paper.

Tom's eyes swung to her in question and found that she'd been watching him. She looked tense for a moment, but then she slouched a bit in her chair. He knew she would tell if he asked, and he was not going to miss this opportunity.

"Is the stack of paper what you've been working on?"

Mackenzie nodded.

"Is it something for work or for you?"

"For me."

Tom's eyes went back to the neat pile and the neat desktop.

"Is it a book?"

Mackenzie nodded, a small smile on her face. "Can I look at it?"

"Sure." Mackenzie stood, went for the manuscript, brought it back, and set it on the table in front of him.

"*Access Denied,*" he read out loud. "A novel?"

Mackenzie sat across from him but didn't answer. Tom looked up at her.

"Come on, Mackenzie. Don't take me this far and drop me."

Mackenzie laughed. "No, it's 502 Micah Bear books. Of course it's a novel."

"All this is one novel, or am I looking at several copies?"

"It's just one."

"And it's finished?"

"Just last weekend."

Tom shifted the stack slightly and flipped through the pages until he was at the last one: 784. He looked up at her again and found her smiling at him.

"I like a challenge now and again," she explained simply. "I had this story in my head and wanted to see if I could write it. And I did."

Tom gaped at her. He knew she was writing and was nearly positive that it wasn't Micah Bear, but he was not prepared for this. He stared at her and then back down at the papers.

"May I read it?" he finally asked.

Mackenzie had been anticipating this, so she was able to answer immediately. "Yes, you can, Tom, but what you can't do is talk about it. This is very private for me."

"Of course. I won't say a word. But tell me, what do you plan to do with it?"

"Nothing. I know that's unbelievable to an editor, but that's the truth. I think it's a pretty good story, and I enjoyed putting it down on paper, but I did it for me, and that's all I care about."

"Does anyone know about this?"

"My sister knows that I started writing, but she doesn't know I finished it. My mother knew what I was doing, but I don't think she even told Jack. I trust you, Tom — you know I do — but I have to say it again: Please tell me you know how private this is for me."

"I do, Mackenzie, and I consider it a great honor that you're letting me read it."

Mackenzie laughed again. "You'd better save the accolades for after you've read it. You'll probably say it's dry as dust or all been done before."

"I'll be honest, shall I?"

"You can be, of course, but don't forget what I said: I did it because I wanted to, and I did it for me."

Tom smiled at her. Once he had gotten to know her, even a little, understanding her was so much clearer. She was incredibly independent, something he very much admired. He wasn't in the habit of comparing her to Brita, but he realized suddenly how tiring that woman had been. She had been helpless with so many things. Mackenzie, on the other hand, didn't seem to need help with anything. He almost wished that she did.

For a moment his love of books got to him, and without thought he turned over the title page and began to read. Mackenzie sat watching him, a smile on her face. He'd actually taken in a few pages when he felt her eyes.

"It's nice that you could come and talk to me, Tom."

He laughed. Her sarcasm was always so fun to him.

"All right. I'll leave it. After all, you're leaving tomorrow, so I'll have plenty of time."

"Oh, yes. I take up so much of your time when I'm here."

"You're such a brat," he told her complacently. "What are you making for dinner?"

"Did you come for dinner?"

"Yes. I'm starved."

"Well, I hope you like canned soup or Cheerios."

"You're kidding."

Mackenzie smiled at him, and not ten minutes later he learned that she wasn't. He even went through her cupboards for proof. They sat down to a meal of bean with bacon soup, crackers, cheese slices, and Twinkies for dessert. Tom enjoyed it but determined to buy her a cookbook for her birthday.

San Francisco

Jack had prayed long and hard about what he wanted to say to his stepdaughter, but now that they were alone and she sat across from him at the kitchen table, he felt strangely tongue-tied. He couldn't think of anything that hurt him as much as this wall that Mackenzie had put up between them. He loved her. She was also Marrell's child, and his thoughts and memories of that woman were some of the sweetest of his life. Mackenzie's not needing him or even wanting to talk to him was a blow almost as painful as Marrell's death.

"How is work going?"

"Okay."

"Are you looking forward to August?"

"Yes and no. I'm still uncertain about my plans, so I don't know what I think right now."

"Well, if you want to work for me, I can use you."

Mackenzie tried to smile. "I don't think the commute would pay off."

This was the first time Jack knew for certain that she would not be returning to California.

"Where will you live?"

"I'm thinking about some place outside of D.C., but I'm not sure yet."

"But not California?"

"No."

"Is it me, Mackenzie? Have I done something?"

Mackenzie's heart broke a little, but not enough to cry. "I just can't do this anymore," she admitted. "I don't know if I can explain."

"Can't do what?" He was desperate for answers.

Anger filled her, but even though it showed in her eyes, her voice was calm. "I can't pretend that I'm not angry anymore, Jack. I can't and I won't. You love a God who can't be trusted, and I don't want any part of it."

It made his stomach roll to know that if she died tonight, she would spend eternity in hell, but he had to be who he always was, even if she hated it or him. The thought gave him another question.

"I don't think I've changed, Mic. What's happened that you can't stand to have anything to do with what your mother and I believed?"

"You don't want to hear it."

"I do, Mic. You won't say anything that will change my love for you."

Mackenzie shook her head. "No, you'll just pray for Mackenzie some more and ask God to reach her poor lost soul."

Jack could have flinched at the bitterness and sarcasm and at the same time was thankful that Marrell didn't have to see it. Thinking of her gave him courage. He took a moment to ask for more wisdom, knowing God would honor his request, and addressed Mackenzie straightforwardly.

"Well, Mackenzie, I guess we know where we stand. I'm who I've always been, and you want nothing to do with that. To the best of my knowledge I've never shoved Jesus Christ down your throat. We asked that you attend church, but no one's ever forced you to pray or read the Word. I'm not going to pretend that I don't pray for you, Mic. I won't do anything just to make you more comfortable or to try to gain what we used to have."

Mackenzie looked at him. She hadn't expected any less, but having Jack say it outright was a surprise. Nevertheless, it was what she wanted. If Jack's face could be trusted, he accepted the fact as well.

"I don't leave for two more days, Jack, and I'd still like to see my sister. Is it all right if I stay?"

"You've misunderstood me, Mic." His eyes were tender even though she wouldn't look at him. He was in pain, but his heart knew peace. "You can stay forever, but I'm going to live out my faith as I've always done. I'm not going to tiptoe around you, not today or ever, but you're welcome in this home, or any home I have, for as long as I live."

"Thank you," Mackenzie said softly, still unable to meet his eyes. She couldn't say she was sorry because she wasn't, but in some ways this was a relief. She knew the next two days would be strained, and indeed, they were very difficult.

Delancey hated the silences and the pain she

saw on Jack's and Mackenzie's faces, but she had no idea what to do. Guilty as the thought made her feel, it was almost a relief to have her sister leave. She took her to the airport without Jack and cried all the way back to the apartment.

For Delancey, things were not as they'd always been with Jack, but she had to admit that it felt easier without Mackenzie. With her sister in the mix, she felt she had to choose, and right now she couldn't do that. She didn't understand, however, that her own quiet distance with Jack was, in fact, choosing, and Jack knew without having to ask that Delancey would not stay the whole summer.

Arlington

"Where are you taking me?" Mackenzie asked when Tom picked her up at the airport but did not take her home.

"To my place. I've got dinner ready."

"Let me guess . . . pizza?"

"Wrong. You'll just have to be surprised."

Mackenzie smiled at him. She was tired and a little achy, but it was nice to see him. She hadn't thought about missing him but now realized she had.

"So what did you do to keep busy these last two weeks?"

"All I've done is work," he told her without elaborating. "How was your trip?"

"It was all right."

Tom glanced at her. "Want to tell me about it?"

"I don't know. It's a long story."

"I have time."

Mackenzie looked at him. "Maybe some other time, all right?"

"Of course."

Mackenzie was glad that he let it go, and they finished the ride in silence. She was as relaxed as a cat, almost dozing, by the time they reached his place.

"Come on," he coaxed her as he opened her door. "I'll get a little Pepsi into you and bring you back to life."

Mackenzie went along with him, and when he finally sat her down at his kitchen table and gave her a huge sub sandwich and several deli salads to choose from, she was glad she had come.

"These are good! Gino's, right?"

"Of course. You wouldn't expect me to welcome you home with anything else."

"Thank you, kind sir."

"By the way, why haven't you asked me if I read your book?"

"Oh," Mackenzie's brows rose. "I thought of it when my plane was leaving San Francisco but then forgot again."

Tom was amazed all over again. He knew she'd been guileless with him about her feelings, but he hadn't thought her this at ease. Most people wanted to know if the other person approved. Mackenzie Bishop honestly didn't care.

"Did you read it?"

"I did, and it's excellent."

Mackenzie beamed. "Well, Tom, coming from you, that's a real compliment. Thank you."

Tom took a bite of his own sandwich and mentally regrouped. This was not going anything like he had planned. He opened his mouth to try again but decided to wait until they were finished with the meal. They did the dishes, talking all the while, and Tom even kissed her when she got suds on her cheek, but she wasn't expecting the move he made after dinner. Taking her hand, he led her to the big chair and pulled her down in his lap. Their relationship was getting physical, but nowhere near this much. Mackenzie's eyes widened, and she wondered if he'd been drinking. She was almost sure of it when he kissed her long and hard.

"Tom, what in the world —"

"Do I have your attention now?"

"You've had my attention all evening."

"No, I haven't. I want you to listen to me, and I'll do anything to make sure you do."

Mackenzie stared at him in confusion before climbing from his lap. She sat on the edge of the sofa.

"You have my attention, Tom, and you can start by telling me what that was all about."

"No, I'm going to start by repeating what I said about *Access Denied.* It's good, Mackenzie, *very* good."

"Thank you, Tom, but I did hear you the first time."

"You're sure?"

"Yes."

"Okay, because I'm serious, Mackenzie. I know he'll make some changes, not to the story itself, it's too good for that, but maybe a little with your grammar. You tend to use the word *just* too much and *that* a little too often, but he's —"

"Who, Tom? I don't know what you're talking about."

"I'm talking about Paxton and what he's going to say."

Mackenzie bolted to her feet. *"You gave the manuscript to Paxton?"*

"No, but I'm going to."

Mackenzie collapsed back onto the sofa with relief, and Tom talked on for some minutes before he realized he'd lost her again.

"Do I need to get you over here in my lap again? I'm trying to tell you —" He stopped when Mackenzie just continued to shake her head. Tom took a deep breath and suddenly realized how emotional he had been. If ever he needed to be calm and professional, it was now. He sat up in the overstuffed leather chair, took a moment to compose himself, and looked at his guest.

"Mackenzie, your book is good. I'm not saying that just because I care for you but because it's true."

Mackenzie only stared at him.

"*Access Denied* is the freshest thing I've read in five years. I was late for work the Monday after you left because I read until four in the morning and overslept my alarm, something I haven't done since I was a teenager. Your book needs to be in bookstores, and Paxton Hancock is the man to put it there."

"I can't," Mackenzie said softly. "I appreciate what you're saying, Tom. It means a lot to me. But you don't understand: I *can't.*"

"Why can't you?"

Mackenzie sat back, and for a moment she studied the white ceiling of the condo's living room. "I met Paxton right after I moved here, and at first he was interested in me, even when he found out I was so much younger. But when I told him I didn't want a relationship, he just became my friend. We did lots of things together over the months before he met Jodi, and if there was one thing I learned, it's that he *hates* aspiring fiction authors. He would moan until I told him

538

to shut up whenever he attended a party and was caught in the corner by some long-winded wannabe who told him every detail of a book that wasn't written yet."

Tom started to shake his head, but Mackenzie went on, so he stopped.

"I also lived in his world for a little while, Tom, and I didn't like it. On top of that, I don't like to use people. Pax is my friend. The only favor I've ever asked of him was to look at Delancey's artwork, and that's how you ended up with Micah Bear. So you see, I can't."

"No one appreciates your not taking advantage of your connection to IronHorse more than I do, Mackenzie, and I mean that. You could have hounded me months ago about this book, but you didn't. You wrote it for yourself, and I love that. But there's more to this story. I may work in children's books, and I may keep more abreast of that market than any other, but books are still my passion. I love them. My bedroom is lined with one bookshelf after another, all packed with books I've read and reread. Paxton would not thank you for keeping this from him just because he doesn't like to be bothered with the wannabes of this world."

"Tom," Mackenzie tried another tact, "it won't work. He'll take one look at my name and laugh."

"We won't use your name."

Mackenzie's mouth opened. "Lie to him? Pretend I didn't write it?"

"Absolutely. I promise you, in the long run he will thank us."

Mackenzie could only laugh. He was serious, and she was incredulous. She sat still while he stood and went into the next room. He returned with a fat folder, obviously her manuscript.

"I'm headed to Paxton's right now to see if he's home."

"What will you say?"

"That my mother spoke out of turn and I've been roped into passing this manuscript on to someone."

"What name will you use?"

She stumped him with that. He walked back to his big chair and sat, the book in his lap.

"Ken Bishop," he suddenly announced with a smile.

"Ken? Where did you get 'Ken'?"

"Mackenzie."

That woman shook her head. "He'll pick up on the Bishop, Tom. It's too obvious."

The man thought some more, his brow furrowed.

"And Ken sounds like a doll."

"Mac then," Tom tried.

"You can't put that with Bishop. He'll know in an instant."

"What's your mother's maiden name?"

"Walker."

A big smile stretched Tom's mouth, and he stood. Mackenzie found herself staring again.

"That mother of mine," he spoke in a singsong voice as he moved toward the door. "Having her old friend's grandson just drop in on her like that. Why, she hadn't even remembered that Mac Walker was still in the state, and here he was all grown up, and me stuck with this manuscript."

Tom dropped the role just long enough to wink at her and tell her to stay put. He was out the door and long gone before Mackenzie asked herself, *What in the world have I done?*

540

Thirty-Two

Jack knew he would cry when she left, but he told himself to hold together until she was gone. It was like losing Marrell all over again. Mackenzie had gone so far as to write to Delancey asking her to send some of her things. Several boxes had been mailed. Now the car they had purchased for Delancey was full of her belongings, far more than she needed for a year at school. Jack wondered if he would ever see her again.

How has it come to this, Lord? How did we get so far away? I know they were never on the same page with us spiritually, but I thought the girls cared. Jack had to stop that train of thought before he sobbed like a baby.

Delancey was coming from her bedroom now, looking a little uncertain, but some of her black-belt training was coming to the fore. Jack had seen it off and on through the years, but not for some time had he seen that resolute expression on her face.

"All set?" he asked softly.

"I think so."

"Listen, D.J., I think you feel that you need to choose between me and Mackenzie. You don't. I

541

don't think Mackenzie will care if we stay in touch." But Jack wished he'd saved his breath. He never thought Mackenzie had so much influence over Delancey, but right now she certainly did. Delancey looked more determined than ever after those words. It was as if she was ready to crumble and had to get out before it happened. Jack didn't want her to stay just because he'd begged her, so he let it drop.

"I'd better go," Delancey said.

"All right. If you think of it, just drop me a postcard so I know you made it. Illinois is a long way away."

"I will, and I'm still going to pay you back for the car, Jack."

"No, you're not, D.J., and I mean it. I'd even cover your schooling if you'd let me."

But she was already shaking her head. "I don't know if I'm even going to school the first semester, Jack. Thank you, but I have the account money from my dad and the advance money from the books. I'll be fine."

"Well, if ever you're not, you know the number."

Delancey trembled as he hugged her but was thankful he didn't walk her down to the car. He was right: She did feel as though she had to choose. Mackenzie wanted nothing to do with San Francisco and Jack, and Delancey didn't know how she could live in both her sister's and Jack's worlds. At times she felt Mackenzie was being unreasonable, but she was still her sister, and in her mind, the last family she had.

It was this thought alone that enabled her to check the map, put the car in gear, and drive away from California with no intention of returning.

Mackenzie hung a childhood photo of her and Delancey on the wall next to her desk and stood back and smiled at the two little girls in poodle skirts grinning at the camera. From there she turned slowly to look at the room, not caring that it had little furniture, and smiled in delight.

Her own apartment. It wasn't the same as living on base by herself. This was her very own, with only the lease to keep track of and not her term of service with the United States Army. It had been a good three years. She wouldn't have traded them for anything. But she was glad to be done, and the apartment helped with that. She could stay as long as she liked. It was quite a ways from Tom's place, but right now that was the only drawback.

Mackenzie sat in her desk chair and thought about Sunday afternoon. They had been in Tom's condo, sitting on the sofa and talking, but when the talking stopped, things grew very intense for the first time. Mackenzie hadn't objected, but Tom had called a halt to things before they had a chance to go very far.

"You don't love me, Mackenzie; I can feel that you don't. You care and so do I, but if we do this, it's going to ruin the friendship we have right now. I'm not willing for that to happen. Someday the time might be right, but not now. Later on I'll be sick that I didn't follow my heart, but right now we can't go any farther."

Mackenzie had not been pleased. She hid it, but she had been irritated. Now she was nothing but relieved. She didn't love Tom — not like she thought love should be. She cared for him more than anyone in the area right now, but that wasn't love. On the sofa she had just been carried away with sensation. Her mother would have called it lust. Mackenzie was working on pushing the painful subject of her mother away when the phone rang. Knowing only a few people had her number, she picked it up with a smile. It had to be Delancey or Tom.

"I'm sorry but you have the wrong number," she told the person who wanted to order a pizza from her, but the thought of food reminded her that she hadn't started anything for supper. Tom had given her a cookbook for her birthday, but she wasn't in the mood to try anything. She was brushing her hair with plans to go out when someone knocked at the door. Tom was no more inside before he took Mackenzie in his arms and kissed her soundly.

"Well, now," Mackenzie gasped. "Hello to you too."

"I just booked a room at the Alexandria for us," he whispered softly, and Mackenzie stiffened.

"Is that so?"

"Yes. You see, Mr. Paxton Hancock wants to meet Mr. Mac Walker in the morning."

Mackenzie gripped the arms that were holding her. "Are you serious?"

"Yes! He tried to stay calm, but I've never seen him so severe."

"Severe? What does that mean?"

"Haven't you ever seen Pax when he's working? When he's thinking, all smiles and banter fade away. He almost looks mad."

"So what does that mean?"

"He'll have to tell you."

"So you didn't tell him?"

"Nope. I'm doing everything I can to protect you, Mackenzie, just as I promised. By meeting at the Alexandria, I can talk with him without anyone listening, and then when the time is right, you can come out of the bedroom."

"Oh, my," Mackenzie breathed. This was such a surprise. Somewhere along the line she had completely panicked. She had told Tom to go get her book and bring it back, but he had talked her out of it, deciding instead to go with whatever she wanted. Her list had been long but not unreasonable. She never wanted to be known as Mackenzie Bishop. Tom and Paxton could tell no one who Mac Walker really was. If anyone was to be told, Mackenzie would do the telling. She would never come to their office for anything but children's books, and if word ever leaked out, she was through with IronHorse forever.

And amazingly enough, Tom believed Paxton would agree to all of it. Tom knew of several other writers who worked with nom de plumes, and no one thought anything of it. In times of doubt, Mackenzie told herself she was arrogant, that no one would read her book anyway. But on the off-chance that it was a success, she had to protect herself. The evening with Carson Walcott was still fresh in her mind.

"What if he's mad?" Mackenzie voiced the horrifying thought.

"He won't be. It's the same as when I wanted to meet you, Mackenzie. If I hadn't wanted the Micah Bear book, I would have given it back to Paxton and that would have been the end of it. He would have done the same with *Access Denied.* Editors don't have time to make long apologies. He's obviously interested in the book. Now, the details I can't tell you, but he wouldn't ask to meet with you just to say, 'No thanks.' "

"All right."

Tom gave her a hug, but she was doubting her "all right" almost as soon as she said it. The next morning, when she stood in the bedroom of the suite Tom had booked, she was sure she was anything but all right. Indeed, "sick to the stomach" was the only description that fit. She had stood for a time and tried to listen to the conversation in the other room, but that had made it worse. She had sat at the table and started a note to her sister. When Tom opened the door and asked her to come out, she nearly jumped from her skin.

Telling herself not to run away, she forced her legs to move toward the door. She walked just five steps into the other room and stopped. Paxton, who had been on the sofa, stood slowly, almost like a doll on strings.

"Mackenzie?"

He looked thunderstruck and her heart sank.

"Please don't hate me, Pax. I know better than anyone how much you hate it when aspiring writers bother you. I just had this story, and then Tom thought it was good. I —" but she couldn't go on. Her hand came to her face and she didn't see Paxton when he came toward her, but went with him when he led her to the sofa.

"I'm sorry," she said at last.

"Sorry is the last thing you should be." Paxton's calm voice broke through her misery, and she looked at him. "I've known there was more to you from the day we met, Mackenzie. I just didn't know what."

"Oh, Pax," she breathed, still upset. "I never wanted to deceive you or pretend to be someone else. It's just that my privacy is so important."

"Tom explained all of that to me, and I understand completely. You'd probably be amazed at the authors I protect."

Mackenzie just stared at him.

"Where did you get that story? No, don't answer that." He looked down at the floor. "Now that I know who wrote it, it makes complete sense. Only someone who's been at the Pentagon would know some of what you wrote. And the characters — they're so believable, the way they respond and think, and even their physical abilities. There was nothing supernatural or unbelievable." Paxton realized he'd been rambling. He looked up at the dark-haired author and grinned. "Mackenzie, darlin', I'm gonna make you a star."

She laughed, not knowing he was very serious. "What's that supposed to mean?"

"It means that IronHorse is frothing at the mouth to publish this book. I thought Hank Darwell would have a fit."

Mackenzie's eyes grew. "You discussed this with your editor-in-chief?"

"He read it and called me in the middle of the night."

Mackenzie started to stand, but Paxton caught her arm.

"Sit down, Mackenzie. I suspected a pen name, so it's all been very hush-hush. You don't need to worry about it. He won't care who wrote it as long you sign the contract."

"What contract?" She looked suspicious. It was all happening so fast.

Paxton went to his briefcase, and Mackenzie chanced a look at Tom, who was wisely staying in the background but still strongly resembling the Cheshire Cat. Paxton came back with the document. Paper-clipped to the top was a check.

"You know the routine, Mackenzie: half on signing the contract and half on receipt of the manuscript, but the book is done, so the check is in full."

Mackenzie looked at the amount. There had to be some kind of mistake. She looked up into Paxton's face.

"I could tell you how good the book is, Mackenzie, but I think the check does that. I wasn't certain you wouldn't be one of my regular writers sitting here and having a joke on me, but on the chance that I was really going to meet a man by the name of Mac Walker, I had to come prepared so he would know we mean business."

Mackenzie was speechless.

"It's a fabulous book, Mackenzie. There's no other way to say it. To be honest with you, I've never read such a good one that had no sex or swearing in it, but I couldn't put the dumb thing down."

"And will IronHorse want sex and swearing, Pax? Because if that's the case, I'm not interested. They wouldn't add anything to the story, and you know me well enough to know that's not my style."

"Yes, I do know you, and no, nothing like that will be added. I want to edit it and work on some of the grammar, but the story and your characters won't change much, if at all."

"And you're not mad?"

"No, I understand why you did it this way."

"Do you really understand how important my privacy is to me, Pax? I can walk away from this right now if you can't keep it quiet for me. I swear to you I can."

Paxton smiled. This was the Mackenzie he knew,

the woman whose convictions were bigger than she was, whose chin came out when she was upset and whose eyes made you tremble with doubt or passion.

"I can do this for you. No problem. There are some legal hoops to go through — Uncle Sam must have his due — but no one needs to know that Mac Walker is Mackenzie Bishop."

Mackenzie started to relax. This was Paxton and Tom — they were her friends. And right now it looked as though her dream was really going to happen: She was going to be a novelist. Just the week before she'd been looking in the want ads for work. Now she had some.

"What happens now?" she asked.

"You go over this contract. Tom, when do we have to be out of here?"

"I booked for two nights since I wasn't sure I'd even get her out of the bedroom. We have all day."

"Good. Let's go over this one item at a time. It's a little different than the other contracts you've had with us, and I want to make sure you understand it all."

"But the check is actually mine?"

Paxton took it from under the clip and handed it to her.

"Thank you, Pax."

"Thank *you,* Mackenzie. You don't by any chance have any more stories up your sleeve, do you?"

"I started one Monday," she answered matter-of-factly, causing Paxton to laugh in disbelief.

"You're kidding?"

"No."

"What's it called?"

"*Seahorse.*"

"Good title. What's it about?"

Mackenzie started to tell him but stopped. While trying to control her nerves in the other room, she had written a teaser paragraph for Delancey. She went to her purse now, dug out the deposit slip she'd been writing on the back of, and brought it to Paxton. She let him read it.

The plans were important, not just important, vital, and not just to the United States, but to the entire civilized world. Monty Forester had to find the link, but the clues were small. If he moved too fast, he could miss them — too slowly and it would be too late. He knew only one thing, had only one lead. If he could uncover the path, it would surely lead him to the *Seahorse.*

Paxton sat back and let his head drop against the seat. "Mercy, woman," he said softly, "you've been sitting in my back pocket for how many years, and I never knew it." He lifted his head and looked at her. "Were you doing this when we met?"

"I'd have to look back on my calendar, but I think it was about the same time." Mackenzie suddenly smiled. "I do remember the night you called me and told me you had met Jodi. I'd been writing that scene around the Eiffel Tower and had a hard time getting into our conversation."

"That was a great scene." Paxton was grinning as well.

"Thank you."

"How long do you think it will take to write *Seahorse?*"

"I don't know. I had to do *Access Denied* after work and on weekends. That's why it took more

550

than two years, but I'm out of the Army now."

"I didn't know that."

"Yes, I have an apartment in Alexandria."

"So you could write full-time?"

"Yes, if I wanted to."

"Don't you want to?" Paxton asked so comically that both Tom and Mackenzie laughed.

It was the very note they needed. Tom gave Mackenzie a hug and ordered some food, Mackenzie used the bathroom and took a moment to compose herself, and Paxton went to the table to set out the contract for their meeting. He'd been in this business a long time, and he knew what the market was hungry for. Mackenzie Bishop, alias Mac Walker, was going to top the bestseller list in the first six months. Paxton Hancock was ready to bet his career on it.

Chicago

Wondering why someone had been in such a hurry to get something to her, Delancey opened the express mail package. Thinking it was probably expensive junk mail, she stared in disbelief as she saw airline tickets with her name on them and the small note attached.

> Don't bother to call if you're coming, Deej. I'll meet flight 786 into Washington National at 8:09 if I don't hear from you. Just throw some things in a bag and please get on that plane. I'm dying to see you.
>
> Love, Mic

Delancey quickly checked the dates and let out a shout that probably woke her neighbor's baby. She didn't care. The dates were perfect. Her flight went out on Friday night and came back on Monday, days when she had no classes. Delancey suspected that her sister had contacted the school and asked. And the flight was in just 28 hours. Delancey wondered how she would stand it.

Mackenzie was no better. The next evening she stood at her sister's gate and paced with excitement. She had sat by the phone from the moment she had sent the tickets, mentally begging Delancey not to call and refuse. Now the plane was landing, and it was just a matter of time.

Mackenzie's breath caught in her throat when she saw her sister, and moments later they were hugging. People rushed past them, but they never noticed. The sisters only knew they were together at last.

"Come over here." Mackenzie tried to speak. "Come by the wall."

Delancey kicked her bag in front of her with one foot and went back to hugging Mackenzie once they were off the main traffic path. She couldn't believe she was there. It seemed like forever since they had been together. Delancey loved no one as she did her sister. There was a bond between them that transcended explanation.

"Thank you for coming." Mackenzie wiped at her face.

"Thank you for the tickets. I could have bought them, but it never occurred to me to come for the weekend. Do you want me to pay you?"

"Of course I do, with interest."

Delancey looked at her. "I miss you, Mic."

"I miss you too. It's funny how life never lets you go backward."

"What would you do differently?"

"Nothing. I would just understand that my

552

childhood and my time with you and Mom were brief and needed to be savored."

Delancey nodded. "Have you talked to Jack at all?"

Mackenzie shook her head. "I can't. I don't hate him, D.J. — I hope he understands that — but I can't take the connection or his beliefs right now," she added softly.

"I called him on his birthday last week. He was glad to hear from me, but it felt strange, and we ended up with very little to say to each other. Shay and Oliver were taking him out for dinner, and I was glad of that." She sighed a little. "He doesn't have my phone number or address, so he can't really contact me. I couldn't let his birthday go by, but it was a relief to get off the phone."

"I got one more letter from him before I moved, but I haven't even been reading them for a long time."

"Pretty soon he'll get 'Return to sender'."

"Yeah," Mackenzie answered, then shook herself. "This is not the way I want to spend the weekend, Miss Bishop. I don't want to be sad. Come on, I can't wait to show you my apartment. It's not fancy, but I like it."

"When are you coming to see mine?"

"Soon. Tell me what it's like."

"It's not fancy at all, and sometimes I get tired of having just one room and so little space, but I wasn't willing to pay for more than a studio right now. And anyway, my neighbors are very nice. One just had a baby, who is an absolute doll."

"Boy or girl?"

"Girl. Adelaide Rose. Isn't that gorgeous?"

"Yes. I love it. How do you like not living at school?"

"It's wonderful. I can go to class and then head home to study in peace and quiet. I'm looking at computers. Right now I use the school's, but that's about the only drawback. As soon as I get one, I'll feel like I have it made."

"I love mine," Mackenzie told her.

"How's the writing coming?" Delancey asked.

Mackenzie smiled at her. "I'll tell you all about it when we get into the car."

Delancey grinned. "Oh, this sounds good."

Delancey didn't know how good. Mackenzie knew the route by heart and was able to talk and drive without difficulty. She gave Delancey the whole story, from Tom's taking the manuscript to her meeting with Paxton the month before. Delancey was silent for just an instant, and then she couldn't stop screaming.

"I can't believe you never told me!"

"It's not something I can talk about on the phone, Deej. It just isn't, and I don't want to write about it in letters either."

"I think I understand, but you could have at least told me you finished it!"

They were at the apartment now, but Delancey hadn't taken any time to look around. She faced her sister in the living room, not even noticing the new furniture.

"I'm sorry, D.J., really I am, but the move here and everything have been nuts."

"Well," Delancey softened suddenly, "I guess I have to forgive you because I just remembered that a children's magazine accepted some of my work and I forgot to tell you about that."

"That's great, Deej. I always knew your stuff was good."

The two women looked at each other.

"I didn't think we would ever lose touch like this," Mackenzie admitted.

"Me either. I don't like it, Mic. We've got to do a better job."

"Yeah, we do."

They hugged again, and Delancey finally noticed the furniture. She loved the dark blue sofa and chair, the oak tables and elegant lamps. She was still touching and admiring everything when she realized something.

"Did you get advance money for *Access Denied*?"

Mackenzie nodded.

"A lot?"

Mackenzie nodded again, and Delancey started to smile. "Do you know what we're going to do tomorrow, Mic?"

"No, what?"

"We're going clothes shopping for you."

"Why?"

"Because ever since you joined the Army, your wardrobe has been sick."

"It has not!" Mackenzie hotly denied.

"Yes, it has. You've been wearing that sweatshirt for ten years, and you can't even read the logo anymore."

Mackenzie opened her mouth to deny it, but Delancey had already headed into the bedroom. She ruthlessly went through Mackenzie's clothes, snobbishly declaring most of her sister's wardrobe a loss and not worrying about how insulting she sounded.

Mackenzie didn't say much, because if the truth be told, shopping was not her favorite sport. She had always admired her sister's taste in clothing, however, and now that she thought about it, Tom always looked nice, and she always felt a bit grubby when they went out. With that in mind, Mackenzie didn't whimper as they headed for Union Station the next morning.

It didn't take long for Delancey to find Mackenzie's style, and when she did, there was no stopping her. Vogue fashions were all wrong for her, but the classics — A-line skirts, plaid blazers, bulky sweaters, jeans, oxford shirts, and slacks — hung on Mackenzie's frame in the most flattering way.

"Wait until Tom sees this."

Mackenzie waited until she'd said it twice and then spoke up.

"It's not really like that, Deej."

"Not like what?"

"You know, like that."

Delancey nodded. "So things aren't real intimate between you?"

"No. We do kiss, but we're friends right now more than anything else. Things got pretty hot one day, but he knows I don't love him, and I don't think he knows what he feels for me. When it was over, I was glad we didn't go very far."

"It sounds as though you did the right thing. I still think about what Mom said to us. She was from a different generation, so I really don't think that waiting for marriage is all that practical anymore, but waiting for true love makes a lot of sense to me."

"Yeah, it does, but right now I can't imagine either one for myself, and since I'm immersed in another book right now, I'm glad Tom and I aren't getting married or anything."

Delancey nodded. "Tell me about the book."

Explaining the plot for *Seahorse* took the next

hour and was discussed over a late lunch. Delancey was amazed at the story and a little in awe of the way her sister could work the plot in her mind. She didn't even make notes.

"Tell me, Mic," Delancey leaned close and asked, "how does it feel? How does it feel to know you're going to have a novel in the bookstores?"

"Right now it doesn't feel like anything since it's so far away. The release date is April, and that's if nothing messes up the schedule. But I will tell you what feels good: not having to go out and get a job. I've tried to make my apartment as homey as possible because I get up and go to work right there. I go for a run every once in a while, but other than going out with Tom or for grocery shopping, the apartment has become my world."

"And you don't feel as though you're going nuts?"

"No. I travel all over in the pages of the book, and I never get cabin fever or whatever you call it."

"Have you already got a contract for *Seahorse*?"

"No. Pax knows about it, but I want to get a little further along before I sign anything."

"Do you ever doubt if you can do it again?"

"All the time."

Delancey nodded. "I get tired of drawing sometimes, and when that happens, I think I'm losing my touch. But then I see something that gives me an idea and bounce right back."

"What are you working on now?"

Delancey beamed. "Well, I just mailed off the pieces that *Rainy Days* requested — that's the children's magazine — but now I have an idea for a regular feature. I'd like to do a one-page picture with hidden things in it. I don't want to put a story with it, just the picture and what to look for. I know some children's magazines run those every month, but most magazines don't. I'd even be willing to shrink the picture for the Sunday comics."

"How about a book of those?"

Delancey looked skeptical. "A lot of those are being done right now, but where I'm not seeing them is in periodicals."

"How about a Micah Bear search book?"

Delancey had not thought of that. "There would have to be a story."

"I could write it. I could write about the things he'd lost, and you could draw them into the picture. Or you draw out the pages, and I'll find the words."

Delancey's dark blue eyes flamed with excitement, and she sat up very straight. "I think it might work."

Mackenzie smiled and suddenly lunch was ended. For fun they stopped by a bookstore and saw their Micah Bear books on the shelf, but then went right back to the apartment to call Tom Magy.

On Sunday morning Delancey poured coffee into Mackenzie's mug and went back to the oven and the English muffins she'd covered with cheese, tiny bits of onion, and some other spices that were a mystery to her sister.

"Maybe I should move to Chicago, and then you can cook for me full-time, Deej."

"I'm not sure I want the job. You're always missing some ingredient I need."

"Well, I can't tell that anything's missing this morning."

And indeed it was not. Delancey had made a breakfast casserole, one her mother used to bake, and a coffee cake, and was just taking the muffins from the oven. Hot coffee and orange juice finished the meal, and Mackenzie felt as though she were in heaven. It was nice to know she would have leftovers for a few days as well.

"So what shall we do today?" Mackenzie asked.

"I think be as lazy as possible, but do you know what? I've never met Tom Magy. He's done the books for us, so we've talked on the phone numerous times, but we've never met."

"Delancey!" Mackenzie was shocked. "I forgot all about that. Let's give him a call. He can give us lunch."

Tom was more than willing to meet with the women, delighted even. They set lunch for one o'clock, and Tom promised it would not be pizza. Delancey was a little nervous on the way over. She believed her sister about the relationship but also realized she could be meeting her future brother-in-law. She need not have worried. Tom made her feel at home and reiterated that he loved the idea of a Micah Bear search-and-find book. Within minutes they were laughing and talking like old friends. Indeed, the women stayed all afternoon, watched sports, and ate.

"I like your sister," Tom told Mackenzie as she was getting ready to leave. "Some artists are weird, but she's just sweet and sensitive."

"Yes, she is. I hate it that she leaves tomorrow, but we've decided that I'm going to Chicago for Christmas, so I think I can survive her departure."

"Especially since you're not really with us these days. You're incoherent every time I call."

Mackenzie only laughed as he kissed her goodbye, but she didn't deny it. Delancey's plane left at 2:00, but the budding author didn't even wait until the next morning to start writing again. As soon as she got back to her apartment, she turned the computer on and worked until midnight.

THIRTY-THREE

Delancey loved to sit next to the window on a plane. Mackenzie liked the aisle, but Delancey loved watching the sky and clouds by day and the lights on the ground by night. At the moment, however, her eyes were closed as she thought back and savored the time with her sister. How wonderful it had been. They hadn't caught up with each other like that in way too long. Some of the days in California at the end of May had been special, but the tension between Mackenzie and Jack had put a damper on everything. Marrell's face leapt into Delancey's mind without warning, and she felt tears coming on, so she kept her eyes closed, even when someone took the seat next to her and the plane taxied and lifted into the air.

It wasn't a long flight, less than two hours, but they would still offer a snack and something to drink. Delancey hoped she could talk the flight attendant into two bags of peanuts and tell him to keep the ginger ale coming. As much as she hated airline food, she didn't know why she never remembered to bring anything to eat.

The captain's announcement that they would be turning off the seat-belt sign finally brought her eyes open. She didn't remove her seat-belt, but she did put the tray table down and reach for

561

her briefcase. A few moments later she had a page she had doodled earlier for the search-and-find book in front of her. The sketch was light, and with a pencil she darkened a few of the details and added a few more hidden drawings. The scene had a lush forest for the background with a clearing in the forefront. The places to hide keys, a watch, a pencil, coins, stamps, and any number of other tiny figures, were numerous. Delancey was working along steadily, dreaming of the story Mackenzie would write to go with the art, when she felt eyes on her. She turned and looked at the person in the seat next to her.

"I'm sorry," the uniformed man said softly and sincerely. "I didn't mean to stare, but you do beautiful work."

"Thank you," Delancey said graciously when she saw his kind smile.

"Is it a hobby, or do you get paid to have that much fun?"

Delancey laughed. "I never thought of it that way, but I am published."

"Would I be familiar with your books?"

"Only if you read Micah Bear books to your children."

He shrugged his shoulders. "No children. Not yet anyhow. Are you published under your own name?"

"Yes. Actually, I'm the illustrator and my sister does the writing."

"I'm so impressed. I've never met an illustrator before. I'm Chet Dobson, by the way."

"Delancey Bishop."

"And that's the name on the front of your books?"

"They say 'Written by Mackenzie Bishop and illustrated by Delancey Bishop'."

"Those are beautiful names. Your mother and father must have known you were going to do something big someday."

Delancey smiled, but that particular subject was so painful that she didn't reply. It still hurt unbearably that her mother never saw the finished books.

Chet saw that he'd blundered. He would have loved to see her smile again but didn't know how to accomplish that. He was very pleased when she spoke to him.

"Is it me, or are you dressed to be flying this plane?"

"Yes, I am."

"Should I be a little worried then that you're in row 18?"

Chet laughed, and Delancey admired the even rows of white teeth that flashed out at her.

"No, I'm just going home."

"Chicago?"

"Yes. My shift ended in Washington, so I'm commuting."

"No first class?"

"No," he smiled. "I'm usually on the flight deck, but if there are seats open, we can come out here."

"And sit in the middle?"

"Yes. Everyone likes the aisle and window."

"But you must like your job."

"I love it. It takes patience and a lot of flight time to get established, but once you arrive, it's nice."

"Where's the most interesting place you've flown?"

"I was in the Air Force, so I've been all over the world, but I love Greece. Greece is wonderful."

"I've never been out of the United States."

"Um, you should get yourself a passport in case the opportunity arrives."

"You make it sound tempting."

"Once you've tried it, you'll be hooked."

"Can you tell me some of the places you've been?" Delancey asked. While he answered, the young artist felt surprised at herself. She was normally rather shy around men she didn't know, and here she was asking questions of a stranger, and answering his, as though they had known each other far longer. It occurred to her that he could be a serial killer, but his uniform looked authentic, and she had watched one of the flight attendants smile at him with familiarity when the refreshments were served. She was still wondering how at ease she felt when she reminded herself that he was married, and knew that this was the reason for her calm.

Since the episode with Tab, who, she learned, had cared far more for her than he'd let on, Delancey had been just plain gun-shy, or rather, guy-shy. She would have enjoyed getting to know someone, but she wasn't sure about anything permanent. Was it possible to spend time with someone and not get too serious? After her relationship with Kyle, she was afraid to find out.

"Well, good luck on your books," Chet said as they landed and taxied toward the gate.

"Thank you," Delancey said, and she meant it. Having someone to talk to had made the time fly.

They didn't speak again as they disembarked. Delancey was already thinking about getting to her car and the drive to the apartment. She also wondered suddenly if she had homework that she had overlooked in all her excitement. It had been like a weekend in paradise, but now it was time to go back to work.

Alexandria

"I'm certainly glad you're going to your sister's for Christmas," Tom told Mackenzie, no smile on his face.

"Why?" Mackenzie asked, her face looking no happier than his.

"Maybe you'll come back in a better mood."

"I don't know what you're talking about." Mackenzie busied herself with the dish in her hand and wouldn't look at him.

"You've been a bear lately, and you know it. I don't know why I put up with it."

Mackenzie's eyes flashed when she turned to him.

"No one's asking you to stay, Mr. Magy."

"Then I won't," he said tightly and put the dish towel down. He said not another word as he picked up his coat and walked from Mackenzie's apartment. She was so angry she could have spit. That he had been right didn't matter; he didn't need to be rude about it or leave in a huff. She finished the dishes in record time and wondered if she had anything for heartburn.

Mackenzie told herself she didn't care if he never came back, but she kept the phone free all evening. The next morning she told herself to forget about him and to write her book, but it didn't work. Not even going for a run helped, so she showered and headed out to shop for Delancey for Christmas. Her flight left in two weeks, and she hadn't bought a thing. She found a dressy watch, not able to remember if Delancey had been wearing one in September. There were some wonderful men's watches too, but she was mad at Tom right now.

She would give him a week to call, and then she would write him off. It occurred to her that she was being childish and should call him, but trying to figure out what to say was miserable to her, so she did nothing.

The misery only increased, easing just a little when Paxton came by to give her a Christmas gift, a pen with her name engraved on it, and to tell her to have a wonderful time with her sister. He was laughingly terrible at playacting as he tried to pretend he wasn't thinking about *Seahorse.*

"Been writing much?" he asked, his hand on the doorknob on his way out, his manner nonchalant.

Mackenzie laughed. "Constantly."

Paxton smiled. "Good. We're going to be right on time with *Access Denied.* I was just talking to Hank Darwell this week. He took the galleys home to his wife, and she went ballistic."

"Did she really?"

"Yep. She wants to meet you and made Hank promise he would invite you to their big Christmas party. He agreed until he could think of a good excuse why you couldn't come."

Mackenzie nodded, her heart suddenly feeling very good. She had done the right thing in keeping her identity quiet, but someone liked her book! Indeed, Mackenzie felt so good that as soon as Paxton left, she went right back to her computer. She wrote like a fiend almost up to the moment it was time to leave for Delancey's. She got a lot done, but the way she treated Tom hounded her almost constantly.

Her heart was so heavy that she nearly called him the day she left, but time was running short.

She felt a bad mood coming on that wasn't helped when someone knocked at the door. Mackenzie was speechless when she opened it and Tom stood there, his eyes intent on her face. He must have been relieved at what he saw because he said, "I thought you might need a ride to the airport."

"Oh, Tom —" Mackenzie was immediately contrite. "I'm sorry about the way I acted."

He took her in his arms and kissed her for a long time. They really couldn't spare the minutes, but Mackenzie didn't care. It was too wonderful to have him back in her world.

"I think we need to talk when you get home," he told her once they started off in the car.

"All right."

"Do you know what I'm referring to?"

"Our relationship?"

"Yes."

Mackenzie nodded but didn't say anything else. She was suddenly glad for more than one reason that she was going away for ten days. Tom was just as glad. He couldn't think when he was with Mackenzie Bishop. She was too distracting, both physically and mentally. She had a way of looking at him that stripped away all pretense, and since he thought his feelings might be stronger than hers, it was a constant battle not to give himself away.

"Have a good trip," he told her sincerely as he pulled into the kiss-and-fly area.

"I will," Mackenzie said as she leaned toward him to obey the sign.

"When you come back, we'll have our own Christmas."

"All right. Shall I call you for a ride?"

"You'd better not call anyone else," he said

lightly, but Mackenzie had the impression that he feared she would do just that. She checked in and went to her gate with the thought that something was very wrong, and that by not calling him, she had let something very precious slip away from her. And the strangest part about it was that she couldn't shake the feeling that he thought she was seeing someone else.

Only Monty Forrester on the pages of Seahorse, Mackenzie could have told him, but she knew it would have to wait at least ten days. She thought about him all the way to Chicago, but once there, her sister and that world consumed her thoughts and time. It was only just before she fell asleep for the first few nights that Mackenzie asked herself what would be the outcome of their conversation when she returned.

"D.J., I have to have eggnog."

"You're kidding." Delancey stared at her.

"No, I have to have some. Let's go to the store."

"Mackenzie, it's the twenty-third. Do you have any idea what the streets are like right now?"

"Isn't there a small market or something in the neighborhood?"

"Not in this neighborhood."

Mackenzie cocked her head to one side. "Why did you rent in this part of town, D.J.?"

"It was cheap."

"Are you really that strapped?"

"As a matter of fact, I'm not, but I didn't realize that until after I moved in and really saw what I would have in monthly income. I should have done more figuring ahead."

"So why don't you move?"

"It's a lot of work, Mic, and I'm busy with my

568

studies most of the time. Not to mention, I haven't gotten close to anyone this year. I can afford more rent per month, but I doubt if I can afford a moving company to move me."

"What have you got that won't fit into your car?" Mackenzie argued next.

Delancey shook her head. "Mic, if you think it's that easy, you find me a place and move all my stuff."

Mackenzie's eyes narrowed. "I'll just do that, Delancey Joy — just see if I don't."

Delancey shook her head in exasperation and grabbed her car keys. "Come on, let's get your eggnog. But don't forget that I warned you. It's going to be a zoo."

Not in Delancey's wildest dreams did she think she would be apartment shopping the day after Christmas, but she learned that Mackenzie had been quite serious on the twenty-third. They had seen three apartments by two o'clock, and Delancey was in a state of shock.

"Mic, I'm still going to end up doing this on my own. Have you figured that out?"

"No, you won't. If you can't get in right now, I'll come back when you can and help you."

Delancey shook her head. Sometimes there was no stopping the woman.

"I think this one has promise," Mackenzie was saying as they pulled up in front of what looked like a warehouse. Delancey, on the other hand, was rechecking the address. There had to be a mistake.

"I'll just leave you two to look around," the woman in gypsy-type clothing said a few minutes later, and the sisters were thrilled to be left on their own. The apartment was one-half of the top floor of an old warehouse. Right inside the door a bathroom had been set up, and next to that was a bedroom, but the rest of the apartment, including the kitchen, was one huge room. The ceilings were at least ten feet up, and since there was no furniture, Delancey thought they could play basketball. The windows that covered most of the exterior walls and went to the ceiling allowed you to look out over the street. It wasn't the greatest view, since all the buildings were other brick warehouses, but Delancey could see herself sitting in a patch of sunlight and drawing for hours. With that thought she came crashing back to earth.

"I have no furniture, Mic. I've been a student, and now I live in a studio apartment. The only thing I own is my easel."

"We'll get you a bed," Mackenzie responded, not to be put off. "The rest will come in time."

"I wouldn't even have a kitchen table."

"So we'll get some TV trays, Deej. You can't let this place go. Think of the work you could get done looking out these windows."

"I'm farther from the school."

"You told me you don't even know if you're going back next semester. With all the stuff *Rainy Days* wants, it doesn't sound like you have time."

"I figured out that I can graduate in the spring if I'll just take on a little more, and I would like to finish, Mic."

Mackenzie finally heard her sister's tone and backed off. "I'm sorry, D.J. I don't want to push you into this. It's just so cool, and I thought you could use some more space."

"You're not pushing me, Mic — well, maybe you are a little. I'm just not up to your speed on this yet."

Mackenzie stayed quiet. She had known she was railroading her but was too excited to care.

"Your place is okay, D.J.," Mackenzie said honestly. "It's just not what I've ever pictured you in, with so little space and light."

Delancey nodded. Her little place was rather dreary, and some of the things she had said to her sister were excuses. She would have loved to find something else but had been too afraid to branch out. She took another look around and scribbled out some questions for the landlady. This place was a little more than the others they had looked at, but the space looked to be well worth it.

"Look at this, Deej," Mackenzie offered, noticing the blinds someone had installed. They came up from the windowsill, and while not covering the whole window, they went up far enough that unless someone was in a helicopter, complete privacy was possible. The ones in the bedroom did go all the way up, and with that, Delancey fell in love with the place.

"Let's go talk to her, Mic."

They ended up doing more than talking: Delancey rented the place that afternoon. They went right back to Delancey's apartment, which she rented on a monthly basis, to speak with her landlord. He had a sweet spot for Delancey, so when she promised to leave it spotlessly clean, he agreed to return half of the month she'd paid ahead. And if he could rent it before the first of January, he would return the other half to her. Things had all moved very quickly, and both girls learned anew what the power of money could do.

Delancey had no references in the area, so Mackenzie wrote out a large check to the new landlady covering first and last months' rent. The check also covered a security deposit that they both suspected was double the norm. The woman was pleased, and Delancey was moved in by the end of the week. She had a bed, one kitchen chair, a desk chair, and her easel, and was as happy as if the place were filled with furniture. Doing homework while lying across the bed or on the floor was sure to be interesting, but Delancey didn't care.

The kitchen and the bedroom at her new place were still in a state of upheaval when Delancey found herself sitting next to her sister in the airport. The end of Mackenzie's visit had come all too soon. She had offered to stay longer, but Delancey had told her no. As they waited for Mackenzie's turn to board, they were strangely quiet.

"It was fun, D.J.," Mackenzie told her.

The younger girl laughed. "I don't know how often I can take this much fun, Mic. I'm just glad that classes don't start for almost a month. Maybe by then I can find my backpack."

Mackenzie smiled unrepentantly. "It's a great place, Delancey. I'd be tempted to move myself if I could find its equal."

"You know," Delancey turned to her, "why couldn't you come and live with me? You can do your writing anywhere, and we could fit another bed in the bedroom."

Mackenzie's brows rose. "I don't know. I'll have to think about it."

"Okay."

Mackenzie suddenly looked at her. "I just realized I'm not going to see you for a while, since you'll be back in school."

"Well, you can come back and see me."

"I know," Mackenzie said, having had a better idea, "let's go someplace for spring break. When is your break?"

"I'm not sure."

"Well, let me know."

"Where would we go? Florida?"

"No, someplace exotic. Europe or something."

Delancey's eyes rounded. "You mean it?"

"Sure. Get a passport so we have the option. I'll do the same. I mean, we could go to Florida, but it would be so much fun to fly to London or Paris for a week."

Delancey laughed and dropped her voice. "You should tell Paxton you need to do book research and that he needs to send you to Istanbul or someplace just as exotic. Make sure there's a beach scene in the book so we can take our suits and get tan."

Mackenzie laughed, but the idea had merit. For *Seahorse* she could use some time in Prague. She was figuring out how she might ask when the final boarding was called. The girls stood and walked slowly, not eager to part.

"Thanks, Mic, for everything."

"I love you, Deej."

They held onto each other for as long as they dared, and then Mackenzie made herself walk to the plane and not look back. As soon as she was out of sight, Delancey went to the window. It was already growing dark out, but she stood and peered through the glass for one more sight of her. She couldn't make out anyone, but she stood there until the plane was pushed back and moved out into position.

"Saying goodbye to someone?" a deep male voice asked from beside her. Delancey was only going to glance, nod, and otherwise ignore the person, but she turned and found a pilot standing six feet away from her.

"Remember me?" he asked, smiling at her.

"Yes, I do." Delancey still felt as though she could cry, so she swallowed hard and concentrated. "How are you?"

"I think better than you are." His voice was very tender. "Did someone just leave?"

"My sister."

"Did you have Christmas together?"

Delancey nodded and glanced down at her wrist. "She gave me a watch."

Chet looked at it. "She has good taste."

Delancey smiled, thinking it would have been nice for Mackenzie to hear that.

"Would I be out of line to ask you to join me for a drink?" Chet asked suddenly.

Delancey's head dipped to one side as she studied him, causing her hair to fall from her shoulder in a thick curtain.

"Why did I think you were married?"

"I don't know," Chet looked surprised. "Why did you?"

Delancey thought a moment. "I think it was when you said that you didn't have children yet — I just assumed."

Chet smiled at her. "Never assume."

Delancey smiled back.

"So how about it, Miss Bishop?"

Delancey knew she was headed back to her new apartment to sob her eyes out and suddenly didn't want that. She heard herself agreeing and then fell into step beside the handsome pilot. He was only a few inches taller than she was, but she had the impression that with his dark blond curls and her very straight pale blond hair, they made a striking couple. They spoke easily as they walked down one concourse and into another.

Delancey had not been to the place he took her. She didn't remember even seeing it before. It was not a large lounge, and with darkness coming on fast, the interior was dim and welcoming. He took her to a table in the corner, and Delancey ordered white wine, something that Lovisa had introduced her to. Chet had a dark beer.

"I take it you're not working," Delancey asked after eyeing his drink.

"I'm just off and headed home."

"You must be tired."

"Never too tired to rescue a damsel in distress."

Delancey smiled. "There must be many of us."

His face grew intent, his eyes on hers. "Since I haven't been able to get you from my mind, I don't know if I've noticed anyone else."

Delancey was stunned.

"I take it you didn't think of me."

"I thought you were married," she reminded him softly.

"Oh, that's right. By the way," he said, seeing that he was moving too fast, "would you care for something to eat?"

"Oh." Delancey felt rescued. "I am a little hungry."

"I'll see what they can drum up."

It was good to have him walk away. Delancey's heart was doing things she wasn't accustomed to. There was something about this man that attracted her to no end. She wanted to stare at him for hours, and when he looked back, she felt flushed all over. She had worked hard at composing herself when he returned and told her he had ordered an hors d'oeuvre plate.

"So what did the two of you do over Christmas?"

"Lots of talking up to Christmas Day, and then two days after Christmas she helped me move to a new place."

"Oh, was the lease up on the old one?"

"No, but it was a little small, and the one we found suits me better."

"I think I can picture you in an elegant penthouse."

Delancey laughed. "Try a converted warehouse."

"You're kidding?" Chet laughed.

"No, but it has character, and all illustrators need that."

"What are you working on right now?"

Delancey filled him in on the *Rainy Days* assignments and the search-and-find books. He told Delancey about where he had been that day and that week, and three hours slipped away like three minutes. It was anyone's guess how long they would have talked, but Chet suddenly reached for his side.

"Excuse me, Delancey. I need to get my pager."

"Sure."

Delancey didn't stare while he consulted the instrument, but she did watch him when he said his boss was calling and he needed to call right back. He left the bar and was gone about five minutes, and even though he sat down again with Delancey, she knew their time was over.

"I've got to go," he told her, very real regret in his eyes. "I want you to take this." He slid a piece of paper toward her. "It's my pager number. I hope you'll call me."

Delancey looked down at it, her heart shouting at her not to assume. She looked up to find Chet watching her.

"Why would I call you?"

"So I can return your call and ask you to dinner."

Delancey told herself to breathe.

Chet studied her face, the high cheekbones and remarkable blue eyes, before his study dipped to her mouth and then back to her eyes. He thought her the most beautiful woman he'd ever seen.

"Goodbye, Delancey," he said softly, his hand touching hers for just an instant. "Don't lose that number."

A moment later he was gone. The waiter came and asked if she wanted something else, but she reminded herself that she had to drive home. She did so very slowly, Chet Dobson's smile and the touch of his hand lingering in her mind all the way.

Alexandria

Mackenzie and Tom did not get together as soon as she got home. They could have, since she got back on the weekend, but Tom took her right home and asked to see her the next Friday night. Mackenzie had never known him to be so formal with her and again wondered what would be the outcome of their meeting.

She dressed carefully for their time together, but she wasted her time. Tom called just before he was to pick her up and asked if she minded eating at his place. Mackenzie didn't mind, but she felt a little like an old shoe.

She drove herself over, and as she did, worked at understanding just what she felt for Tom. She wasn't in love, but he had been on her mind lately, and she didn't think it would take too much encouragement for her to fall for him.

By the time she arrived, Mackenzie had decided to tell Tom how she felt. She would tell him she wasn't in love but that she did care deeply, and ask him if he would like to pursue something more. She felt very good about what was in her heart, right up to the moment he answered the door. Something was wrong, and Mackenzie told herself to do lots of listening.

"Would you mind if we talked before we ate?"

"Not at all," Mackenzie told him, going to the sofa. It didn't pass her notice that he didn't touch her at all.

Tom sat in the big chair and looked right at her.

"I need to start by telling you, Mackenzie, that I've never had a relationship like ours before."

Mackenzie didn't know this, but neither did she comment.

"I've never had a friend who I hugged and kissed the way I do you, and I've never had a girlfriend who I didn't sleep with. For that reason, I can't decide whether I owe you an explanation or an apology."

"I take it something happened?"

"Yes. The type of thing that if you're my girl-friend you've got to know about it. If not, it's really none of your business."

Mackenzie was floored. After all, he'd asked her over; she hadn't pushed her way in. She might have been irritated, but Tom looked as though he was hurting. Mackenzie felt compassion for him.

"Don't tell me anything you don't want to tell, Tom. I guess I don't know how I'd label our relationship either, but don't tell me if you don't want to."

Tom knew he couldn't live with that. He didn't

want to talk about this to anyone, but neither could he pretend that nothing had changed.

"The weekend after our fight I went to a bar. I met a woman and we spent the night together." It was out. He was so relieved that he almost sat back with a sigh.

Every drop of her military training came to the fore, even as Mackenzie felt the color drain from her face. If it hadn't been for the paling of her features, she would have looked as calm and collected as any person could be.

"Are you still seeing her?"

"She's called a few times, but I haven't actually seen her."

"But you would like to."

Tom didn't answer, but Mackenzie didn't take that as an immediate yes. And just what was she supposed to say to this?

"Do you feel better now that you told me?" She groped for a reasonable question.

"That depends."

"On?"

"On whether you walk out that door and I never see you again. That wouldn't make me happy at all."

Again Mackenzie was at a loss. She didn't want a man who couldn't be faithful, but he had a fine point: Were they a couple? Mackenzie would have said yes, but not without reservations. What if they had been married and he'd gone off in a huff and done this? The question chilled Mackenzie to the bone.

"Trust is such a major factor. I know that," Tom was saying, and Mackenzie tried to attend. In truth, her mind was on the fact that he had been with many women, at least two that she knew of.

Was that really what she wanted in a husband? If she became intimate with Tom, she also became intimate with every partner he'd ever had. She wasn't sure why that hadn't been clear to her before, but the films about sexually transmitted diseases she'd seen in high school suddenly came back to mind.

"Mackenzie?" Tom's voice finally got through.

"I'm sorry, what were you saying?"

He stared at her, telling himself not to cry. "I've lost you, haven't I?"

Mackenzie was miserable, but she had to tell the truth. "I wish I could say no, Tom, but to be honest, I don't think I can do this anymore. I hope we see each other often, but I don't want our relationship to get any deeper."

She almost added that he didn't either. No man, no matter how angry he gets, runs off and sleeps with another woman because of one fight. Or was that the way it was? Mackenzie didn't know if she was naive or idealistic. Right now she was just miserable. Tom's face told her he was no better off.

"I think I'll go now," Mackenzie said. Tom made no comment to detain her. "Thank you for telling me, Tom. Thank you for being honest."

He nodded and stood when she did.

"I forgot to tell you that the next two books will be out next month and that the layout for the first search-and-find is coming along beautifully."

"Great," she said, trying to sound sincere. He looked so hurt. "I'll let Delancey know."

"Okay."

She was quickly at the door, hating the way this was ending and asking herself if it really had to. She left before she had her answer, went straight home, called her sister, and sobbed like a baby over the pain inside her heart.

THIRTY-FOUR

Chicago

The phone rang and Delancey jumped with nerves, even though she had been staring directly at it. She had put a call in to Chet Dobson's pager 24 hours before, regretting it almost immediately. Now it rang five times, and still she debated. She waited for a few more seconds and finally picked it up.

"Hello."

"Delancey? It's Chet Dobson."

"Hi," she said softly, trying not to sound winded.

"Did I get you at a bad time?"

"No, not at all."

"I'm glad you called."

"Are you?" She sounded as young and unsure as she was.

"Ohhh —" His voice was soft and smooth. "I can tell you doubted my sincerity at the airport. I'll have to think of a way to convince you that I'd just about given up hope and was ready to hire an investigator."

It was just what Delancey needed to hear. She laughed in delight and felt herself relaxing as they talked about nothing in particular but became familiar with each other again. The relaxation remained until Chet mentioned going to dinner.

"Are you free this Friday night?"

"I think so." Her hand gripped the phone.

"Give me your address, and I'll come for you at 7:00."

"Chet."

"Yes?"

"Would it be all right if I just met you?"

"Of course," he answered so swiftly that she felt herself relaxing again. "Do you know where the Palmer House is?"

"The hotel? I've heard of it."

"They have a great restaurant. How does that sound?"

"It's fine." She relaxed a little more.

"Okay. I'll see you there at 7:00, or maybe you'd better make it quarter of. Will that work?"

"Yes."

"I'll see you then," he said softly but didn't say goodbye. "I can tell you it feels much longer than five weeks since I sat with you at the airport."

"It does, doesn't it?" Delancey answered, but she barely managed the words. He had been aware of the weeks!

"I'll see you Friday night. Don't be late."

"I won't. Thank you for calling."

"Thank *you*. Goodnight, sweet Delancey."

"Goodnight."

Delancey hung up but didn't move. She felt as though she were floating on a cloud. The paper that was due in the morning was only half done, but Delancey forgot all about it. She eventually floated into her bedroom to figure out what to wear.

"What are you hungry for?" Chet asked Delancey when they had been seated at their table.

"Oh, I don't know," Delancey told him softly. She didn't want to let on that she was too nervous to eat. Delancey thought she remembered everything about him, but when she walked into the elegant lobby of the Palmer House and his eyes met hers, she was amazed all over again at how warm and tender they were and how they looked at her. She felt cherished and desirable all at the same time.

"Did I tell you how beautiful you look?" Chet asked without even looking at her this time.

"Yes." Delancey smiled. He'd said it at least twice. "But thank you again."

He glanced up just long enough to wink at her, and Delancey made herself look down and study the menu. She thought she might be able to eat a little chicken, but when the waiter brought someone's steak past, she changed her mind to beef. What she hadn't planned on was the drink waiter coming back first.

"White wine, Delancey?" Chet asked kindly.

"No, just Pepsi please," she said and smiled at the man who hovered near the table.

"Very well. And for you, sir?"

Delancey heard the drink he ordered and wondered what it was. She also wondered if he had far to drive home.

"Delancey, are you worried about getting yourself home? Did the wine at the airport give you trouble?" Chet asked when the waiter left. Delancey wondered if he could read her mind.

"No, but I only drink if I'm in the mood, and I'm not tonight."

"I'm impressed. Most people are not that levelheaded about it."

Delancey shrugged one slim shoulder. "I didn't

584

grow up with it. My parents never drank, and my father warned us against it so strongly that I didn't even try it until my first year in college."

"Is he proud of you now?"

"He died the month before I turned 13."

"I'm sorry, Delancey. That must have been awful for you."

"It was, and ironically, he was hit by a drunk driver."

"Wow. You just never know, do you?"

"Isn't that the truth."

"How did your mom handle it? I mean, were there a lot of you?"

Delancey shook her head. "Just my sister and me, and my mom was remarkable. She went out and got a job and just took care of us."

"That's great. Has she remarried?"

"Actually she did, about two years after my dad died."

"Is your stepfather all right?"

"He was wonderful to us," Delancey said softly, realizing she did not want to talk about this. "But my mother's gone now, and I don't have a lot of contact with him."

Her wonderfully expressive face had closed off, and Chet knew that he needed to back off. She was hurting about something, and he suddenly remembered his comment on the plane about the name her parents had given her. The thought made him wonder when her mother had died, but he kept it to himself.

"What did you decide on for dinner?" Chet asked and saw instantly that he'd said the right thing.

"I think a steak. What are you having?"

"The same. Did you want an appetizer or

anything first?"

"No, just the salad before the meal will be fine, thank you."

The tense moment was over, and they relaxed into conversation again. Chet had Delancey laughing within minutes. The tall blond had heard of love at first sight but thought it all nonsense. Looking across the table into Chet Dobson's smiling eyes made Delancey ready to believe in fairy tales. He was warm and sensitive and funny. Delancey felt herself slipping away.

Chet was in the same boat. All the women he had known before were suddenly fading from view. He had to work hard in order to advance in the airline, and he was willing to do that, but he was already working on how often he could be with this woman and still meet all his responsibilities. It might take some juggling, but he would find a way.

The evening lasted for hours but felt like minutes to the young couple. When Chet finally walked Delancey to her car, he did so slowly, his hand holding hers. Delancey turned to him with plans to thank him for a wonderful evening, but his head was already bending. It was not a deep, passionate kiss, but one that made Delancey feel loved. She sighed very softly when he straightened.

"I've wanted to do that since I saw you on the plane, sweet Delancey."

"I'm glad you did."

"Thank you for a wonderful evening. Shall we do it again?"

"Oh, yes," she said as a smile stretched her mouth.

"I'll call you," he whispered before turning and moving to his own vehicle. And he did call, but not for two weeks. Nevertheless, Delancey was sitting right by the phone.

Alexandria

It took some time to get over Tom, more time than Mackenzie had figured. She would have said that the first burst of tears was enough, but she was wrong. Always so busy with a book, she was suddenly at loose ends. She didn't want to write, and she didn't want to call him and risk getting hurt again. He called once on a business matter but was off the phone so fast that Mackenzie knew he was ready to move on as well.

For a time she did nothing. She didn't run, write, or even eat very often. Never was she more aware of the fact that she didn't make friends easily. Family had always been at the core of her heart, but Delancey was the only one left, and she was busy so much of the time.

Consequently, she was way behind on the writing schedule she had set up for herself. She had to call her sister.

"Hi, Deej."

"Hi, Mic. What's up?"

"Delancey," she wasted no time in getting to the point, "are you going to be really bummed if we don't go away for spring break?"

"No," Delancey said honestly, her voice kind. In truth, she had been having a hard time with the idea of being so far from Chet. "What's up? You're not sick, are you?"

"No, but I've just been so down about Tom, and I'm only just now getting back into my writing. The story's going so well that I'm afraid to stop. Do you know what I mean?"

"I know just what you mean, and we'll go some

587

other time. Maybe this summer. Then we'll have all the time in the world."

"Thanks, D.J. I was so worried about what you would say."

"Well, you shouldn't have been. If I get a chance to come and visit, I will. Or if you can come here, you know you'll be welcome."

"All right. How's Chet?"

"He's wonderful."

Mackenzie smiled at the tone in her sister's voice. She had never tried to figure out who would fall in love first, but now that it had happened, it was fun to watch.

"I'll have to come and meet him."

"Oh, Mic, I wish you would. He's so special, so sensitive to my feelings."

"He sounds too good to be true."

"But he isn't. He's real, and he's all mine. I wish you could meet someone just like him."

"Sometimes I wish I could meet *anyone,* but most of the time I'm too wrapped up in the book to notice."

"Is the release date still intact?"

"Yes. April 9. I can't wait."

"And how close are you to being done with *Sea-horse*?"

"Within a hundred pages I would guess, but I never know for sure. If it keeps going well, I should be done in just a few weeks."

"Great. I want to read it. When you're finished, why don't you box it up and send it to me?"

"Okay. I'd love to have your input. D.J., are you really okay about spring break?"

"I am, Mackenzie, I promise you. I've got so many projects going that have had to wait while I do schoolwork. Or I just might sleep the whole week."

"Okay. Well, take care of yourself."

"I will. You do the same."

The girls rang off but neither one lingered over the call. Delancey headed back to her easel, and Mackenzie returned to the keyboard.

Chicago

"What's this?" Delancey asked Chet after he had arrived at her apartment. He had kissed her and said hello but then immediately handed her an envelope.

"You'll have to open it and see."

Delancey looked at the smug expression he wore and smiled. He loved surprising her, and surprised she was. The envelope held an airline ticket in her name.

"Jamaica?" Delancey gawked at it and then at him.

"That's right. You did tell me you got your passport, didn't you?"

"Yes, I did, but I never dreamed —"

Chet smiled, loving her response. "To be honest with you, I have to work some of the time, but it's a special chartered flight, and while I'm off, we can be together."

"Oh, Chet. It sounds wonderful. What are the dates?"

"Right after school lets out. It's your graduation present from me."

Delancey reached over to kiss him but in the process had a sudden thought. "Will I have my own room?"

Chet's eyes were direct. "If you want that, yes."

Delancey swallowed hard. This was new ground for her. "May I let you know?"

589

"Of course." His gaze was tender. "I haven't pressured you before, Delancey. I'm not going to start now."

Just his saying that made her want to say yes, but she didn't. She waited another week to say it and was very glad she did; Chet said he loved her for the very first time.

Alexandria

"It's as good as your first," Paxton told Mackenzie. "I wasn't prepared for that, but *Seahorse* is as good as *Access Denied.*"

"Well, I'm glad to hear I'm not losing my touch," Mackenzie said lightly, but she was very pleased.

They were in Farrell's for dinner. Paxton had called her just the day before to say that he was finished reading and needed to meet with her. Mackenzie had been a bit fearful of his response but need not have worried. He was ecstatic.

"The ending is such a surprise," Paxton went on. "I think that's what I like so much. I love it when I don't see something coming."

"There were several ways I could have gone, but this ending won out."

"I'm glad it did. I think I would have figured out anything else."

They ordered their food when the waiter came, thankful for the private booth, and went right back to talking.

"I started another story, Pax," Mackenzie told him in between bites of salad and bread. "It's different from the other two, but I'm excited about it."

"Tell me about it."

"It all takes place in the United States — nothing out of the country this time — and centers on a police commissioner. I know it's been done before, but I hope to add a few new twists to it."

"What's the driving force?"

"A serial killer."

"You're right." Paxton's voice was flat. "That has been done before."

Not put off, Mackenzie sat thinking. Like her first book, she did this for herself. She had a story in her head and had to write it, even if Paxton didn't want to publish it.

"Do you even want to hear about it?" Mackenzie finally asked.

"Yes, I do, but I felt I should be honest. By the way, what's it called?"

"*Blue Crayon.*"

"*Blue Crayon?*"

"That's right," Mackenzie teased. "Want to know more?"

Paxton nodded and smiled, keeping in mind that she hadn't let him down yet. He sat transfixed for the next 20 minutes and listened until Mackenzie gave him the wrap-up.

"The commissioner is completely stumped by now. Sixteen people in the Chicago area are dead — children, women, and men — all from different walks of life, but all killed in exactly the same way, and each is left with a blue crayon in his or her hand. The commissioner is so perplexed that he's getting ready to turn in his badge. He's lost weight and his hair is falling out, and the governor is breathing down his neck to solve the worst set of crimes in the state's history. He's beside himself, but he's so tired he can't think, so he takes a day off. He spends the day with his children, and that's when he sees it: his daughter's crayon box. The blue crayon is a completely different brand. When he questions her, she says she got it from Mrs. Edmondson. Mrs. Edmondson is an adorable middle-aged woman who has lived with them for five years — she's nanny to the commissioner's children."

"What is the woman's problem?"

"She's obsessed with the commissioner's youngest child. Anyone who even looks at her cross-eyed is removed from the picture."

Paxton nodded, feeling more impressed than he'd planned on. "I like it, but I'm still going to warn you that it's been done quite a bit."

"What hasn't been, Pax? But if I put my own slant on this and keep the reader guessing, then I've done my job."

Again the man looked at her. "I know I've said this before, Mackenzie, but you really are a surprise."

The writer laughed. "I'm glad. I wouldn't want you to be bored. By the way, how is Jodi?"

Paxton beamed. "She's pregnant."

"Congratulations!"

"Thank you," he said as he bowed his head modestly.

"Are you two ever getting married?" Mackenzie boldly questioned him.

"Yes, we will, in another few months when things slow down at work. It will be very private, but we'll have you to dinner sometime."

"I'll enjoy that."

"Will you be bringing anyone along?" Paxton asked with no work at subtlety.

"No, I'm afraid things are pretty quiet in that area of my life."

"Tom told me he blew it but didn't elaborate."

Mackenzie nodded. "It's taken me some time to get back on my feet, but I think I'll be all right. I hope Tom is too."

"I'm glad you don't hate him."

"Me too."

"How's your sister these days?"

"She's fine. At the moment she's in Jamaica with her boyfriend."

"Sounds nice."

"Yes. He's a pilot and has to work part of the time, but she needed to get away."

"She graduated, didn't she?"

"Yes. Made me wish I'd gone to school."

"For what?"

Mackenzie opened her mouth, shut it, and shrugged. "I don't know."

Paxton laughed. "Listen, Mackenzie, there are people who have college degrees and study for years to do what you do naturally. Don't ever take it for granted."

"Thank you, Pax. I'll try to remember that."

Dinner ended on that warm note, and Mackenzie went back to her apartment. She was tired and had no plans to write but got an idea while watching TV. She ended up as she often did — writing until her eyes couldn't focus on the screen anymore.

Delancey was in the shower when Mackenzie called, but she had left a message, and as soon as Delancey was dressed, she called her back. The younger sibling was glad that she had a few minutes to compose herself or her voice would have given her away. About the only person she wanted to hear from these days was Chet, but the summer had brought more work than ever, and she had never felt so alone.

"Hi, Mic," Delancey worked at being cheerful.

"Oh, you're home. I just called."

"I was in the shower."

"Oh, okay. I'm calling to tell you that I'm taking a trip."

"You are? Where?"

"Europe."

"Oh, Mic, how fun! When are you going?"

"Two weeks."

"Where to?"

"All over. Wanna come?"

"Oh, Mic!"

"You're welcome, Delancey, and I mean it. I have to get out of this apartment or go crazy, and I think it's time I see a little of the world. I know you have deadlines, so I don't want you to feel pressured, but I'm going for a month, and you're welcome to join me."

The first thing Delancey wanted to say was no, at least until she talked with Chet. He had talked about their going away again since they got back from Jamaica, but the summer had slipped past and it had never happened. Even their dates and phone conversations had started to slow down. When Chet was with Delancey he was remarkably attentive, but when he was working, she might as well not exist. Delancey suddenly didn't care if he wanted to go somewhere with her or not. It was already September, and she hadn't seen her sister since Christmas.

"Name the date, Mic, and I'll be there."

"Do you mean it, D.J.?" Mackenzie's voice changed with her excitement. "You'll come?"

"Yes."

Mackenzie was so elated that it took her a moment to speak. "I already bought your tickets, just in case, Deej. You fly here on the fourteenth and we both fly out on the fifteenth. When we return, we both fly into National on the thirteenth, and you go home the fifteenth of October. Will that work?"

"Oh yes, Mic! A whole month together! Do you know how long it's been?"

"Too long. I can't believe how long it's been since we've even been able to hug each other. Virginia just isn't that far, but all I ever do is write."

And all I do is wait for Chet to call, Delancey thought, but she kept still.

"Well," she said instead, "you deserve this getaway. Where do we start?" Delancey was getting into it.

"We fly in and out of London, but in between, we go anywhere we like."

Delancey nearly squealed with delight. It was a dream come true. The sisters ended up talking for more than an hour, plotting and planning how they would visit places they had only dreamed of going.

Delancey got off the phone feeling buoyant with the thought of doing this with her sister. She loved the fact that it would be private, just the two of them. Not to mention the fact that Mackenzie was always so fun. They hadn't spent a month together all in one stretch since Mackenzie joined the Army.

The mood, the excitement, and even the need for privacy held Delancey for the next several days, even through one phone call from Chet. By the time he called she was scheduled to leave in four days, but since he'd called to cancel a date,

Delancey was irritated and didn't tell him of her plans. She left Chicago without a backward glance, her landlady giving her a ride to the airport and also promising to tell all visitors that Miss Delancey Bishop was on an extended vacation, and nothing more.

London

Neither one of the Bishop sisters had ever been in a store like Harrods. Floors and floors to wander through and all of them filled with the most gorgeous merchandise either one of them had ever seen. They walked around almost speechless for the first hour and became uncorked in the lingerie department.

"Look at this." Mackenzie held up a camisole so soft and white that it looked like snow.

"They have the same fabric in other pieces," Delancey pointed out, holding up some panties. The girls went slightly mad until Delancey realized something.

"Mic, we're going to have to lug all this around if we shop now."

"We'll have it shipped home," she said simply.

"But no one's there to get it."

Mackenzie had not thought of this complication. And with that, they slowed down, knowing they were going to end their trip in London as well.

"We'll just take a little more time at the end than we planned."

"That works for me."

Since shopping was cut short, sight-seeing began early. They took a double-decker, open-air bus to see some of the sights and to get a feel for what they would do later. Trafalgar Square, Buckingham Palace, and the Tower of London looked inviting, and Mackenzie made a mental note to spend some time in those spots, even as they took a five-hour train ride to Glasgow, Scotland.

They stayed in a bed-and-breakfast inn, saw the Glasgow Cathedral and the Botanical Gardens, took in a show at the Theatre Royale, walked for miles, ate at small pubs for dinner and lunch, and talked almost nonstop. Feeling as though they had years to catch up on, both women pulled out all the stops.

"How are things *really* going with Chet?" Mackenzie wanted to know. They had left Scotland, gone back through England, and were now on a ferry crossing the English Channel with plans to go to Brussels, and then on to Frankfort and Prague.

"You know that phrase, 'love is blind,' Mic? Well, there's a lot of truth to it. I can't believe how much I wait for him to call, and even when he cancels our dates, I usually stuff down my feelings so he won't feel guilty."

"Why is it so hard for him to see you?"

"Work. He's low man on the totem pole, and he has to take the hours he can get. Sometimes it's two weeks before he can even call me."

"Maybe you should move in together — then at least he would see you when he's home."

"I hadn't thought of that."

"Your place is great for work. Maybe you could live at his place and work at the warehouse. Would that work? Is his place nice?"

"I've never seen it."

Mackenzie didn't need to comment on this. Her face said it all.

"He works so much, Mic," Delancey said, but it

sounded lame even to her own ears. "He comes when he can. It doesn't ever feel as though we have time to go to his place."

Mackenzie tried to swallow the feelings of anger toward this man she had never met. Did he know how sweet Delancey was? Did he know that she would never abuse his love but cherish him as she longed to be cherished? Mackenzie mentally shook her head. She had to get her mind off of this or she was going to tell her sister she was a fool.

"What did he think of this trip? Was he put out?"

"I didn't tell him." D.J.'s chin came up a little.

Mackenzie let out an incredulous little laugh. "You didn't tell him?"

"Nope. He called a few days before we left, but it was to cancel another date. I was irritated."

"Won't your landlady tell him where you are?"

"She's a man-hater, Mic. When I told her I wanted it kept silent, she was delighted."

Mackenzie really laughed at that, and Delancey couldn't help but laugh too. When they sobered, however, Delancey's face showed her pain.

"You feel used, don't you?"

"I do, Mic." Tears filled her eyes. "Sometimes he can only come by for a few hours, but we always end up in bed. I even fell asleep one time and woke to find him gone. I felt like an old coat."

"Do you even enjoy it, D.J.?"

"The sex? Yes, I do, but the guilt is awful. When I'm with Chet I can't see anyone but him, but as soon as he leaves, I think about the way Mom warned us. All the days and nights I spend alone make me think about the way she waited for marriage. I thought waiting for love was good enough, but now I'm not so sure."

For a moment Mackenzie had no idea what to say. Telling her sister to break up with Chet was not the answer. She was clearly in love, and feelings didn't change that swiftly.

"It sounds to me like the relationship is all on Chet's terms," Mackenzie suddenly realized.

"It is that. And since I love him, I put up with it."

"Would you put up with it if he knocked you around once in a while?"

"He would never do that."

"But would you?"

"No, never." Delancey frowned at her.

"What if he cheated on you? Would you just look the other way?"

"Of course not." Delancey was getting testy.

"So you do have your limits, Delancey. I think when you go home, you need to tell Chet Dobson that the limits have been adjusted. You deserve better than you're getting, and you're the only one who can demand it. If he doesn't want to do this on your terms, or at least on both of your terms, I think he should take a hike."

Easier said than done was Delancey's first thought, but she didn't immediately discount what her sister had to say. She thought about Chet almost constantly, but what fun was it being in love alone? Oh, he told her he loved her, but lately there was little action behind the words. For a moment she tried to imagine life without him and felt so bereft that she could hardly breathe.

Seeing that her sister needed time, Mackenzie was quiet. It was amazing, really. They had watched their mother in two wonderful relationships, but Delancey wasn't lucky enough to find one of her own. Without warning Mackenzie could hear her father saying that luck had nothing to do with it. She hadn't thought of that in years and didn't want to think of it now. It was with relief that she realized it was almost time to disembark.

THIRTY-FIVE

Prague led to a trip through Switzerland, into Paris, and then to southern France where it was remarkably warm. For several days the sisters lay on the beach at Saint-Tropez. After all the cathedrals, small shops, art museums, and trying to be understood, it felt wonderful to lie around, talk, and eat. Delancey was approached by at least ten different men, and Mackenzie had her share of offers, but the sisters had time only for each other.

They slept in in the mornings, and after a leisurely brunch were usually on the beach by noon. It wasn't extremely crowded, but some of the other hotel guests were interesting, and their swimwear was nothing short of outrageous.

"I wish I'd known I would need my bikini," Delancey commented as one tan, very scantily clad woman strolled by.

"That wasn't a bikini, Deej. That was a few scraps of cloth and a little dental floss."

Whenever Mackenzie made these outrageous comments, her sister was her best audience. She ended up burying her face in her towel in order to muffle her laughter.

"That's what I love about you, Delancey," Mackenzie laughed at the other woman's response.

"You always laugh in all the right places."

The sisters smiled at each other before Delancey turned over. "Could I possibly be tired again? We just got up."

"I think it's the sun — it drains you."

They were silent for a time, Delancey sunning her back and Mackenzie sitting up scanning the beach.

"You really should draw this, D.J.," Mackenzie said as she ran her fingers through the sand. "It's so beautiful."

"I took some pictures," Delancey answered with her eyes closed, "so even if I can't remember, I can always get out my pictures and draw a little something."

"Be sure and send me copies of the photos."

"I will," Delancey said on a huge yawn and proceeded to fall asleep. Mackenzie, on the other hand, was awake and thinking.

I could live on the water, she thought, her eyes on the glorious Mediterranean. *I could wake up every day and see the water and be calmed and feel at peace.* Mackenzie thought back to her years of living at the Presidio. At some point almost every day she had a view of the ocean or San Francisco Bay, and it never ceased to delight and amaze her.

It wasn't long before Mackenzie joined Delancey in sleep, but a seed had been planted in her mind and was swiftly growing. She said nothing to Delancey, since she was not ready to talk about it, but she thought about it nonstop. It was on her mind as they left Saint-Tropez, went back through Paris, and ended their trip in London as planned. It was hard to believe that the time was over, but four weeks after they arrived, they were rested, tanned, loaded with souvenirs and memories, and on their way home.

As soon as Delancey headed for Chicago, Mackenzie wrote day and night for two solid weeks, but just 18 days after arriving home from Europe, the older Bishop was back on a plane, this time headed toward the West Coast, her dream of living on the water still strong in her mind.

Chicago

Delancey was home for two days when someone knocked on the door. She had done a lot of thinking while on the trip and was taking her sister's words to heart. She did deserve better than Chet was giving her, and having not spoken to him for a month, she could already see that continuing on his terms, with all the waiting and wondering, was worse than not seeing him at all. It was for this reason that she was able to answer the door, find him standing there, and not throw her arms around him or apologize for not being in touch.

"Hello, Delancey," he said tersely as he came in without permission.

Delancey said nothing. She shut the door, which was cold on her bare legs — she'd been working out — and stood and looked at the man she loved.

"Where have you been?" he demanded as soon as he turned to her, making no effort to hide his anger.

Delancey's brows rose with shock, but she was calm. "I beg your pardon?"

"Yes, you should beg my pardon. How dare you leave like that and not tell me!"

Delancey's mouth opened in surprise, and anger swiftly leapt into her eyes. "Let me get this straight, Chet. You're only available to me when *you* say you're available; I can't even call you at home — only on your pager — and you want to know where *I've* been? I don't think so." Her voice ended on a frigid note before she moved to the door and opened it. "Get out!"

Chet's hand came to his mouth. He was shaking, but Delancey didn't notice.

"I said get out," she repeated.

"I'm sorry, Delancey." His voice grew soft. "I shouldn't have said that. I've been worried sick and just wasn't thinking. I didn't know you felt that way, or we could have talked about it. I'm sorry. Please don't throw me out until you've heard my side."

Delancey couldn't handle his face. He looked utterly crushed. And he was right on one point: She hadn't told him how utterly tired she was of not seeing him. She slowly closed the door, walked past him into the living room, and sat on the futon chair she had purchased with her last check from IronHorse. She deliberately avoided the matching sofa so he could not sit next to her. She was silent as he sat on the sofa. Taking the end closest to her chair, he scooted to the edge and leaned toward her.

"How are you?" he asked tenderly, and Delancey told herself not to melt.

"Fine."

Chet nodded. He had been in complete confusion when a week went by with nothing but her answering machine to talk to. When it got to be two weeks, then three, then four, he thought he would go out of his mind. Now she was back and clearly angry at him. Delancey had never been angry at him, and he hated it.

"Did you go on a trip?" he tried.

"Yes."

"Have a good time?"

"Very."

He worked at keeping his voice even and said, "We're not going to get anywhere if all you're going to give me are monosyllabic answers, Delancey."

"And just where are we trying to go, Chet? Tell me that."

"I'm trying to find out why my girlfriend, the woman I love, would go away for a month and not tell me. And I'm also trying to figure out what I've done wrong. I have to work a lot, and I thought you understood that."

"I do understand it, Chet, but I'm not willing to live like that anymore, even if it means never seeing you again." Delancey watched him pale but kept on. She was dying inside, but her mind was made up.

"Do you know what my sister asked me?"

Chet shook his head no. In desperation he had called her sister but gotten only her answering machine as well.

"She asked me what your place was like. I had to tell her I've never seen it. Sometimes you come over here, and all we have is an hour together, but no matter how little time we have, we end up in the bedroom. I'm sorry, Chet, but that's not good enough anymore. I'm not going to be your plaything. I'm ready to commit myself, and all you can do is work. You say you love me, but you have a funny way of showing it."

"Oh, Delancey, I didn't know you felt that way. I hate being away from you. You do understand that, don't you?"

Delancey didn't answer. She thought the pain might kill her. Was this really all she would ever have? A man whose work meant everything to him?

"I'll do better," Chet was saying. "I'll call every day, even if I can't see you. And we'll do more things together. I told you we would go on that trip, and I promise you we will. Just give me another chance, Delancey. Don't ask me to let you go. My heart can't take it."

With that Delancey was in tears, and Chet came to her side. He held her tenderly and let her cry, telling himself he was every kind of fool for treating her this way and then wondering at what love could drive a man to do.

They talked for the next six hours. It was the most time Delancey had had with him since Jamaica. Her heart was on the way to healing by the time he left. She told herself that if things didn't change she was through, hoping all the time that she wouldn't have to find out. In the weeks and months to follow, however, Chet made a real effort. They even began spending the night at his apartment and dining there just about every week. And as always, as long as Delancey was with him, the world was bright. It was only after he left her or she went home alone that she could feel the hole in her heart.

Alexandria

Mackenzie dropped the finished manuscript for *Blue Crayon* on the kitchen table and said to her editor, "I'm moving, Pax, so I wanted you to have this now. I leave at the end of the month."

"Where to?"

"Lake Tahoe. I've bought a house on the lake."

Paxton's mouth opened. "Tell me you're kidding."

"I can't, because I'm not."

For a moment he didn't say anything. His mind searched around for an appropriate reply but came up blank. For some reason he had terrible regret that he and Jodi had never had Mackenzie over again. Her first two books were still spending time in the top ten of the *New York Times* Bestseller List, but he wondered just how much fun she was really having.

The surprise was not that she had bought a house. With her money he would have done so months ago. He was startled that she was moving so far away. Of course, if she didn't really have friends here, what did it matter where she lived? That, however, was the last thing he could say to her.

"Is this the entire manuscript?" he asked, having finally slowed his mind down.

"Yes. It's about 200 pages shorter than the other two books, but the story is complete, and I thought that was more important than the length."

"You're right. The story is more important."

"Is that all you can say, Pax?" she asked, her tone a little wounded. " 'Is this the whole book?' Nothing about my move?"

"I'm sorry, Mackenzie," he said sincerely, seeing how thoughtless he'd been. "I think it's great. I mean, it'll be rotten to have you so far away, but having to fly to beautiful Lake Tahoe to talk with one of my top authors might not be so bad." He ended this with a smile.

"How did you know?" Mackenzie leaned forward and suddenly asked, her face serious and intent. "How did you know that people would like my books, Pax?"

He smiled. "I've been in the business a long

time, and before that, all I did was read. I had a teacher in school who caught on to my love of literature. He started on me when I was a freshman in high school, so that by the time I went to college, I concentrated on English and literature classes. When a job editing the campus newspaper became available, I took it, but the short length of the articles and the way everything had to be done so swiftly every month just about drove me to drink.

"For a while I thought I'd missed my calling, but then I got a job with a small publisher who was always overworked and understaffed. It was almost as bad as the editor's job but with one major difference: I got to read books. I hated the constant rush and having to do jobs I wasn't trained to do, but the reading made it all worthwhile. From there I went to IronHorse, and because I've recommended that we publish some of the biggest names in the business, Hank Darwell thinks I'm invaluable. I love my job, and I'm still able to collect the cream, as your books prove, so it's a perfect combination."

Mackenzie was impressed. She had known that IronHorse was not in the habit of publishing books just because they felt sorry for the author, but not even when Paxton promised to make her a star did Mackenzie imagine how popular her books would be. IronHorse had already been approached for information on MacWalker so movie rights could be negotiated, but since she didn't want anyone else writing the scripts, and she didn't want to take the time to go back over a book that was already done, Mackenzie said no. She had too many new ideas for that.

As if he could read her mind, Paxton suddenly

asked, "Are you working on something right now?"

"No. I've got a story idea, a good one, but all I've done lately is pack. I'll start it when I get out there and settled."

"All right, but how about telling me about it now?"

"It would take a while, but the title is *Shibboleth,* and it's centered in and around the Pentagon and deals with weapons and national security."

"*Shibboleth,*" Paxton said softly. "As in a password to prove who you are, like in the Bible?"

"Exactly. I don't have all the details worked out, but much to the interest of the whole world, there's a new fabric on the market. It's as thin as a piece of plastic wrap, but there's not a bullet in the world that can penetrate it. A French scientist created it, but he's angry at his own government and the way they've treated him. He comes to America, thinking they will give him help and protection, which they plan to do, but then the President's dog is poisoned, and something frightens a child staying at the British consulate so badly that she hasn't spoken a word in two weeks. To say the least, things fall all to pieces."

"Do you have any of this written down yet?"

"Like notes? No, I do better when I just keep it in my head."

Paxton couldn't stop the smile that crossed his mouth. "I'll miss you, Mackenzie."

"Why is that?" she honestly wanted to know.

"There aren't many people who can write as effortlessly as you can. Tom was just telling me that Micah Bear books are the hottest thing this Christmas, and I know from the *Times* list that Mac Walker is one popular fellow."

Mackenzie didn't know what to say to that. She

609

could have reminded Paxton that they didn't see each other that often, but he might take it wrong. In truth, the last thing she wanted to do right now was watch him and Jodi frolic in wedded bliss. She recognized her own cynicism but had no idea how to feel differently.

Paxton didn't stay that much longer, which was fine with Mackenzie. She still had packing to do. The moving van didn't come for another few weeks, but she was eager to have everything ready. Bodily she was in Virginia, but as far as her mind and thoughts were concerned, she was already living on the lake.

Zephyr Cove, Nevada
February 1991
Mackenzie walked out on the deck of her home on Lake Tahoe and picked up a fat pinecone that lay at her feet. Sticky with sap and smelling just heavenly, it was at least nine inches long and the color of the dried-out pine needles that lay everywhere in the summer, or like now, mixed with snow during the winter. The cone was so plump it made her smile. Such things she now saw every day and knew she would never tire of. In her opinion there wasn't another place in the world like Lake Tahoe.

As to the lake, some people said the color was sapphire, but that depended on where you were. The blue along the shoreline was lighter, but as the water's depth increased, so did the deepness of the blue. And if that wasn't enough, having the Sierras rising up around her like protective hands just made Mackenzie want to smile. And smile was something she did often since the move. It took the moving van a little longer than she figured, and Mackenzie laughed at how poorly her small amount of furniture fit into the huge home she had bought, but it was all hers, and that was what mattered.

Somewhere along the line it occurred to her that her parents had never had this. They had lived in homes, but never their own. Mackenzie wished they could see her now, and for the first time in over two years, she was able to think of her mother's death without anger. Her parents had loved this lake, and Mackenzie knew they would have loved her house as well.

Her coffee was getting cold and so were her feet. She kept her deck cleared of snow, but that didn't change the freezing temperatures. She headed back into the huge living room and to the fireplace where she had built a fire that morning. From her place on the sofa she sat looking around, never tiring of the view.

The front door came directly into the living room, but the ceiling in the area was not vaulted since there were three bedrooms above: a luxurious master suite and two other bedrooms with their own bath. Exactly opposite the bedrooms, on the lake end of the house and up another set of stairs, was a huge loft that Mackenzie had made her office. It was wide open to the living room below and had windows toward the lake, the likes of which she had never seen.

The dining area was on the far end of the living room, and the kitchen that sat off to one side behind the garage even had great windows and a view of the lake and trees; both rooms exited onto the deck that ran completely along the lake side of the house. There was a powder room tucked away near the kitchen where the door led to the garage, and next to it was a spacious laundry room. The house was on a dead-end road that bordered a state park. Mackenzie had a neighbor across the street and one to the north, but to the south was the park and to the west — her "backyard" — lay Lake Tahoe. Life was as sweet as she could imagine.

That she had no one to call, no friends to do anything with, escaped her for a time. She had already started looking for furniture to fill the rest of the house, and between trips to do that she worked on *Shibboleth* and two more Micah Bear books. For the moment she was keeping busy. There was no time to think about what might be missing in her life.

Chicago

Delancey stared at the blank paper but had no desire to draw. She was behind on her work for *Just for Kids,* the second magazine that had commissioned her art, but all she could think about was Chet. Lately it seemed that only if they had a huge fight and she threatened never to see him again would he make the effort to spend more time with her. And even with that, it would last only a few weeks.

What kind of relationship is that? she asked herself. *All I do is sit here and wait for the phone to ring. I don't want to play games anymore. Going away and not telling him was a high school trick, but that's what it takes to get his attention. I thought by now we would be married, but he's never mentioned it. I just don't know if I can go on like this. Maybe I should go and visit Mic.* But the thought had no more than formed when she pushed it away. Hard as it was to wait for him to call, Delancey didn't want to be that far away. She nearly ran when the phone rang in the midst of all these thoughts, but it was only Tom Magy.

"How are you?" Delancey asked when she recovered from her disappointment.

"I'm fine. I'm in Chicago, and I want to take you to dinner.

"Oooh, I would like that. When and where?"

They set up plans to meet that night, and Delancey arrived in a very good mood. She and Tom hugged, and moments later they were talking about everything.

"I have something for you," he said as he pulled out the new Micah Bear search-and-find book.

"Oh, Tom!"

"It's just in, so I grabbed it on my way out the door."

"Thank you. It's beautiful."

"We just used your artwork for the cover, and we can't miss with that."

"I love it when a new book comes out. This one ran late, so I've been anxious."

"Yeah. It's a shame we didn't pick up the Christmas season, but if this is anything like the others, it won't matter."

"Did you send any to Mic?"

"That's on my list to do when I get back. How is she, Delancey?" Tom asked sincerely.

"She's doing well," Delancey told him, her voice kind. He had hurt her sister, but Delancey felt she understood. "She loves living on the lake, and most of the time she's buried in a book and doesn't remember how far apart we are."

"And how about you, do you remember?"

Delancey smiled a little. "I think I usually have more time on my hands than she does, but I am up to my ears in work right now."

"Still in love with . . . was it Chad?"

"No, Chet, and yes I am."

"Will I be in trouble for asking you to dinner?"

Delancey grinned. "Not from me. In fact, you did me a big favor. He called at the last minute, and I'm always too available. It felt good to tell him I had a date and know that he was wildly jealous."

Tom laughed, assuming that the relationship was an open one, not understanding that Delancey was completely serious. It had given her no end of satisfaction to tell Chet he couldn't stop by on his way home from the airport because she was going out. He wasn't happy, and Delancey left no doubt in his mind that she didn't care.

She could just about predict the days to follow. Flowers and champagne would arrive, and after that, Chet himself, a gift of some type in his hand. Delancey asked herself why she put up with it. Her standard answer — that she loved him with all her heart — was starting to wear thin. She knew that she didn't want to think about it right now.

"I think I've lost you," Tom said, breaking into her thoughts.

"I'm sorry." Delancey was instantly contrite. She would not give Chet the satisfaction of ruining her evening. "Just woolgathering. How's work going for you?"

"Fine."

"I forgot to ask you why you're in town."

"Things are not as busy right now, so I'm headed to a children's writer's conference. We've picked up some of our best authors at those conferences, and my boss thought it would be a good idea."

"Sounds fun."

"Have you never been to one?"

"No, never."

"I think you would enjoy it."

"But why would I go — I mean, aren't they meant to help you get published?"

"They are, but you can also learn new things and see what's going on in the market." Tom stopped and blinked. "On second thought, I've stolen a few authors from other publishers when I've been at those conferences. I don't think you'd enjoy it all that much, Delancey. Don't go."

Delancey found this highly amusing and teased him for some time about where it was and how she could get in without registering. They talked until almost 11:00, and at the end of the evening she was slightly surprised not to find Chet on her doorstep. She went to bed, however, with a smile on her face. He had left five frantic messages on her answering machine.

Zephyr Cove
Why can't anything last? Why do You have to ruin everything? I don't want to think about my mother, and I don't want to think about Jack! In her mind the words were loudly shouted at God, but as Mackenzie sat on her deck, a book open across her lap, not a whisper could be heard.

It had been going so well. The winter had ended, she had gotten in more skiing than she had ever dreamed of, and then she had been there to watch spring arrive and the earth sprout with new life. It had been delightful.

Now it was mid-July, and summer vacationers were crowding the lake, but she didn't care. She

615

had her own little world, and she was happy — happy right up to the minute a young couple moored their boat not far from her house and spent the day eating, laughing, and holding each other close, a day Mackenzie had planned on spending out on the deck with her laptop. She tried not to look, but even turning away did not stop the romantic rock music they played or allow her to miss the sound of their laughter and fun. After just 20 minutes she gave up, heading into the house to pace in frustration until she changed into workout shorts and tank top.

Not even shooting buckets into the basketball hoop the previous owner had put over the garage helped. Noon already on top of her, she cleaned up, climbed into her Jeep, and headed toward Reno.

Every time she drove the Jeep lately, she thought of Jack, and she had no plans to continue with that. However, she didn't bank on the way she would be treated as the car salesman took in her Jeep — in good shape but not brand new — her cutoff jeans, and her T-shirt. She hadn't told the man she could buy his job, let alone one of his cars; she only thought it, and stalked out with her head high. Leaving the Ferrari dealership in disgust and rage, Mackenzie felt as though the whole day was shot.

She wasn't in the mood to write or even go home. For the first time she drove right past the Skylark turnoff that led to her street and headed through South Lake Tahoe, down Highway 50 toward Meyers. She was somewhat calm by then and realized she didn't really want to go anywhere. She grabbed the road that led out to Christmas Valley with plans to turn around and head home, but by then she was driving the speed limit and finally able to enjoy the incredible trees and mountains. The cloth top was off, and the smell of pine floated around her. It was hot, but she loved it, her mood improving by the moment.

She drove for a long time before turning around, and when she did, she decided to pull over and walk awhile. She hadn't worn shoes for that purpose and didn't plan to go far, but the trees, chipmunks, birds, and fresh smell of everything was so inviting that she couldn't resist. She was just climbing from the seat when there was a loud burst, and she jumped out to see her rear tire go flat on the rim.

For a moment she was so angry she couldn't move. The Jeep was tipped over at an odd angle, and had Mackenzie been wearing boots, she would have kicked the offending tire. All of this was made worse by the fact that her spare was sitting in her garage.

For a moment she told herself this could not be happening. If she just stayed still and woke up, the nightmare would be over. She closed her eyes and tried to think straight.

"Are you all right?" A woman's voice startled her.

Mackenzie's head whipped around, and she watched a woman emerge from the trees, step onto the edge of the road, and walk toward her. She stopped a little ways off and spoke again.

"My name is Roz Cummings, and I live through the trees there. Is there anything I can do?"

For the stupidest reason, Mackenzie felt tears come to her eyes. It might have been because Roz's voice had the same sweet tone as her mother's.

"May I use your phone?" Mackenzie asked, not able to stem the flow.

"Of course." Roz smiled kindly, not commenting on the tears. "Come this way and we'll go through the backyard. I heard the pop. Was it your tire?"

Mackenzie could only nod before she reached for her keys and followed the other woman through the trees, through the gate in the fence, across the green grass, and into a dining area right off the kitchen at the back of the house.

"Here you go," Roz handed Mackenzie a cordless phone. "Do you need the phone book?"

"I don't think so." She couldn't believe how teary she was. "I think the number is in my wallet." It wasn't until right then that she realized her purse was in the Jeep. Mackenzie's hand came to her mouth in an effort to stop crying. Roz stood in surprise and then compassion as she wondered whether she might be hurt. It was such a helpless feeling to have this stranger crying in her kitchen. She finally went for the box of tissue and pressed one into Mackenzie's hand.

Mackenzie used it and tried to speak. "I'm sorry," she gasped. "I just need to go get my purse. I'm sorry."

"It's all right," Roz said and meant it. "I'll stay here and make you something cold to drink. You go get whatever you need."

Mackenzie nodded and moved out the door. It was just plain stupid to leave her purse, but right now she was making a fool of herself, so that action seemed rather par for the course. Sniffing and dribbling all the way, she retraced her steps, grabbed her purse, and by the time she was back in Roz's kitchen, had the number out for the auto club and her emotions somewhat in control.

"Tell them to honk when they get there, so you can stay in here out of the heat until they arrive," Roz told Mackenzie while she dialed. The younger woman was still explaining where she was when Roz put a tall, frosty glass in front of her. The club said it would be close to an hour before help arrived, and Mackenzie cringed at the thought of imposing on this woman's hospitality for that long. She pushed the off button on the phone, set it down, and opened her mouth to explain.

"Drink up," Roz cut in, and Mackenzie glanced down, suddenly so parched she could hardly talk. She was still drinking when a teenage girl entered the room.

"Hey, Mom." She seemed not to even notice the other woman. "The Cantrells want me to babysit tonight. Is that going to work?"

"I think so. How late?"

"Not very. They're going shopping and out to dinner is all."

"Okay. Are they picking you up or are we taking you?"

"Oh, I'll call and ask, but they usually pick me up."

"Okay."

"Hello," the teen said, her smile as warm as her mother's.

"Hello."

"This is my daughter Sabrina," Roz was swift to explain.

Mackenzie smiled at her and then remembered she had never given her name. "I'm Mackenzie Bishop."

"Mackenzie Bishop?" the teenager questioned, leaning a little closer.

"Yes."

"*The* Mackenzie Bishop who writes the books?"

Mackenzie blinked. She had never been recognized before, but then she was not very social.

"Yes, I write books, but they're a little young for you."

Sabrina shook her head. "I read them to the kids I babysit, and they love 'em. We've spent more time on the Micah Bear search-and-find book than any other they own."

"Who is this, Rina? Jonathan Cantrell?"

"Yes. He'll be so excited to learn that I've met you."

Mackenzie felt herself smiling. The teen's praise was so genuine and warm, and with a little cold tea inside of her, she was feeling much better.

"It is exciting," Roz was saying. "An author right here in our kitchen. I won't gush though." She put her hand up. "You must get that all the time and hate it."

Mackenzie laughed in spite of herself. "As a matter of fact, I don't. This is the first time."

"Oh, wow, can you believe that, Mom? I've seen your books everywhere. That's so cool."

"Well, we are honored then," Roz said with a huge smile. Small talk followed, punctuated by the honking of a truck. "That'll be them," the hostess spoke as she stood.

"Come on, Rina, let's walk Mackenzie back to her Jeep."

They did this quietly and stood back while Mackenzie spoke with the auto club man and showed him her card. They waited with her while he prepared to tow the Jeep to the nearest station for repair. Mackenzie would ride along in the cab of the truck.

"Thank you, Roz," Mackenzie said when it looked like he was almost done. "Can I pay you for the call?"

"No, no, don't worry about that. We were just glad to help." Roz touched her gently on the arm. "You take care of yourself and stop back anytime."

Mackenzie thanked her again, smiled at Sabrina, and went to the truck. It had started out as an awful day but hadn't ended so badly. Roz Cummings was the nicest person she had met in a long time. Mackenzie finally felt at peace with her thoughts, so much so that she was ready to write again, something she did until late that night.

THIRTY-SIX

It took much longer than normal, but Mackenzie thought she might have a decent batch of cookies. She had overslept because of her late night but still got up with Roz Cummings on her mind. She had been remarkably kind and the first woman in a long time to whom Mackenzie felt drawn. She had never been a person who couldn't accept gifts, but the way Roz had not mentioned the way she had blubbered in her kitchen made her want to do something for her in return.

Baking and cooking had never been her strong points, but at this point Mackenzie was willing to give it a try. Her mother used to make an iced oatmeal molasses cookie that was wonderful, and Mackenzie was now at the icing stage. Not able to resist, she popped one into her mouth. A moment later she was at the sink, spitting it out and getting a drink to wash the taste from her mouth. Still swishing away the bitter taste, she stood with one hip propped against the counter and stared out the French doors that led off the kitchen to the deck.

The cookie hadn't been sweet at all. Could she have actually left out the sugar? Mackenzie couldn't believe it, but there was no denying that the cookie had been awful. The sugar was the only logical conclusion she could draw. What else could it be? She ended up dumping the whole batch down the garbage disposal, telling herself it had been a sappy idea anyway. She went up to the loft with the intention of writing, and she got a lot accomplished, but the next morning Roz Cummings was still on her mind.

It was only a little after nine o'clock when Mackenzie headed out the door to drive to Christmas Valley. The road where the tire went flat was familiar, but it took a moment to find the exact street Roz's house faced. Mackenzie felt her palms grow damp as she climbed from the Jeep, but she knew she had to do this. Her face flamed at the thought of Roz thinking she was some kind of weirdo, and she was relieved when Sabrina answered the door.

"Hi, Mackenzie," she said as if it were an everyday thing. "How are you?"

"I'm all right. I just wanted to drop this off." She held out the second Micah Bear search book. "It's for Jonathan. That was his name, wasn't it?"

"Yes! Oh, cool. Come on in," Sabrina stepped back and invited. "Mom! Mackenzie Bishop's here, and she brought a book for Jonathan Cantrell."

"Well, Mackenzie," Roz came around the corner as Mackenzie stepped over the threshold, "this is so nice. And look at this gorgeous book. Come in and have a cup of coffee."

"Oh, I don't want to be in the way. I just wanted to thank you again for Tuesday."

"Well, you're welcome," she said as she walked away. "I'll just get you a cup of coffee."

Mackenzie felt she had no choice but to follow.

"Cream or sugar?"

"Both," Mackenzie heard herself say, even as Sabrina was introducing her to her older brother, Josh.

"Hi." He smiled and went back to his breakfast. Mackenzie had eaten hours ago and was uncomfortable that she had intruded. Roz, on the other hand, thought nothing of it. She delivered Mackenzie's coffee, made just the way she liked, invited her to take a seat at the table, and settled down to talk to Mackenzie as if she had all day.

"How long did it take to fix your tire?"

"About an hour."

Her look was compassionate. "Did it make you late for anything?"

"No. I was just headed home when it happened."

"Where is home?"

"Across State Line. Zephyr Cove."

"Oh, that's a pretty area. Have you lived there long?"

"Since January."

Roz nodded but stayed quiet as many more questions crowded her mind. She did not want to appear nosy. There was something very vulnerable about the woman she had seen two days ago. The woman today was composed, confident, and sure of herself, but the woman she'd seen earlier would not leave her mind.

"I wanted to check with you, Mackenzie. You weren't hurt the other day, were you?"

"No." Mackenzie's cheeks heated slightly, thinking of the way she had cried. "It had just been a long, frustrating day."

"I've had those." Roz smiled and took a sip of coffee.

Mackenzie then remembered hers. She glanced

at Josh and found his eyes on her. He smiled and ducked his head a little.

"You're going to be late, Josh," his mother told him kindly. "He mows the lawn at the church," Roz informed Mackenzie. "It's nice that he can pick his own hours, but sometimes I think it's easier to have a set schedule."

Mackenzie nodded. "My sister would agree. She's an illustrator, and unless she has a deadline breathing down her neck or is really excited about an idea, she leaves it until the last minute."

"She does the illustrations for the books you write, doesn't she?"

"Yes, and also some freelance work for a few children's magazines."

Roz was paging through the book Mackenzie brought, slightly awed that she knew the author.

"Has your sister sold any of her work on its own?"

"You mean framed prints? No. She's had some of her originals framed, and I have a few of them, but other than the Micah Bear posters that our publisher puts out, all her work is in books or magazines."

"At the risk of sounding rude, Mackenzie, you seem very young to be so established."

"I am young." Mackenzie was not offended. "I was just 23 last month, and Delancey won't be 22 until next week. And of course when we started, we were quite a bit younger."

"What a special gift."

It was so much like something her mother would say that Mackenzie stiffened to keep her emotions at bay. Roz didn't notice. She was drinking her coffee again.

When Mackenzie later tried to recall exactly

what happened next, she couldn't quite do it. But before anyone could say anything else, both Sabrina and Josh went on their way, Josh saying how nice it was to meet her, and Sabrina telling her she would give the book to Jonathan as soon as she saw him. Roz saw her family off. They were no more out the door when the bell rang.

"That'll be the gang for Bible study, Mackenzie," Roz said as she pushed to her feet. "Don't feel that you have to rush off. We're studying the life of Christ, and you're welcome to stay."

Mackenzie nearly bolted for the door. The kindness the woman displayed to her was the only thing that kept her from slipping out the back patio door and running for the Jeep.

"Come on in," she heard Roz say, and moments later Mackenzie was being introduced to Margie, Kathy, Susan, and Gary. They all greeted her as if she were one of the gang, set their things aside, and gathered in the living room with their Bibles. Mackenzie felt she had no choice but to follow.

"We're in the book of Mark," Roz explained to Mackenzie, before Gary, clearly the leader, took over.

"I think I'll pray before we get started," he said, and Mackenzie bowed with the others, her gaze focused wide-eyed on her lap.

"Father in heaven," she heard Gary say, "thank You for this time we can meet around Your Word. Open our hearts and help us to listen. Amen.

"Let's get right into chapter 3 where we left off. Oh, Roz, maybe you could get Mackenzie a Bible."

"You can share with me." Since she was on the sofa next to Mackenzie, Kathy offered and shifted the Bible until it sat between them.

"Thank you," Mackenzie replied automatically,

thinking she had to get out of there before she suffocated.

"Okay, I want you to follow along as I read verses 13 through 15," Gary said. " 'And He went up to the mountain and summoned those whom He Himself wanted, and they came to Him. And He appointed twelve, that they might be with Him, and that He might send them out to preach, and to have authority to cast out the demons.'

"What do we see here that we've been seeing since the beginning of the book?"

"Christ's authority," Margie answered immediately.

"Exactly," Gary said with a smile. "It's amazing. Demons fall on their faces in His presence. A man's hand — withered and useless — is suddenly healed. Christ's authority is unmistakable in every chapter. Some people come for healing and some come out of curiosity, but His authority leaves them all without excuse. This *has* to be God's Son.

"Now in the three verses I just read you, there was a certain order of things that I see as significant. Do you see in verse 14, the first requirement of the disciples is that they be with Christ? Did you catch that? Now what's the second one?"

In spite of herself, Mackenzie read verse 14 in Kathy's Bible and saw the words, "that He might send them out to preach." She had only just finished reading it when Roz gave that very answer.

"That's right," Gary confirmed again. "Before the preaching and before He gives them authority of their own, He wants them to be with Him. Isn't that interesting? Remember back in chapter 1, verse 35, when early in the morning Jesus goes off to a lonely place to pray? Now you know me well enough to know that I'm not saying the only time we can meet with the Lord is in the morning, but don't miss the significance of these verses. This God-Man, this Jesus Christ, He knew where to start. He knew what He needed, so He met with His Father before the day began. He knew what the disciples needed — they needed His example and teaching above all else — so the first thing He required of them was to be with Him.

"I think about these passages when I hear myself telling the Lord that I'm tired of being a father to three active teens and that I don't want to make the effort anymore, or when I find myself wondering why I can't seem to say no to a persistent temptation. I ask myself if I've taken care of first things first. Have I been in the Word and prayer like I need to be? Above all else, are they a priority?"

His eyes moved around the room, but Mackenzie didn't feel singled out, only fascinated at what she was hearing. The authority of Christ had never before occurred to her. Gary was almost through with the hour-long study before she remembered that she wanted nothing to do with this God-Man, His authority, or anything else.

And in fact, Gary and the women didn't hang around. They thanked Roz and were swiftly on their way, leaving Mackenzie alone with her again. She didn't get comfortable but stood in such a way that Roz knew she wanted to go.

"I'm so glad you could join us, Mackenzie."

"Thank you for your kindness, Roz, but I have to tell you that I really don't want anything to do with Jesus Christ."

"Can you tell me why, Mackenzie?" Roz asked

openly.

"I just —" she began but couldn't find the words. She struggled for a moment, but Roz cut back in.

"I shouldn't have asked that, Mackenzie. I'm sorry. You're welcome here even if you don't want to talk about Christ, but I would like to tell you something."

Mackenzie steeled herself for Roz to tell her she was praying for her, but that didn't happen. Roz simply put a hand on Mackenzie's arm and spoke softly.

"You're a different person today than you were yesterday. Yesterday you were crying and upset, and even though you're confident and collected today, I can still see that you're hurting. You hide it very well, but I can see it. You're welcome back to Bible study. We meet every Thursday morning at ten o'clock, and I hope you'll come, but I also hope you'll come back and hear *my* story. Five years ago I was not the person I am today, and I'd like to tell you about it. If you don't leave with anything else today, Mackenzie, I hope you leave knowing that I like you and that you're welcome here anytime you wish."

Mackenzie wanted to cry all over again but managed not to. She thanked her hostess yet again and moved out the door. Almost in a state of shock, she drove home. She was not angry, just alone and confused. It was hours before she realized she desperately needed to talk with her sister.

Chicago
Chet tenderly kissed Delancey goodnight and slipped out the door. They had spent a wonderful

evening together, and for the first time ever, he had spoken of the future. He was growing tired of being on call at the airline and had gone so far as to ask Delancey what she thought of France. He had heard about a small airline there that favored American pilots. Delancey had loved France when she was there with Mackenzie, and without much encouragement, she saw herself married to Chet and living in a little French villa where she could paint and draw to her heart's content.

If the phone hadn't rung, Delancey might have merrily dreamed all night, but hearing the sound of her sister's voice was worth coming back to earth.

"What have you been up to? Writing like mad?"

"Off and on. I've been lying in the sun like a lazy fool, so I'm tan but dry as a bone. One of these days I'll get writing again. Pax keeps calling, and I never return his calls. I wouldn't be surprised to open my front door one of these days and find him standing there."

"I'm sure you're right," Delancey laughed. "He's not about to let his top novelist stray too far. By the way, Chet just told me he read *Access Denied* and loved it. It was all I could do not to tell him."

"But you didn't."

"No. After all this time, it's become almost a habit to stay quiet about it."

"I'm glad you did, Deej. I'm not ready for anyone to know. By the way, is he taking you out for your birthday next week?"

"Yes." Delancey filled her in, but in truth Mackenzie was only half attending. When there was a slight lull, she finally found the courage to say what she had called about.

"Hey, D.J.?"

"Yeah."

"Do you know what I did this morning?"

"What?"

"I went to a Bible study." Mackenzie's voice was lighter than she felt, and her hand gripped the phone so hard that she was getting a cramp.

"You're kidding." Delancey's voice grew rather cool.

"No. It was so weird. I mean, not the people, but I was at this lady's house — I just met her Tuesday — and then her Bible study group showed up and there was no way to leave."

"Was it awful?"

"No," Mackenzie answered, surprised that she was able to say so. "It really wasn't. I mean, I don't agree with it, not personally, but this man made it very interesting."

"You're not thinking of going back are you?" Delancey sounded so horrified that Mackenzie took a moment to answer.

"Well, I don't know. It was kind of interesting."

Mackenzie was not prepared for her sister's anger.

"You can't be serious!"

"Well, I haven't decided or anything like that," Mackenzie said, trying to defend herself.

"I can't believe what I'm hearing." There was no disguising Delancey's ire. "I have never known you to be a hypocrite, Mackenzie. What's come over you?"

"Why does my going make me a hypocrite?" Mackenzie asked in genuine confusion.

"You've never wanted anything to do with God, Mic, and you know it. Anytime I've ever brought it up, you said that's fine for me but to leave you out."

Mackenzie felt stunned. Why had she thought she could talk to her sister about this? Her heart felt so crushed she thought it might break. She didn't say anything for some time, and Delancey finally heard herself.

"I'm sorry, Mic. I didn't mean that." Her voice was soft and hurt as well. "I don't know why I said it. I'm just so surprised."

"It's all right, Delancey. I understand."

But things were not all right, and neither sister understood. For the first time either woman could remember, there was a barrier between them. Delancey felt threatened that her sister might turn to a God that she had always hated. It was so inconsistent with who Delancey knew her sister to be that she was shaken. Mackenzie felt as though she was all alone on a desert island. They hung up after five more minutes of uncomfortable conversation, but things did not feel good.

A week later, when Mackenzie called her sister to wish her a happy birthday, she decided against mentioning the Bible study again. Delancey loved the CD player Mackenzie had sent, and they managed to find things to say to each other for almost ten minutes, but there was still a strain. Mackenzie was holding out, and Delancey knew it. Guilt or not, the older sister had been off the phone for only 20 minutes when she headed out the door for Roz's house, hoping she would be on time.

"How old were the kids then?" Mackenzie asked Roz, some six weeks after she had started to attend the study. It had taken weeks for Roz to learn much about her, and she was only able to accomplish this because Mackenzie would usually visit at some other time during the week. On

632

Thursday at 10:00, the young author sat silently for the entire hour and was the first one out the door. Today she stayed.

"Well, let's see. Five years ago Rina would have been 10, Josh, 12, and Devon, 15. They well remember my drinking and not coming home for days. Adam would go looking for me but wouldn't always find me. The kids would be terrified until I came in the door and then throng me, but I was usually hungover and pushed them away. Their dad would be left to comfort them."

"He was already a Christian?"

"Yes. He'd come to Christ four years ahead of me."

"And you haven't had a drink since?"

"As a matter of fact I have, not for more than three years now, but prior to that I stumbled several times. Adam forgave me, and I knew the Lord did, and even though I'm tempted today, I count the cost and choose to obey."

Mackenzie glanced around and tried to think. Roz was nothing like she first believed. Her life looked like a charmed one with three great kids, a loving husband, and many friends. It was hard to imagine her drunk or running around on her husband.

"I don't want to slam what happened in your life, but I'm no drinker," Mackenzie said at last. "And I just don't feel I need to be saved from anything, Roz."

"What about hell, Micki? It's a very real place."

"Okay," her hand went up, "I would be a fool to tell you I want to go to hell, but Roz, I can't live my life as a Christian. I know I can't. God can't really be trusted to do the right thing, or my parents would still be alive."

Roz's head bent to one side as she thought. "We're very earthly-minded creatures, aren't we, Micki? We want God to make everything perfect right here and right now, but that would be inconsistent with what happened in the Garden of Eden. Sin entered the world through one man, and because of that, the whole world is under Satan's rules.

"There is no perfect here-and-now. I, for one, don't want it perfect now. I don't want to get too comfortable here. Sin hurts and makes us sad, but it also reminds believers that we have something better waiting for us. Drunk drivers do hit servicemen and take them from their families. Cancer does enter the bodies of our loved ones and take them away, but I'm going to say what you've certainly heard before: God is sovereign. Nothing happens without His hand."

"And you can love a God like that? A God who allows those things to happen?"

"With all my heart," Roz said softly. "I was headed to hell the fast way. My life was falling apart. And you can tell me that you don't drink and you don't have the same needs, and all I can say to that is boloney. You're a sinner just like I am. Are there sacrifices? Yes. Are there heartaches? Yes, but there's also joy and the knowledge that God is not going to let anything happen to me that He doesn't want to happen and that I won't be able to handle. I might get hit by a drunk driver or I might get cancer, but I don't have to worry that it was an accident or that I'm alone. Do I want Adam or the kids to die? Of course not, but I have a God in whom I can trust. I want that for you too, Micki. I want it with all my heart."

How have I come to this place? Mackenzie sat in

Roz's kitchen asking herself. *I wanted nothing to do with my mother's beliefs, yet here I sit, fascinated with Roz and wanting to be close to her. I couldn't get away from Jack fast enough, and now I wish he were here and I could talk with him. How I wish Jack would take me in his arms and hold me and tell me God could still love me — might still want to forgive me.*

Roz watched Mackenzie's face, but she stayed quiet. Never did she imagine that walking to the road to see whose car had broken down would lead to knowing Mackenzie Bishop. More alone than Roz had ever been, she was as independent and savvy as any woman Roz had ever met. Her heart was tender toward children, but it wasn't at all unusual to see a cynical light gleam in her eyes, and that was only if she was letting her emotions show — something she was very adept at hiding.

It would be so easy to beg this younger woman to fall to her knees and repent, but Roz wouldn't do that. There were sacrifices in the life of a believer — nothing that outweighed the peace God gave, but they weren't something someone could talk you into. "Love-prompted obedience" was the way one of the pastors described it. On her own, Mackenzie would have to come to a point of wanting and needing what only God could offer. Until then, Roz could do nothing for her.

"I think I'll head home now," Mackenzie said softly.

"All right. Are you sure you won't stay for dinner? Adam and the kids will be home in just a little while."

"Is it that late?"

"About 3:30."

"The time slipped away, Roz. I hope I didn't ruin your day."

"If you think that, then you haven't been listening."

Mackenzie smiled at her but still said, "I'm not sure if I'll see you next week or not."

"All right. You know you're welcome."

The women hugged, and Mackenzie went on her way, wondering not for the first time over the fact that Roz never said she would pray for Mackenzie. She somehow knew she did, but it was funny to her that she didn't mention it. Her mother and Jack, and even her father, had said it often.

Mackenzie went straight to the phone when she got home and dialed Delancey's number, but when she got only the answering machine, she hung up. They had talked very little in the last several weeks, and when they were on the phone, Delancey had so little to say that Mackenzie was at a complete loss. She had asked her sister if she was angry, and Delancey insisted she wasn't, but Mackenzie had stopped believing her.

I need you right now, Delancey, she spoke to the phone. *Why can't you be there for me? Why can't I talk to you about this?* But there was no answer.

Mackenzie didn't know when she had been so tired, but at night sleep took hours to claim her these last few weeks. She could lie down now but knew it would be no use.

"I don't need You." She suddenly said the words out loud as she paced in the kitchen. "I have everything, do You hear me? I am Mac Walker! I don't need You." Mackenzie sank into a chair and her voice softened. "If I don't need You, then how come I'm desperate to talk to Jack?"

Before she could change her mind, she went back to the phone. The number, her home phone for years, was dialed with ease, but she listened with dread to the mechanical recording stating that the number was no longer in service.

"No," Mackenzie whispered to the machine that could not hear her. "You have to be there, Jack. You have to be. I need you. I don't deserve your forgiveness, but I need you."

Not until the words were out of her mouth did Mackenzie realize what she had said. Her face dropped into her hands.

I can't believe it would be true. You have to remember all the things I've said to You, how much I've hated You. You can't forgive me, God. You just can't! But Mackenzie knew better. She had never allowed her heart to soften, but she had heard many of the things her parents and Jack had said over the years.

She cried until she thought she would be sick. Somewhere along the line, the confident and arrogant Mackenzie Rose Bishop had become a pathetic mess. The woman who rose from the table, face puffy and eyes swollen, to search her numerous bookshelves for the Bible her mother had given her felt as though she'd been clubbed and beaten. Her body ached with the weight of her sin and pain.

The Bible finally in her hand, Mackenzie went to her bedroom. It was a huge room without much furniture, but Mackenzie took little notice. She lay across the bed, turned on the lamp that sat on her bedside table, and turned to the book of Mark. She read from the beginning, going slowly when she got to the parts that Gary had gone over on Thursday mornings. She didn't understand all of what she read, and in fact didn't make it through the whole book but rolled over on her back and tried to talk to God.

I can't handle myself anymore. I'm so miserable that I don't even want to go on. I thought I had it all. I thought I could take care of myself.

Mackenzie stopped as she remembered her father's same words. He had come back from Germany and said to them that he believed he could do everything on his own but then saw his own inadequacies and admitted to God that he needed help — he needed saving.

I would give anything to have my father or Jack here right now. I need a father right now, God, and I don't know where to turn.

With sudden clarity Mackenzie remembered a verse her mother had shared with her, a verse where God was referred to as "Papa God." Just the thought of it brought on fresh tears. She sobbed until she was utterly spent and didn't remember falling asleep, but the phone's sudden ringing told her she'd been out hard.

" 'lo." She cleared her throat and tried again. "Hello."

"Micki?" It was Roz's voice.

"Yes. Hi, Roz."

"Are you all right? You sound as though you were sleeping."

"I must have dropped off."

"I haven't been able to stop thinking about you, Micki. Are you sure you're all right?"

Mackenzie sighed. "I don't know what I am, Roz. I can't remember what I'm supposed to say to God. I need my dad but he's not here, and I can't find the way."

"Mackenzie, can Adam and I see you?"

"Oh, Roz, if only you could. I need you, but my eyes are so swollen that I don't think I can see to drive."

"We'll be right there."

It felt like forever to Mackenzie. Typically, lake homes were built with a view to the lake, so Mackenzie was not able to see the street unless she was in one of the upstairs bedrooms. But she didn't want to be that far away when they came. She ended up hovering around the front door and just barely controlling her tears when she saw Roz.

Roz was tender and hugged Mackenzie as soon as she got in the door. They were both thankful for Adam, a man whom Mackenzie had come to respect and care for. He took charge.

"Let's sit here in the living room," he suggested, and then waited for his wife to lead Mackenzie to a chair.

"How are you doing?" he asked when Mackenzie looked at him.

"Just awful. I can't do this anymore, Adam. I've been running and pushing God away for so long. I thought I would never want anything to do with Him, and now that I do, I can't think clearly."

Adam nodded, his heart asking God to give him the words. "Mackenzie, I have some things I want to say to you, and you need to be listening."

Mackenzie nodded, her puffy eyes on him. Roz remained very quiet, but her heart was petitioning God that Adam might have the right words, and also that Mackenzie would humble herself before God.

"The gospel is very simple, Micki," Adam told her, "but it's also very serious. When the gospel is explained to us, we can't just give an intellectual nod of the head. We have to embrace it with our

639

hearts. God is not interested in anything less than that. Does that make sense?"

"Yes, it does."

"You haven't wanted anything or anyone to rule you, Mackenzie. You've been rebellious and willful. You can't come to God still determined to have your way. Do you understand that, honey? I don't want to talk you out of this, but this is a serious step, and I would be lying to you if I said otherwise."

"I understand, Adam. Please don't spare me," Mackenzie said quietly. "I've been sparing myself for years, and now I'm miserable."

"Could you hang Jonathan Cantrell on a cross to die, Mackenzie?"

"No." She bit her lip and cringed at the thought.

"He's precious, isn't he? But far more precious than we can imagine is the Son of God. And God's love for us can't even be compared to our love for Jonathan or our own children, yet He sent His Son. Do you believe that, Micki?"

"Yes. I've just always been so arrogant about not needing to be saved, and then when my mother died, I was so angry . . ."

"There's a very simple word for those things, and I think you know that too."

"Sin."

"Yes. It's all about belief, Mackenzie. It's all about understanding that we have nothing to offer and can do nothing to save ourselves. God's Word says that we must believe on His Son alone to save us from our sin."

"I want that, Adam. I didn't until now, but now I'm afraid that it's too late — that I've waited too long. I can't remember what my mother used to say."

"True, heartfelt belief is just what God is looking for, Micki. Romans 10:9 says if we confess with our mouth that Jesus is Lord and believe in our hearts that God raised Christ from the dead, we will be saved. And that's just what I did, Micki. I called Pastor Dave. I know that God would have heard me on my own, but I wanted Pastor Dave to hear and hold me accountable. He met with me, and I gave my life to Christ right there in his office. And you can do it right now. You can tell God that you've run from your sin and now you want to stop. You can tell Him you believe in His Son and need His salvation. His gift never runs out. All who ask may have it."

Mackenzie took a huge breath. It was suddenly so clear. "I want to, Adam. I want to right now."

His smile was very tender. "Roz and I will listen, all right?"

"All right." Mackenzie's gaze took in both of them before she closed her eyes.

"Father God," Mackenzie addressed God as her mother always had, "I've been running, but You know that better than anyone. I don't want to run anymore. I want to be saved. I want to thank You for sending Jesus to die for me. My mother thanked You for that until the day she died, and I never understood until now. I am a sinner, and You are God Almighty. The only reason I could even approach You is because You've allowed me to." Mackenzie was amazed at what she was remembering and couldn't stop talking to the Lord.

"I want You to take me, Lord God, and make me Yours. I've lived for myself, and I'm so full of sin and pain that I can't stand it anymore. Delancey didn't understand. She was angry at me, but I know, Father God, that You understand and will forgive me. Look into my heart, Father God, and take away my sin. I trust You to do this, God, just like You promised in the book of John. Thank You for saving me from sin and eternity in hell. Amen."

Mackenzie looked up and sighed. She knew nothing but profound peace.

"I'm tired," she said softly, and Roz chuckled.

"You probably will be for several days, if not weeks. It can be very draining."

Mackenzie looked at her. "Thanks, Roz."

"Oh, Micki," Roz said on a relieved laugh, "do you know how much I've prayed for you?"

"You never told me that you did."

"No, I didn't. I used to hate it when Adam told me he was praying for me. It only made me more angry, so I didn't say it to you."

Mackenzie hugged her. Adam was next.

"I don't know what to say."

"You don't have to say anything," Adam said with a smile. "It's our privilege. We're just thankful that we could be here when you needed us."

They stayed for another half an hour because Mackenzie had questions. She didn't have many — she was too drained for that — but Adam wrote out some passages for her to study and hugged her again when he left. Roz asked her to come to lunch the next day so they could talk some more, and eventually they went on their way.

Mackenzie had plans to eat some dinner and read her Bible all evening. She started with good intentions but hadn't reckoned on just how tiring it had all been. She went to bed at 8:30 and slept the night through.

THIRTY-SEVEN

Mackenzie was calm as she dialed Delancey's number the next morning, somehow certain that now that the decision was made, all would be fine between them. She knew better than to think no rain fell into the lives of Christians, but neither did she believe that her first time of testing would be 24 hours after her time of belief.

"Hi, D.J.," Mackenzie said softly, excited about the change in her life and so eager to say the right thing.

"Hello, Mackenzie." Delancey had the same cool voice she'd had for several weeks.

"I wanted to talk to you about something. Do you have time now?"

"Yeah," she replied, but she sounded reluctant. "I guess now is a good time."

It was not the way Mackenzie would have chosen to start, but she didn't want to wait. "I think you know that I've been, well, you know, doing some searching, and, well, I wanted to let you know that I came to Christ last night. Roz and Adam came over and prayed with me. I was so confused about a lot of- —"

"I really don't want to hear about it," Delancey said shortly, cutting her off midsentence.

"Oh."

Delancey had managed to shock her sister speechless.

"Was there anything else?" Delancey sounded impatient now.

"No, I mean, I would like to tell you about it."

"If that's all you called about, Mackenzie, I have to go. I'll talk to you later."

Mackenzie's hand shook as she replaced the phone. It would have shook more if she could have seen her sister as she immediately called Chet's pager. She was terribly relieved when he called her right back. He'd been busier than ever these days.

"Hi. What's up?"

"Nothing really. I just want you to know that if you get my answering machine, it doesn't mean I'm not here, so leave a message since I might not pick up."

"Okay. What's going on?" His tender tone made her want to sob.

"It's my sister," she told him, a catch in her voice. "She's just acting so weird, and I don't even want to talk to her right now."

"What did she do?"

"She became a *Christian*. Can you believe it?"

"Oh, Delancey, you poor kid. I have an aunt who's one of those fanatics, and she drives us all crazy."

"I grew up with all of that, and I was nothing but relieved when I left it. I don't know why she has to ruin everything. I think she's depressed about things. If she would have just asked me, I'd have told her she needed a counselor, not a pastor."

"Maybe you should tell her that."

"I don't want to talk to her."

"Write to her. If she writes back, you don't have to answer her letter or phone calls, but you'll feel better if you set her straight from your side of things."

"Maybe I'll do that," Delancey responded thoughtfully.

"I gotta go."

"Okay. Thanks for calling back. We're still on for Friday?"

"I think so." It was his standard reply, but Delancey barely noticed. Mentally, she was already telling her sister a few things and not choosing her words very carefully.

Christmas Valley

"She didn't even say goodbye," Mackenzie told Roz just a few hours later. She was trembling so badly that she could barely talk. "Roz, tell me that God wouldn't ask me to give up my sister. Please tell me. She's all I have."

The pain in Roz's face confirmed Mackenzie's worst fears.

"Oh, Roz," she cried, "it's all my fault. I've been her teacher. She's mimicked me from the time we were small, and I've made it clear to her that we just needed each other, that God could keep His nose out of our business."

Pain and regret overcame Mackenzie. With her face in her hands, she couldn't speak for a long time, and Roz waited, sitting close to her on the sofa. She couldn't tell Mackenzie that everything was going to be fine with her sister. She wished it could be so, but relationships far more intimate than that of sisters had been split in two because someone chose to follow Christ. Roz sat still and prayed for this baby in Christ, well aware from

645

her own life that just because God saved people didn't mean they didn't have to live with their past choices.

"Mackenzie, I need to tell you some things, all right?"

Mackenzie nodded, thinking that the pain in her head was going to split it open and that her heart was going to break.

"When very painful things or temptations come into my life, I try to remember several passages of God's Word. The first one, in 1 Chronicles 29, explains the sovereignty of God. Do you know what that is?"

"I think so."

"It means God is completely in control at all times," Roz explained anyway. "He rules over all creation at every moment. He's all-knowing, all-powerful, and completely free to do as He wills. He knew you were going to call Delancey, and He knew she would reject you. He's in control. And that brings me to the second verse. Because God is in control, we can trust that He's not going to let anything happen to us that we can't handle. First Corinthians 10:13 says that God is faithful and will never allow you to be tempted beyond what you can stand.

"You might be tempted to be angry at Him or with Delancey, but those would be sinful responses. You might be tempted to be sorry you ever got into this, but that would be wrong. The time has come for Mackenzie Bishop to surrender herself to God, even if your relationship with Delancey is changed forever. We can pray for Delancey, and if He chooses, God can do a great work in her heart, but Delancey can't save you. Keep reminding yourself that you need the relationship with God more than you need the relationship with Delancey. God may give you both someday, but for now, you can choose to trust Him to take care of both of you in His own way."

Mackenzie so appreciated the fact that Roz kept emotion out of it. Never once did she mention feelings, but instead just gave her the facts.

"Thanks, Roz."

"You're welcome. Don't make the mistake of thinking that God expects you to skip through life when you're hurting, but even amid your pain, you can choose to be thankful. You might experience something akin to mourning over this situation, Micki, but God can give you peace and work in your life if you don't stiff-arm Him. Does that makes sense?"

"Yes."

Mackenzie stayed for the next two hours, and they talked about the situation some more, but Roz also asked Mackenzie about the Army and the things she saw while living on the East Coast. Amid all of this, she fed her a big lunch. And before Roz let her leave, she made sure she still had the verses that Adam had given her.

Roz told Mackenzie to call anytime and that she would see her soon, but it never occurred to her that she wouldn't be at the Meyers Bible Church on Sunday. When she didn't come, Roz was on the verge of calling her. Adam stopped her, telling her that for the time being he thought it was all right that she keep meeting with the women and Pastor Gary.

Roz greatly appreciated his advice, a needed reminder not to overwhelm the younger woman. However, she prayed that Mackenzie would grow hungry to have more fellowship and be with the entire church family on a regular basis. She also asked God, as she knew Mackenzie was, to reach into Delancey's heart and do a work. Roz knew that He was the only One who could make the change.

Mackenzie's decision had been made on September 5. The rest of the weeks that passed in that month, and into October, were ones that brought growth and more understanding of the Word for Mackenzie.

Knowing that her sister needed more time, Mackenzie stopped calling Delancey by the end of September, but in an attempt to open up the lines of communication she still wrote to her every week. The letters weren't returned, but Mackenzie strongly doubted that they were read.

The one letter that Delancey did send was so angry and accusatory that it rocked Mackenzie back on her heels. She met with Roz and Adam several times to discuss it and her response, and although she ached to have contact with her sister, she realized at that time that the Cummings were becoming her family. They loved her as one of their own, including her in many family celebrations.

Mackenzie spent hours in the Word every day, taking pages of notes and writing down questions about anything she didn't understand. But there was something almost frightening to her about attending church on Sunday. She was starting to strongly believe that she needed to be there, but so far she was only attending Bible study and minichurch on Wednesday nights. The Cummings were patient, and since they saw steady growth and interest, they continued to wait on this issue.

In the midst of all of this, Mackenzie had put her writing completely on hold. In a difficult session — breaking her silence had proved to be more difficult than she thought — she told Roz and Adam about her career. They were very understanding when Mackenzie told them she simply had no interest in finishing *Shibboleth* at present. It was a great story and still in her head, but her discovery in the Bible of all the things that never applied to her before now made it the most exciting book she had ever read or been interested in. She worked at not being impractical with it, but even that was hard. She didn't want to clean the house or cook. She wanted only to read and study her Bible.

This went on until the first of November when she had a surprise visit from Roz.

"Come in," Mackenzie said with pleasure. They visited weekly, but it was usually at her house in Christmas Valley.

"Bad time?"

"Not at all. Come on in."

As she walked in, Roz glanced around and almost smiled. Things looked just as she knew they would.

"I need to talk business with you," Roz said once they sat at the kitchen table with glasses of cola.

"What kind of business?"

"Well, I need to explain a little something first. Before we came to Christ, Adam and I spent money as though there were no tomorrow. Then even after we came to Christ, it took years to get on a budget and do things well."

Mackenzie nodded, getting ready to offer Roz any amount she wanted. She was in for a shock.

"I clean houses on Mondays and Tuesdays to pay off the debt. Now one of my ladies has made other arrangements. We don't live on my money — it all goes to pay off the debts — but I want to pick up another house so it doesn't take us any longer. That's where you come in."

Roz knew that Mackenzie was a very bright woman, but she could see that she was not catching on at all. She felt she had no choice but to take a breath and plunge in.

"Mackenzie, you need a cleaning lady."

The look on Mackenzie's face was comical. She even glanced down at herself and made Roz smile.

"I don't mean you personally; I mean your house."

"Oh, Roz, of course!" Understanding dawned. "I was just noticing how gross the carpet is in my bedroom and that I should lug the vacuum up, but I got sidetracked and didn't do it."

Roz tried not to smile, but it peeked out. Seeing it, Mackenzie started to laugh. The two women went into a fit of giggles.

"I was so afraid to ask you," Roz admitted. "I thought you would think I was trying to take advantage."

"Not at all." Mackenzie was still chuckling. "My apartment in Alexandria was so small that just a quick sweep with the vacuum made it look brand new. Not to mention that I was on a city street with apartments all around. The dust here is awful, and with the fireplace I just —" Mackenzie shrugged, and Roz laughed a little more. She was on the verge of saying something when the phone rang.

Always hoping it might be Delancey, Mackenzie did not let the machine get it. She almost groaned

650

when she heard Paxton Hancock's voice. She had nearly forgotten about the man.

"Long time no talk to, Mackenzie," he said, obviously in a good mood.

"Hey, Paxton," Mackenzie replied, trying to think fast. Should she tell him everything now, write a letter, or set up another phone conversation?

Roz was using her hands to question if she should leave, but Mackenzie shook her head no.

"How's the book coming?"

"It's not right now, Pax. I've got other things going on."

"Micah Bear?"

"No, I just —" She stopped short, thinking of the way Delancey had responded and dreading the same from her editor.

"Mackenzie, what is it?" Paxton's voice was so compassionate that she relaxed.

"I will finish the book, Pax, but I've made some changes in my life. Things were pretty miserable for a while for me, and when I did some searching, I found that my needs were spiritual."

"Okay . . ." Paxton's voice was still open.

"I trusted in Jesus Christ about two months ago. That doesn't mean that I'll never write again, but for right now, my interest is in other areas. Am I making any sense, Pax? I would hate it if I sounded like some kind of nut, because it's not like that."

"I don't think that at all. To tell you the truth, you seemed pretty unhappy even before you left. If you found a religion that's a help to you, I'm glad for you."

"It's not a religion, Pax; it's a way of life. Religion is something you do on Sundays. Life

651

lived in Jesus Christ is something you do every day of the week."

"Wow, you're really into this."

"I am, Pax, and I'm sorry I didn't call and let you know. Time just got away."

"Well, good luck. You know that I still want that book and anything else you can crank out, but I'm glad to hear you're doing so well."

"I haven't forgotten the deadline, Pax. I will get it to you."

"Aren't we past that deadline?"

"I thought it was February 1."

Mackenzie could hear papers rustling.

"You're right. I had a spot open up and wanted to put *Shibboleth* in it, but if you don't have it done, you don't have it done."

"I'll tell you what," Mackenzie said, reaching for paper and a pen, "I'll call you in a month and tell you where I am."

"That's fine. And Mackenzie, I mean what I said. Even if you never write another word, I'm happy for you. IronHorse wouldn't thank me for saying that, but they weren't the ones that saw your sad face and how alone you were."

"Oh, Paxton." Mackenzie was overjoyed. "I can't tell you what that means. I don't know if the future holds any more books, but you've been a good friend, and I thank you."

"Take care, Mackenzie."

"I will. Tell Jodi I said hi and hug that baby for me."

Mackenzie hung up, so glad that Roz had stayed.

"He was the man who launched Mac Walker's career," she explained.

"Your editor?"

"Yeah. We met a long time ago. It took more

than two years to write my first book, and then the man I was dating gave it to Paxton to read without his knowing I wrote it. He's taken everything since then."

"I've never read any of Mac Walker's books, but Adam and Devon have. They love 'em."

Mackenzie nodded in true modesty. Writing was not an effort for her; the words and stories just poured out.

"Do you know that I can see the hand of God on me even then, Roz? My books have nothing in them that I'm ashamed of. My father was a moral man, even before he was saved, and most of my heroes are patterned after him. Not even the violence is graphic. I could have three books on the market totaling millions of copies, all of which I'm ashamed of, and even the one I'm working on now could be something I would want to put into the fireplace, but I don't feel that way."

Roz smiled. She loved this woman like one of her own. Her growth and hunger for the Lord were wonderful to see.

"God is good, Micki. You'll be learning that for the rest of your life."

This news suited Mackenzie, who wanted nothing more right now. The women talked a little more business, settling on the day for weekly cleaning and how Roz was to be paid. When Roz left, Mackenzie took a good look around. Things were pretty bad. She didn't even have to get close to see the dust and dirt patterns on the carpet. Now that she was more aware, she felt that Monday could not come soon enough.

Chicago
It was all Delancey could do not to skip through

the airport. She didn't know why she had never thought of it before, but meeting Chet's plane was the most exciting thing she had done in a long time. She couldn't wait to see his face. Most of the time she didn't even know his schedule, but one night he'd had to call his boss from her apartment, and just his side of the conversation had given her enough to go on.

She arrived at Gate C-38 and stood way back in the shadows. Other people were milling around but came to attention when the light over the door flashed. Someone with the airline went to open it and make ready. Delancey could see that it had been a large plane: Many people disembarked. She knew she would have to be patient since he would be one of the last people off.

She almost stepped forward when the crowd thinned but then decided to hang back until the last minute. At last she saw him. Her face lit up as she moved forward, but she stopped before taking two steps. A petite brunette had gone up to him, and Delancey watched as Chet put an arm around her and kissed her. She turned slightly, and Delancey could see that she was very pregnant. She watched as Chet took the woman's face in his hands and tenderly kissed her twice more on the lips. Only then did she see the little girl at their feet. The child leapt for attention until Chet reached down and scooped her up. She was the image of Chet Dobson, but with her mother's dark hair.

Delancey was incapable of moving. As though someone had suddenly plunged her heart into the icy waters of the sea, she stood frozen as Chet's arm went around the woman and the three of them walked down the concourse. She had no idea how long she stood there. A child running from his mother darted into her legs, causing her to look down. She saw the hunter green wool pants set she had just bought, Chet in mind all the while.

As sure as she knew her name was Delancey Bishop, she knew that woman was his wife. So many things made perfect sense. Like blinds opening on a covered window, understanding flooded in like sunlight. Almost in automation, she began the walk back to the parking garage and her car. Her surprise had backfired. Not a tear was shed; however, her heart felt utterly cold to the man she had been ready to spend the rest of her life with. She left the airport but didn't go home, at least not for a while. She suddenly had quite a bit of work to do.

It was almost bedtime one week later, but as soon as Chet's pager showed Delancey's number, he made an excuse to get out of the house. He hadn't been able to get her for a week and wanted nothing more than to talk to her. On the way to "buy milk," he tried to think if she had been upset with him at all but thought things were going fine.

"Hi." His voice was smooth when he heard hers.

"I need to see you, Chet."

"Okay. I've been trying to call."

"I need to see you," Delancey repeated, so cold inside was she that she didn't even need to tell herself to be strong.

"We have a date tomorrow night, don't we?"

"I need to see you now."

"I can't, Delancey."

"Now, Chet." Her voice became cold, and he became alarmed. She hadn't pulled any games lately, but that didn't mean she wouldn't.

"Okay. I'll come over."

"No, I'll meet you at Clancey's in an hour."

"Clancey's?" he questioned. They never went there.

"That's right. One hour."

"Okay." He sounded weary and impatient, but Delancey knew he would show up. She was there long ahead of him. The waiter, $20 richer and with strict instructions to leave them alone, was ready to keep an eye on the man joining her and to call the police if he acted at all threatening.

Delancey didn't smile or move when he approached the table, and Chet, knowing her look, sat opposite her in the dark corner booth and didn't try to touch her.

"What's so urgent?" he asked, knowing from experience that if he could keep control of the conversation, he could settle her down much sooner.

"I met your plane last week," Delancey said simply.

Chet paused but recovered quickly. "I didn't see you."

"No, you were too busy kissing a short brunette and hugging a little girl."

It gave Delancey no end of pleasure to see him pale. If she could have acted out her fantasy, the waiter would be calling the police to have *her* removed for violence.

"Delancey, I —" but she let him get no further.

"Don't even try." Her voice was so calm it was frightening. "I know everything. Do you hear me, Chet? *Everything.* I know you're married to Kari Anne and have been for six years. I know you have a daughter named Jennifer who was four in

656

September, and that your wife is scheduled to have a little boy in five weeks."

Chet licked his lips but still managed to speak. "If you only found out a week ago, how —"

"It's amazing what money can buy in this town. I told the man I wanted information fast, and I got it. I kept my phone unplugged unless I was calling him so you couldn't reach me. I know that you live in a beautiful home on Shady Oak Drive and that your wife's family is loaded. I know that there is no airline in France and that you share the apartment we were in with another married pilot who likes girlfriends as much as you do."

"Delancey, it doesn't have to end like this."

Her smile was bitter and brief. "You're wrong, Chet, very wrong. It's over, and if you ever try to contact me again, I'll make a little visit to Kari Anne."

It was the worst thing she could have said. He knew it was over, but he wasn't about to let her go while she was still holding all the cards. He forced himself to sit back, his eyes going into the sexy droop that she loved.

"You won't go, Delancey. It's too good between us." His voice was low and inviting. "You'll pout for a few weeks, but then my pager will go off, and I'll see your number."

Delancey stopped her movements to leave.

"Have we ever talked about my black belt, Chet? No? How silly of me to have forgotten. I hope you do come by. I'll be sure to invite you in. But be prepared to hit the floor fast. I'll take great satisfaction in breaking your spine in three places. Even if you do live to tell about it, I'll know that you'll never fly another plane, and you'll never lie to your wife or anyone else again." She picked up her purse. "You think I won't go? Watch me."

Delancey moved from the booth and headed directly to the waiter she had spoken with earlier, another bill and a piece of paper in her hand.

"I just broke up with my boyfriend. These are our names, my address, and the plate numbers on our cars. If he follows me inside of ten minutes, call the police and tell them you suspect a possible attack."

"Of course, madam. Anything else?"

"No. Thank you."

Delancey was fine all the way home, her cynical thoughts keeping her company. Indeed, it had been easier than she thought. Why, she hadn't even kept him that long. He would still have time to pick up ice or whatever lame excuse he had given his poor wife.

Delancey's buoyant mood lasted until she had all the shades pulled, the door secured, and the phone unplugged again. It lasted right up to the moment she went to the bathroom and was violently sick. It took a moment for her to realize that she was sobbing, and when she did, one person came to mind. She nearly fell across the bed and dialed the number.

"Hello," Mackenzie said as she picked up the phone.

"Micki," Delancey whispered.

"Delancey?"

"Yeah, it's me."

"Hi." Mackenzie told herself to stay calm. "Are you all right?"

"I need you, Mic." She said the words so softly.

"What's that?"

"I need you."

"I'll come." Mackenzie needed nothing more,

her voice turning to business. "I'll get on a plane as soon as I can."

"Thank you."

"Will you be picking me up, Delancey?"

"I don't want to leave the apartment, Mic. I can't."

"All right. Are you hurt? Should you call your landlady?"

"No. I just need you."

"I'm on my way. I'll call you from the plane and tell you exactly when I'll be there."

"All right."

"Hold on, Delancey. I'm coming."

Delancey couldn't say any more, but Mackenzie didn't need her to. In less than half an hour she had booked a flight and was on her way to the Cummings'. Roz was surprised but glad for her. She left the housekey with her and said she would call. Roz and Adam promised their prayers and stopped to pray for her the moment she left.

I want to beg You for mercy, Father, Mackenzie prayed as she belted herself into her seat on the plane. *I want to beg You to spare my sister, but I have no right. You know best. Whatever this is, You are in control. Thank You that she called me. Thank You that she knew I would still care. The last months have felt like a year. I love her, Father. I need my sister. I hope it's in Your plan that she be with me again. If not, Lord God, give me strength, because I'll surely need it.*

Mackenzie made herself stop. There was no one next to her in the posh leather seat, but it was late in the day, and fatigue, along with the emotional outpouring of hearing from her sister and rushing to the airport in Reno, was suddenly on her. The flight would take three-and-a-half hours, and she needed to be strong when she arrived. Just 20 minutes after takeoff, she was sound asleep, Delancey still lingering on the edge of her mind.

"Is that you, Mic?" Delancey called through the door after hearing the knock.

"Yes, I'm here."

Delancey opened the door, and Mackenzie had all she could do not to respond to her sister's appearance. She seemed to have dropped weight, and her eyes were red and swollen. They didn't touch, at least not at first. Wanting to be sensitive, Mackenzie tried to feel her way along. The women stood just inside the door and turned to each other. Delancey looked like a wounded animal, and Mackenzie had to physically restrain herself from hugging her.

"You came." Delancey stared at her.

"I wouldn't do anything else."

"Chet's married," Delancey said softly. "He's been married for six years."

"Oh, Delancey, no!" Mackenzie quietly wailed.

"He has a little girl, and his wife is going to have a baby."

Mackenzie could hold back no longer. She grabbed her sister and held on with all her might. Delancey wrapped her arms around Mackenzie's back and sobbed. They sank to the floor in grief and pain, still holding each other and crying. Nothing in all of their lives hurt like this. Mackenzie felt as if she couldn't breathe, and Delancey wanted to die.

It was close to an hour before either one could utter a word, and by then it was only to agree to sleep. It was coming onto five o'clock in the morning when Delancey climbed into bed and Mackenzie took the sofa. Tired as she was, Mackenzie fell asleep praying for her sister and asking God to give her the words when they faced each other in the morning.

THIRTY-EIGHT

The Bishop women slept only until eight o'clock. Mackenzie was up first, took a quick shower, and started some coffee. Delancey also used the shower and then came to the kitchen table.

"Do you hate me?" she asked quietly.

"Why would I hate you?" Mackenzie said softly, turning from the counter.

"Because I wanted nothing to do with you until I needed something."

"I'll never hate you, Deej, not as long as I live, but I can't help you either, not the way you need to be helped. You can call me anytime, and I'll listen, but I can't make any lasting changes or help your pain very much."

Delancey looked at her. "I should have asked you this a long time ago, Mic, but what happened? What changed your mind?"

Mackenzie forgot the coffee and came to the table.

"I want to tell you, Delancey, but I don't want you to feel guilty."

"I already do."

"Why?"

"Because if you needed God, then I wasn't there for you. I wasn't a good sister."

Mackenzie had suspected as much but had never

been given a chance to ask.

"You can't do that to yourself, Deej. Even if you had called or come to visit, the help would have been temporary. I needed permanent change, the kind Dad and Mom always talked about and I wanted nothing to do with."

It was as though Delancey had finally caught on. "You believe it now, don't you? You believe what Mom and Dad did?"

"Yes. With all my heart."

Delancey could only stare. The change in Mackenzie was amazing. Even tired and her hair still dripping from the shower, the peace in her face was unmistakable. Mackenzie had grown very hard. Delancey hadn't realized how much. The change in her enabled Delancey to see things clearly. For an instant Delancey had hope, and then she remembered where she had been.

"I'm glad for you, Mic," she said sincerely. "I'm glad that you didn't go where I have and that you have peace now."

"But you don't believe you can."

Delancey shook her head no. "I knew better, Mic. I told you that. I've always felt guilty. I think forgiveness can extend to sins of ignorance, but not to sins when people know full well what they're doing."

"That's not what we heard for all those years, Deej — just the opposite. If the death of Christ was just for some sins, then the whole thing is a lie. I've found out that there are no lies involved except the ones Satan tells me or I tell myself. Everything God says is true. I'm sorry I took so long to understand that, Delancey. If anyone is to blame for your hurt, it's me. You've been following me since you could walk, and I led you astray."

Tears had filled Mackenzie's eyes, and Delancey's own mouth trembled.

"I've been a big girl for a long time, Mic. I have no one to blame but myself."

"I'm sorry he hurt you, Deej. I'm so sorry."

"I was ready to spend my life with him, Mic." Tears streamed down her face. "I was ready for us to settle down, have babies, and grow old together, but he belongs to someone else. I feel so awful, Mic. I was with her man. I feel just sick about that. I would love to tell her how sorry I am, but I don't want anything else to do with Chet. Everything he ever said to me was a lie, and the whole thing has made me feel so cheap and used."

Mackenzie went to her and put her arms around her. She asked God to work a miracle in her life, because that's what it was going to take. She knew she couldn't stay forever. Her trip home would come in two weeks, and after that, Delancey would be open and vulnerable to anything.

Mackenzie heard the direction of her thoughts and reminded herself that she was not God. He had to do the work, and He was the one who could protect and take care of Delancey — no one else.

"I have something I want to say to you, Deej, but before I do, you need to understand that I'll always love you. My love is not conditional on your agreeing with me."

"You want me to become a Christian."

"Yes, I do, but I have a lot of things I want you to think about first. I'm new at this, but I keep thinking of things I read in the Bible and things Roz, Adam, and Pastor Gary have said."

"Have you told me about them?"

"Roz is the woman whose Bible study I went to

664

that first day, and Gary leads the study. Adam is Roz's husband."

"Okay."

"Tell me if this makes sense to you. Chet was unfaithful to his wife. He sinned against her, right?"

"Yes."

"But what if he went around and told everyone else. Maybe he confessed it to a coworker, his neighbor, his children, and even his wife's parents, but never talked to her. Would that take care of it?"

"No, of course not."

"That's right. He sinned against *her,* and any apologies that need to be heard, need to be heard by *her.* It's the same way with our sin toward God. All our sin is against Him. It was wrong of you to be with Chet, and without knowing it you sinned against his wife, but the bigger picture is the way you sinned against God. He's the one to whom we need to confess. He's the one with whom we need to make things right. A holy God cannot tolerate our sin, any sin. Now, I want you to get up and make us some breakfast."

Delancey gawked at her. *"What?"*

"I have a headache from not eating, and you need to think about what I just said." Her voice became dry and chagrined. "I would offer to cook, but you know how bad that would be."

Delancey laughed for the first time in eight days. Mackenzie chuckled a little, but Delancey really laughed, a little hysterical fatigue thrown in for good measure. She started breakfast, however — a meal she'd been skipping, along with most meals, since that day at the airport. While she baked and cooked, they talked.

"How do you *know*, Mic? How can you be sure there's been a change and you're not just imagining things?"

"Because of what I've read in the Bible. It's an amazing book, Deej. I try not to go on feelings, not that they never play a part, but they can't be trusted that often. I'm a writer, Delancey, so things don't escape my notice. If the Bible is some made-up work of man, then a group of geniuses got together and created a masterpiece. Either that, or the whole thing was preordained by a holy, mighty God. I choose to believe the latter.

"On top of that, there's no describing the peace I have. I didn't know I could be at such rest. I'm even writing again, and it's flowing beautifully. I'm not sure I'll keep it up after this book, but I'm fulfilling my contract with IronHorse because right now I think that's important. When I told Paxton about my decision for Christ, he was very happy for me. He could tell before I moved that I was unhappy."

"But I thought moving was your dream; you know, living on the water and owning a home."

Mackenzie shook her head as she remembered. "You didn't see me after I moved out there, Deej. I was a maniac. I ran like a fool. At first the house was enough. Then I wanted more furniture, so I started buying everything in sight. Finally, I went to Reno to buy a Ferrari, but I was treated like trash, and in my anger I took a long drive. I got a flat tire and met Roz Cummings.

"I was drawn to her, D.J. She's special. Her voice is just like Mom's. I see now that it was the Lord's hand on me even then."

"Oh, Micki," Delancey's said softly. "To have what you have would be wonderful. I can't tell you how much I envy you."

"You might not believe it today, D.J., but you can have it. It's not without a price. I nearly lost my sister, but the price God paid, the death of His Son, puts all my little hangups in the dark. It hasn't been easy, D.J., but it has been worth it.

"I even had to go so far as to understand that I needed my relationship with God more than I needed one with you. Right now you're dying for Chet, but you need God more than you'll ever need any man. No man can keep you from hell for all of eternity. And no man can give you a peace that no one can describe. I can hardly handle the thought of living forever in heaven without you, Deej, so I'm going to tell you what we always hated to hear: I'm praying for you."

Delancey was on the verge of tears, and Mackenzie could see she didn't want to cry. She fell quiet when her sister went back to her mixing bowl, but just as she stated, she prayed as she had been every day since September 5.

The sisters were back to sleep by noon. They had talked and eaten, but the late night was catching up. Again, Mackenzie was the first to waken, and when she did, she made a few calls home. She talked with Roz to touch base but then called the church and tracked down Pastor Gary to ask a few questions. By the time Delancey got up, she had pulled out the map the car rental place had given her and studied it.

"I'd like to take a drive, Deej. Are you up to it?"

"I think so. Where to?"

"The North Avenue Bible Church. I just called home, and Pastor Gary told me that Pastor Dave knows the pastor there. I want to know that you have some place to turn when I leave."

"When are you going home?"

"Not for two weeks, the day after Thanksgiving."

"Two weeks?" The younger woman's face lit up. "You're staying two weeks?"

"Yeah. Can you put up with me that long?"

Delancey only sighed. "I don't deserve you, Mic."

Mackenzie stood. "That's a subject we need to keep talking about, but right now let's get to the car."

Mackenzie did the driving. She always enjoyed it more than Delancey, and Delancey was a good map reader. Some 20 minutes later they parked on the quiet street in front of the church. Mackenzie reached for the door handle.

"Are we going in?" Delancey asked, panic in her voice. Mackenzie turned to her.

"You've been following me your entire life, Delancey, from the time you were tiny. I never gave it much thought, but it's true. You said you're a big girl and have been for a long time. I understand that, but if you never follow me again, Delancey, follow me now. You need someone here in Chicago with you. You and I can fax each other or talk on the phone every day, but if you're not moving to Tahoe at the end of these two weeks, you've got to have someone here." Mackenzie studied her sister's pale face. "I've never deliberately done anything to hurt you, D.J., and I'm not starting now. Trust me on this."

Delancey nodded and got out of the car. The nap she'd had earlier had been good but oh so brief. She hadn't risen but lay there thinking about Chet until she heard Mackenzie moving around. The ice around her heart was beginning to melt.

Even remembering his mocking face telling her she would weaken and call did not stiffen her spine. She desperately wanted to talk with him. What she would say put a damper on the thought, but she still ached to be with him.

"Good afternoon." A man's voice startled both women. They hadn't seen him or the woman standing with him as they opened the door to the church and moved into the foyer. Mackenzie had been intent on the bulletin board and possibly gaining some brochures concerning the church.

"Hello." Mackenzie was the only one to reply and knew she would have to take charge. "My name is Mackenzie Bishop. I'm a part of the fellowship at Meyers Bible Church in California."

"Pastor Dave Brinker?" the man asked with a smile.

"Yes. He gave me the name of this church and told me to ask for Pastor Woody Carlisle."

The man put his hand out. "You found him. It's nice to meet you, Mackenzie. This is my wife, Paula."

"Hello." Mackenzie smiled warmly. "This is my sister, Delancey."

"I thought the name was familiar," Paula spoke up. "You write books, don't you?"

"Yes," Mackenzie confirmed. "Delancey does the illustrations."

Paula turned to her. "Our children love your books. They pore over them for hours. The illustrations are remarkable."

"Thank you." Seeing her sincerity, Delancey felt herself relaxing a little.

"Can we help you?" Pastor Woody offered.

"Well," Mackenzie responded, picking up the ball again, "I'm just here in town for a brief visit, but when I leave, I want to be certain that my sister has someplace she can come."

"I'm glad you chose us," Woody said, taking the lead. "Can you come and sit down a moment?"

"Thank you," Mackenzie replied as she followed the pastor and his wife into the sanctuary. Delancey hesitated, and then somewhat reluctantly went along as well. They sat in the pews, Woody and Paula in front turned to talk, and Delancey and Mackenzie directly behind them. Paula questioned Mackenzie a little about the books, but it wasn't long before they fell silent. Woody, his eyes on Delancey's pale face, watched as she studied the room. He couldn't be certain, but he thought she might be trembling. She suddenly turned to him.

"I shouldn't be here," she whispered. "I've done awful things. I shouldn't be in this place."

Woody, who had been praying since they arrived, smiled very tenderly.

"It's easy to be mistaken about that, Delancey. It's easy to think that we have to fix ourselves up before we can meet with God or be in His house, but that's not what the Bible says. The Bible says Jesus Christ came like a doctor. Well, we all know the healthy don't need a doctor, only the sick. If you're sick with sin, Delancey, then you're just where you need to be."

"You don't know what I've done."

"You're right, I don't, and I don't need to, but God knows every detail, and He's still willing to forgive you."

"My mother tried to tell me, and so did my father, but I wouldn't listen."

"And now? Delancey, will you listen now?"

"I am ready to listen, but He doesn't want me. I

670

know He doesn't."

"Then you're not ready to listen," Woody said softly, surprising Delancey. She stared at his calm, sure face and understood what he meant. She was still trembling, but her voice was calm.

"Have you been studying the Bible for a long time?"

"Since I was 14."

"My sister is a new Christian." Delancey turned to her. "You won't be hurt if I ask him some questions, will you, Mic?"

"No," Mackenzie told her, honestly.

"I want to tell you what I've done, Pastor Carlisle, and then I want you to tell me if God can still forgive me."

"All right."

"I had a boyfriend, and we slept together when we weren't married. And then last week, I found out that he has a wife and a child, and also another baby on the way." Delancey was trembling so strongly now that there was no missing it. "I broke up with him as soon as I found out, but before that, I knew my actions were wrong, and I did it anyway. That's what makes me think God can't forgive me."

Woody nodded. "Sexual sin is very serious, Delancey. I won't mince words with you over that. But understand this: Sexual sin is no less forgivable than any other sin." The pastor reached for a pew Bible, turned to the New Testament, and kept the Bible open as he talked.

"I've turned to the fourth chapter of the book of John and an account of a woman who met and talked with Jesus. She was a sinner, and on this day it was just the two of them. They were out by a well at the edge of the city, so there was nothing for her to hide behind. But you see, He's the Son of God, so looking through wells or into people's hearts is no difficult thing. And do you know what He saw in this woman's heart? Five husbands, and at the time, she was living with a man to whom she wasn't married.

"She thinks He's a prophet, but we, the readers, understand more. She's so excited about what He said, about the way He explained her life to her, that she rushes back to the city and tells everyone about Him. But that's not the most significant part. The most significant part is when His disciples return. He's just spoken with this woman whose life is full of sexual sin, and He tells His men that the harvest is ready. It doesn't say that she turned to Him for forgiveness, but knowing all she had done, He was still ready to forgive her on the spot. He said that the field was ready for harvest. He saw her as part of the harvest and was ready to winnow that field.

"So now you sit here today, Delancey, and you think your sin is beyond His reach. The Bible says it's not. I could give you account after account of people whose sins have far outweighed your own, but then you would miss the point. If you committed only one sin in your whole life, you still wouldn't be good enough to come to God. Stop looking at what you've done, and see what God did."

Delancey couldn't believe what he had just said. She sat for a moment and then shook her head in wonder.

"Tell me Delancey, would you like to make things right between you and God, once and for all? I don't want you to think that life is going to become perfect. But you don't have to leave here alone, Delancey. You don't ever have to be alone again."

"I want that so much, but I'm still thunderstruck that He's willing."

"Thunderstruck or not, are *you* willing to take Him at His word and trust that His forgiveness is complete? This is the telling point. Are you willing to trust God and turn your life over to Him? Only you can decide."

Delancey nodded after just a few moments of thought.

"Should I pray out loud or to myself?"

"I think that accountability is a good thing," Woody said, echoing Adam's words to Mackenzie. "Praying so we can hear is a good thing, but whether or not your prayer is verbalized, it's your heart's attitude that makes the difference."

Delancey nodded, and the three waited until she bowed her head before following suit.

"Father God —" Like her sister, she started as her mother always had. "I've tried to talk to You before but never followed through. I want more than anything to know that I can come back to You. I hate the shame I feel before You. You're a holy God, and I have sinned and sinned often against You. I've known for years that Jesus died for sin, but my pride was too big to turn to Him. Please take me now. It's so much worse than if I'd come to You before, but if I'm understanding this correctly, it's never too late. Thank You for dying for my sin and for bringing Mackenzie to me when I didn't deserve either of you. In God's name I pray, Amen."

Delancey looked over at Mackenzie and waited no more than a half a second before throwing her arms around her. The women clung to each other.

Paula ran for Woody's office and the box of tissue there.

"Thank you, Micki. Thank you." Delancey could not stop saying that words. "Thank you for coming to me."

"I love you, Deej. I love you too much to do anything else." She pulled back a little. "Sisters, D.J. — sisters twice!"

"Oh, Micki." Delancey had been drying up a little but was gone again.

Paula returned and passed the box, but not before Woody grabbed one to take care of his own needs.

"Thank you, Pastor," Delancey now said, several soggy tissues balled in her hand. "It was so clear to me once you explained it. Thank you."

"You're welcome, Delancey. Tell me, do you live close enough to join us here for services?"

Delancey nodded. "Only about 20 minutes."

"Great. Let me give you a card with the times and such. Do you have a Bible?"

"I do, but I'm not sure where it is right now."

"I can find you one."

"Actually," Mackenzie broke in, "I think that's something I'd like to give her."

Woody and Paula smiled at her.

"There's a Christian bookstore about two blocks from here," Paula offered. "I can give you directions."

"Thank you."

The four of them talked a while longer and a church schedule was found. Paula invited both women to join her Tuesday morning for a women's Bible study, directions were given to the bookstore, and goodbyes were said with the sweet thought that they would see each other again on

Sunday.

It was a quiet pair that left the church. Peace and emotional exhaustion sometimes looked that way. Inside the church, Pastor Woody Carlisle was holding his wife, their own wonder at God's goodness causing some speechlessness of their own. They both prayed that the Bishop women would be in one of the pews on Sunday.

"I have a confession to make to you," Mackenzie said to Delancey much later that day. Delancey was reading a brand-new study Bible with a beautiful teal green cover. They had eaten dinner and cleaned up afterward, and the women were sitting on Delancey's comfortable furniture.

"What's that?"

"I've never been to church in Meyers. Only Bible study and minichurch."

"Why, Micki?"

"I don't know. It somehow scares me. That sounds so lame, but that's the way it feels."

"It doesn't sound lame. When we got to that door this morning, all I could think about was Mom. I almost ran."

"But that's just it, D.J. Mom would be thrilled, so why am I so scared?"

"The emotion. It's overwhelming. Mom wanted us to *want* to go to church for years, and we never did. Now that we do, she's not here." Delancey suddenly sat up. "Mic, we've got to call Jack."

"I already tried." Mackenzie's eyes were sad. "The number is out of service."

"He's moved," Delancey said, stating the obvious and sitting back with a sigh.

"Most of the time I can't think about the way I treated him," Mackenzie admitted. "It hurts too much."

"I can't picture him alone." Delancey said, her voice soft. "I just can't."

Burdened with the choices of their past, the women were silent for a time.

"Do you suppose his move was recent?" Delancey finally asked. "And if we sent a letter, it might be forwarded to him?"

"We could try." Mackenzie was more than willing. The pain and regret was so strong. It took a moment for her to realize Delancey was asking a question.

"What's that?" Mackenzie had to bring her mind back to the present.

"Did you say whether or not you're going to church this Sunday, Mic?"

"I'd like to, and I plan on it." Her face was thoughtful. "I think I'd feel better if I had something nice to wear. All I brought are jeans."

"Let's check my closet."

Mackenzie took in Delancey's tall willowy frame and snorted. "My backside gets a little more shelf-like every year, Delancey. Nothing you have is going to fit me."

"I have a few skirts that might work."

Mackenzie wasn't convinced but went with her to the bedroom anyway. The skirts did work, but the blouses and sweaters that matched them were tight on her arms and across her bust. Delancey's shoes were too big.

"We'll go shopping tomorrow," Delancey proclaimed. "We'll get you all set."

"All right."

It wasn't until that moment that Mackenzie noticed a few hangers with men's attire. They were in the back and not very noticeable, but Delancey caught the direction of her sister's gaze.

"Would you like some help getting rid of those?" Mackenzie asked gently, trying not to hate the man who owned them.

"I'll get a garbage sack," Delancey said quickly and rushed from the room.

Mackenzie stood very still. *How are we going to make it, Father God? The pain is so great. Why must we hurt so much before we learn? Will it ever be easier? Will we ever be wiser?*

Delancey didn't go back into the room but passed the bags to Mackenzie, went to the sofa, and picked up her Bible. Half an hour later when Mackenzie put her shoes on, gathered the rental car keys, and picked up the bags, Delancey didn't ask where she was going. She told her she would watch for her, and in an effort to survive the pain, kept studying the passage in the fourth chapter of John.

It was hard to believe it was over. Delancey had followed Mackenzie's rental car to the airport so she could see her off. Mackenzie told her she didn't have to, because she might run into Chet, but Delancey said that she would have to face the possibility.

They had done nothing but talk about Scripture, how to deal with sin and temptation, and what God expected of His children, for two solid weeks. They attended services on both Sundays and minichurch on Wednesday night, along with Paula's Bible study on Tuesday morning. Pastor Carlisle had even fielded some calls when Delancey had asked questions that Mackenzie couldn't answer.

"Tell me something, D.J., would you ever

consider moving to Tahoe?"

The other airport patrons were forgotten as Delancey looked at her sibling.

"Or, I could move here," Mackenzie suggested. "I could sell my house or rent it and move here to be near you."

"You would do that? Sell your house to move here?"

"I want to be near my sister," she said softly. "It's been way too long. I know you need the church body here, and I think you're going to get very close to them, so, yes, I would move. But if you ever hanker for California, I would be the happiest woman on earth."

Delancey thought her big sister, Mackenzie Rose Bishop, was the most wonderful person she had ever known. Micki was not a Chicago-type person, but she was willing to leave California to be near her.

And why would I stay here? I came for school and remained for Chet, but California is home.

"I'm sorry, Delancey," Mackenzie broke into her thoughts. "You have so many changes and hurts to work through right now. It was insensitive to ask you."

"No, Mic, it wasn't. I've just never thought of it, that's all."

"Are you trying to say you'll think about it?"

"Yes."

Big sister or not, Mackenzie leaned over and put her head on Delancey's shoulder. The younger woman was taller, so she fit nicely. Delancey leaned her head against Mackenzie, and they just sat together until Mackenzie's row number was called.

"I love you, Micki," Delancey said with tears

in her eyes.

Mackenzie couldn't speak at all. They held onto each other as long as they dared.

"I'll pray for you, Mackenzie," Delancey said at last.

In sheer delight, Mackenzie laughed through her tears. "And I will for you."

"Oh, Mic, it's so sweet to be able to say that. Please think of me often. I can tell I'm going to be weak in one particular area."

"Keep in touch with the Carlisles. They'll help you to think clearly. Be in the Word every day."

"Call me," Delancey said as she watched her move away.

"I will."

Delancey moved to the window, much as she had done before when Chet approached her. It was daylight outside, and that helped dispel the images, but she well remembered the quiet drink they'd had that night.

I thought he was married. Do You remember that, Father? There was something about him that made me doubt even then, but I ignored it and thought about no one else from that time forward. Help me get through this, Lord. Help me to think clearly and to believe that You can heal me and ease the pain.

The plane finally backed up and moved on its way. The sisters had spent a few hours with Carlisles the day before, and Paula had made a point of telling Delancey that if she needed to come over after Mackenzie left, she was welcome. With the invitation still fresh in her memory and before she could change her mind, she drove from the airport straight for their house, thanking God all the way that she hadn't seen Chet.

679

THIRTY-NINE

Zephyr Cove

The calendar read March 24, 1992, when Mackenzie faxed a page to her sister and stood by the phone in anticipation. The ring didn't take long, and feeling rather smug, Mackenzie picked up the receiver and said, "Hello, Delancey."

"Have you actually been in this house?" Delancey demanded.

"As a matter of fact, I have."

"Oh, Mic! Tell me about it."

Mackenzie laughed. She hadn't been looking for a place for her sister. They'd talked about her making a move, but nothing was definite. Then on the way home from church the past Sunday, she spotted a house, one she had seen many times, except now it had a Realtor's sign out front. The house nearly waved its chimney and shouted Delancey's name. She met with the woman who had the listing and had been able to look at it just that morning.

"Mackenzie," Delancey said again, "start talking."

"It's wonderful, Delancey. The only reason the owners are selling is because the husband has been transferred out of state. They built it themselves only two years ago. The walls are white pine and still smell fresh. They don't smoke or have pets. The main room has everything — living room, dining area, and L-shaped kitchen. There's a loft."

"Oh, Mic!"

"The stairs to it are open and go right off the living room. The mud room that you use to get in the door off the kitchen is very spacious. On the opposite side of the house is a four-season porch. It's gorgeous! And then across the front of the house is an open deck."

"How many bedrooms?"

"Two with a bath in the middle. They're not huge but very homey."

"Oh, Mackenzie, it sounds wonderful."

"If I thought you would forgive me, I'd have bought it on the spot."

"It says here 'priced to sell,' but this number is pretty steep."

"Not for this house, Deej. It's just wonderful. The woman from the real estate office says they're in a hurry, so I thought I could buy it. That way we would avoid going through the banks, and you can pay me back."

"I have the money."

"You do?"

"Yeah. I've never touched the money from Dad's insurance."

"I've never spent mine either. I don't know about you, D.J., but I think Dad would be delighted to buy you a house in Christmas Valley."

"I'm going to be crying if you keep that up."

"That's all right, isn't it?"

"It would be if I hadn't been so weepy lately."

"What's going on?"

"Just so many wonderful things. I'm still thinking about our Colorado ski trip last month. I had such a good time with you, Mic. Then that award when I got back, you know, from *Just for Kids.* Then there's Paula and Woody. They've taught me so much, and I know they love me, but just last week they asked if I should move to be closer to you. I've never even discussed our conversation with them. Then this weekend I find out that my landlady's brother wants my place, so she's asked me if I can be out by the first of June. And now you send this. Oh, Mic, God is so good."

Mackenzie could have shouted. Her sister was coming! It was too wonderful to be real.

They were in almost constant touch for the next few days as more contacts were made about the house. Mackenzie asked more questions and saw the house again, this time taking Adam with her. He checked things she had not thought of and asked that the cost to have the fireplace and furnace inspected be shared by both parties. He even negotiated the price down for her, and after the offer to purchase was accepted, closing was scheduled for May 1.

Mackenzie walked on a cloud for days. She spent many hours at the Cummings' house, as well as seeing Roz every Monday, and knew that if God asked her to stay in Tahoe and serve Him for the rest of her life, she would count herself blessed beyond measure.

She had even started writing again, but not for IronHorse. In the weeks that followed her departure from Chicago, Delancey had done two more search books for Micah Bear. Mackenzie had taken a month and put words to the illustrations, but shortly after that, she had an idea that she thought might work for a Christian novel, *The*

Parchment Soldier. She didn't know exactly what was out there in that market. She just knew that the character in her mind was a little like herself, running hard, but learning in the end that eternal things were the most important.

Did Christians read such things? she asked the Lord only, because she wasn't ready to talk to anyone else about it, at least not until one Saturday in the middle of April. She had been writing but stopped so she could drive over to talk with Adam Cummings. He wasn't visible when she got to the redwood-sided house, but Josh was out front, shooting baskets by himself in the driveway. Mackenzie, still not sure she was ready to discuss it, was glad for the distraction. She stole the ball from him and did a nice layup.

"What's it going to be? Horse or pig?" he asked.

"You're too easy to beat at pig. Let's go horse."

"If I recall, I beat you last time," Josh said indulgently. "But then at your advanced age, the memory goes."

"That does it, Joshy boy. No mercy."

The teen only grinned at her and made his first shot. No one missed for a while, but then Mackenzie did what she always did to Josh — moved into three-point land and swished it. He didn't allow himself to groan, but it took effort. He had his first letter a few seconds later. Mackenzie didn't want the game to end too swiftly, and by the end she did have H and O, but a few more nicely timed three-point shots, and she had complete control.

"How do you do that?" Josh asked in dismay.

Mackenzie shrugged and laughed. "I don't know. Delancey hates it too. Of course, she can jam like you can, so when we go one on one, I'm at her mercy."

"I'll have to keep that in mind."

"I'm going in the house now, Joshy. Is your dad in?"

"Yeah, he's replacing the garbage disposal. Rina got it in her head to shove a whole head of cabbage down there and added her bracelet to boot."

Mackenzie knew Josh's penchant for teasing, so she took his words with a grain of salt. However, she did find Adam just rising from the kitchen floor. Roz called a hello from the bedroom where she was ironing.

"Hey, Micki girl," Adam greeted her. "You're just the lady I want to talk with."

"About what?"

"A little something I've been thinking about. Let me wash up, and we'll sit in the living room."

Mackenzie couldn't imagine what he was talking about, but she did as she was told. It took a little longer than she expected, and by the time he came back, her mind was working on her story again.

"I've been thinking," Adam began, "but before I explain, I want you to understand that I'm just making a suggestion, not telling you what to do. All right?"

"Sure."

"Are you aware that Meyers has a planted church in Kingsbury?"

"I think I've heard that. I mean I've heard of the Kingsbury church and seen their sign, but I guess I've never made the connection to our church."

"The Kingsbury Bible Church was planted by our church about five years ago. We were getting quite big, and some of our people were coming from very far away, so two of our pastors went

684

there. They now have a strong leadership group and their Sunday attendance is only about 75 people fewer than our own. Just like us, their emphasis is on male leadership, accountability, blamelessness, evangelism, and discipleship."

"Okay."

"I'm telling you all of this because I think you should start attending there."

Mackenzie blinked at him and was surprised by how instantly angry she felt inside. Even after attending church with Delancey, it had taken until the middle of January for Mackenzie to start attending all the services at Meyers. Now that she was settling in and getting to know people more each week, he wanted her to leave!

Adam had come to know Mackenzie very well in the past eight months and knew the expression she used to cover her feelings. She was either angry or shocked, or quite possibly both. Roz joined them just before Adam began to speak again.

"What are you thinking?"

"I'm trying to think what your reason could be."

"I'm sorry, Mic. I should have explained. You could have neighbors that are believers. You might be shopping at the grocery store with people who attend Kingsbury. The close proximity from your house just makes it something I think you should consider. The fellowship could be very special."

Mackenzie no longer hid her feelings. She turned angry eyes to Roz.

"Did you know he was going to say this?"

"He told me, yes."

"And what do you think?"

"I think we'll still see you almost as much as we do now, but you'll have a chance to fellowship closer to home."

"I have to go." Mackenzie stood, completely bent out of shape.

"So there are areas of Mackenzie's life that we have to tiptoe around," Adam said quietly, and Mackenzie stopped but didn't look at him. She could see his face in her mind. He wouldn't be angry — just looking at her with those dark, thick-lashed, direct eyes.

"I never said you had to do this," Adam reminded her, his voice as kind as his expression. "I just wanted you to think about it."

"Delancey's coming, Adam," Mackenzie turned to remind him. "What about that?"

"Delancey's house is one mile from ours and two miles from the church. You're a 40-minute drive in good weather. As I said, I just want you to consider it."

Mackenzie returned to her seat, apologizing for her outburst and trying to strip the feelings away so she could think well. She felt so let down and rejected that it hurt. Roz had begun to say something, and Mackenzie made herself attend.

"The pastors at Kingsbury are wonderful, Micki. The churches used to get together for functions, but we're both too big for that now. We can't find a hall to hold us. I know dozens of people at Kingsbury, and you ought to know Adam and me well enough by now to see that we would never suggest something that would hurt you."

Mackenzie felt ashamed, and her face showed that.

"I need to repeat, Micki, that you don't have to go anywhere," Adam reemphasized. "Just keep it in mind. Be open to what the Lord might have for you."

"All right. I'll do that." And she planned on it, not knowing how hard it would be.

"Why did you come by, Micki?" Roz suddenly wanted to know, but Mackenzie no longer wanted to talk about *The Parchment Soldier.*

"I mostly needed to get out of the house," she said, telling a half-truth and then mentally wondering whether there was any such thing as a half-lie. Wasn't any lie a complete lie?

"Can you stay for dinner?"

"No," Mackenzie declined. She was no longer irritated, but she didn't want to think about Adam's suggestion either. She cut her stay short and argued with the Lord the whole way home.

Do You know how many years it's been since Delancey and I have lived in the same area? I can't believe You would ask this of me. She's the reason I started attending on Sundays, hoping that she would come someday and knowing I would need to be a good example. Some weeks I want to bawl my eyes out, but I still go, and now Adam wants me in a different church. I want to run and hide at the thought of trying to make new friends. Don't they understand how hard that is for me? I don't exactly have friends breaking down my front door, You know. I just can't do it, and that's all there is to it! In Mackenzie's mind, the matter was settled. She put the subject conveniently into a far corner in her mind and left it there.

Delancey came at the end of May, and all thoughts of changing churches faded from view. Mackenzie was living her dream. Her sister's house was 40 minutes away, and they saw each other weekly. It had been so long since they were this close, and their relationships with the Lord only enhanced the bond they had always shared.

They spoke of spiritual matters often, and neither sister could think of anything else they needed. It seemed to them that God had blessed them for life.

The cool October air pulled at Delancey's lungs as she ran. Her lungs were starting to ache, but her mind was so intent on Chet that it took awhile to notice. Almost a year ago she had stood in the airport in Chicago and watched him with his wife. It still hurt to think of that scene. Before leaving Chicago, however, and on the advice of Woody, she'd written him a long letter, telling of her own conversion and how she hoped he would someday see his need for Christ and would make things right with his wife. When she left, she did so without giving the post office her forwarding address. The Carlisles had suggested this and also that she route her mail through them. If Chet did come looking for her, he would have to face Pastor Woody Carlisle. Delancey hoped he would, only because she knew what a help Woody and Paula could be.

Wrongly as he had treated her, having Chet leave her life was like experiencing the death of a loved one, and at times she still grieved. But not in a hundred years did she believe she would be doing so well a year after that fact. She didn't think she would ever love again, not because she still pined for Chet, but because she didn't honestly believe that there would be a man out there who would understand. It would seem that God would want her to be alone and enjoy only Him. When she ached for things that she could not have — a man's touch and someone to hold — she applied the truth of the Scripture and did her best to deal with it when it came.

Her lungs finally got her attention, and she slowed to a walk. Five minutes later she caught sight of her house. Seeing its neat frame and perfect setting always made her smile. She jogged up the steps of her front porch and opened the door to the ringing of the phone. She dashed to get it.

"Hello."

"Hello, Delancey? This is Rachel Brinker. Am I getting you at a bad time?"

"No, this is fine." She worked to catch her breath. "How are you, Mrs. Brinker?"

"I'm fine, but I'm calling for a favor, and I'm afraid you'll feel I'm taking advantage of you."

"I don't think I will," she said honestly.

"Well, if you have other things going on, deadlines and such, and can't do it, just tell me."

"I will."

"Good. Gary and Mary Beth O'Hara have been married 25 years, and we're giving them a party on the first Saturday in December. Gary was the first pastor here at Meyers, even before Dave. We'll have a general announcement and so will Kingsbury, but we want to do up some invitations since there will be folks — you know, family and such — who don't attend either church. We have someone with a scanner and all that fancy computer stuff to put the invites together, but we all thought it would look so nice if the invitation had a little floral design or something, maybe even pinecones to go with our trees. What do you think, Delancey?"

"I think it sounds wonderful. I would feel honored to help. I work best when I know just what a person wants, so if you could be specific

689

with me, I'll put something together."

"Oh, all right. I'll talk to the committee and get back to you. From there, however, could you go directly to the person with the scanner? That will make for fewer phone calls, I think, and things will be smoother."

"Of course. Whom shall I check with for approval of what I come up with?"

"I've seen your work, Delancey," she said with a smile in her voice. "We'll love whatever you draw."

"Thank you, Mrs. Brinker," Delancey said warmly.

The women were off the phone not long afterward, but Delancey thought about the conversation for a long time. Her mother had commented often about God's gifts, and even said as much about Delancey's art, but Delancey had never taken it in until recently.

It's such a privilege to do something for You, Lord. I wish that every Micah Bear book told children about Your love. I'm glad to do this for the O'Haras, Lord. I feel I'm honoring You with my work.

Delancey climbed into the shower then, her heart still thankful for all God's blessings. It would take a little more time before she understood that whenever she gave God the glory, even for a Micah Bear book, she was honoring Him. And it would be several weeks more before she saw that she could do other children's books, books that would tell about the love of God.

Having not bothered with a very accurate shopping list, Mackenzie threw a box of rice pilaf into her shopping cart, trying to remember if she had any in the pantry at home. She looked down into the basket at the odd selection of food and mentally shook her head.

I could help you pay off your debts real fast, Roz. You can cook for me as well as clean — even once a week would be welcome. I tell You, Lord, she said changing her thoughts to prayer, *cooking is just not my strong point. That's no excuse, but it's so hard when I ruin everything I make. I've also decided I don't like eating alone. I do so much better at Delancey's or when we go out.*

"Mackenzie?" a voice called so softly that for a moment she thought she imagined it. She was going to move down the aisle but thought she'd better look. Her hands still holding the bar on the basket, she glanced behind her and froze. Jack Avery was standing ten feet away from her. His hair and mustache were grayer now, but he was still remarkably youthful for a man who had just turned 50. Not even remembering why she was in the store, Mackenzie turned and walked slowly toward him. She stopped when they faced each other.

"I tried to call you," she whispered, thinking of all the things she'd mentally said to him since coming to Christ. "I've wanted to talk to you for so long, but the phone — the number was a recording." He wasn't saying anything, only staring at her. "I'm so sorry, Jackson," she finished. "I'm so sorry about the way I treated you."

Too emotional to speak, Jack reached and pulled her into his arms. Mackenzie wrapped her arms around him and held on for dear life. Jackson! She'd found Jackson.

"I'm sorry," she said again.

"It's all right." His voice was hoarse and choked.

Mackenzie looked up to see tears coming down his face which started her own.

"I'll never treat you that way again, Jack. I promise I won't."

"It's over now, Mackenzie." He smoothed the hair from her face. "We don't need to talk about it anymore. All is forgiven."

"Jack," Mackenzie grabbed his arms. "I believe now. Jack, I came to Christ a year ago in September."

Mackenzie watched him work to maintain control.

"Delancey too," she managed. "She made a decision a few months after I did. She just moved here."

"Delancey lives here?" He said, wishing he carried a handkerchief. Every day since he met Marrell and her daughters, he had prayed for Mackenzie and Delancey, and since Marrell's death, he often asked God to reunite them. But the event happening in a grocery store in Lake Tahoe never occurred to him.

"We both live here," Mackenzie was saying.

Jack took a breath and tried to think. "Do you live together?"

"No. D.J. is at Christmas Valley. I'm at Zephyr Cove."

Jack stared at her. "I live at Kingsbury."

Mackenzie's mouth opened. "Do you go to the Kingsbury Bible Church?"

"Yes. Are you and D.J. at Meyers?"

Mackenzie could only nod. *You tried to tell me, didn't You, Lord? but I was so stubborn. If I'd changed churches I would have seen Jack months ago!*

"I want to talk to you, Micki. I want to know everything."

"Sure."

"Let me make a phone call, and, well, we could sit in my car."

"Or go to my place. I'm just up the road."

"Okay. Wait for me, and I'll follow you. What does your car look like?"

Mackenzie smiled. "I'm still driving the Jeep."

"I've gotta get out of here." Jack was tearing up again. "Wait for me up front. Oh, do you need to finish?"

"No, I made a horrible list, and I don't even know where it is right now."

Jack laughed. She was still the same Mackenzie.

They split up then, Mackenzie going right to the check-out and then standing like a child, head craned to see the store. Jack showed up out of nowhere about five minutes later, checked out, and came toward her. She didn't know if he'd used the phone or not, but he walked right out to the parking lot and spotted her Jeep.

"I'm in the green Benz, so give me a minute to get pulled around."

"Okay. If I lose you, go to Skylark, then down to Lake Street, and I'm the last house to the south, next to the park."

"Okay," Jack nodded, and again they split up.

Leading the way, Mackenzie was spared from hitting someone only by God's protection. She spent more time with her eyes on the rearview mirror than on the road. She had found Jack. God had let her find Jack, and she hadn't even been looking. It was too wonderful to even take it in. Mackenzie's euphoric state lasted until she pulled into her garage, jumped out, and came to Jack as he climbed from his car. The look on his face reminded her of how far apart they'd been. Not until that moment did she realize how much explaining she had to do.

"This is where you live?" he asked softly.

"Yeah," she said gently, not wanting to laugh at his thunderstruck face. "Come on in."

Jack's heart filled with dread. The girls had gone off in anger, their hearts worldly and closed off to the things of the Lord. Many were the times he had to rein in his imagination as to what might have become of them. Now, as he walked into this fabulous lake home, he asked himself if Mackenzie was married or what type of work she'd gone into. Could she still be in the Army and living here? He had kept track of all the new Micah Bear books. There were a lot of them, but he didn't think children's books paid that well.

"Sit down, Jack," Mackenzie invited as she knelt to build up the fire. Without even looking at him, she could feel his eyes moving around the room. It had an odd effect on the author. By the time she took the other stuffed chair that flanked the fire, she was as nervous as a cat.

"Are you all right, Micki?"

"I'm fine, Jack, really. I just need to explain all of this. The problem is you can't talk about what I'm going to tell you, Jack, not to anyone. I think that's an unfair thing to ask a person, so if you'd rather I not tell you, I won't."

Jack thought about this a moment. He was not a naturally curious person — it was easy for him to stay out of other people's business — but this woman was special. It was like watching Marrell with dark hair. Mackenzie had the same graceful movements and some of her expressions. And they lived five minutes away from each other! Jack wanted to be involved again with no barriers. For this reason he said, "Tell me."

"All right." Mackenzie was relieved. She wanted him to know. "Did Mom ever mention to you that I was writing on my own, without D.J.?"

"I think she might have, but she didn't go into great detail. I remember now that she said it was something you wanted kept quiet, so we never spoke of it even to each other." He shrugged. "Then I forgot all about it."

Mackenzie nodded. "I'm published, Jack," she said simply. "Very successfully."

"Okay . . ." Jack drew the word out as understanding dawned. "You mean, more than just the Micah Bear books?"

"Yes."

"I haven't seen any of them."

Mackenzie took a breath, knowing how widely read her stepfather was, and said, "Yes, you have."

Jack frowned at her.

"I'm Mac Walker."

Understanding was not long in coming. His eyes grew huge before he threw back his head and laughed in delight. A moment later he was up, pulling her from her chair and into his arms.

"Mackenzie! I can't believe it!" He tried to squeeze the life out of her, and all Mackenzie could do was laugh. "They're fabulous!"

"Have you read one?"

"I've read *every* one. Everyone I *know* has read them!" He looked down at her in delight. "I'm so proud of you. But tell me, why Mac Walker?"

"It started almost as a joke," she began but went on to map out all the events. By the time she was finished, Jack understood completely. Living in San Francisco, he had occasions to see how the public acted around celebrities. It was pretty awful. A name as big as Mac Walker's would not go unnoticed.

"Now," he said as he sat back down, "tell me the rest. Tell me about your conversion."

Mackenzie smiled and talked nonstop for the next 90 minutes. Jack cried with her, laughed with her, and felt his heart overflow time and again. It was nothing short of a miracle. Both women had gone so far away before God brought them to Him.

"Now you, Jack," Mackenzie said at last. "How have you been?"

"I've been very well," he told her warmly and sincerely. "But I need to start by telling you something important. I'm married again, Mackenzie."

Nothing could have prepared Mackenzie for this. She stared at him and then gave a short, breathless laugh.

"Well, congratulations," she said softly, gasping a little to keep the tears at bay. "I mean that, Jack."

"I know you do, Mic, and I would like to tell you about it."

"Of course." But she was biting her lip now, tears in her eyes. "I'm sorry, Jackson. I still think of you as my mom's and now you belong to someone else."

Jack took her hand and led her to the sofa so he could put his arm around her. She and Delancey were the daughters he never had. He would choose to cut off a limb before he would deliberately hurt one of them, but her response was natural.

"Tell me," Mackenzie said. She was a bit teary, but she desperately wanted him to know she cared.

"It started when Bayside Architecture decided to put an office up here. That was late in 1989, the same year your mother died. They approached me, and at first I said no, but I came up here that Christmas, looked around, and met a pastor I really liked."

Mackenzie smiled. "Kevin DeLong or Harris Redick." She named the men at Kingsbury.

"Kevin DeLong. We met several times over a few days, and then I went home to discuss it with Pastor Mickelson, Oliver, and Shay."

"How are Oliver and Shay?"

"They're great. The kids are huge."

"I don't know why I never thought to call them to track you down."

Jack smiled. "That would have taken away from the fun of the grocery store. Anyway, as it turned out, almost one year from the date of your mother's death, I moved up here, got an apartment, set up the office, and started attending Kingsbury Bible Church. That was when I met Joanne Stone.

"At first we just talked. It reminded me of your mother and me, only the roles were reversed. She was interested, although I didn't know it, and I was still in love with my wife. But we still saw each other at church, and we would talk at the different functions. She's a widow with grown children and a little older than I am, so I just never made the connection. Then she went to Kevin, told him how she felt, and asked if he would talk to me. To make a long story short, when I got over my shock, Joanne and I started to get to know each other in earnest. We were married this last March and just moved into a new home in Kingsbury."

"I'm happy for you, Jack; honestly I am. Angry as I was at everything, whenever I pictured you alone, it just about killed me."

Jack leaned close and kissed her brow. "Thank you. I want you to meet her."

"Oh, Jack —" Mackenzie hesitated. "Could I wait a little while for that?"

"Of course." He understood completely. "Whenever you want. You and Delancey can both come, okay?"

Mackenzie nodded. "I do need to meet her soon, Jack, because the Lord's made it clear that He wants me to start attending Kingsbury. Meyers is too far, especially in bad weather, but I've been digging my heels in like an idiot and haven't gone."

Jack grinned. "The change in you is amazing."

Mackenzie laughed. "It was too long in coming, I can tell you that, and sometimes I think I haven't learned a thing." Her face grew serious. "I was a fool to run from what you tried to teach us, Jack. It's so clear now."

"That's one of the things I love most about our heavenly Father, Mic — His persistence. He never lets us go."

Mackenzie looked at him in wonder. "I just needed a few groceries. I never thought I'd find you."

"Shall we call Delancey?"

"Let's do one better, let's go see her. Do you have time?"

"Yes. Let me make one quick call, and we'll go."

The two were off just minutes later, this time in Jack's car. They talked nonstop all the way to Delancey's, at least Jack did, as he remembered to tell her that over a year ago he had lost his sisters within two months of each other. He also said he still had boxes of her mother's things for her to go through.

Once at Delancey's, Mackenzie was able to stand back while Delancey renewed her relationship with this special man. Watching them talk, seeing the love in Jack's eyes when he looked at both of them, only served to remind Mackenzie of the blessings God had for her.

I underestimate You, Father. I can't do that anymore. Thank You for blessings we don't even know we need.

FORTY

Delancey muttered to herself over the mistake she just made and frowned at the drawing in front of her. For some reason, she couldn't get it right. It was the same little bear she had been drawing for years, but she kept messing up his face. She continued to study it, castigating herself for several minutes. It was a relief to have the phone ring and take her mind off of Micah Bear.

"Hello."

"Hello, this is Richard Wilder. May I speak with Delancey Bishop please."

"This is Delancey."

"Oh, hello. Rachel Brinker gave me your name and number. She said you're doing some artwork for the O'Haras' invitation. I'm the person with the scanner."

"Oh, of course. I've got everything all done. Shall I bring it this Sunday?"

"Actually, if you had something completed, I was hoping to work on it this Saturday. Could I stop by and get it from you?"

"Or I could meet you," Delancey suggested, not wanting to mention that she was not married and didn't like telling strangers, even people from the church, where she lived.

"All right. What's good for you?"

"Um. Do you know where Mountain Mocha is?"

"Yep."

"I could meet you there just about any time."

"Okay. How about 1:30 today?"

"That's fine. It's not that big in there, but so you'll know, I'll be wearing a Donald Duck baseball cap."

Richard laughed. "I'll find you."

"Okay. I'll see you then."

They rang off, and Delancey checked the clock. She wouldn't need to leave for three hours but in the meantime needed to get something done. Picking up the phone, she called Mackenzie.

"Hi, Mic."

"Hey, Deej. What's up?"

"Nothing. I can't seem to draw a thing today, and I'm mad at myself."

"Take a break."

"That feels lazy to me."

"Come on, Deej, all you do is work."

"No, I don't. I took all that time to move out here and get settled."

"Delancey, that was months ago, and moving is not restful!"

Silence.

"What's really going on?"

"I don't want to hurt you."

"You won't."

"I'm sick to death of Micah Bear."

Mackenzie laughed so hard that Delancey would have pinched her had she been close.

"Stop it, Mic."

"I can't! I've been sick of him for a year but didn't want to tell you."

"You're kidding!"

"No."

Delancey finally saw the humor. She laughed with her sister until they were both giddy.

"It was stupid not to talk about it," Delancey told her.

"I know. Sometimes stupid is what I do best."

"I think I will take that break."

"Good. Head into the kitchen, cook a lavish dinner, and invite me over tonight."

This gave Delancey more giggles.

"I'm serious, Delancey," Mackenzie cut in. "I haven't eaten well since the last time you had me to dinner. Actually, since you're sick of Micah Bear, just give up illustrating all together and become my cook, okay?"

"You might be a slave driver."

"True."

"You can come to dinner, though, about six o'clock."

"You're an angel, Deej. Oh, I have another call coming in; it's probably Pax. I'll see you tonight."

"Okay, 'bye."

Delancey thoroughly enjoyed turning away from her easel, taking her sister's advice, and giving herself a break. She picked up the book she was reading and let herself get immersed, so much so, that if a pinecone hadn't hit the roof, she might have been late to meet Richard Wilder. Remembering at the last minute to grab her hat, she shot out the door to the garage.

Already the air was promising snow. They had had a few flurries, but nothing stayed on the ground. It would come, however, and Delancey thought she just might ski every day the whole winter. She was so busy dreaming about that sport that she almost missed the driveway to the

Mountain Mocha cafe.

It was a fairly new restaurant, or so she'd been told, and when she got inside, almost all the tables were open. She sat down by a window, ordered a peach Smoothie, and opened her art portfolio. She certainly hoped everyone would like what she had come up with. The tiny blue flowers were ones she copied from pictures she had taken in a hotel lobby in France. The vines were the basic garden variety, but the rest of the flowers were from her memories of living at the Presidio.

Delancey was so intent on what she had done that it took a moment for her to realize she wasn't alone. She glanced up, but her head had to just keep going. An incredibly tall man with dark brown hair, brown eyes, and horn-rimmed glasses was standing at her table. He smiled at the look on her face, and Delancey blushed and hurried to stand.

"Don't get up," he said in a deep voice. "I'm Richard Wilder, by the way. I'll just join you."

"I've seen you at church," Delancey said with surprise. "I mean, across the way."

"I think I've seen you too," Richard told her, wanting to be polite but using the word "think" because he didn't believe he would ever forget this woman if he had seen her.

"I need to tell you," Delancey immediately began to apologize, "that if any of this isn't going to work, I can do some more."

"Okay."

Delancey hesitated, suddenly afraid that her work would ruin the whole invitation.

"I won't have hurt feelings," she went on. "Just tell me, okay."

"I will," Richard told her, hoping it wouldn't be

too difficult to be honest.

Delancey, feeling resigned, pushed the folder over to him.

"Would you care for something?" a waitress suddenly appearing at their side asked. Richard ordered an entire meal, and Delancey felt badly for interrupting his lunch hour. She noticed that he was already looking inside the folder.

For a moment Richard had all he could do not to ask her if she'd been joking. Knowing she was anxiously looking on, he made himself not glance up until his examination was complete.

"These are wonderful," he said, finally meeting her eyes.

"I can do some others," Delancey said as if she hadn't heard him.

"No, these are perfect. I have their wedding photo, and I'll just put it on the front and border it with these." He pointed to the vines and dainty blue flowers. "Then on the inside I'll use these flowers along the top and bottom. You see this one big rose? I'll take it to put right in the middle on the back."

Delancey smiled, feeling herself relax. "Wow, you're a quick study."

"I think your artwork makes it easy."

The waitress brought his coffee, chicken sandwich, and fries, and Delancey was quiet while he prayed.

"Do you mind if I eat?"

"Not at all."

"Do you mind if I get a little nosy?"

Delancey shrugged in surprise. "I don't think so."

"Do you do this for a hobby or for a living, because you're good enough to do something with this, Delancey."

"I am published," she said with quiet modesty, "and I do a little freelance work."

"I'm glad someone has seen how good you are."

"Thank you. Did you have to come far?"

"Very far, all the way across the street."

Delancey smiled as she looked out the window.

"The real estate office?"

"No, the dentist's office."

"Are you a dentist?"

"Yes."

"Let me see your teeth."

Delancey was able to inspect them because Richard laughed long and loud before giving her an exaggerated grin.

"Very nice," she told him, feeling very satisfied that her work was going to be acceptable.

"Thank you. You look as though you've had perfect teeth all your life."

"I never needed braces, if that's what you mean. Both my parents had great teeth."

"Are they gone now?"

"Yes."

"Any family at all?"

"My sister."

Richard smiled. "Sisters are nice. I have three."

"Any brothers?"

"No, and I'm the baby, so I grew up with four mothers."

"Grew *up* is putting it mildly," Delancey told him and watched him laugh again.

"They just kept feeding me and I just kept shooting up."

"Is it hard to work over a dentist's chair?"

"No, the chairs these days adjust easily, and most of my length is in my legs. If I can find a place to put those, I'm fine."

"I'd better let you eat," Delancey suddenly realized.

"All right. How about another smoothie or something to eat?"

Delancey looked thoughtful. "I was noticing those cookies."

"One cookie coming up."

It was one of the nicest interludes Delancey had had since she arrived. Dr. Richard Wilder was easy to be with, and they talked nonstop until he had to go back to his office an hour later. Delancey drove home, ready to call Rachel Brinker and tell her things were in the works, but Mackenzie's Jeep was in her driveway.

"Well, hello," Delancey called when Mackenzie climbed down from the seat. "Dinner isn't ready yet."

Mackenzie laughed. "I was going to give you ten more minutes and then go see Roz. I've got something to show you, or rather read to you."

"Sounds interesting."

"Okay —" Mackenzie paced a little when she got inside, and Delancey could see that she was very excited. Delancey sat on the sofa and watched her.

"You're tired of drawing Micah Bear, right?"

"Right."

"Well . . ." she said, drawing the word out, "how about some other animals?"

"Like?"

"I thought you'd never ask." Mackenzie whipped a piece of paper from her pocket. "How about a baby tiger named Casey? Dexter is a baby boa, Lambert is a baby wolf, Arlo is a baby elephant, and Wilson is a baby owl. I call them the Jungle

Buds."

"Mackenzie!" Delancey had come to edge of the futon sofa. "Those are adorable names. What are the stories?"

"Lessons from the Bible. The first one is forgiveness, about when Wilson thinks he's better than the others because he can fly. I've got that partially written, and after that I have thankfulness and praise, sharing, prayer, and witnessing."

Delancey sank back in amazement. "You're incredible, do you know that?"

Mackenzie only smiled. "Think you can draw them?"

"Yes, but I want us to do something first. I want us to talk to Jack and Adam and see what they think."

"I was thinking of them too. We'll see Jack Friday night."

Nothing could make the girls so quiet so quickly. Having Jack back in their world was like a dream come true, but meeting his wife was proving to be a real issue of trust. They were invited to the house to meet Joanne this Friday night.

Would some of their mother's things be out? Would Jack and Joanne touch each other? And if they did, how would it feel? Jack had waited so long to kiss their mother, and by the time they began to touch, the girls were ready for it. But it wasn't the same now. Jack was theirs, or rather he had been. It didn't seem right to see him with another woman. What if Joanne Avery looked like their mother? What if she didn't like them? Questions threatened to overwhelm them, and since there were no answers, they accomplished nothing.

When Friday night rolled around, the girls drove

separately to the house in Kingsbury, but Mackenzie didn't get out of her Jeep until Delancey arrived. Both wishing they could put this off, they walked up to the door together, a strained silence between them.

Jack answered the door and knew in an instant that they were both tense. Had the girls known, Joanne wasn't much better, so desperate was she to show them she cared. Jack wondered what the evening would bring. He hugged both women, took their coats, and asked them into the living room. The house was beautiful, designed by Jack, but Mackenzie and Delancey took little notice. They stood even when Jack invited them to sit, both of them coming to complete attention when a short, dark-haired woman came into the room. She was neat and trim in a sweater and slacks, her hair just a little bit gray, but overall, very young looking. She stopped at the edge of the room and beamed at them.

"Oh my," she said softly, "Jack said you were lovely, but I had no idea. Not even the pictures I've seen have done you justice." She continued to smile at them, and surprised as they were by her appearance and warmth, the sisters didn't answer.

"I'm sorry you lost your mother," she went on so kindly that Mackenzie's and Delancey's throats closed. "I love Jack, but I wish for your sakes that you hadn't lost your mother, even if it meant I could never have him."

Mackenzie's hand went to her mouth, and Joanne went to Mackenzie. Without permission, she put her arms around her and the women hugged.

"I'm sorry I didn't say anything," Mackenzie told her. "I was just afraid."

"I understand. It's all right. Are you all right, Delancey?" Joanne turned to her.

"I could use a hug."

Joanne smiled, and the women embraced until Delancey looked down at her in wonder. "I've never considered myself possessive of Jack, but I was nervous on the way over here. I can see I was just being ridiculous."

"When I was 15, my father remarried. The woman couldn't stand me. My parents were divorced, so I was only there two weekends a month, but they were torture. I understand your fear very well."

Standing off to the side, Jack could not stop the sigh that escaped him. All three women turned with a laugh.

"Can we eat?" he asked Joanne. "I need a little sustenance if things are going to be so emotional."

"You poor baby," Mackenzie teased him, and Joanne found great amusement in that.

"Everything is ready," she told him, touching his arm on the way by. "I think I want to give the rolls a few more minutes, but we can sit down."

"Is there anything we can do?" Delancey asked, following her through the living room to the formal dinning room that sat off the kitchen.

"Don't volunteer me, Deej. You know what that's like."

"Is there anything I can do?" Delancey rephrased the question, with Jack laughing in the background.

"I don't think so, but I'll let you know if I think of something."

"How are you two?" Jack asked when they stopped in the dining room. The table was set with a linen cloth and what appeared to be the best china. The women glanced at the lovely table, but then at each other before looking at Jack.

"What does that look mean?" Jack still knew them well.

"Well, we probably should wait until after dinner," Mackenzie said.

"For what?"

"A little project we have going," Delancey explained. "We want your opinion."

"Give me some hints."

"Okay," Delancey started. "Not Micah Bear, but like that."

"And with a spiritual emphasis," Mackenzie added.

"Oh." His eyes lit up. "Sounds interesting. Did you bring anything with you?"

Mackenzie looked at her sister.

"Yes, we did," Mackenzie told him.

"In the car," the younger woman said.

"Okay, Jack, I'm ready for you," Joanne called from the kitchen, and Jack went to her. Mackenzie and Delancey looked across at each other.

"We were so stupid," Mackenzie said softly. "As if Jack would marry someone who would hate us."

"She hugged us, Mic. I think that was so sweet."

"Yes, it was."

The hosts and food arrived a few seconds later, and an evening of wonderful food and fellowship began. The guests heard Joanne's side of her courtship with Jack, and her love for him was more obvious by the minute. If Jack's gaze could be trusted, he was rather smitten himself.

Not until they'd had dessert in the living room did anyone offer a tour of the house. It was wonderfully laid out with a wide living room, elegant kitchen and dining area, and three bedrooms, one of which was a lush master bedroom suite. The girls were also taken down the hall for a full introduction to the "family."

"Matthew is my oldest," Joanne said as she pointed to the first picture. "He's a doctor in Reno. This is his wife, Jasmine, and their two children, Brady and Logan, ages seven and five. Then this is my daughter, Gemma, and her husband, Andy Phillips. They have two as well — Ashley, who's four, and Caleb, who's 14 months. And in this family picture, right next to Matthew, is my youngest son, Tucker. He's not married."

"These children," Delancey began, "are adorable. I would love to get my hands on them."

"Thanksgiving," Jack stated. "I think they'll all be here."

"The Cummings have asked us," Mackenzie told him.

"Christmas then," Joanne suggested. "Can you come then?"

"Yes," Delancey said a little too loudly. "I've got to hold this little boy. What was his name?"

"Caleb. Isn't he a doll?"

"Yes. Do they live close?"

"Gemma and family live in Placerville, so we probably see them at least twice a month — not as often if the roads are bad."

"Have you lived here your whole life, Joanne?"

"Since I was a teenager."

Such questions were the order of the evening. The Bishop women got to know Jack's new wife so well that they felt utterly relaxed with her and even set up a day to go out to lunch. They talked and laughed until very late, and Jack did not remember the project until they were headed out the door after midnight.

"We'll come by with it sometime," Delancey told him, knowing she had quite a little drive home and should be on the way. "Maybe tomorrow or Sunday."

"Okay, give me a call."

Hugs were given all around before Mackenzie and Delancey headed to their cars. Snow was just starting to fall, and as it had in the past, it caused both women to drive home with visions of skiing dancing through their heads.

Mackenzie and Delancey were standing together Sunday morning in the foyer of the church when Richard Wilder approached. Mackenzie saw him first and looked up in surprise. He was clearly headed their way, but she never remembered meeting him before.

"Hello, Delancey," he said kindly. "I thought you might want to see this."

"Oh, Richard," she exclaimed as he handed her the invitation. "It looks like I drew the flowers right on here. You do wonderful work."

He smiled down at her enthusiasm and then saw the brunette at her side. He put his hand out to Mackenzie.

"I'm sorry for barging in. My name is Richard Wilder."

"Mackenzie Bishop. It's nice to meet you, Richard." She smiled and looked at the card in her sister's hand. "Did you do the flowers, Deej?"

"Yes. Richard has a scanner and put it all together."

"What's a Deej?" Richard asked, his face so comical that they laughed.

"Deej is short for D.J., which is short for

712

Delancey Joy," Mackenzie explained.

"Ahhh." His face cleared. "And what does Delancey do with Mackenzie?"

Mackenzie looked at her sister, who answered.

"Mackenzie goes down to Micki and then Mic."

" 'Hey stupid' works too," Mackenzie mouthed off, and Richard laughed.

"Thank you for showing this to me, Richard," Delancey said as she handed it back to him. "Even the back looks wonderful."

"Computers are amazing things."

"Did you have to adjust the color?" Mackenzie was very interested.

"I did, but not manually. The computer has an automatic adjustment that does a pretty good job."

"Let me know what Mrs. Brinker says, will you, Richard. I want to be sure she's pleased."

"She is. I just talked to her. Be prepared to be thronged and gushed over. She hugged me, and I didn't do much of anything."

"Where are your glasses?" Delancey asked, suddenly noticing their absence.

"I'm wearing contacts today."

"May I be very rude?" Mackenzie asked out of the blue.

Richard laughed again. She seemed so gutsy and forthright. "I think I can handle that."

"Just how tall are you?"

"I'm a hair under 6'5"."

"I thought you had to be. It's not very often that Deej can wear those three-inch spikes of hers and still look up to a person."

Richard smiled kindly, but for some reason Delancey blushed to the roots of her hair. Mackenzie noticed it and grew very serious.

"I guess we should go in."

"I'll see you later," Richard said as he moved away, not letting on that he'd seen her face heat as well.

"I'm sorry," Mackenzie whispered when they were alone.

"It's all right. I don't know what came over me."

The women went inside, but Mackenzie was still thinking. She was starting to notice something and wondered if her sister had. She tried to think back to attending church with her folks but couldn't recall knowing very many of the young men. Was it her, or were the men at church much more respectful of women than any others she had known? If they were, it wasn't any surprise, since most of them were probably new creatures in Christ, but not until just now did she think she ought to be appreciating it. The organ finished with the prelude, and the praise group that started the service was standing at the front, songbooks in hand. It was time to put other thoughts away and get into the service.

Mackenzie and Delancey planned to go skiing on Thanksgiving morning, but a better offer came along: three-on-three basketball at the Cummings'. Devon was home from school and said it was either that or football. Knowing that Mackenzie and Delancey were coming, Roz asked him to go with basketball.

"And if you're smart," she told him, "you'll grab Delancey; Micki says she can jam."

"That works for me," Josh filled in.

"Yeah, but who gets Richard?" Sabrina wished to know. "I think it's only fair that Richard and I end up on the same team, since I'm the shortest one."

714

"Only if Mom doesn't play."

"I probably won't," she told Josh, "but if I do, I expect to be on Richard's team as well."

Adam sighed dramatically, more than happy to sit inside with the newspaper all morning. "They all used to fight to have me on their team."

Roz kissed the top of his balding head. "I'll be on your team, dear. Does that help?"

His brows went up in a mischievous way. "That depends on what we're playing."

Husband and wife exchanged a warm smile before Roz went back to her work in the kitchen. There was plenty of time, but she liked to have everything ready ahead. The basketball players were coming at 10:00 to play until noon. The plan called for them to then use the Cummings' bathrooms or go home and clean up to eat at 1:00.

Along with Richard and the Bishop sisters, they were being joined for dinner by Pete and Margie Woodhouse — Margie attended the Thursday morning Bible study — and Adam's mother and stepfather, Corrine and Lloyd Newhart. It was sure to be a fun time, and Roz always loved it when Adam had a long weekend off. The next day they would shop for a Christmas tree. It was going to be wonderful.

The doorbell rang in the middle of all these thoughts, and she was glad Sabrina went to answer it. She could hear the basketballs on the driveway already, and with a word to her husband, Roz slipped out of the kitchen to her bedroom to spend a few moments in prayer. There probably wouldn't be another minute for the rest of the day when she could do this, and she wanted a little thankful quiet time with her Lord on this Thanksgiving morning.

"We have got it made," Mackenzie said to Sabrina, Richard at her side. "The doc's on our team; we can't lose." Mackenzie feigned a great startle and looked up at him. "Why, Richard, I didn't see you standing there."

He told himself not to laugh, it would only encourage her, but he couldn't help it. Her eyes and voice could be hysterical.

"You are going to have to win this for us, Richard," Sabrina told him.

"You'll do fine," he told the younger woman before turning to Mackenzie. "Micki," he asked, using her nickname for the first time, "what are your strengths?"

"Definitely the outside. I'm helpless under the basket." Again she used her eyes to express herself, and he was smiling when he said, "Sabrina?"

"I can dribble pretty well, and my passing is okay, but my shooting is awful."

Richard smiled hugely. "Ladies, we've got this in the bag." He leaned over to huddle with them until the other team, Delancey, Devon, and Josh, called to say they were ready.

The game started slowly. It was a little colder than had been forecasted, but the pavement was nice and dry, thanks to Devon and Josh, and in no time at all, the players were hot. Delancey had jammed a couple, and at 6'2", Devon had taken several home, but Richard was making most of his team's baskets. Play was hot underneath when Sabrina passed to Mackenzie, who took it out wide. Both Delancey and Josh yelled to Devon to block her shot, but seeing where she was, he took his time. A few moments later, they had three points.

"Well now," Richard came back to give her five. "You *can* hit from the outside."

"You doubted?" she said, putting her hands on her waist.

"I won't anymore."

"Enough talk, Bishop," Delancey shouted. "Take it out."

"Yeah, yeah, Deej," she mouthed right back, doing as she was ordered but talking all the while. "Like all I have to do today is watch you fly through the air."

The game was on again, but even with Richard's height and Mackenzie's good shooting, the other team took it by two points. Devon cut Richard off, and Josh drove in for a layup, putting his sister on her back. She wasn't hurt, and he helped her to her feet, but she was disappointed about the loss.

"Come on," Mackenzie comforted her, "we'll beat 'em this time."

Until that moment, Sabrina had not realized she was among fanatics. None of them seemed to tire. At one point she went for her father just so he could give her a break. Coming in fresh, Adam tipped the scales in their direction and they won by seven points. They switched the teams all around for the third game, and by the end, it was quarter to twelve. They agreed to cool down and clean up.

Roz came out long enough to speak to Mackenzie and Delancey, who were headed to Delancey's to change, telling them to be on time, since she had everything planned for one o'clock sharp.

FORTY-ONE

"How did you come to Christ, Richard?" Adam's mother asked several hours later. The meal was eaten and dishes were cleaned up. The younger people were either watching a football game or playing on the computer. The adult Cummings, Pete and Margie Woodhouse, the Newharts, the Bishops, and Richard Wilder were sitting in the living room talking about every topic under the sun.

Corrine Newhart, a fairly new believer, found this the most fascinating question anyone could ask. Adam had already asked his stepfather and Pete to share their stories, and now Corrine, ready to hear everyone's, looked to Richard.

"I was seven," the young dentist started, smiling over the memory. "It was a communion Sunday. I had not remembered sitting through one before that day, and suddenly they were handing out 'juice and crackers,' or so I thought. I was such a little piglet. They passed them right over my head, and I never heard another word. All I knew was that they had shared a snack without me. I waited only until we were in the car to mention it, and as soon as my parents got home, they sat me down and talked to me about belief and salvation through grace.

"So you grew up in a Christian home?"

"Yes. I have three older sisters who all came to the Lord ahead of me and now have Christian husbands."

"That's marvelous," Lloyd spoke up. His hair was fully gray, and although he wasn't related to Adam by blood, he had the same full face and smiling eyes. "Delancey, can you go next?"

"I can, but it might work better if Mackenzie did. She was saved first."

"Do tell, Micki," Roz teased her.

Mackenzie laughed and related how she had thought she had everything and just kept trying to run from the emptiness in her life. She recounted the story of the flat tire and meeting Roz. Remembering it well, Roz was beaming when Mackenzie finished. Mackenzie, on the other hand, was feeling a little tense. What would her sister say when it was her turn? She remained quiet and prayed for her.

Delancey gave a bit of background but swiftly came to the present. "I had spent so many years running from the truth that when Micki came to Christ, I wouldn't speak to her. At the time I was in a relationship, and since I had a boyfriend, I decided I didn't need a sister all that much.

"But then the relationship broke up, and I was devastated. I called Mackenzie. She didn't slam the phone in my ear but came to me in Chicago. She knew she couldn't stay forever, so she found me a church. It was a Friday, but the pastor and his wife were in the foyer of the church; I know God's hand was involved. As though they had all the time in the world, the Carlisles sat down and we talked. Pastor Woody Carlisle brought me to the Lord." Delancey looked at her sister. "It was just a year ago this month." Mackenzie's eyes met Delancey's and they smiled over the sweet memory.

Since Delancey had never heard Roz and Adam's stories, those were shared, and before anyone had noticed, the day had slipped into evening. Leftovers were brought out for the next meal, and the fellowship carried on. By the time the Bishop women left, it was nearly nine o'clock. Dropping her sister at home before going on to Zephyr Cove, Mackenzie was dead-tired but filled with delight over the wonderful friends God had put into her life.

These thoughts were dimmed only when she thought about the future. She had made a decision to go to Kingsbury the following Sunday. At the moment, nothing could rob her of her joy faster. Even knowing she would see Jack and Joanne, her argument with the Lord continued. All of this anxiety occurred before knowing about the huge snowstorm that would hit on Saturday night and make her very glad that she had only a five-minute drive to church.

Mackenzie told herself she was being ridiculous, but it didn't work. She was literally sick to her stomach by the time she got to church on Sunday. And because her nervous stomach sent her into the bathroom several times, she was very late. She told herself to buck up but couldn't stop shaking.

Stomping the snow from her high-heeled boots, she slipped into the door of the church and found the foyer empty of all but one man. He smiled kindly, his hand full of bulletins, and Mackenzie forced herself to walk toward the closed sanctuary doors.

"Good morning," he said softly, handing her a paper.

"Good morning. I'm so late. Is there a place in the back?"

She watched him glance through one of the little windows in the double door. "There is, in the back pew right there. If you find a Bible, just move it."

"Oh, I don't want to take anyone's seat."

"Don't worry about it. I'm sure whoever's there will shift over."

"Okay."

Mackenzie, unaware of how tense she looked, wrung the man's heart. She had a Bible, but he couldn't help but wonder if this was all very new to her. He watched her take a deep breath, like a woman forced to face a firing squad, and walk through the door as he opened it. He hoped she wouldn't see the smile on his face and think him laughing at her.

Mackenzie, mentally kicking herself, could have used a little laughter just then. With one phone call last night or even that morning, Jack would have been waiting for her. *But no, Mackenzie, you had to be sick in the bathroom, and now you're all alone.*

Mackenzie was so preoccupied in her pity-party that she went on autopilot. She got to the pew, which had more room than she thought, scooped up the Bible sitting there, and sat gripping both copies of Scripture as if her life depended on it. They sang one more song before the sermon, but Mackenzie never did let go of the Bibles.

A man stepped to the front, and Mackenzie's attention was riveted to him. Was this Kevin De-Long or Harris Remick? She was still trying to figure it out when the dark-haired man from the foyer came to the end of the pew.

"Is there room?" he said softly, and Mackenzie moved over. There was room to spare.

Her eyes went back to the front, but before she could get too involved, the man leaned close. Mackenzie stiffened before she heard him say, "May I have my Bible?"

Mackenzie glanced into her arms and put a hand over her mouth to smother a sudden laugh. He was laughing as well, his eyes brimming with amusement. She mouthed an apology as she handed him the large black leatherbound volume, and only after she turned to the front did she feel her face heat. It didn't last. The sermon was starting, and as soon as she found out they were in the book of Proverbs, she was captivated. She was finding this book difficult when she tried to study it.

An outline was included with the bulletin, the kind with lots of blanks to fill in, and just like at the Meyers church, she was hearing things she had never even considered, let alone studied. Verses that she'd read briefly took on new meaning as they were explained, and she suddenly found them more relevant to her life than she ever suspected.

"Look at verse 10 of chapter 4," the pastor said. "These are the words of a father to a son, but if you're sitting there today and you're not a son, or you're 75 and your own father is gone, this still applies to you. Catch the depth of these thoughts as I read. I'll emphasize some of the words for you. 'Hear, my son, and accept my sayings, and the years of your life will be many. I have directed you in the way of wisdom; I have led you in the upright paths. When you walk, your steps will not be impeded; and if you *run,* you will not stumble. *Take hold* of my instructions, *do not let go. Guard her,* for she is your life.'

"Are you catching the action words? This father is warning his son to be on guard to grow. Our fathers, either earthly or heavenly, cannot shove wisdom down our throats. We have to be willing, alert, and on our guard to remember what we've heard from them."

Mackenzie closed her eyes for a moment, her thoughts full of regret. *I have been angry at You since Thanksgiving night. I didn't want to come here. I didn't want to obey, and when I did, I did it with the worst attitude. I'm sorry. Please help me to fit in here and reach out. I still want to run and hide. Please calm my fears and help me to let You lead.*

"Why do we choose to disobey?" Mackenzie came back to the sermon to hear those words. "Look at verse 18, and the description of the righteous path, 'like the light of dawn that shines brighter and brighter until the full day.' Isn't morning wonderful? I can tell you that if you were caught in that storm last night, this morning, white as it is, must have looked pretty good. But verse 19 reminds us of what the other path looks like: darkness, and people unable to see what they stumble over, repeating the same sin time and again.

"God has better for us. God has the paths of righteousness for children who listen. I read to you about the path of the wicked: They drink the wine of violence, they can't even sleep unless they do evil. I'll say it again: God has better for you, my dear friends, and it can start today."

Mackenzie watched him bow his head and pray for the very things he had just taught them. He asked God to touch the hearts of the congregation and help them obey and want the righteous path God offered.

Mackenzie opened her eyes and sat there, amazed at all she had learned and how much she had enjoyed the service. The people all around her were moving, and even though she had just asked God to help her reach out to others, she kept her eyes on her Bible and took way too long putting her pen in her purse. She had just stood when Jack's voice spoke from behind.

"Good morning, Mic."

Mackenzie turned and smiled, relief flooding her.

"If we had known today was the day, we would have saved you a place."

"I waited until too late to call you."

"Well, at least you met Tucker."

Mackenzie looked at the man still standing close by. He had moved to the aisle but had not left. Mackenzie looked back at Jack, who smiled as he read her look.

"This is Tucker Stone, Joanne's son. Tucker, this is my daughter, Mackenzie Bishop."

Tucker smiled. "Well now, sitting right next to my sister, and I didn't even know it."

Mackenzie stood in shock when he gave her a huge hug — he was not a small man — but then relaxed when he gave one to Jack as well.

"Where's Mom?" he asked.

"Coming right behind me. I didn't want to miss Micki."

"You didn't tell me she stole Bibles," Tucker said, his brow lowered.

Mackenzie laughed as she had wanted to do during the service.

"I can see you didn't listen to the sermon," Tucker went on, "if you think theft is funny."

"Who's going to fill me in?" Jack asked just as Joanne slipped next to him. He put an arm around her.

After greeting his mother, Tucker told the story, and Mackenzie laughed again at his description. "And you should have seen her face before she lifted my Bible. You would have thought she was headed to the gallows. She took a deep breath and walked through the door as though it was the end of her life."

"I did not," Mackenzie denied, but she still laughed. "I was just nervous about being late, that's all."

"That's all," Tucker mimicked, his eyes wide. "You looked like a ghost with mink-colored hair."

Mackenzie's mouth fell open. "Mink-colored! The mink is related to the weasel!"

Tucker laughed at that, and Mackenzie shook her head in mock disgust. She had never had anyone tease her with so little prior association. She did it often and found it rather interesting to have the table turned.

"Come to lunch," Joanne said when there was a break. "I made a big pot of soup yesterday, and I have a pie from Barbara Ann's."

"I was hoping you'd ask," Tucker wasted no time in saying.

Mackenzie was still on the pie. "Who's Barbara Ann?" she questioned.

"How have you missed the best bakery on the lake?" Tucker asked, looking shocked. "Barbara Ann's Bakery. Her cherry pies have won awards."

"I had no idea I was so deprived," Mackenzie replied drily.

"We're just so thankful that you won't be any longer," Tucker said, his face and tone very grave as he looked at her with pity. Mackenzie told herself not to smile. She could see that it would only encourage him. But it didn't work: She was barely holding her laughter. Tucker's blue eyes were wide with innocence when she turned to Jack and Joanne, a smile still on her face.

"I think I'll run home and change. Will that work?"

"That's fine," Joanne assured her.

"You look very nice though," Jack put in.

Mackenzie pulled a face. "Thank you, but you know me. If I stay dressed up for too long, I get a rash."

Jack laughed because he did remember very well. Jeans and a sweatshirt would be her attire, of that he was certain. And 30 minutes later he saw that he had been right. Mackenzie came through the front door in well-worn jeans, and a navy sweatshirt over a white turtleneck. The colors were wonderful on her, and she looked as good as she had in the red and black plaid skirt, white blouse, and red cardigan that morning.

Joanne had changed as well, so Mackenzie felt right at home. She felt even more at home to walk in and see that the 49ers game had already started. Without even thinking to ask Joanne if she needed help in the kitchen, she sank into a chair, her ski jacket unzipped but still on her back.

"Roughing the kicker," she said softly just moments later. She didn't catch Jack's smile as he watched her, but it was very loving. Tucker caught it and felt something squeeze around his heart. This man who had come into their mother's world had not been someone they had been looking for, but he'd been oh-so-welcome. Jack had walked into their hearts when he talked openly and freely to them about where he had been and what he had done, his wife and stepdaughters included. Jack had not been obsessed with the Bishop sisters, but their names were mentioned from time to time, and his pain was always evident. To find them would have been sweet enough, but to find them and learn that they now shared his faith was like a precious gift from God.

Tucker's eyes swung to Mackenzie. She certainly was pretty, and a good sport in the bargain, but there was something almost vulnerable about her. He could see that she was independent and also what he would call street-smart, but amid the laughter, Tucker saw something he couldn't put his finger on. His mind going back to the game, he told himself it was because she had looked so upset that morning.

"Okay," Joanne called from the edge of the room, "it's all on — soup, sourdough bread, cheese slices, and crackers. Help yourself and sit where you want. And don't forget — pie for dessert."

"I'm sorry I didn't lend a hand, Joanne," Mackenzie apologized, just now remembering to remove her coat.

"It was a very simple meal, Mackenzie, and I never suffer in silence," she smiled. "If I had needed something, I would have hollered."

"Amen to that," Jack teased her. "Nag, nag, nag. The things some men have to put up with."

"I think that just earned you kitchen duty, Jackson Avery," she told him, but he only kissed her before asking everyone to pray with him.

Mackenzie didn't hear much of the prayer. She

727

was still getting over the fact that Jack was back in her life, had a wife he loved, and that they both loved her. It was something of a miracle to her. She spent most of the afternoon with Jack, Joanne, and Tucker, and sat with them in church that evening. By the time she crawled into bed that night, all she could say to the Lord was *How could I have doubted that You would take care of me?*

"Well now," Jack said softly as he climbed into bed that night, "what's this about?"

Joanne tried to stop the tears, and she did, but it took a few moments. Jack waited, his elbow on his pillow, his head propped in his hand to look down at her. It was so clear to him now. Marrell had said she never dreamed that she could love two men, but she did. She loved Paul Bishop and she loved Jackson Avery. Jack now understood. He would never forget Marrell, and at times his heart still missed her, but this woman, so different from his first wife, yet so special, warm, and loving, filled his heart completely.

"Have I done something?"

"No," she replied as she moved her dark head against the pillow and used the flannel sheet to dry her eyes. "I'm thinking about Mackenzie. I just love her, Jack. She's so special. But why does it break my heart when she drives off alone in her Jeep? She doesn't act lonely or ever make comments, but I didn't like being alone all those years, and so I naturally think she's lonely too."

Jack kissed her.

"You do have a tender heart, especially in that area."

"I know I do." She sounded disgusted with herself. "You didn't want anyone until you met

Marrell, so why do I have to have everyone paired off?"

"Because you're so social. But I think what you feel for Mackenzie goes deeper than that. She's a very bright, talented woman, and when she makes the effort, she interacts well with people. It's very hard to see that type of woman living her life without someone special to share it."

"I don't know how much she'll talk to me, Jack. And she doesn't need to talk to me — it could be anyone — but I want to take care of her. The girls and I had a great time at lunch the other day, but Mackenzie is more reserved than Delancey, and I know she's already shared things with you." Joanne paused, feeling that she was making a mess of this. "Just keep a close eye on her for me, all right?"

"I will. Be encouraged by how well she did today."

"It was fun to have her here."

"She is fun, and she seemed to enjoy Tucker." Jack thought a minute. "Why do you never ache to have Tucker marry?"

"I do," Joanne admitted, "but not as much. I wonder how much he still thinks about Celia, and I know from experience that until he's over her, he won't even see other women. And on top of that, he doesn't need anyone, Jack. He's very content with his work, and he's grown in the Lord so much in the last few years. I wouldn't be surprised if he never married."

"And you're okay with that?"

"Yes, I am. Probably because he doesn't seem vulnerable. Micki does."

She had given Jack much to think about. He wondered if it might help her to know how successful Mackenzie was as a writer but then put the thought away. He would not tell. Mackenzie had not told him he couldn't talk to Joanne, but his new wife was not a naturally curious person, and although they spoke of the fact that Mackenzie had a very private area in her life, Joanne had told him she didn't need to know about it. Both had felt a peace about the way they left it.

"How are you?"

"Hi, D.J.," Mackenzie smiled. "I'm fine."

"I thought about you nonstop yesterday and even tried to phone you in the afternoon."

"I was at Jack and Joanne's. I even met Joanne's son, Tucker."

"What's he like?"

"Funny, a terrible tease, but nice, just like Joanne."

"And the services. How did they go?"

"Wonderful. In the morning we were in Proverbs, and in the evening we discussed the roles of women in the church. It's a lot of food in one day, Deej, but I learned so much. Did you miss me?"

"I admit that I did, but Richard sat with me. I tell you, Mic, he's one of the nicest guys I've ever known."

"Isn't he sweet? He's so unassuming and gentle. Kind of a gentle giant."

"I'll have to tell him you said that. He'll laugh."

"Did you get notes for me on the dating series?"

"Yes. I'll fax them to you every Monday until the series is over."

"Good. I hate to leave that study on Sunday nights."

"Hey, before I forget . . ." Delancey interjected,

730

and the talk turned to business. She'd had a call from Tom Magy that morning, and he had been very disappointed that the women were turning to other things. He talked to Delancey for a long time about publishing Jungle Buds with them. Delancey told him she would fax him a few pages but knew that he wouldn't want anything with such a strong biblical emphasis.

"I hope I didn't overstep myself, but I laid it on the line to him."

"It's more than that, D.J. Even if IronHorse puts it under its inspirational line, I think it might lose something coming from a company whose books are mostly in the general market. Even if Tom wants it, I think I'd like to keep pursuing Christian publishers."

"I agree. I've already told myself not to feel guilty. I may do another Micah Bear someday — who knows?"

"Sure. By the way, if someone publishes this series and the first five or six books do well, I'd like to highlight each character in future books. I can even see the covers, just from the work you've done so far."

"What would their stories be?"

"I would like to tell how all of them came to Christ. Maybe the stories wouldn't be diverse enough to do each one, but I'd like to give it a try."

"Oh, I can't wait to see what you come up with. By the way," Delancey continued in a voice dropped low out of habit, "how is *The Parchment Soldier* coming?"

"Good. Sometime after the first of the year, maybe February or March, I'm going to go back to Colorado. The end is turning just a little bit romantic, and that part takes place at Beaver Creek. Wanna come?"

"Like I would pass up skiing in Colorado?"

Mackenzie laughed. "We'll plan on it."

Delancey said she had work to do and rang off just after that, but Mackenzie's mind was still on the snow in Colorado. Right out her windows was a land so capped with snow that the trees were barely green. Roz had a cold and wasn't coming to clean that morning. She could take a few hours off and ski right now, right here. That was all the convincing she needed. Twenty minutes later she was headed to Heavenly Valley, but she forced herself to make it brief and was back before noon and settled in at the computer.

Delancey went to minichurch at the Davis home each Wednesday night. The Cummings were regulars, and Richard Wilder had recently started to attend. They were studying a book on the holiness of God, and Delancey was enjoying it, but tonight she was preoccupied. They didn't always take time for prayer requests, but tonight Pastor Dave, who led their study, wanted to spend most of the time in prayer. They went around the room praying for the nation's leaders, the local government, and their own evangelistic outreach, but then he asked for requests from the group. He and Delancey had had a few minutes alone before they started, and she had shared something with him. He turned to her immediately and asked her to start things.

"I think you all know that Mackenzie and I write children's books together." A little embarrassed to be the center of attention, she spoke softly before her eyes scanned the room and found everyone listening. It would have been easier if they hadn't been attending so closely, but Richard's kind face, along with the small smile Rachel Brinker gave her, helped her to go on. "The books have been successful, but we started all of that before we came to Christ, and we'd really like to do something with a biblical emphasis.

"Our stepfather has seen what we've got so far, and he's encouraged us, but lately I'm trying to do God's job." She made a little face and everyone smiled. "I find myself saying things to the Lord like, 'This is for You; of course You'll bring us a publisher.' I know that's not true — I mean, I don't know what God has for us, and I'm starting to obsess about it. I think this talent that Mackenzie and I have is from the Lord, but I keep taking it back and telling Him how I want things to be. I would like your prayers, so that I would get rid of the emotions and be willing for whatever God has."

"Okay. Thank you, Delancey," Pastor Dave nodded as he wrote. "Anyone else?"

Someone else immediately spoke up, and Delancey was pleased to be finished. She had started to feel emotional at the end, even as she was asking for prayer to conquer that very thing, and knew that if someone had questioned her, she might have broken down. It was good to go back to prayer a few minutes later and focus her mind on the other needs and concerns of the group.

It took quite awhile for everyone to share and pray. They ran overtime, and parents with children had to leave swiftly to pick up the kids in junior and senior youth groups held at the church. Others weren't in such a hurry, however, and Delancey suddenly looked up to see Richard and Pastor

Dave both coming from the kitchen area toward her.

"Delancey, I hope you don't mind, but I asked Richard to share something with you."

"Oh, of course not," Delancey said, staying in her seat while they took chairs close by.

"I thought of him when you shared with the group tonight. He's been in the same situation."

Delancey's eyes swung to the tall man on the sofa beside her chair, and for a moment she was distracted by how good he looked in glasses.

"I came to the dental office here in Meyers about two years ago as a junior partner. I had no more than arrived when they decided to extend the office hours. The one night some of the partners wanted to stay open late was Wednesday night. Others of us wanted it to be Thursday. I wasn't worried, though. After all, God wouldn't want me to miss church. I was convinced it would be voted down. It wasn't. With a month's notice I was being booked with Wednesday night patients.

"I was so angry at first that I considered leaving, but God kept reminding me that He's sovereign. At first I said, 'If You're sovereign, then how come I'm working on Wednesday nights instead of having fellowship?' I knew that attitude was wrong, however, and I started to ask myself questions about who God is and what kind of authority He has. I discovered that He can ask me to do anything, and I need to be swift to say yes. I began to do that and to praise Him for my job, even on Wednesday nights. Now, almost 18 months later, we've changed things around again, and my late night is Tuesday."

Delancey smiled at him but looked a bit lost. Seeing her face, Richard's heart broke. He

734

couldn't remember the last time he wanted to take someone in his arms and just hold her.

"It's hard, isn't it?" His voice was as tender as his feelings, and Delancey nodded. She took a deep breath and tried to quell her emotions.

"I can't stop thinking about it. I mean, we haven't even pursued it that much, but I've decided how it should be. I think God must be sick to death of me talking about it."

"No, He isn't," Dave spoke up. "You need to think about who God is when you look at this issue, Delancey — not be clouded with what you want. God may want you to stop thinking about it all the time, especially since it sounds as though you're worrying to God, not praying to Him. But never think that He's tired of you, Delancey. Don't stop giving Him a chance to show you how much He has in store for you."

Delancey thanked both Dave and Richard and thought on their words for a long time that night and in the days to follow. She would have done just as Richard had in his place, assuming that God wanted her in minichurch. The other thing that struck her was Dave's comment about worrying to God. She was definitely doing that, and she didn't have to ponder long to know it.

In the weeks that followed, the worry did not simply disappear, but she got a letter of encouragement from the Carlisles in Chicago and also started to read her Bible every time she felt herself telling God what to do. The joy and peace she knew in that time was indescribable. So new in the Lord the year before, Delancey was headed into a Christmas the likes of which she would never forget.

FORTY-TWO

The Saturday before Christmas, Richard called Delancey. She was up but still trying to get herself going. It was for this reason that she had a hard time convincing Richard that he had not awakened her.

"No, you didn't. I just haven't talked to anyone today."

"I didn't wake you?"

"No." Her voice croaked a little. "I've been awake for about 15 minutes."

"Well, I'm still not convinced that I didn't blow it, and here I'm calling to ask you a favor."

"Oh, what is it?"

"Can you meet me at Mountain Mocha or, better yet, the cafe next to my office?"

"That depends on whether you want to meet this morning or this afternoon."

"Since I'm the one asking the favor, you tell me. If it won't work at all, I'll catch you another time."

Delancey looked at the clock. "If I can meet you in 45 minutes or so, I'll have an hour. Will that work?"

"Yes. That will be plenty of time."

"Okay. I'll see you then. The cafe or Mountain Mocha?"

"Come to the cafe, and I'll buy you breakfast."

"Oh, in that case, I'll only be a half an hour."

"Okay. I'll see you there."

Delancey was on time, but Richard was running a little late. She ordered coffee, smiled at a group of children who appeared to be sitting with their grandfather, and wished she had asked Richard what he wanted. It might have given her more time to think about saying yes or no. She was still trying to figure it out when he walked in.

"I'm sorry," he apologized as he slid into the booth, her portfolio going to the table. "The phone rang as I was headed out the door. My sister called from Washington, and we don't get to talk that often."

"The state or D.C.?"

"Washington State. All the kids have colds, and she's just glad that school let out yesterday so they can recuperate on Friday before Christmas."

"How many nieces and nephews do you have?"

"Ten."

"Ten! Oh how fun. How many girls and boys?"

While Richard was giving her a rundown, she had a sudden thought. That it was none of her business didn't occur to her until he had stopped talking and she had asked him.

"Richard, why have you never married?"

"Oh, I plan on it," he said with a smile. "I plan on it."

The change in Delancey's face was startling. Richard had been stirring his coffee but stopped when he looked up and read the panic in her eyes. He was opening his mouth to question her when she spoke in a strangled little voice.

"Richard, if you have a fiancee, why do you never speak of her?"

Richard's mouth dropped open. "I don't,

737

Delancey," he said softly. "I, um, that is, I mean, I said that all wrong. I just meant that I have peace about being married someday. I think God has that for me, and I plan on it because I think He'll give me the perfect woman."

Delancey was so humiliated that she could have died. She stared at him in mortification before shifting in the booth so that her gaze went out the window.

"What can I get you, Doc Wilder?" the cafe's regular waitress asked as she came up, her smile accommodating.

Richard only glanced at Delancey before saying, "I think we'll both have the special, Mary."

"Okay. How do you want your eggs?"

"Scrambled."

"And the meat?"

"Ham."

"How about some juice?"

"Yes, orange juice, please."

"Okay. Coming right up."

It was all the time Delancey needed. She turned back and made herself face the man across the booth. Her face was pale, but her voice was calm.

"I'm sorry, Richard. I had no business asking you that. I'm very humiliated, and I hope you'll forgive me."

"There's nothing to forgive. I can see how you could have misunderstood me. I need to be more careful and not so arrogant with the way I say things."

He was so sweet that Delancey wanted to slip over to his bench and lay her head on his shoulder. She came so close to admitting that to him that when she caught herself, she sat up a little bit straighter, and took a sip of her coffee.

"This man," Richard started softly, desperate to understand, "this man that you talked about in your testimony, Delancey — he hurt you, didn't he?"

Delancey nodded, somewhat glad that he remembered and understood her behavior.

"We went together for a long time. I was ready to marry him, but I found out he was already married and had been the whole time."

Richard had to work to keep the anger from his face. How could anyone treat her like that?

"How did you find out?" he asked to keep his mind moving.

"He's a pilot, and I went to the airport to meet his plane. I'd never done that before, but before I could show myself, he'd taken another, very pregnant, woman into his arms. Their little girl was with her. To say the least I was devastated, but that led me to Christ, and for that reason alone, it was worth it."

Richard could see that she meant every word. "That's incredible, Delancey. What a wonderful testimony you'll be to your own children someday."

"I won't be marrying," she said simply, her face neither resigned nor upset.

Mary chose that moment to bring their plates. Delancey laughed at what she got.

"You have good taste. Thank you."

"Actually, I wasn't sure what it was either," Richard admitted. "I just ordered the special."

Delancey smiled at him before he prayed. Richard kept the prayer brief and let Delancey start her food, but he was not about to abandon the subject.

"Why don't you think you'll ever marry?"

"It's a little hard to explain because it comes out sounding as though I don't care about his wife, but the more I've thought about it over the months, the more I see that I was in great sin long before I found out he was married. That was awful, as you can well imagine, but I knew I was too intimately involved with this man, Richard. I knew it very clearly, but I didn't care and kept on."

"And you don't think God can forgive that?"

"Oh, I know He can and has, but I don't expect another man to put up with that. Why should he?" She shrugged a little. "There are consequences to sin, Richard, and sometimes we have to live with them."

"But what if a man came along —" he began, but Delancey was already shaking her head, so he fell quiet.

"I couldn't stand that," she said softly. "I might start to like him, and then the time would come when I would have to tell him what I really am — second-hand goods." She shook her head a little and picked up a piece of toast. "When I think of him looking at me in revulsion, I just want to be sick. I don't want to put myself through that, Richard. And I don't think God would ask it of me."

Richard was at a complete loss for words. He didn't think that Delancey noticed, at least he hoped not, and he thought himself rescued when she spotted the portfolio he had laid beside him when the food came.

"Oh, Richard, did you want to meet with me to return the artwork?"

"I almost forgot." He reached for the folder. "I wanted to ask you if I could use these drawings again. My parents' fortieth wedding anniversary is in February, and I'd like to try to do the same type of invitation for them. I'd be willing to pay you, Delancey. Or if you don't want them used again at all, just say the word."

"I think it's wonderful. Can I do some more for you, or will those work?"

"These are perfect. I'm going to use them differently this time, but I shouldn't need any more."

"Have at it. I hope they like it. Where did you say they lived?"

"Santa Rosa."

"Oh, I know Santa Rosa. We used to have some friends who lived in Sebastopol."

"I grew up in Sebastopol. My parents only moved to Santa Rosa a few years ago."

"Did you ever go to Lacys' Apple Orchard?"

"The Lacys went to our church. I've known them for years."

Delancey's mouth opened, and Richard laughed. She went on to explain the connection with Shay, her mother, and Oliver. In the process, the time got away.

"I'm so sorry to eat and run, but I'm meeting some of the women from Bible study, and we're doing a little shopping for Christmas decorations for the church. I'm sorry. Thank you for breakfast."

"You're welcome. Thank you for the artwork. I'll get it back to you sometime after the first of the year."

"Okay. I'll see you tomorrow."

Richard watched her dash out, her straight blond hair pushed behind her ears and curved against her neck. He left a tip, paid the bill, went to his car, and automatically drove home, but he got no farther than the garage. He shut off the car and put the door down but sat staring through the front windshield.

You never promised life would be easy, Lord, his heart prayed. *I think she's the one. I think You put her in my life to keep, but she doesn't have a clue.*

Richard let his head fall back against the seat. *She thinks she's second-hand goods, Lord.* He felt his throat close just at the thought. *I will never think of her that way, Father. I will never see her in that light. I wish she had saved herself for me, for us. I wish she had honored her body before You, but I will never throw it in her face or make her feel unforgiven. If I'm wrong, Lord, and You don't want us to be together, then I pray that You'll bring another man along to show Delancey she's wrong. You've forgiven her, Lord, and she can have a husband and children. Please help her to see that Father, and give me the patience and tenderness I need to be her friend, even if I can never be her husband.*

All Jasmine Stone could do was cry. "It's the baby," she explained, gesturing toward her extended waist. "Pregnancy always does this to me, and now to have you here — Jack's daughters — I just can't stand it."

Her husband, Matthew, seated beside her on the sofa, put an arm around her and smiled. Perched on the sofa arm by his brother, Tucker spoke to the Bishop sisters.

"You'd be surprised at what a normal person she really is. None of the tears or that weird twitch in her cheek. She even —"

Tucker cut off when Jasmine hit him in the stomach with a sofa pillow.

"Learn her technique," Andy Phillips said. "It's handy where Tucker is concerned."

The Bishop women smiled at him and then at Tucker, who was clearly the family clown.

"I don't know why I'm always picked on," he protested, but then 15-month-old Caleb Phillips waddled his way into the room and stole the show. He had a book and put it on the first lap he came to. The lucky person was Delancey.

"Shall we read this?" she asked, lifting him carefully into her arms. He looked up into the strange face for just a moment, but then Delancey opened the book and his eyes went downward.

For a few moments everyone in the room watched. Her touch was so gentle and her voice so soft. Even Mackenzie thought it was the sweetest thing she'd ever seen. The reading went well until the story had the word "mommy" in it. Caleb looked up, found Gemma, made a noise, and moved to climb from Delancey's lap. She let him go. He made a beeline for his mother and sat looking back at Delancey.

"Don't you want to finish the book?" Delancey asked, smiling at him, but he lay back against his mother, happy where he was.

"My loss," Delancey said softly, still smiling.

"Just wait until about eight o'clock tonight, Delancey," Gemma comforted her, "when Ashley has played with cousins all day. She'll be looking for any lap she can find."

"That goes for Logan and Brady too," Matthew added. "By the way, where are they?"

"I think they're still burying Jack in the snow."

"The man must be frozen," Andy put in. "I'd better go rescue him."

"I'll come with you," Matthew offered.

Mackenzie listened to all of this in amazement. They were so warm and open, and they loved and accepted her and Delancey just as if they actually were Jack's daughters. The last time she had been in a large family setting had been in Florida. It had been a long time ago, but she would never mistake the two families. She had called her grandmother about nine months after her conversion, but there had been no answer. She reminded herself to call again.

"I was hoping to get you two alone for a few minutes," Tucker said suddenly as he pulled a chair close to Delancey and Mackenzie. And indeed he was right, the room had momentarily emptied. "Can we talk a little business?"

"Sure," Mackenzie answered but had no idea what he was talking about.

"Great. Jack showed me your Jungle Buds book, and I think it looks fabulous. I've got a call into —" He saw their faces and came to an awkward halt. Any number of joking remarks came to mind about the way they stared at him, but he could see that the timing was all wrong.

"I've done something wrong — I can see that — but I have to be honest with you," he said, putting his hands out, "I don't know what."

Delancey answered. "We don't like to take advantage, Tucker. We knew you were a freelance editor, but Jackson never told us that he was going to check with you about Jungle Buds. We would have told him no."

"May I ask why, Delancey?"

"Yes. For one thing, you have better things to do than take your valuable time finding us a publisher, and secondly, we're either good enough to do this or we're not."

Tucker nodded in understanding. "I appreciate your sensitivity on my behalf, but I'm not acting

744

as agent for you. I do have close contact with three different publishers, none of whom would thank me for not telling them when I've seen someone's work that needs their attention. That brings us to your second point. Being introduced by me won't gain you anything if the work isn't good, so rest assured on that."

There was still no comment from either woman, and he was reminded that when the subject was the publishing world, these women knew their way around the block, at least in the ABA market, the general market.

"We don't mean to be rude, Tucker," Mackenzie spoke up, "or unthankful. As a point of fact, the only reason Micah Bear was published is because I had a friend in the business. We are new to the Christian market." She shook her head. "*New* isn't the word — we don't exist in the Christian Booksellers Association market, so we're still trying to feel our way. Maybe if you tell us what you have in mind, it will clear the air."

"Well, first of all, Jack didn't tell me that you didn't want anything done, so I already have a call in to two publishers." He watched as Delancey looked at Mackenzie, but that woman never took her eyes from him. It crossed his mind that she would be very good at poker or across the desk negotiating a book contract. He suddenly wondered if she might not be in the wrong business. As an agent she would be impressive.

Tucker reined in his wayward thoughts, still thinking he would have given much to know what was on her mind, but as it was, they weren't even able to finish the conversation. Jack came in from the yard, proclaiming that he was frozen through, and almost on his heels were the children and

745

their only half-frozen fathers. By the time people dried out and warmed up, it was time to put dinner together. And after that the fun began: the Christmas story, traditionally read by Matthew, and gift opening around the tree in the living room.

Not for the first time in her life, Mackenzie found herself very thankful that her sister loved to shop and had fabulous taste. Jack's stepdaughters had brought gifts for everyone, and since Delancey had made the selections, they were all appropriate. They gave Jack and Joanne matching cable-knit sweaters in a deep hunter green, toys in just the right age group to each of the children, and small hampers of fruit, cheese, and chocolates to the other adults. Mackenzie had footed most of the bill, which she was more than happy to do since Delancey had done all the footwork.

As for the Bishop sisters themselves, they made out like bandits. Jack and Joanne gave them both Lake Tahoe sweatshirts; the Matthew Stone family gave Mackenzie a beautifully engraved pen and Delancey a leatherbound sketchbook; Gemma and Andy added Lake Tahoe desk calendars for the new year; and Tucker bought them new ski mittens.

The Micah Bear books that Jack had bought for the children were brought forth and, with Mackenzie's new pen, duly autographed. The adults were more impressed than the children, although Brady, Logan, and Ashley all thanked them. By then it was quite late, so the children were carted off to bed, all clutching some cherished new toy.

Just to prove to herself she could do it, Mackenzie helped Joanne make cocoa and popcorn and only burned one bag in the microwave. In the midst of the preparations, one of the grandchildren wanted Joanne, so Mackenzie was left on her own. She continued to pull mugs from the cupboard until she realized she had twice as many as she needed. Preoccupied with counting how many adults were left, she didn't catch the teapot until it whistled good and loud for several seconds.

Joanne had left marshmallows out for the cocoa, and after the teapot was calm, Mackenzie attempted to put them in a bowl. Some rolled onto the floor before Mackenzie could stop them. She heard a chuckle and looked up to find Jack watching her.

"Still as competent in the kitchen as you always were."

Mackenzie shook her head. "Why is it that some people can do this so normally, Jackson, and I'm all thumbs?"

"Those little cream cheese and pickle things you brought were good."

"That's because I threatened Delancey with bodily harm if she didn't give me a fool-proof recipe. A two-year-old could have made them."

Jack smiled but didn't comment. He pitched in and helped her put the rest of the snack together. They were still working along quietly when Mackenzie said, "My mother was always a little bit off when it came to cooking, and two very different men loved her."

It took a moment for Mackenzie to hear what she had said. Her eyes went to Jack, who was again watching her.

"I don't know why I said that. I'm not even looking to get married."

"Maybe you should be."

"So I can poison him in the first year?"

But Jack didn't laugh or even smile. "How lonely are you, Mackenzie?"

He watched her sigh.

"Right now, not at all, and most of the time, not at all, but when it hits, it hits hard."

"Do you believe God can bring someone into your life?"

Mackenzie bit her lip. "I'm not sure that I do. I'm not even sure I've ever thought of it."

"Is there a little fear involved?"

Mackenzie looked down at the table. "I think there is. To love with that kind of intensity puts a person in a very vulnerable position." Mackenzie looked up. "But then you would know that better than anyone."

"Yes, and I chose to marry again — take the risk, if you will. And do you know why? Because even if I have Joanne for only a short while, it will be worth it. My life has been richer and my world a bigger place because of her."

The words were no more out of his mouth than Joanne walked back in.

"How's it going?"

"We were just talking about you," Jack informed her.

"And well you should! I left Mackenzie here to work all alone. She'll never want to come back."

Joanne smiled at her and started to load the tray for the living room. Mackenzie pitched in to help her, but her mind was still on Jack's words. It occurred to her suddenly that they really hadn't needed to give her a Christmas gift; seeing their love and being included in their family was more gift than she could ever hope for.

The Top of the Tram restaurant at Heavenly Valley was packed the next day, but the family still managed to get a table. A babysitter had been called in so that Jasmine could shop and the rest could ski. Delancey had not been aware of the family tradition of skiing the day after Christmas, but it was something she would never have missed. They had hit the slopes early and were now ready for some lunch.

Family surrounding him, Tucker was in his element. He and Matthew had started on college roommates and had the whole family laughing until they cried.

"Mom'll remember this one," Tucker kept on. "I had this roommate named Christian. We called him Chrish." Tucker smiled when Joanne started to laugh. "I have never met anyone like Chrish's mom. She was an incredible practical joker. I went home with him to San Diego one time, and as soon as we got there, Chrish asked his mom if she had been behaving herself. I thought it was kinda weird but then didn't give it too much thought.

"The next morning, I go to use the bathroom. I'm kinda groggy and out of it, but I'm getting ready to take care of things when this voice — I know it came right out of the toilet — yells at me, 'Don't do that, I'm working down here!' "

The table dissolved into laughter, but Tucker did not let up.

"I didn't go to the bathroom for the rest of the weekend. I was even afraid to use the bathroom when we got back to school."

Gemma was begging him to stop, and Delancey

had tears streaming down her face.

"Did that really happen?" Mackenzie demanded, having just found her breath.

"Yes. It was some little mechanical box that sounded off whenever the seat was moved. Chrish told me his grandmother nearly collapsed when his mom used it on her. And his mom had more little gadgets. In Chrish's closet she had put a fake owl whose eyes lit up before he hooted at you. Chrish was completely nonplused, but I nearly had a heart attack with that one."

"And this went on all the time?" Jack asked.

"Yeah. He'd been away at school for the first time and that gave her all kinds of time to find new pranks for him. I guess she's always been that way, so Chrish took it in stride, but I'll never forget her smile when I shot out of that bathroom as if my pants were on fire."

"Something tells me you deserved anything you got, Tuck," Matthew told him. "If I recall, you pulled a few in those days."

Tucker managed to look innocent, but no one was convinced.

"You cried your eyes down your cheeks, Deej," Mackenzie told her.

"Did I? I'd better head to the bathroom. Don't tell any more before I get back, Tucker."

Delancey had no more excused herself, weaving her way through the tables, when a table full of men stopped her. The family couldn't hear what was being said, and Delancey moved on after just a few words, but for some reason they all looked to Mackenzie.

"Do you know them?"

"No." Her face was calm. "But men have always been attracted to Delancey's looks, and in the

750

process some forget their manners. She's never rude to them, but I could tell she kept it pretty short."

"And how often does it happen to you?" Gemma asked in all honesty. She found Delancey beautiful but didn't think any man could resist Mackenzie's dark hair, fascinating eyes, and straight-talking manner. She was remarkably gutsy, as Gemma had witnessed on the slopes, and Tucker's sister was captivated by her.

"I don't think it ever has," Mackenzie said. "D.J. and I have talked about it. She's more approachable. I tend to stand back a little. I don't mean to — it's not anything I plan on — but I'm just not as sociable."

"Until you get to know someone," her stepfather added.

"True. Then you have to tell me to put a sock in it."

"And I think the funniest part," Jack continued, "is that Delancey is the one who could do someone real harm."

Mackenzie laughed. "Yes, she could. Because of my Army training, I can protect myself, but Delancey could do major damage."

Delancey was coming back to the table then, and the family all watched as male eyes followed her every move. For some reason, Tucker's eyes were drawn to Mackenzie. She sounded as though she took her sister's attention in stride, but he wondered if it didn't hurt a little. He let the matter drop when he watched the two sisters smile at each other, not an ounce of malice or jealousy between them.

"Are they ever bringing the food?" Joanne asked suddenly, her stomach growling. The table erupted with laughter again when the orders arrived just moments later.

FORTY-THREE

"How was your Christmas?" Richard asked Delancey when he saw her the following Wednesday night.

Delancey smiled with remembrance. "It was so nice. Our stepfather is married to Joanne Stone."

"I think I met them at the O'Haras' twenty-fifth."

"That's right, you did. Joanne's family is so special. They just took Mackenzie and me in."

"Good. You look as though you got a little skiing in."

"Yes," Delancey responded, her hand moving to her peeling nose. "We skied the day after Christmas with Jack and Joanne and everyone, and then Mackenzie and I went yesterday." She smiled up at him. He wasn't a lot taller when they were sitting, but he was still above her. "How was your Christmas, Richard?"

"Great. It's hard to be out of the snow, but everyone came here last year, so we went to the folks' house this year. My great grandmother was there as well. She's 96."

"Oh my. How is she doing?"

"Very well. Not so strong physically, but she hasn't lost anything upstairs. She took me on in chess and almost beat me."

Delancey laughed, and Richard reached into his Bible and pulled out a piece of paper.

"Before I forget, I want to give you this. I hope you won't find me presumptuous, but after our last conversation I did some studying and wrote out a few notes. You can read it or throw it away; it's up to you."

"I'm glad you mentioned our last meeting, Richard." Delancey's expression was contrite. "I want to apologize for that morning. I argued with everything you said, and I'm sorry."

"Delancey, I didn't take it that way. I was asking you some very personal questions, and you didn't seem defensive to me at all. If you were out of line, you kept it very well hidden."

She nodded. "Thank you for this," she said as she tucked the envelope in her Bible. "I will read it and get back to you."

"You don't even have to do that. I just wanted you to have some verses to think about."

"Thanks, Richard."

Pastor Dave was ready to start things, so they fell quiet. He started by telling the group about a man he had encountered that week. His wife, Rachel, sitting right beside him, had heard the story right after it happened, but her reason for not paying attention to his story stemmed from something else. She was too busy asking God to help Delancey Bishop see what Richard Wilder kept so carefully hidden. She felt relieved when her husband asked her to go to the piano and play the hymn they wanted to sing.

Are you part of a minichurch?

Those had been Jack's words to Mackenzie just two days earlier when he had asked her to join

754

him for lunch. Now, on the first Wednesday of 1993, she stood outside the home of strangers and told herself to grow up and go inside.

One of our minichurches meets right around the corner from your house. I think you should go.

More of Jack's words came back to mind. Mackenzie had known for some weeks that it was time to get more involved. She had spoken with both Adam and Jack about staying in Roz's Bible study, since the study on Mark was so exciting to her, and they felt it was a good idea. But staying home on Wednesday nights was no longer an option. Because minichurches were more than Bible studies or prayer meetings, they were small congregations of believers, she needed to be involved in one from Kingsbury.

Several cars were parked in front of the house, but it didn't look like it would be too crowded. She was wrong. Eighteen people were in the Bradfords' spacious living room. To a person they smiled and greeted her, but if she hadn't seen Tucker's familiar face, she might have turned and run. He was even sliding over on the sofa to make room for her. He beckoned with one hand, and Mackenzie slipped in beside him.

"Welcome, Mackenzie," Titus Johansen, the elder in charge, greeted her.

"Thank you."

"You'll all have to introduce yourself to Mackenzie Bishop. She's been going to the Meyers church, but she lives closer to Kingsbury and is coming here now. I have an extra book, Mackenzie, but I don't have it with me. I'll get it to you this Sunday. Maybe for tonight you can share with someone."

"Okay."

"You have that ghosty-mink look again," Tucker leaned over and whispered. Mackenzie's eyes brimmed with amusement as she turned her head to look at him. She didn't know how he managed to look angelic when he was being so outrageous.

"Don't worry," he finished. "There's nothing to be afraid of. We don't make you bite the head off of a live chicken until the second time you attend."

Mackenzie could have hit him. The last thing she wanted to do in front of all these strangers was burst out laughing. Had she but known it, she could have laughed. The group, Tucker's regular minichurch, knew that he had that effect on people. She was glad when it was time to open with a song from the chorus book. By the time they finished, she had her laughter under control.

Mackenzie enjoyed the evening, although the study — she had come in in the middle of Genesis — proved to be a bit difficult at times. She thought it might help to get the study guide Titus had mentioned. The group itself, however, was very encouraging. There was a diverse group of ages, and a good mix of men, women, couples, and singles. Many people spoke with her, some of whom she did not know, and all generally made her feel welcome. Luke and Megan Bradford were very gracious, seeing her to the front door and even warning her that they were planning a minichurch party at the end of the month.

"We have something special every other month and usually try to include the children and any guests people want to invite. This time it's a sledding party to Camp Sacramento and then to the church to thaw out and eat."

"Sounds fun." Mackenzie loved anything with snow.

"We'll be talking about the details in the weeks to come, but if you miss anything, just give me a call. We're in the church directory."

"Thank you, Megan. I had a wonderful time."

"I'm so glad, Mackenzie. We'll see you Sunday."

"Okay. Goodnight."

Mackenzie was only a few steps out the door when it opened again. She didn't turn, feeling that it wasn't her business to know who was leaving, so she was already on the street when Tucker said, "Where's your Jeep, Mackenzie?"

Mackenzie turned. "I walked. I live just around the corner."

"I'll give you a ride."

"It's just around the corner," she repeated.

"It's dark out, Mackenzie. Humor me."

Mackenzie came back to where he was standing and climbed in when he opened the door of a small gray four-door.

"Around which corner?" he asked as the engine came to life.

"Behind us and then to the left."

"Okay. So how did you like it?" he asked as he turned around in the Bradfords' driveway.

"I liked it a lot. Titus has some real insight. I wish I'd been there when you got started."

"Well, don't hesitate to ask questions if something doesn't make sense to you. If you stay quiet, it's going to only get worse as we move on. How far down, by the way?"

"To the end. We're almost there, five more houses."

Tucker slowed as they neared. "Left or right?"

"On the right."

Tucker pulled up to the last house on the street, sure he had misunderstood, but Mackenzie's hand was on the door handle. Tucker bent down some to see out Mackenzie's side.

"*This* is where you live?" he asked, his mouth hanging open.

Mackenzie smiled at his look, took her closed fist, and pushed his jaw up until his mouth closed.

"Better keep that shut, Tuck, something might get in. Thanks for the ride. Goodnight."

He never said a word. In silence he watched her get out, go to the door, open it, wave to him, and disappear inside. Tucker pulled his car around at a snail's pace, now able to see from his own window. He drove away very slowly.

Inside, Mackenzie leaned on the front door and laughed. She knew he might ask questions that she would have to field, but his face made it worthwhile. She didn't think that Tucker Stone was speechless very often. She was still chuckling when she locked the front door, climbed the stairs to her office loft, sat down at her desk, and turned to the verses they had studied that night.

They had been in chapter 20. Mackenzie read it over again, amazed at the unrest. *Why did I think things were a little more peaceful in those early times?* she asked the Lord. *I've known for years that sin came into the world in the first few chapters of Genesis, but things went down hill so swiftly. I can't believe Abraham would do such a thing to his wife.*

Mackenzie's opinions on the matter weren't quite so strong when she read ahead to chapter 21 and learned of Sarah's attitude and actions toward Hagar. She sat back in her desk chair and thought about man's sin. It was all-encompassing.

No one escaped it.

It's more amazing that You would forgive us at all, Mackenzie said softly to the Lord, her throat closing a little. *I don't know if I've thanked You today for what you did, and I'm sorry. Already I take it for granted. Thank You, Lord for dying for me. Thank you for snatching me off the destructive path I was on.*

Mackenzie reached for the light on her desk, shut it off, and walked to the windows. With no light behind her she could see the lake, even though the moon was a sliver. Lights shown from her neighbor's house, and far across the surface of the water, nestled in the trees and hills beyond, she could see tiny flickers of lights.

How many people who live on this lake know You created it and that You died for their sins? How many have I tried to tell? Mackenzie didn't have to search very hard to know that answer. When she had first moved there, she didn't care, and now for the last year and four months she had been so self-absorbed that she hadn't even seen them. She didn't even know the neighbors' names.

It's time for things to change, Mackenzie told herself as she headed to bed. Her only regret was that she hadn't started a long time ago.

It was past the middle of January before Delancey had a chance to study the verses Richard had given her. They all spoke of God's forgiveness, and light was beginning to peek through very slowly. She had agreed with Richard that God had forgiven her but not that she could go on with her life. *What kind of forgiveness is that?* she ended up asking herself and finally seeing what he meant.

759

Understanding this, however, did not immediately solve the problem of the man himself, whoever he might be. Just exactly how did a woman tell a man about her past, and at what point? The theme of the Sunday night messages was dating. The five steps Pastor Gary had worked out were fascinating. They didn't answer every question but sure helped along the way. Delancey got out her last handout and looked it over.

1. GTKY (get to know you) in a group. This is not a group date.
2. GTKY on a date or two. Avoid becoming boyfriend/girlfriend at this point.
3. GTKY in a group again.
4. GTKY on some dates, spend lots of time with the family.
5. Boyfriend/Girlfriend.

Pastor Gary's strongest recommendation was that all of this move very slowly and there be no physical contact. Delancey, who knew very well the dangers of being alone with a man, couldn't have agreed more, but at what point did a woman tell where she had been and what she had done?

Delancey hated herself for it, but tears that would not be stopped filled her eyes. There were so many lies out there. Television loved to glamorize sex, but the shows she used to watch never dealt with the heartache. Yes, God's forgiveness was complete, and Delancey believed that with all her heart, but to have listened to her mother when she told her to wait would have been the sweetest thing of all.

You can get me through this, Lord. I know that. I

still think of Chet. I wonder about his wife and children and if he's still cheating on them. He wasn't the one You had for me. I think deep in my heart I knew that all along. And the guilt was so awful. Please take him from my mind, Lord. Help me to move on. If Richard is right, Lord, You are able to send me someone who would understand. I can't quite see how that could happen, but I'm willing to learn. Help me to wait on You and to understand that no man can meet my needs and be there for me the way You can.

Delancey wrestled with the subject for days. Part of her wished that Richard had never given her the paper. She had been at peace about not having someone, false as her impression had been, and now she was filled with anxiety as to how it would all work. She felt herself obsessing and had yet another sin to take care of. When Mackenzie called to see how she was, she honestly admitted her exhaustion. She was even too tired to explain it to her.

"You almost sound as if you're coming down with a cold," Mackenzie commented.

"I think I'm just so emotional these days, and I'm not sleeping all that well."

"This is harder work than I ever thought it was, Deej. Is it the same for you?"

"Yes. I can't say that Mom made it look easy, but I don't think I ever knew the battles that went on inside. Mom didn't explode with temper at us or drink like a fish, so I have to assume that her battles were internal, like mine. Some days my thought life wears me out."

"Isn't it easy to say no one will know? I fall into that trap," Mackenzie admitted. "But one little slip is all it can take to send me off. I never think that one sin will do it, and when it does, I ask myself when I'm going to learn."

"I hear you." Delancey covered a huge yawn.

"I'd better let you go. Get some rest."

"All right."

"By the way, I booked some flights but haven't picked up the tickets. How do these dates sound to you?" Mackenzie gave her the dates of February 19 to February 26. Delancey said they were fine.

"I need this kept quiet, D.J., unless we're going to tell people we're going on vacation, all right?"

"That's fine. We are vacationing for part of it," Delancey said, "but I won't tell anyone who doesn't have to know. How is it going?"

"Well. I'll fill you in when we go next month."

"Okay. Pray for me, Mic. I really am tired and emotional these days."

"I will, Deej. I love you."

"I love you too, Mic."

Confirming their love for one another wasn't anything new; they told each other often. But two days later, when Delancey woke with a chest so tight she could barely breathe, the confirmation was a comfort to her as she dialed Mackenzie's number.

"You sound terrible." Mackenzie's voice was soft with compassion.

"I feel terrible. Mic, have you needed a doctor here?"

"No, I haven't. I should get in for a routine physical but haven't done it."

"I guess I'll check with Roz."

"I wonder if you shouldn't go to the emergency room at the hospital."

"Oh, I don't know. Maybe I'll think on it for a

while."

"I'll come and get you," Mackenzie was saying, hearing the bossiness in her voice and not caring.

"I'm not that bad, Mic," she began, but her sister cut her off.

"It's starting to snow, and I have the Jeep. I'm leaving here in about 15 minutes. Get ready to go, and if that's too hard, I'll help you when I get there."

Delancey was too tired to argue, but she thought Mackenzie was being overly protective. After hanging up the phone, however, she just sat and stared into space for the next half an hour. Too achy to eat or even shower, Delancey was moving very slowly in the bedroom when Mackenzie arrived.

"Delancey?"

Delancey came to the bedroom door and stared at her. Mackenzie was alarmed at the red in her cheeks and the blue tinge around her lips.

"Do you need some help getting ready?"

"I haven't showered."

"I don't think we'll worry about that right now. Where do you keep your overnight bag?"

"Why?"

"Because even if the doctor says you're all right, you're coming home with me."

Again, Delancey was too tired to care. She sat on the edge of the bed, ancient sweat pants on, and watched her sister take over. Mackenzie found a bag, threw some clothes and toiletries inside, and then came to her.

"Do you want to change into jeans, or are these all right?"

"I slept in these," Delancey said, looking at her dully.

Mackenzie dressed Delancey and took her to the Jeep. A little over ten minutes later they were pulling into the emergency parking area of Barton Memorial Hospital. Leaving the duffle bag but grabbing Delancey's purse, Mackenzie took her inside.

Lots of red tape and questions later, they saw a doctor. Mackenzie's heart slammed in her chest when the doctor's look became serious and the nurses were sent here and there with terse orders.

"Delancey?" The doctor's voice was kind for her. "You have a severe case of bacterial pneumonia. We're going to admit you."

"I think I'll be all right," Delancey said. She'd grown progressively worse since Mackenzie's arrival, and that woman was barely holding herself together.

"Are you Delancey's sister?" a nurse asked.

"Yes."

"We're going to get her set up in a room now. You can come in as soon as she's settled."

"Her breathing's worse," Mackenzie said, her own face strained and frightened.

"Yes, but we're going to stay right with her, and we'll be starting her on an antibiotic in just a few minutes."

The bed was being moved out of the emergency room, and Mackenzie followed.

"Micki," her sister croaked.

"I'm right here, D.J. — right behind you."

"Do I have to stay?" she gasped.

"Yeah, you do," she spoke through her fear. "They'll take good care of you."

"It hurts to breathe."

"That's why you have to stay," Mackenzie made herself say. They had stopped for a moment, and

764

Mackenzie was able to come right to the bed. Delancey reached for her.

"It hurts, Micki. What's the matter with me?"

"Pneumonia, D.J., but they're going to start you on the medicine you need, okay? It's going to be all right."

Sensitive to the frightened woman on the gurney, the nurses moved Delancey but allowed Mackenzie to stay close. They even allowed her in the room as long as she remained against the wall. Mackenzie watched the proceedings for a time but knew she was going to need help.

"Just put your hand up if you can hear me, Delancey."

Delancey's fingers rose.

"I'm going to call Jackson. I'll be right back."

Delancey waved again and Mackenzie slipped from the room, telling herself to hold together. The sign for the phones was overhead, and she followed the arrow. Joanne picked up after just two rings.

"Joanne, it's Mackenzie. Delancey has pneumonia. Can you get word to Jack? We're at Barton Memorial. They've just admitted her." Mackenzie's voice broke. "Please ask Jack to come."

"I will, Mackenzie. I'll call him right now. Are you all right?"

"I just need Jack."

"Okay, dear. I'll call him now."

Ten minutes later Mackenzie was in the hallway outside Delancey's door when Tucker stepped in front of her. She stared at him for a moment.

"My sister is sick," she said softly.

Tucker nodded. "I was at the house when you called."

Tucker's voice was almost too much for her. It

was deep and comforting, but he wasn't Jack.

"I need Jackson." Her voice had grown ever softer.

"Mom was calling when I left. He's probably on his way."

Mackenzie could only nod. Tucker moved until he was beside her and leaned on the wall as well. He turned to study her but thought if he touched her, she might crumble. As it was, just the sight of Jack coming down the hall a few minutes later was too much for her. She burst into tears when his arms went around her.

"She's so sick, Jackson. She can't breathe."

Jack held onto her while asking God if people died from pneumonia in the nineties. He honestly didn't know, and neither did he want to play with the possibility right then. Losing Delancey was a little beyond his thinking at the moment.

"What did the doctor say?"

"That she's very sick and they're putting her on an antibiotic."

"Someone named Micki?" the nurse coming from the room asked the group.

"That's me," Mackenzie called out.

"She's asking for you."

Mackenzie went without a backward glance. Jack asked whether he could go in and the nurse said yes. Jack followed but held back a little.

"Hi, Deej," Mackenzie said softly when she neared the bed.

Delancey coughed weakly, and Mackenzie was scared. Her chest sounded like a rock in a tin can.

"You gotta get better, Deej." She made a valiant attempt to hide her tears. "We're going skiing next month."

"So tired. I wish Mom were here."

"Me too."

Hearing this, Jack's hand went to his eyes. He stayed still for a few minutes, trying to gain control, before joining Mackenzie by the bed.

"Hi, D.J."

"Hi, Jack."

"Pretty bad?"

"It hurts."

"Just try to rest," he told her. "We'll take care of everything. You just take care of Delancey."

"I need to sleep."

"Okay." Mackenzie felt it was the best thing for her, but the doctor arrived, and it had to be put off. He questioned Delancey, made her breathe into a little tube, and then listened to her chest again. Jack had turned away for this but still heard Mackenzie say, "You're hurting her."

"I'm not actually," came the doctor's clipped reply. "She's already in pain."

"Would it be possible to get a doctor who has taken a little more time with his bedside manner?"

The doctor only looked at her. Mackenzie didn't protest when Jack took her arm and led her out.

"Why did you do that, Jack!" she snapped when they got outside. "Did you see him? He probably doesn't even have a pulse."

When the doctor followed them out a few seconds later, Jack turned Mackenzie around toward Tucker. Before she knew it, Tucker's arm was around her shoulders and he was walking her down the hallway. They turned into a small, empty waiting room, and Tucker directed her to a chair. Mackenzie dropped into it, let her head fall back, and closed her eyes.

"I shouldn't have said that."

"No, you shouldn't have," Tucker agreed, his voice kind. "You're feeling emotional and you're frightened for Delancey, but he is the doctor."

"It looked as though he was hurting her. It just slipped out, and then when he stared at me, I got mad." Mackenzie looked at Tucker. "I'll have to apologize."

"I was hoping you'd decide to do that," he said, his voice still compassionate.

The opportunity came sooner than she expected. Both Jack and the doctor came to the small waiting room just a few minutes later. Using the kind manner Mackenzie believed he should have used on her sister, the doctor explained that Delancey would remain hospitalized until her breathing became easier. He said that Mackenzie could stay in the room with her and even graciously accepted Mackenzie's apology when she made it. The doctor left less than ten minutes after he came in the room, and the three were left alone.

"I'm sorry, Jackson." Mackenzie made this apology as well.

"You did the right thing in apologizing," he assured her. "I somehow think the doctor understood, but your testimony is at stake, so I think you did well."

"Is there anything he's not telling us?"

"I don't think so. She's anxious for you to be near, so he's more than willing to have you stay. He thinks she'll be improved in just 24 hours, but since her breathing is so labored, he wants to keep an eye on her."

"I'd better get back down there."

Tucker hugged her and said he would slip out and give his mother a call before spreading the news to Delancey's church family. Jack saw Mackenzie back to the room and found Delancey sleeping. He took a house key and a list of things Mackenzie needed from home and called Joanne to ask her to be ready to go with him.

Mackenzie went back into the room alone, sat in a chair by the bed, and looked at her sister, whose body looked too thin under the sheet and light blanket. It reminded her just a little of her mother's hospital room, and for a moment panic clawed at her throat. Asking the Lord to help her keep all of this in perspective, she prayed and began to find things to thank Him about.

Delancey could have collapsed or needed to be rushed here, but she called me early so the doctors could get right on it. She knows You, Lord, so Your Spirit can comfort her. Thank You that it can comfort me. Mackenzie couldn't say any more. She was overcome with emotion for some minutes. She was still crying when Tucker slipped quietly into the room, came over by her chair, and bent down to talk with her. Mackenzie thought he had gone and said as much.

"I made the calls from here," he whispered. "I called the church and talked to Pastor Dave, and then I called Roz. She's going to spread the word. I'm sure she'll be here before the day is over."

"Thanks, Tucker," Mackenzie said through several sniffs.

Tucker stood long enough to grab some tissues from the bathroom and came back to hunker down next to her again.

"Are you going to be all right?"

"I think so. I'm so arrogant, Tucker. Just the other day I told the Lord that I thought I had things pretty together. I'm such a fool."

Tucker's smile was gentle as he put his hand on

her arm.

"It's easy to be lulled into a false security, Mic, and Satan knows that. You couldn't have known about this, so being specifically prepared wasn't possible, but we do need to work to be ready for anything the Lord might bring. As you're seeing, circumstances can change in the blink of an eye."

Mackenzie nodded. She hadn't thought about any of this. Other than Delancey's being upset with her well over a year ago, life had been pretty smooth sailing since she'd come to Christ. Was God still there when the hurts came? It was a question she knew she would explore. She knew that answer was yes, but she wanted verses to prove it to herself.

"Can I bring you something right now?" Tucker offered.

"No, I'm fine."

"Okay. I'll check in on you later, and I know Jack and Mom are bringing your things."

"Thanks for everything, Tucker."

"You're welcome." He touched her arm and smiled.

Mackenzie watched him leave, smiling when he turned back to wave at the door. Her sigh was very soft. Jack's new family was one more thing for which to be thankful.

FORTY-FOUR

Delancey woke up to coherency more than 24 hours after she was admitted. She was groggy and weak, but the person next to her bed was recognizable.

"Hello, Richard," she croaked softly.

That man, who had been reading the paper, looked up and beamed at her.

"Hi, yourself. How are you feeling?"

"Sore," she answered and coughed weakly.

Richard immediately stood and raised the top half of her bed so she could sit up. She had to cough some more, but as soon as she was finished, Richard was waiting with a cool washcloth to bathe her face. Delancey thought it felt like heaven. He began to talk gently as he worked.

"Mackenzie's gone to your house to take a quick shower, so I told her I would wait and keep an eye on you."

"Are you missing patients?" she rattled.

"No. I was off this morning." He didn't tell her that he'd been planning for weeks to take the morning off so he could get some work done at home — phone calls that were hard to accomplish on Saturdays.

"Are you ready for some breakfast?"

"Oh, I don't know, maybe just something to

drink."

"Okay. I'll head out and see what I can drum up."

Delancey thought about him after he left. It was so sweet of him to be there, and he had his glasses on. He looked so cute in his glasses. She moved a little in the bed and thought about what she had said to him. That she was remarkably sore had not been an exaggeration. It occurred to her that she should take something for the pain but had no idea how ill she had been. She tried to think back to getting to the hospital and Mackenzie being angry at someone in her room, but it was all so fuzzy. Richard came back when she was still working it through.

"Richard, when did I get here exactly?"

"Yesterday morning."

"Oh, was it just yesterday?"

"Yes. Have you lost track of things?"

"Yes. Oh, 7UP." She saw the can in his hands. "That sounds good."

Richard poured it for her and helped her with the straw. Her color was better, but she had no energy at all. The first time Richard had seen her had been at four o'clock the afternoon before. She had been pale, her breath coming in gasping little puffs, and he had been frightened for her. It was even scarier to learn that she had been worse around noon. This morning when he arrived, Mackenzie told him that she had improved through the night. Even if he'd had patients scheduled for that morning, he would have been strongly tempted to cancel them.

Realizing his thoughts had wandered, he looked up to find Delancey's eyes on him. She smiled when their eyes met.

"It was so nice of you to come, Richard."

"Well, I couldn't leave you here alone," he smiled, his eyes slowly growing serious. "My mind wandered to some pretty scary things."

"Like what?"

"Like Delancey not being here. I thought about how nice that would be for Delancey — she would be in heaven — but I'd be stuck here knowing that I never told her how I felt."

Fuzzy as she was, understanding was long in coming. She stared at Richard Wilder as if she'd never seen him before, a million denials running through her mind. Richard read her look without effort.

"And before you tell me that I've got the wrong woman," he said, his voice soft and gentle, "I'll tell you that I haven't. I know exactly who I love."

"Oh, Richard, you can't; not knowing what you know."

He leaned close and said softly, "*Especially* knowing what I know. I'm not asking you to marry me — it's too soon for that — and you may never want to marry me, but you will know one thing: There are men much different than the pilot in Chicago, and you're looking at one. If you give me a chance, I'll spend the next 50 years proving it to you."

"Oh, Richard." Delancey was amazed. "You're so sweet. I just want so much better for you."

Richard smiled. "Now isn't that a fun co-incidence! I want the same for you, and I think I'm the perfect one for the job."

Delancey laughed a little and coughed again. "I've never had a conversation like this in my life."

"Well, this sounds like someone who feels a little better," a nurse said as she came in with a tray.

"Are you up to a little breakfast, Delancey?"

"I guess I could try."

"Okay. Are you going to be staying?" she asked of Richard.

"Yes."

"Well, we're short-staffed this round, so I think I'll take advantage of you and let you help Delancey."

"That's fine."

The nurse set the tray down, checked Delancey's vital signs, made notes on the chart, and went on her way. Richard stood up and uncovered Delancey's food. It was pretty bland fare, but he put milk and sugar on her hot cereal and moved everything closer to her. Not until he looked over did he realize how closely he was being watched. He felt himself blushing but didn't try to hide it.

"Have I ruined everything between us, Delancey?"

Already growing tired, she moved her head on the pillow. "I didn't know men like you existed. I'm afraid I'm going to wake up and find that I dreamed the whole thing."

"Don't try to keep it all in your mind. I probably should have waited to tell you. We have lots of time to talk about it."

"How does it go — 'Get To Know You in a group'? Isn't that the first step?"

"That's it," Richard smiled, but she was fading. "Here, Delancey, try to eat a little something."

He held the bowl for her and even coaxed a few more sips of liquid down her throat. One bite of Jell-O went in, but she didn't like the lime flavor. He actually managed to get half the cereal into her by the time Mackenzie showed up, but by then, Delancey was almost out.

"Oh, Micki," she said, her voice slurred. "Richard loves me. Can you believe it?"

Mackenzie's eyes flew to Richard's and saw the confirmation there.

"I should have waited to tell her."

Mackenzie looked shocked.

"Are you angry with me?" the big man wanted to know.

Mackenzie shook her head no but couldn't speak.

"Come here, Mackenzie," Richard said but had to go to the other side of Delancey's bed himself to hug her. Mackenzie hugged him back. They looked at Delancey, but she was out cold. Richard moved to lower the bed and dim the light, and Mackenzie moved the food tray out of the way. They both sat in the chairs by the window.

"I've done this all wrong," he said softly. "I know you're not supposed to tell the woman you love her before you spend time getting to know each other. It just sort of came out."

"But you do love her?"

He turned to look at her. "Very much."

"Why, Richard? When have you been with her enough to know?"

"Every Wednesday night at minichurch, and it's not unusual for us to sit together or near each other in church and talk when the service is over. She's also loaned me some of her artwork, and because of that, met me for coffee and for breakfast once."

"When did you meet?"

"At the end of last October. It isn't a lot of time, Mackenzie, but I'm not in a hurry here."

"Richard," Mackenzie warned, laying her hand on his arm, "Delancey's been hurt — very hurt."

"She told me."

Mackenzie shook her head, not sure he understood. "She's made some bad choices as well, and that hurt her, but the relationship she spoke of in her testimony really hurt —"

"I'm not like him," Richard interrupted, cutting her off quietly. "I'm not hiding a wife and children somewhere."

Mackenzie's relief was incredible. She had no idea her sister had talked to him about that. She was no longer worried that Richard would rush things with her sister. Clearly his feelings were stronger, which could pose very real problems, but it also looked as though he was willing to give Delancey time.

"Mackenzie," Richard suddenly went on, "I understand from Delancey that you're the only family she has left, so I need you to know that your approval means a lot to me. I want to court your sister, to use an old-fashioned term, but I'm not headstrong on this. If you have any doubts about this, or me, just say the word."

"I don't, Richard. If my sister is willing, I couldn't be more pleased."

Richard nodded and sat back in his chair. Mackenzie relaxed as well. Their eyes, when not checking on Delancey, were on the snow-covered pines out the window. It was too much to take in right then. Both sat quietly in the chairs, Richard only slightly more rested than Mackenzie, and Delancey out for the count.

Richard had to be at the office at 11:30, so he was gone before Delancey woke. Mackenzie stayed awake for only a few minutes after he left. The cot they had brought her for the night was still against the wall. She crawled onto it and slept again herself.

When Delancey woke again, her sister, Jack, Joanne, Roz, and Sabrina were in her room. They had been speaking quietly among themselves but now came close to talk with her. She smiled at their caring but knew she wasn't going to be able to stay awake for long. Roz and Sabrina had been there for a while, so they left soon afterward, and when Delancey had a chance, she motioned Mackenzie to come closer. Mackenzie bent low to talk with her.

"Was Richard here?"

Mackenzie smiled. "Yes."

Delancey stared at her for several seconds. "So, it's true?"

Mackenzie could only nod her head.

"Is it me, Mic, or is he the sweetest man in the world?"

"He's a doll," Mackenzie agreed with her.

"I want to talk all about it, but I'm so tired."

"We'll have time when we get to my house."

"Your house?"

"Yes. They might let you go tonight, and I'm taking you home. You know what a good nurse I am."

Delancey smiled.

"We're going to go, D.J.," Jack came close to tell her.

"Thanks for coming."

"Mic says she's going to take you home."

"Yeah. You'd better pray for me since I'll be at her mercy."

Jack bent to kiss her before talking to Mackenzie.

"Call me whenever they release her, and I'll

meet you at the house."

Delancey heard this but didn't understand it. She wanted to ask, but the nurses were coming in and shooing everyone out so they could get her vitals and help her clean up before the doctor came.

She didn't recall the conversation between Jack and Mackenzie until she arrived at Mackenzie's that evening, her breathing slightly easier and not a drop of energy in her system. Jack was at the side of the car the moment Mackenzie pulled into the garage, lifting her in his arms and carrying her into the house and all the way upstairs to one of Mackenzie's spare rooms. Joanne was already there, adjusting the pillows and tucking her in.

"You look a little winded. The ride home can do that."

"I have no energy, Joanne. It's the weirdest feeling."

"That takes time, dear. Antibiotics are amazing things, but you just rest and let someone else take care of you."

Thinking of Mackenzie's cooking and nursing skills, Delancey wondered if she shouldn't have remained in the hospital. She smiled, not able to help herself.

"What does that smile mean?" Mackenzie had come in and seen it.

"I was wondering what we're going to eat for the next few days with you in the galley."

Mackenzie's hands went to her waist in mock outrage. "I'll have you know, Delancey Joy, that I have more cans of soup and more frozen micro-waveable entrees than the grocery store."

"I can hardly wait."

"Well, you've shown me no respect, but I'll still

offer you something hot to drink."

"Like what?"

"I have tea, coffee, hot chocolate, or spiced cider mix."

"Spiced cider, please."

"Coming right up."

Mackenzie passed Jack on the stairs and proceeded to the kitchen. Joanne joined her a few minutes later, however, to cancel the order.

"Is she asleep?" Mackenzie guessed.

"Yes. She didn't even hear us say goodbye."

Jack came into the kitchen right behind his wife.

"Mackenzie, while we're still here, do you need to get anything from the store? You can give me a list."

"Maybe I'd better. The doctor wants her to drink lots of fluids, and if she can ever stay awake, she'll drink me dry in no time at all."

"Put together a list," Joanne told her, "and we'll go right now."

"Okay, and could you possibly come back sometime tomorrow and stay for an hour or so? I need some fresh air and exercise."

"Of course," Jack spoke up. "We'll come in the morning. Will that work?"

"Yes, it will, and I don't think you need to rush back with the groceries. We'll be fine for tonight."

They waited while Mackenzie made her list.

"Thank you for understanding," she said as she handed it to them. "I don't think she's in that much danger now, but I would feel better not leaving her alone right away."

"She was a pretty sick lady," Joanne said softly. "I can see why you don't want to take a chance."

"Thanks for everything, Joanne."

The older woman hugged her. "Get some rest,

Micki."

"I will."

Jack was next, hugging her warmly before going on his way.

Mackenzie closed the house up, since it was already dark, and went to check on Delancey. She was sleeping soundly, albeit noisily, and Mackenzie knew she would be up in the night to check on her. She prepared a tray to put next to Delancey's bed that included juice, red Jell-O, and on impulse, a small dinner bell. She left the light on in the hallway and went back downstairs. She had only just arrived when the doorbell rang. It was Richard.

"Hello," Mackenzie greeted him as she stepped back.

"Roz gave me your address; I hope you don't mind."

"Not at all."

He pressed a bouquet into Mackenzie's hands when she shut the door. "Can you give these to Delancey?"

"Certainly. She's asleep right now."

"I suspect that's all she'll do for several days." He looked down at Mackenzie, taking in the dark smudges under her eyes. "I hope you can get some rest tonight."

"I plan on it."

"I'll go." He glanced around, feeling a bit uncomfortable about staying but wishing he could be close to Delancey. "Please keep me informed, Micki. Just call, and I'll come if you need me."

Mackenzie smiled at him. "I will, Richard. Goodnight."

"Goodnight."

It was nice to be able to add the flowers to

Delancey's tray. Mackenzie hoped she would see the card. She double-checked the locks and then looked at the clock. Tired as she was, she didn't want to miss anything. She didn't like to turn in before nine, but tonight she would make an exception. She was asleep five minutes after settling the covers in place.

Delancey drained the tall glass of juice she found on her tray the moment she woke, only then realizing she had slept through the night. She then turned her face into her pillow to cough, not wanting to wake Mackenzie. Light was just beginning to peek through. She was too lazy to reach for the lamp, so reading the card that sat with the flowers would have to wait. Like a child, she checked it again every few seconds until she could see it clearly.

Get well, D.J.
I'm thinking of you.
Richard

Delancey smiled at the sight of his neat pen. He wasn't the typical doctor in that respect; she could read every word. She lay looking at the ceiling for a long time, her mother on her mind. Delancey was finally able to understand what her mother had felt when Jack confessed his love to her. Her mother hadn't been in love with Jack — they had just been friends — just like her and Richard. Delancey decided it was a very special thing to have someone love you. It was vulnerable and a little bit scary but also warm and secure.

I can't lead with my heart on this, Lord. It's too big an issue. I've got to think clearly. I'm still a little surprised that Richard wants marriage, but even with that, I need to hear him out in case I misunderstood. I was pretty sick, Father. Maybe I misunderstood that whole thing.

Delancey caught sight of the perfect bouquet on the tray and knew she was fooling herself. He had all but proposed, and probably would have if he had felt she had been ready. She thought back to the afternoon Jack had come to the house and said he loved their mother. It had been such a shock. But then nothing happened. Delancey remembered thinking that he would be over every day and call nonstop, but that wasn't the case. Jack and her mother had moved slowly.

In the midst of this Delancey remembered that her mother had worked for Jack. They saw each other five days a week and had become good friends before Jack had said a thing about love.

Delancey looked at the card in her hand. Was Richard now sorry he had said anything? Delancey didn't know where the thought came from, but it would not go away.

It was a relief to hear water running. No longer fearing she would wake Mackenzie, Delancey took herself to the bathroom. Mackenzie was waiting for her in the hallway when she emerged.

"Do you suppose you could help me shower, Mic? I can't stand the hospital smell in my hair."

"Sure."

Delancey sat down to catch her breath for a few minutes while Mackenzie readied the water and towels. She finally called Delancey in, fussing over her like a mother hen. It wasn't without its hilarity, but the job got done.

"Did you see your flowers?" Mackenzie asked, the blower on low, the hairbrush moving gently. She watched her sister smile.

"Yes. I wish I could smell them better. I'm still too plugged up."

"I'll make sure they have plenty of water so you can smell them in a few days."

"I'm sleepy again. Have you ever been tired of being tired?"

"Yeah. You can get back into bed, and I'll bring you some breakfast."

"I'll probably fall back to sleep."

"Well, I'll just wake you long enough to put some food into you."

And she did. Delancey returned to her bed, fresh pillow slips and all, and fell sound asleep until Mackenzie woke her for breakfast. She slept again right afterward, leaving Mackenzie time to get a few things done and time to pace until Jack and Joanne showed up.

Mackenzie had been on the road for less than five minutes when Tucker came by in the car. Still walking fast to warm up, she slowed down as he pulled to a stop.

"How's the patient?" he asked.

"A little better. Jackson and Joanne are at the house right now."

"So you're skipping out for a little air."

"Exactly. I can still smell the hospital."

"Want some company?"

"Sure."

"Let me park at your house and I'll come back and catch up with you."

"Okay."

Mackenzie took it easy until he jogged up beside her, slowing down to her walking pace. She glanced down as he came up beside her and noticed how much longer his legs were.

"Will it drive you crazy to walk with someone whose pace doesn't match yours?"

"No, not at all. I like any excuse to be outside." Tucker didn't add that Mackenzie's company only added to the pleasure. He hadn't expected to like her so much, but Jack's stepdaughters were both delightful.

"What do you do to keep in shape?" Mackenzie asked suddenly.

"I ski in the winter and play tennis in the summer."

"No running or walking?"

"Some running, but I prefer to ski."

Mackenzie sighed. "I think I could be on the slopes every day. I make myself stay home and work on lots of days when I want to be out there."

"I tend to get up early and work so I can go in the afternoon. Or ski early and work later."

"May I ask you a question, Tucker?"

"I was hoping you would," he told her outrageously.

Mackenzie smiled and asked, "Can you tell me about your job? I don't think I really know what you do."

"I freelance edit for a few publishers."

"I knew that, but not the specifics. Do the publishers contact you? Do you have certain authors you work with or someone new all the time?"

"Most of the time I work for a publisher, but on occasion an author will personally hire me. I have regular authors, but I also get new authors every year. Some come back time and again, and some for just one book. Once in a while someone will come on the scene with a great idea and no writing skills. Other times I just polish the manuscript a little and send it on its way."

"And what about you? Do you have a book inside of you?"

Tucker smiled. "I don't think I do. I love working with words and helping others see their full potential, but I don't want to rewrite anyone's story or do one of my own."

Mackenzie nodded. He was perfect editor material all right.

"What are you working on these days?"

"Jungle Buds," she said a little too swiftly, and when she glanced up, she found Tucker watching her. They had nearly come full circle and were almost back to the house, but Tucker, who had started to lead the way, headed into the park.

"Why do I get the impression that there's more to you than meets the eye?" Tucker asked conversationally.

"I don't know, why do you?" Mackenzie evaded, wondering whether she was being deceptive. She was working on Jungle Buds, as well as *The Parchment Soldier.*

"All right, Miss Bishop, I'll come right out and ask you. Are you working on something in addition to Jungle Buds?"

Mackenzie came to a complete stop and faced him. She looked up, surprising him with how swiftly her face showed her confusion and misery.

"Tucker, if I'm not ready to answer that question, am I being deceitful?"

"Of course not, Micki. You did the right thing in telling me. I shouldn't have asked you."

She still looked upset and spoke quietly to his chest. "It's not you, Tucker. I don't talk to anyone about it — well, just Delancey, but she's different."

Tucker bent slightly at the knees to catch her eye.

"It's fine, Mackenzie, just fine. If ever I can help you with anything, just call, but I won't ask again or tell anyone that we spoke of it."

She looked up at him. Tucker looked right back. For a few seconds neither of them spoke. Not for the first time Mackenzie noticed his size. He wasn't extremely tall, but he was broad, and not just his shoulders — his whole frame was wide. He looked very solid. She hadn't planned on liking him so much, but she had to admit that she did. For an instant her mind wandered to a place it shouldn't be, and she swiftly pushed the images aside and thought about the gentle way he had just treated her. For the strangest reason she wanted to go up on tiptoe and kiss his cheek. She pushed that urge away as well.

"Thank you, Tucker," Mackenzie said at last. The silence between them was growing uncomfortable.

"I don't think I did anything."

"Yes, you did" was all she would say before she swung down the path and kept walking. Thankfully the conversation shifted, and Mackenzie wasn't forced to think anymore about it.

Mackenzie looked at the food on her kitchen counters and shook her head. When word got out that Delancey was ill, folks from Meyers as well as Mackenzie's minichurch brought cookies, muffins, casseroles to be frozen or eaten on the spot, a cake, and two loaves of homemade bread. Delancey had feared what they would eat, but clearly it wasn't going to be a worry. Indeed, she would probably go home before they ate it all.

And in the midst of the food's arrival, Richard called and asked if he could visit and bring lunch on Sunday afternoon.

Still wanting to stay close to home, Mackenzie skipped Sunday school, so she'd only been home for half an hour when he arrived, laden down with a large cardboard box that smelled as though he'd been busy.

"I hope you like lasagna and garlic bread," he said as he came in.

"Oh my, yes. Can I take something?"

"No, just show me to the kitchen."

"Over that way," Mackenzie pointed, shutting the door behind him, the aroma lingering in his wake. She was headed across the room when he came back from the kitchen and began to speak to her. His attention, however, was suddenly diverted. Delancey was coming down the stairs. Mackenzie watched him smile up at her sister.

"How are you?" he asked, watching her descend.

"Much better, thank you. How about yourself?"

"I'm fine. I made lasagna. Are you up for any?"

"Oh, yes. I'm starved."

"Whenever you're ready . . ." Richard let the sentence hang.

Both women were. The meal was delicious, though not very long. Delancey had been ready to take the world by storm when she arrived downstairs, but by the time she had cleaned her plate, she was fading. She wouldn't go upstairs as Mackenzie suggested, so Richard went with her into the living room, and they settled in to talk. It wasn't five minutes, however, before he was back in the kitchen ready to help with the dishes.

"Asleep?" Mackenzie asked.

"Yes."

She nodded. "Should I be worried about how much she needs to sleep?"

"No. She's improving, and it's going to be slow, but be in touch with the doctor if you're worried."

"She has an appointment to see him on Wednesday."

"Tell him all your concerns, but I think he will say she's doing fine."

Mackenzie turned away from the dishes to look at him.

"I'm glad you came by. I could tell Delancey enjoyed it."

"That's good to hear. I might be out of line, Micki, so don't feel you have to answer, but is there someone special in your life right now?"

"No," she said softly.

"Would you like there to be?"

Mackenzie looked at him. His care of Delancey, and her for that matter, could not be faulted. Having him around made Mackenzie ache for male companionship.

"At times," she answered honestly, although she had to admit to herself that those times were getting to be more constant.

"I haven't visited Kingsbury in a long time. Are there many single men?"

"There are quite a few, but I'm not the most social of creatures. I think that God will have to drop the man in my lap."

"Maybe He will drop you into the man's lap."

Mackenzie laughed. "Either way, it'll have to be obvious."

"God is capable of that," Richard said softly, and Mackenzie smiled at him and went back to loading the dishwasher.

Delancey was still sleeping when they finished in the kitchen. They sat with her in the living room and talked some more, but she did not wake up. Richard eventually left, and Mackenzie went to her office. Delancey slept on for the next hour.

FORTY-FIVE

"Mackenzie, are you in the office?"

Mackenzie stood, went to the open railing, and looked down at her sister where she still lay on the sofa some 12 feet below.

"Hi."

"He's gone, isn't he?"

"Yes."

Even from that distance, Mackenzie heard her sigh.

"I was afraid of that."

"He understood, D.J., and I know he had a good time."

Mackenzie made her way to the stairs and crossed the living room to sit in a chair. Delancey looked discouraged.

"I asked him if it was normal that you sleep so much, and he said yes."

"That's all well and good," Delancey began but stopped. She was upset, but there was no point in taking it out on Mackenzie, not to mention the fact that she had no right to be angry in the first place.

You bring someone into my life, Lord, and instead of being thankful, I'm snapping at You for not moving things faster. If I could just remember that I didn't think anyone would ever care, it might help to keep all of this in perspective.

"He did understand, Deej."

"Thanks, Mic. I never thought anyone would love me, but instead of being thankful, I'm torqued out of shape and mad at the world."

"What do you mean you didn't think anyone would love you?"

She shrugged. "I just thought that part of my life was over."

"Because of Chet?"

"Yeah. I didn't think anyone would want me once they found out."

"Oh, Delancey," Mackenzie said, looking pained, "I didn't know you felt that way."

"Part of me still does. I keep thinking that I'm imagining all of this."

"I might agree with you if I hadn't just watched Richard over lunch."

Delancey nodded. She had noticed it as well. When they rested on her, Richard's eyes were as tender as any she had ever seen. He was courteous and kind to Mackenzie, but where Delancey was concerned, everything was stepped up a notch.

"I don't want to patronize you, Delancey, or downplay sin, but there are all levels of purity. The man or woman who doesn't come to marriage a virgin has not chosen the best, but the man or woman who has all but engaged in the physical act is not entirely chaste either.

"Not that God can't forgive, we both know that He can and does, but when I think back on the books I've read and the movies I've seen, many of them with graphic scenes, I can't tell the man I marry that I've come to him completely pure. I think purity starts in the mind, long before we

791

have a boyfriend."

"I hadn't thought of that. I still tend to beat myself up over Chet, but in truth I have watched what I read and see. Roz calls it a second virginity, and I've really worked at practicing that."

"I know just what you're saying. You wouldn't believe the stack of books and videos I carried from this house after I came to Christ. I felt clean when I was done."

"What did you do with them?"

"Most went to charity, but some were so bad that I put them in the trash."

"I'm so glad you never wrote books like that, Mic. Think of the shame you would feel."

Mackenzie's wonder was as great as Delancey's. "God was taking care of me even when all I did was stiff-arm Him away. It's been interesting to write *The Parchment Soldier* because it's almost autobiographical. Mason Coltrane shoves God away for a long time, accomplishes many things, but then finds himself empty and alone."

"How is the book coming?"

"Very well."

"Can I read it?"

Mackenzie brightened and said, "Do you want to?"

Delancey nodded and watched her move to the stairs. Her sister was so good at what she did that Delancey took it for granted. *Mackenzie needs validation too. I ask her every so often how the writing is going, but I don't show enough interest.* Delancey was fairly certain that if she voiced these thoughts out loud, Mackenzie would snort and tell her she was being ridiculous, but she knew she wasn't.

"This is just the first 500 pages," Mackenzie

spoke when she brought in the manuscript.

"How long do you think it'll be?"

"Oh, maybe between 600 and 700 pages. I'm never sure."

"I was hoping to get home tomorrow," Delancey said as she settled deeper into the sofa and turned to the first page, "but maybe I'll stay here and read all week."

Mackenzie smiled. If Delancey had been looking at her, she would have known that her suspicions were correct: Mackenzie did need encouragement in her life; not just where her writing was concerned, but in every area. Right now she was working hard to be the strong older sister and would not let on otherwise. She left Delancey to her reading and tried not to be anxious about what she might think of the book; a good thing, since Delancey could read for only so long before falling back to sleep. Mackenzie determined, however, that when her sister felt up to it, she would have to tell her she really needed her right now.

It was a good thing for Mackenzie's sake that she didn't know the future, or she might have become very discouraged. Taking the manuscript with her, Delancey did go home by Tuesday. She even took herself to the doctor on Wednesday. He confirmed what Richard had said: She was going to be weak for some time. That factor was going to alter Mackenzie's plans in a way she wasn't expecting.

I can't make Colorado, Mic; I don't have the energy. I don't want you to change your plans. The Parchment Soldier *is a fabulous book. Go to Colorado on your own so you can finish it. You and I will go*

793

another time.

Delancey's words floated through Mackenzie's mind as she boarded a plane for Denver on the nineteenth of February. It had never been her plan to go alone, but Delancey had been insistent. And she was right about one thing: Mackenzie did want to finish her book and needed to visit Colorado to do it.

The flight left on time and was uneventful. With no one beside her, Mackenzie enjoyed being left to herself to continue with her notes. She wasn't outlining the book, but since she was traveling all this way with no publisher's promise of reimbursement, she didn't want to leave anything out. She had a map handy and the addresses of several condos she needed to inspect. She didn't write with extreme detail, but if she could see a place, it helped to motivate her and make the story come alive in her mind.

She thought about the story. At the end of *The Parchment Soldier,* Mason returns to a woman he had met briefly in a clinic in Colorado. He had been injured, and her care of him had been wonderful, but more than that, they had talked about God. In the process, Mason's life had been profoundly touched.

Caitlin, who was divorced with a small son, didn't believe that God was who man made Him, something Mason had always believed. She believed that the Bible was absolute truth and that man, who deserved nothing, must come to God as He required.

It was many chapters later before Mason saw what she meant and believed for himself. At the end of the book, Mackenzie planned for him to go back to Colorado to visit her church and see if she might still be around. Mackenzie had tears in her eyes as she thought about the ending and the sweet scene between Mason, Caitlin, and her little son, Sawyer. Mackenzie's head went back against the seat, and she reclined her chair.

Maybe I shouldn't be doing these romantic scenes, Lord. They throw me out of whack. Why do I feel so lonely and uncertain these days? It's like I need more, but You've made it clear that You're to be my everything. Where does someone else fit into my life? Delancey and Richard are seeing a little of each other and moving so carefully. It would be very surprising if they weren't married someday. Jackson didn't marry Mom until he was over 40, but he also didn't want anyone before Mom. What about me, Lord? I have a yearning inside but no one special in my life. What exactly does that mean?

Without warning a face popped into Mackenzie's mind, but she didn't take that as any sort of sign. Indeed, she fell asleep just moments later and slept until it was time to prepare for landing.

Beaver Creek, Colorado

Even living in the Sierra Nevadas as Mackenzie did, it was hard to top the Rockies for beauty. The drive from the airport in Denver was two hours straight up into the mountains, and since Mackenzie was living the story in her mind, she looked at everything with new eyes but did not allow herself to stop along the way. She planned to get in some skiing, relaxing, and reading, but she also planned to work hard and go home with all the info she needed to finish this book.

Located in a high, bowl-shaped valley ten miles west of Vail, Beaver Creek was her destination. Mackenzie checked into the Hyatt, impressed that she was recognized from past visits. She knew she would be safe during her stay, and it didn't hurt her feelings in the least to know she would live in the lap of luxury as well. The hotel offered the best in ski-in/ski-out accommodations that included personalized attendants who clicked you out of your bindings, put your boots in an Air Dry rack overnight, and gave you a pair of slippers before sending you on your way. Cider and hot chocolate were optional.

Mackenzie had seen dozens of places that would need to be explored before she went home the following week, but for now she just wanted to settle in. She unpacked her bag, double-checked that her ski equipment was delivered to the right spot, set up her laptop, and, notebook in hand, went in search of food.

She ordered a good meal at one of the hotel restaurants, her hand moving on the pad the moment the waiter walked away. Once in a while she sat back and envisioned a scene, almost laughing in delight at how special Mason Coltrane had become after he came to Christ. He was like her father in some ways: strong, warm, and romantic. It took some time for Mackenzie to realize she had created a Christian dream-man, but then she frowned at the description. Mason wasn't a dream-man. He still sinned, had doubts, and was oftentimes stubborn when God asked for something.

"Sounds more like Paul Bishop's daughter than it does Paul Bishop," Mackenzie said softly to herself, and she shut the notebook to concentrate on her food. A wave of loneliness hit her before the meal was over, but she forced her mind to remember that with Christ she was never alone, praying as she did that God would give her a wonderful week, even without Delancey.

Meyers
"Good morning," Richard said softly to Delancey when he joined her in the pew on Sunday. They hadn't sat together during the sermon, but Richard had sought her out as soon as the service was over.

"Good morning. How are you?"

"I'm fine, but I don't need to ask how you are — you look great."

"I do feel good. I suddenly came out on top yesterday. I told Mackenzie that I wasn't up to going with her to Colorado, but now I think I could have."

"I'm kind of glad you're here," Richard said.

Delancey smiled at him.

"Why did Mackenzie go to Colorado?"

Delancey hesitated. Richard saw it and waited.

"I have things in my life, Richard — you know, in the past — that I don't like to share. Well, Micki hasn't done anything that she's ashamed of, but her life now, her present situation, is very private."

Richard nodded. "That house is pretty spectacular."

"Yes, it is. I would like to tell you about it, Richard, but I can't do that unless I talk with Mackenzie."

"Is it something you're involved in?"

"No."

"In that case I can't say as it's really any of my business."

"But you would feel it was your business if I was involved?"

"Only on the point that if we're trying to get to

797

know each other better, having secrets isn't going to help."

Delancey nodded. For a moment it had felt intrusive, but this made sense.

"Does that mean I can ask you questions?"

"Yes. Anything you wish."

She looked embarrassed but managed to ask, "Does your family know about me?"

"My parents have known for some time that I met someone I thought was pretty special, but since I hadn't spoken to you, I didn't feel it was my place to say more."

"And now? Have you told them we've talked?"

"I called my mother in the middle of last week to ask for an address, and she asked me. I told her only that you and I had talked some and that you were the woman who did the artwork for their invitations."

Delancey looked surprised. She had forgotten all about that. She also noticed how cleared-out the church had become.

"I guess we'd better go."

Richard walked her outside to her car, but they began to talk again. They were both rather cold by the time they parted some ten minutes later, but neither took much notice.

He's so special, Lord, Delancey said as she started the car and gave it a few minutes to warm up. *He's so caring and easy to talk with. Let me see what I need to see. I don't want to go off on an emotional cloud. Don't let me do that.* Hunger finally hitting, Delancey put the car into drive and went home.

In his own car, and waiting to make sure Delancey's started, Richard did some praying of his own, his thoughts much like Delancey's. She was such a special person, and the fact that she asked about his family made him think she was seeing how serious he was. He finally took himself home, his own car warm, but hunger hadn't hit him yet. He was still too busy asking God to continue helping him move slowly.

Beaver Creek

Mackenzie was standing in the hallway of the Hyatt near the shops, thinking about whether or not she wanted something sweet to eat, when she spotted him. She blinked, shifted her head a little to be sure, and then approached.

Looking in the window of one shop, Tucker Stone took a moment to realize that someone had come to stand close to the window right next to him, someone who smelled very nice. He didn't want to stare but did glance down even as he stepped away. Mackenzie's familiar face looking up at him stopped all movements.

"Hi, Tuck," she said softly.

"Mackenzie!" Tucker gave her a hug. "What a surprise!"

Mackenzie laughed and said, "I was a little surprised myself. What are you looking at?"

"I'm trying to find something for Jack and Mom's anniversary next month."

"Oh, this shop isn't very big. Have you tried Golden Beaver Dry Goods? Delancey loves it."

"Is Delancey here?"

"Not this time."

Tucker was about to ask how often she came to Colorado to ski but realized he hadn't even covered that she was there at all.

"Mic, did I know you were coming to Beaver Creek?"

"I don't think I mentioned it. Did you say you were coming?"

"No, because I didn't know. It was all very last-minute. One of my authors has a condo here, and when part of his family couldn't join him for the week, he asked me."

"How nice. Did you just arrive?"

"On Sunday. How about you?"

"Last Friday. I'm almost ready to go home."

A million questions came to mind, but Tucker didn't voice them.

"Are you free to meet Rudy Norton and his family tonight?"

She couldn't stop the stiffening of her body. "Oh, Tucker, I don't want to intrude on them."

"They wouldn't think it intrusive. We're making tacos and having a great feast. He's here with his wife and kids. You'll love all of them."

Mackenzie didn't know what to say. It did sound like fun, but she was not good with strangers. *You're not going to get better if you don't practice.*

"Say you'll come," Tucker pressed her.

"I'll come," she told him before she could change her mind.

"Good. Now come with me and help me find something for Mom and Jack. Oh, wait a minute," Tucker said, remembering something suddenly and looking down at her. "I have something I need to show you."

"Okay." Mackenzie looked uncertain but went with him as he moved two shops down and pointed through the window.

"When I saw this suit earlier, I thought it would be perfect for you." He looked down to see that she wasn't even looking in the window, but right at him.

"Tucker, are you one of those men who likes to shop?"

He grinned. "Yes. How about you?"

"I hate it."

He only grinned again. "I'll have to convert you."

Mackenzie only laughed.

"Come on now," he hustled her toward the door. "Look at this wool suit."

Mackenzie had to admit that he was right. It was beautiful: a gorgeous plaid in deep navy and teal with a tiny yellow stripe.

"I think you should buy all three pieces, the teal turtleneck and all."

"Do you now?" She looked amused.

"Yes." He was undaunted. "Get your size and try it on."

"What's the hurry?"

"Well, we still have to get something for Jack and Mom and be back at the condo by 5:00 to help with dinner."

"Oh. All right."

Mackenzie did as she was told, finding her size and disappearing into the small dressing room. Tucker was right: It was a perfect color and style for her. She could have looked at it for half an hour but remembered the time.

"How was it?" Tucker asked as soon as she emerged.

"It's beautiful. Thank you for finding it."

Tucker smiled, obviously very pleased.

"I think you might be in the wrong business. You and Delancey should be professional shoppers," Mackenzie said just before she went to pay for the outfit.

Not until she asked the clerk to have it delivered to her suite did Tucker realize she was staying right in the hotel. He still didn't comment but hustled her out the door to help him find some other shops. They ended up wandering down through what was called the Pedestrian Plaza and over to the Beaver Creek Lodge. For just an instant Mackenzie wished that Delancey had been there to go with him, but it wasn't long before she realized she was having fun. It was strange: The only other person who could make shopping fun was her sister.

"What is that smell?" Tucker finally said when they had looked through the dry goods store and found nothing he wanted.

"That would be the Rocky Mountain Chocolate Factory. We haven't looked there."

Tucker's brows went up in an adorable way. "Let's go."

They found the perfect gift for Jack and Joanne, and Tucker even bought dessert for the meal that night. He didn't give Mackenzie time to freshen up but hustled her to his car.

"Tucker, I at least need to comb my hair."

"You look wonderful," he said simply but sincerely, and Mackenzie, not wanting to be teased and wishing she hadn't agreed, fell silent. The drive was just minutes long and made in silence as well. Tucker didn't think anything amiss until they climbed from the car and a streetlight showed Mackenzie's strained features.

He stopped completely and asked softly, "Mackenzie, what is it?"

"Nothing," she said, trying to make it true in her heart.

"You look upset."

"No — I mean, not really . . ." She stopped, trying to be honest. "I'm just not good with people,

Tucker. I have to work on that."

"I'm sorry I pushed you into this."

"It's okay. I just don't want to intrude. I mean, you haven't even checked with them."

"That won't matter. That's the kind of people they are. You'll like Rudy and his wife, Jacki. Honestly you will."

Mackenzie nodded, shaking a little and hoping it was just the cold. She followed Tucker to the door and made herself stay behind him when he opened the door and walked right in.

"Is that you, Tuck?" a man's voice called from inside.

"Yes. And I've brought a guest."

"Good. We need someone to grate the cheese."

Mackenzie smiled when Tucker turned to wink at her. No wonder Tucker liked this man. They sounded much alike.

Rudy came to meet her just moments later, and he was as nice as Tucker had claimed. She had read one of his books — he wrote nonfiction Bible studies — and it was something of a privilege to meet the man. His wife, Jacki, was next, and then his two sons and two daughters, Sam, B.J., Cassie, and Lydia, ages 23 to 17.

They all treated Mackenzie as though she were part of the family, and when over dinner they discovered she wrote, they were more excited for her than she would have imagined.

"I think that's wonderful," Jacki exclaimed. "Lid is interested in children's books. Who does your illustrations, or do you do them?"

"My sister does."

"How fun," Cassie said. "Too bad I can't draw, Liddy."

"B.J. can," Lydia countered.

"That's true." This came from Rudy. "How does it work, Mackenzie? Does your sister give you pictures and you work out a story, or just the opposite?"

"For us, the story comes first. Delancey draws beautifully, but she needs words to get her started. As soon as I describe a scene, she can run with it."

"And where did she study?"

Mackenzie explained but also felt a need to tell them that Delancey's work was good enough to be published before she had studied anywhere.

"How did you learn to write?" they asked next.

Mackenzie smiled. "As a kid I took a correspondence course, but I think a lot of my situation is just an overactive imagination."

They all loved this, and Mackenzie realized she was having a wonderful time. Rudy was not at all put off when she had some questions for him. She was careful not to mention fiction, but some of what he said gave her information about Christian publishing that she hadn't known.

"I think cake is in order," Jacki said about an hour after the meal. "Did you kids know that Tucker brought chocolate cake?"

"That's redundant," Mackenzie couldn't help but comment.

"What is?" Tucker asked.

"Chocolate cake."

It took the younger people a few minutes to get the joke, and Rudy had to explain it to Lydia, but Jacki was still laughing when she asked B.J. to come and help her serve. Rudy continued to smile when his wife left, thinking that their guest fit into the family very nicely. He noticed that both his boys seemed to find Mackenzie Bishop quite interesting, and he understood why, but his eyes were on his good friend, Tucker Stone. They probably wouldn't need to work together on the next book for several more months, but he needed a little time alone with Tucker before they parted company again. He had something that needed to be said.

"So what's the plan for tomorrow?" Tucker asked when he drove Mackenzie back to her hotel.

"I'm going to ski all day and then lie in the hot tub. Want to join me?"

"I was hoping you would ask." His voice was dramatic enough to make Mackenzie smile. "The Nortons are going to be with family, and I was going to bum around on my own. I'll even buy you dinner tomorrow night."

"Well, I won't pass that up."

"What time shall I meet you?"

"The lifts open at 9:00. Come right to my suite, and we'll head down."

"All right."

"By the way, just bring your equipment in and leave it with someone at the desk. Tell them you're with me. They'll give you a day pass and put your gear out for pickup." She gave him the number of her suite, and by then they were back at the door.

"I had a great time, Tuck. Thanks for inviting me."

"Thank you for coming. I'll see you in the morning."

"Okay. Goodnight, Tuck."

"Goodnight, Micki."

And it was a good night, both sleeping soundly and waking ready to ski. They were headed to the slopes by ten after nine. Tucker had heard about the service at the Hyatt but not experienced it. He found it to be quite a treat. On top of that was skiing with Mackenzie. She was gutsy and smooth in her technique, and just as if they were waltzing, she "danced" with him down each slope.

"When did you learn to ski?" he asked her over lunch, both a little flushed from the morning's activities.

"We used to go to Tahoe when I was a kid and even as a teen. My mother grew up in Colorado Springs, so even when we lived in San Francisco, she always had a hankering to head for snow. We skied whenever we had the chance and money. I suppose you've been skiing since you could walk."

"Just about. I can't ever remember *not* being on the slopes. And being the youngest of three, I had to keep up."

"You must have had a blast with Matthew and Gem."

"Oh, we did. My folks too."

"My dad never skied as well as my mom."

"It was just the opposite for me; my dad was the best." Tucker's voice grew soft as he said this, causing Mackenzie to get more personal.

"When did you lose him?" she asked gently.

"I was in high school. Matt took over, or I don't think I would have made it."

"He's how much older?"

"Six years, and Gem is only two. I can't remember — are you older than Delancey?"

"By 13 months."

"That must have been fun for your folks."

Mackenzie's brows rose. "So fun they didn't have a third."

"Did you miss that?"

"Not really. Deej and I have gotten along well

for most of our lives. I tend to be bossy, and she tends to be a follower. It's a winning combination until I give her the wrong advice."

"*You* give wrong advice?" His face was shocked.

"Well, I did once," she conceded mischievously, before stealing a fry from his plate.

They skied for two more hours after lunch, spent some time in the hot tub, went their separate ways for a few hours, and then met back for dinner in the Patina Ristorante located in the Hyatt. Tucker was there first and watched Mackenzie approach. She had changed into jeans, a western shirt, and boots. Her thick chestnut hair bounced loosely on her shoulders, and her movements were naturally graceful. Tucker thought she looked fabulous.

"All set?" she asked as he came forward to meet her.

"They said it'll be ten minutes."

Mackenzie nodded. "Do you want to go elsewhere?"

"No, I'm not that hungry. How about you?"

"I can wait."

They took seats in the waiting area, Mackenzie noting absently that they never ran out of things to talk about. She even had a question about a verse she was studying in the book of James, and Tucker was able to help her with it.

Once they were seated in a comfortable booth, a waiter, looking ready to give up the shirt off his back, appeared with menus that sported everything from light entrees to gourmet fare. Both Mackenzie and Tucker wanted something on the lighter side and settled for the day's special of French onion soup and Mediterranean salad. Mackenzie wanted coffee, but Tucker went with lemonade.

"You don't really want the coffee as much as you do the cream and sugar," Tucker commented at he watched her. "I've noticed that before."

"That's about it," Mackenzie agreed without shame. She also made a face. "I don't actually want to taste the real stuff. Don't you take anything in yours?"

"Oh, a little cream and sugar, but I'm not in your league."

Mackenzie smiled, but his words made her mind wander. In truth, she would have admitted that it was *she* who was not in Tucker's league. He was so special. Mackenzie couldn't help but think that the woman who claimed his heart would have to be special as well.

All at once she needed a moment alone and was almost glad that she needed to excuse herself. Hoping that Tucker had not read the sadness in her eyes, she quietly eased out of the booth and left the table.

Forty-Six

Tucker watched several male heads turn when Mackenzie reentered the restaurant and crossed to their booth. She looked completely unaware of anything as she sat down, and without planning on it, Tucker said something.

"Do you ever notice how many men watch you, Micki?"

Mackenzie blinked at him as if he'd spoken another language, shook her head a little, and started to open her mouth.

"If you're about to tell me," Tucker cut in, "that you're Mackenzie and not Delancey, save your breath. I know exactly which woman is having dinner with me."

Mackenzie had never been so surprised. Having stayed in the bathroom until she regained control, she now had the sensation that her world had tipped and righted itself again in the space of several seconds. She stared across at Tucker for several heartbeats before softly speaking.

"Tucker, how did you know I was going to say that?"

His smile was full of warm compassion. "Being six years older, Matt entered his medical internship when I was still in high school. My father hadn't been gone that long, and suddenly I was faced with everyone asking if I was going to be a doctor too. I had no interest in that area but suddenly began to doubt myself. Matt never said anything to pressure me, but I was cast in his shadow repeatedly; sometimes I still am.

"I don't see Delancey doing anything like that to you, but something tells me that *you've* compared yourself to her for your entire life. I think she looks up to you in a very strong way, and you're a great role model for her, but I think you somehow feel inadequate when it comes to your looks. The Bible repeatedly tells us that the most important part of man is on the inside, so maybe I shouldn't have said anything, but the truth is, Micki, you're a beautiful woman. Delancey is very attractive too, but there's no reason for you to stand in her shadow."

"It's hard not to, you know. She's taller than I am." She was more comfortable making a wisecrack than being serious, but Tucker would not let her get away with it. He reached over and laid his hand on hers.

"Just think about what I've said. The next time I compliment you, I don't want you to mention D.J. or get that skeptical look on your face."

Not accustomed to being ordered around, Mackenzie took a moment to respond. She opted to close the subject.

"I don't think it's that bad, Tucker."

"That blouse is beautiful, Mic. Did you get it up here?"

"No." Her tone and expression were instantly dismissive. "I think Delancey found it somewhere."

Tucker only stared at her, and with that look, Mackenzie caught herself. Not believing compliments had become as natural as breathing. In the next instant she was angry. She hid it fairly well, but her voice was on the cool side when she asked Tucker a question.

"If the most important part of us is our hearts, why are we even talking about this?"

"Because a certain intimacy is established when a compliment is given, especially between a man and a woman. You have to get a little bit close to do it honestly, and, by your own admission, that doesn't come easily to you."

Mackenzie did remember saying that, but it was so long ago — she would have doubted that he remembered. She didn't realize that she didn't have to say a word: Tucker had seen her in action many times; strangers were very hard for her.

The waiter brought the first part of their meal just then, and Mackenzie hoped that the other conversation was over. Tucker prayed briefly before asking Mackenzie a question about skiing at Beaver Creek that made her feel like she could breathe again. The topic then ranged to skiing at home and how often Mackenzie went.

She answered, and he said, "I'm impressed. I thought only the natives went that often."

Maybe that's what I'm trying to become, Mackenzie thought, ignoring the ache in her heart over still not fitting in. Was that true, or was it an emotional response to a long day and a conversation she had found painful and exposing?

She might have been surprised to find that Tucker thought the day long as well. They didn't linger over the meal, and although Tucker asked Mackenzie if she wanted to take a walk, he was glad when she declined. He was quite tired. He walked Mackenzie to her suite, told her to have a good flight home, and took himself down the hall.

Mackenzie thanked him, shut the door, but didn't move. Her mind was swarming with emotions as she tried to sort through truth and fiction. What had started as a wonderful day had turned rather sour. With a shake of her head, she pulled her boots off. She was turning for the bathroom to ready for bed when there was a knock on the door. She opened it to find Tucker in the hall.

"I'm sorry to bother you, Mackenzie." His voice was very soft. "I need to apologize."

More than a little surprised, Mackenzie blinked up at him but stayed quiet.

"I had no business doing that to you. If I want to tell you that I think you're beautiful, then I should do that instead of telling you that men stare at you and then scolding you for not believing me. I'm sorry I did that, and I hope you'll forgive me."

"Of course, Tucker, thank you," Mackenzie said softly. "It's true that I need to think about what you said, so I wasn't angry at you."

"Be that as it may, I handled it very poorly."

Mackenzie wasn't sure what to say, but her look was open.

"Have a good trip, okay?" Tucker took a step away.

"You do the same, and I'll see you when you get home."

Tucker nodded, bid her goodnight, and went on his way. Mackenzie was in bed 20 minutes later, still not sure how she felt about the day. She fell asleep before she could decide.

"Gem!" Tucker exclaimed when he opened his front door the morning after he returned and found his sister standing there. He gave her a great hug, invited her in out of the cold, and offered her a cup of coffee.

"Where are the kids?"

"With a sitter," she said with pleasure, taking a satisfying sip from the steaming mug he pressed into her hands. "Andy told me to take the day off and run away. I'm here to have lunch and shop with Mom."

"Is it a surprise?"

"No. I called yesterday."

"Well, I'm glad you stopped in. I don't suppose I'm invited to lunch?"

"No. It's a girls-only thing. Tell me, Tuck, have you ever thought about marrying Mackenzie?"

Tucker nearly choked on the coffee in his mouth. He swallowed with an effort and stared at his sister in amazement. She was looking remarkably calm and as though she expected an immediate answer.

"Do you know," Tucker finally replied, "you're the second person to ask me that in the last few weeks."

"Who was the other?"

"Rudy Norton."

"While you were in Colorado?"

"Yes."

"How does he know Mackenzie?"

Tucker explained the way they had run into each other, and Gemma looked more pleased than ever. She also still looked as though she expected an answer. She waited just a few minutes before giving him a pointed look and saying, "Well,

813

have you?"

"Gem, for mercy's sake."

"Don't for mercy's sake me, especially if Rudy said something to you. If that's the case, you must have the subject on your mind — at least a little."

Brother and sister stared at each other.

"She fascinates me," Tucker admitted softly.

Gemma's eyes grew tender. "She's so special, Tuck. I love Delancey so very much, but there's something about Mackenzie that —" Gemma gestured with her hands, a helpless move since the words were not there.

"I think I know what you mean, but I hope you're not expecting me to drive to Zephyr Cove and propose."

"Well, not today, but maybe next week." Gemma's smile was cheeky.

"Thank you."

"Seriously, Tucker, I know I sounded off-the-wall, and I don't know if God has this for you or not, but I can't stop thinking about you two at Christmas. I had to tell you."

"What happened at Christmas?" Tucker frowned in thought.

"Nothing in particular; there was just such a chemistry."

Tucker's raised brows told Gemma she had surprised him again.

"You didn't notice it?"

"No, but I'd like you to tell me about it."

"It's just the type of people you are. You have such a zany sense of humor, and some women would spend all their time laughing at you. Mackenzie laughs, but then she gives as good as she gets. I would have been stunned if you had told me you haven't thought of her at all."

"Why?"

"Because most men don't want a woman who sits and looks at them with adoring eyes; they want a woman they feel is their equal on most levels."

"And you think Mackenzie is?"

"Oh, Tucker, I wish you could watch the two of you. It doesn't matter what you're doing: skiing, talking, or joking. She matches you so well."

"Tell me, Gem," Tucker said indulgently, "what am I doing if Mackenzie's interest lies elsewhere?"

Gemma sat up very straight at Tucker's kitchen table, her look turning stubborn.

"Well, it just can't, that's all. You'd better say something soon to make sure, but in the meantime, she can just wait for you."

Tucker got a good laugh over this one. "I'll let the Lord know He can take the week off since you're in control."

Gemma took her mug to the sink.

"If I'm going to be laughed at, I'm leaving, but you mark my words, Tucker Stone, you should marry Mackenzie Bishop, and I don't mean maybe. Now, see me to the door."

Tucker did, hugging her and thanking her with a warm smile on his face. He hoped she would have a good time and thought it very wise of Andy to tell her to take a day for herself. Tucker had work to do, lots of it, but Gemma had him thinking. He'd all but gawked at Rudy when he took him aside, and now his sister . . .

Well, Rudy and Gem, I'm interested, I can tell you that, but there's something else here that I can't put my finger on. If I could discover that, I might be ready to show my hand.

Tucker forced his mind back to the computer and the manuscript that needed his undivided attention, but a pair of incredible greenish-gray eyes that kept coming to mind made it no easy task.

"You're just the lady I was hoping to see," Tucker said to Mackenzie the next evening at minichurch. The group had just been dismissed, and most of the people were still in small clusters talking. Tucker had been across the room, but when the seat next to Mackenzie vacated, he took it.

"What have I done?" she teased him.

"Many horrible things I'm sure, but it's what I've done that I'm afraid of."

"What's that?"

"Do you remember back at Christmas when I told you I had already talked to someone about your work?"

"Yes."

"Well, I never heard back, so I thought it was water under the bridge. I completely forgot that I left a voice-mail message, and now that things have slowed down from the holidays, someone had time to listen. Are you going to hate me?"

"Probably, but tell me the rest anyhow."

"Johanna Joyce — she's an editor with Candlelight Press — called me today all excited about my knowing the Bishop sisters. She's very familiar with your work and desperately wants to know if you've sold your Jungle Buds idea to someone else."

Mackenzie was stunned. She had never counted on someone in the Christian market knowing about their general market titles but then realized how foolish that had been. It was perfectly logical that an editor would make the connection. But was this what they wanted? Did they have a choice? It wasn't as if they had told Jack and

Tucker to use other names. Mackenzie had enough of that with Mac Walker.

As though the room were empty, Mackenzie sat mulling it over. She was quiet for so long that Tucker interrupted her thoughts.

"You're doing your poker look now."

"My what?" This brought her eyes to his.

"Your poker look. You did it to me when I first mentioned to you and D.J. that I'd talked to someone about these books."

Mackenzie had no remembrance of this and continued to watch him to see if he was joking. He wasn't. Mackenzie, however, wanted to laugh.

"I can honestly say, Tucker, that you're one of the most fascinating people I've ever known."

He looked startled. "What did I say?"

"It's not just now. There are times when your compliments have turned my head and other times when you've called me a rodent. Now I have a poker face."

"I have never called you a rodent!" he protested.

"Maybe not in so many words, but —" she let the sentence hang.

"Tell me about this time I called you a rodent."

"So what does she want you to do exactly?" Mackenzie parried, neatly ignoring his command.

"Who?" Tucker was momentarily at sea.

"Johanna Joyce. Does she want my phone number or does she want us to send something?"

Tucker looked at her, his sister's words about the way she matched him coming to mind. He made himself look away to answer.

"She mostly wanted to know if you've gone elsewhere. I had to tell her that I honestly didn't know."

"No, we haven't, but now what happens?"

"I call her back. If you want her to see your work, I'll tell her or say no thank you. I suppose you'll want to talk to Delancey."

"I will," Mackenzie replied absently, "but I wouldn't have to; she usually wants me to handle this end."

"More experience?"

Mackenzie's eyes swung to his. "As a matter of fact, yes."

Tucker's eyes narrowed ever so slightly. "One of these days I'm going to figure you out, Mackenzie Bishop."

Insecurity rolled over Mackenzie without warning, and she shifted her gaze.

"Don't look too deep, Tucker. You'll probably be very disappointed."

Tucker cocked his head as he studied her profile. "Why would you say that?"

Mackenzie could have ripped her own tongue out. She refused to look at him.

"I'd better get going." Like a coward, she scooted to the edge of the sofa.

"What do I tell Johanna?" Tucker asked quickly, letting the other subject drop when he didn't want to.

"Oh." She looked as flustered as she felt. "Can I call you, Tucker? I guess I should at least mention it to Delancey."

"That's fine."

"Okay. Thank you, Tucker. Goodnight."

"Let me give you a lift."

"It's all right."

But Tucker wasn't going to be put off. He rose to follow her, not anticipating being stopped by someone needing to ask him a question. Mackenzie talked to Titus and his wife for a moment, but she was still out the door ahead of him. She was nowhere to be seen when he got to his car, but he still drove around the corner to check on her. She was just getting to her front door when he got to the house. Satisfied that she at least got home, he had no satisfaction over her comment.

I've got to leave this with You, Lord. I don't have any idea what the future holds, but I can't let that worry me. Thank You that You know it all. Thank You for Mackenzie. Please bless her. Help me to be blameless in the relationship, to encourage her, and to always glorify You with my actions and thoughts.

Tucker prayed all the way home, giving the relationship to the Lord. Mackenzie was heavy on his mind the rest of the evening and again in the morning. He didn't want to speculate on what that meant.

"You don't seem yourself, Micki. You seem discouraged."

"I think I am. I'm not thankful these days, Jack. I'm restless and anxious, and I just have such a hard time giving things to the Lord." She gave him a direct look. "Jack, how did you know about Mom or Joanne? If God is supposed to be my everything, why am I so lonely?"

"Oh, Micki," Jack said tenderly, "that's a hard one. All I can tell you is that God doesn't play games with us. If He gives us a longing to be married, He will provide the mate. I can't say that I was never lonely before I met your mother, because for brief times I was. I had to learn to go to the Lord and seek Him first. It wasn't a sugar pill, Mic. I couldn't just use prayer or Scripture whenever I was down, but I had to have a steady diet of it. That way, when the loneliness came, I knew just where to turn. I never dreamed that your mother would walk into my life, or Joanne for that matter, but I could be alone again tomorrow."

He watched her nod and then let her think for a moment. It was on the tip of his tongue to ask whether she had met someone, thinking this might be the reason for her loneliness, but something made him hold off.

He needed to check on her more often than he did. It wasn't at all unusual for him not to talk to her all week. He couldn't feel guilty about that since she had a phone too, but he knew how hard it was for her to share from her heart and how equally hard it was for her to get close to others.

Joanne came to the edge of the living room and softly announced that lunch was ready. Thanking her, Jack and Mackenzie went to the kitchen, but Jack was still thinking about ways he could help Mackenzie grow.

Delancey saw Richard across the room and turned away with a small smile. The church was having a spring party with lots of good food and fellowship, and although they hadn't spoken of it, Delancey hoped Richard would be there.

She liked him a little more each time they spoke; indeed, he was on her mind almost all the time. It was so easy to put on and be someone else when you were on a date, but at church and at special functions like this, it was impossible to keep up a false front for very long. Delancey had been given numerous opportunities to watch Richard, and she liked what she saw. He was caring and kind, and his attention to the details in Scripture was a great example to her.

"Hi, D.J." Sabrina had come up and was now talking to her. "How are you?"

"Just great. How are you?"

"I'm fine."

The women hugged, and before they broke apart, Delancey noticed people approaching. Releasing her young friend, she stood to full height to see it was Richard and two others.

"Hi, Delancey; hi, Sabrina."

"Hi, Richard," they both greeted him.

"I'd like to introduce my parents to you. Dad and Mom, this is Sabrina Cummings and Delancey Bishop. Delancey, Sabrina, these are my parents, Bill and Marlowe Wilder."

"How nice to meet you," Delancey said kindly, hoping no one could see that she was shaking inside.

"It's nice to meet you too, Delancey, and you, Sabrina." This came from Bill before he turned to the younger woman. "Now, how old would you be, Sabrina?"

Sabrina answered, and since Delancey was listening, Marlowe took a moment to catch her son's ear. After she put a hand on his arm, he bent low to hear her.

"Delancey looks terrified, Richard. Please make sure she knows we're not here to inspect her. We just wanted to see you."

"I will. I thought maybe I'd ask her to dinner tomorrow night. What do you think?"

"Oh, do!" she urged him softly. "I'll make whatever you're hungry for, and we'll just have a relaxed time, but make sure she knows she doesn't *have* to come."

Richard smiled warmly at his mother and touched her shoulder. He well remembered the way she talked about his father's family. They had been wealthy at one time, and even though the fortune was dwindling, for years they'd had illusions of grandeur. Sweet little Marlowe Doyle had been put on display every time she visited until it was almost the death of the relationship. She had finally asked William Wilder, with whom she was very much in love, whether she was marrying him or his whole family.

Bill's father had very progressive views about women, saying they should wear slacks everywhere and work out of the home. Completely against his own viewpoint, his wife was never seen in pants and was a homemaker as well. One of Bill's aunts had very definite ideas about child raising, and another thought that having more than one child was a complete waste of a woman's time. Each time Marlowe visited, she was subjected to a different "interview."

Growing up in the atmosphere of these vocal, opinionated people, shy Bill Wilder, a new believer, took some time to gain the courage to tell Marlowe what he wanted from a marriage, but when he did, he learned that Marlowe wanted the exact same things.

"How are you?" Richard was suddenly next to Delancey. His parents were still talking with Sabrina and a few others who had come up, so Richard grabbed a moment with Delancey.

"I'm fine. It's nice that your folks could be here."

"My doorbell rang yesterday afternoon, and I opened the door to find them standing there."

"They surprised you. How fun."

"Are you free to join us for dinner tomorrow night?"

"Oh, Richard, don't your folks want you to

themselves?"

"No, they would love to have you. My mother is just afraid that you'll see it as some sort of inspection."

For some reason Delancey found this highly amusing.

"Would they want to see my teeth?" she asked with a laugh.

"I'm the one who wants to see your teeth," Richard admitted softly. "Don't you ever need a checkup so I can have an excuse to see you?"

"I'll see what I can do."

Richard had all he could do not to touch her. She was so sweet, and when she smiled up at him, his heart slammed in his chest.

"So you'll come?" he asked to divert his thoughts.

"I'd like to. What should I bring?"

He almost said "nothing" but thought better of it.

"You know that salad you made for Thanksgiving, the one with the pudding and fruit? Will you make that?"

"Oh, no problem. Can I bring anything else?"

"Just yourself."

It was said so softly that Delancey's eyes found his. What she saw there melted her heart. They stood still, just watching each other for a moment, before getting back into the group's conversation.

The rest of the afternoon and evening was spent playing games, enjoying food, and sharing fellowship. They weren't together constantly, but they were aware of each other. Delancey prayed that she would think clearly. Richard asked God to help him give her as much time as she needed.

FORTY-SEVEN

"How are you, my dear?" Roz asked as soon as she arrived at Mackenzie's house Monday morning. "You look like you've been crying."

"I have been, but they're good tears. I've been struggling with so many things, but Jack and I talked yesterday, and then Joanne, Jack, and I talked, and by the end of church last night, I knew I had to surrender my stubborn will and pride. I need to serve the Lord the way He wants to be served."

Roz hugged her again. "I've been thinking about you a lot. I haven't called anywhere near as often as I had planned. Tell me, Micki, is there a woman at Kingsbury you can be calling?"

"I go to minichurch around the corner from here, at the Bradfords'. Megan has talked about our going to lunch, but it hasn't happened yet. I think she's only about three years older than I am, but she has three kids under the age of seven. I know how time-consuming that can be."

"But in the meantime, you don't talk to anyone."

"Well, I —" Mackenzie began, but she had to shake her head no. "I call Delancey sometimes, but I tend to think I have to do this on my own."

"We're going to start praying for a friend for you, Micki girl. We're going to ask God to bring someone very special into your life, all right?"

Mackenzie nodded. She needed to talk with friends more often and believe that God had great and wonderful things for her.

"Thank you, Roz. I needed to be reminded of how good God is and how much He wants to do for me."

"What are you studying right now?"

"I'm doing a topical study about the early church. Pastor Kevin feels so strongly that God's big ideal is the local church, and I'm starting to see what he means. All through the New Testament, you can't miss the references to things being done under the church's leadership. I've got a notebook that I keep writing in, and in the midst of that, I'm trying to learn my own role as a single woman."

"In light of that, Mic, you must be seeing how important fellowship is. We can freely ask God to bring someone into your world. It's what He wants for you."

Mackenzie nodded, working to take it all in. She had to keep reminding herself that she was not to be overwhelmed by all of this. God's burden was light, and that was the only burden He wanted her to have.

Roz started her work a short time later; she still enjoyed coming to Mackenzie's house once a week. Mackenzie went back to her office. She was writing along very well with her book, laughing often at how Mason Coltrane was learning the same lessons the Lord was teaching her. The ending had been somewhat fuzzy in her mind, but on this day, the vacuum droning on in the living room below, it all came together for Mackenzie. Using her Bible and her own gift with words, she began the wind-down of the book, thinking that if it was a quiet week, she might actually finish. Excited to see the end in sight, she was typing at a breakneck speed when the phone rang.

"Hello."

"Hello, Mackenzie, this is Cria."

"Oh, hi, Cria."

Mackenzie saw Cria Johansen, Titus' wife, every week at Bradfords' but had never spoken to her on the phone. She had asked about her unusual name, however, and learned that it was a nickname for Christina.

"Am I catching you at a bad time?"

"Not at all."

"I have a favor to ask you."

"Okay."

"I have the two- and three-year-olds for Sunday school, and my helper, Lissa Horn, had her baby this morning, so I was wondering if you could fill in for a few weeks."

"Oh, I think so. I've never helped in Sunday school before. Is that going to matter?"

"No. I mostly need you to take children to the bathroom, hand out papers, and keep the peace if a fight breaks out."

Mackenzie laughed. "I just read an article that said children are born innocent."

Cria laughed with her. "I've read stuff like that too. If ever a person doesn't want to bother reading what God has to say about that subject, he can just visit our nursery class and see what a myth that is. So how about it? Do you want to help?"

"I'd love to. What classroom is it?"

Cria explained how to find her and told her when to be there. As Mackenzie hung up, she suddenly felt very excited and told the Lord so.

I never thought about helping in Sunday school. Maybe this will lead to something permanent. I would love that. I would love to serve You in some special way in this local body, Lord. I pray for the church family, but in my heart I want to learn to do more. Help me to follow Your lead and to be ready with a servant's heart.

The phone jangled in the middle of this prayer. This time it was Delancey. She was having dinner with Richard and his parents that night and was a nervous wreck. She asked Mackenzie to *pray.*

Can you make something that goes with fruit salad, Mom? Delancey wanted to know what to bring, and I told her fruit salad.

Richard's question from the night before lingered in Marlowe's mind as she watched her son with the woman he loved. It hadn't taken an hour before Marlowe knew that Richard wanted to marry this girl. He had said there was someone special, and knowing that Richard was not the type to throw his feelings about, she should have known it was serious.

She praised God that Delancey Bishop was a believer and that her spirit seemed as gentle and quiet as a woman's could be. Marlowe knew that you couldn't know a person in such a short time, but she was given a marvelous first impression as Delancey shared the sofa with Richard and talked with natural grace and ease. If the smile on Bill's face was any indication, he was feeling the same.

"Did you say your father was in the Army?" Bill was asking Delancey.

"Yes, for more than twenty years. He was killed in an auto accident at the Presidio."

"How old were you, Delancey?" Marlowe asked.

"My thirteenth birthday was seven weeks away."

"Oh, my," Marlowe said softly. "So he never knew about your books."

"No, I guess he didn't."

"Tell them your good news from last week," Richard urged her.

"Oh, yes, we heard from a Christian publisher who wants to see our new series."

"This is something different from Micah Bear?"

"Yes. Mackenzie had the idea."

"What is it about?"

"It's called the Jungle Buds, and it's about some little animals that hang out in the jungle together. In the process they learn things the Lord would want them to know."

"Give them the names, D.J."

Delancey smiled at him. "They're all babies. Arlo is an elephant, Casey is a tiger, Dexter is the boa, Lambert is a wolf, and Wilson is a baby owl."

Marlowe laughed in delight. "Those names are adorable."

"That was all Mackenzie's doing."

"But the illustrations are pure Delancey," Richard said with pride. "I would never have believed that anyone could make a snake cute, but Dexter the boa constrictor is amazing."

Delancey looked very pleased, but she also felt her face heat. She was glad when Bill said he was ready for dessert. She offered to help prepare it, but the older Wilders said they would do the honors. Delancey watched them leave the room before looking back to Richard. His eyes were on her.

"My parents like you."

"I like them. They're very kind, and your dad is

828

a sweetheart."

"Does it make you think of your own folks?"

"A little. I don't have anyone for you to meet. I don't think that occurred to me until last night when I got home. Sometimes that feels funny."

"Will you ever want me to meet your grandmother in Florida?"

"I don't know. Mackenzie calls her from time to time, and I write to her, but even when she writes back, it's clear that things aren't normal. My grandfather died suddenly, I guess; Mackenzie wasn't able to get a real clear picture. She thought of writing to one of our uncles or our aunt, but we're not sure we want to have any contact with them. None of them seems very normal."

"My father has some aunts like that," Richard said. "They're elderly now, which has only made it worse. When my folks were first married, they saw more of them, but once my sisters and I came along, they didn't want to subject us to their bizarre view of things."

"You're going to think I'm nuts, but I'm kind of glad."

"That I have weird aunts?"

"Yes. Sometimes your life seems so perfect; I wonder how we'll ever find anything in common."

"My life hasn't been perfect, Delancey — not even close."

Delancey looked at him. "You'll have to tell me about it sometime. I'm glad you haven't had to live through the mistakes I have, Richard, but I do wonder how this could possibly work. I do ask myself how a man like you could care for a woman like me."

Richard leaned close and speared her with his eyes.

"Please don't see me as some type of paragon. I'm anything but. I have some areas of sin that I battle every day. Don't put me on a pedestal. It'll be all the harder when you understand that I have feet of clay."

Delancey stared at him, her look a little stubborn. Richard leaned a little closer on the sofa.

"I can hear my folks coming back, and that's a good thing, Delancey Bishop."

"Why is that?"

"Because when you get that stubborn look, I want to kiss you."

Delancey blinked, and Richard simply sat back and watched her. Not until he did that did she react. Coming in ahead of Bill just a few seconds later, Marlowe took in Delancey's beet-red face and tried not to speculate as to what might have caused it.

Mackenzie sat for a while after the service ended on Sunday. She hadn't sat with anyone, so it was a good opportunity to take her time putting her notes away and think about some things that Pastor Kevin had said.

Roz just said it to me Monday, but I still fail to take it in. You have things for me, Lord, but I never ask. You want to comfort me and love me, but I feel I must do it on my own. This independence is getting to be a major sin area in my life. Now today, Kevin explains how much You love to give to us, and still I don't ask. Help me, Lord, help me to be willing to take risks, step out, and believe You.

Mackenzie was no more done praying about this than she looked up and saw Tucker across the way. She had been asking the Lord's help with something during the week. Now sitting here, trying to give God her all, she realized the answer, at least the start of the answer, might be in front of her. With a prayer for wisdom to deal with her fears, Mackenzie made her way over to him. He was talking to someone, so she hung back, but he saw her approach and waved her closer.

"Okay, Tuck," the other man was saying, "I'll wait for you to get back to me."

"Will do. Thanks, Drew."

"Hi, Mackenzie," Drew Campbell said as he moved away, and Mackenzie smiled and greeted him.

"Did I interrupt, Tucker?"

"Yes. I'm very angry."

Mackenzie instantly felt better. He was still Tucker.

"Well, when you're over your fit of temper, let me know. I need to set up a time to discuss a little business with you."

"Oh, what kind?"

"The business kind."

Mackenzie found herself under his scrutiny. She stood still, telling herself she was not going to talk about it here. This was not the place.

"What are you doing right now?"

"Right now?" she shrugged. "Going home."

"I'm hungry for something from Marie Callender's. Come with me, and we'll talk business."

"Oh," Mackenzie said inanely, and Tucker's look became amused. "I mean, are you sure you want to do that?"

"Very sure. Come. I'll even let you pay."

It was out of the way for Tucker to bring Mackenzie back, so she followed him in her Jeep to the restaurant. Her palms were slick on the wheel as she thought about asking him to help her, but a plan was forming, one that she hoped would give her the courage to speak.

Tucker was praying for the same thing. He had learned that with Mackenzie, a little gentle steamrolling was necessary at times. He thought he was just the man for the job. The waitress had no more walked away with their order than he started.

"So what can I do for you?"

Taken off guard, Mackenzie thought fast. "Well, I'm not exactly sure. I want to ask you something, but I'm a little afraid of, well, being insulting."

"I'm not easily insulted," he told her.

Mackenzie nodded, seeing how that would probably be true but not wanting to be the one to find out otherwise.

"I want to hire you, Tucker," she said softly.

"To do what?"

"I don't want to get into a 'favors thing,' " she went on as if he hadn't spoken. "Your time is valuable, and I want this to be a business arrangement, nothing less."

"What if I want to do this *thing* as a favor?"

Mackenzie's mouth compressed, and she shook her head. Tucker wanted to smile. She was one determined lady when she planned to be.

"Well, why don't you tell me the details, and we'll work out the business arrangements, if we need to, after that."

Mackenzie didn't want to do it that way, but she thought she had held off long enough.

"I want to hire you to read something I've written, Tucker, and I want you to be brutally honest."

"All right," he agreed immediately. "But I have to tell you, Mic, you don't need to pay me for that."

She was already shaking her head. "Your time is valuable, Tuck, and I don't want to take advantage."

"Mackenzie, I appreciate that, but I don't think we're talking that much time — what is it, a few chapters?"

Mackenzie stared at him, and although he wasn't sure what, he knew he'd said something wrong. Her look uncertain, she was opening her mouth to say something when their salads came to the table.

Tucker prayed for the food, and Mackenzie began to eat. So good with words on paper, she asked herself why she couldn't explain herself to this man. The whole thing was such an effort for her; she wondered why she bothered. It was looking easier and easier to call Paxton and ask him if he was interested. He surely wouldn't like the way she wove Christ into the plot, but Paxton was looking better all the time.

"Will you do something for me, Micki?" Tucker asked.

"If I can."

"Tell me what this looks like to you. If you and I had the ideal business arrangement, what would it look like?"

"Well, I guess I would give you my manuscript to read."

"Would you want me to edit it or just read it?"

"I think for now just read it and tell me if you think it has promise or if it needs a lot more work. I would want to know if the plot makes sense, or if it's totally lame — you know, all that kind of stuff."

"It's a novel?"

"Yes. I would also want you to keep track of

833

your time, the page count, or however it works, and let me know so I can pay you."

"How many pages are we talking about here?"

"Eight hundred and fifty."

Tucker's head came up. "Eight-fifty?"

"Yes."

Tucker took a moment to respond. "I owe you an apology, Micki. You're talking, and I'm not listening. I'm sorry."

Tucker went on to name an hourly salary he thought she would be pleased with. He assured her he was quite willing to do it for free and left the decision in her hands.

Mackenzie nodded. "I think that sounds good. There is one other thing, Tuck." Her voice was soft. "This is very private for me."

"I'll remember that and be very discreet."

Mackenzie nodded. "How will I get it to you?"

"Bring it tonight to church and leave it in the Jeep. Afterward I'll come and get it. It'll be dark by then, and no one will be the wiser."

"Okay. Thank you, Tucker."

"You're welcome. I'm glad you asked me."

Mackenzie felt a little shaky now and tucked into her food in earnest.

"Did I see you with the nursery class today?"

"Yes," Mackenzie smiled. "Cria asked me to help since Lissa Horn just had her baby."

"How long will you fill in?"

"For at least a month. Do you have a class, Tucker?"

"Yep. My boys are eighth graders now."

Mackenzie stared at him. "What do you mean, eighth graders *now?*"

"We have a program for Sunday school that's set up more like discipleship. I've had the same boys since the sixth grade, and I'll have them until they graduate from high school."

"That's fabulous. Does it work that way for all the classes?"

"Starting in the sixth grade. We've been at it for about four years, and so far it's been very good. The teachers try to do more than just see the kids for one hour on Sunday morning. Some months I have more time with them than others, but overall, we're getting very close."

"And you serve as an usher too, don't you?"

"Not on a regular basis. I was filling in that first day you saw me, and I'm on the list to help out, but I'm not a full-time usher anymore."

It was news to Mackenzie just how many people it took to keep things moving in an active church body. Her study on that subject was opening her eyes to many things, so Tucker's jobs were of great interest.

The rest of the lunch was fun. Business talk fell away, and they became silly and laughed at outrageous things.

Tucker was good at his word and waited for Mackenzie to leave the church that night, drove his car close, and took the manuscript. She made herself not ask how long it would take him, but something told her she would be on pins and needles until he called.

As though someone were playing a huge April Fool's joke on Mackenzie, she greeted that month with the worse case of flu she had ever had. She wasn't often sick and thought that this bug must be making up for lost time.

Looking for sympathy, she put a call in to Delancey but got only her answering machine.

Not wanting to call anyone else, she took two aspirin, went back to bed, and slept for the better part of the day. Every muscle in her body ached when she woke after one o'clock. She hadn't eaten anything, but she felt rather sick to her stomach. The kitchen and something cold to drink seemed a long way away, so she lay still for some time and tried to drum up the energy to go downstairs. The phone rang as she was on her way back to sleep.

"Delancey?"

"No, it's Tucker. Are you all right, Mackenzie?"

"Oh, Tucker, I thought you might be D.J. I have the flu."

"When did that hit?"

"In the night. I feel so sick to my stomach, and my throat is on fire."

"Your throat hurts?"

"Yes. I think it's because I haven't had much to drink."

"Are you in bed?"

"Yeah."

"Mackenzie, I want you to get up, get dressed, and wait for me downstairs. I think you need to go to the clinic."

"Oh no, Tucker, it's just a flu."

"Not if your throat hurts. Strep is going around. I'm going to come and take you, so get ready and wait for me downstairs."

Mackenzie felt as though she was going to be sick, so she agreed and hung up. She wanted to go back to sleep so she wouldn't vomit but made herself do as she was told. A hot shower sounded nice, but there was no time for that.

With purse in hand, she was ready and dressed when Tucker arrived. She looked very sick indeed, but Tucker didn't comment; he only got her to the car and buckled her in. They hadn't gone a half a mile when she groped for the doorhandle and said Tucker's name in a muffled voice. He swiftly pulled to the side. Mackenzie proceeded to be very sick on the side of the road. Tucker stood next to her and pulled her hair back from her face.

"I'm sorry," she gasped miserably. "I'm sorry."

"It's all right. Just go slow."

Mackenzie stood and took the tissue Tucker had grabbed from the car. She wiped her face and tried not to sway on her feet.

"Can you manage the car again?"

"I think so. I'm sorry."

"It's all right. We'll see a doctor, and he'll get you all set."

Back in the car, Mackenzie realized she did feel better. The urgent care clinic was not too far down the road, and five minutes later, Mackenzie was filling out a form and waiting to see the doctor.

Tucker's large, quiet presence beside her was a comfort. At one point he put an arm around her and she let her head go to his shoulder. She was almost asleep when her name was called. Tucker waited until she was in a nurse's care before using the phone. When Mackenzie emerged some 40 minutes later, he was glad he had made the call.

"I have strep," she told him, looking more pale than ever. "I have to get some medicine."

"I'll get it for you. Let's get out to the car and up to Mom and Jack's."

"What are we doing there?"

"Just getting you settled in where someone can look after you."

Mackenzie was too out of it to even comment. She had been sick again before the doctor came and felt totally drained. She did as she was told for the next few minutes as Tucker helped her into the house, sat her in a chair, and tenderly brushed the hair from her face.

"I hate to throw up, Tucker."

"I'm sure you do. Mom's got some 7UP; that might help you feel better."

Joanne was already coming with a glass.

"Give me your prescription, and I'll go fill it. Mom'll be here for you."

"Thank you."

By the time Jack got home from work that night, Mackenzie had had her first dose of penicillin and was sound asleep in one of the bedrooms upstairs. It was decided that Joanne and Tucker would go to Mackenzie's and get some of her things. While they were gone, she woke and talked with Jack.

"Hi," he said softly as he bent and kissed her.

"Hi, Jack. Tucker brought me over. Was that okay?"

"I wouldn't want you anywhere else."

"I left a message for D.J. earlier today but never talked with her. Can you call her?"

"I think Joanne already did, but I'll check when she gets back."

"She's gone?"

"She and Tucker went to get you some things to wear."

"I feel awful."

"Just rest," he told her sweetly.

Staying awake was not an option. She fell in and out of sleep until Joanne came back with her clothes, helped her take a shower, and then put her back to bed. Tucker waited in the living room, the Winnie-the-Pooh slippers he had seen at her house still hanging from his hand. He had spotted them as they were leaving and thought they might cheer her up. Jack had come down to put dinner on, but Tucker waited where he was. The urge to go up and take care of Mackenzie was surprisingly strong. She was so miserable, and as much as he trusted his mother, he wanted to see for himself that she was all right.

I'm falling, Lord. I know I am. Don't let me go there by myself. I don't know what she thinks of me, not specifically, but You do. You're able to do anything, Lord, and I praise You for this. If You want this for us, it will happen. If we're to find each other, Lord, let it happen in Your time and help us not to leave You out of the picture.

"Staying for dinner, Tucker?" Jack asked, sticking his head around the corner.

"If you have enough."

"Sure."

"Thank you," Tucker said. Staying allowed him to be close to Mackenzie just a bit longer.

When Mackenzie woke in the morning, Delancey was in her room. She sat in a chair reading a book as though she'd been there for hours. The movement of the covers brought the book down, and she looked at her sister.

"Welcome back." Her voice was soft and kind.

"Thank you. What time is it?"

"Almost nine."

"How long have you been here?"

"Since about 8:15. How are you feeling?"

"Sore, but I don't think I need to be sick."

"How's the throat?"

"It hurts."

Delancey stood and went to the nightstand, dragging her chair with her so she could be closer.

"Here, take your next pill."

Mackenzie was grateful for the drink she was offered and drained the glass once the medicine was down. She lay back thinking someone with large boots had been kicking her.

"Is Tucker here?" she asked suddenly.

"I don't think so. Why?"

"I don't know if I dreamed about him or just thought of him every time I woke up."

"Well, at least you pick your dreams well," Delancey said softly, a small smile on her lips.

Mackenzie looked up at her.

"Speaking of which, how is Richard?"

"He's wonderful." The smile grew. "I didn't know men like that existed."

"I know what you mean. All the men at church are so different from any we've ever known. I never catch anyone checking out my body, D.J. It's so special."

"Yes, it is. Richard told me he wants to kiss me, but he's not even held my hand."

"How do you feel about him these days?"

"I'm in love with him, but we're going to move slowly. His parents were wonderful, but I still want to meet his sisters. I was afraid of that until just last week, and then I gave it to the Lord. He's given me a real peace."

"What happened?"

"I was not using logic, and when I did, it was a big help. I've met Richard's parents, and I know the person he is, so why did I think his sisters would be scary and not like me? It was just foolish." Delancey looked at Mackenzie. "I think sometimes that my past sins are written all over me. Like I said, I just needed to think biblically about it, and the Lord was able to help me see."

"I'm glad, Deej. I've prayed for you about the

whole thing."

"I'm sorry I wasn't there when you called, Mic," Delancey said very soberly. "I feel like I'm never there for you. I thought that would all change when I came to Christ, but sometimes I'm as self-centered as always."

"I do need more fellowship with women, Delancey, but that doesn't mean you have to be the only one. I need to work on reaching out."

Delancey looked upset. "You always make excuses for me, Mic. I'm trying to apologize, but you won't let me."

Mackenzie lay looking up at her, thinking how true that was.

"I'm sorry." Delancey started again. "I'm sorry I haven't been there for you, and I'm sorry I snapped at you just now. If you need to reach out more, that's between you and the Lord, but I know I could be doing a better job as your sister. So again, I'm sorry."

"Thank you, D.J."

Delancey leaned over and hugged her older sister.

"I don't tell you enough what you mean to me, Mackenzie. I don't tell you enough how much I love you."

"I love you too, Deej."

The women hugged for a long time, both having missed this simple act. Mackenzie's body ached, her throat was raw, and she was hollow inside, but suddenly she felt much better.

FORTY-EIGHT

Mackenzie had not planned to stay at the Averys' all day, but Joanne had other ideas. She clearly relished playing the role of nurse, and in truth, Mackenzie enjoyed her so much she ended up staying, which meant being pampered all day. Both Delancey and Tucker were returning to have dinner with them that night, and Mackenzie knew that with the easy day she'd had, she would feel more than well enough to go home by morning.

That night Delancey was in the kitchen helping Joanne when Tucker arrived. Mackenzie was settled in the living room, Pooh slippers in place, watching the evening news.

"Hi," Tucker greeted her as he took a seat. "You look like you feel better."

"I do. Thank you for everything, Tucker."

"You're welcome. How's the throat?"

"Better — much better."

"And your stomach?"

"I'm starved."

Tucker smiled. It was nice to have her back to normal.

"Who brought my slippers?" Mackenzie asked.

"I saw them by the stairs and grabbed 'em. I didn't know you liked Winnie-the-Pooh."

"Not just Pooh Bear," Delancey called from the

dining room. "Any and all cartoons. Her office is filled with them."

Tucker looked at Mackenzie. "Is that true?"

She nodded, a smile on her face. "I even watch them on Saturday mornings."

Tucker laughed. "They're not as good as they used to be."

"No, the best ones are gone, but sometimes I see reruns of Bugs Bunny and Elmer Fudd, or Foghorn Leghorn, and that gives me my fix for the week."

"I love the Coyote. I'm hoping that one of these days he'll eat the Road Runner."

"I feel the same way. I want Sylvester to eat Tweetie too."

"This sounds intellectual," Jack commented, having just showered for the evening.

"It is! Cartoon watching has become an art, Jackson. I can't believe you don't understand that."

"You're feeling better," he commented. "You didn't care what you watched about 24 hours ago."

"Dinner is ready," Joanne called to all of them.

"Okay," Jack answered, making his way from the room.

Mackenzie stood and suddenly found Tucker right next to her. He spoke quietly.

"The reason I called you yesterday was because I read your book."

Mackenzie felt excitement shoot through her. "Did you really, Tucker?"

"Yes. I finished it. I'd like to talk to you about it after dinner. Does Delancey and everyone know about it?"

"Only Delancey does, but I don't mind if Jack and Joanne find out."

"Okay."

"Tucker —" Mackenzie put a hand on his arm and waited for him to look at her. "I don't want you to spare me."

"Okay," he said softly, a tender smile covering his mouth.

"Come on, you two," Joanne urged them. "Food's getting cold."

Mackenzie told herself not to panic. In the midst of being ill, the book had been forgotten. Now the time had come. She told herself she had done her best and couldn't ask more of herself. That Tucker's approval meant a great deal to her had not sunk in yet. It would be some time before it did.

"What's the book about?" Joanne wished to know. Dinner was over and everyone was gathered in the living room.

"Shall I tell her, Mic?"

"That's fine, Tucker. Delancey has read most of it."

Tucker gave a quick rundown of the story. He didn't go into detail, but clearly he had read every word. He did a nice job explaining.

"And what did you think?"

"It's excellent," he said seriously, his eyes on Mackenzie, even though the question had come from Jack. "It's one of the best books I've read in a long time." Tucker's praise was sincere, but he was not at all surprised to see Mackenzie's inscrutable look in place. He realized now that it was her business face, her look of concentration.

"What would you change?" she finally asked.

"Maybe a little of Mason's ability. Sometimes fiction gets to be bigger than life, and lots of times

844

that's all right, but at times Mason seems too good to be true with his physical ability, like his shooting and such."

"What part exactly?" Delancey asked.

"Well, he goes from no experience to being the best shot. That was a little hard to swallow."

"Mackenzie," Delancey said softly, her voice telling her sister she was waiting for something.

Mackenzie looked at her. "It has to be believable, Deej, no matter what."

Delancey did not look happy. She exchanged a glance with Jack, whose brow was lowered in thought as well. Tucker missed none of this.

"What's going on?" he asked.

"Mackenzie was an excellent marksman, Tucker," his stepfather told him kindly.

Tucker looked at the woman across from him. "I tend to forget that you were in the Army and not just your father." His eyes narrowed in thought. "And you picked up a rifle without prior experience and shot well?"

"Yes. I was awarded the expert badge for the rifle range." She shrugged a little. "It's just like that for some people, Tucker. There were women in my unit who were terrified of the thing. I wasn't. I wasn't as strong with maps, and I was taken apart on a weekly basis for the shape of my footlocker, but there was never any criticism of my job with the M-16."

Again Tucker looked at her in thought, his head nodding slowly.

"Were you by any chance stationed at the Pentagon?"

"Yes."

His face dawned with understanding. So much made sense now. The book was almost autobiographical, but because Mason Coltrane was such a masculine protagonist, no one would ever make the connection unless they knew the details. Tucker had not been kidding; the book was wonderful. He knew several publishing houses that would jump at the chance to publish it. If he was editing it, he would polish a few areas but leave the rest alone.

"What else, Tucker?" Mackenzie pressed him.

"Let me see," he said, coming back to the present. "I think you use a verse out of context toward the end. There are several other verses you could use, so you might want to look into changing that, but other than a few scenes with Mason that I didn't find as believable as the rest of the book, I thought it was fabulous. The ending is such a surprise and so satisfying. I didn't feel that it had to go on and on, but I did feel as though I could read it again. The plot makes such nice turns. I lost some sleep getting through it."

Mackenzie felt short of breath. He liked it. He really liked it!

"If you want, I can go over it again and edit it."

"Do you have time?"

"I can work it into my schedule. It's pretty long, so I probably won't have it back to you for a few months. Will that work?"

"Yes."

"Okay. I'll plan on it. I'll write directly on the manuscript to indicate the changes. Do you want it back a little at a time or all at once?"

"All at once," Mackenzie said softly and just sat there.

Delancey smiled as she watched her.

"You didn't think it was any good, did you, Mic?"

Mackenzie hated to admit it. "I wanted to think it was good, but I was afraid."

"Oh, Micki," Tucker said sincerely, "it is good. The plan of salvation is woven seamlessly into the plot. The characters are so likable. I cried at the end. *The Parchment Soldier* is a great book and so believable."

"Whom should she talk to about publication, Tucker?" Joanne wanted to know.

"Candlelight has a good selection of fiction, and they're not such a big house. They make their authors feel like family. I'll think about it, okay, Mic?"

She nodded and smiled at him, suddenly feeling very tired. This was emotionally draining stuff.

Mackenzie was exhausted. It didn't help that she'd been so ill. Her lids drooped, and she let her head fall back against the seat. She was unaware of the way Delancey and Tucker made their exits. Not until Jack woke her to ask if she wanted help getting upstairs did she remember that she hadn't really thanked Tucker, at least not well enough, in her mind.

"You'll see him Sunday," Joanne told her as she lovingly mothered her charge into bed. Mackenzie didn't comment, but the thought of not seeing him the next day made her sad. She was still thinking about his smile and the way he had sat with her in the waiting room when she drifted back to sleep.

Easter Sunday was a delight. The praise group sang a cantata at the morning service. The fellowship was very sweet before church families parted to gather and eat. Andy and Gemma went to Andy's folks, but Richard joined Delancey and

Mackenzie at Jack and Joanne's. Matthew and Jasmine were there with the boys and their new little Charlotte, who went from one set of arms to the next. Tucker was also included, much to Mackenzie's enjoyment.

Ham was the main entree for dinner, along with a feast of side dishes, and when it was time for dessert, Delancey and Mackenzie surprised everyone by producing a gorgeous cake and announcing that Candlelight had called that week. The company wanted their Jungle Bud series and was thrilled to join with them on this project.

"When do the books come out?"

"Not until Christmas," Delancey answered as she handed out large slices, Mackenzie dropping ice cream next to each piece. When Tucker's came along, they gave him extra.

"What's all this?"

"Well, Tuck," Delancey explained, "you were the one who got us going."

He shook his head. "I told you, if your work wasn't good enough, it would never fly. I can't take credit for this."

"All right," Mackenzie said with resignation, "we'll have to take the cake back."

Tucker moved it out of her grasp just in time. Giving her a playful warning look, he snatched a fork and went on his way. For a moment the women were alone at the table — long enough for Delancey to softly say, "Oh, Mackenzie."

"I know." Her voice was just as hushed. She didn't look at her sister. "Just pray for me, Deej."

Brady came looking for seconds just then, and nothing more was said on the subject.

"Did you see this?" Cria asked Mackenzie before

the service began.

Mackenzie looked down at the announcement in the bulletin, the one for women's softball, and then back at Cria.

"No. What is it?"

"Our church has two softball teams. We play Meyers and two other churches. I'm on one of the teams. You should join us."

"I haven't played since high school PE."

"What position did you play?"

"Usually pitcher."

Cria's smile started slowly and got very wide. The organ began to play.

"I'll get back to you," she whispered.

At the time Mackenzie had nodded in complete innocence. Now it was the end of May, and Mackenzie found herself driving to her first Monday night practice.

She was told that it was not an intensely competitive group — the players were mostly out to fellowship and have fun — but for some reason Mackenzie was nervous. She felt a little better when she parked and realized Tucker was in the car right beside her.

"Hello," he greeted her as they climbed from their vehicles. "All set?"

"I think so. Tell me, Tuck," she moved to his side and spoke softly, "is this really just for fun, or does the competition get rather intense?"

"No, the women have a great time. They like to win and they play hard, but rarely does anyone get angry. There's a lot of laughing."

Mackenzie looked up at him and suddenly felt self-conscious.

"Actually," she said, her head dropping until she was studying the toe of her cleat, "I don't know why I'm bothering you with this."

"As a matter of fact, I'm the perfect person to bother with it."

Mackenzie looked back up. "Why?"

"I'm your coach."

Mackenzie's mouth dropped open. Tucker smiled as his hand came up. With two fingers he caught the underside of her jaw and shut her mouth.

"Keep that closed, Mic," he said softly. "Something will get in."

Mackenzie didn't comment.

"Come along," he ordered, putting a hand on her back and pushing, all business now. "It's time to play ball."

Mackenzie groaned. She and Tucker walked to the ball field together. From the outside, all looked fine, but Mackenzie wanted to run for her life. Pleasing Tucker had become very important to her lately. Every time she saw him, she wanted to ask about the manuscript, but not wanting to become a pest or make him regret his decision to edit for her, she made herself keep quiet. She dressed for Sundays and Wednesday nights with extra care. On the Sundays she wore the suit from Beaver Creek, she worked hard not to expect him to notice but was thrilled when he did. Now she was on his softball team, a game she hadn't played in far too long, and dreaded how foolish she would look.

A quiet mental pep talk helped a little. She told herself to do what she was told and play her best. That was all anyone could expect from her or any of the other women. That they all knew each other was clear the moment she walked up, but Mackenzie told herself to take things one practice at a time.

"Hi, Mackenzie," Cria greeted her.

"Hi, Cria."

"Ready?"

"I think so." Mackenzie smiled at her and waved at one of the moms whose little girl was in her Sunday school class.

"Okay," Tucker called. He had dropped the bag of equipment and now stood with a clipboard in his hand. "Is everyone here?"

Someone said, "I think so."

"We'll warm up with a little batting practice. Brian's team is going to come over in about an hour, and we'll have a little game. We both play Meyers in two weeks, so this will help us get ready." He looked out over the field and then to the women. "All right, you know the drill."

Mackenzie watched in near panic as they all started toward the field. Her new mitt in hand, she followed Cria.

"Mackenzie," Tucker said, stopping her.

"Yeah?"

"Why don't you try your hand at catching? That way you'll see how the drill rotates."

Mackenzie nodded willingly. This she could handle. Tucker pitched to the woman at home plate while the rest were in position about the field. The bases, as well as the outfield, were covered, and each woman took six pitches and then rotated from the outfield to the infield. Mackenzie was almost the last one up, and having thrown enough balls back to Tucker, her arms felt warmed up. She tried to remember if there was any trick to batting but couldn't recall. Tucker threw and Mackenzie swung hard. It was a nice connection, and Cria cheered her on from first base.

"Nice hit," Tucker complimented her, giving her another pitch. This one was just as good, and by the sixth, she was smacking them well into center field. Tucker had all he could do not to go hug her. She had looked so uncertain, something he didn't often see on her face, but it would have embarrassed them both if he'd singled her out. When the other team arrived, he called the women in for a huddle.

"Okay, ladies," he began. "Other years we've been kind and fair. This year we're going for blood."

The women all smiled.

"Mackenzie, can you pitch for us?"

"It's been a long time, Tucker. Does the other team know they need extra medical insurance?"

Tucker smiled as the group laughed.

"You'll do fine."

You haven't seen me was all Mackenzie could think. Tucker, who had watched her sail balls back to him from home plate, handed her the ball without comment, fairly certain that her pitching would be more than adequate.

"Nancy," Tucker ordered, "catch a few for Mackenzie."

What followed was an hour of the most fun Mackenzie had had in a long time. Once the other team arrived, the banter back and forth was hysterical, especially between Tucker and the other coach, Brian Pankratz. Mackenzie's pitching was not very consistent. It was a comfort that the other team's pitcher was worse. She didn't hit anyone, and that was what she cared about most. When it was her turn at bat, she smacked a line drive into left field, and since she was fast, she made it to second and sent two others home. In the midst of this she realized both Cria and Tucker had been right: The league was more for fellowship than expertise.

"Well, what did you think?" Tucker asked on the way back to the car.

"I think I have a pound of dust in my hair, but I had fun."

"You did well."

"I'm just glad I didn't break anyone's nose."

"You're too hard on yourself."

"Micki! Tucker!"

They both turned to listen to Cria.

"I've got the makings for root beer floats at my house if you're interested."

"Sounds good to me," Mackenzie told her.

"Count me in!" Tucker shouted as well. "I was hoping she would ask," he told Mackenzie in a softer voice.

Mackenzie looked up at him and pulled the bill of his hat over his face, hoping he wouldn't notice that all she wanted to do these days was stare into his face.

"I'll see you there," Tucker told her.

"Okay. Thank you for tonight, Tucker."

"My pleasure."

His voice was more casual than he felt. He thought it might be time to get a little closer to Miss Mackenzie Bishop, and he had to work at not rushing ahead full steam. She hadn't shown interest in any other men, and if his eyes could be trusted, he thought she might be looking at him a little more often these days. He was doing plenty of his own looking, so it would have been near to impossible to miss hers. He started his car and headed to the Johansens' house with a very light heart. Any time he could spend with her, no matter how many other people were around, seemed to do his heart a world of good.

I'd say it's time to figure out a way to make this work, he told the Lord. *Please help me to know just the right time and place.*

Richard got slowly out of the car at Delancey's house, his movements deliberate and measured. It wasn't often a man proposed marriage, and he found that his heart would not beat normally in his chest.

Delancey loved him. With a soft voice, her face flushed, she had told him two weeks ago. Richard had immediately scheduled an appointment with Pastor Gary and had a long talk with him. The questions Pastor asked had been good ones, many Richard had already considered, but they forced him to do even more searching than he already had. In the end, all paths led back to marrying Delancey Bishop. Richard couldn't have been more thrilled. She was the woman he had prayed for for a very long time.

Richard was on his way to the front door of Delancey's house when he heard a thump. He thought it might be coming from around the back, so he left the porch to investigate. He found Delancey on the rear deck, broom in hand, sweeping like a madwoman. She hadn't heard him come up and, when she spotted him, started so violently that she dropped the broom.

"Oh, Richard, you startled me!"

"I'm sorry. I heard a thump and thought I should check it out."

So glad to see him, she recovered swiftly. "Well, you're just in time. Things are all clean. Can I interest you in something cold to drink?"

"That sounds good."

In truth, Richard didn't think he could drink anything. His courage was suddenly deserting him. He knew she loved him, but the moment of truth was upon him. Would Delancey agree to be his wife? And what would he do if she said that no, she wasn't ready yet?

"Have a seat," she invited, slipping through her screened porch to head to the kitchen. She was gone just long enough to make Richard's palms sweat. Delancey saw nothing amiss, however, and returned with two glasses of Pepsi, ready to settle in for a nice chat. Richard couldn't even hold his. He took a sip and reached to put it on the picnic table.

"Are you off work early, or has the time gotten away from me?"

"I'm off a little early. I was rather hoping you might want to go to dinner tonight. I should have called and asked you earlier this week but didn't."

Delancey was more than ready to spend the evening with him, but for the first time she noticed a tenseness about him.

"Richard, are you all right?"

"I will be," he said softly.

Delancey stared at him, trying to work through this cryptic reply. She watched as Richard moved his chair closer to hers and leaned over the arm to speak to her.

"I picked something up today that I've had on order for about two weeks." Richard looked into her wonderful blue eyes and smiled. "I hope the one I've chosen is not a disappointment to you. I guess in my mind I've pictured candlelight and soft music, but then I realized I just wanted to be

855

alone with you when I asked."

Heart pounding, Delancey watched him reach for his pocket. The diamond ring, surrounded by tiny sapphires, was the most beautiful thing she had ever seen.

"Will you do me the honor, Delancey, of becoming my wife?"

"Oh, Richard," she breathed, tenderly putting her hands on his cheeks. "I would love to be your wife."

He leaned into her hands and they kissed for the first time. Richard then captured her left hand and slipped the ring on her finger. She laughed with delight when it fit.

"It's so beautiful. And sapphires — I would never have dreamed!"

"They're for your eyes."

Delancey leaned her forehead against his. It was harder to see him this way, but she wanted to be close.

"Do you have any idea how much you mean to me?" she asked him.

"I think I do. I was just about sick with nerves that you might say you're not ready."

"I'm ready. In fact I'm free tomorrow."

Richard laughed and kissed her again. He sat back and looked at her. "I have to be careful how much I do that," Richard admitted softly.

It was just the type of thing she would expect him to say. She wanted to kiss him for it but knew that was playing with fire.

"So tell me," he said as he leaned close and spoke without touching her. "When can we be married?"

"Well, I don't know. I guess I'd rather not have anything too grand. What do you think?"

Richard reached for the calendar in his wallet.

"Four weeks from tomorrow is June 26. How does that sound?"

"Micki's birthday is the twenty-fifth. If we're married then, we'll always be tied up around her birthday. I don't want that, plus, I'm not sure four weeks is enough time."

"Okay. Six weeks from tomorrow would be July 10. Is six weeks enough time?"

"I think it might be," she said slowly.

"But —" Richard started for her.

"Richard, is it terribly important to you to be married on a Saturday?"

"No, I just thought it was the logical time. What do you want?"

"A Friday night. Six weeks from tonight."

"Oh," he said taking a moment to catch up. "I like the idea."

"Do you really?"

"Yes. I wouldn't have thought of it, but it sounds fun."

"Good. There's one other thing. I think we should have talked about this before, but I didn't want to be presumptuous."

"What is it?"

"Your house."

"You don't like it?"

"I love it. I just don't like the location. I can't imagine living in town like that. I think I would miss the woods terribly."

"I've thought of that, and I have an idea. How do you feel about adding onto this house?"

Delancey's eyes grew. "How would we?"

It was as if he came uncorked. He rose to his feet and moved around the outside of the house, pointing and explaining his plan. He had clearly given it great thought, and when he was done, Delancey was in a state of shock.

"That sounds wonderful. I would never have thought of it, especially the way to add a second bathroom."

"That's a must."

"Why is that?"

Richard looked down at her. "I can't take the chance that you'll present me with a group of daughters."

"Would that be so bad?"

"Not if we have two bathrooms."

"Oh, come now, Richard."

He was still looking at her. "I grew up with three older sisters. It's a miracle I ever saw the interior of the bathroom."

Delancey only laughed, and Richard captured her hand.

"We'll probably have to live at my house until construction is completed, but I think it might work."

"Oh, Richard." She hugged him tightly when they were back on the deck. "I love you."

He gave in again and kissed her, told her he loved her before releasing her, and moved across the deck to stand.

"Does dinner sound good?" he asked softly.

Delancey nodded. "Yes, I'll get ready. Richard, can we go see Mackenzie tonight? I want to tell her in person."

"That's fine. We'll do that."

Delancey started inside but turned back and looked at him. She started to speak but stopped. She slipped inside to change, knowing that if she didn't determine to walk blamelessly right now, the next six weeks were going to feel like a year.

FORTY-NINE

"How are you doing?" Cria asked Mackenzie before the children arrived one Sunday morning.

Mackenzie looked at her friend and knew she could be honest.

"I'm doing well now, but I really had some battles yesterday." Mackenzie sighed softly. "I have such a hard time agreeing with God on certain things, Cria."

"Like?"

"His timing for one, and also who He is and what He expects from me."

"What was going on?"

"Just me wanting my own way. I mean, is God who He says He is or not? How I answer that question determines how I respond to dozens of issues. If He's the one and only God of the universe, then He does have the right to expect me to go the speed limit, to give to Him out of a cheerful heart, and to not . . ." Mackenzie took a moment to compose herself. "To not be angry at Him because He's given someone special to my sister but decided I must wait."

Cria came over and hugged her. Mackenzie would have welcomed the release of tears but knew they would be joined at any moment by parents dropping off little ones.

"I'm happy for her, Cria, with all my heart, but what woman doesn't dream of some man coming right out and admitting that he loves you? It was like something out of a storybook, and Delancey needed that; she's been hurt so badly." Again she sighed. "He asked her to marry him Friday night, and in their joy they came right over to tell me, but now all I can say to God is, how could You have forgotten me?"

"He hasn't," Cria said softly. "God knows your heart, Micki. He could very well have put this desire in you. If He did, He'll bring someone. Maybe the man won't walk up and say 'I love you, Mackenzie,' but God is always faithful. His faithfulness doesn't always look the way we expect it to, but He's promised to finish the work He's started in us, and He will do it. I can't promise you that you will not be alone in this life — you might be — but if God asks that of you, He will be sufficient."

"Thanks, Cria," Mackenzie said softly as the first children arrived.

I have so much to be thankful for, Lord. Mackenzie hugged the children and helped with chairs and little purses, but her heart was in prayer. *Just keep reminding me, Lord — keep showing me how to please You and what You want of me. Thank You that Cria reminded me that You're enough and You'll always be enough. I just need to keep that in my mind and You on the throne of my heart.*

Early on in their relationship, Roz had quoted John 3:16 to Mackenzie but put her name in the verse. Without warning, God brought it to mind. *For God so loved Mackenzie that He gave His only begotten Son, that if Mackenzie will believe in Him, she will not perish, but have eternal life.*

"Okay," Cria said excitedly to the group of children that surrounded her. "Let's sing 'Jesus Loves Me.' "

Mackenzie was more than happy to join in. She had just been reminded of how true it was.

Tucker knocked on Mackenzie's front door the first morning in June, hoping he wasn't too early. She didn't answer, so he took a chance and rang the bell. Manuscript in hand, he began to turn to his car but remembered something she once told him. He went ahead and put the manuscript back in the car before he moved into the park that bordered Mackenzie's property. He came around the side of the house in time to see Mackenzie come up out of the water, walk across the dock, and slip into a heavy white toweling robe. She spotted him as she wrung her hair out to one side and used a hand towel on her face.

"Well, good morning," she greeted him with a smile.

Tucker came down the path to her dock and smiled at her.

"How was it?"

"Brisk, but then that's why I do it. What brings you out this morning?"

Before even talking about it, they sat on the wooden bench that was built into the dock.

"I finished the manuscript."

"Did you, Tuck?" Mackenzie touched his arm. Her hand was cool. "I hadn't wanted to nag you, but I've been a little anxious."

"I'm all done editing."

"What did you think after the second time through?"

"I liked it even more. It's a great book."

861

Mackenzie bit her lip. She had worked hard and found such a compliment very exciting. She looked down and played with the tie on her robe, a small smile on her face.

"Mackenzie, what cologne do you wear?" Tucker asked as if it had been a great mystery.

"Chanel No. 5."

"You always smell good."

"It must be on the robe," she told him, trying not to dismiss the compliment. She did feel self-conscious, however, and a little flustered with his nearness. She glanced out over the water, telling herself not to blush.

"This would be an easy view to wake up to in the mornings."

"It is," Mackenzie agreed, relaxing with the impersonal subject. "All these homes have good views."

"How well do you know your neighbors?"

"I'm getting to know them. I bought this house before I came to Christ, and I was so angry in those days that I didn't want anything to do with anyone. Then for a while after I believed, I was wrapped up in myself. I have a real burden for them now. I've found one of the best things I can do is go shoot baskets on my hoop. There are several kids who join me every time."

"That's great. I have kids who come to my door and ask if I can come out and play."

Mackenzie had a good laugh over this one but knew he meant it.

"May I ask you a question, Micki?" Tucker said suddenly, his voice thoughtful.

"Sure."

"Have you ever been engaged to be married?"

"No," Mackenzie didn't hesitate to tell him. "I

was involved with someone when I lived on the East Coast. I think things could have gotten pretty serious, but we had a big fight, and while we were not speaking to each other, he met some woman at a bar and slept with her. I didn't want to see him anymore after that."

Mackenzie looked over at Tucker, who was watching her very carefully.

"Is there a reason you asked?"

He nodded. "You handled Mason's broken engagement very well."

"Are you speaking from experience?"

"Yes," Tucker admitted, his eyes now going to the water. "I am."

"Where is she, Tuck?"

"She's dead," he spoke as his gaze swung to meet hers. "We met in college. Her name was Celia. We fell in love and wanted to be married. We were both young and knew we had a lot of school ahead of us, but we were determined to make it work. We weren't really accountable to anyone, and that became a problem, but out of the clear blue, two months before the wedding, Celia broke up with me.

"She had been having headaches, and I thought she was just stressed over school and not feeling well. I tried to talk to her, but she wouldn't return my calls or even see me. I was frantic. It got worse when her roommates told me she had left school. It became a nightmare when I found out she wasn't speaking to her own parents; they couldn't even find her.

"Three weeks before we were to be married, they called me and said that the sheriff had just found her. She'd driven the car down an embankment and was dead behind the wheel. Her parents

863

were utterly crushed, but her father was thinking clearly enough to order an autopsy. Celia had a massive brain tumor. At the end, the doctors didn't think she could have been in her right mind. It helped a little to know that I hadn't done anything, but it took a long time before I didn't think of her all day, every day."

"I'm sorry, Tucker," Mackenzie told him softly, tears in her eyes.

"Thank you, Micki. I have only one regret, but it's a big one." His gaze had wandered, but he looked her in the eye again. "We weren't pure in our relationship. We planned on waiting, but we had too much time alone, and things went too far. Once we had slept together, we never stopped. We were both believers and felt horrible every time, but since we didn't turn to anyone for help, there was no one to hold us accountable."

Mackenzie didn't say anything but knew that had to have made his pain even worse.

"It's made things so much worse," Tucker confirmed her thought. "I think my grief over her loss was so much deeper. I know things an unmarried man shouldn't know, and worst of all, I can't tell the woman I marry that I waited for her."

"You didn't make the best choice, Tucker, and I don't want to excuse sin. But if the woman loves you enough to marry you, then she'll be as ready to forgive you as God has been." Mackenzie's tone was almost angry in its firmness.

Tucker smiled at her. "Thank you, Mackenzie."

"For what?"

"Just the encouragement you are."

This made her feel very nice inside and lessened the disappointment when, about five minutes later, he said he had to go home and get to work.

He scooted back through the park and met her at the front door with the manuscript.

"How do I pay you, Tucker?"

"I'll figure it out and let you know."

"Okay. Thanks again."

"When you have it ready to go and find you want some help with a publisher, feel free to check with me."

"Thank you."

"We'll see you tomorrow night."

"Okay. 'Bye."

Mackenzie shut the door but didn't stand still. She laid the manuscript on the stairs that led to the office and turned and took the other stairs to her bedroom so she could shower and dress. She wasn't all that anxious to go over the manuscript, but right now it was the best thing. If she didn't get busy, she was going to do little but think about Tucker Stone for the rest of the day.

"Oh my," Mackenzie breathed softly as the woman at the bridal shop brought out the fifth dress.

"Do you like it?" she kindly asked the two women who occupied the beautiful gilt chairs.

Delancey could only stare in awe. It was an incredible creation of silk, satin, and lace. The neck was high lace and the sleeves three-quarter length. The skirt wasn't overly full, but that didn't detract from the elegance since the tiny lace and satin insets caught the eye before anything else.

Mackenzie had to stop herself from singing out, "This is the one!" She knew it had to be Delancey's decision, but the dress was perfect for her.

"I think I'll try this one on," the younger woman said softly, a dreamy smile on her face.

"Of course. If you'll come this way."

"Come with me, Mic, please."

"Sure."

Ten minutes later it was Mackenzie's turn to stare. Her sister looked like something out of a magazine. Not overly tight, the dress fell perfectly over Delancey's long torso and legs. Mackenzie could only think of how pleased Richard was going to be. Delancey didn't look capable of any coherent thought.

"What do you think?" Delancey asked, still staring at herself in the room's huge mirrors.

"I think it's perfect. You look beautiful." The moment she said this, however, practicality crept in. "What does it do for your budget?"

Delancey consulted the tag on the sleeve. "It's a bit much." They were alone, so Delancey felt free to add, "I can't believe what wedding dresses cost."

"It's a beautiful dress, D.J., but if you don't want to spend this much, don't. You'll look wonderful in whatever you wear, and Richard won't care if you're in a gunnysack."

Delancey looked at herself. The dress was perfect, but she had asked God to help her be wise and a good steward of what He had given her.

"Maybe I'll keep looking."

The saleswoman checked back, and Delancey told her she was going to keep looking.

"That's fine. I do think I should mention to you, however, that the reason this dress is on sale is because it's been discontinued. We only have this one and a size three left. So you won't be able to order it later."

"This dress is on sale?"

"Yes. Thirty percent off."

Delancey burst into tears, and the woman turned to Mackenzie.

"That means she'll take it," Mackenzie said and had them both laughing.

Tears were nothing new to a woman who worked in a bridal boutique, so she found the box of tissues and told Delancey to wait while she got her measuring tape. The dress needed some minor alterations.

"I made a fool of myself," Delancey complained when the woman left, the tissue still at work on her face.

"No, you didn't." Mackenzie was sporting one of her "looks." "I always cry when things go on sale. I was a regular watering pot in front of the V8 display at the market last week."

"Stop, Micki." Delancey's face was already turning red.

"And then when I saw that the ground chuck was marked down, well, it was Niagara time."

Delancey's tears had turned to silent, red-faced laughter. The salesgirl came back and smiled at the sight.

"It looks as though she made you feel better."

"She has that effect," Delancey admitted, the tissue at work again. "You need to go look for a dress, Mic."

"All right." Mackenzie pushed to her feet.

"Keep in mind," the woman told her, "that most dresses can be ordered in a variety of colors."

"Okay. I'll come back if I find something."

Mackenzie was not as successful. She was the only one who would stand up with Delancey, so she could have any style dress she wanted, but many of the gowns had scooped necklines.

She finally gave up and went to join Delancey at the bridal desk. The woman was taking down all details, including the wedding date. Pastor Gary had wanted Richard and Delancey to counsel with an older married couple before the vows were said, and that meant moving the wedding back. The date was now planned for July 30.

Delancey's example to Mackenzie about the date being changed was fabulous. She had been disappointed but not angry, and the couple they were going to work with were two people who had known Richard for years. Delancey chose to be thankful for this opportunity to get to know her future husband's friends. The extra weeks, weeks when she thought she would already be a bride, would be something of a trial, but the work on the house was going to start on time, and if it got to where she couldn't live there, Roz and Adam had invited her to live with them until she could move into Richard's.

Delancey, who kept telling herself not to expect everything to be perfect, was finding that it was turning out to be quite perfect to her. She had only been home from shopping with Mackenzie about ten minutes when the doorbell rang. She had been on the verge of calling Richard to say she'd found a dress and hoped that it was he. She was surprised to see Jack at her door.

"Well, hello," Delancey said as she smiled and hugged him. He usually called several times a month, but he hadn't visited in a long time.

"Hello, yourself. How are you?"

"I just found a wedding dress," Delancey told him, "so I feel pretty good."

"Do you have it here?"

"No. It needed a few alterations. They'll call

when it's done."

"Well, it's interesting that you found one, since that's the reason I'm here."

The two had sat in Delancey's living room, Jack in the big chair and Delancey on the sofa.

"You want to make my wedding dress?" Delancey teased him. "I had no idea you were that talented."

"Close," Jack grinned. "I want to pay for your wedding dress."

Delancey blinked.

"And everything else."

"You can't be serious."

"But I am. When you and Richard asked me to give you away, it was crystal clear in my mind. It took my wife to remind me that you probably wouldn't be under the same assumption."

"I don't know what to say."

"There's nothing to say. You're my girl."

Delancey closed her eyes to stop them, but the tears would not stay back. She loved Joanne — she loved her more than she could have imagined — but Jack was the closest tie to her mother, and the ache was still huge.

"I can't believe how much I miss her," she said as she looked at him, not having to explain the shift in thought. "It was so fun to have Mic there today — she's just nuts — but I couldn't help but ache for Mom when I tried that dress on."

"She would be so proud of you." Jack's voice was soft with remembrance. "I remember the different things she talked about at the end, and her daughters' weddings were some of them. She didn't want you to feel you had to wear her dress since it was so yellowed and old-fashioned, but she did hope that you would stay in a wonderfully romantic place the first night, and she wanted to pay for it."

"I didn't know that," Delancey shook her head.

Jack smiled. "Well, it's not the type of thing you bring up over dinner."

"Richard is taking care of the honeymoon, but I'll tell him what Mom would have wanted."

"I think that's wise. Something tells me you won't be disappointed."

Jack didn't stay a lot longer, but they did talk finances. Mackenzie had already offered to pay for the cake, which had been ordered at the beginning of the week, and now Jack went on to question Delancey and get an idea of what else she would need. She had not been in financial trouble with the wedding, but it was nice to know that most of her savings would remain intact. She was so wowed by the offer and the way everything was coming together that she called Richard as soon as Jack left.

"I found a dress," she blurted out when he answered.

"Already?"

"Yes. Mic says you'll like it."

"I'm sure she's right."

Delancey told him about Jack's visit as well, and Richard laughed.

"What's so funny?"

"Oh, I just remember a certain lady who thought that sharing her life with someone was a privilege she would have to forego."

Delancey sighed. "It was so clear in my mind."

"Now people are coming out of the woodwork in support of us. It's pretty special."

"It is, isn't it."

"Did Micki find a dress?"

"No, we'll have to keep looking."

"Too bad she couldn't just get a wedding dress of her own."

"I know. I was going to ask her how it was going, but we never got to that."

"It's such a temptation to play matchmaker."

This was such a funny statement from Richard. She couldn't quite picture him interfering with anyone else's relationship, but his love for her sister gave her a very secure feeling.

When Delancey hung up quite a while later, she realized that she and Richard had never discussed *who* they wanted Mackenzie to marry. It didn't matter — they both had one man in mind — and only hoped that he and Mackenzie could figure it out someday soon.

"Do you know what I just found out?" Tucker asked Mackenzie after they'd just won a softball game.

"No, what?"

"We share a birthday."

"Do we really?" Mackenzie was very surprised. "June 25?"

"Yep. And do you know what else it means?"

"What?" Mackenzie smiled. He was really enjoying himself.

"We're going out to lunch."

"Well, now. Do I have to pay this time?"

"No. This will be my treat."

"My, you are in a good mood."

"You can bring me a present."

Mackenzie had a good laugh over this, but in truth, buying him something would have given her a great amount of pleasure. *Anything* to do with Tucker gave her pleasure.

"So where are we going?" Mackenzie asked as she threw her gear into the Jeep.

"That's a secret."

"How will I know what to wear?"

"Dress casually, but wear long pants and have a jacket."

"Tucker, we're talking about the end of June, right?"

"Yes. You don't have to dress for warmth exactly, just the possibility that you might get cool."

Mackenzie stared at him, wanting to laugh at the childish gleam in his eye. He was such a character.

"What time shall I be ready?"

"I'll pick you up around 10:15."

"This is for lunch, right?"

"Yes. Now just be ready on the twenty-third and no more questions."

Mackenzie stared up at him and smiled.

"Are you coming to the pizza parlor?" Tucker asked, not able to look away from those eyes of hers. They had gone for pizza after every game and even sat at the same table, but Tucker had never come out and asked her.

"Yes. I'm starved. How about you?"

"I'll be there."

"Good," Mackenzie told him.

"Why is that good?" he teased her.

"You're always good for a laugh, Tucker, and sometimes you pick up the tab."

"Thanks," he replied dryly as he moved off to his car. "It's nice to know I'm so loved."

Mackenzie laughed at his tone and face, but her heart was beating swiftly in her chest. *You're loved, Tucker — very loved. And someday I might be able to tell you that.*

■ ■ ■ ■

She told herself it was foolish, but Mackenzie was almost sick with nerves the morning of her birthday. She was going to dinner on Friday night with Delancey and Richard, but today it was lunch with Tucker. Just the thought made her want to skip around the house like a child. She had never felt for anyone the way she felt for Tucker Stone. Standing in her living room, trying not to be nervous, she almost jumped from her skin when the bell rang.

"Happy birthday," he said, the moment he saw her.

"Thank you. Happy birthday to you."

"Thank you. Are you all set?"

"Yes."

"Let's go."

To Mackenzie's surprise, he drove only a few miles down the road to the Zephyr Cove Marina. He parked without speaking, and Mackenzie climbed out when he shut off the car. The marina had a small restaurant, but he had parked over by the boats. She glanced up at the huge paddle wheeler docked in the bay, the *M.S. Dixie II*.

"Are we headed out to sea, Tucker?"

"Yes, we are."

Mackenzie laughed. "I've never been on this boat."

"I know. You mentioned it one day, and because I think that's a crime, we're going to go."

"Oh, Tucker." She couldn't hide her delight. "This is so exciting. I've seen the paddle wheeler from the house so many times and just never —"

She shrugged and Tucker laughed. It felt good to

know he'd chosen the right thing.

"Come on. We leave at 11:00."

"How long will we be out?"

"Well, we'll eat lunch on board, go out to Emerald Bay, circle the small island, which will give us a view of the Vikingsholm Castle, and head back. It all takes about two hours."

Mackenzie bit her lip in excitement. How fun to see Emerald Bay up close! She had never done that either and could hardly wait. They opened the gate a little before the time to board, and to Mackenzie's surprise, stopped each group for a picture. Tucker slipped an arm around her while they posed, and Mackenzie knew that however the picture looked, her smile would be genuine.

The boat was so fun. The upper deck let you see forever across the lake and into the mountains, and the lower deck, filled with tables and chairs, let you look out at the amazing sapphire-blue water that, had it not been for the window, you could have reached out and touched.

After enjoying the view from up top, they took a table in the lower deck, sitting across from each other and talking. A waitress came by and took their order for burgers, fries, and root beer. They never ran out of things to talk about, and the conversation ranged to many topics. They had been out almost an hour when Tucker suggested they go stand on the prow. They slipped into their jackets and stood at the front of the ship, the water not far below them.

"Now look down," Tucker told her as they cruised along.

"Okay. What am I looking at?"

"Just the water," he replied, looking down as well. "Don't take your eyes from the water."

Not ten seconds later he heard her gasp and knew that she had seen it. He turned when she grabbed his arm.

"Did you see? It was amazing! The water just went from blue to green in an instant. It looked as if someone drew a line."

"Pretty cool, isn't it?"

"Oh, Tucker, I never knew."

He smiled at her.

"They show that video inside," she said softly, "that talks about the way it all came together millions of years ago, and I feel sad for those who believe it. If you take the Creator out of the creation, there's not much to be excited about."

"That was nicely put, Micki."

She smiled.

They circled Emerald Bay, gazed across at Vikingsholm, and cruised back out across the lake. Both were thirsty for something to drink and headed back inside. Not paying attention, Mackenzie bumped into Tucker's back.

"I'm sorry, Tuck, I wasn't watching where I was going."

"That's all right, Mic. You can bump into me anytime you like."

"I'll bet you say that to everyone."

"No, I don't." He had turned back so swiftly that Mackenzie stopped. She gazed up at him, realizing that something had been different about his voice. There was no teasing in his eyes. They were just watching her in a way she hadn't noticed before. As she stood there, he brushed a piece of hair from her face before shoving his hands in his pockets.

"Shall we go in?"

Mackenzie wasn't capable of anything more than

a nod. Tucker opened the door and held it for her. After showing her to a table, he asked what she wanted and went to order it. The few moments apart did them good. By the time Tucker returned, Mackenzie was composed and noticed that Tucker seemed normal as well. She was against speculating on what might have happened, so she didn't know if she was disappointed or not when nothing more was said on the subject.

FIFTY

The time between Mackenzie's birthday and Delancey's July 30 wedding flew by. The Fourth of July had been held at Mackenzie's and was declared a hit by all. The fireworks on the lake had been spectacular, as had been the food and fellowship with many of the minichurch family, Tucker included, as well as Richard, Delancey, the Cummings, and the Averys.

Just a few days later, Tucker had left for a Christian publishers' convention, and Mackenzie was amazed at how much she missed him. They usually saw each other only a few times a week, but even at that, Mackenzie felt a hole in her world. Now the wedding day was here, and rather than consider the crowd of people she would have to see, all Mackenzie could ask herself was whether Tucker would like the rose-colored dress they had found for her to wear. She was rather preoccupied with the thought until it was time for her to attend Delancey, who ended up needing all the attention she could give.

"You're sure everything is ready?" the younger sister asked for the fifteenth time.

"Yes, I'm sure. Roz, Joanne, Rina, and I covered all the bases."

"Have you seen Richard? He is here, right?"

"Yes," Jack answered, coming in the door in time to hear this, "he's here."

"I just wish I could see him."

"Why can't you?" Mackenzie asked.

"Oh, I don't know, bad luck and all that stuff you hear."

"Delancey Joy Bishop! What has luck got to do with it?" Mackenzie's hands were on her waist, and she looked ready to take her sister apart. Delancey wanted to laugh for the first time since she arrived at the church.

"I've always thought that was the stupidest thing!" Mackenzie was ranting now. "You're going to commit the most intimate act a person can by joining your life to his, but you can't see him if you want to. What rot!"

Delancey's smile was huge.

"What are you laughing at?"

"You should see yourself." Delancey shook her head.

"And you should see Richard if you want to!"

Jack, who had wisely remained silent, watched as Mackenzie stormed her way to the door and went in search of the groom.

"Richard." She put her hand on his sleeve when she found him in the foyer and was glad when he accompanied her as she moved down the hallway. She could feel eyes on them but didn't care. Her sister's face was pale and her eyes anxious. She needed to see this man. Mackenzie spoke when Richard leaned low to listen to her.

"Can you come and see D.J.?"

"Of course."

"You're not going to give me any of that stuff about not seeing the bride, are you?" Mackenzie was frowning at him, and Richard smiled much as

Delancey had.

"Pass up a chance to see Delancey? You don't know me very well."

"I like you, Richard." She grinned cheekily at him and led the way.

Just moments later, he slipped into the Sunday school room where Delancey was waiting, and Jack came out.

"Hi," Delancey said softly.

"She was right," Richard told her as he crossed the room.

"Who was?"

"Mackenzie. I do like your dress."

"Disappointed that when I walk down the aisle, you'll have already seen it?"

"Not in the least."

He stopped in front of her and bent to kiss her forehead.

"Was there a reason you wanted to see me?"

She shrugged. "It's all become such a big thing. I sort of wish we had run away and been married privately."

"How long have you felt that way?"

"Since they put me in this room and made me feel that I couldn't see you."

"Your sister did the right thing. There isn't any reason why we shouldn't see each other, and in a few hours we'll say our goodbyes and run away just the way you wanted."

She knew she was being a baby, but her heart felt so much better.

"I'm better now," she told him.

"All right. I'll see you down front in about . . ." Richard held his wrist up, "twelve and a half minutes."

Delancey smiled. "I can hardly wait."

Richard stole a quick kiss before giving her a wink and slipping back out the door. She was still smiling when Mackenzie came back in. She went right to her and hugged her.

"They're almost ready for you. Are you all right?"

"Thanks to you, I'm more than ready."

Jack was on hand to do the honors, and just as planned, Delancey walked down the aisle to marry Dr. Richard Wilder. They were both radiant during the ceremony and at the reception to follow.

Tucker enjoyed the ceremony and time after, but if someone had asked him, he would have been forced to admit that he found the bride's maid-of-honor much more distracting than the bride. Indeed, it felt as though someone had put a band around his chest when Mackenzie preceded Delancey down the aisle in that beautiful gown, her face a mixture of fear and excitement.

They had a few minutes together during the reception, but for the most part, she was across the room. He had been overloaded with work the entire month and missed her terribly. She had told him that Delancey and Richard would be gone for ten days. He didn't think that Mackenzie would be lost without her sister; indeed, he knew she would not be, but he thought that the next ten days might be a nice chance to spend some time with her. It would take him a few more days of work to finish the manuscript he was currently working on, but then he would be free. The evening ended without his ever having an opportunity for more than a few words, but he went home at peace. He would call Mackenzie first thing the following week.

■ ■ ■ ■

Richard and Delancey Wilder's *"run away"* was a small lodge on the north shore of Lake Tahoe. They would be there two nights before driving on to the coast, and their honeymoon would include a trip to see the Lacys in San Francisco. They would arrive home about a week later. No one had decorated their car, so the getaway was made in a very quiet fashion, husband and wife both sighing with content.

"It was a wonderful wedding," Richard said as he reached for her hand. "You did a great job."

"I had lots of help. I just love your family, Richard. Your mother couldn't do enough, and I know she stayed around to clean up afterward."

"She's like that. My sisters too."

"They're so fun."

They drove in silence for a time, and somewhere along the line Delancey fell asleep. She woke to the sound of her husband's voice and his hand on hers.

"Shall we go up to the room?"

"Did I fall asleep?"

"Yes, you've been working hard."

She loved the understanding in his voice and smiled at him before rolling her eyes in self-directed disgust. They were in their room just a sort time later, a wonderfully cozy place with vaulted ceilings and a superb lake view. Delancey was taking in the room, the big bed, and lovely wall hangings when she spotted them. On the table was a bouquet of roses, the likes of which she had never seen. The florist had used every color imaginable. Delancey went to the vase, pulled out the card, and read, "No one else on earth colors my world the way you do. All my love, Richard."

Delancey turned to her husband, who had come close behind her, threw her arms around his neck, and laughed.

"I love you, Richard Wilder."

"The feeling is quite mutual," he returned as he smiled and kissed her. "There's a huge tub in the bathroom," he told her when they came up for air. "How does a hot bath sound?"

"If you'll join me, it sounds like heaven."

Richard didn't need to be asked twice. Like children whose hearts were young and untroubled, they shared an evening of love and discovery, a perfect start to their honeymoon. It wasn't a full "moon" that they planned to be gone, but certainly ten of the sweetest days either of them could ever imagine.

"How busy is your week?" Tucker asked Mackenzie when he saw her on Sunday.

"Not too bad."

"How about a game of tennis?"

"Oh, I'd like that. Do you play often, Tucker?"

"Yes."

Mackenzie hesitated.

"Changing your mind?" His voice held a hint of challenge.

"No," Mackenzie began, but didn't go on. "Although, I just remembered I don't have any balls or a racket."

"I have an extra I'll bring for you. And I have two new cans of balls."

"Okay," Mackenzie shrugged. He would probably slaughter her, but she had to admit that any time with him would be worth it.

"Where are we playing?"

Tucker named the time and place but then offered to pick her up. Mackenzie accepted and laughed when on Tuesday she found herself pacing just like she had on her birthday. She checked her shorts and shirt five times and her hair at least twice that. By the time she started chasing tennis balls, she would be a sweaty mess, but she wanted to look her best when he arrived.

They talked about Tucker's latest project all the way to the courts. He had just finished editing a Bible study book on Job and found it quite interesting.

"I've learned a lot of things."

"I never thought about that, Tuck — that you would have a chance to study while you worked."

"Yes, indeed. I've had some challenging projects this year and two new authors so far."

They were at the courts then, and Mackenzie went with Tucker to get the rackets out of the trunk. He pulled out a beautiful graphite racket and handed it to her.

"This is your extra?" Mackenzie asked incredulously.

Tucker grinned. "No, I was being chivalrous."

Mackenzie shook her head and held out the tennis racket. "I don't think it's going to help, Tuck, so you take the good one."

He didn't argue but smiled at her as she accepted the trade. The other racket was still in good shape. Fifteen minutes later, Tucker had returned all of Mackenzie's hits with ease. She was running her legs off but missing most of the balls he put back across the net. It was her turn to serve, but she walked to the net. Seeing her, Tucker came forward as well. She held out the racket without a word. He traded her back, his eyes brimming with laughter. Silently he went back to the baseline while she turned away.

The racket was no help. Mackenzie's serves were accurate but not very fast. It was during this time that she realized Tucker must be falling asleep on his feet. It was her serve again, but as before, she headed to the net.

"Tucker, are you having fun?"

"Yes," he said sincerely.

"Why?"

"Because you're fun to be with."

"But I'm no challenge."

That wasn't the least bit true, but he knew she was talking about tennis.

"I'm having fun," he repeated.

Mackenzie looked unconvinced and regarded him for several heartbeats before going back to serve. She stayed on the baseline until it was Tucker's turn to serve and another thought occurred to her. Heading back to the net, she looked him in the eye.

"You're going easy on me, Tucker. I can tell. I want you to serve the way you would normally serve. I'm not going to improve unless you do."

"Micki, you're doing fine," he began.

"No, Tucker," she cut him off. "Give it your best shot."

Having spoken, she turned away, missing Tucker's large but very tender smile.

Mackenzie positioned herself for his serve and waited. Seconds later she barely kept her mouth shut. His serve had rocketed past her in a frightening manner. Without even bothering to go after the ball, she moved once again to the net.

"I didn't mean that," she wasted no time in telling her opponent.

Tucker could not hold his laughter. She was the most delightful person he'd ever known.

"How about we sit for a while?" he suggested, taking in her flushed face.

"Oh, I would like that," she admitted.

The courts were next to the Douglas County Library, and the park sat nestled among the tall trees that were a hallmark of the area. Tucker had thought to bring water, and after locating a bench, they sat in the shade with their drinks.

"You do fine," Tucker said honestly.

"It's been too long, and you obviously play all the time."

"We'll just have to get you out more."

"That would be nice," she said softly.

They fell silent then. The air always smelled of pine, and in the heat, the water only emphasized the dryness of the ground and foliage.

"I was playing tennis the day my father died."

Tucker turned to look at his companion.

"We were living at the Presidio then. Dad had just driven to the commissary, and then we looked up and Mom was calling us in. Dad's CO was there when she told us. Everything after that felt like slow motion and did for a long time."

"Do you still think about him a lot?"

"Not as much as I do my mom," Mackenzie admitted. "She was the most wonderful mother anyone could ask for. She wasn't a great cook — we have that in common — but she made a home for us. She sewed and cleaned and came to cheer at all our games. She never desired to be anything but a wife and mother and was proud of that. She didn't leave the home to work until Dad died.

And above all else, we knew we were loved."

"What a great memory for you," Tucker said softly, trying to imagine her as a little girl or young teen.

They eventually went back to their tennis game, playing until the heat got to them, and Tucker announced that Jack and Joanne had invited them to dinner. They stopped by Mackenzie's long enough to let her clean up, and then they headed to Kingsbury. Tucker dropped her off at the Averys', then went home for his own shower. Jack was grilling outside, and after hugging Joanne, Mackenzie went out to see him. She was there when Tucker came back, his hair still wet. Content to move to the patio doors and watch, he didn't join Jack and Mackenzie in the backyard. Joanne noticed his arrival and went to stand next to him. Tucker put an arm around her. She studied the direction of his gaze and felt free to speak.

"You look as though you could close your eyes and head into dreamland, Tuck."

Tucker smiled. "These days I do all my dreaming with my eyes wide open."

Joanne smiled. "And this dream woman, is she a warm, talented, mahogany-haired beauty?"

"One and the same," Tucker smiled down at his mother. "Did you know, Mom? Did you know I would fall for Micki?"

"We haven't spoken of Celia for so long, Tuck, so I wasn't sure where you were, but I did hope. And of course Gem planted ideas in my head. Your sister was so determined."

Tucker laughed. "After she came to see me, I really got to thinking."

"She'll be glad to know she had a hand. Tell me, Tuck, have you spoken with Mackenzie?"

"No. There's something still there that concerns me," he admitted. "I can't put my finger on it, and I don't feel comfortable just coming out with it."

"Talk to Jack."

Tucker looked at his mother.

"He knows?"

"Yes. I don't think he will tell you, but I think he can put your mind at ease."

"You don't know?"

"No, and I don't need to, but I do think you should talk with Jack."

Tucker knew he would take her advice, not tonight, but soon. For the moment, however, he could let it drop and enjoy the evening with three of the people he loved most in the world.

"What have you done with your manuscript?" Joanne asked Mackenzie over dinner. "Have you sent it to anyone yet?"

"No," she said with a smile. "I'm not sure why I'm hesitating. I went through all of Tucker's changes, and I've made a copy, but I guess there's a little fear of rejection involved, so I'm just sitting on it for the moment."

"In that case," Jack spoke up, "you should write another."

"Well, I did start one," she said.

"Did you really?" This came from Tucker.

Mackenzie nodded, still working on her food.

Tucker asked himself when he would stop being amazed by this woman. At this time he honestly felt God moving them in the direction of marriage, but he couldn't help but wonder when he would know everything about her. Of course it went two ways: She had things to learn about him as well. She wasn't very good about asking him about his life, and he wondered whether she would feel more free to ask if they were actually courting.

"Tell us about the book you're on," Jack encouraged Mackenzie, effectively breaking into Tucker's thoughts.

Mackenzie mapped out another story, and all Tucker could do was grin at the great plot and characters.

"How far are you?"

"Oh, about 150 pages."

"Want an editor?" he smiled.

"Sure."

"Do you want to feed it to me a little at a time or wait until it's done?"

Mackenzie's head tipped to one side as she thought.

"What would you want?"

"A little at a time, and then a final read-through when you're finished."

"Okay." Mackenzie laughed at how he knew just what he wanted. "When should I give you the first part?"

Tucker smiled. "When I drop you off tonight."

His smile was so warm that Mackenzie blushed and went back to her food. She knew that he hadn't meant anything intimate by it, but the exchange felt very personal to her. She hadn't thought of their outing as a date, but that's what it was. She finished the evening with that thought on her mind and a prayer in her heart that it would be the start of something very special between them.

"Why don't you all come in?" Mackenzie suggested some weeks later when the group arrived back at her house. Richard, Delancey, Tucker, and Mackenzie had spent the day together and were now going out to dinner. Mackenzie had a gift certificate for a steak house in town that was going to expire if they didn't use it.

The other three joined her inside, and Mackenzie went up to the office to look for it. She wasn't gone very long before calling down that she had found it. No one had changed from their casual clothes, since they were all very hungry, so she came swiftly down the stairs. They were almost to the front door when the phone rang.

"The machine will get it," Mackenzie said as she kept moving. She froze, however, when the machine picked up before she thought it would. Paxton Hancock's voice came over the line, loud and clear.

"Mackenzie, darling, love of my life, how are you? I miss you, love. I can't tell you how much, and the children, they ask for their mommy every night. Please come back to us, darling. I beg of you." His tone changed to a dry command before he said, "Call me, Mackenzie."

Mackenzie turned to find Tucker, Richard, and Delancey staring at her. Delancey was barely holding laughter, but the men in the group looked thunderstruck. Unfortunately, both women began to babble in unison.

"It's this crazy friend."

"East Coast, you never know."

"He's been around forever."

"We just ignore him most of the time."

Both women stumbled to a painful halt, and Tucker, bless his heart, came to the rescue, his voice holding no censure.

"Do you need to call someone right now, Mic?"

"No."

"So we can go eat?"

"Sure."

Mackenzie didn't dare look at Delancey as they left, or they would have laughed themselves to tears. Indeed, they didn't really speak at all until they used the women's bathroom at the restaurant.

"I'm going to have to tell Richard who that was, Mic."

"You mean you've never told Richard?"

"No."

Mackenzie's mouth hung open. "You married this man, but that never came up?"

"It did come up, but not the specifics. When he learned that I wasn't really involved, he said he didn't have to know. And let's face it, Mic, you get in the habit of not talking about it, and you just don't."

Mackenzie nodded in understanding, glad that Delancey had Richard, but she couldn't help but wonder what Tucker must be thinking. She shook her head at the thought and wondered if she would ever hear from him again.

"Mackenzie met Paxton Hancock when she was still in the Army. He works for IronHorse, and that's how Tom Magy got the Micah Bear series."

Richard was listening attentively, but Delancey stopped, seeing how long this could take. She finally went to the bookshelf in the other room, came back to their bed, and handed him *Blue Crayon.*

"Mackenzie wrote this."

Richard started visibly, but Delancey just stood by the bed.

"Mackenzie wrote this?"

"Yes, and all the other Mac Walker books."

Seconds passed, and his face grew thoughtful. Delancey waited to hear what he would say.

"Why the pretense?"

The question surprised her a little, but she sat back down on the bed and answered.

"Two reasons. Mackenzie met Paxton before she was published and saw a little side of that lifestyle before she was involved: the glamor and glitz that's not so glamorous up close. The name itself was really more of a gag — that's the second reason. Well, maybe there are three, since Mackenzie also decided she didn't want her privacy destroyed."

"Do you really think it would have been so bad?" Richard looked doubtful.

"Tell me, Richard," she asked, trying not to be angry that he didn't understand, "what would your patients be like on Monday when they find out you wrote four bestsellers that people want to make into movies?"

Understanding wasn't long in coming. People would probably have so many questions that he would never have a chance to look inside their mouths.

"Does Tucker know?"

"No. I don't think she knows where they stand yet, and I must tell you, Richard, we're so used to *not* talking about it that it even feels funny to discuss it now. It all happened before we came to Christ, and in some ways it feels unreal."

"What do you suppose Paxton wanted?"

"He was genuinely pleased for Micki's decision about Christ, but I'm sure he'd like another book from her. She's not ashamed of what she's done,

891

but she's past all of that now."

"She should do a Christian novel."

"She has. I'm sorry I didn't tell you. It's as I said, we just don't talk about it, and she hasn't tried to market the new one yet."

Richard smiled. "I really have no one to blame but myself. I told you if it didn't involve you and me, then I didn't need to know."

Delancey smiled. "You'll have to learn to be more nosy."

They laughed about it, but a certain man they knew could have used their prayers. He was about to ask questions that he feared were none of his business or might take him away from the woman he loved. He didn't feel he had a choice. Whatever he found out, he had to start somewhere.

FIFTY-ONE

"Your mom talked to me, Tuck, so I'm not surprised you wanted to get together, and even though I may not be able to tell you everything, I want you to ask about whatever is on your mind."

The men were out for lunch on Monday, and Jack only waited until they had ordered to open conversation.

Tucker nodded and said, "I care for Micki, Jack, I want you to know that right up front."

"Of course you do. I can see that."

Tucker's hand went to the back of his neck. "You're going to think I'm nuts, but I can't get it out of my head that she's been married."

"I don't think you're nuts, but no, there's nothing like that in Micki's life. In fact, I honestly think she'll talk to you when she feels you're going to be a permanent part of her life."

Tucker nodded.

"Or have the two of you already talked along that line?"

"No. I've been hesitant as to what I'm missing in her life — not sure that I really was missing something and halfway hoping she would just open up and talk to me."

"Sometimes not talking about something gets to be a habit, Tucker. In Mackenzie's situation, it's become a way of life, and the very way she lives her life hangs on discretion."

Tucker blinked. It was so hard to be in the dark on this issue. He honestly had no idea what his stepfather could be speaking about, but the older man was right: He had never told Mackenzie how he felt or suggested they look into getting to know each other on a new level.

"It's time, I think," Tucker said softly. "I need to tell Mackenzie how I feel and see if she feels the same."

"You doubt?" Jack asked with a smile.

Tucker looked at him. "You know her so much better, Jack — what do you think she's thinking?"

"I think she's in love and terrified that you only want to be friends. I think she doesn't want to lose your friendship, so she's willing to go along and be your buddy for as long as she needs to, just so she can be a part of your life."

Tucker closed his eyes. The words made him think of a starved child who was thankful for whatever crumbs she was thrown.

"This weekend," he said softly. "I'll talk to her this weekend. Even if you and I are both wrong about what we've seen, it will be good to have it out in the open."

"Mackenzie doesn't spill her feelings at the drop of a coin, but if you talk to her, ask her questions. She'll open up. I'm sure of it."

"May I tell her that we talked?"

"Certainly. She knows I won't say too much without her permission. As your mother has pointed out to me, I'm rather protective of her. If the issue were immoral, I wouldn't be willing to do that, but it's nothing like that."

Those were the best words Jack could have used.

The lunch ended on a positive note since Tucker was certain of his next course of action. He went home and worked for several hours before calling Mackenzie to ask her out on the weekend. Getting her answering machine didn't bother him. He was at peace about trying her later, after he went for groceries. God was going to work this out in a way that would please and honor Him. No matter what, Tucker knew God would give him the strength needed for the days ahead.

Tucker had been completely normal at dinner on Saturday night and when Richard and Delancey had dropped her off, but in truth, Paxton's call was giving Mackenzie nightmares. She had seen Tucker across the way at church Sunday morning, but for the first time she could remember, they hadn't spoken all day at church. Mackenzie found herself just wanting to be with him.

This was the reason she was in her car headed to his house. Though she had never been there, she thought she could find it. She didn't know what she would say, except that she wanted to ask him to take a walk with her to gauge whether things had changed. She had no agenda or rehearsed speech, she just desperately needed to be near the man she loved. Was it wrong to do it this way? She wasn't sure, and right now was afraid to examine it too closely.

Her concentration was taken up with driving when she neared his house. He didn't live too far off the lake, but the streets and houses were numerous. She maneuvered the Jeep here and there until she spotted it: a blue ranch-style house that sat on the corner of Oakland and El Dorado Streets. Mackenzie pulled into the double-wide driveway, cut the engine, and sat for a moment. Her courage finally boosted, she was climbing from the seat when the garage door began to rise.

Tucker, who already had the driver's door open on his car, stopped when he noticed a vehicle in his driveway.

"Well, hello," he said with a smile, walking to the edge of the garage.

"Hi, Tuck," Mackenzie responded, working like a Trojan to keep her feelings at bay. "I should have called, but I took a chance you'd be home and might want to go for a walk."

"I'd love to, but I'm completely out of food. Come to the market with me."

"Oh, that's all right," Mackenzie began, stuffing down her disappointment. "If you have plans . . ."

"Come on," he ordered, ignoring her protest. He hadn't thought he would see her before Wednesday and wasn't going to let her get away now. "Climb in."

Mackenzie did as she was told, telling herself not to examine everything he did. He was acting normally and she needed to do the same.

"How are you?" Tucker asked as he backed from the garage.

"I'm fine. How about you?"

"As soon as I get some food, I'll be better."

"You love to shop. I'm surprised you ran out."

They were on the street now, and Tucker smiled. Mackenzie glanced back at the house.

"That's a nice house, Tucker. Have you lived there long?"

"With the exception of college, all my life."

"Really?"

"Yes. I grew up there, and now I'm buying it from my mom."

"And you work there too?"

"Yes. I've set up one of the bedrooms as my office. It's nice because it has three bedrooms. If an author needs to come and work with me, I have a place for him to stay."

"What do you do if it's a woman?"

"If she can't bring her husband, I try to go to her. It all depends on the book. It's not that often that I actually need to see the author — most of the work is done by phone — but when I need to fly somewhere, it makes for a nice change."

Mackenzie went on to ask him what he was working on now. They arrived at the market right after he finished filling her in.

It was clear in the first few minutes of shopping that Tucker liked to cook. Mackenzie always headed for the frozen foods. Not Tucker. They made their way to the spices, meats, fresh fruits, and vegetables. With the exception of some tomato sauces and cans of soup, there were very few canned foods. They moved along easily, Mackenzie growing more relaxed by the minute. He was the same as always.

Tucker pushed the cart down the aisle where the store had light bulbs and household supplies. Mackenzie walked contentedly beside him. This aisle also had a full display of glossy magazines and a few dozen paperbacks. Mackenzie glanced over to see one of her books. Without stopping to form a plan, she picked it up.

"Did you ever read this, Tucker?"

He glanced down. "*Access Denied*? Yes, it's a good book."

"I wrote it," Mackenzie said softly.

Tucker was on the verge of teasing her when he looked into her eyes. Time came to a stop. Things fell into place so swiftly that it took his breath away.

"Mac for Mackenzie," he said softly, "and Walker is your mother's maiden name."

Mackenzie nodded and just watched him.

Tucker didn't care that they were in the grocery store. He moved close and put his arms around her, lowering his face just enough to kiss her temple.

"I love you, Mackenzie."

"Oh, Tucker." Mackenzie looked up at him, her heart in her eyes. "I've loved you for so long."

The back of his hand came up to tenderly stroke her soft cheek. For a moment, so many things ran through his mind that he couldn't speak.

"Let's get this list done and get out of here so we can talk," he suggested.

"I'd like that."

Because they kept stopping to look at each other, the shopping took longer than it should have. Tucker's gaze was very tender, and Mackenzie thought him the most wonderful man she'd ever met. They didn't say much as they drove back to his house, and Mackenzie didn't even go inside when Tucker took the perishables to the kitchen. When he returned, locking the house on the way, he took Mackenzie's hand in his and started toward the lake.

The beach area wasn't too crowded. August was rushing toward September, and many families had gone home. But neither were they alone. They walked for a time before finding a quiet bench. Tucker let go of Mackenzie's hand so he could sit at an angle to look at her. Mackenzie did the same.

"You can imagine how many questions I have."

"I think I can. I hadn't planned to tell you about

MacWalker, but when I saw the book, it just came out."

Tucker smiled at her, his eyes alight with pride. "You're a great writer, Micki. I'm amazed at the stories."

"Thank you, Tuck. It means a lot to hear you say that."

"How did it all happen, and why MacWalker?"

"Do you remember the phone call Saturday night?"

Tucker nodded, without telling her how much it had been on his mind.

"That was my editor, Paxton Hancock. We didn't start out as editor and writer. I met him in a bar, and when Delancey gave me some of her work, I showed it to him. He passed it on to a children's editor by the name of Tom Magy, who was the one to publish the Micah Bear series for IronHorse. Tom is also the man I ended up involved with, the one I mentioned to you that day on my dock." Mackenzie waited for Tucker to nod before continuing.

"I got an apartment after I left the Army, and one time when Tom came to see me, he saw a manuscript on my desk. He asked to read it. I was going out of town right then, but I left it with him. By the time I returned, he was ready to take it to Paxton. I could have died."

"Why?"

"Pax hates wannabes, and even though we saw each other regularly for a while, I never told him I was writing a book."

"But Tom told him anyway?"

"Indirectly. I told Tom that Pax would see my name on the manuscript and just laugh, and that's when Tom came up with the pen-name idea."

Mackenzie shook her head as she remembered. "Tom made up this story about his mother and some old family friend, and Pax actually agreed to read it."

"You and Delancey were already published by then?"

"Yes. We had been for some time."

"Okay."

"Well, I don't know how many weeks went by, but Tom came to me and said that Pax wanted to meet Mac Walker. Tom booked a hotel suite, and I waited in the bedroom while he met with Pax. I was just about sick with nerves, so afraid that Pax would think we were trying to deceive him."

"But he didn't."

"No. He just said he'd always known there was more to me than I let on."

"Had you and Paxton been involved?"

"Not intimately. He wanted us to be, and we did date some, but his world was so phony that I didn't want anything to do with it. Then he met a woman, and I was relieved. They're married now and have two children."

Tucker nodded, trying to take it all in. So much made sense — the way Mackenzie lived, her private lifestyle, Jack's comments during lunch. This story of how she became published, however, was fascinating. He wanted to know more.

"I take it Paxton offered you a contract."

"He had it with him and wanted to know what else I had up my sleeve."

"Had you started another book?"

Mackenzie grinned. "*Seahorse.*"

Tucker's laugh was loud and full before he shook his head in wonder and just stared at her.

"I had no idea. I hope you know that."

"I'm afraid that's the point."

Tucker nodded, his face serious now.

"Do you feel that I've lied to you, Tuck?"

"No, not at all. I tried to call you today."

"You did?" Mackenzie was pleased.

"Yes. I was going to ask you to go out with me this weekend. What would you have said?"

"I'd have said yes. Was there something special you wanted to do?"

"I wanted to talk to you about my conversation with Jack. I went to him because I knew I'd fallen in love with you, but I had the sense there was something in your life that we should talk about."

"What did he say?"

"He said I didn't need to worry; that yes, you had something in your life that you would probably talk to me about someday, but I didn't need to fret that you had a husband and children hidden away somewhere."

Mackenzie chuckled. "I can barely keep my own life together some days without hiding a family."

"But you're not opposed to having a husband and children should God bring them into your life?" Tucker's look was a mixture of fun and intensity.

"No," she answered softly. "I think I would like it very much."

His heart swelling with love, Tucker stood and held out his hand. Mackenzie let her fingers twine with his, and they started back down the beach.

"Are you against my telling someone that we're getting to know each other?" Tucker asked.

"No, not at all."

"Good, because I need help, Micki. I've told you that I was not at all accountable in my relationship with Celia, and I want it to be different for us. You know that I struggle with sexual issues. I know from Scripture that God takes it seriously. If I don't have someone asking me how I'm doing, I might be tempted to go too far."

They weren't back to Tucker's house yet, but he still stopped and looked down at her.

"Do you understand what I'm saying?"

"I think so. It's a pretty powerful temptation."

"Yes, and I find you quite desirable, so I'm really going to have to watch myself."

Mackenzie nodded.

"I also want to thank you for the way you dress. You always look lovely, but you don't dress seductively, and your modesty has been a big help to me."

Mackenzie smiled up at him. "I'm glad, Tucker. I've been rather preoccupied of late about what you think of my clothes and such."

"I think your clothes *and such* are gorgeous."

Mackenzie looked away, but she was smiling.

They walked on, this time not saying much until they arrived back at Mackenzie's Jeep.

"I'd better let you go," Tucker said. He had dropped her hand and now stuffed his own hands in his pockets.

"This is hard for you, isn't it, Tucker?" She had noticed before but now understood more.

"Yes. I'm trying not to touch you. I haven't earned that right."

"Because we're not engaged."

"Because we're not married, and I need to be as careful as possible."

Mackenzie nodded, but the idea took some getting used to. She didn't think now was the time to pursue the subject, but it was on her mind.

Other than planning to see each other at minichurch, they didn't talk further. Tucker smiled warmly at her, and Mackenzie's grin was as sincere as her heart, but she left his place with questions piling up inside. It was still fairly early when she got home, and once there, remembered she hadn't eaten dinner. While absently spooning in something she'd heated in the microwave, she sat with paper and pen, listing concerns and questions about her relationship with Tucker Stone.

It's so simple in the movies, she told the Lord with a small shake of her head. *They see each other and live happily every after. But it doesn't work that way in real life. I've asked for wisdom in the past, Lord, and You've always provided. I must ask again, this time for one of the biggest things in my life.*

Mackenzie was up late, not anxious but thinking. By the time she went to sleep, a plan was taking shape. First thing in the morning she would go to see Mrs. Richard Wilder.

"And he told you he loved you right in the grocery store?"

"Yes!"

Delancey laughed with delight and leaned across the sofa to hug her older sister.

"Did you tell him back?"

"I did, and then we went back to his house, walked to the lake, and talked for a long time. He naturally wanted to know all about Mac Walker, so I did a lot of the talking. It was on the way back to his house that he stopped me with something, Deej, and I want to know what you think."

"Okay."

"He says we can't touch until we're married —

903

not engaged, *married.*"

Delancey nodded in understanding. "I have to tell you, Mic, Richard and I couldn't handle it."

"Couldn't handle what?"

"Touching while we were still engaged. Things would start with a simple kiss, but that was never enough. Before something happened we had to stay apart because we were not husband and wife. It was especially bad during those weeks when we had already planned to be married. We talked on the phone a lot, but we didn't see each other much, and we had almost no physical contact."

Mackenzie was surprised. Why did she think that simply because her sister knew better and that she and Richard were believers, this would not be an issue?

"You look like you're thinking," the younger woman commented.

"I am. I've been a little hard on Tucker, even though I said that love would let you forgive. I mean, I know it will, but —"

Delancey stared at her. "Mic, what are we talking about here?"

"There was someone else in Tucker's life. You've helped me to see how easy it is to have things go too far, but I can't help but wonder how often he'll touch me and think of her."

"First of all," Delancey said firmly, "you must talk this over with Tucker. He's got to know what you're thinking, Mackenzie, or this is never going to work. Second, I can tell you from my own experience that God is able to do incredible things when we let Him. I can't tell you that I never think of Chet, and when I do, I pray for him, but Micki, I'm not kidding when I say that when Richard touches me or I touch him, I think only of us."

Mackenzie stared at her in thought, and Delancey remembered something else.

"I have seen the way Tucker looks at you, Mic. He isn't thinking of another woman."

"No, I don't think he is either; I just suddenly had all these doubts."

"And now is the time to have them so they can be discussed. Chad and Marcy Cline taught us so much in our premarriage class. We studied a book that was very good, but mostly they let us talk and ask questions. It was invaluable. You have to discuss everything: how many babies you want, where you want to live, does Tucker plan to stay in this area or is it his dream to farm chickens someday — everything."

Mackenzie laughed, but Delancey's point was well taken.

"Oh, D.J., I feel better."

"Good. How about some breakfast?"

"Haven't you eaten?"

"No. I slept in this morning."

"Well, you know me. I won't say no if you're doing the cooking."

They talked nonstop while Delancey cooked, and it was close to noon before Mackenzie said her goodbyes. They weren't long apart, however, since Mackenzie's Jeep wouldn't start. She came back inside to use the phone. It wasn't the first time it had happened, and Mackenzie knew it was time to do something.

"I just realized something, Deej," Mackenzie said before the auto club tow truck arrived.

"What's that?"

"I'm going to go car shopping."

Delancey blinked. "Today?"

"As soon as I can. I'm treating Tucker's declara-

905

tion as though the world has come to an end. I've got to be clear-headed, and although we have a lot of things to talk about, I suddenly realized that I've had my life on hold while I waited for something from Tucker. Now that I have it, I still have to keep moving."

"So you're going to buy a new car?"

"Yes, and have the house painted, send out queries for my book, get my hair cut, do something with the bushes on the north side of the house, and then ask Drew Campbell, the elder over our Sunday school program, if he'd be interested in a play I'm working on for Christmas."

Delancey smiled. "I love you, Micki."

"I love you too, but why did you tell me now?"

The younger woman shrugged. "I'm just not as practical as you are, and I wish I were."

"It can be very boring." She had her "look" on. "Do you have any idea what I do before I go to bed each night? I'm like a little old woman. The pillow has to be just so and the window open a little. The toilet lid has to be up so I can go in the night and never wake up. And my nightshirt — I like a certain one. Did I mention the tissue box that has to be close by in case I sneeze? I'm very dull, Delancey. I just want you to know."

Delancey was still laughing when the tow truck arrived. She stood with her sister while the Jeep was hitched up and taken away. She remained there for a few minutes in the driveway and thought about her morning. Her heart was suddenly compelled to pray for Tucker Stone. The reason was simple: No matter what she said, Mackenzie Bishop was anything but boring.

Tucker's conversation with Titus Johansen was

the highlight of the week for Tucker. It wasn't that he hadn't enjoyed hearing Mackenzie say she loved him; it was because Titus' words of encouragement to him were further confirmation that God would bring him and Mackenzie together as husband and wife. Added to that was knowing that he would see Mackenzie at the Bradfords' that night. He had tried calling her Tuesday morning but only gotten her answering machine. After that he had worked nonstop the rest of the day.

The next night when he had walked into the Bradfords', Mackenzie was already there. Other people had already taken the seats next to her, but she smiled when he caught her eye. Titus, who was the soul of discretion, didn't say anything, but he smiled hugely at Tucker before starting the night's worship.

Right now they were in Genesis 45 and studying Joseph. Tucker had heard much about Joseph, but the close look they were taking was giving him new insights into this man of God. Mackenzie had never looked at Joseph in depth, and she was captivated. Some of the questions she asked were very insightful, and as Titus led the discussion each week, she was like a thirsty sponge. She was especially moved over the way Joseph dealt with his brothers. It was a wonder to see the compassion and forgiveness in his heart. Mackenzie knew she could learn a lot from Joseph. She was still thinking about his life when Titus closed and Cria sat down beside her.

"Hello," she said softly.

"Hi, Cria." Mackenzie smiled at her and wondered at the gleam in her eye.

Cria bit her lip in uncertainty. "Didn't Tucker tell you he was going to talk to Titus?"

Mackenzie shook her head. "He just said he was going to ask someone to hold him accountable. He didn't say who."

"I hope you know it's taking all my will not to leap about and tell everyone."

Mackenzie laughed. "I'm glad you're able to restrain yourself. I don't think I could handle that just yet."

"But you are excited?"

"Now what do you think?"

Cria laid a hand on her arm. "He's so special, Micki. Titus and I have come to love him so much, and if we could have picked anyone for him, it would have been you."

Mackenzie smiled, wanting to talk more about it. But the other groups in the room suddenly fell quiet, and as Mackenzie said, she wasn't ready yet for a big announcement. That most of the occupants of the room had watched these two falling in love never occurred to her. They were not big teasers, and since Mackenzie was so good at keeping her feelings from her face, none would have taken the risk of being wrong.

Tucker eventually made his way to Mackenzie's side, joining the conversation with Cria, and, when it was time to leave, driving Mackenzie home. The only difference on this night was that he parked the car and walked around the house with Mackenzie so they could sit on her dock.

"What did you do today?" Mackenzie asked him.

"I spent most of the day on the phone with an author from Oregon, but before that I had an appointment with Titus."

"Cria told me you'd talked to him."

He clicked his tongue. "We just can't keep any secrets from you women. What did you do today?"

"I went car shopping."

"Car shopping?"

"Um hm."

"Mackenzie, how many cars do we need?"

Mackenzie blinked at him. "We?"

Now it was Tucker's turn to be surprised. He looked down at her, searching eyes that were searching his in return. His voice was soft and thoughtful when he questioned her.

"On Monday did you think I was saying 'I love you, let's be buddies forever'?"

"No, Tucker, I didn't, but unless we're married by the weekend, I need a more dependable vehicle."

"The Jeep's not dependable?"

"Not these days. I have the auto club phone number memorized."

Tucker sat for a minute. "You're one independent lady, did you know that?"

"Both of my parents are gone, Tuck. I've had to be."

He nodded in understanding, but it still bothered him a little that he hadn't known about her vehicle. "I realize we haven't been talking about our relationship for very long, but I think it would be good if we surprised each other as little as possible."

"That's a good point."

"So tell me, how are you going about this?"

Mackenzie filled him in on having the Jeep restored. It was such a nice winter vehicle. Then she described her search for a car similar to the one he drove.

"I'm also having the house painted, sending out a query to Candlelight for *The Parchment Soldier,* writing a children's Christmas play, and having my hair cut on Friday."

Tucker laughed until he had tears in his eyes. When she told, she told all.

"What's so funny?" she smiled as she watched him.

"Just you."

"Well, you asked."

"True. Why everything right now?"

"Because it's all needed to be done for a long time, but I've been sitting on my hands waiting for you to notice me."

"Is that true?"

"Yes, it's played hob with the rest of my life, and now I need to get back to work. I'm sure Cria thinks that I rushed out today and bought every bride magazine on the rack, but that's not my style, Tucker. I hope that'll be all right."

"It will be fine. We don't need fancy — just lots of family and friends."

"That sounds nice."

"Do you feel cheated, Micki, that I haven't asked you to marry me yet, but we're making plans?"

"No. I figure you'll get around to it, and before then we have things we need to discuss."

"That makes it sound as though you're not sure."

"No, I'm sure, but I saw my sister today, and when I told her some of my fears, she said we have to talk about them."

It was almost fully dark now, so Mackenzie's face was fading from view. Tucker wasn't about to discuss serious issues with the woman he loved when he couldn't see her face.

"I'll tell you what, we'll get together this weekend and talk about things."

"All right."

"Mackenzie," he said, taking her hand in his, "you do understand how serious I am, don't you?"

"Yes, Tuck, I do, and I'm serious in return. I was just telling the Lord on Monday night that the real thing is so different from what you read in books. When you join the lives of two sinful people, doubts, selfishness, pride, and any other sin you can name come strongly into the picture. I'm just not clear on some things, Tucker, and I want to be before we go much further."

"There's nothing I want to hide from you, so that's fine with me."

They were silent then, Mackenzie loving the way his hand was larger than hers. She loved the way *he* was larger. It wasn't just his broad shoulders — Tucker Stone was broad all over. She knew Delancey loved Richard's tall slimness, but Mackenzie preferred a little more man to hold. The thought of holding him close made her face flame with anticipation, and she was glad that Tucker was not taking any chances in that area.

"Walk me out front?"

"Sure."

They said goodbye next to his car before Mackenzie let herself inside. She would have loved for him to stay so they could talk for hours, but her witness before her neighbors was more important than that. She let herself inside and took herself to bed.

I don't want to rush this, Lord. I want to enjoy it, but I am anxious to know exactly where we stand. Give me a heart for You, Father, that will help me to be the woman Tucker needs. She then thought about the things she wanted to ask and prayed for those questions as well, trusting that God would move all things in His time.

911

FIFTY-TWO

"How is it going?" Titus asked when he called Tucker on Thursday night.

"It's going well. We talked for a little while on Wednesday night, but we're going to head out Saturday and talk about some things that are on Micki's mind."

"Did she say what?"

"No, but she's glad I haven't actually asked her to marry me because she wants to settle some questions first."

"It sounds as though she's thinking well. Why don't you come by after dinner?"

"We won't be going in the evening. Darkness makes it harder for me. We'll probably go for lunch somewhere in a very public place."

"Good thinking. I'll check with you Sunday to see how it went."

"All right. Thanks for calling, Titus."

"I'll be praying, Tuck."

The men rang off, and Titus immediately sought out Cria. He took her in his arms and just held her.

"Are you okay?" she asked.

"Yes, but I can't hug Tucker right now, so I'm coming to you."

Cria smiled at him. "Why would you want to

hug Tucker?"

"He's working so hard on his relationship with Micki. I know he loves her, but he's not letting it get physical. Do you know how hard that is for a man?"

"Only from what you've told me." She framed his face with her hands and kissed him. "I'll pray for him, Titus — Micki too."

Their toddler chose that moment to drop a cup of orange juice on the floor, so all conversation and cuddling ended, but the Johansens did pray — they prayed for Tucker and Mackenzie every time God brought them to mind.

"I think about Celia more than I thought I would, Tucker," Mackenzie admitted. It was Saturday afternoon, and they were at the Zephyr Cove Marina, sitting on the beach and watching the speedboats and jet skis bobbing in the water. They had eaten a picnic lunch and talked of light, fun things, but Tucker waited only until lunch was over to find out what was on Mackenzie's mind.

"For a while I was pretty hard on the two of you, but then Delancey talked to me, and that helped."

"What do you mean by 'hard on you'?"

Mackenzie looked uncomfortable but still admitted, "It bothers me that two people who call themselves followers of Christ could go too far."

"It should bother you," Tucker said softly. "For myself, I'm deeply ashamed. It didn't matter that Celia and I loved each other and planned to be married — it was wrong. I've confessed it, Mackenzie, and I can ask for your forgiveness, but that type of thing never completely goes away. Even if Celia had lived and we'd been married, I couldn't have told my children that we'd been pure."

Mackenzie nodded but didn't comment. Watching her, Tucker instinctively knew there was something more. He asked her about it and waited.

"What you said in Colorado, Tucker — it turned out to be true." She had been playing with the sand, her eyes averted, but now she looked at him. "I do look at Delancey and feel that I don't measure up. It's nothing she does. It's all inside of me. When I'm thinking well, those thoughts don't enter in, but if I let my emotions take over, Satan has a heyday with me."

"How has it been lately?"

"Awful. And now I'm comparing myself to Celia. I tell myself that she was beautiful with willowy curves and that I'll never satisfy you. God has reminded me that my heart is the place that matters, but I keep forgetting.

"I don't even want to see a picture of Celia, because the way she looks shouldn't make any difference. I keep telling myself that our love is what matters, but I'm more insecure over the subject than I would have imagined."

"I'm so glad you told me, Micki. I can tell you're on the right path, even though you're discouraged about it right now. I need to keep reassuring you. For the record, I thought you were drop-dead gorgeous long before I fell in love with you."

"When did you, Tuck?"

"Fall in love? I think it was at Beaver Creek." He smiled at her. "I looked up to see you there," he sighed, "and my heart nearly beat out of my chest. And then you were so scared to meet the Nortons, but you came in and did it anyway. You

914

talked to me about that verse you were stuck on, your face so intent as I explained it to you. And then Rudy talked to me."

Mackenzie's brows rose.

"It's true. It seems you quite captivated his sons — not that I blame them — but he thought you were perfect for me."

Mackenzie's mouth opened, and Tucker grinned.

"When I got home, Gemma came to see me and told me I should marry you."

Mackenzie looked out over the water, amazed at what she was hearing.

"Mackenzie." Tucker waited a moment before drawing her back. "I will not be thinking of any woman but you when I hold you in my arms. Do you understand?"

Mackenzie nodded.

"I can't say that I'll never be tempted, but I'll work hard to be all yours for all of our lives." He stopped and stared at her as he weighed his next words. "And if I can be very blunt, your face and figure give me the shivers."

"I like the way you're put together too. I love you, Tucker."

"And I love you," he said as he put his arm around her and drew her close for a few moments.

"Are you feeling better about things?"

"Yes." Mackenzie looked into his face as he drew back. "But Delancey said we also have to talk about how many babies we want and whether you plan to raise chickens some day."

Tucker shouted with laughter. It was going to be so much fun to be married to this woman.

"Tucker, will we live at your house?" Mackenzie asked out of the blue.

"*My* house? You would give up your place on the

lake?"

"If you want me to, yes."

"I appreciate that, love, but do you know what?"

"What?"

"I've dreamed my whole life of living on the lake. I think it would be wonderful."

"What will you do with your house?"

"Well, if it works out to live at your house, I would keep mine for an office. That way, when someone comes to work with me, he could really stay in comfort, you know, with no one else there."

"What do you mean, if it works out?"

"I'm not sure I can afford the taxes and mortgage on your home. We'll have to talk about some numbers."

"Mac Walker royalties more than covered the house."

"The house is paid for then?"

Mackenzie nodded, and Tucker's brow lowered.

"How are you paid, Micki?"

"Mac Walker is a business. Paxton has everything set in a special account back East. If I need funds, I make a phone call and money is transferred."

"How do the taxes work?"

"The only income in my name is from the Micah Bear books, and I pay my taxes quarterly on that. Mac Walker, the business, pays taxes out of the special account. I get a full statement each quarter from the accountant."

"And you keep all those?"

"The statements? Yes. Would you like to see them?"

"I would, yes." Tucker went on to tell Mackenzie approximately what he made a year and why it varied with different projects. "The only reason I would want to give up the house would be if it's going to hinder our giving to the church and help-ing others. Do you know what I mean, Mic?"

"Yes. I worry a little about raising children on the water, but I guess we would learn to deal with it."

"We'd probably close off the deck, for starters."

Mackenzie nodded. "That would work."

"By the way, how many children do you want?"

"I don't know. My father had three siblings and my mother had none. I always thought it would have been fun if there had been at least four of us, not that I would trade Delancey." She paused a minute. "I do know one thing, Tuck. Cria was really sick with all three kids, so I guess I'd like us to wait until we've been married a year to try. I might not be sick at all, but if I am, I don't think that would be a fun way to spend our first year."

"Okay. What method of birth control should we use?"

Mackenzie looked at him. "I don't know. Oh, Tucker, there's so much to decide."

"There is," he took her hand. "But we'll talk to others, research issues, and use the wonderful minds God gave us."

Mackenzie smiled at him.

"And right now, we need to change the subject before I attack you."

Mackenzie laughed at his dry tone but knew he was somewhat serious. She watched his eyes a moment.

"Did you know that you have great legs?"

Mackenzie didn't answer immediately, and before she could say anything, Tucker came to his feet.

"Come on. Let's put this stuff in the car and take a walk. I need to get some of this energy

917

worked out."

For the next hour they walked through the park that led back to Mackenzie's house. They didn't go far because the car was waiting at the marina, but they discussed several more things.

"I want a big wedding," Tucker announced at one point.

Mackenzie stopped on the trail. "What do you mean by 'big'?"

"Lots of everything — people, cake, food, fellowship, you name it." He paused when he saw her face. "I'll help pay for it, Mic."

"It's not the money, Tucker. It's me. Have you ever heard what Delancey says about me?"

"No."

" 'The only domestic thing about Mackenzie is that she lives in a house.' I'm not into all that stuff, Tucker, and I wouldn't even know where to start."

"I'll help you, and so will my mom."

Mackenzie was not thrilled, but she didn't let on. Tucker was ready to go see his mom on the spot, but Mackenzie was rather quiet.

He's so different from most men, Lord. He likes to shop and wants a big wedding. I'm amazed and overwhelmed. I'm not good with crowds. I just want to run away and be married quietly.

"You're awfully quiet."

"I was just thinking."

"About?"

"How nice it would be to run away and be married privately."

Tucker stopped and put his hands on her shoulders. "I love the thought of a huge noisy wedding; I will admit that. But there is a factor that's bigger than all of that: I grew up here. This

918

has been my home church for years. Celia and I met in southern California, but everyone still knew that I was engaged and that she died. There are literally hundreds of people who will want to come out, wish me well, and meet my bride. And quite frankly," his face lowered as he whispered, "I'm dying to show you off."

"I'm being selfish, aren't I?"

"No, but we are different people. After we get married I'm going to need to be willing to sit at home with you, and you're going to need to be willing to put on your dancing shoes and be social with me."

Mackenzie nodded as Tucker bent and kissed her brow before stepping away and taking her hand again.

"I have a feeling that Titus will be talking to Kevin pretty soon and they'll be looking for a couple to work with us on the premarriage class."

"Do you know who it will be?"

"No, but I hope it's Titus and Cria."

"I would like that," she told him fervently. "I would like that a lot."

Mackenzie's words gave him great pleasure two weeks later when Titus did call and tell him they would be meeting with him and Cria if they became engaged, and even if they wanted to put off the engagement for a time. Tucker did not want to put it off. He had been working on the perfect time and place to ask Mackenzie to marry him, remembering that she didn't like crowds but at the same time wanting to share their news with the people in their world. He thought he had just the plan. He called and asked her to a late lunch on Wednesday. They met at Marie Callender's, since the restaurant was halfway between their homes, and Tucker asked for a booth in the corner.

The lunch special of beef pot pie was one of Mackenzie's favorites. They feasted and laughed for about an hour before Tucker picked up the folder next to him.

"I brought the last chapters you gave to me. I'm sorry it's taken so long."

"That's all right. I'm putting the polish on that Christmas play, so that's taking all of my time."

"Are you putting music in that too?"

"Yes, but strictly the traditional hymns like 'Silent Night,' 'Away in a Manger,' 'What Child Is This' — you know, all those."

"Sounds wonderful." He opened the folder. "I want to go over one of these chapters with you. I made quite a few changes and want to make sure it makes sense."

"Okay."

Tucker scooted closer in the booth and turned to the page.

"Just read this over and see if you like the idea."

Mackenzie began, not noticing the way Tucker watched her. It all made complete sense, which made her wonder a little why she needed to check it. She almost put it down early but decided to read to the end.

Don't worry if you can't make sense of it was one of the last lines. *What I really want to know is if you'll be my wife.* Mackenzie blinked and read again. She slowly looked up at the man next to her, first at his eyes, and then at the ring he held between two fingers.

"Oh, Tucker," she breathed softly.

"Is that a yes?"

"Definitely."

"I was hoping it was."

Before he could put the ring on her finger, Mackenzie cupped his face in her palms, loving the feel of his strong jaw and the slight scratch of his beard.

"I love it that you love me."

"And I do love you, with all my heart," he whispered before pressing a soft kiss to her mouth. "Here," he whispered, sounding like a child on Christmas, "try it on." He picked up Mackenzie's hand and slid the ring into place.

"Oh, Tucker, it's beautiful."

A large marquise-cut diamond stood alone on an intricate filigree setting. Mackenzie had never seen anything like it.

"The band is filigree too and goes right here," he pointed to the side. "How does it fit?"

"It's wonderful." Mackenzie stared at her hand before looking at Tucker. "Almost as wonderful as you."

Tucker smiled at her. "Now, I must tell you two things."

"Okay."

"I want to tell everyone at minichurch tonight, and I want to be married before Christmas."

"That's fine, but why before Christmas?"

"I think Christmas is a very romantic time of year. I think it would add to the celebration to have a new wife and every year be able to remember being married not long before Christmas."

Mackenzie smiled. "There's hope for you, Tuck."

"How's that?"

"I always thought my father was the most romantic man I'd ever known, but I think you just might give him a run for his money."

"What did he do?" Tucker asked, frankly curious.

"I'm sure I don't know everything, but he loved to brush my mother's hair. He also loved big band music, and he and Mom would slow-dance in the living room." Mackenzie suddenly smiled. "He also liked to paint her toenails."

"Oh my," Tucker smiled, his look rather intimate. "That's romantic stuff all right."

Mackenzie laughed. "My mom was just like him. Every year for *his* birthday she bought a special nightie to wear."

Tucker sat back with a huge sigh, his eyes on a distant spot. The waitress came by asking if they wanted coffee, and Tucker said yes. He took his time adding cream and sugar and then took a few sips. He finally looked back at Mackenzie.

"We'll finish this conversation *after* we're married. All right?"

Mackenzie smiled. "All right."

"But just so we have the plan straight," Tucker went on, "You get the nightie, and I'll come up with the nail polish."

Mackenzie laughed so hard she had to put her napkin over her face.

That night, just as Tucker had wanted, he made an announcement to the minichurch family.

"Something happened today, something wonderful, and I wanted you all to share in it with me. I'm going to need your prayers and your support." He paused but didn't let himself look at her yet. "Mackenzie Bishop did me the honor of agreeing to become my wife."

Tucker turned and smiled at her. Mackenzie bit her lip. His voice had been so humble and sweet.

"When, Tucker?" Megan Bradford asked.

"We're hoping to set a date before Christmas."

Tucker had called Titus earlier to ask him if he could share, so Titus had been able to plan a special time of prayer. He asked God to build a new home in Tucker and Mackenzie and to bless them with years of service for Him.

After study Tucker drove Mackenzie home but didn't stay to talk. Mackenzie was all right with this, as she was feeling emotionally drained. She went to bed as soon as she got in the door but lay with the light on so she could see her ring. Delancey had all but screamed over the phone when she called her, and they were going to lunch tomorrow. Joanne and Jack had been just as ecstatic, as had Matthew and Gemma.

There have been so many times, Lord, when I didn't trust. Yet even when I ran and tried to hide from You, You were there and in control. Thank You for never letting go and never giving up.

Mackenzie fell asleep thanking the Lord, the light still on. She didn't discover it until she needed the bathroom at 2:00 A.M. She fell back to sleep dreaming about Tucker Stone.

December 4, 1993, Tucker and Mackenzie's wedding day, was upon Mackenzie before she could blink, but she still managed to be ready. Delancey had come in like a trooper and helped out, giving the bills to Jack and pushing forward until Tucker had the wedding he had always dreamed of.

While going through her mother's things, Mackenzie found Marrell's wedding dress and fell in love with it. Delancey made her sister's day when she located someone who could restore the simple, old-fashioned gown. Both Tucker and Mackenzie thought it beautiful.

Joanne, Delancey, Roz, and Gemma planned to

meet at Mackenzie's the morning of the wedding. Her living room was spacious, and she wanted to get dressed at home. They were planning to turn her entire living room into a boutique. Looking at her list, Mackenzie was thinking about what else needed to be done when the doorbell rang.

"I knew you would be early, D.J.," she smiled as she opened that portal. It was Matthew Stone.

"How are you?" Matthew smiled at her.

"Matt! Hi. Come in."

Matthew came forward, hugged her, and stepped back to study her. They had just been together the night before at the rehearsal dinner, but he wanted a few minutes alone with her.

"Can you sit down?"

"Yes, until the hens show up. Mom warned me that they'll be breathing down my neck any minute."

Mackenzie laughed.

"Do you want coffee?"

"No. I just want to talk to you."

"Okay."

He sat for a minute and then began to share. "I don't usually get choked up, Mackenzie. As a doctor, I can't wear my heart on my sleeve, but this wedding has had an odd effect on me." He stopped, his eyes a little moist. "I miss my father right now in such a powerful way." His voice dropped even lower. "I tried to be there for Tuck when Dad died, and to a degree I think I was, but so many times I knew I fell short. Now he's marrying you, and I —"

Seeing how emotional he was, Mackenzie's own eyes filled with tears.

"It's not fair that I make you cry on your wedding day, Micki, but I wanted you to know that my brother means more to me than I can say. And if I could pick any woman in the world for my brother, it would be you."

"Oh, Matt," Mackenzie whispered. "Thank you."

"Thank *you* for loving him and being the woman that he needs."

"He's wonderful, Matt. I can't believe how wonderful he is."

"Yes, he is. He's a true man of God, and I know he'll work like a dog to make this marriage work. You'll be happy together."

Mackenzie went for the tissue box and then hugged her soon-to-be brother-in-law.

"I'm going to be in big trouble with my mother if your nose swells up."

It felt good to laugh.

"Where are you two headed tonight?"

"We're coming back here, turning off the phones, and ignoring the door."

Matthew smiled. "No trip?"

"Not now. We'll drive to San Francisco tomorrow or Monday, but we'll probably be back by Wednesday. We'll go away later."

"And that's okay with you?"

"That's fine with me. One change at a time is more my speed."

They both heard a door slam, so Matthew stood.

"They're here."

"Sounds like it. Thanks, Matt."

He hugged her again and made his way to the door. "Oh, I almost forgot." Matthew came back, a small package coming from his jacket pocket. "Tuck sent this." He didn't stay around but went to the door and was on his way.

Mackenzie had just a few moments to open the

small bag before the family arrived. She smiled in delight at the bottle of fire-engine red nail polish. Taking the stairs two at a time, she dashed up to put the bottle by the bed. She came back down in time to see Delancey sail through the front door, the others behind her. She beamed at them, glad they were too busy to notice the secret smile in her eyes.

Much later that night, Mr. and Mrs. Tucker Stone, still in their wedding finery, made their way into the house on Lake Street. Jack had left the reception for a time to come to the house, close all the drapes, and light a fire. Mackenzie walked over to look down at the flames, and Tucker joined her. She turned to him.

"Hello, Mrs. Stone," he said softly as she went into his arms.

"Hello."

"Oh my." His voice was hushed as he pulled her close. "You are a nice fit."

"I think so too."

Tucker kissed her as he had longed to do so many times.

"Where's the nail polish?" he teased.

Mackenzie smiled. "On the nightstand upstairs."

"That far away?"

The bride only laughed as they sank on the sofa to kiss some more. At one point Mackenzie looked at him, her eyes taking in every detail of his tux.

"You look very good in a black tux. I don't suppose it's practical to add this to your wardrobe?"

"I would say no. You, on the other hand, can wear this dress for me anytime you want."

"Thank you."

Tucker's voice dropped. "Or if you're too warm,

you can always slip out of it."

Mackenzie's smile was warm and intimate as she leaned to kiss him again.

People in various places all over Tahoe were still talking about the wedding: what fun it had been, the great food, how lovely Mackenzie had looked, and the love they'd seen in Tucker's eyes. Jack and Joanne were talking about it as well. Matthew, Gemma, and their spouses were visiting in the Avery living room. The grandchildren were in bed, and Mr. and Mrs. Avery were retiring as well.

"And you left the house all ready?" Joanne asked.

"Yes. All the curtains were drawn, and I started a fire."

"Good. It sounds like just the right setting."

"With the way those two look at each other, I'm not sure they'll notice where they are."

Joanne laughed as she hugged him. "We did it, Jack! All five kids are married, two to each other."

He kissed the top of her head. "I would say that God has blessed us."

Joanne smiled up at him. "I couldn't agree with you more."

EPILOGUE

Mackenzie and Tucker honeymooned at Beaver Creek about two months after the wedding. Tucker had his heart set on going back there with his wife, and reservations had been impossible until then.

Now early summer had come, and their routine was already established. Tucker left the house most days and went back to what was now termed "the office." Mackenzie worked at home, Roz still coming in on a regular basis, and by the time they had been married about four months, Mackenzie's cooking was beginning to show signs of improvement. She made an effort to stay in the kitchen and concentrate, and most nights they had something edible to eat.

Richard and Delancey were already trying to have a baby, but Tucker and Mackenzie were sticking to their plan to wait one year. Nearly every day started with a walk or a run before Mackenzie took her swim, and those were some of the most precious hours of the day for the newlyweds. On this day they had run for a time, but Mackenzie's leg was aching a little, so they slowed to a walk. As they did, she began to tell Tucker a new story idea. He listened in silence and wondered when her creativity would stop amazing him.

"It's not really a mystery, but there are unknown aspects."

"Who's the main character?"

"Well, it's sort of a story within a story. The first person you meet is Marrell Brockmont. She's in her early 70s. Her husband is dead, and her two grown children live far away. One summer, however, her granddaughter, Amy, comes for a visit. She's 15. Amy notices that Marrell goes to her desk and writes for a long time every morning. Amy is naturally curious about it, so they start talking. Marrell admits that she's writing a story.

"It's a novel, and at first Amy thinks her grandmother is a little whacked, but as she listens and gets into it, she really starts to enjoy it. She wakes up every morning eager to hear more."

"What is the story?"

"It's a story about a woman named Alma Freed. Alma has grown up in a small midwestern town and has her first taste of city life when she goes off to college in Chicago. Not having any prior interest in science, she's amazed with her grades and understanding of scientific matters. One of her professors notices her grades and starts to keep an eye on her. She's not a flashy person. Her hair and clothing are nondescript, and he thinks she might be just the person he needs."

"The professor needs her?" Tucker questioned his wife.

"Yes, he has friends who are in trouble."

"What year does this take place?"

"About 1953."

"Okay, go ahead."

"Well, he needs someone to go to Europe, someone unnoticeable. He sends Alma. Posing as a maid, she's able to obtain a document that will eventually save the lives of several men who are currently under investigation at this point in the story. The plan is perfect until the man she works for chooses that night to tell her he's fallen in love with her. He proposes and wants an answer from her on the spot. She manages to put him off, but she lives in this mansion he owns. She asks for a few hours on her own, and he grants it. She escapes with the document hidden in her hat.

"She ends up in a horrible mess, which I'll explain in more detail in the book, but if it wasn't for a woman she met at some revival meetings, she would have been killed. The woman's name is Danika. She helps Alma escape and loses her own life for it. When Danika's brother, Andrej, who happens to be a new believer, finds out why his sister died, he's ready to turn Alma in or murder her himself. He has to leave the country before he can make a decision about what to do, so he drags her along."

Tucker and Mackenzie had arrived back at the house. They sat on the sofa so Mackenzie could tell him more.

"The book has a fun chase scene as Andrej drags Alma with him everywhere. At first he thinks she's nothing better than a murderer, but then he starts getting to know her, finds out she'd been attending the revival meetings too, leads her to Christ, and they end up falling in love. He believes her story, and now they only have to find a way back to America so Alma can finish the job the professor gave her.

Mackenzie twisted on the sofa a little to stretch her back. She felt as though she'd been talking all day. She couldn't get comfortable, so she stood and rotated her shoulders a little.

"I'm going to go for a swim now."

"Now? What about the end of the story?"

"Oh, Tucker, you'll enjoy it more when I put it down on paper."

"No, I won't. Tell me the end."

"I'm going to go for a swim," Mackenzie said, barely managing to keep the smile from her face.

"Mackenzie Rose Stone, you sit down here and tell me!"

Mackenzie ignored him, and Tucker made a grab for her. Mackenzie eluded him, standing on the opposite side of the sofa, a smile on her face. Tucker was not long in catching on.

"Come here, Mackenzie," he crooked a finger in her direction.

"No. I'm going for a swim."

Tucker came to his feet and moved toward her, but he wasn't fast enough.

"Tell me the story," he said as he stalked her.

"No."

"You leave me little choice." He shook his head in regret. "I'll have to resort to the tickle torture."

"You will not! Now you just get ready to go to work, Tucker."

He continued to pursue her, making threats all the while, but Mackenzie would not give in. He chased her around the furniture, and Mackenzie might have been able to keep it up for some time, but she dashed up the stairs toward the bedrooms. She realized her mistake about halfway up, froze, and turned back, but it was too late. Tucker was already standing calmly at the bottom.

"Are you going to tell me the rest of the story, Micki?"

"No. Now go eat breakfast so you can get to work."

He started up after her, taking each step very slowly and deliberately. "Have I told you lately that you have great legs?"

Mackenzie tried not to smile as she backed away. "Not since yesterday."

"Um." He studied them now. "Very nice."

"Go to work, Tucker."

"Tell me the story, Micki."

This time she just ran. She tried to get the bedroom door closed, but he was too fast. He caught her in the middle of the rug and they wrestled like bear cubs. Mackenzie was no wraith-like creature to be thrown about at will, but Tucker outweighed her by a good bit. When he had her pinned, both her wrists manacled in one of his hands, he put a hand on her waist and asked one more time.

"Are you going to tell me?"

Mackenzie pressed her lips together and tried to get away, but he only tickled her until she called uncle.

"You promise?" He made sure before he let go.

"Yes," she gasped, too spent to fight anymore.

On the bedroom floor they sat with their legs crossed, knees touching, as she told him the rest.

"Well, they eventually get back; it's not easy, but they do it. They keep having to stop and set up housekeeping in order to keep a low profile. They come down through Canada, already married by now. Pregnant, Alma is so sick she wants to die. Certain government officials are after her, so they have to travel by night. They head right back to Alma's university in Chicago and nearly scare the college professor into a heart attack when they go to his home in the middle of the night.

"He forgives Alma when he sees who it is, and

she gives him the paper that releases five men from prison. Our government had put them in jail for suspicion of communism. Alma agrees to take the stand, but that puts her all over the front pages of the newspaper. The book ends with Andrej and Alma taking on new identities. They'll never see their families again, but they have each other and their baby."

"And all of this is what Marrell Brockmont is telling her grandchild?"

"Yes. Amy loves it, leaps to her feet, hugs her grandmother, and leaves to go to the mall with friends. After she leaves Marrell pulls out the drawer of her desk and moves a piece of wood that opens a slim compartment. From there she pulls out a copy of the document that freed the men, to this day believing that she did the right thing."

Tucker blinked. "It's her story! Marrell has been telling her granddaughter her own story!"

"Yes."

Tucker laughed. "You love the touch of pretense, don't you?"

"I do," Mackenzie smiled and admitted.

Tucker's sigh was huge as he leaned his forehead until it touched hers.

"You're good; do you know that?"

"Thank you," she said softly, staring at him as the love she felt burgeoned in her heart. "I like being married to you, Tucker Stone," Mackenzie admitted very quietly.

He stroked her cheek and kissed her softly, but not before he smiled into her eyes and said, "I was hoping you would."

ABOUT THE AUTHOR

Lori Wick is one of the most versatile Christian fiction writers in the market today. Her works include pioneer fiction, a series set in Victorian England, and contemporary novels. Lori's books (more than 4 million copies in print) continue to delight readers and top the Christian bestselling fiction list. Lori and her husband, Bob, live in Wisconsin and are the parents of "the three coolest kids in the world."

The employees of Thorndike Press hope you have enjoyed this Large Print book. All our Thorndike, Wheeler, and Kennebec Large Print titles are designed for easy reading, and all our books are made to last. Other Thorndike Press Large Print books are available at your library, through selected bookstores, or directly from us.

For information about titles, please call:
  (800) 223-1244

or visit our Web site at:
  http://gale.cengage.com/thorndike

To share your comments, please write:
  Publisher
  Thorndike Press
  295 Kennedy Memorial Drive
  Waterville, ME 04901